ICHIRO

Written & Illustrated by Ryan Inzana

ETCH
HOUGHTON MIFFLIN HARCOURT
BOSTON   NEW YORK

ALL RIGHTS RESERVED. ORIGINALLY PUBLISHED IN HARDCOVER
IN THE UNITED STATES BY HOUGHTON MIFFLIN, AN IMPRINT OF
HOUGHTON MIFFLIN HARCOURT PUBLISHING COMPANY, 2012.

ETCH IS AN IMPRINT OF HOUGHTON MIFFLIN HARCOURT PUBLISHING COMPANY.

LYRICS TO "NEW YORK IS GONNA BURN" BY THE DON'T STOP RECORDED 2002 AT
FUNHOUSE STUDIOS, BROOKLYN, NEW YORK, REPRINTED WITH PERMISSION.

VERSE FROM "FLOWER OF SUMMER" ("NATSU NO HANA") BY TAMAKI HARA REPRINTED
WITH PERMISSION.

FOR INFORMATION ABOUT PERMISSION TO REPRODUCE
SELECTIONS FROM THIS BOOK, WRITE TO TRADE.PERMISSIONS@HMHCO.COM
OR TO PERMISSIONS, HOUGHTON MIFFLIN HARCOURT PUBLISHING COMPANY,
3 PARK AVENUE, 19TH FLOOR, NEW YORK, NEW YORK 10016.

HMHBOOKS.COM

THE TEXT WAS SET IN TIMSALE.
THE ILLUSTRATIONS ARE MIXED MEDIA.

LIBRARY OF CONGRESS CATALOGING-IN-PUBLICATION DATA IS ON FILE.

ISBN: 978-0-547-25269-8 HARDCOVER
ISBN: 978-0-358-23840-9 PAPERBACK

MANUFACTURED IN CHINA
SCP 10 9 8 7 6 5 4 3 2 1
4500799698

For Yuko

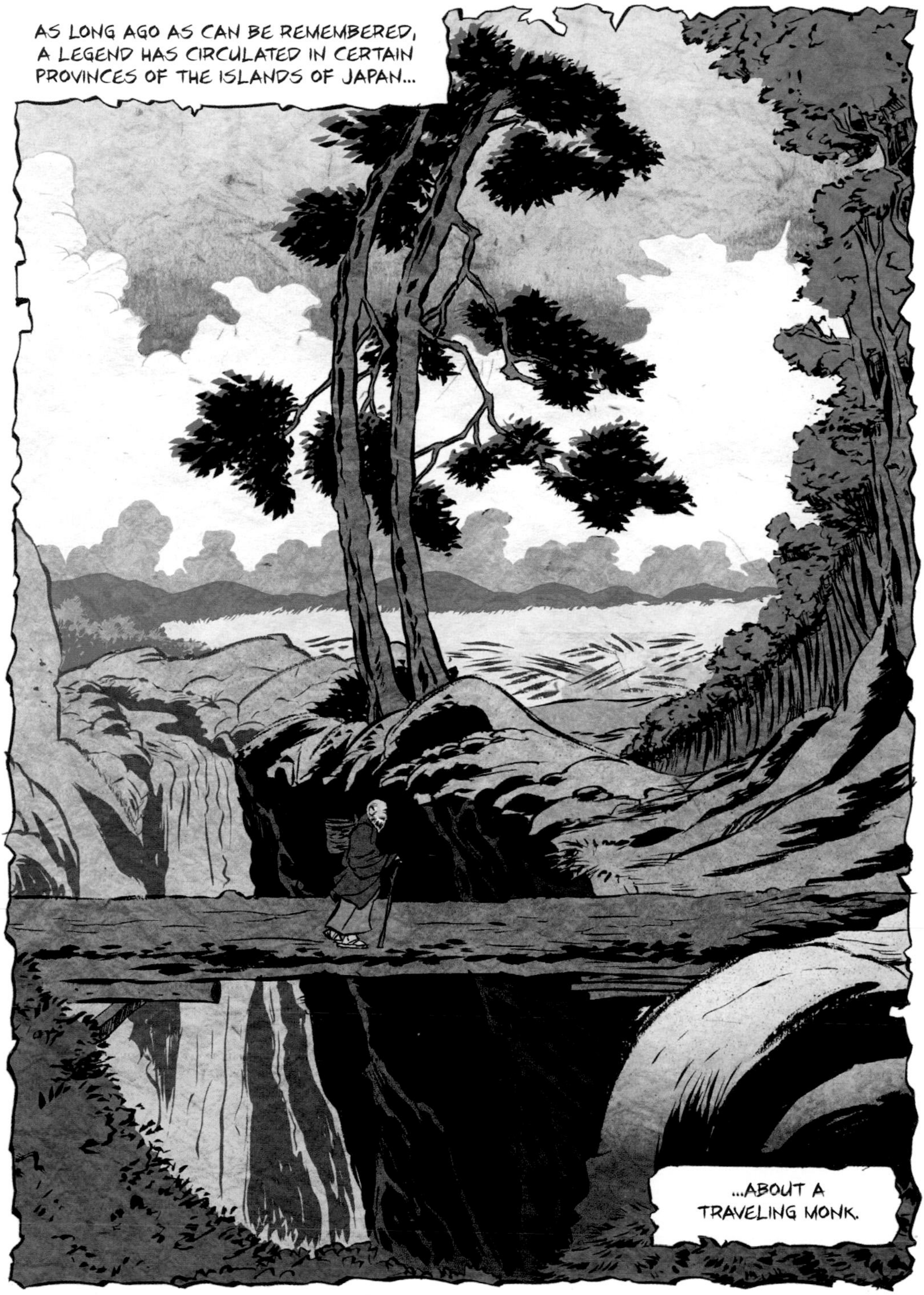
AS LONG AGO AS CAN BE REMEMBERED, A LEGEND HAS CIRCULATED IN CERTAIN PROVINCES OF THE ISLANDS OF JAPAN...
...ABOUT A TRAVELING MONK.

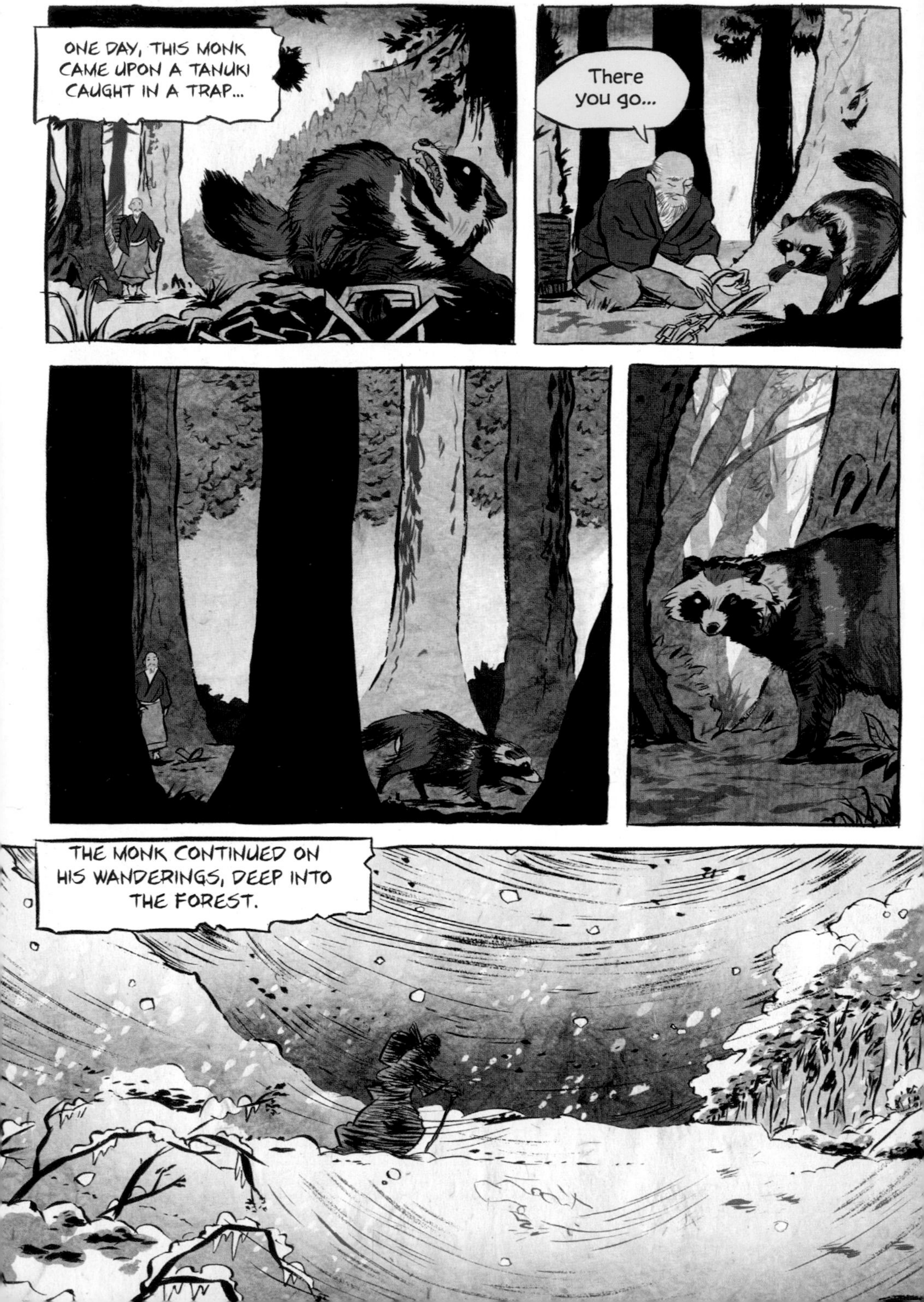
ONE DAY, THIS MONK CAME UPON A TANUKI CAUGHT IN A TRAP...
There you go...
THE MONK CONTINUED ON HIS WANDERINGS, DEEP INTO THE FOREST.

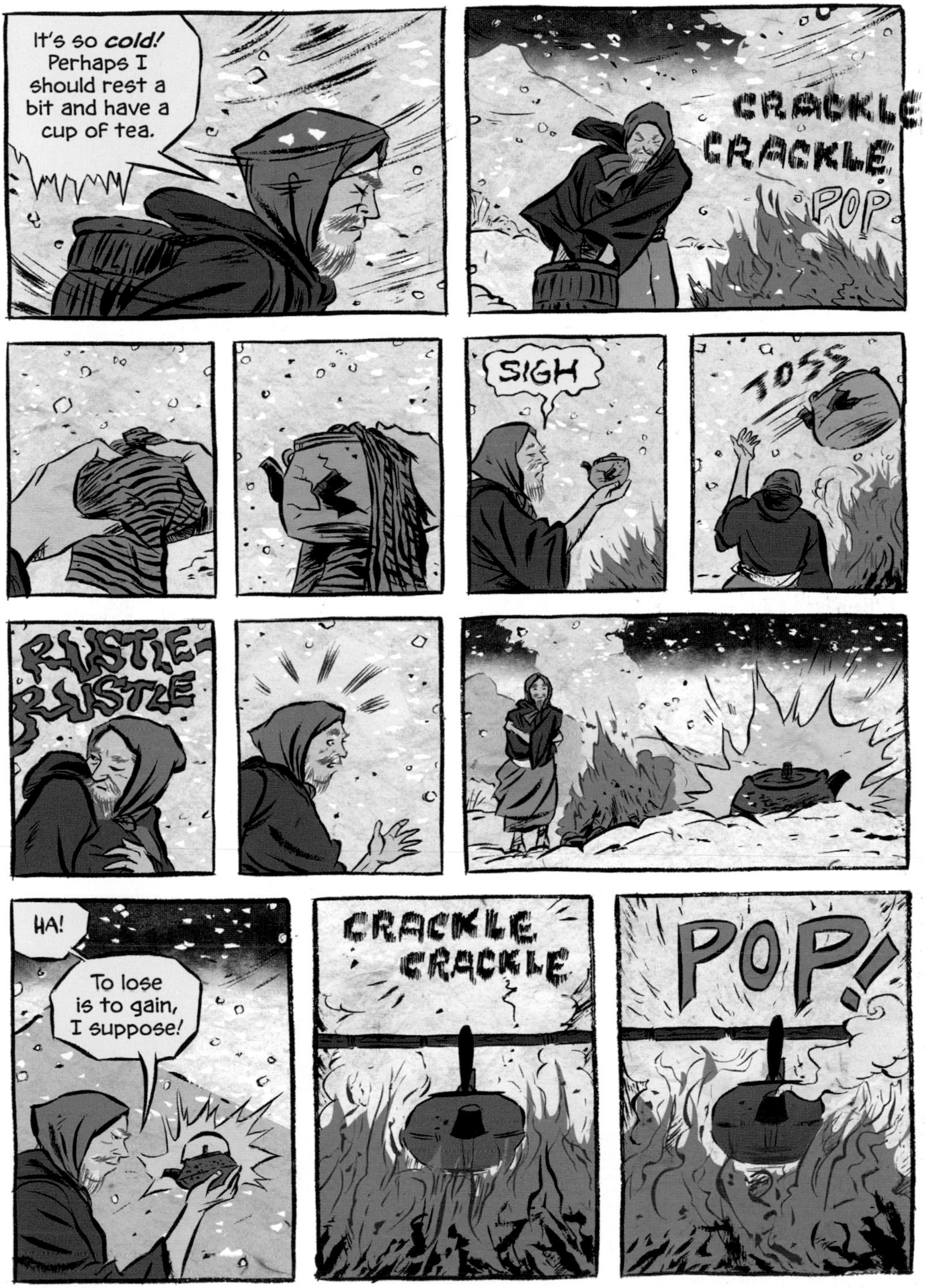
It's so *cold!* Perhaps I should rest a bit and have a cup of tea.
CRACKLE
CRACKLE
POP
SIGH
TOSS
RUSTLE-RUSTLE
HA!
To lose is to gain, I suppose!
CRACKLE CRACKLE
POP!

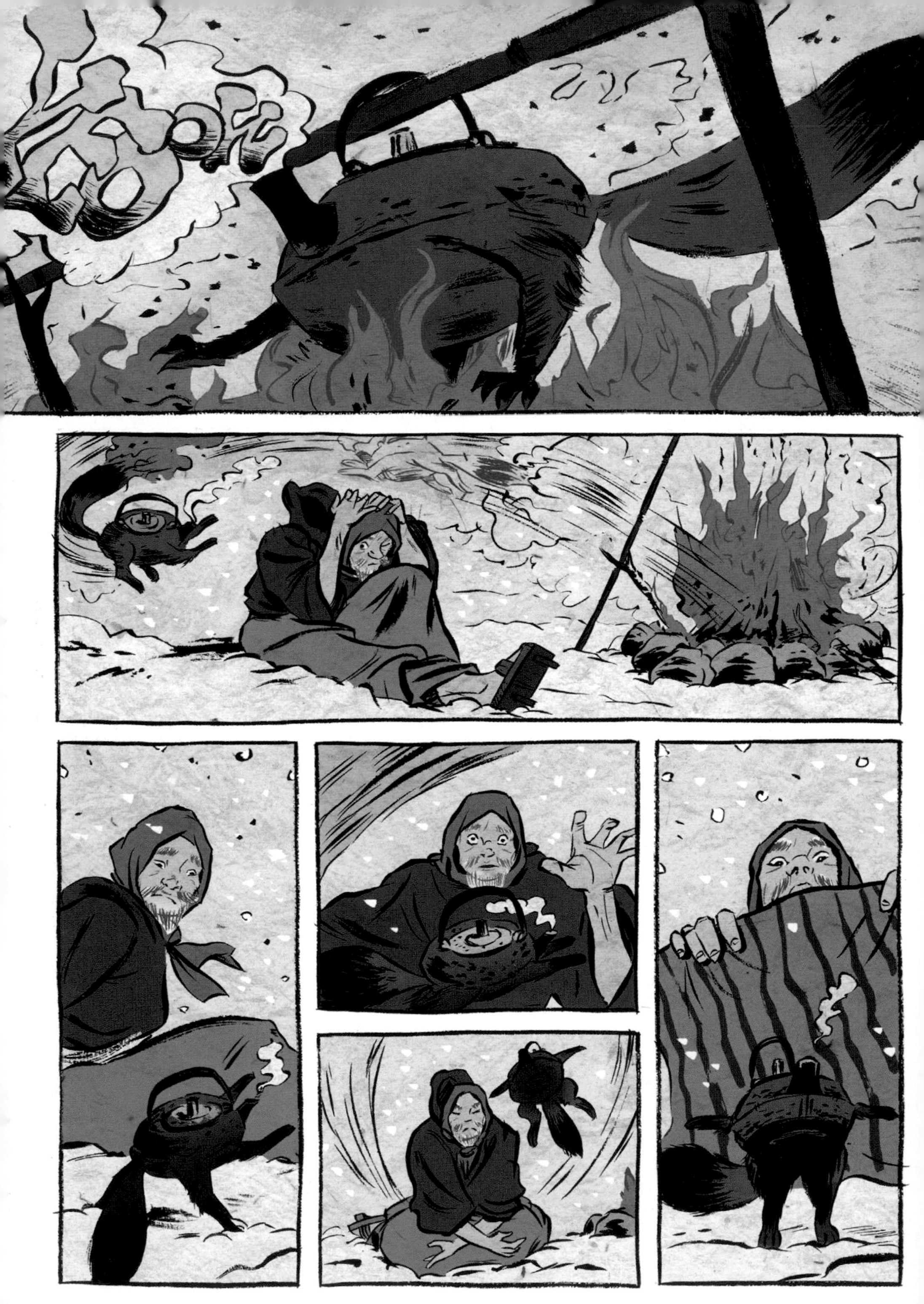

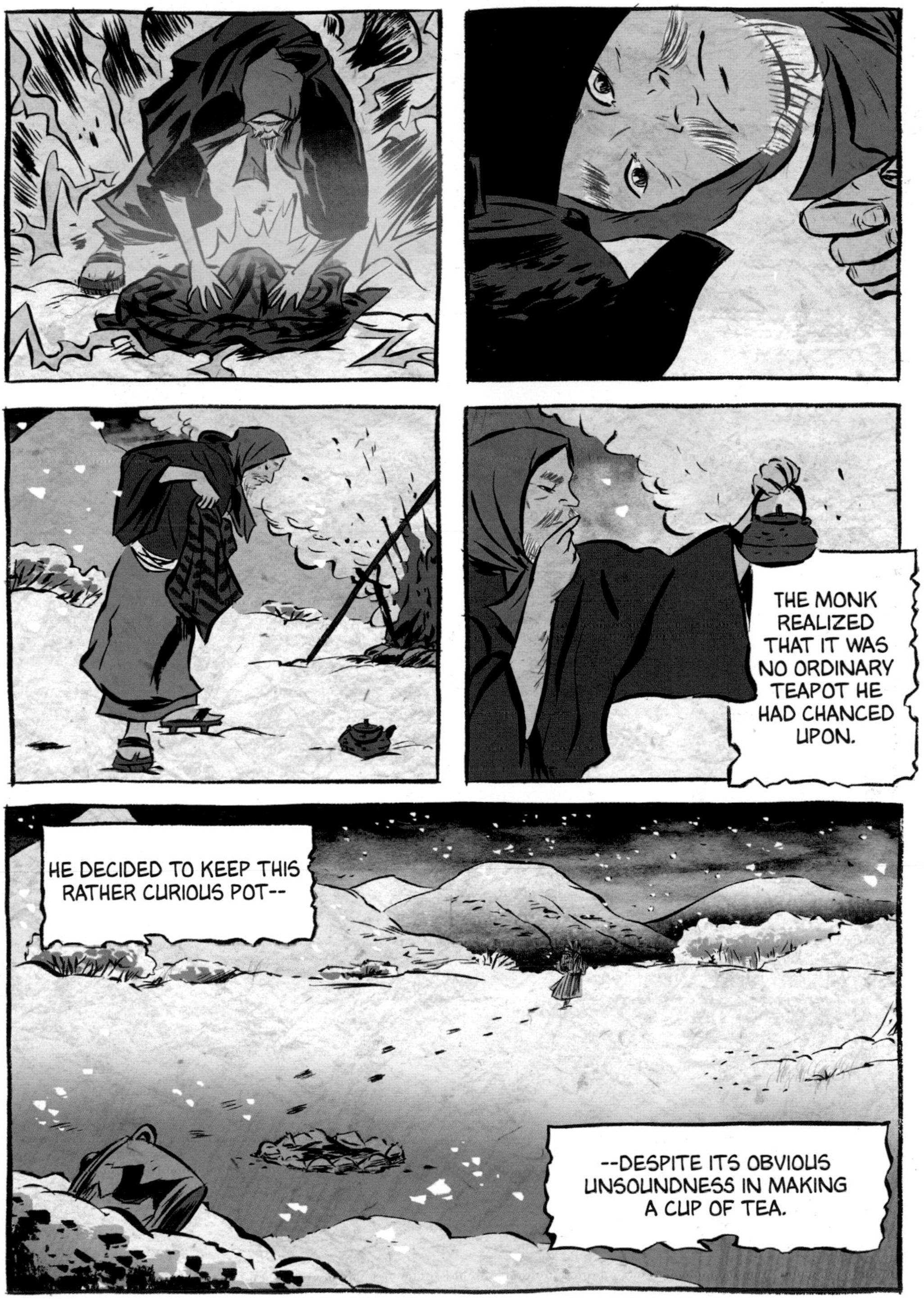
THE MONK REALIZED THAT IT WAS NO ORDINARY TEAPOT HE HAD CHANCED UPON.
HE DECIDED TO KEEP THIS RATHER CURIOUS POT--
--DESPITE ITS OBVIOUS UNSOUNDNESS IN MAKING A CUP OF TEA.

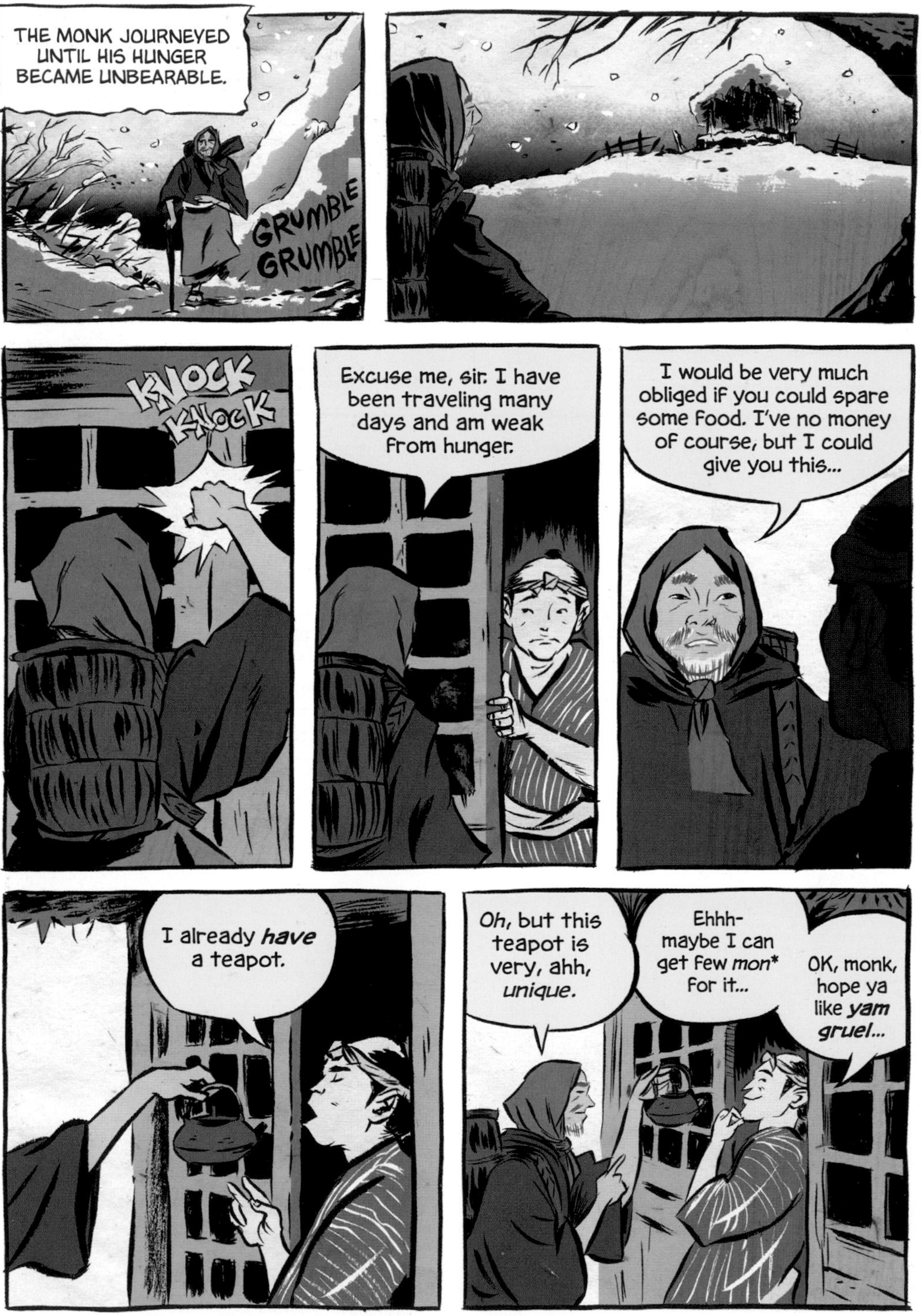
THE MONK JOURNEYED UNTIL HIS HUNGER BECAME UNBEARABLE.
GRUMBLE GRUMBLE
KNOCK KNOCK
Excuse me, sir. I have been traveling many days and am weak from hunger.
I would be very much obliged if you could spare some food. I've no money of course, but I could give you this...
I already *have* a teapot.
Oh, but this teapot is very, ahh, *unique*.
Ehhh- maybe I can get few *mon** for it...
OK, monk, hope ya like ***yam gruel***...

**Mon* were copper coins used in feudal Japan.

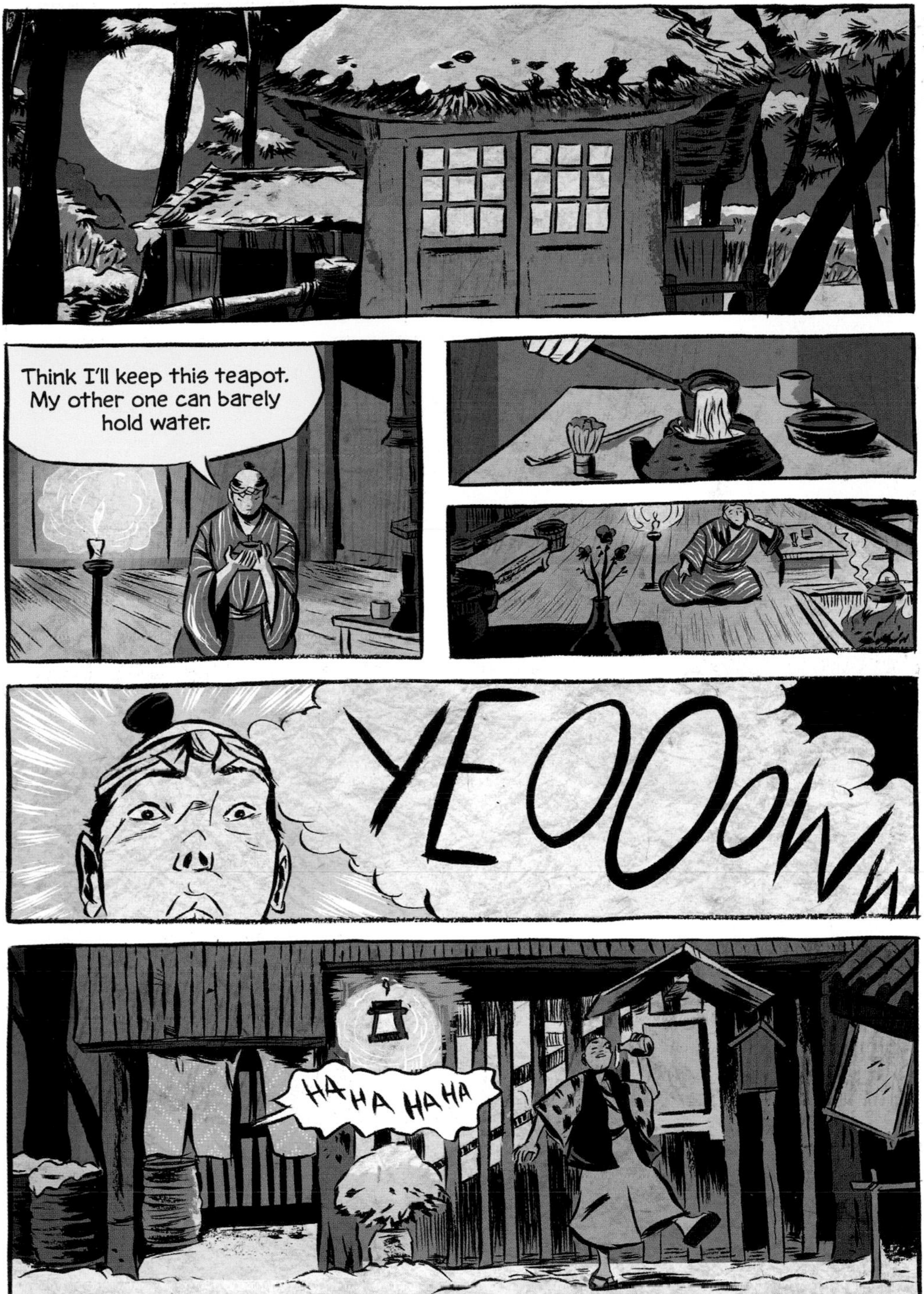
Think I'll keep this teapot. My other one can barely hold water.
YEOOOWW
HAHA HAHAHA

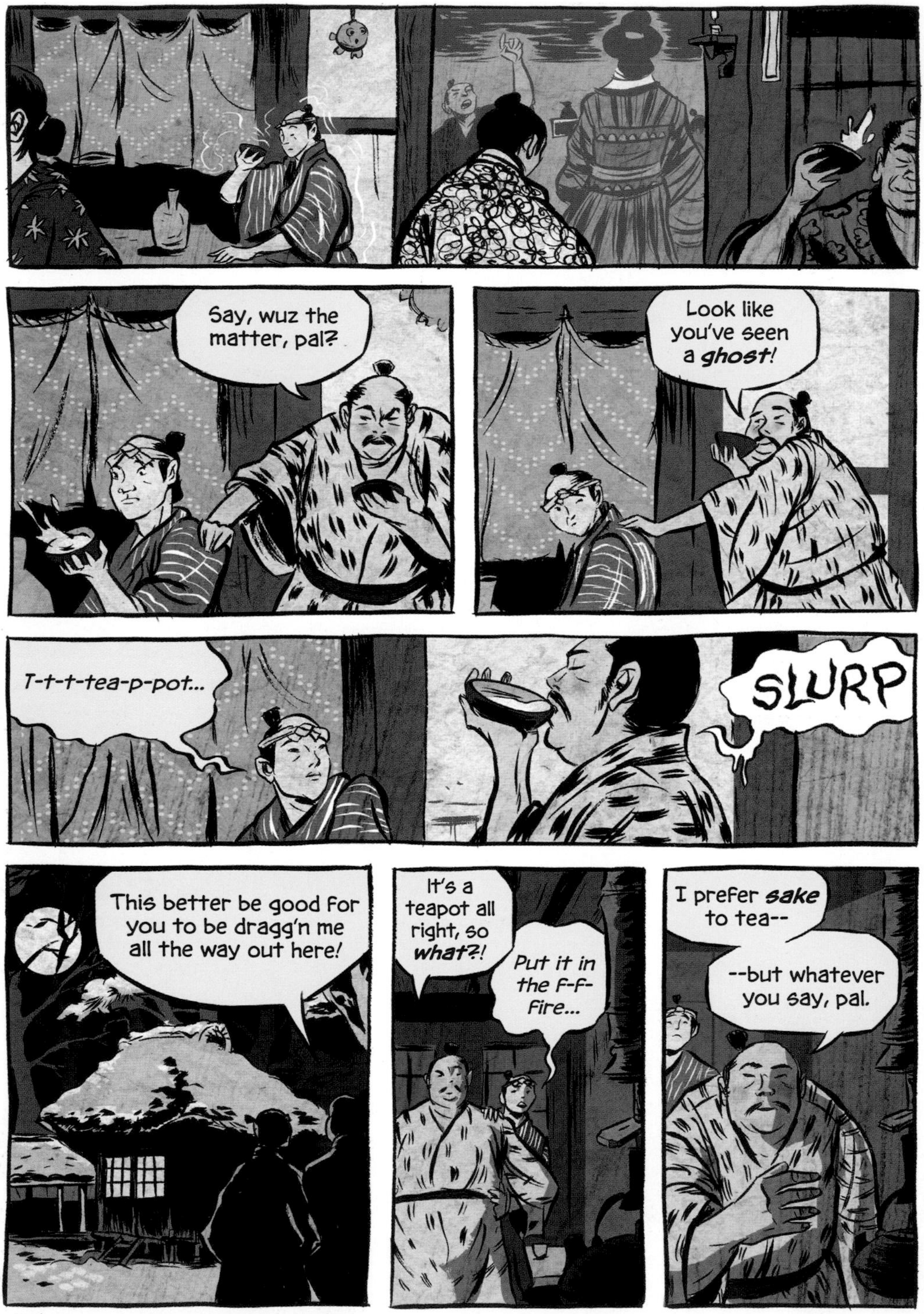
Say, wuz the matter, pal?
Look like you've seen a ghost!
T-t-t-tea-p-pot...
SLURP
This better be good for you to be dragg'n me all the way out here!
It's a teapot all right, so what?!
Put it in the f-f-fire...
I prefer sake to tea--
--but whatever you say, pal.

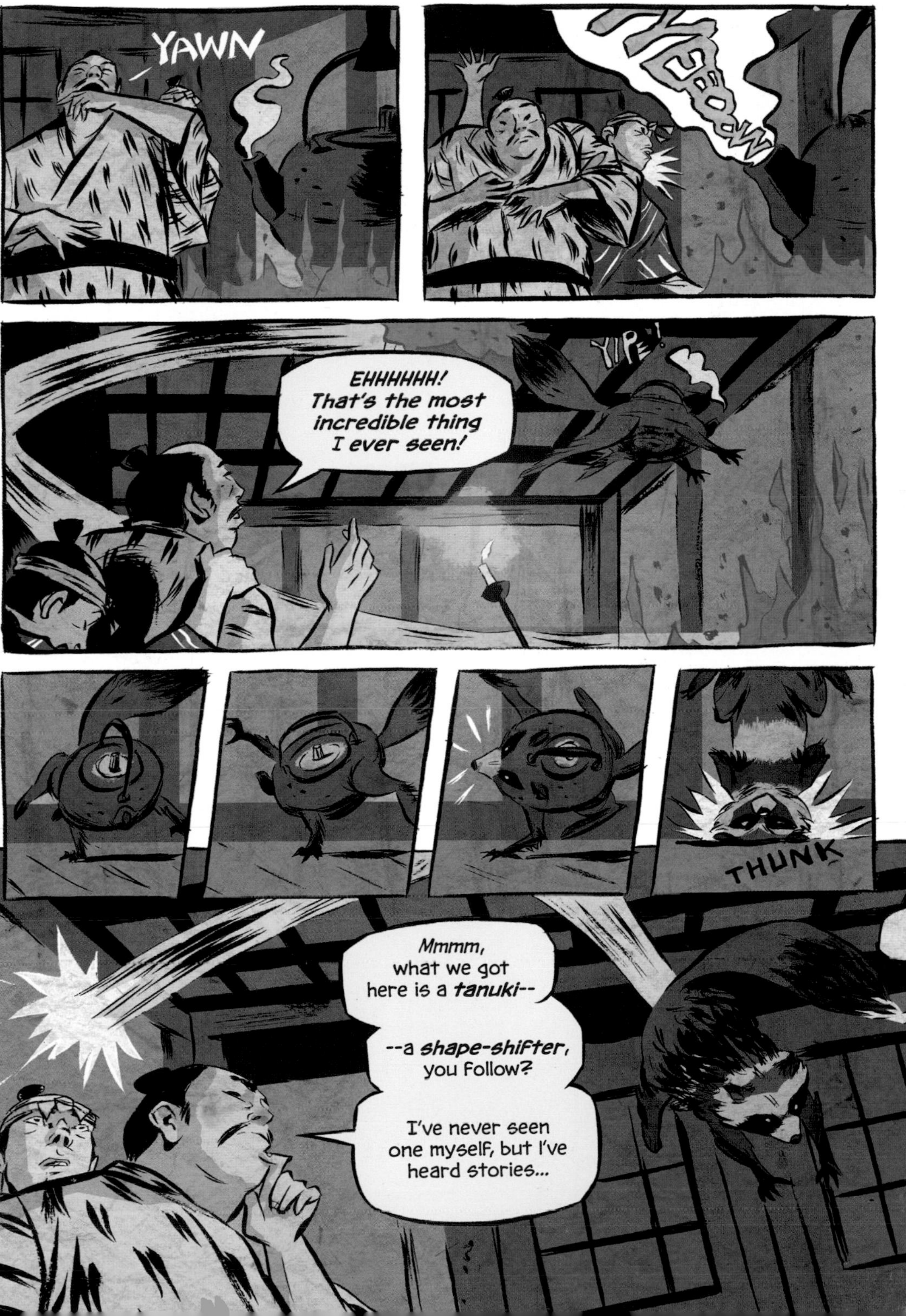
YAWN
EHHHHHH!
That's the most incredible thing I ever seen!
YIPE!
THUNK
Mmmm, what we got here is a *tanuki*--
--a *shape-shifter*, you follow?
I've never seen one myself, but I've heard stories...

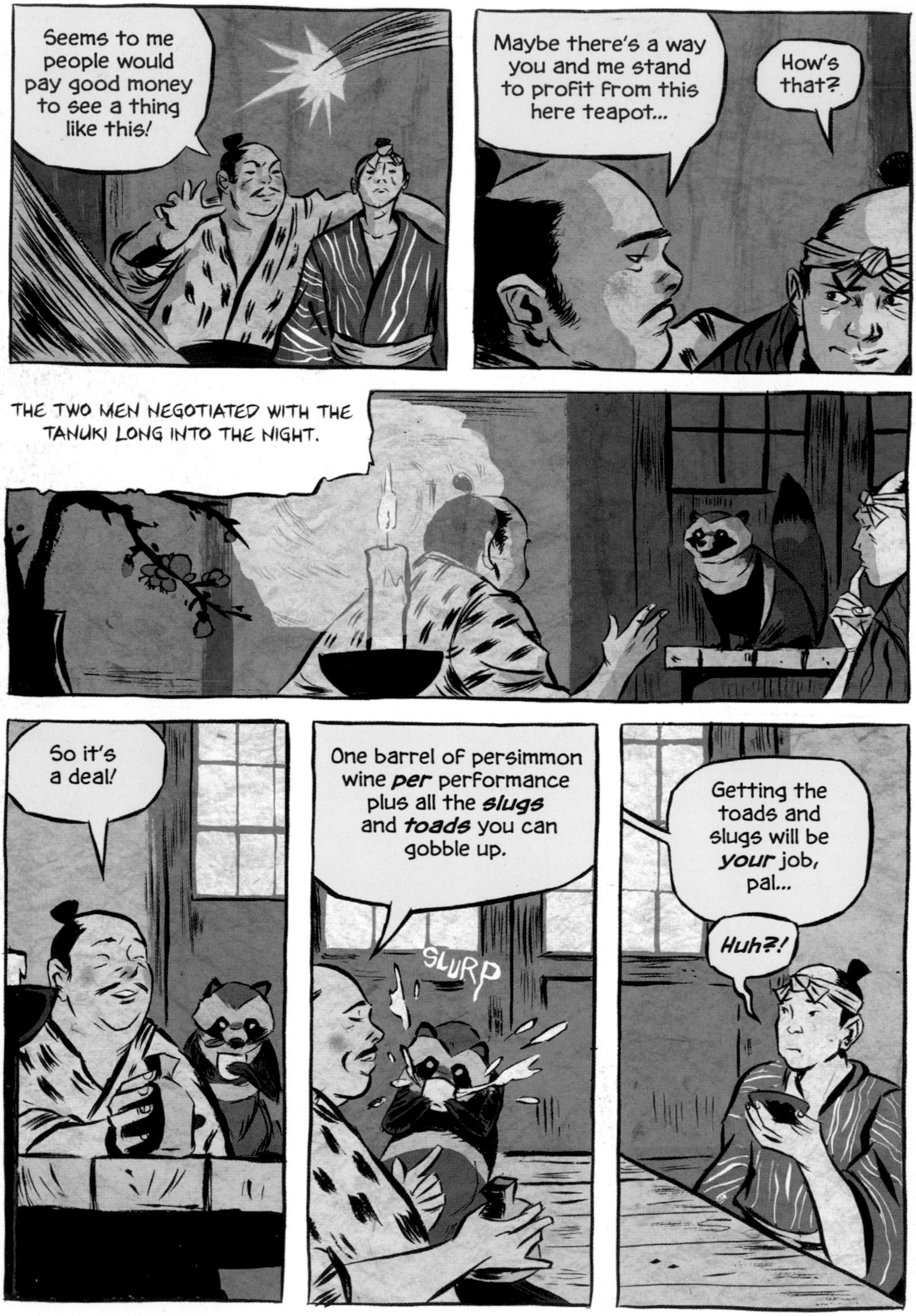
Seems to me people would pay good money to see a thing like this!
Maybe there's a way you and me stand to profit from this here teapot...
How's that?
THE TWO MEN NEGOTIATED WITH THE TANUKI LONG INTO THE NIGHT.
So it's a deal!
One barrel of persimmon wine *per* performance plus all the *slugs* and *toads* you can gobble up.
SLURP
Getting the toads and slugs will be *your* job, pal...
Huh?!

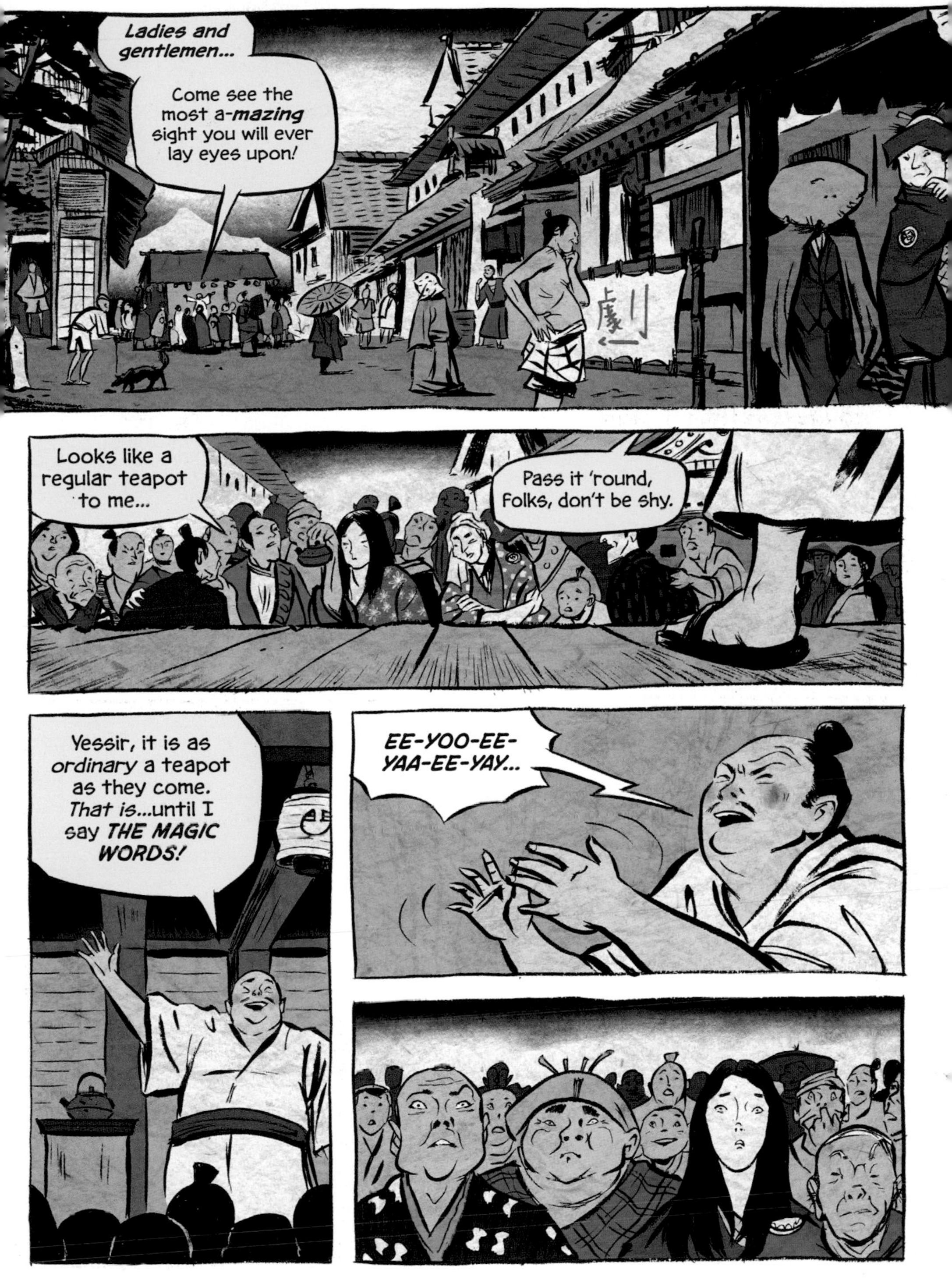
Ladies and gentlemen...
Come see the most a-mazing sight you will ever lay eyes upon!
Looks like a regular teapot to me...
Pass it 'round, folks, don't be shy.
Yessir, it is as ordinary a teapot as they come. That is...until I say THE MAGIC WORDS!
EE-YOO-EE-YAA-EE-YAY...

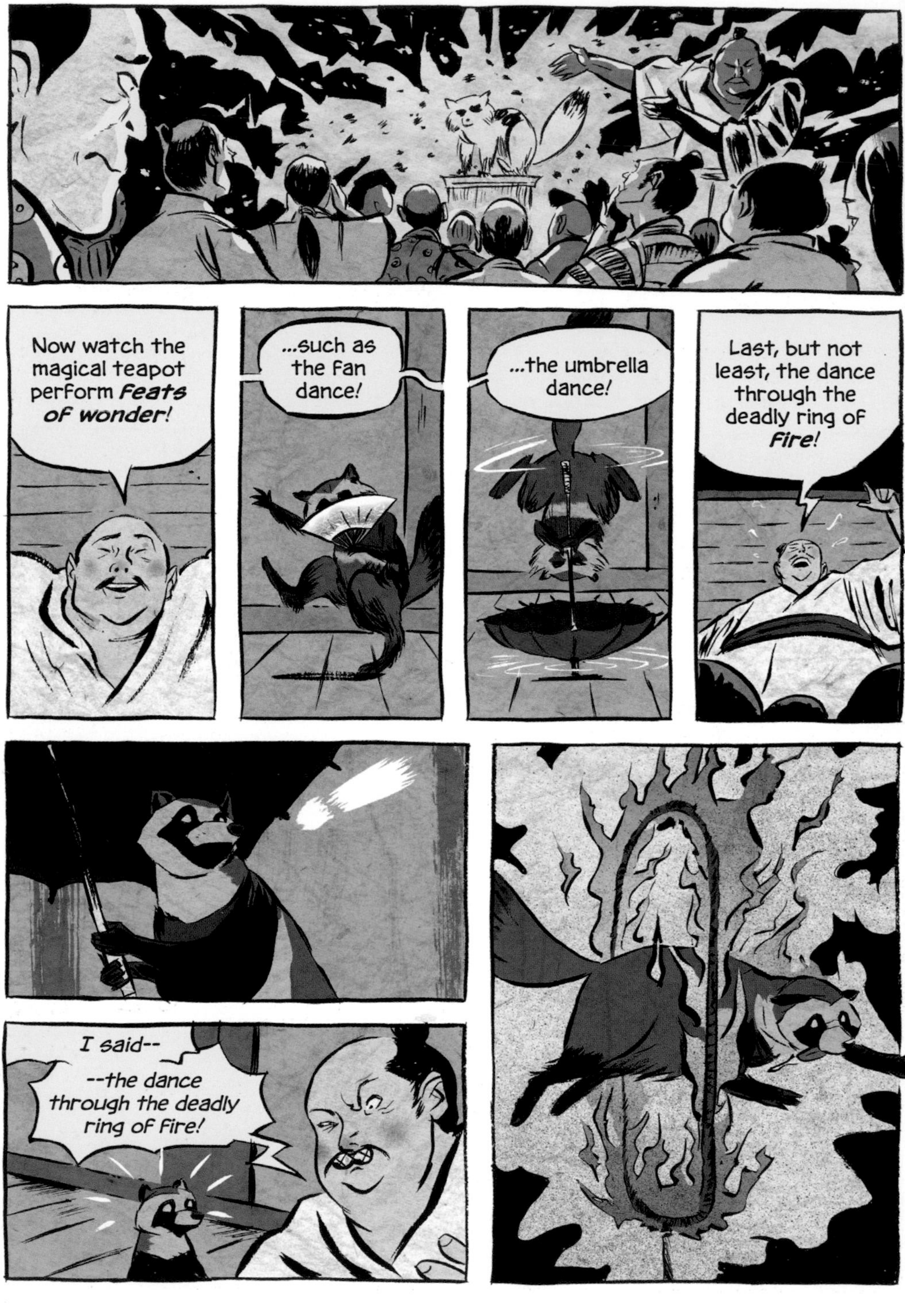
Now watch the magical teapot perform Feats of wonder!
...such as the fan dance!
...the umbrella dance!
Last, but not least, the dance through the deadly ring of Fire!
I said--
--the dance through the deadly ring of Fire!

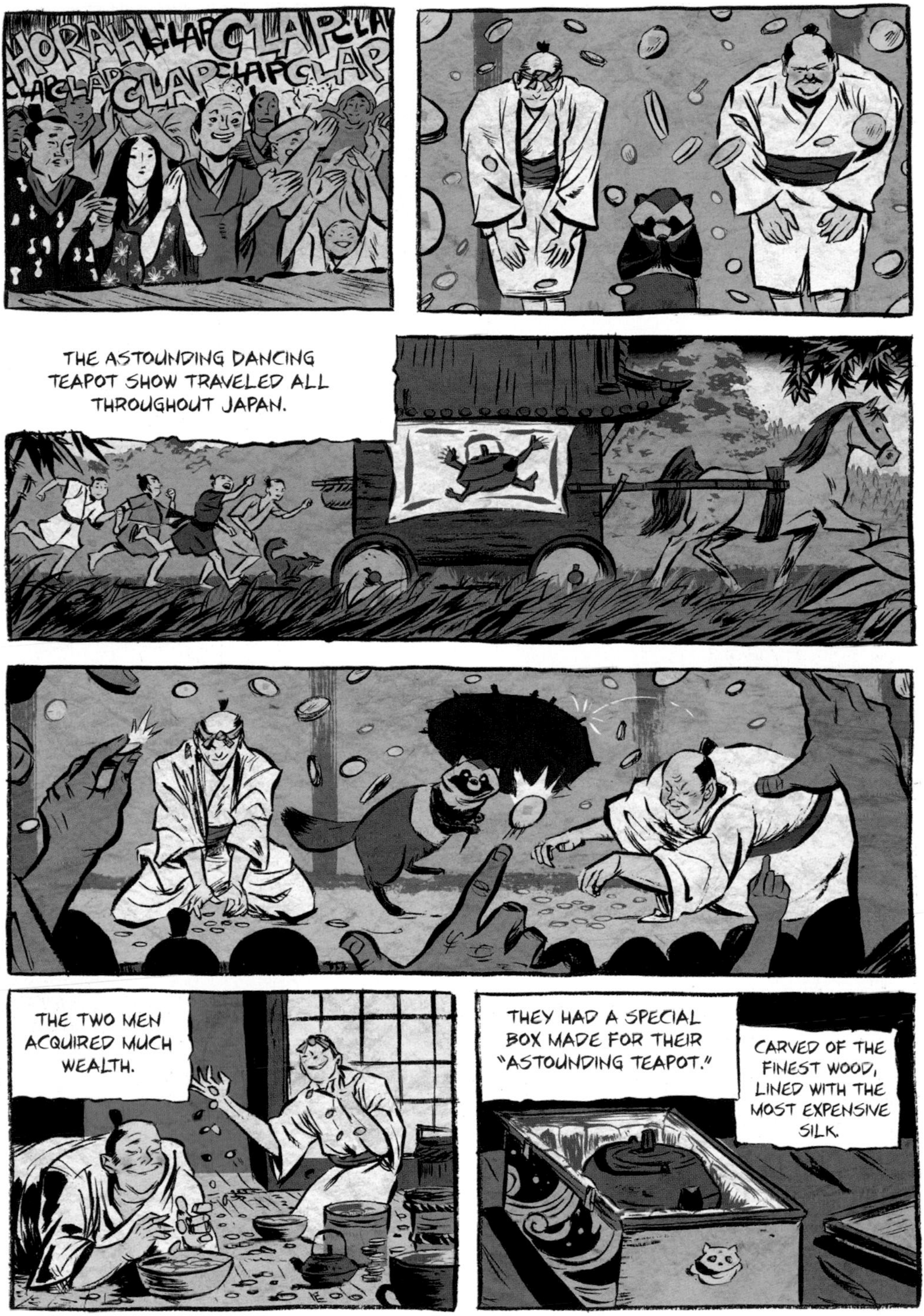
HORAH!
CLAP CLAP CLAP
CLAP CLAP CLAP CLAP CLAP CLAP
THE ASTOUNDING DANCING TEAPOT SHOW TRAVELED ALL THROUGHOUT JAPAN.
THE TWO MEN ACQUIRED MUCH WEALTH.
THEY HAD A SPECIAL BOX MADE FOR THEIR "ASTOUNDING TEAPOT."
CARVED OF THE FINEST WOOD, LINED WITH THE MOST EXPENSIVE SILK.

IN TIME, THE MEN GREW WEARY OF TRAVELING ENDLESS NIGHTS ON THE ROAD. CONTENT WITH THE FORTUNE THEY HAD GATHERED, THE PARTNERS DECIDED TO CALL IT QUITS. AND SO ENDED THE ASTOUNDING TEAPOT SHOW.

AS TALES OF THIS SORT USUALLY END...

...THEY LIVED HAPPILY EVER AFTER.

BUT THAT WAS *NOT* THE END OF THE TEAPOT.

YEARS OF PERFORMING HAD TAKEN THEIR TOLL ON THE TANUKI AS WELL.

SO HE DECIDED TO TAKE A LONG, WELL-DESERVED NAP.

OF THE TWO MEN, ONLY ONE HAD SURVIVED TO TELL THE TALE OF THE TEAPOT'S MAGICAL PROPERTIES.

BUT THE ONLY THING "ASTOUNDING" NOW WAS HOW RIDICULOUS THE OLD MAN'S STORY SOUNDED.

YARNS OF ENCHANTED DANCING NOT WITHSTANDING, THE TEAPOT WAS STILL REGARDED AS A FAMILY HEIRLOOM.

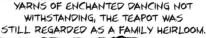

AND SO, WHEN THE OLD MAN DIED--

--IT WAS PASSED DOWN TO HIS FAMILY...

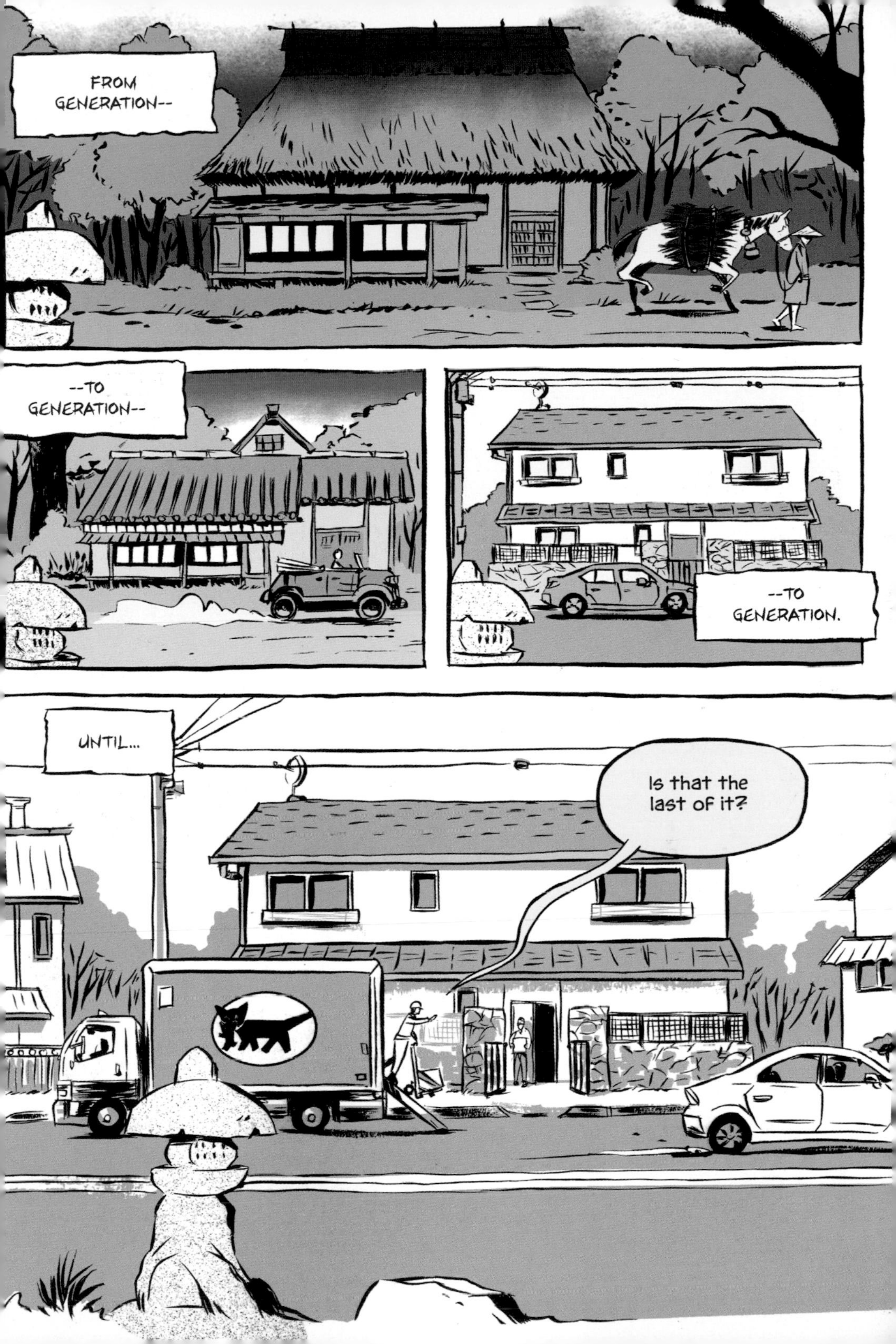
FROM GENERATION--
--TO GENERATION--
--TO GENERATION.
UNTIL...
Is that the last of it?

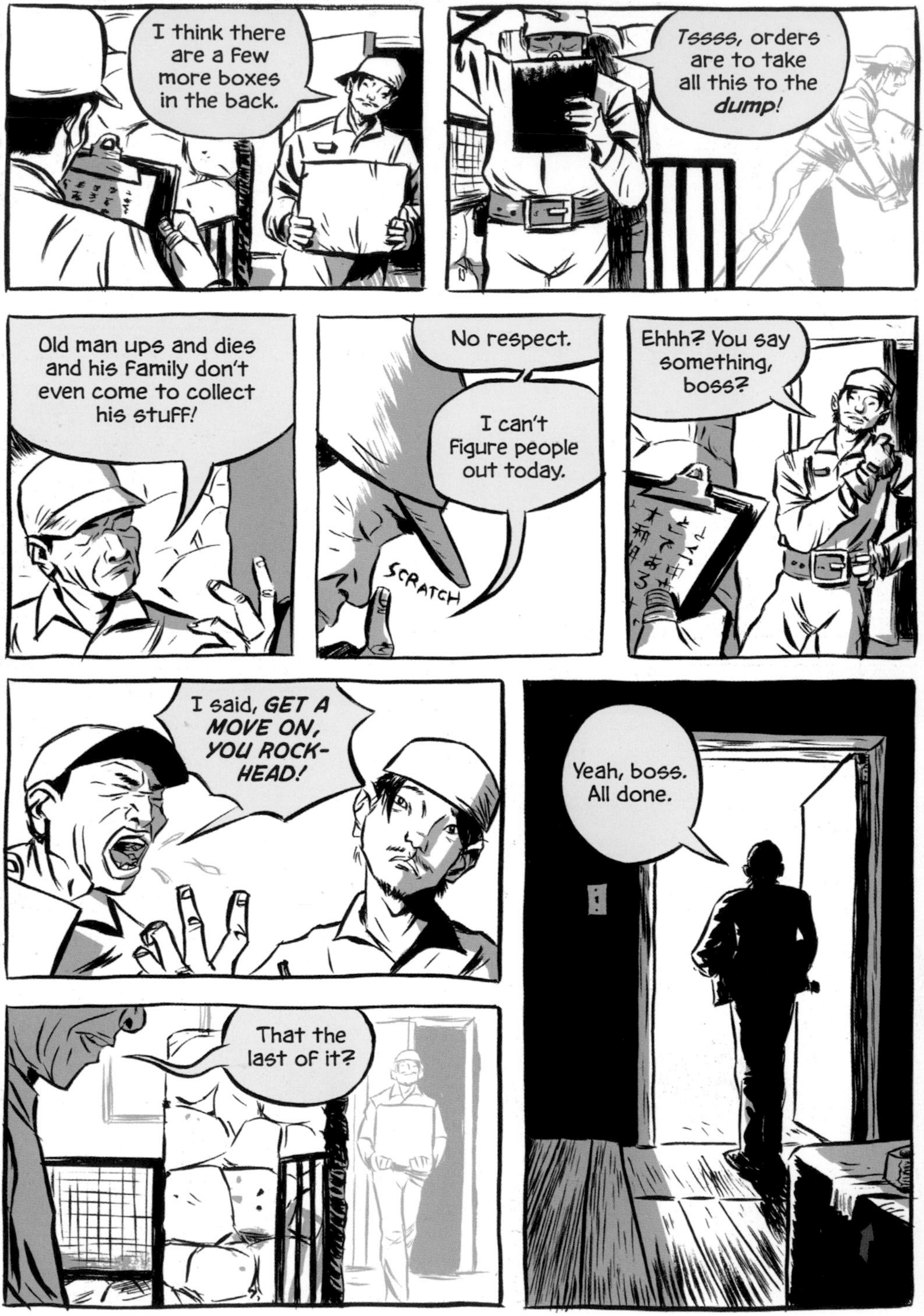
I think there are a few more boxes in the back.
Tssss, orders are to take all this to the dump!
Old man ups and dies and his family don't even come to collect his stuff!
No respect.
I can't figure people out today.
SCRATCH
Ehhh? You say something, boss?
I said, GET A MOVE ON, YOU ROCK-HEAD!
That the last of it?
Yeah, boss. All done.

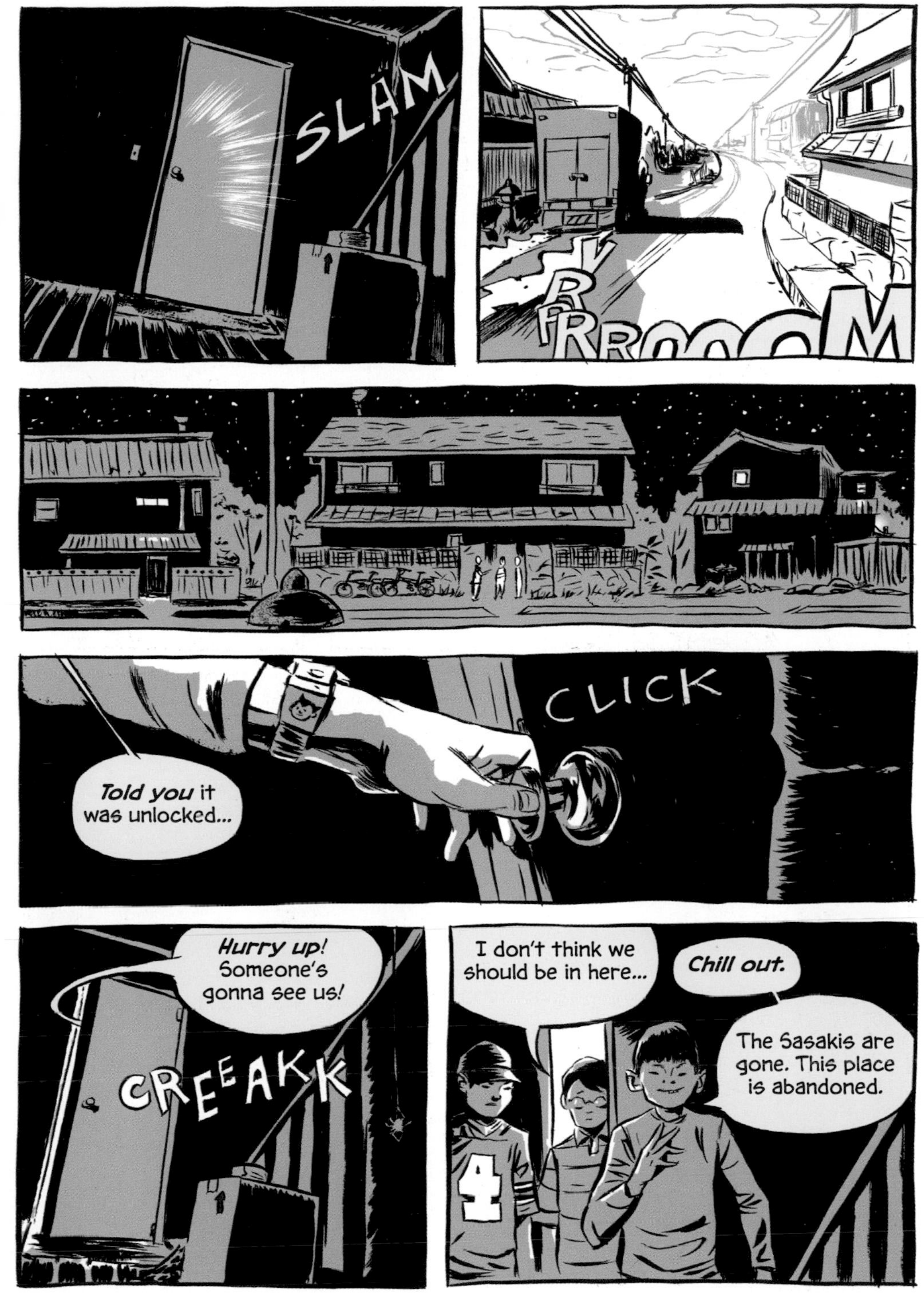
SLAM
VRRROOOOM
CLICK
Told you it was unlocked...
CREEAKK
Hurry up! Someone's gonna see us!
I don't think we should be in here...
Chill out.
The Sasakis are gone. This place is abandoned.

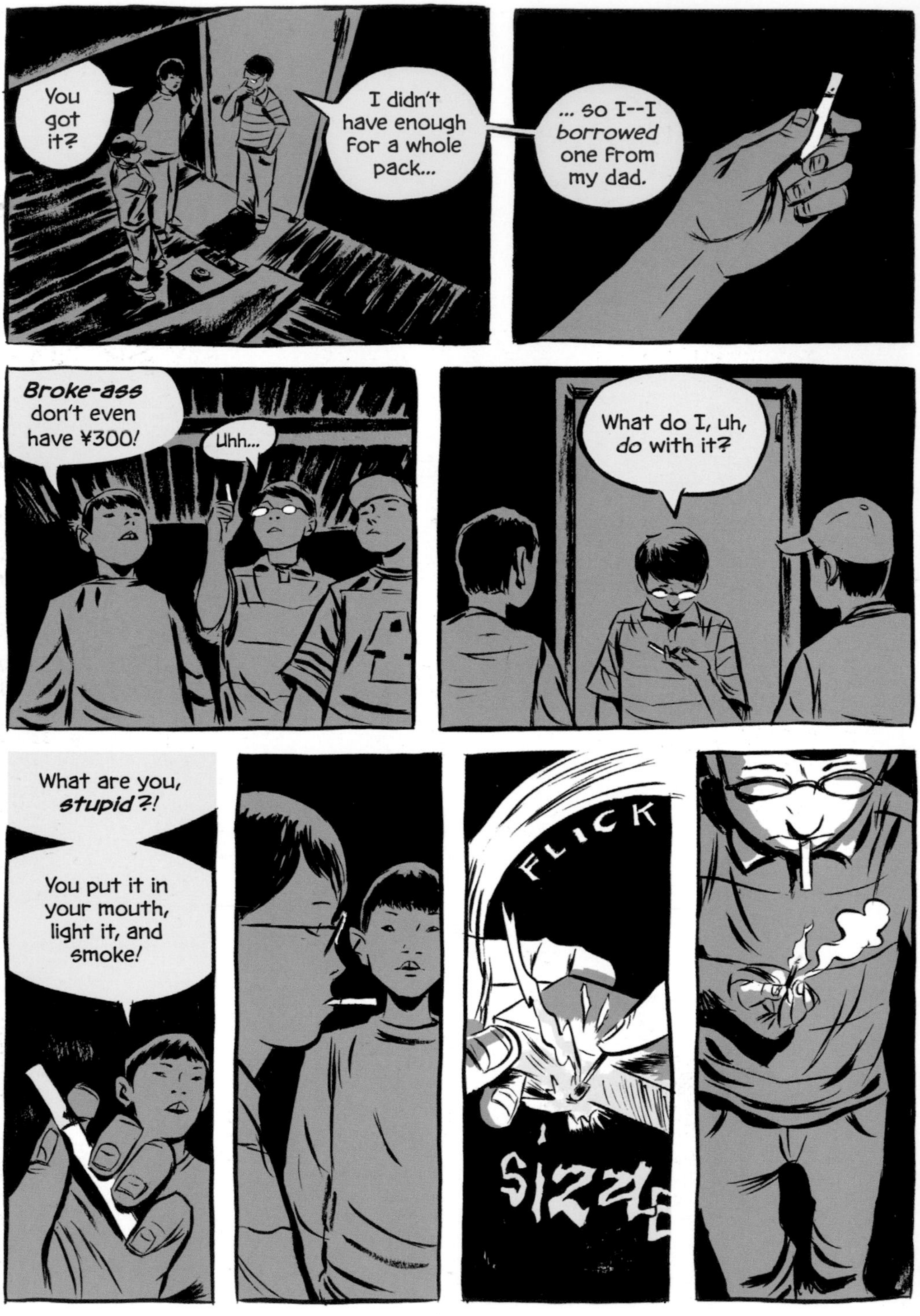

You got it?
I didn't have enough for a whole pack...
... so I--I *borrowed* one from my dad.
Broke-ass don't even have ¥300!
Uhh...
What do I, uh, *do* with it?
What are you, ***stupid***?!
You put it in your mouth, light it, and smoke!
FLICK
SIZZLE

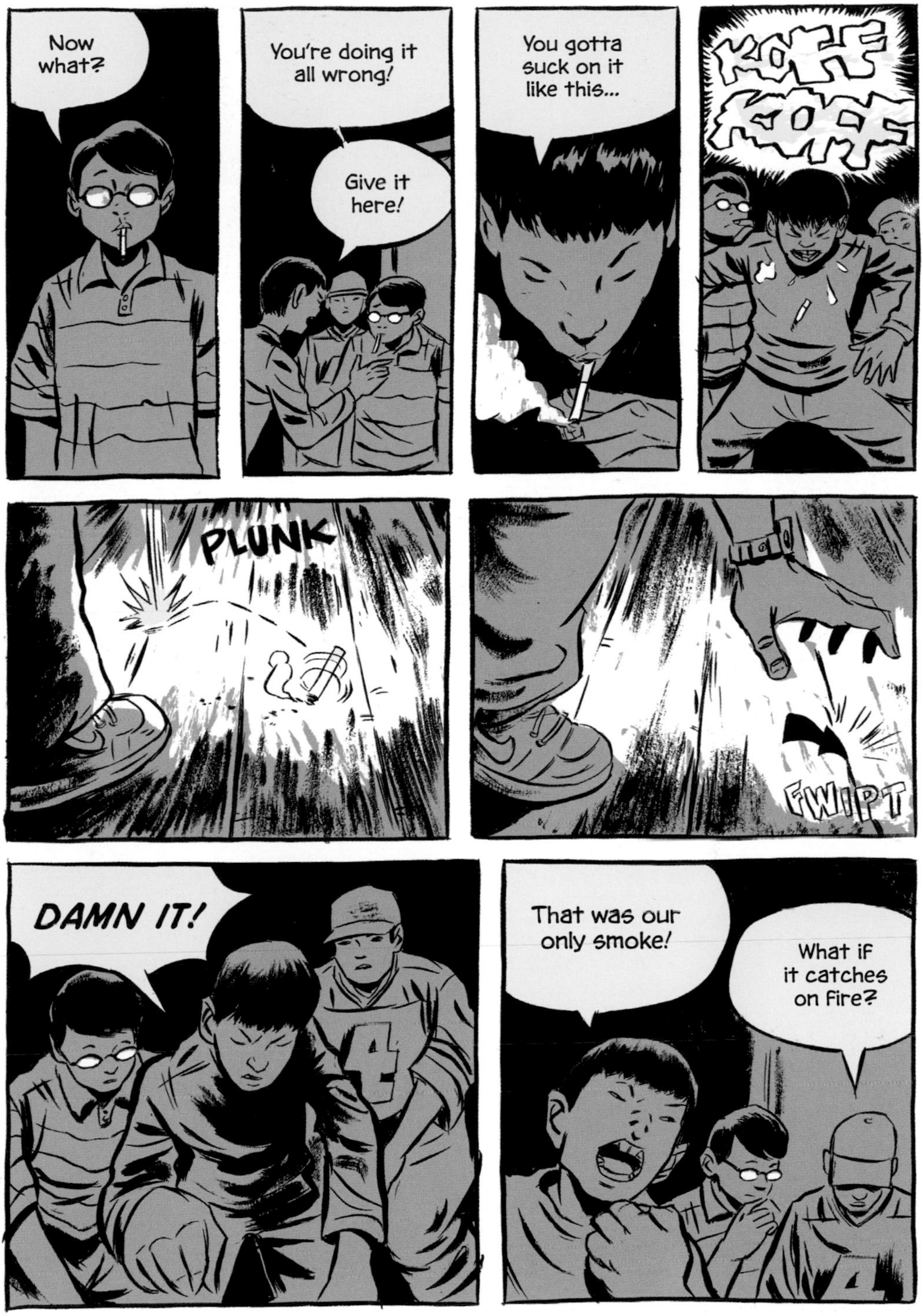
Now what?
You're doing it all wrong!
Give it here!
You gotta suck on it like this...
KOFF KOFF
PLUNK
FWIPT
DAMN IT!
That was our only smoke!
What if it catches on fire?

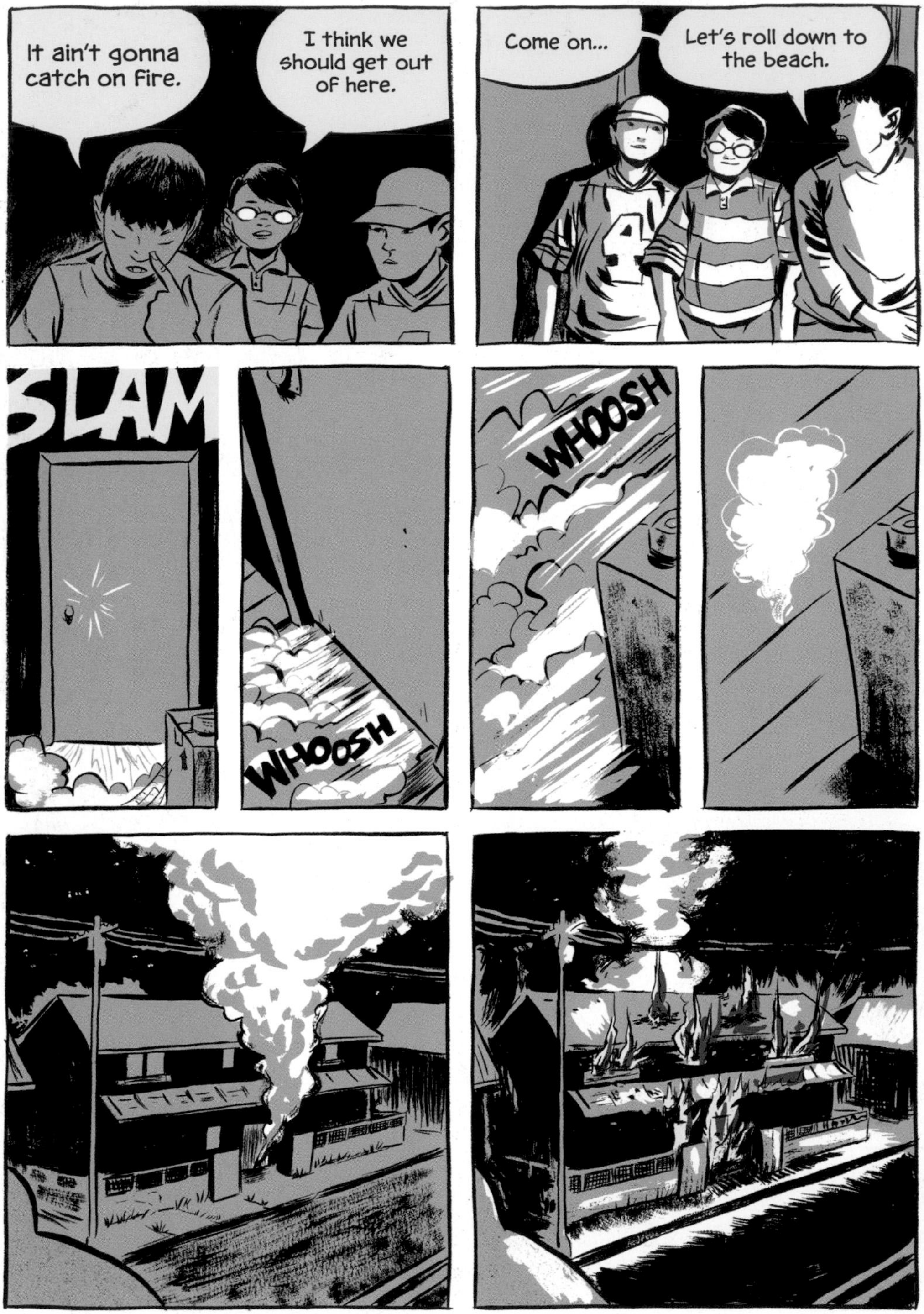
It ain't gonna catch on fire.
I think we should get out of here.
Come on...
Let's roll down to the beach.
SLAM
WHOOSH
WHOOSH

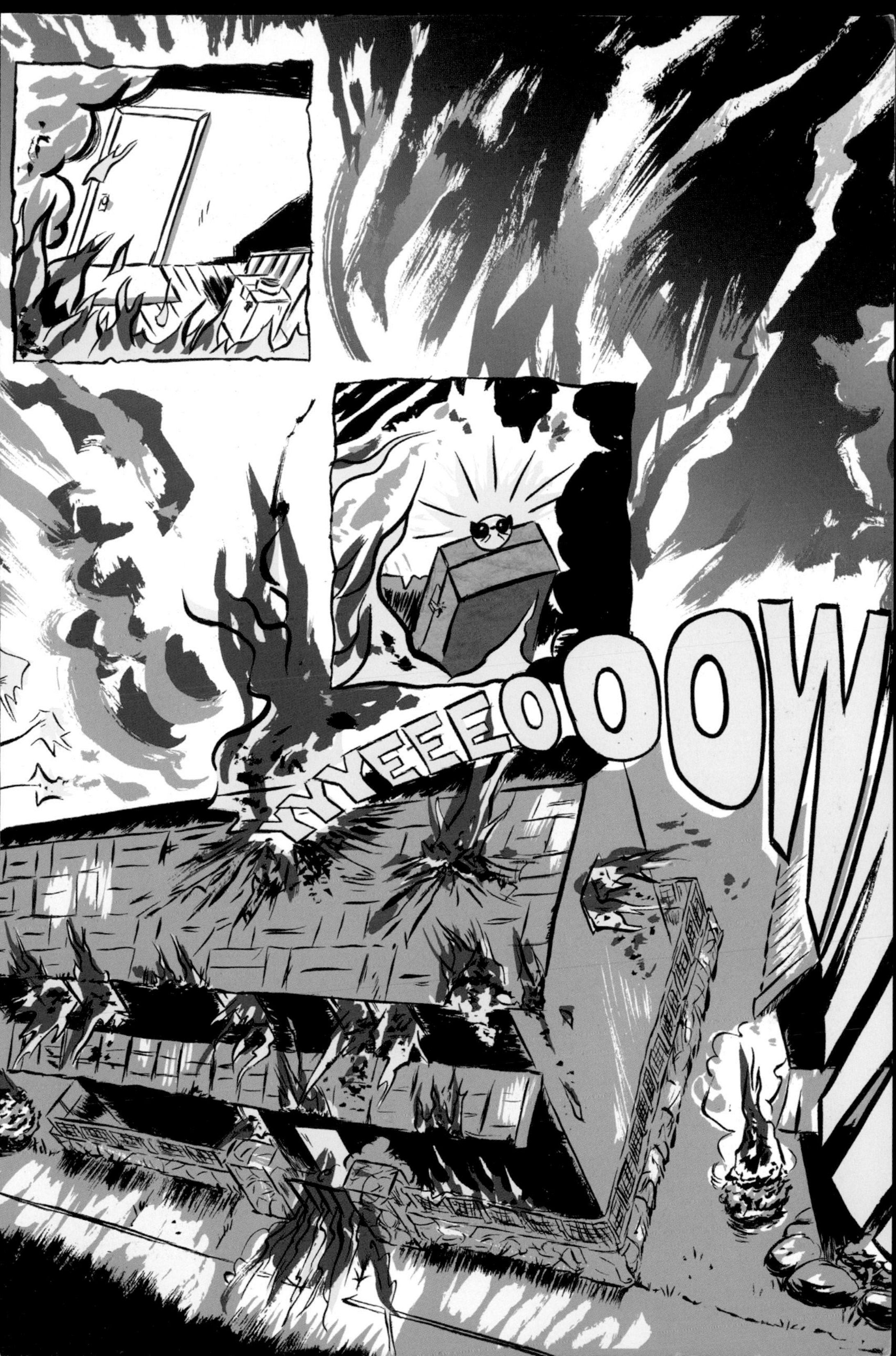
YEEEOOOOW

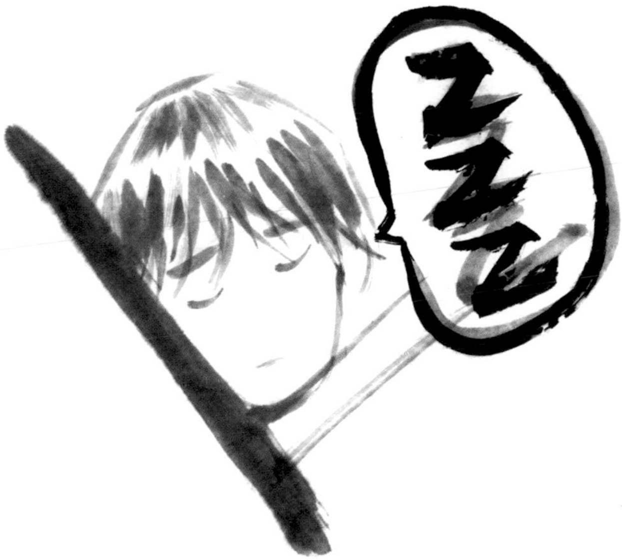
ZZZ

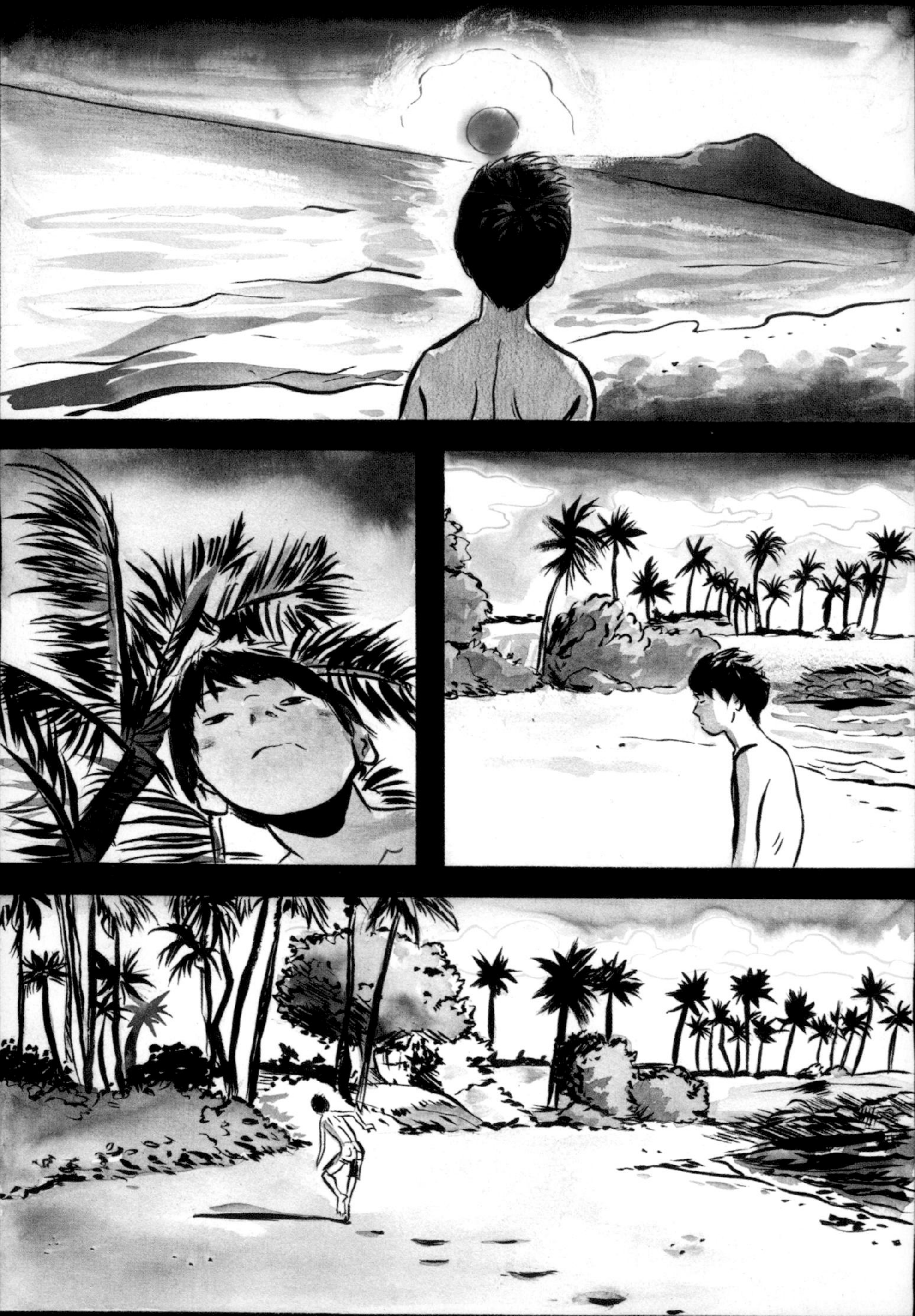

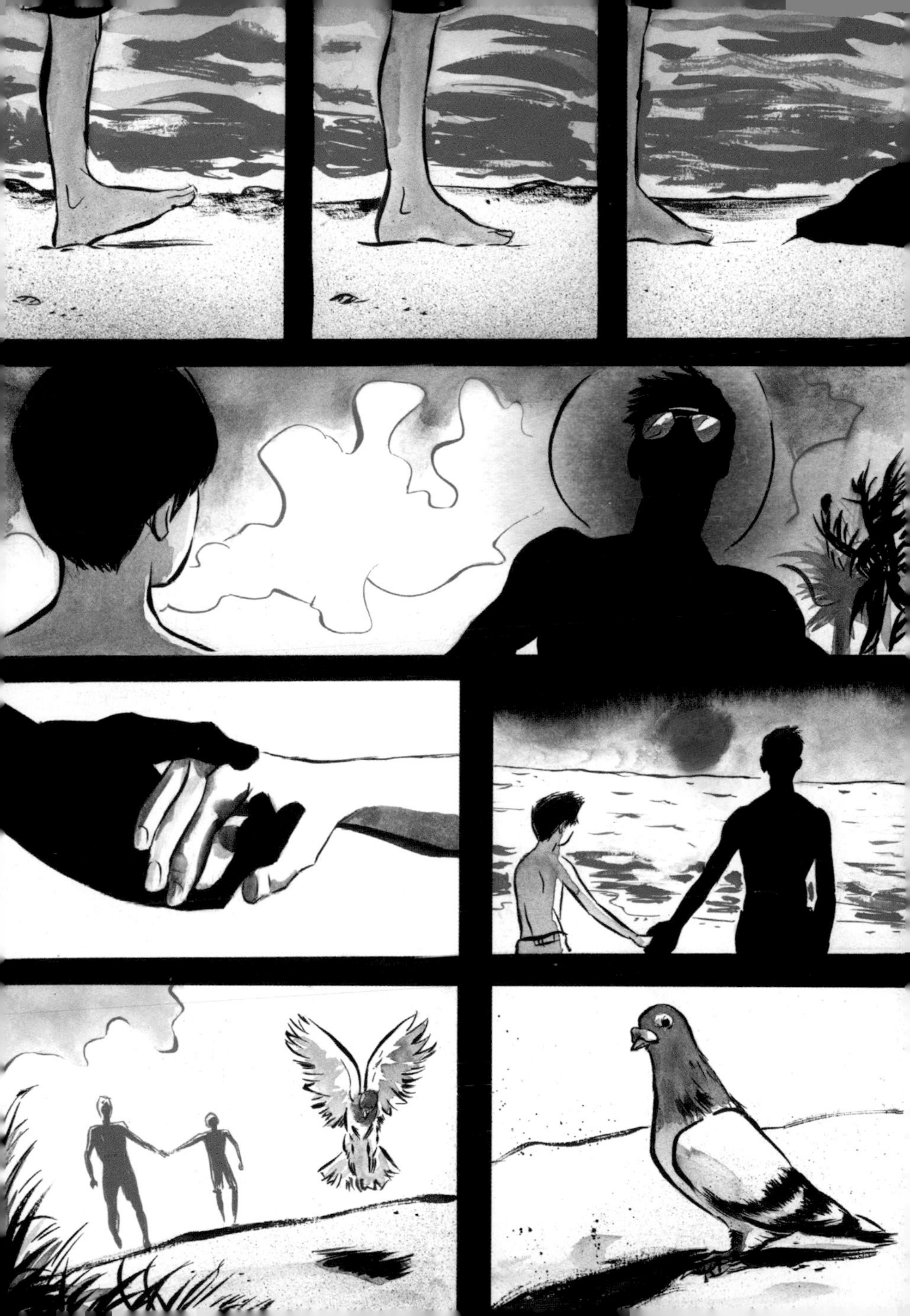

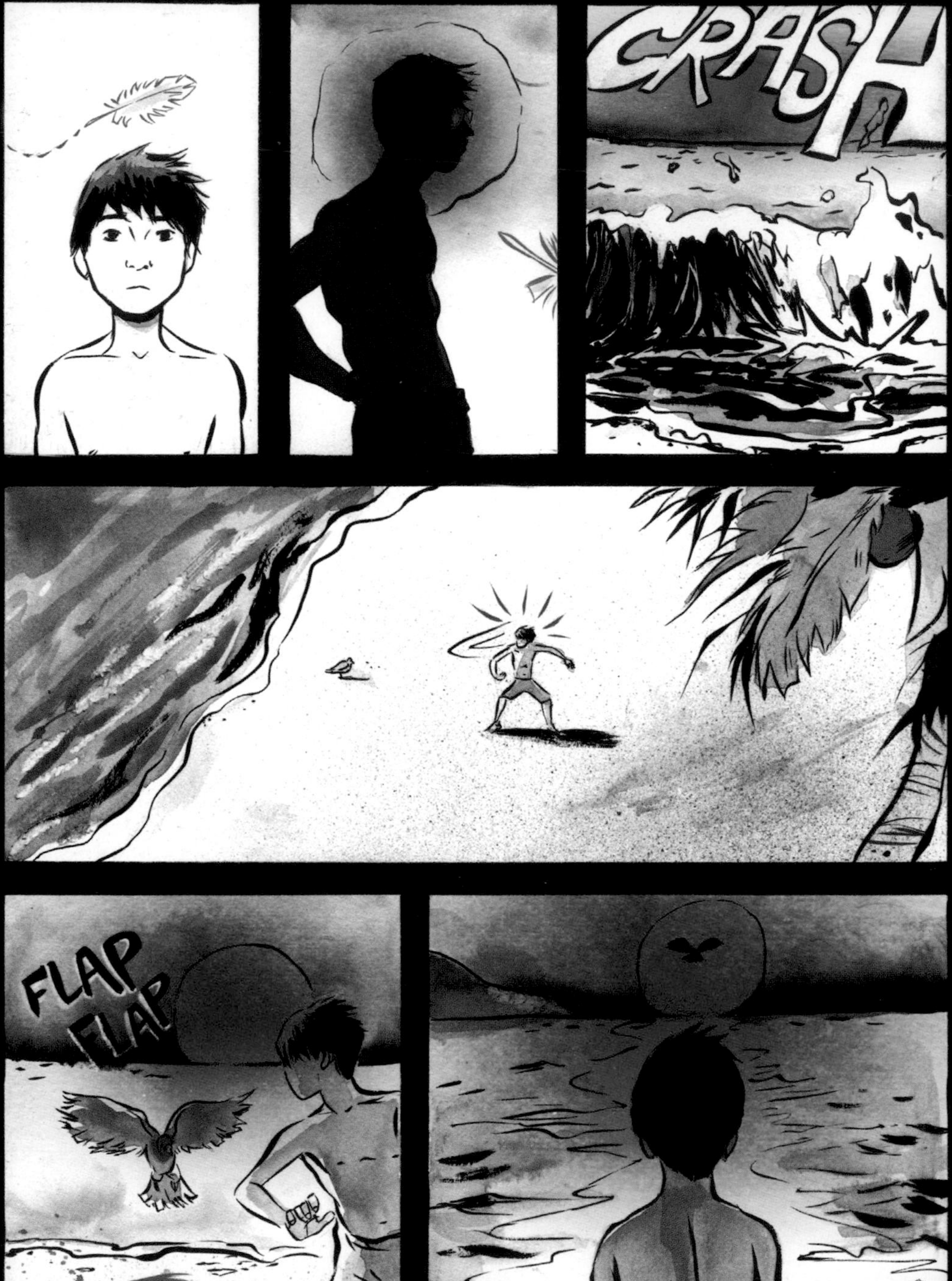
CRASH
FLAP
FLAP

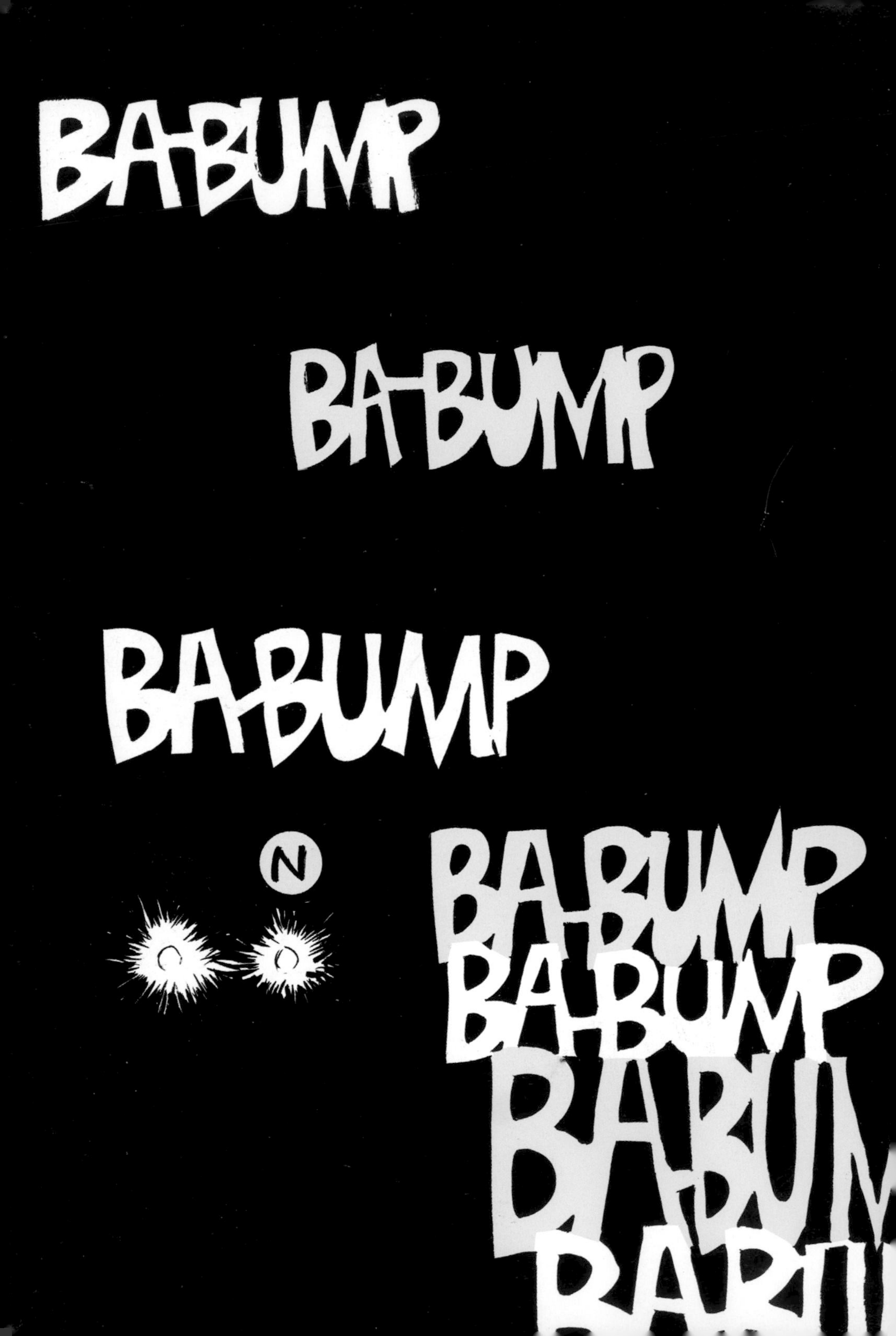

BA-BUMP

BA-BUMP

BA-BUMP

BA-BUMP
BA-BUMP
BABUM
BABUN
BABU

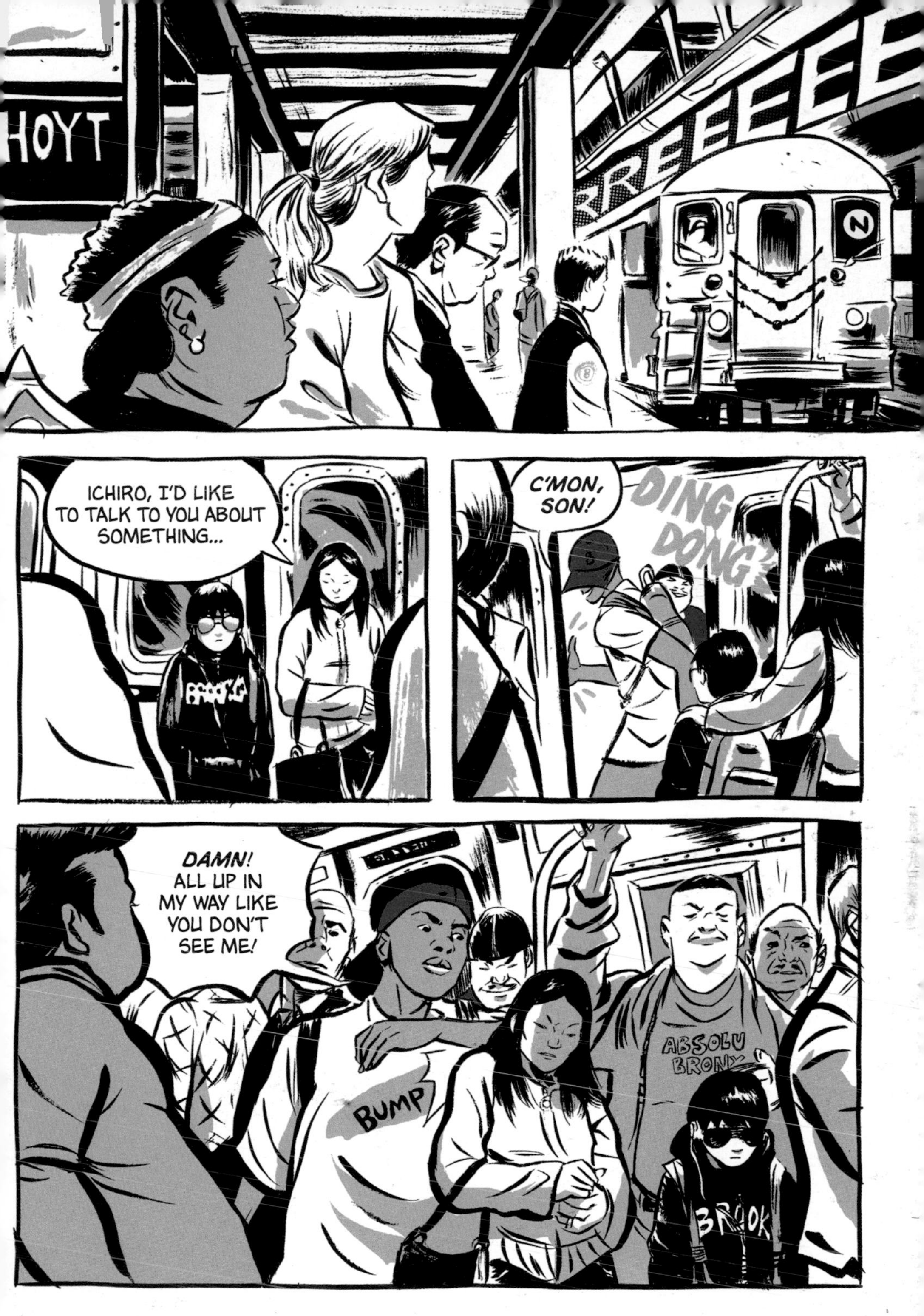
HOYT
REEEEEE
ICHIRO, I'D LIKE TO TALK TO YOU ABOUT SOMETHING...
C'MON, SON!
DING DONG
DAMN! ALL UP IN MY WAY LIKE YOU DON'T SEE ME!
ABSOLU BRONX
BUMP
BROOK

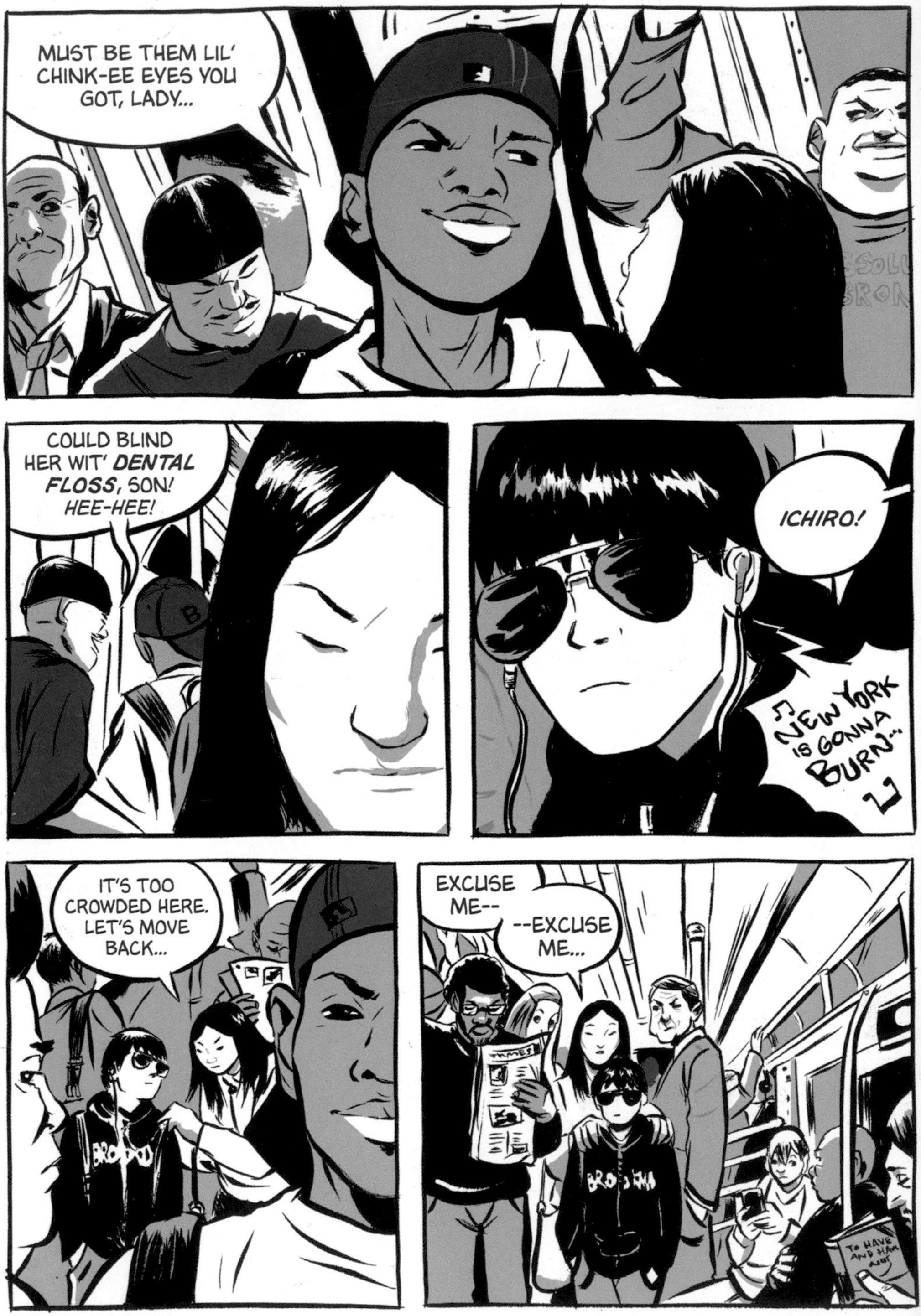
MUST BE THEM LIL' CHINK-EE EYES YOU GOT, LADY...
COULD BLIND HER WIT' DENTAL FLOSS, SON! HEE-HEE!
ICHIRO!
NEW YORK IS GONNA BURN...
IT'S TOO CROWDED HERE. LET'S MOVE BACK...
EXCUSE ME--
--EXCUSE ME...

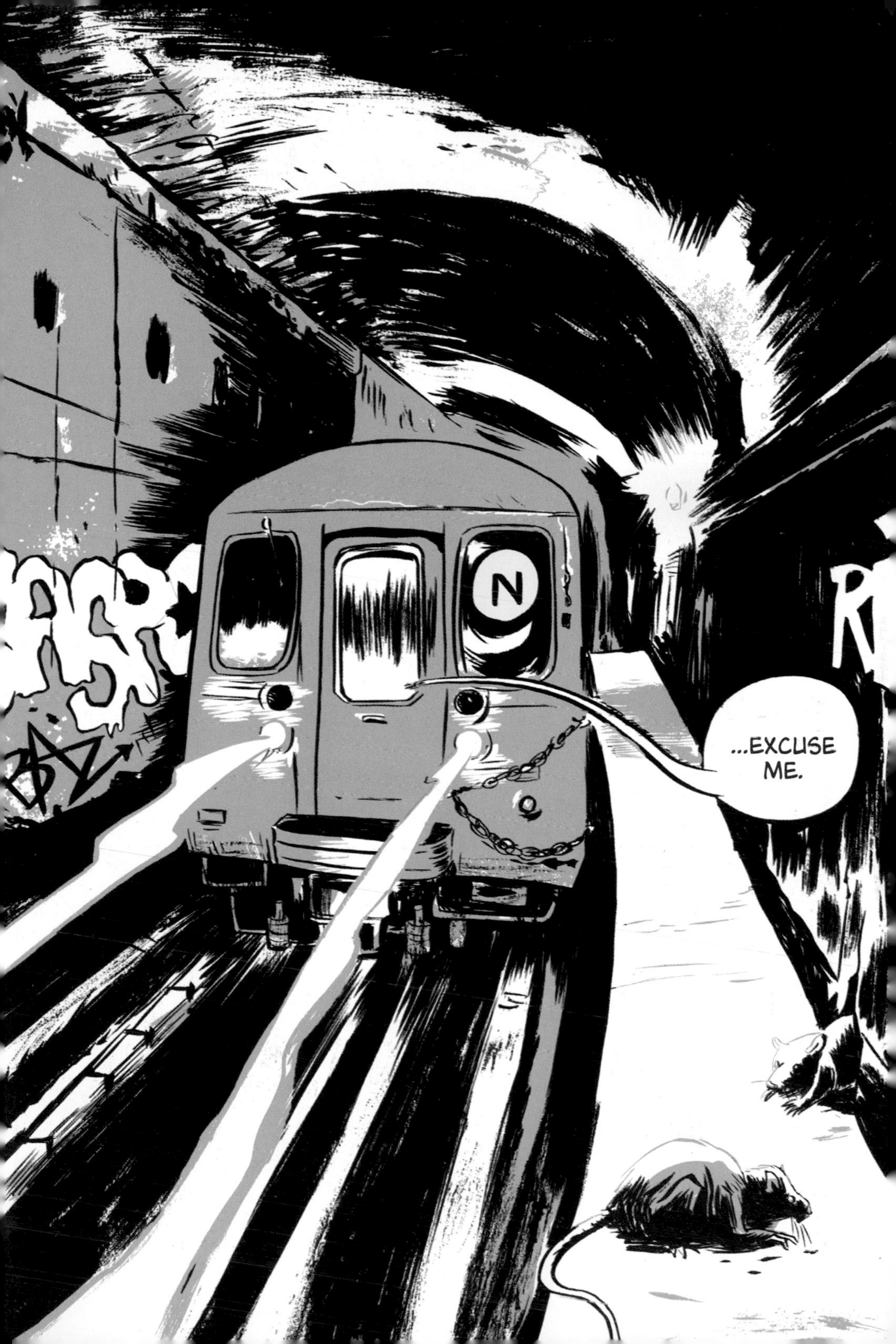
...EXCUSE ME.

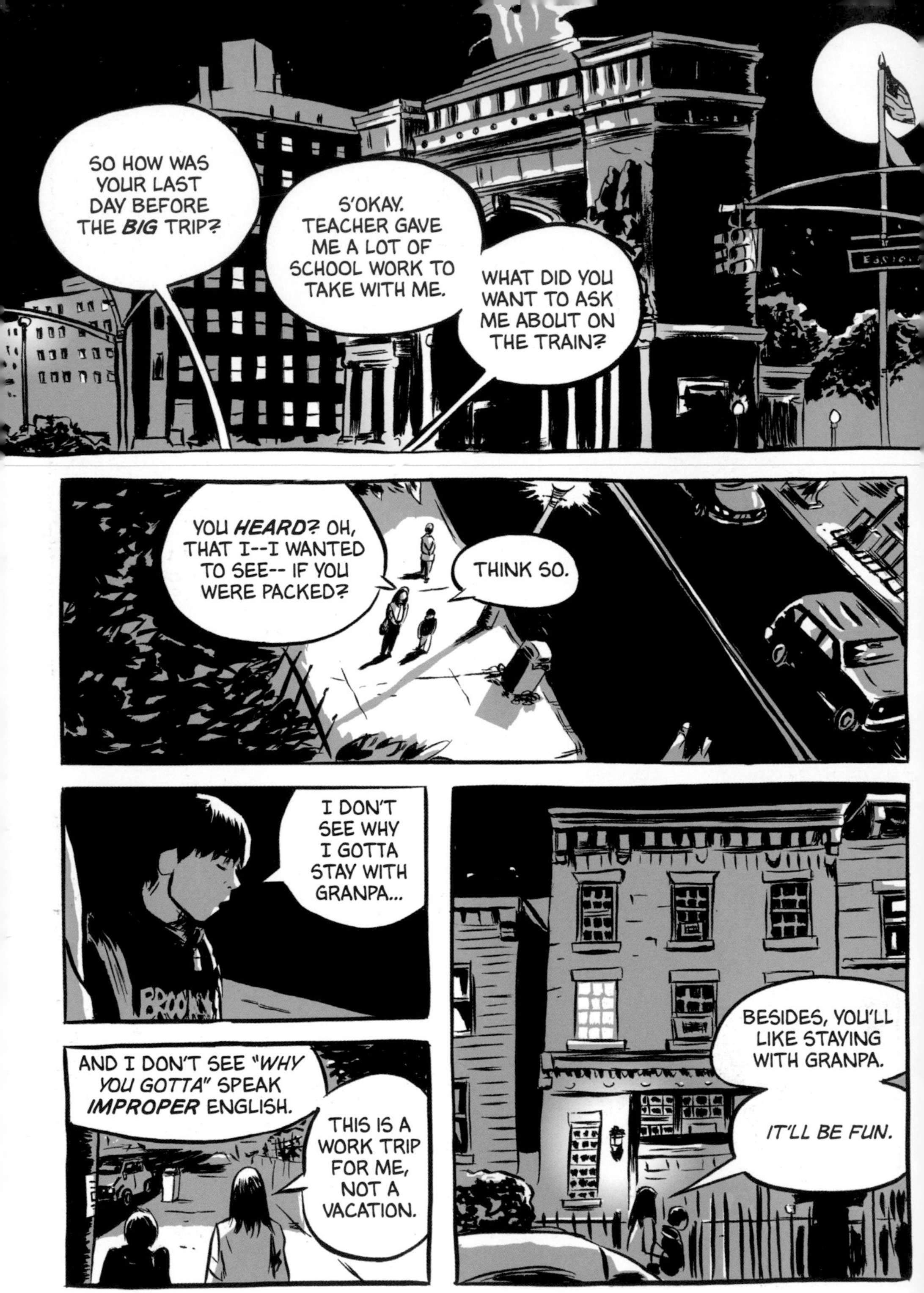

SO HOW WAS YOUR LAST DAY BEFORE THE *BIG* TRIP?
S'OKAY. TEACHER GAVE ME A LOT OF SCHOOL WORK TO TAKE WITH ME.
WHAT DID YOU WANT TO ASK ME ABOUT ON THE TRAIN?
YOU *HEARD*? OH, THAT I--I WANTED TO SEE-- IF YOU WERE PACKED?
THINK SO.
I DON'T SEE WHY I GOTTA STAY WITH GRANPA...
AND I DON'T SEE "*WHY YOU GOTTA*" SPEAK *IMPROPER* ENGLISH.
THIS IS A WORK TRIP FOR ME, NOT A VACATION.
BESIDES, YOU'LL LIKE STAYING WITH GRANPA.
IT'LL BE FUN.

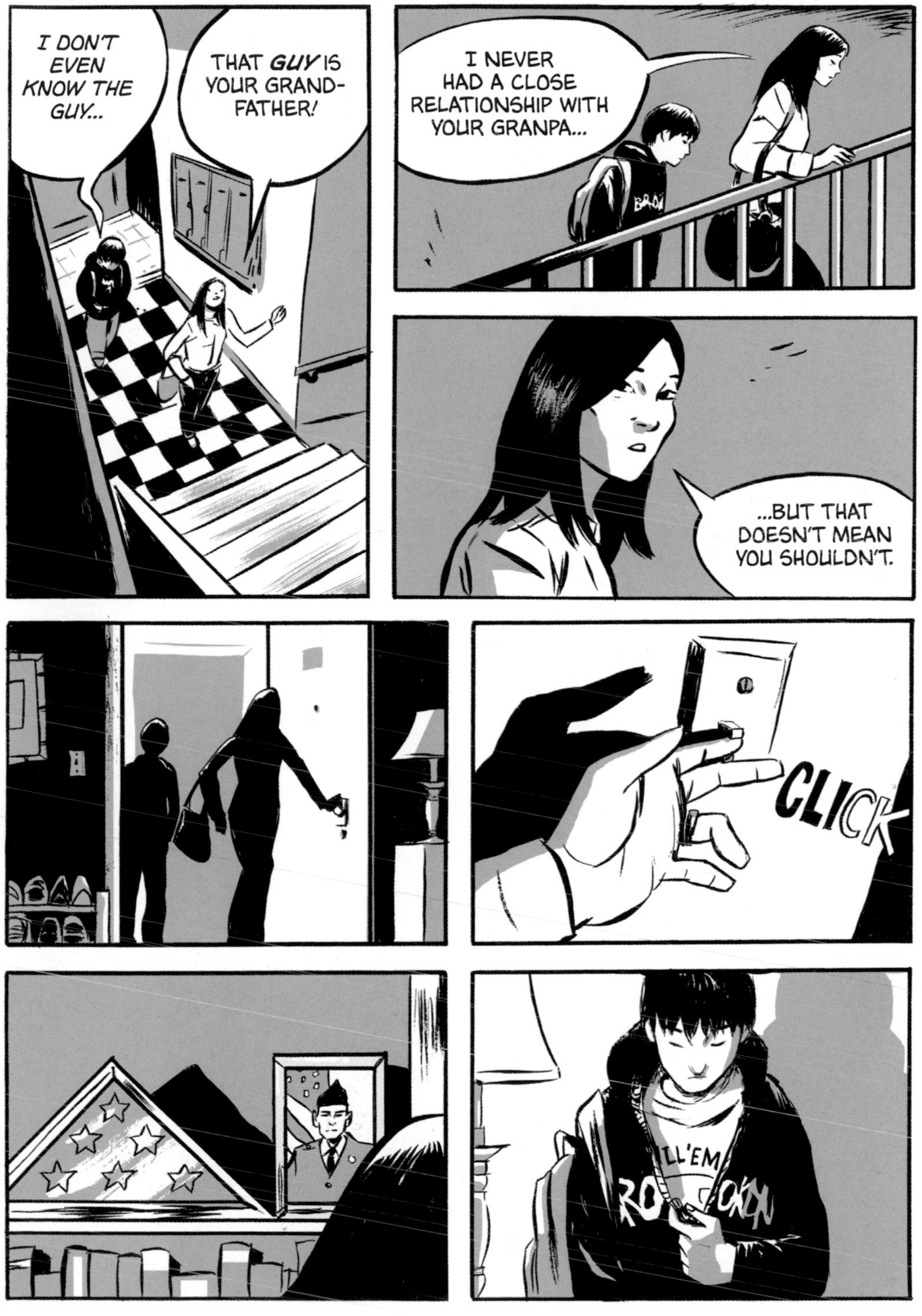
I DON'T EVEN KNOW THE GUY...
THAT *GUY* IS YOUR GRAND-FATHER!
I NEVER HAD A CLOSE RELATIONSHIP WITH YOUR GRANPA...
...BUT THAT DOESN'T MEAN YOU SHOULDN'T.
CLICK

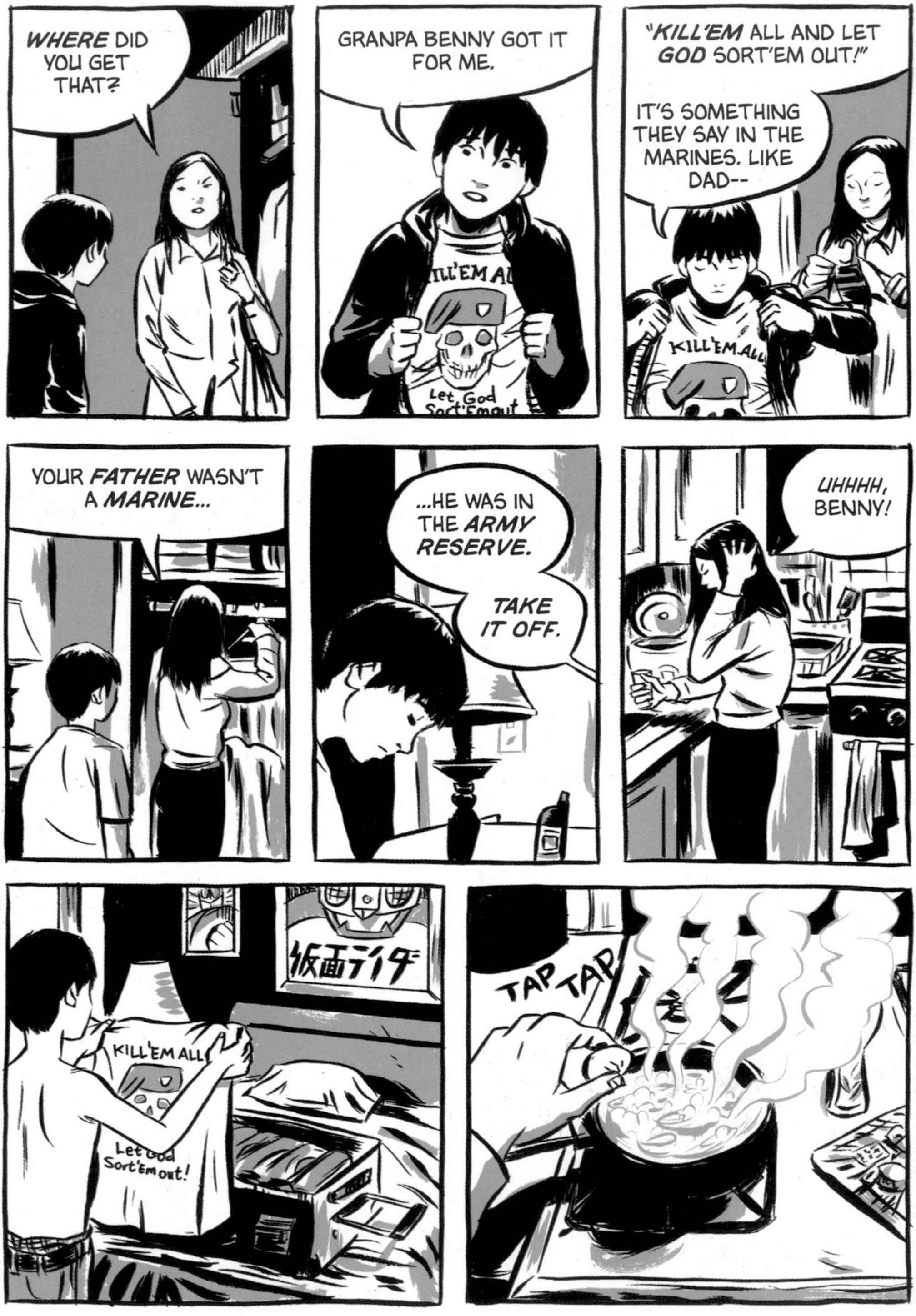
WHERE DID YOU GET THAT?
GRANPA BENNY GOT IT FOR ME.
KILL'EM AL
Let God Sort'Em out
"*KILL'EM* ALL AND LET *GOD* SORT'EM OUT!"
IT'S SOMETHING THEY SAY IN THE MARINES. LIKE DAD--
KILL'EM ALL
YOUR *FATHER* WASN'T A *MARINE*...
...HE WAS IN THE *ARMY RESERVE.*
TAKE IT OFF.
UHHHH, BENNY!
KILL'EM ALL
Let God Sort'Em out!
仮面ライダ
TAP TAP

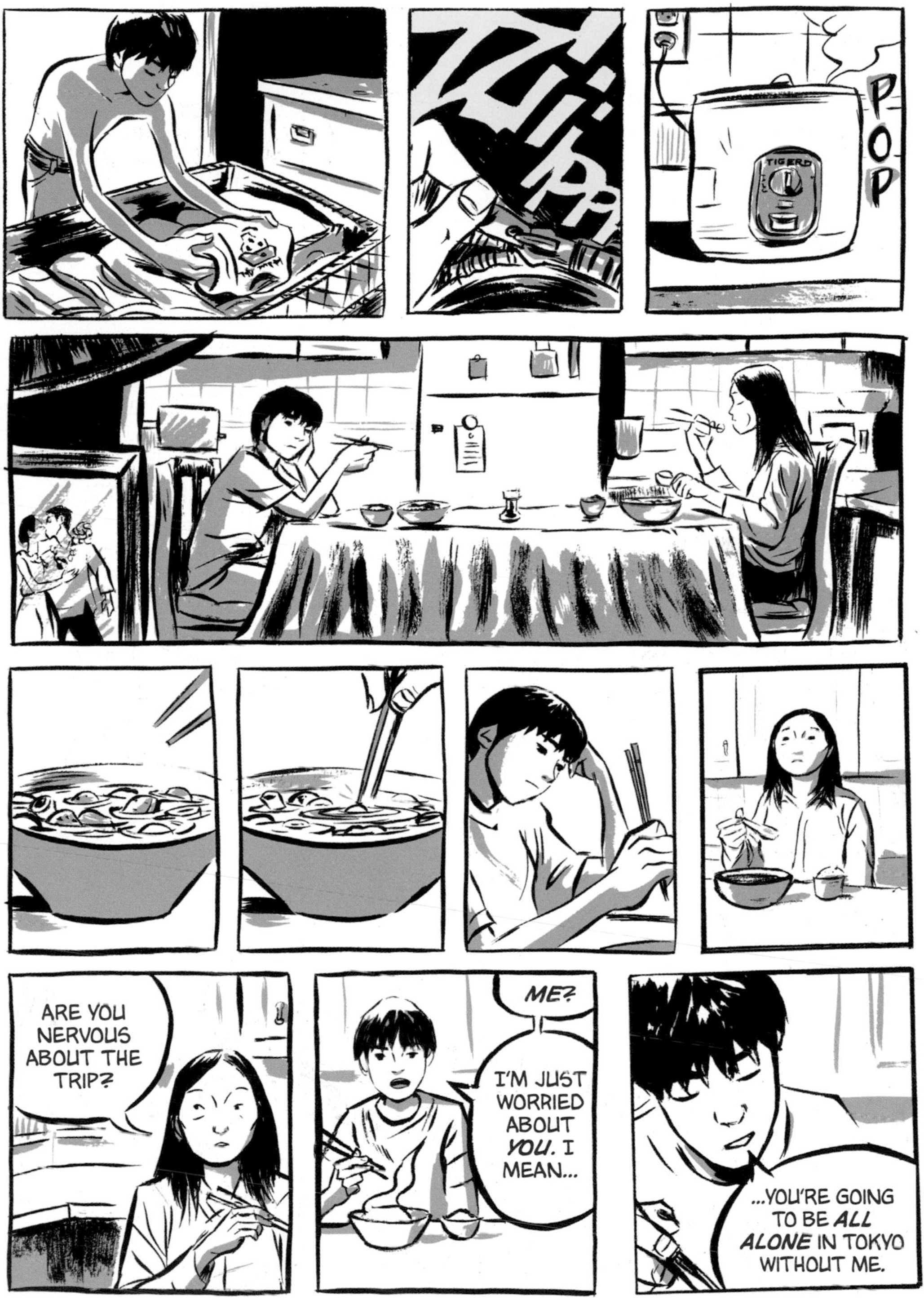
ZIIIPP
TIGER
POP
POP
POP
ARE YOU NERVOUS ABOUT THE TRIP?
ME?
I'M JUST WORRIED ABOUT YOU. I MEAN...
...YOU'RE GOING TO BE ALL ALONE IN TOKYO WITHOUT ME.

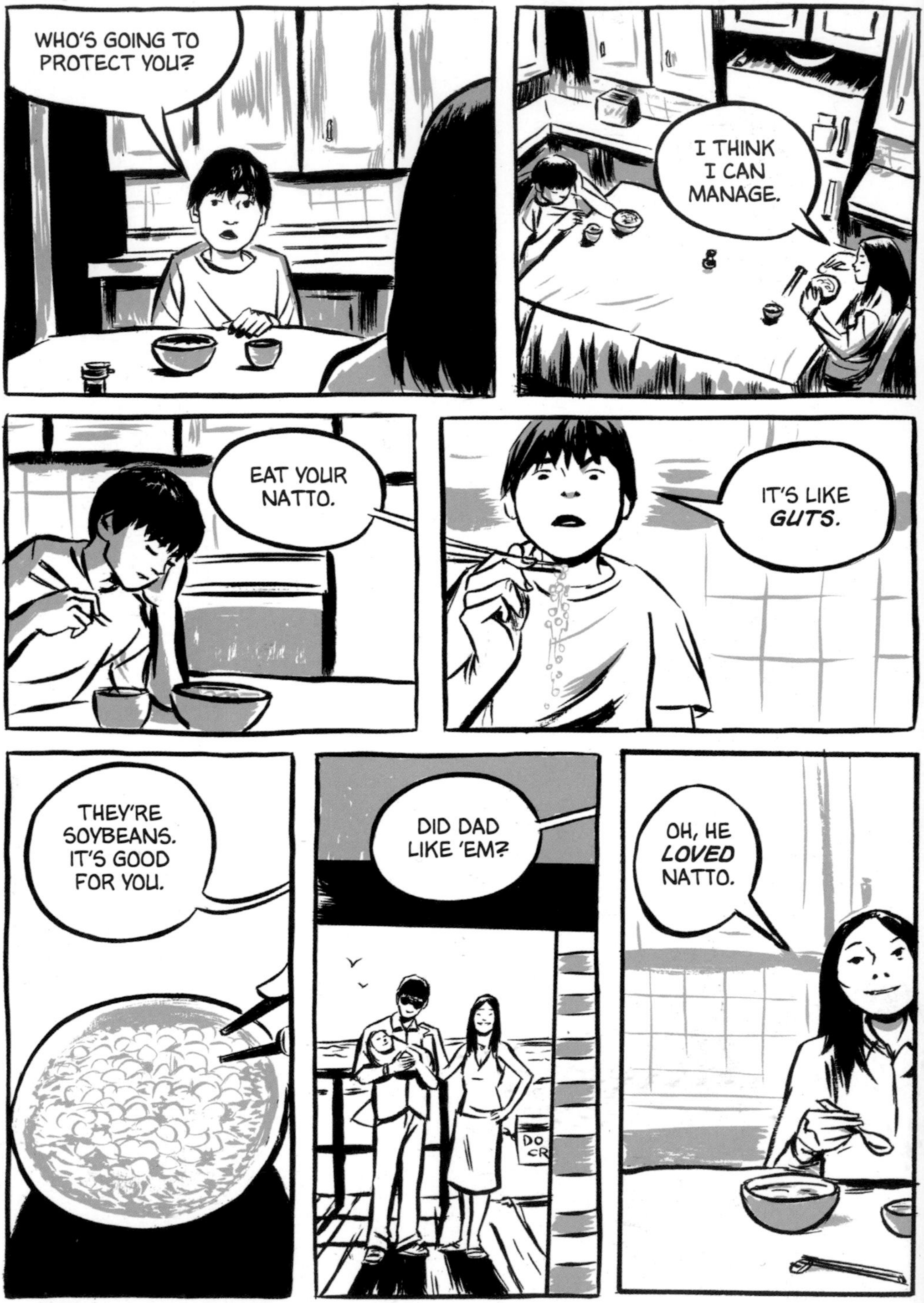
WHO'S GOING TO PROTECT YOU?
I THINK I CAN MANAGE.
EAT YOUR NATTO.
IT'S LIKE *GUTS*.
THEY'RE SOYBEANS. IT'S GOOD FOR YOU.
DID DAD LIKE 'EM?
OH, HE *LOVED* NATTO.

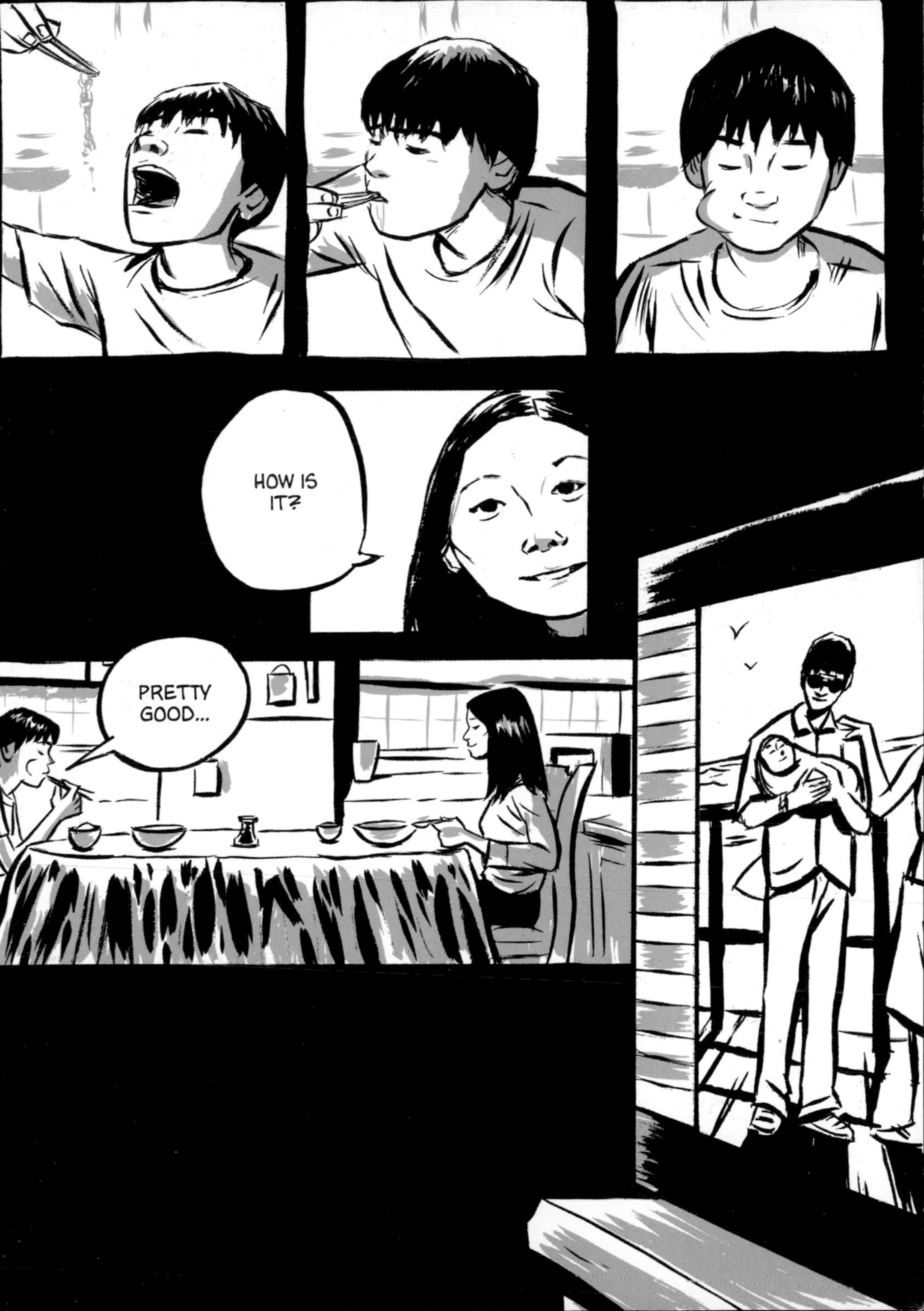
HOW IS IT?
PRETTY GOOD...

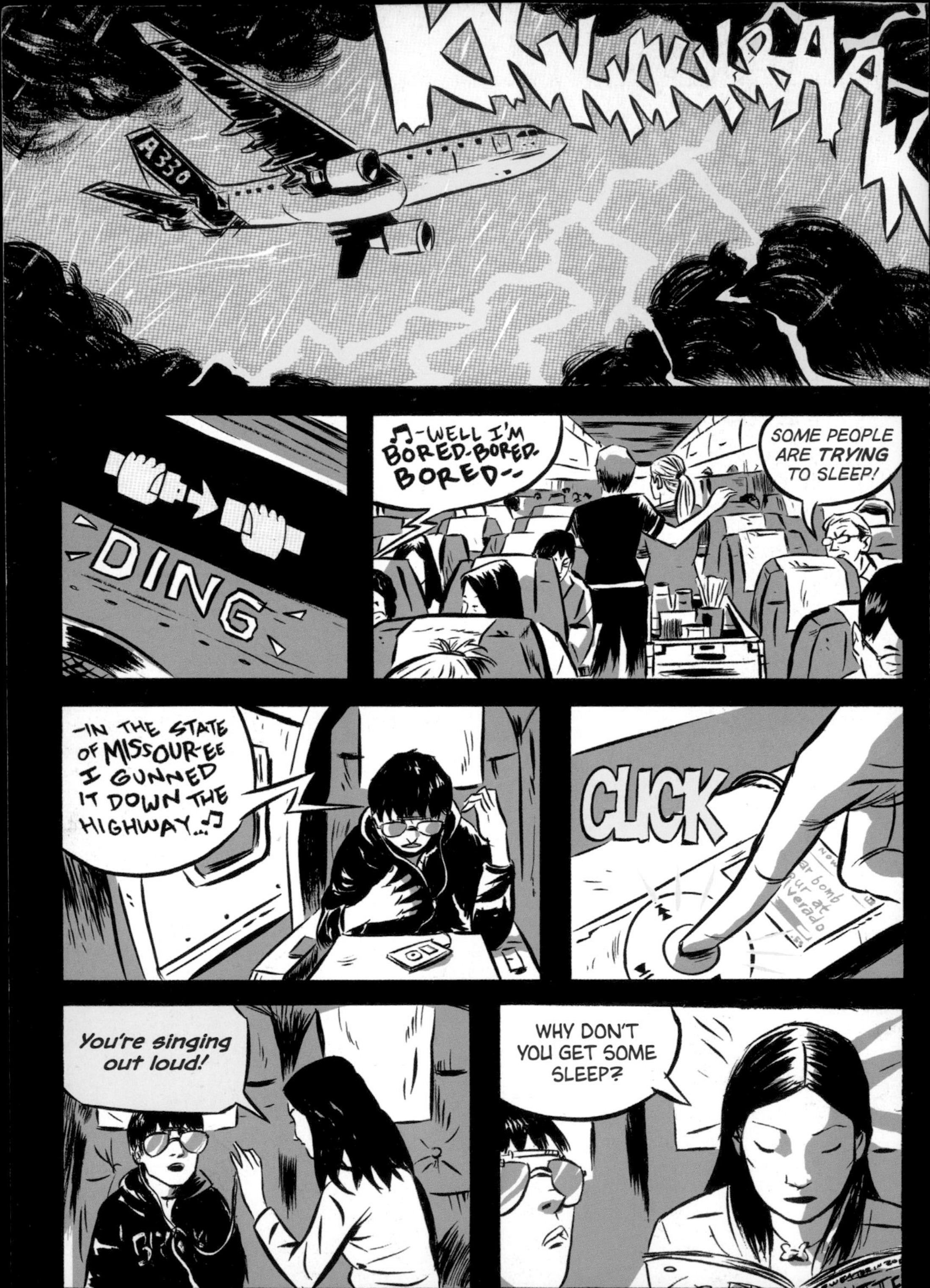
A330
DING
♫-WELL I'M BORED-BORED-BORED--
SOME PEOPLE ARE TRYING TO SLEEP!
-IN THE STATE OF MISSOUR-EE I GUNNED IT DOWN THE HIGHWAY...♫
CLICK
You're singing out loud!
WHY DON'T YOU GET SOME SLEEP?

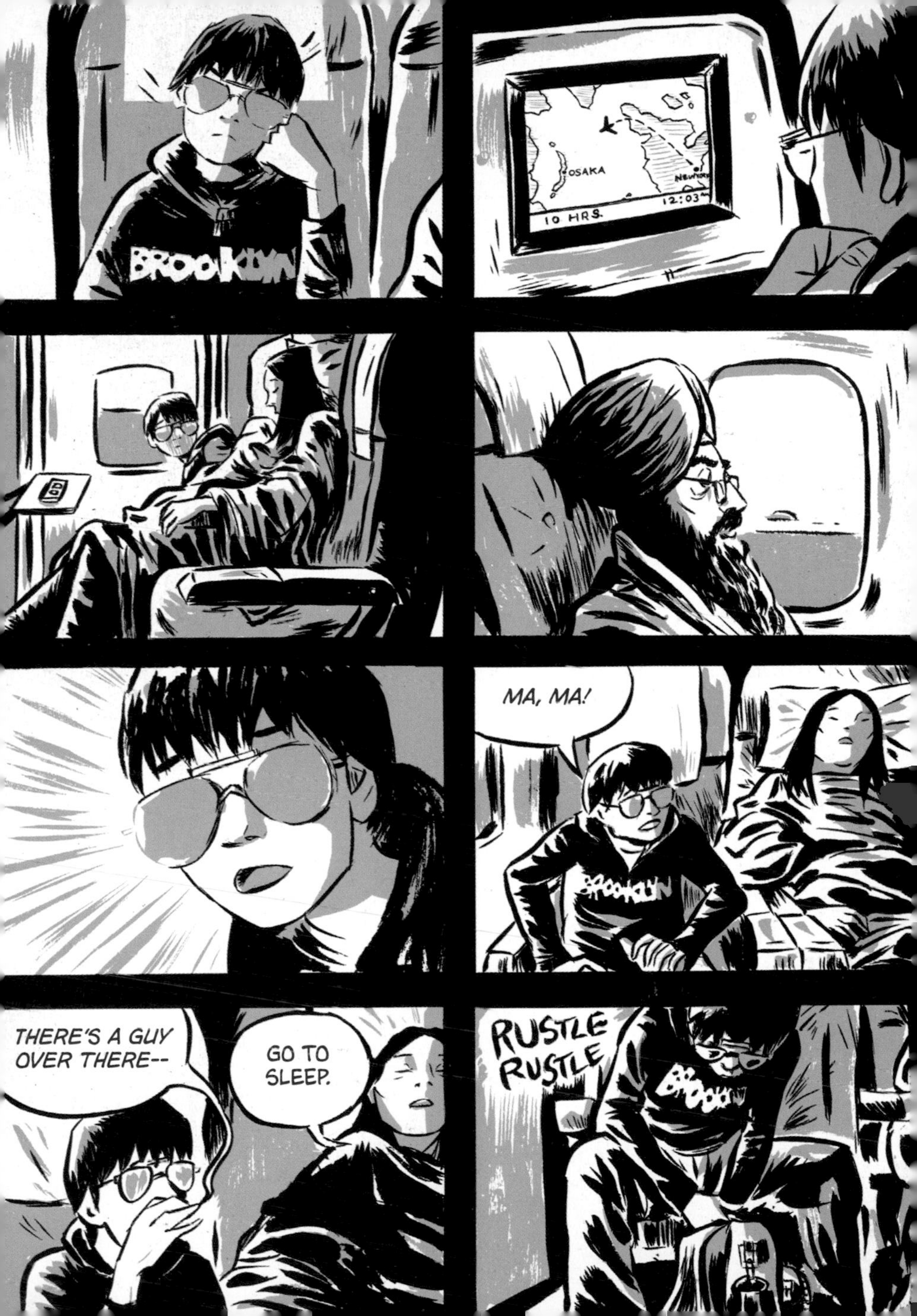
BROOKLYN
OSAKA
NEW YORK
12:03
10 HRS.
MA, MA!
BROOKLYN
THERE'S A GUY OVER THERE--
GO TO SLEEP.
RUSTLE RUSTLE

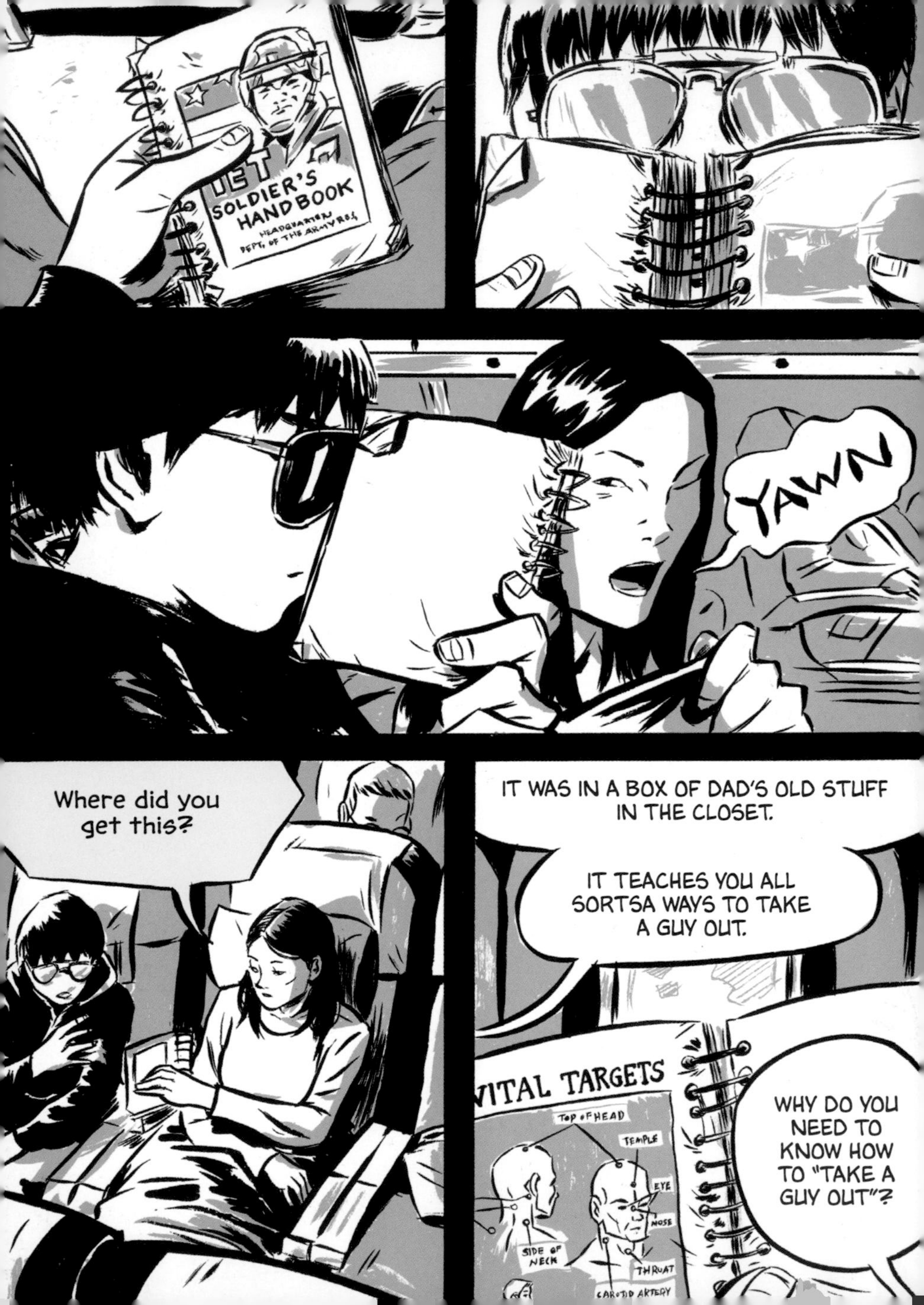
SOLDIER'S HANDBOOK
HEADQUARTERS DEPT. OF THE ARMY
YAWN
Where did you get this?
IT WAS IN A BOX OF DAD'S OLD STUFF IN THE CLOSET.
IT TEACHES YOU ALL SORTSA WAYS TO TAKE A GUY OUT.
VITAL TARGETS
TOP OF HEAD
TEMPLE
EYE
NOSE
SIDE OF NECK
THROAT
CAROTID ARTERY
WHY DO YOU NEED TO KNOW HOW TO "TAKE A GUY OUT"?

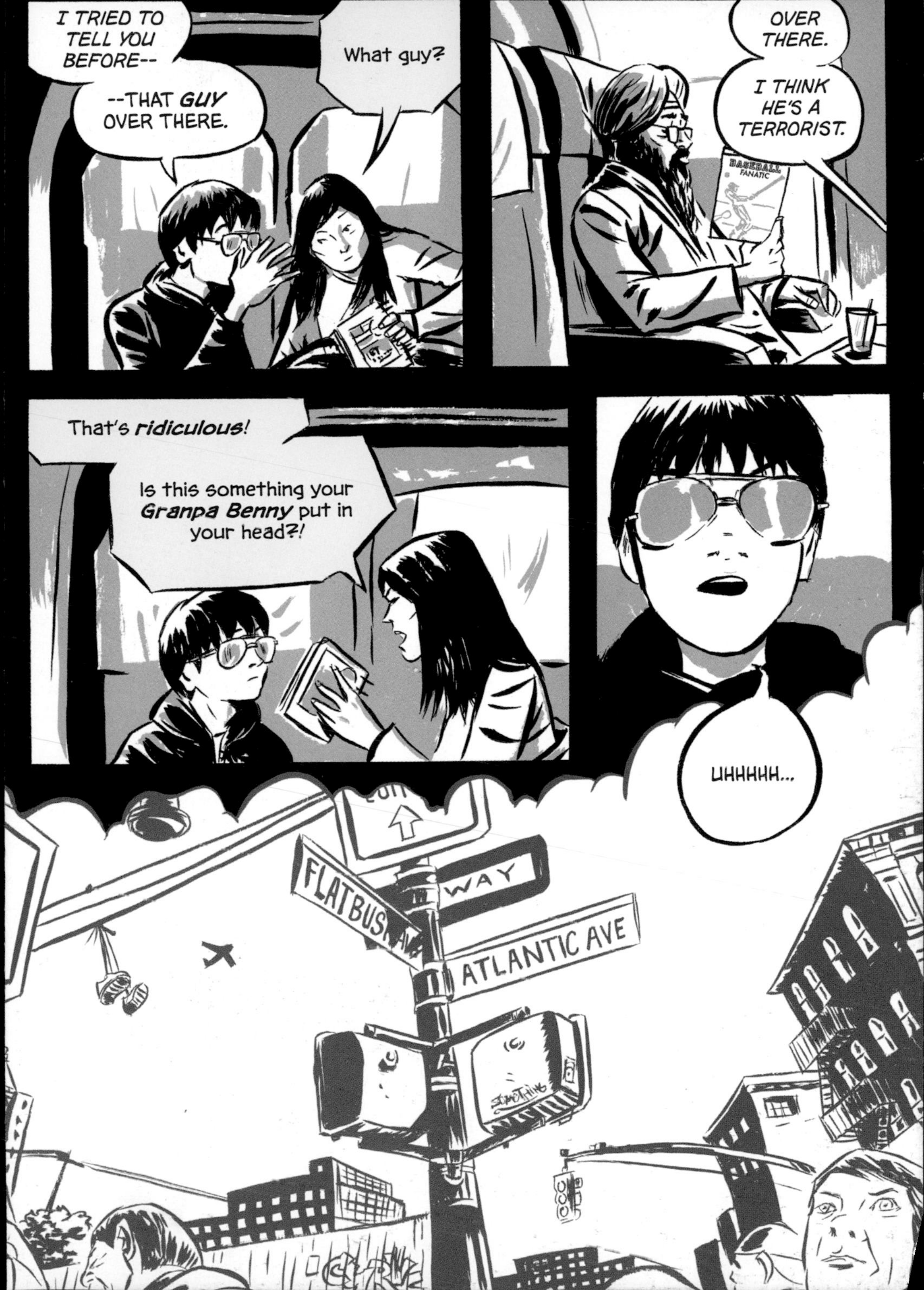
I TRIED TO TELL YOU BEFORE--
--THAT GUY OVER THERE.
What guy?
OVER THERE.
I THINK HE'S A TERRORIST.
BASEBALL FANATIC
That's ridiculous!
Is this something your Granpa Benny put in your head?!
UHHHHH...
FLATBUSH AVE
WAY
ATLANTIC AVE

FASHION
I CAN'T BELIEVE HOW MUCH THIS NEIGHBORHOOD HAS *CHANGED*!
COME ON, GRANPA.
GUITAR WORLD IS RIGHT DOWN THE BLOCK.
MEATS
SPECIALTY
ATM
INSIDE
THIS BAKERY USED TO HAVE THE BEST *SFOGLIATELLE*...
...AND ***STRATOCASTERS***. IT'S SO COOL, AND YOU CAN PLAY THEM RIGHT IN THE STORE!
HOLD ON.
I WANNA PICK UP A PAPER.
CRESCENT DELI
•SNACKS
YOU KNOW, MY BIRTHDAY IS COMING UP...
YOU DON'T ***HAVE*** TO GET ME ELECTRONIC DRUMS, BUT IT'D BE EASIER ON MOM.
HEY!
WHAT'S ***THIS?***

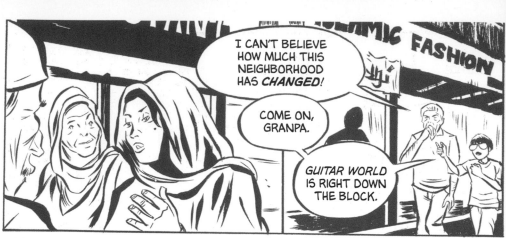

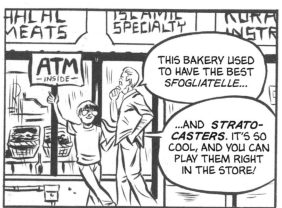

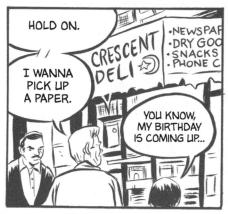

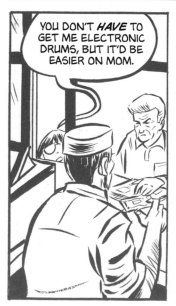

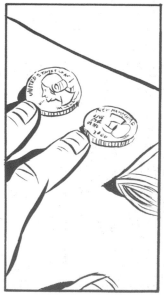

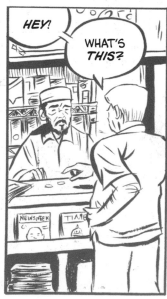

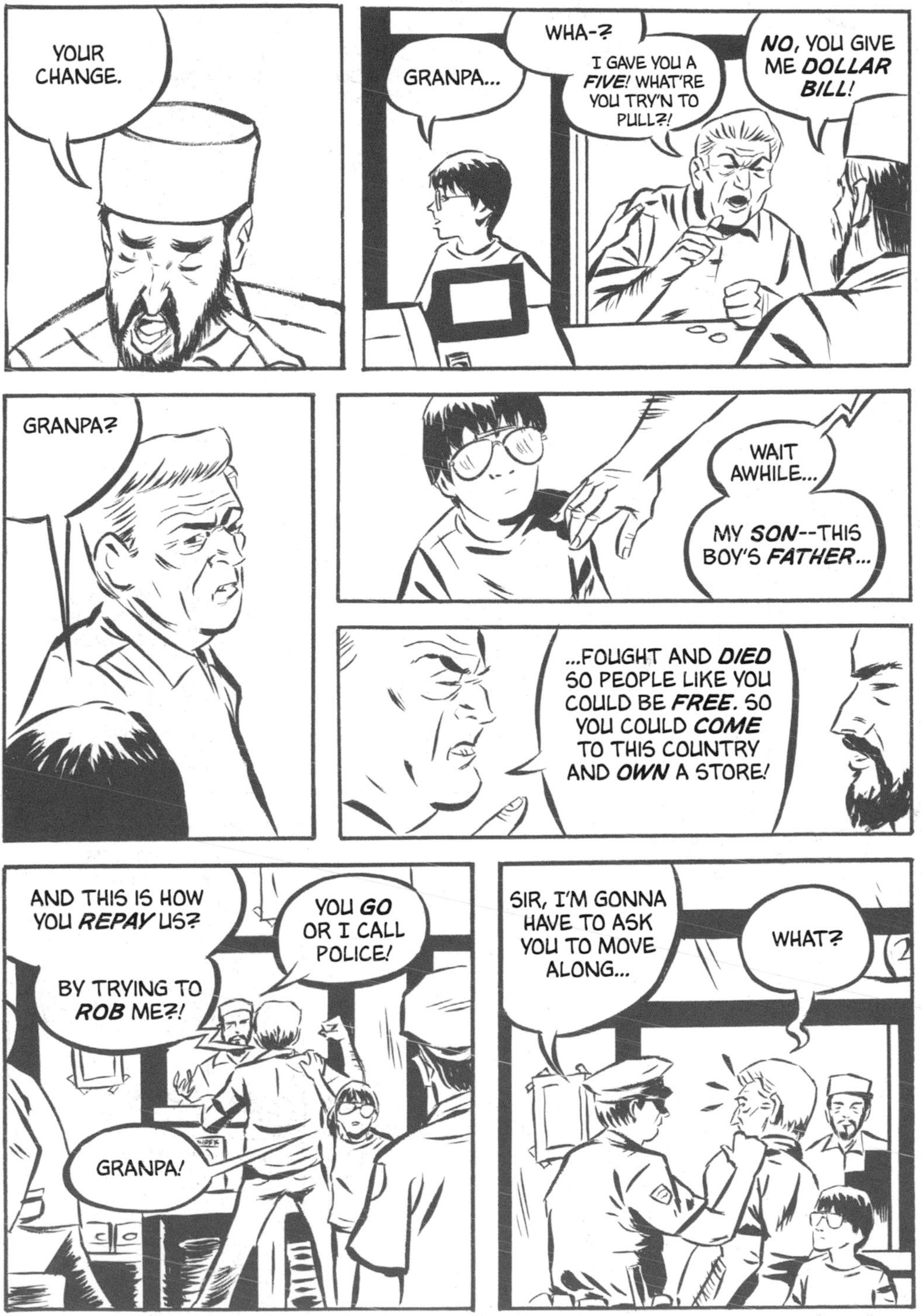
YOUR CHANGE.
GRANPA...
WHA-?
I GAVE YOU A FIVE! WHAT'RE YOU TRY'N TO PULL?!
NO, YOU GIVE ME DOLLAR BILL!
GRANPA?
WAIT AWHILE...
MY SON--THIS BOY'S FATHER...
...FOUGHT AND DIED SO PEOPLE LIKE YOU COULD BE FREE. SO YOU COULD COME TO THIS COUNTRY AND OWN A STORE!
AND THIS IS HOW YOU REPAY US?
BY TRYING TO ROB ME?!
YOU GO OR I CALL POLICE!
GRANPA!
SIR, I'M GONNA HAVE TO ASK YOU TO MOVE ALONG...
WHAT?

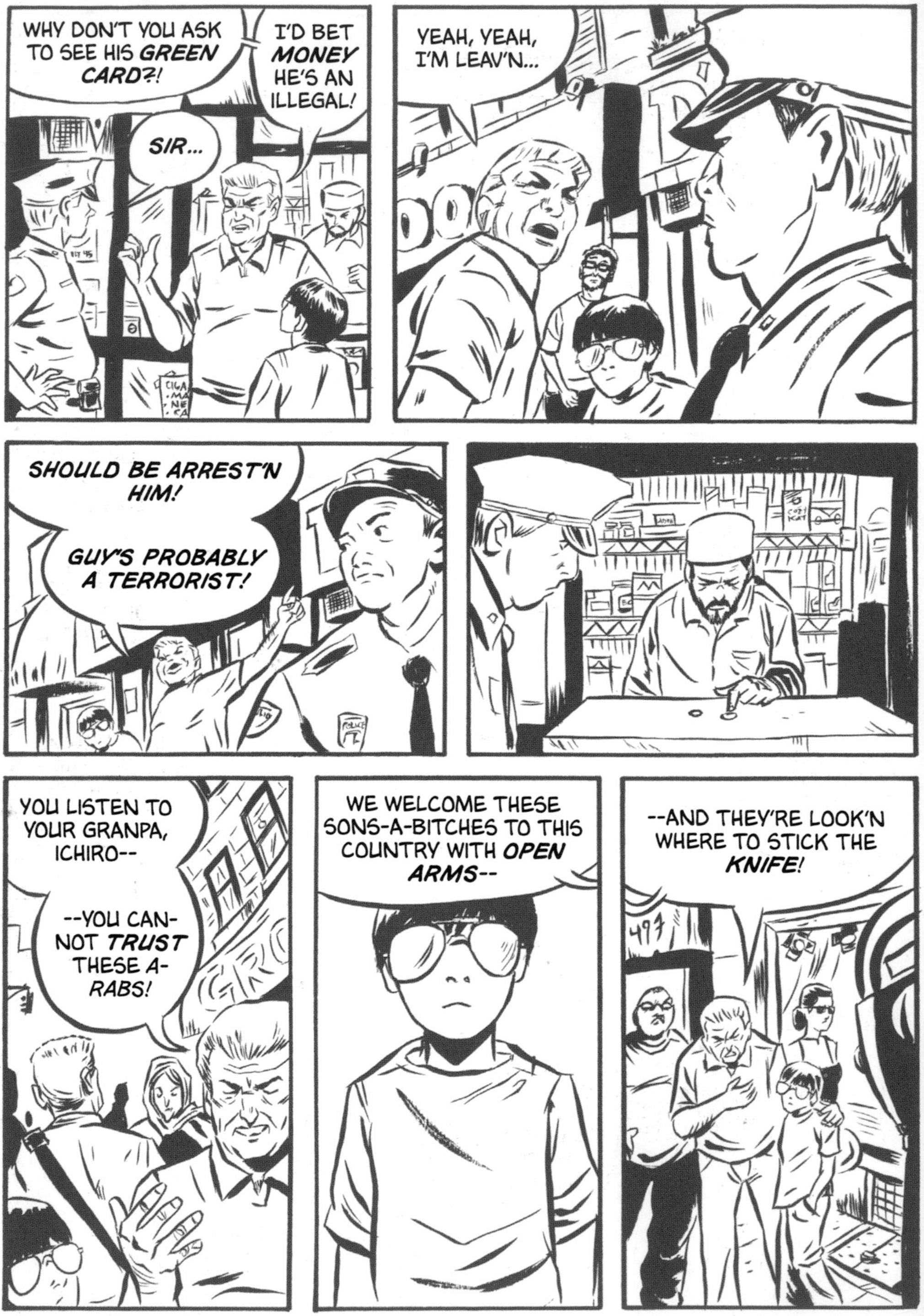
WHY DON'T YOU ASK TO SEE HIS GREEN CARD?!
I'D BET MONEY HE'S AN ILLEGAL!
SIR...
YEAH, YEAH, I'M LEAV'N...
SHOULD BE ARREST'N HIM!
GUY'S PROBABLY A TERRORIST!
YOU LISTEN TO YOUR GRANPA, ICHIRO--
--YOU CAN-NOT TRUST THESE A-RABS!
WE WELCOME THESE SONS-A-BITCHES TO THIS COUNTRY WITH OPEN ARMS--
--AND THEY'RE LOOK'N WHERE TO STICK THE KNIFE!

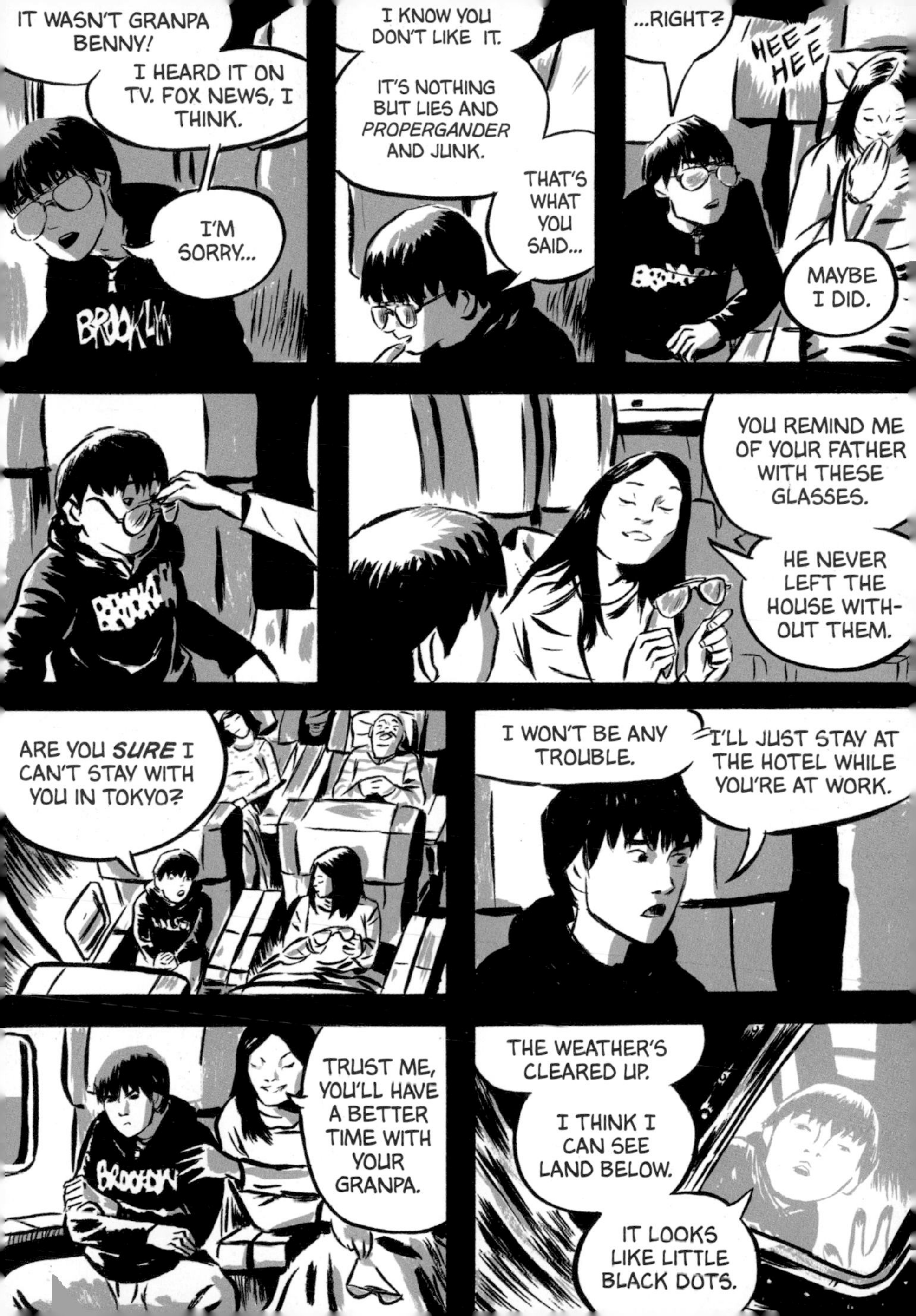
IT WASN'T GRANPA BENNY!
I HEARD IT ON TV. FOX NEWS, I THINK.
I'M SORRY...
I KNOW YOU DON'T LIKE IT.
IT'S NOTHING BUT LIES AND *PROPERGANDER* AND JUNK.
THAT'S WHAT YOU SAID...
...RIGHT?
HEE-HEE
MAYBE I DID.
YOU REMIND ME OF YOUR FATHER WITH THESE GLASSES.
HE NEVER LEFT THE HOUSE WITHOUT THEM.
ARE YOU *SURE* I CAN'T STAY WITH YOU IN TOKYO?
I WON'T BE ANY TROUBLE.
I'LL JUST STAY AT THE HOTEL WHILE YOU'RE AT WORK.
TRUST ME, YOU'LL HAVE A BETTER TIME WITH YOUR GRANPA.
THE WEATHER'S CLEARED UP.
I THINK I CAN SEE LAND BELOW.
IT LOOKS LIKE LITTLE BLACK DOTS.

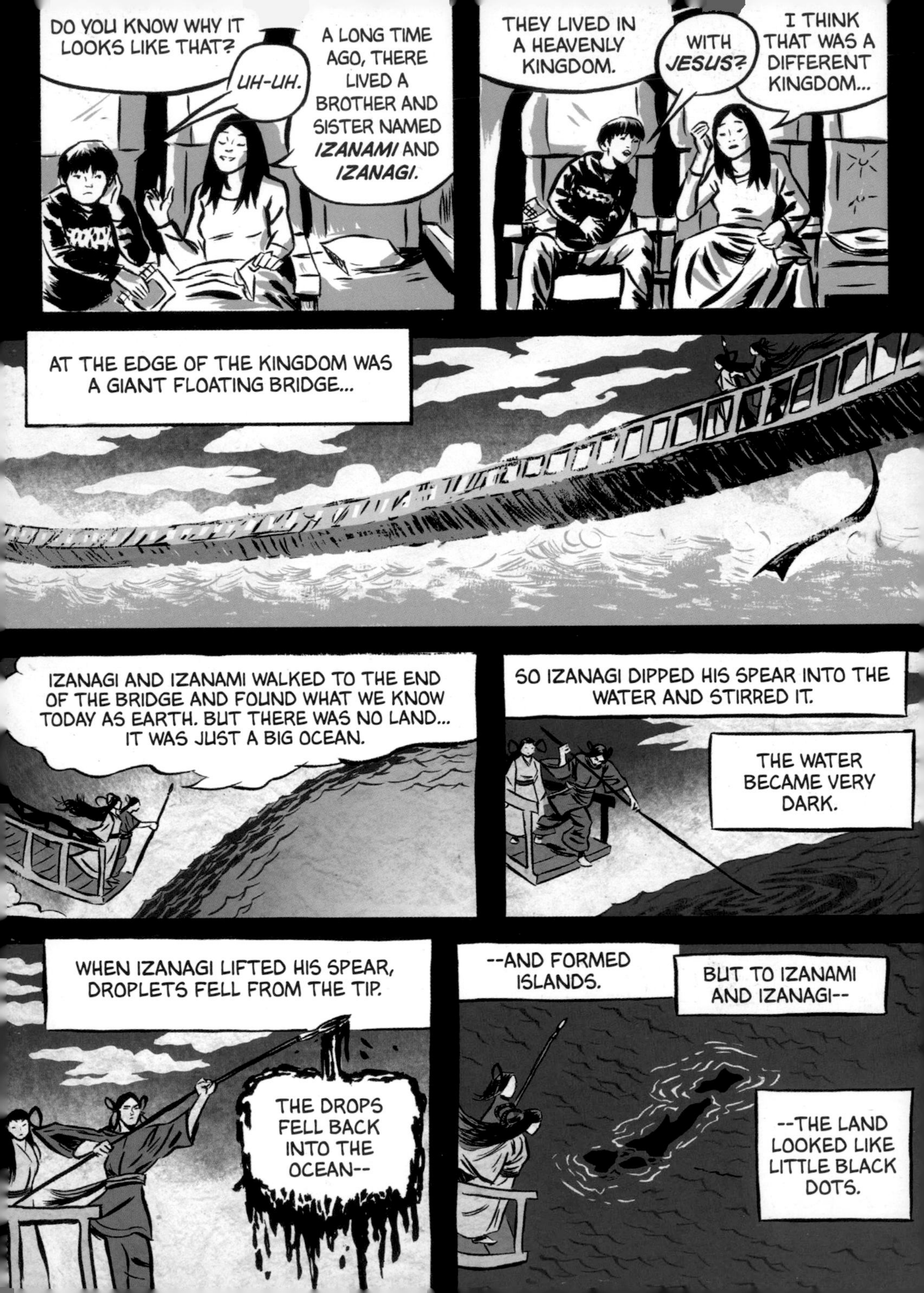
DO YOU KNOW WHY IT LOOKS LIKE THAT?
UH-UH.
A LONG TIME AGO, THERE LIVED A BROTHER AND SISTER NAMED *IZANAMI* AND *IZANAGI*.
THEY LIVED IN A HEAVENLY KINGDOM.
WITH *JESUS*?
I THINK THAT WAS A DIFFERENT KINGDOM...
AT THE EDGE OF THE KINGDOM WAS A GIANT FLOATING BRIDGE...
IZANAGI AND IZANAMI WALKED TO THE END OF THE BRIDGE AND FOUND WHAT WE KNOW TODAY AS EARTH. BUT THERE WAS NO LAND... IT WAS JUST A BIG OCEAN.
SO IZANAGI DIPPED HIS SPEAR INTO THE WATER AND STIRRED IT.
THE WATER BECAME VERY DARK.
WHEN IZANAGI LIFTED HIS SPEAR, DROPLETS FELL FROM THE TIP.
THE DROPS FELL BACK INTO THE OCEAN--
--AND FORMED ISLANDS.
BUT TO IZANAMI AND IZANAGI--
--THE LAND LOOKED LIKE LITTLE BLACK DOTS.

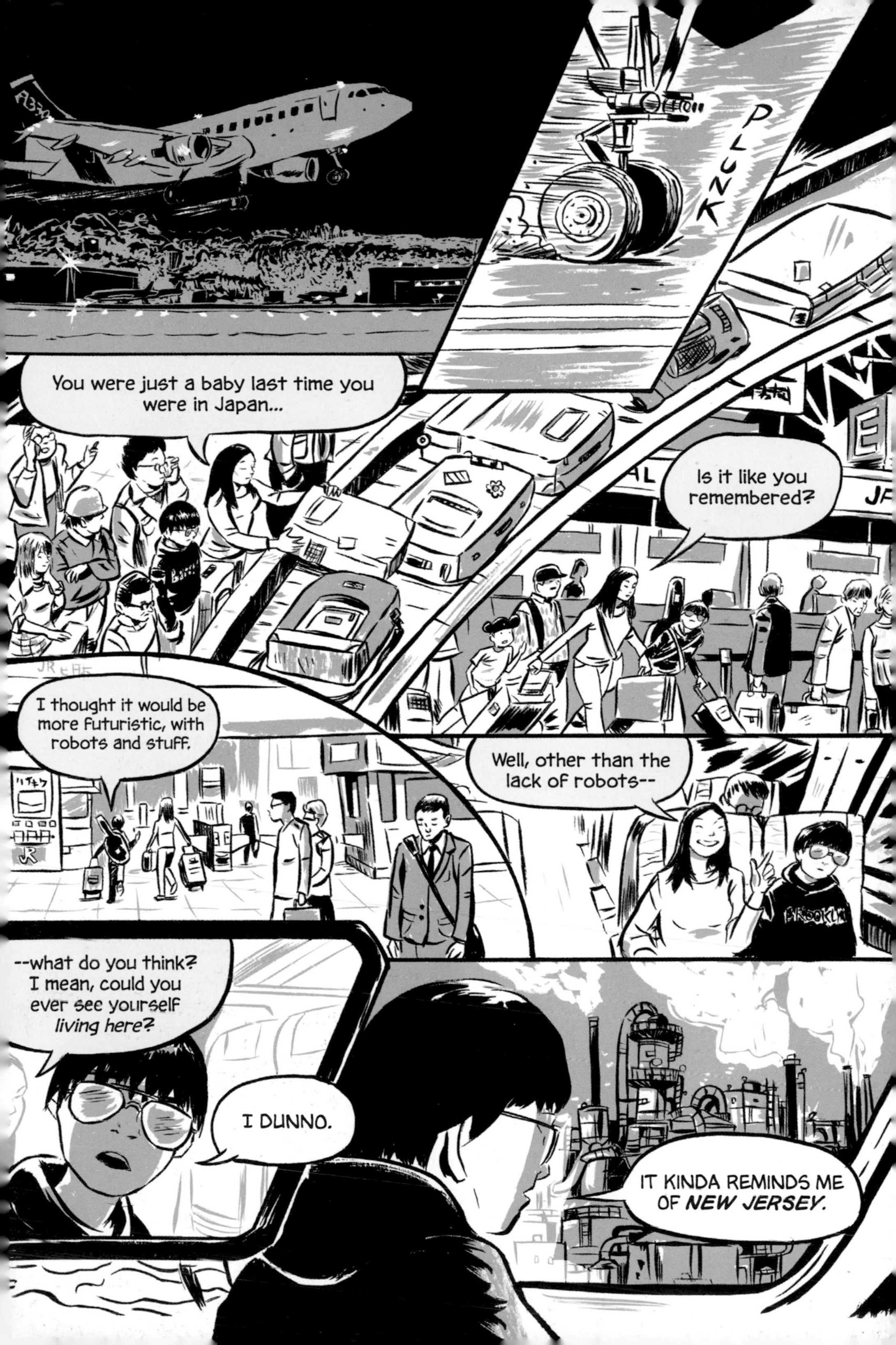
PLUNK
You were just a baby last time you were in Japan...
Is it like you remembered?
I thought it would be more futuristic, with robots and stuff.
Well, other than the lack of robots--
--what do you think? I mean, could you ever see yourself *living here*?
I DUNNO.
IT KINDA REMINDS ME OF ***NEW JERSEY***.

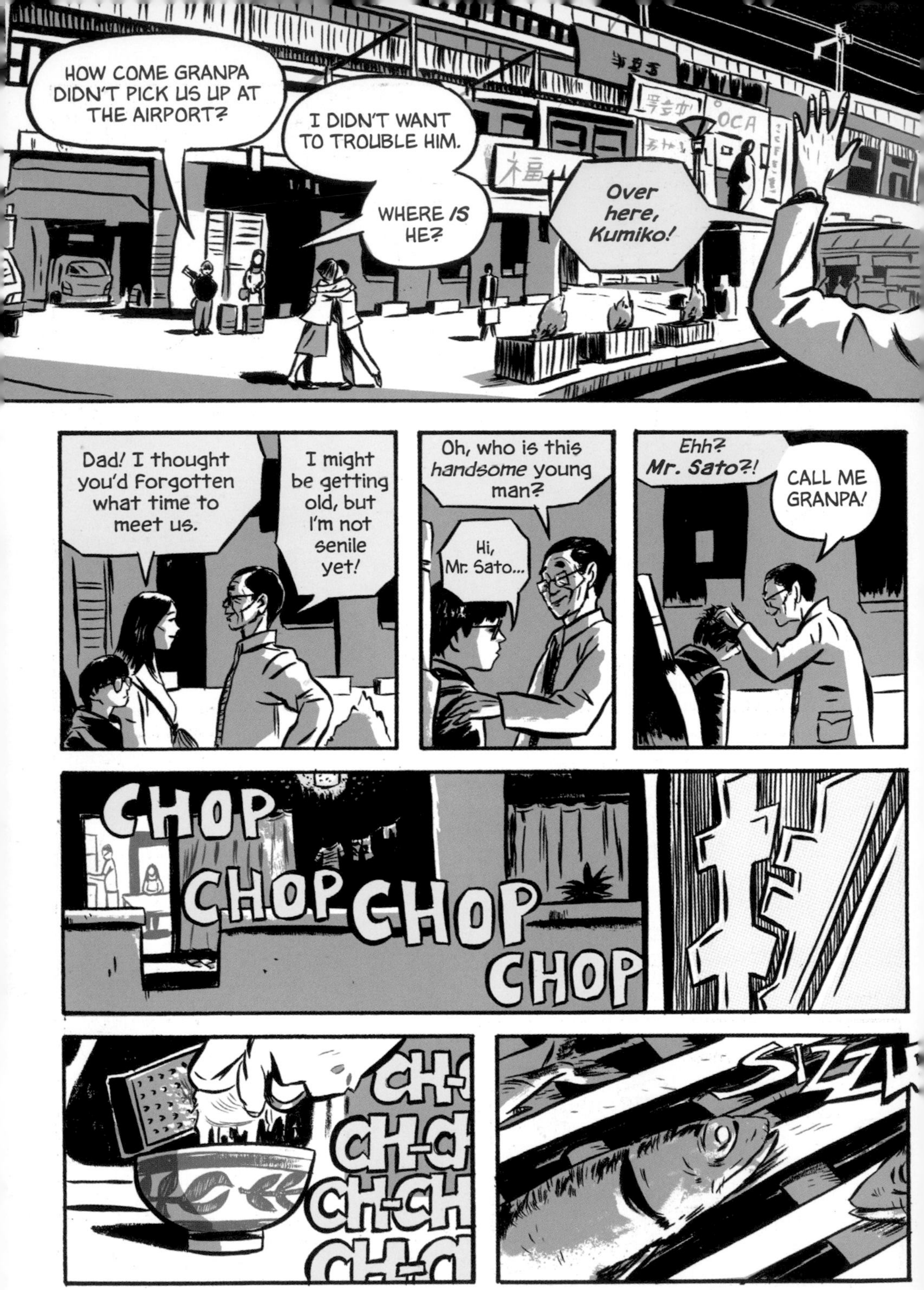
HOW COME GRANPA DIDN'T PICK US UP AT THE AIRPORT?
I DIDN'T WANT TO TROUBLE HIM.
WHERE IS HE?
Over here, Kumiko!
Dad! I thought you'd forgotten what time to meet us.
I might be getting old, but I'm not senile yet!
Oh, who is this handsome young man?
Hi, Mr. Sato...
Ehh? Mr. Sato?!
CALL ME GRANPA!
CHOP
CHOP
CHOP
CHOP
SIZZL

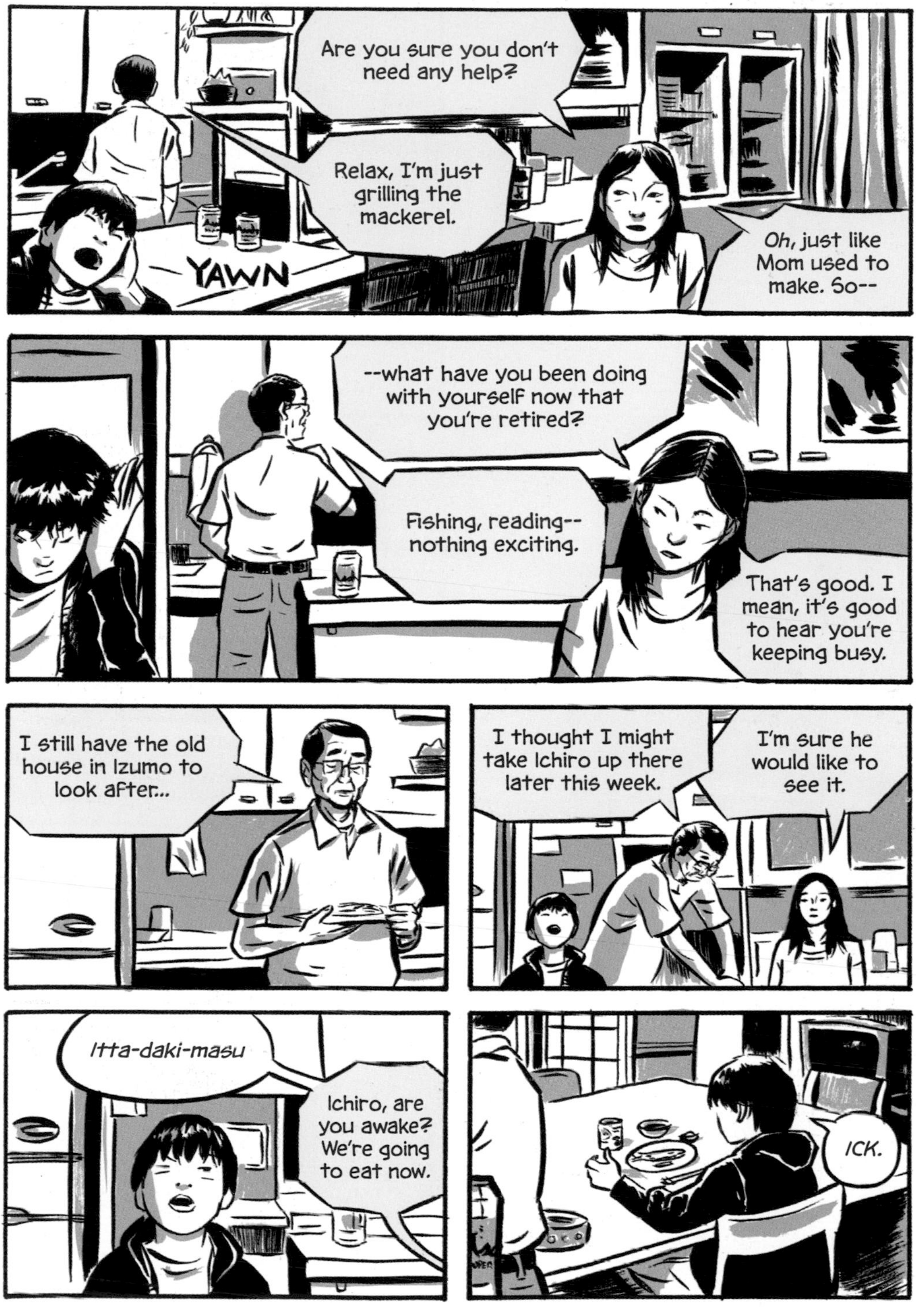
Are you sure you don't need any help?
Relax, I'm just grilling the mackerel.
YAWN
Oh, just like Mom used to make. So--
--what have you been doing with yourself now that you're retired?
Fishing, reading--nothing exciting.
That's good. I mean, it's good to hear you're keeping busy.
I still have the old house in Izumo to look after...
I thought I might take Ichiro up there later this week.
I'm sure he would like to see it.
Itta-daki-masu
Ichiro, are you awake? We're going to eat now.
ICK.

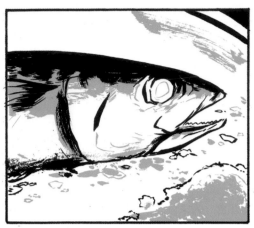

I'M NOT HUNGRY.

I JUST WANT TO GO TO BED.

OK, BRUSH YOUR TEETH FIRST.

UUUGGGHHHH!

I'LL COME TUCK YOU IN BEFORE I LEAVE.

No dinner?

He's tired from the flight.

Hmm, so, how are you both doing?

I mean, are you OK--

--financially?

We're fine. In fact, this teaching position in Tokyo is paying me pretty well. I guess they really value my experience...

It might be a--

--permanent position.

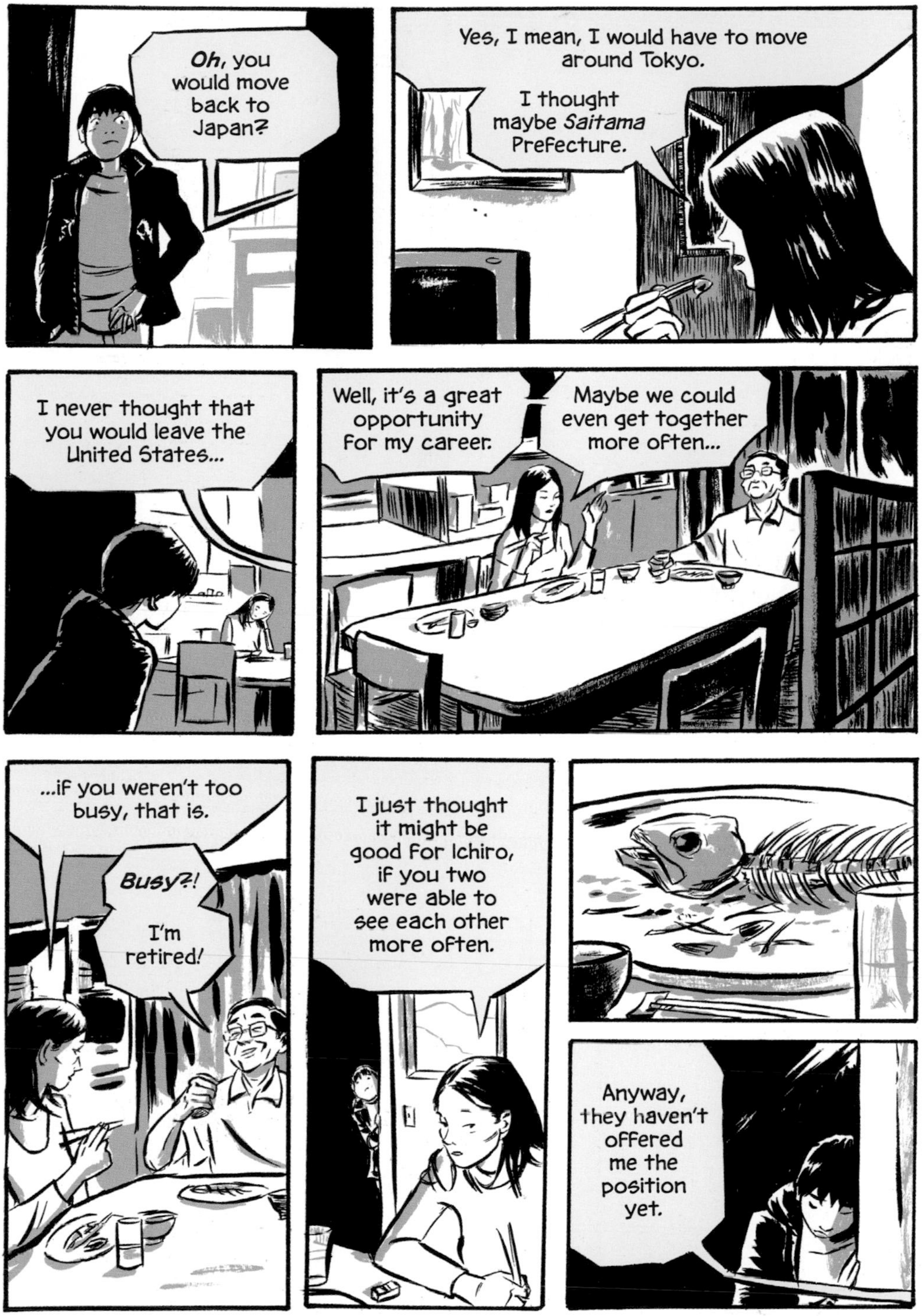
Oh, you would move back to Japan?
Yes, I mean, I would have to move around Tokyo.
I thought maybe Saitama Prefecture.
I never thought that you would leave the United States...
Well, it's a great opportunity for my career.
Maybe we could even get together more often...
...if you weren't too busy, that is.
Busy?!
I'm retired!
I just thought it might be good for Ichiro, if you two were able to see each other more often.
Anyway, they haven't offered me the position yet.

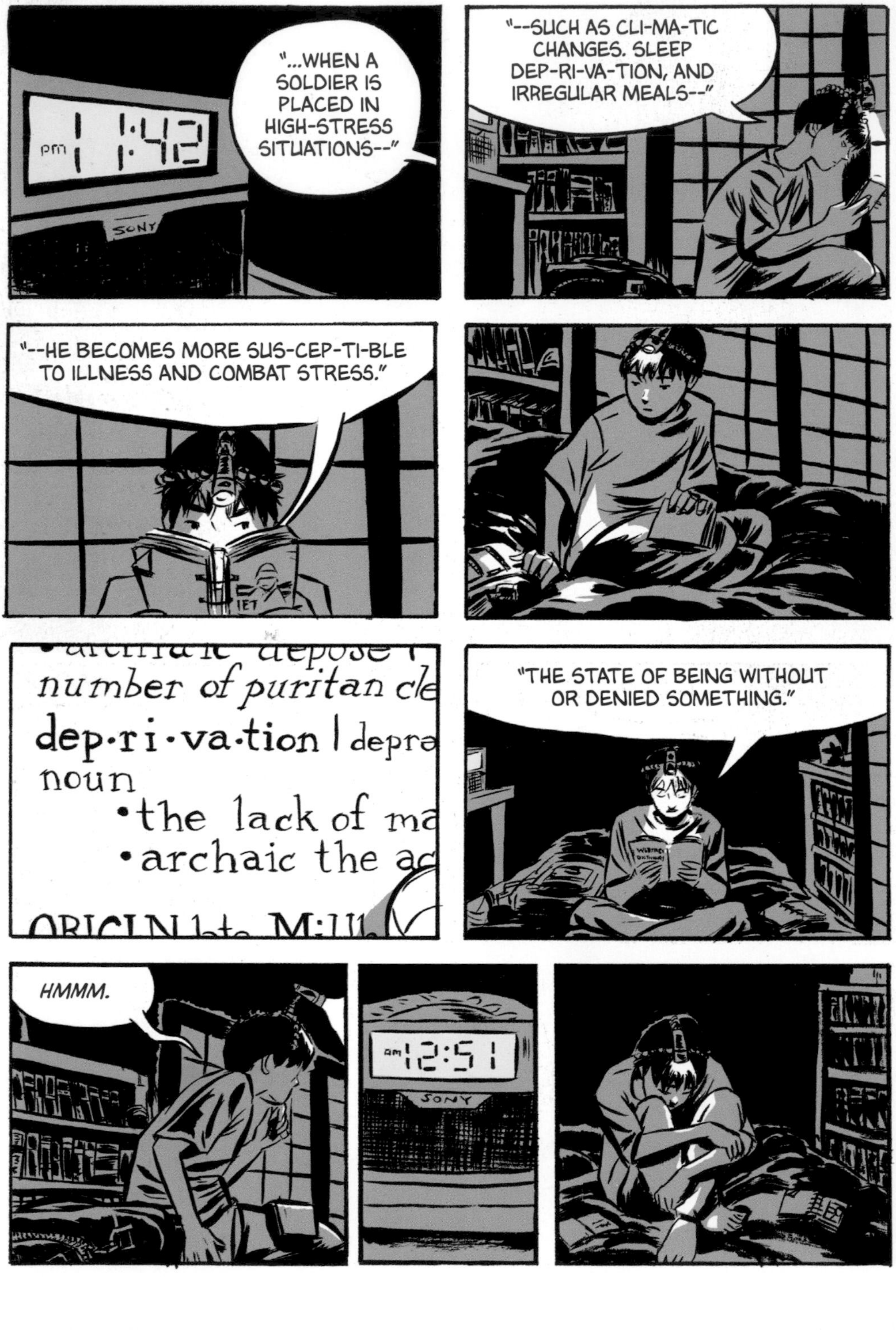
pm 11:42
SONY
"...WHEN A SOLDIER IS PLACED IN HIGH-STRESS SITUATIONS--"
"--SUCH AS CLI-MA-TIC CHANGES. SLEEP DEP-RI-VA-TION, AND IRREGULAR MEALS--"
"--HE BECOMES MORE SUS-CEP-TI-BLE TO ILLNESS AND COMBAT STRESS."
number of puritan cle
dep·ri·va·tion | depra
noun
•the lack of ma
•archaic the ac
"THE STATE OF BEING WITHOUT OR DENIED SOMETHING."
HMMM.
am 12:51
SONY

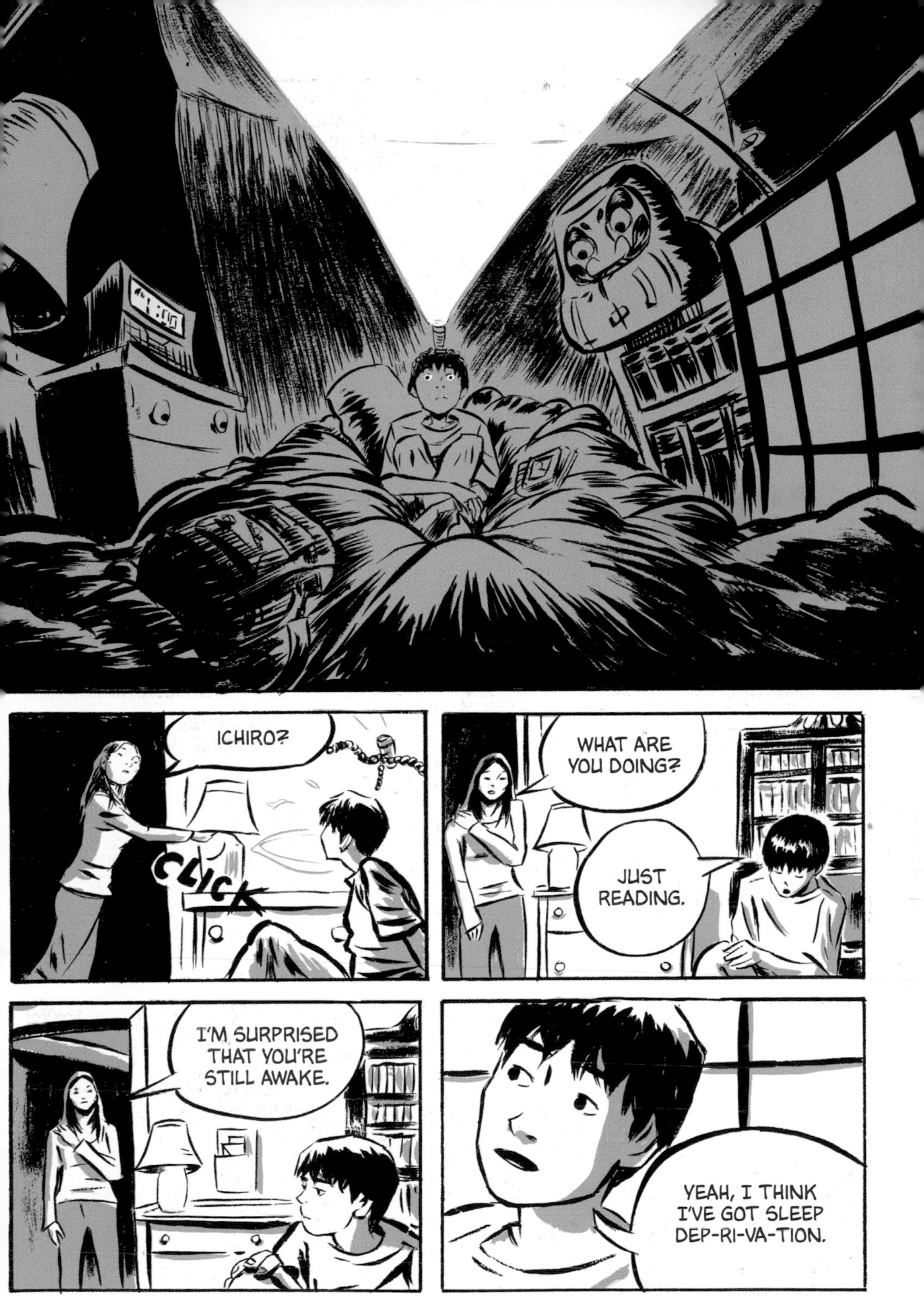
ICHIRO?
CLICK
WHAT ARE YOU DOING?
JUST READING.
I'M SURPRISED THAT YOU'RE STILL AWAKE.
YEAH, I THINK I'VE GOT SLEEP DEP-RI-VA-TION.

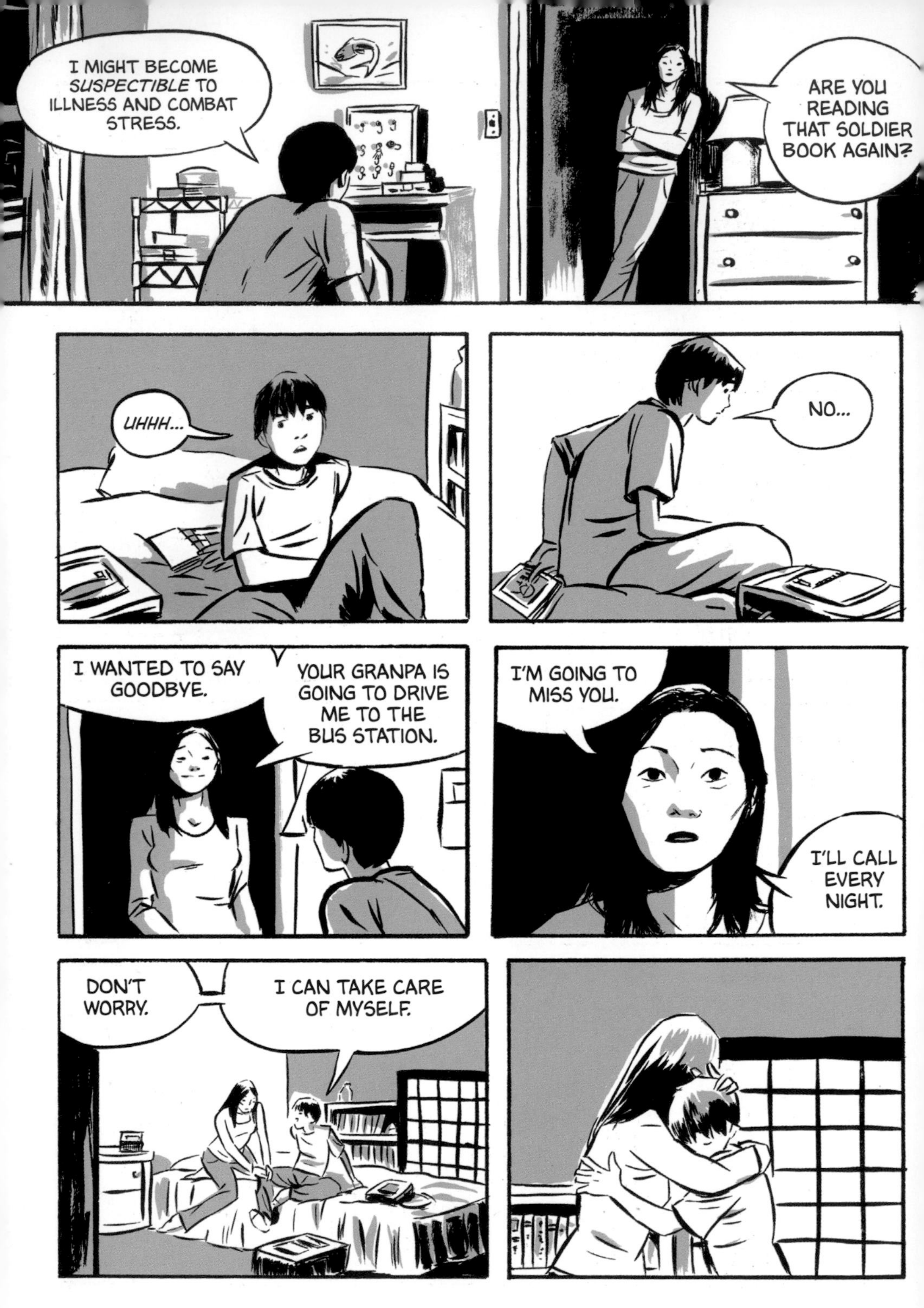
I MIGHT BECOME *SUSPECTIBLE* TO ILLNESS AND COMBAT STRESS.
ARE YOU READING THAT SOLDIER BOOK AGAIN?
UHHH...
NO...
I WANTED TO SAY GOODBYE.
YOUR GRANPA IS GOING TO DRIVE ME TO THE BUS STATION.
I'M GOING TO MISS YOU.
I'LL CALL EVERY NIGHT.
DON'T WORRY.
I CAN TAKE CARE OF MYSELF.

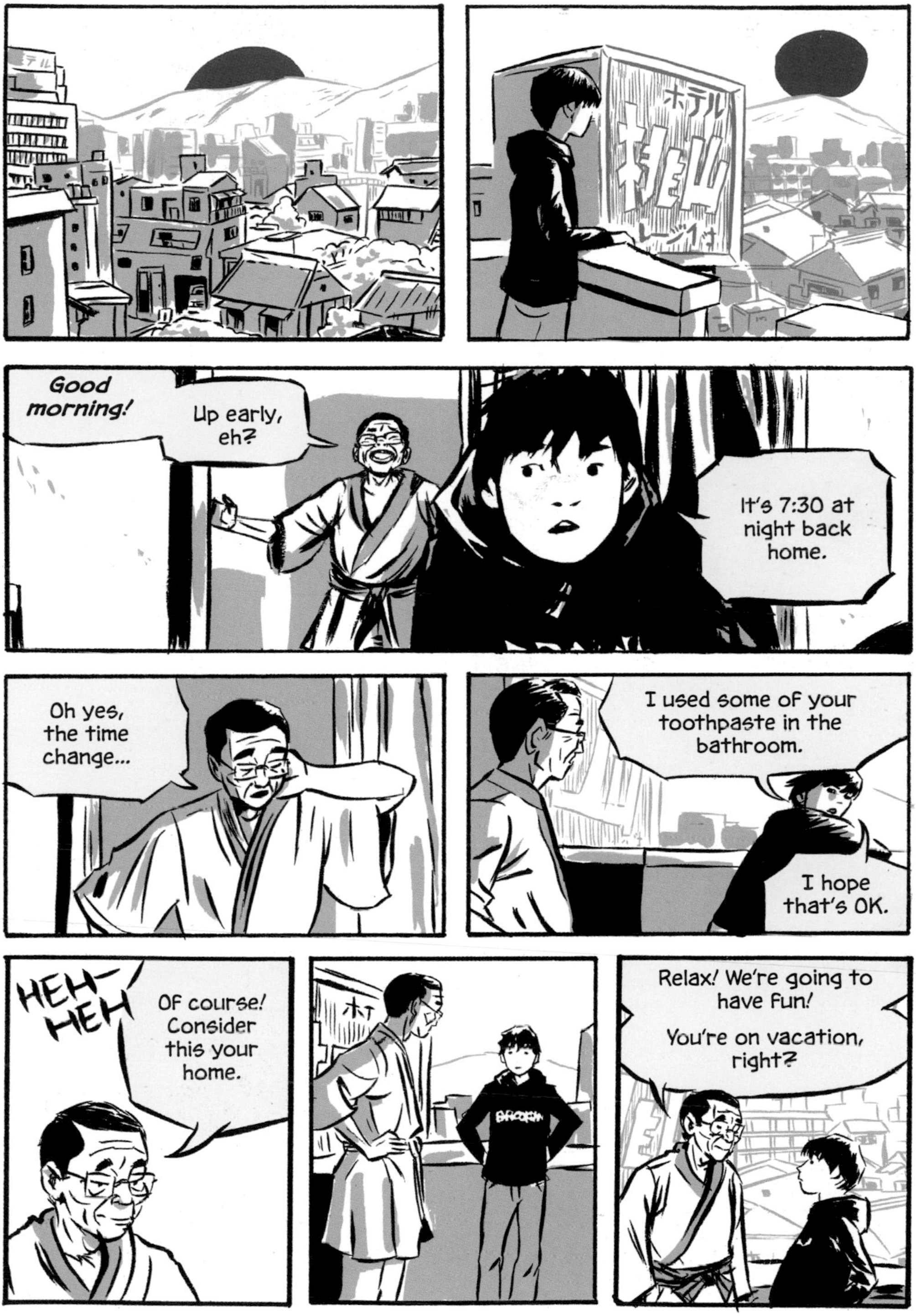

ホテル
Good morning!
Up early, eh?
It's 7:30 at night back home.
Oh yes, the time change...
I used some of your toothpaste in the bathroom.
I hope that's OK.
HEH-HEH
Of course! Consider this your home.
Relax! We're going to have fun!
You're on vacation, right?

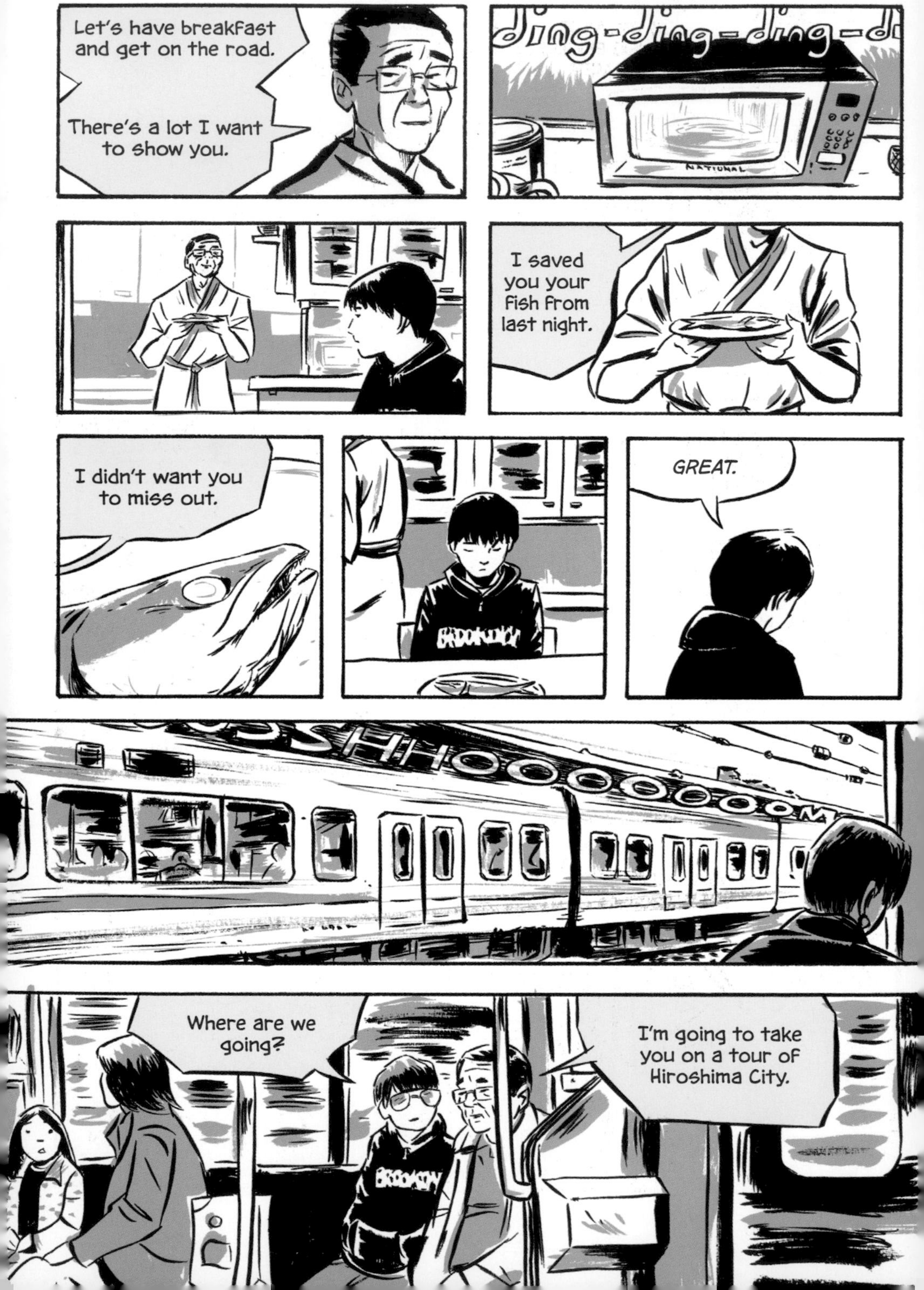
Let's have breakfast and get on the road.
There's a lot I want to show you.
ding-ding-ding-di
NATIONAL
I saved you your fish from last night.
I didn't want you to miss out.
GREAT.
Where are we going?
I'm going to take you on a tour of Hiroshima City.

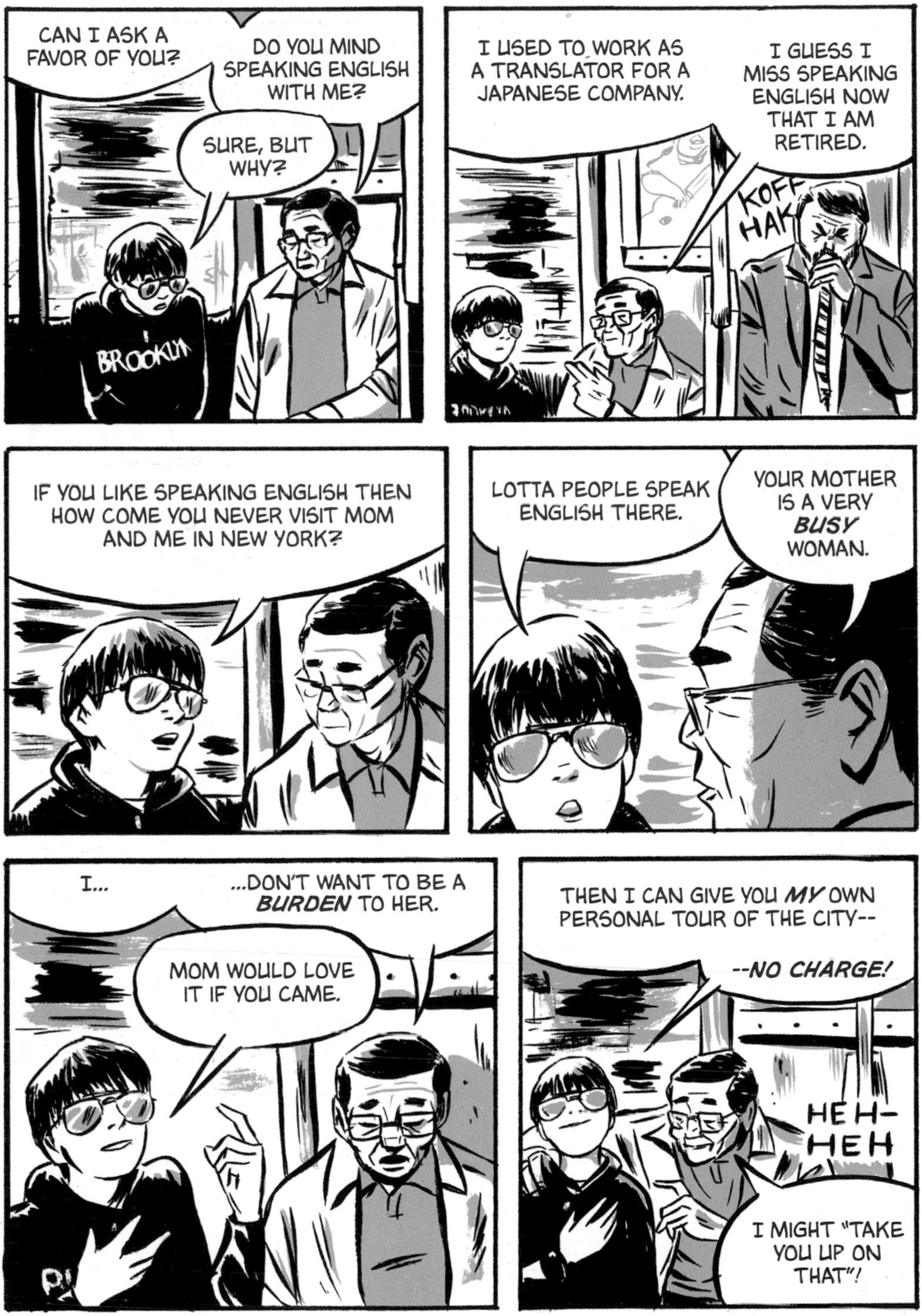
CAN I ASK A FAVOR OF YOU?
DO YOU MIND SPEAKING ENGLISH WITH ME?
SURE, BUT WHY?
I USED TO WORK AS A TRANSLATOR FOR A JAPANESE COMPANY.
I GUESS I MISS SPEAKING ENGLISH NOW THAT I AM RETIRED.
KOFF HAK
IF YOU LIKE SPEAKING ENGLISH THEN HOW COME YOU NEVER VISIT MOM AND ME IN NEW YORK?
LOTTA PEOPLE SPEAK ENGLISH THERE.
YOUR MOTHER IS A VERY *BUSY* WOMAN.
I...
...DON'T WANT TO BE A *BURDEN* TO HER.
MOM WOULD LOVE IT IF YOU CAME.
THEN I CAN GIVE YOU *MY* OWN PERSONAL TOUR OF THE CITY--
--*NO CHARGE!*
HEH-HEH
I MIGHT "TAKE YOU UP ON THAT"!

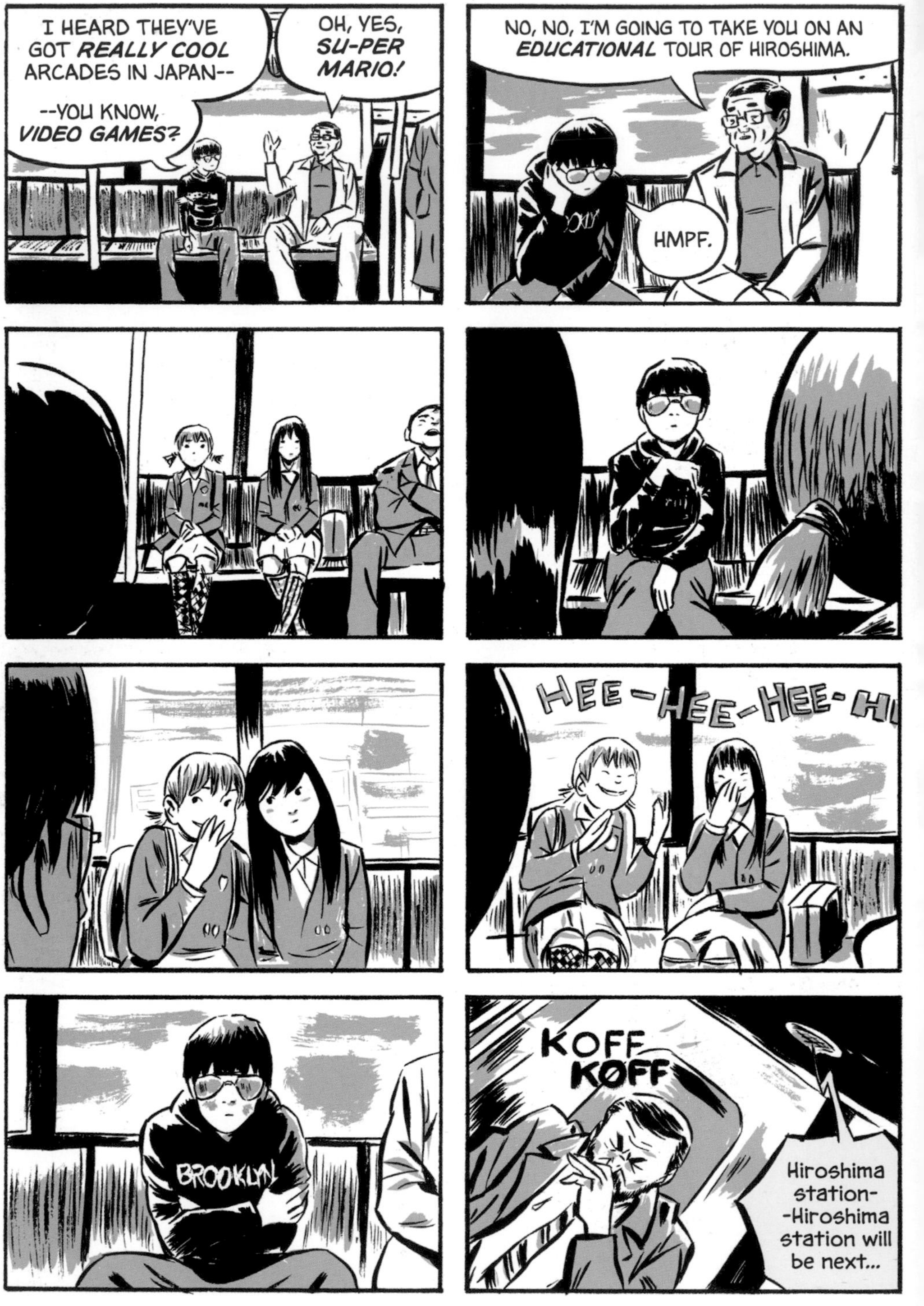
I HEARD THEY'VE GOT REALLY COOL ARCADES IN JAPAN--
--YOU KNOW, VIDEO GAMES?
OH, YES, SU-PER MARIO!
NO, NO, I'M GOING TO TAKE YOU ON AN EDUCATIONAL TOUR OF HIROSHIMA.
HMPF.
HEE-HEE-HEE-HEE-H
BROOKLYN
KOFF KOFF
Hiroshima station--Hiroshima station will be next...

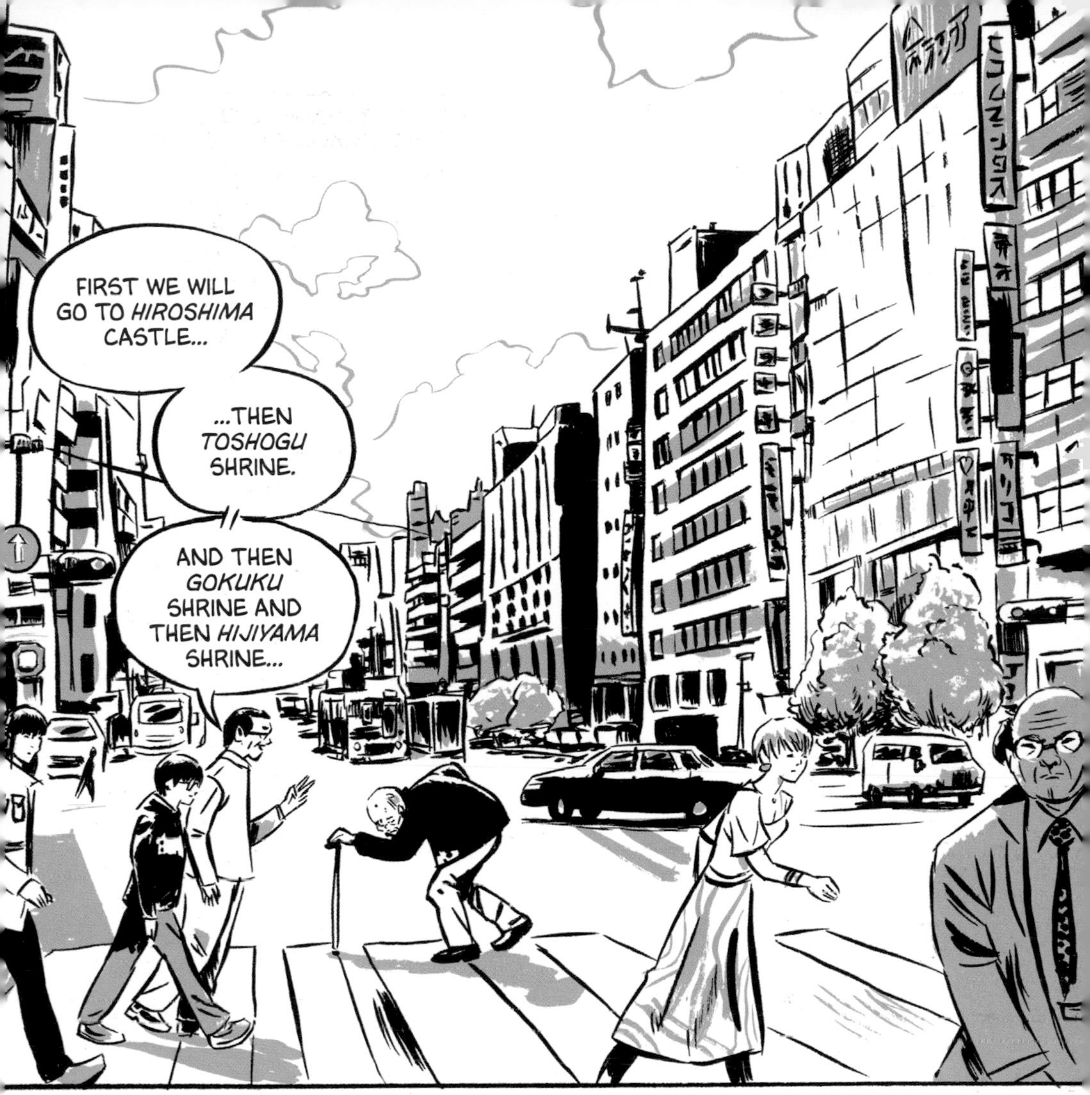
FIRST WE WILL GO TO *HIROSHIMA* CASTLE...
...THEN *TOSHOGU* SHRINE.
AND THEN *GOKUKU* SHRINE AND THEN *HIJIYAMA* SHRINE...

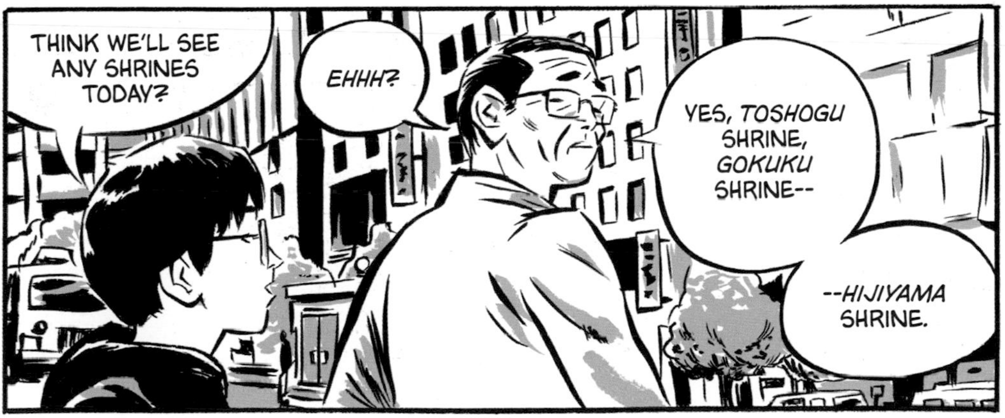
THINK WE'LL SEE ANY SHRINES TODAY?
EHHH?
YES, *TOSHOGU* SHRINE, *GOKUKU* SHRINE--
--*HIJIYAMA* SHRINE.

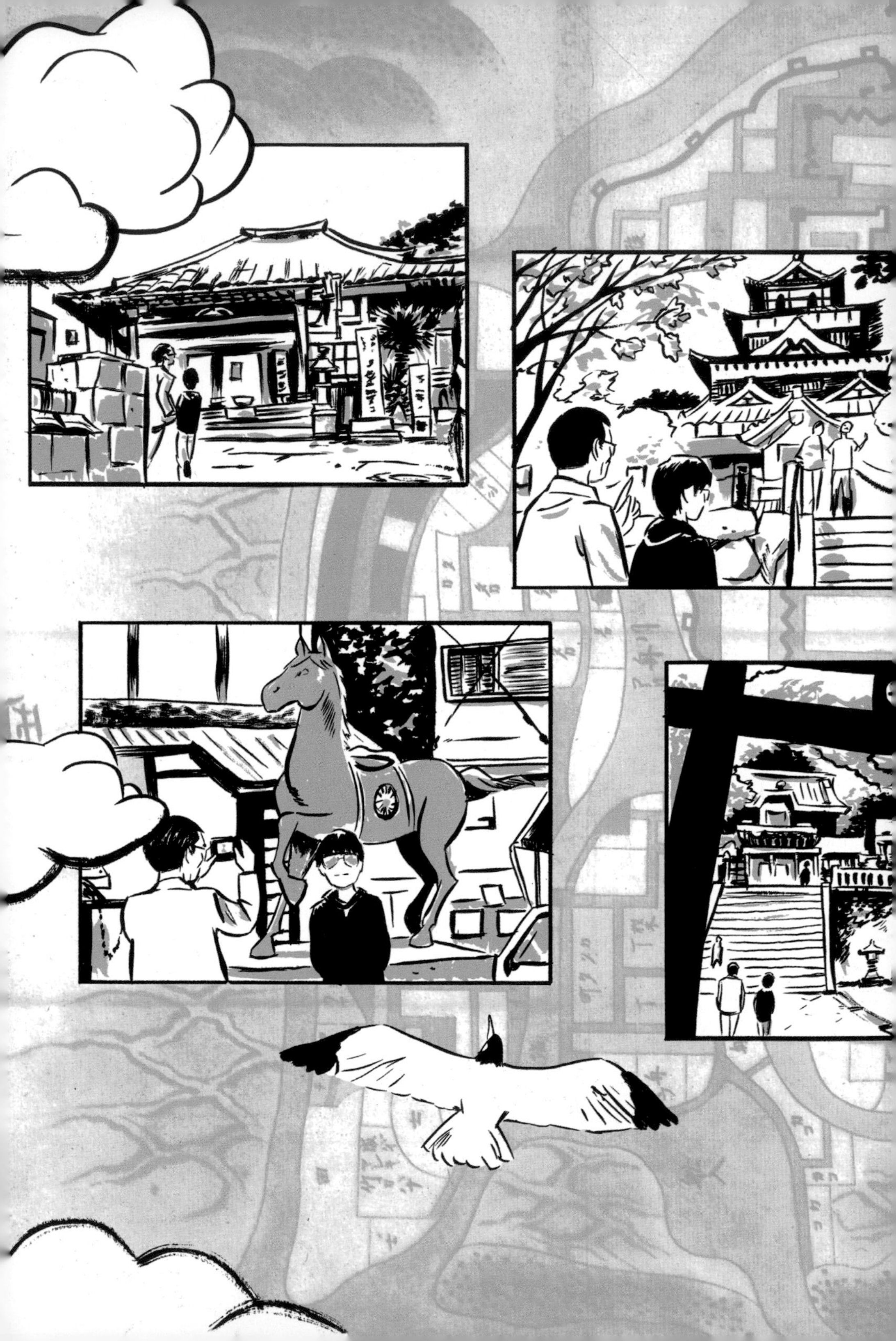

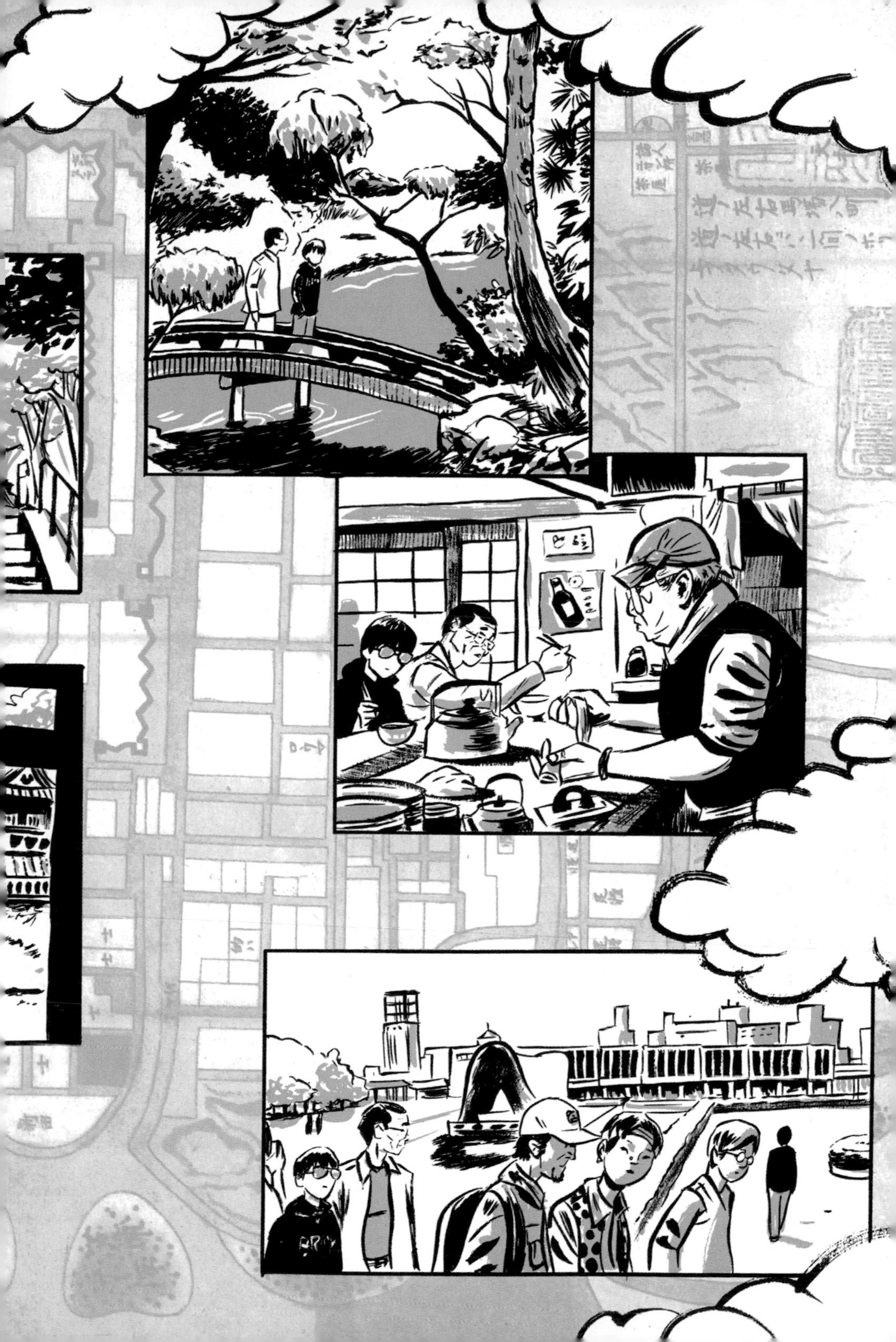

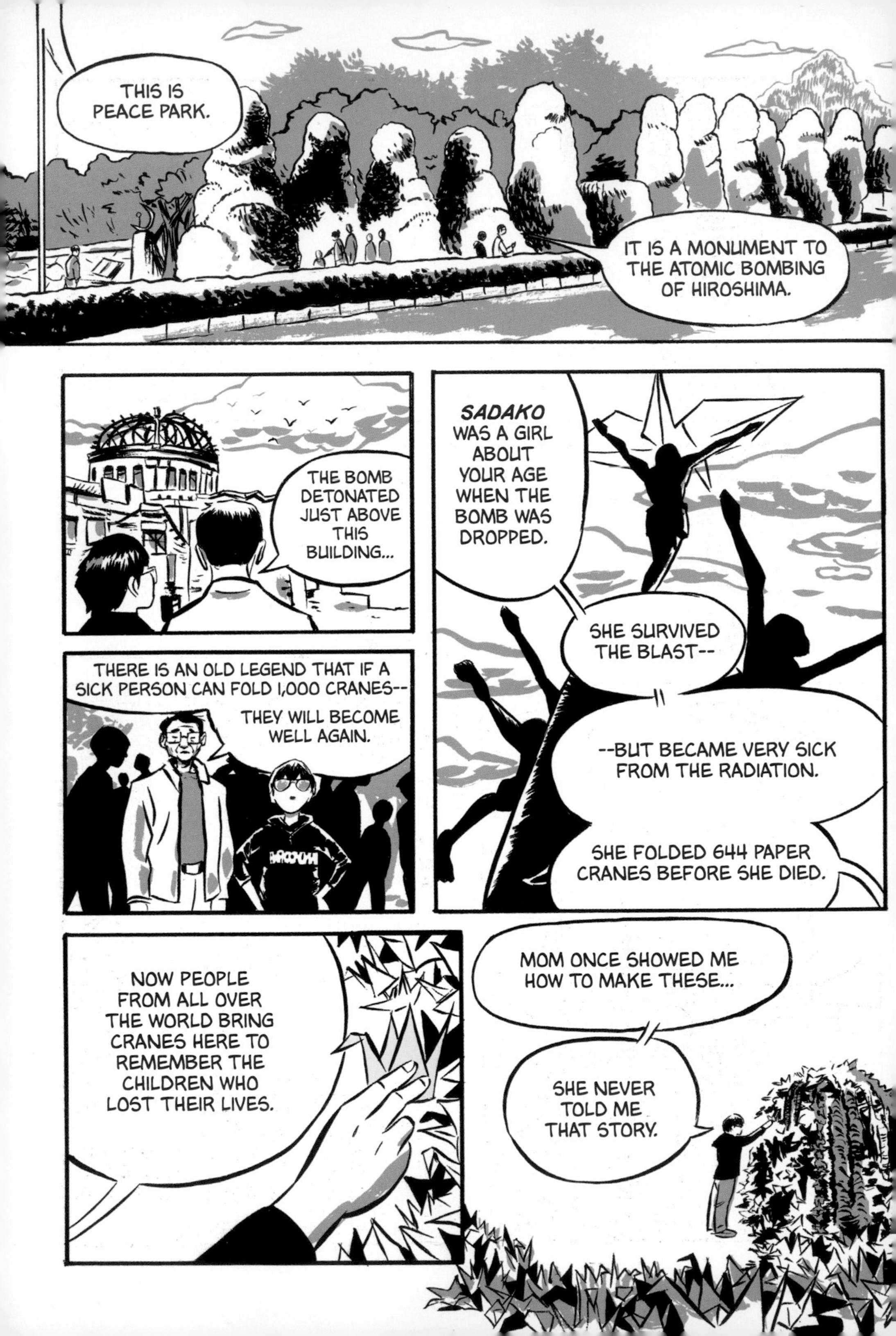
THIS IS PEACE PARK.
IT IS A MONUMENT TO THE ATOMIC BOMBING OF HIROSHIMA.
THE BOMB DETONATED JUST ABOVE THIS BUILDING...
SADAKO WAS A GIRL ABOUT YOUR AGE WHEN THE BOMB WAS DROPPED.
SHE SURVIVED THE BLAST--
--BUT BECAME VERY SICK FROM THE RADIATION.
THERE IS AN OLD LEGEND THAT IF A SICK PERSON CAN FOLD 1,000 CRANES--
THEY WILL BECOME WELL AGAIN.
SHE FOLDED 644 PAPER CRANES BEFORE SHE DIED.
NOW PEOPLE FROM ALL OVER THE WORLD BRING CRANES HERE TO REMEMBER THE CHILDREN WHO LOST THEIR LIVES.
MOM ONCE SHOWED ME HOW TO MAKE THESE...
SHE NEVER TOLD ME THAT STORY.

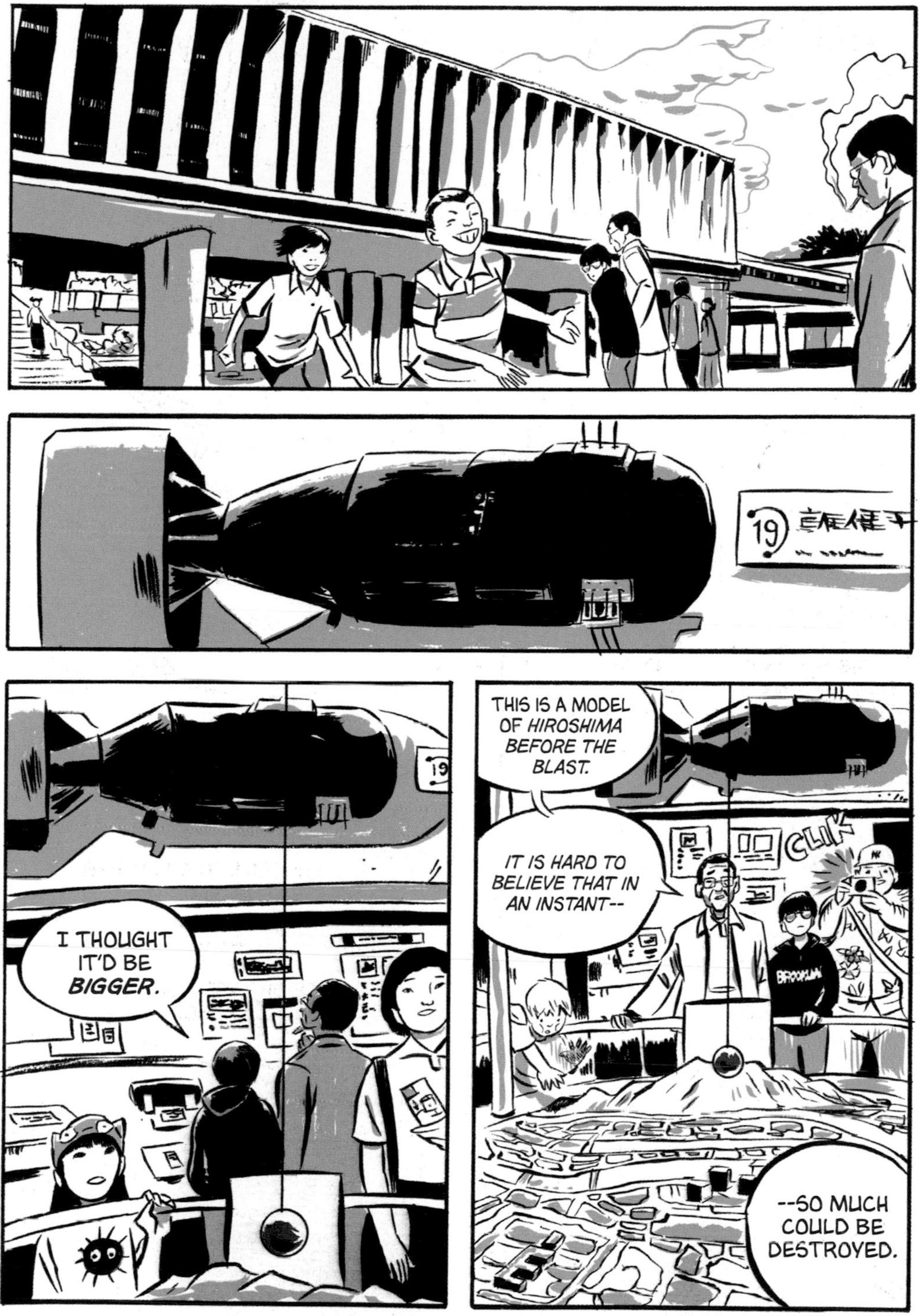
19
I THOUGHT IT'D BE *BIGGER*.
THIS IS A MODEL OF *HIROSHIMA* BEFORE THE BLAST.
IT IS HARD TO BELIEVE THAT IN AN INSTANT--
CLIK
--SO MUCH COULD BE DESTROYED.

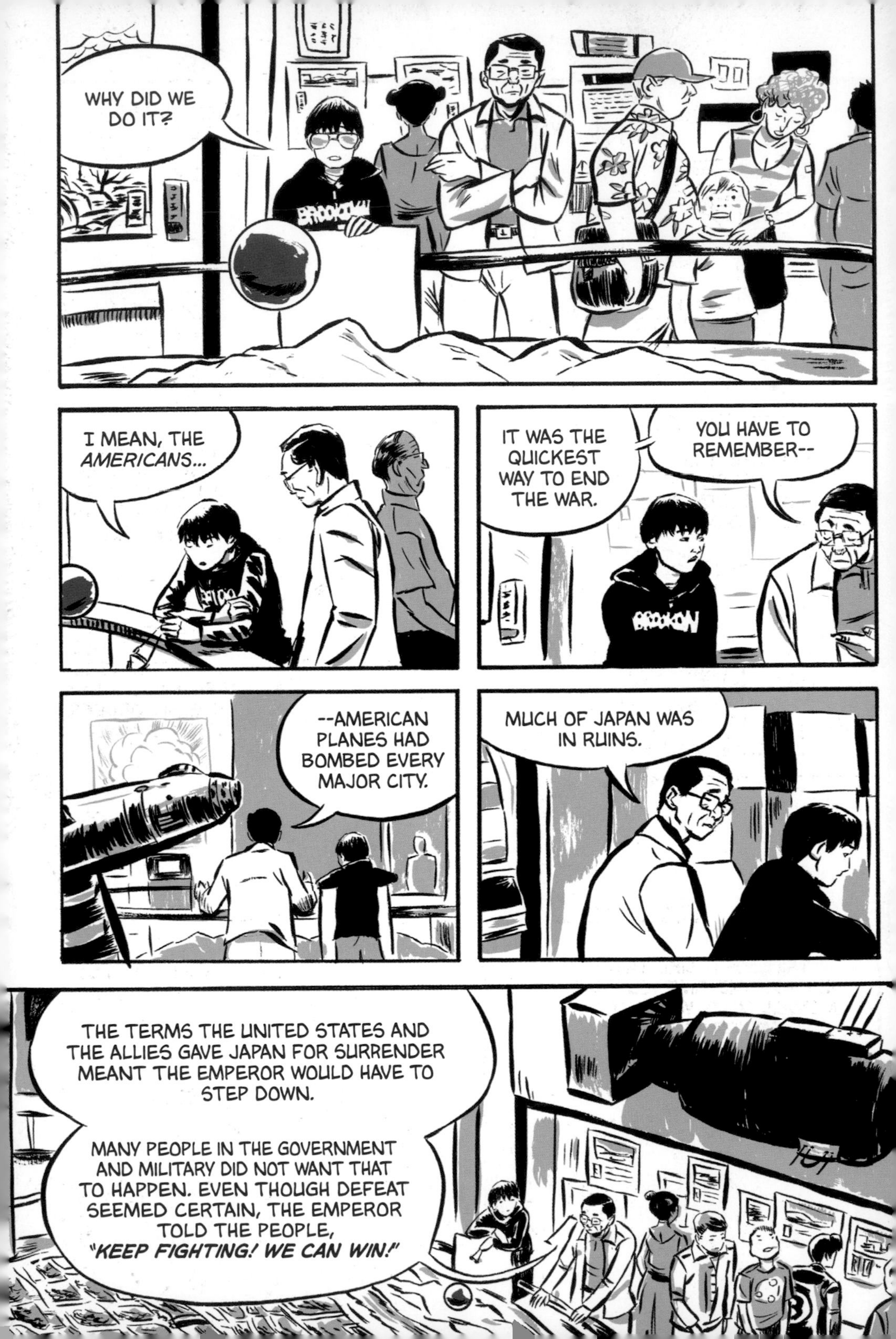
WHY DID WE DO IT?
I MEAN, THE *AMERICANS*...
IT WAS THE QUICKEST WAY TO END THE WAR.
YOU HAVE TO REMEMBER--
--AMERICAN PLANES HAD BOMBED EVERY MAJOR CITY.
MUCH OF JAPAN WAS IN RUINS.
THE TERMS THE UNITED STATES AND THE ALLIES GAVE JAPAN FOR SURRENDER MEANT THE EMPEROR WOULD HAVE TO STEP DOWN.
MANY PEOPLE IN THE GOVERNMENT AND MILITARY DID NOT WANT THAT TO HAPPEN. EVEN THOUGH DEFEAT SEEMED CERTAIN, THE EMPEROR TOLD THE PEOPLE, ***"KEEP FIGHTING! WE CAN WIN!"***

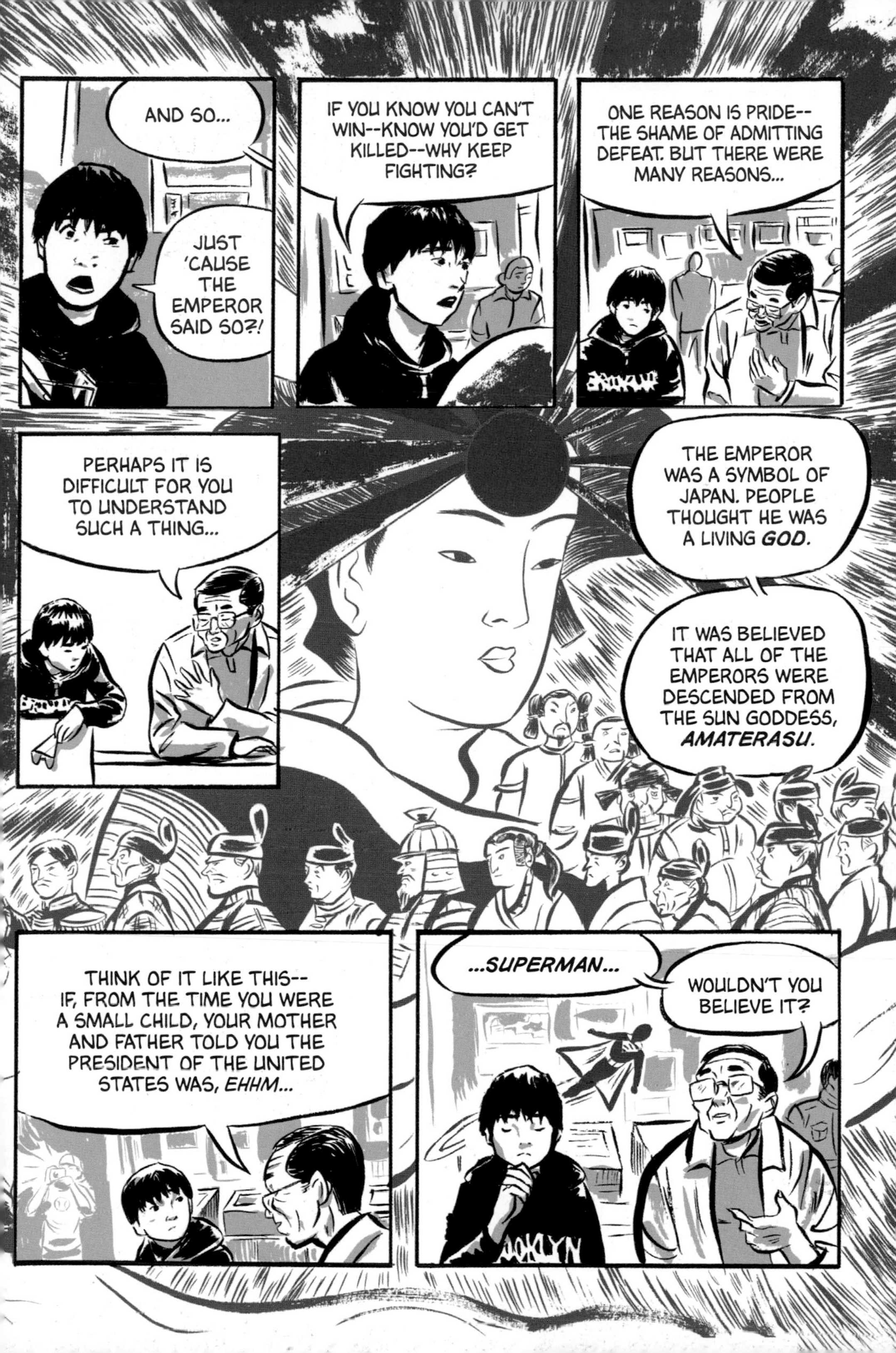
AND SO...
JUST 'CAUSE THE EMPEROR SAID SO?!
IF YOU KNOW YOU CAN'T WIN--KNOW YOU'D GET KILLED--WHY KEEP FIGHTING?
ONE REASON IS PRIDE-- THE SHAME OF ADMITTING DEFEAT. BUT THERE WERE MANY REASONS...
PERHAPS IT IS DIFFICULT FOR YOU TO UNDERSTAND SUCH A THING...
THE EMPEROR WAS A SYMBOL OF JAPAN. PEOPLE THOUGHT HE WAS A LIVING GOD.
IT WAS BELIEVED THAT ALL OF THE EMPERORS WERE DESCENDED FROM THE SUN GODDESS, AMATERASU.
THINK OF IT LIKE THIS-- IF, FROM THE TIME YOU WERE A SMALL CHILD, YOUR MOTHER AND FATHER TOLD YOU THE PRESIDENT OF THE UNITED STATES WAS, EHHM...
...SUPERMAN...
WOULDN'T YOU BELIEVE IT?

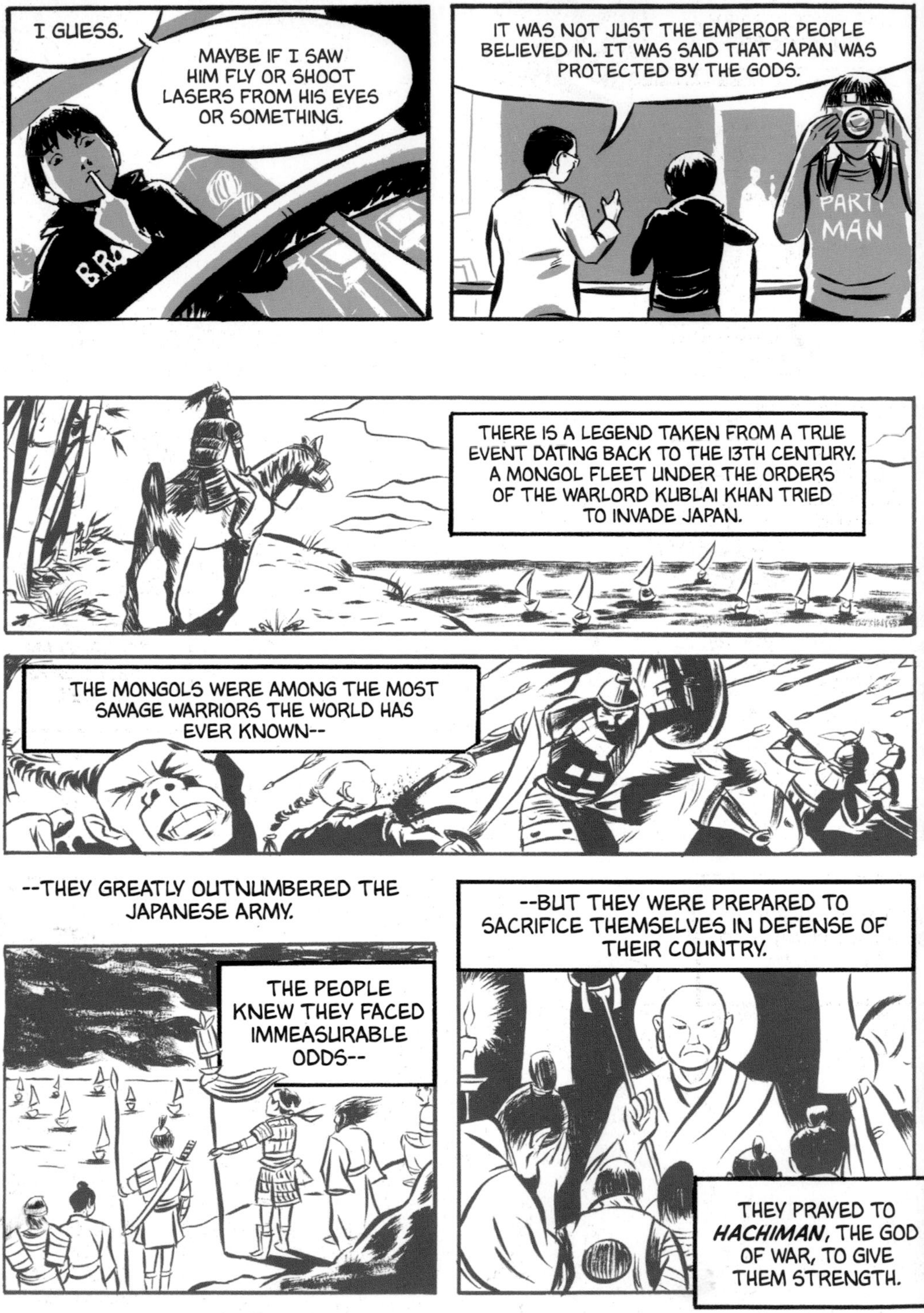

I GUESS.
MAYBE IF I SAW HIM FLY OR SHOOT LASERS FROM HIS EYES OR SOMETHING.
IT WAS NOT JUST THE EMPEROR PEOPLE BELIEVED IN. IT WAS SAID THAT JAPAN WAS PROTECTED BY THE GODS.
THERE IS A LEGEND TAKEN FROM A TRUE EVENT DATING BACK TO THE 13TH CENTURY. A MONGOL FLEET UNDER THE ORDERS OF THE WARLORD KUBLAI KHAN TRIED TO INVADE JAPAN.
THE MONGOLS WERE AMONG THE MOST SAVAGE WARRIORS THE WORLD HAS EVER KNOWN--
--THEY GREATLY OUTNUMBERED THE JAPANESE ARMY.
THE PEOPLE KNEW THEY FACED IMMEASURABLE ODDS--
--BUT THEY WERE PREPARED TO SACRIFICE THEMSELVES IN DEFENSE OF THEIR COUNTRY.
THEY PRAYED TO ***HACHIMAN***, THE GOD OF WAR, TO GIVE THEM STRENGTH.

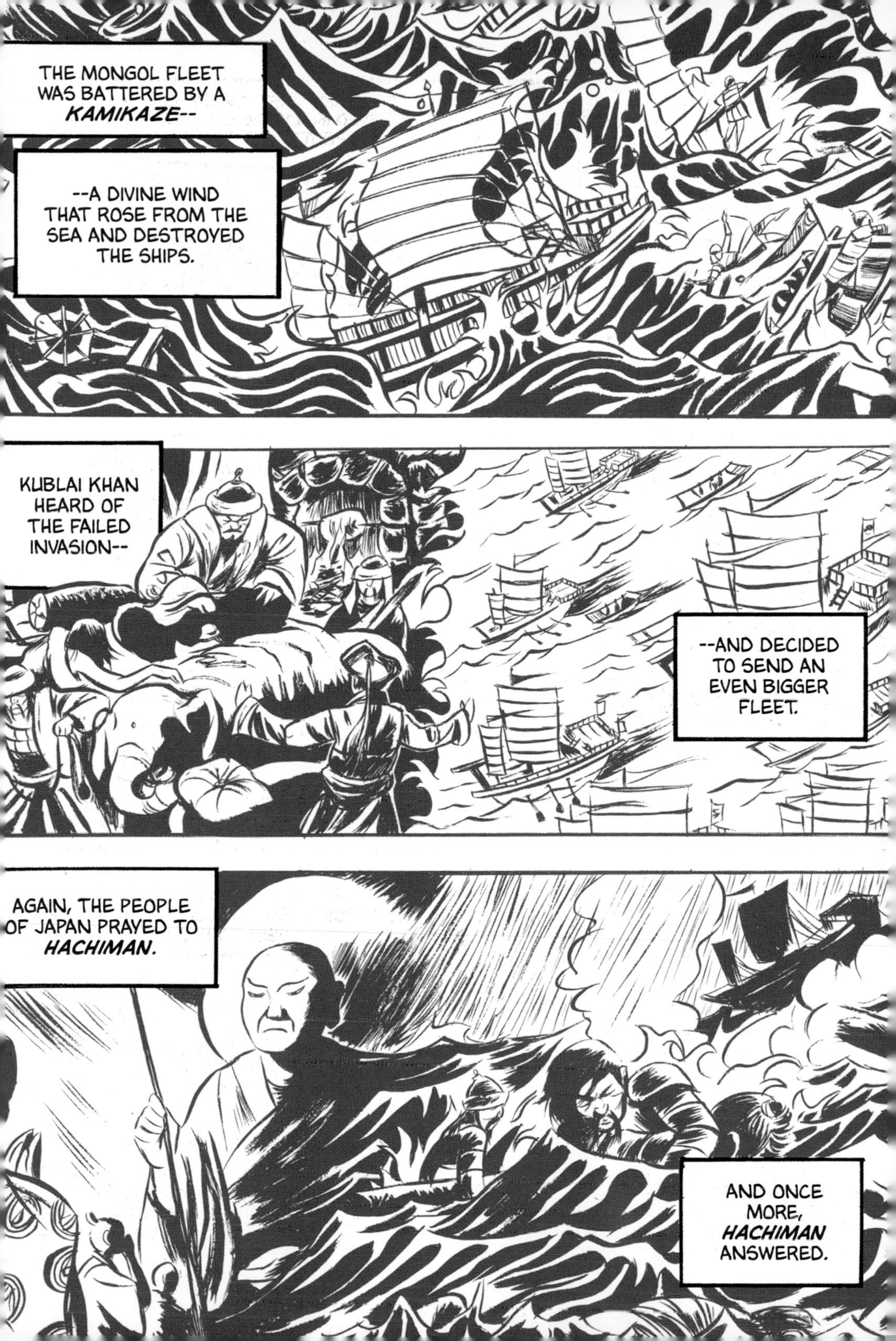
THE MONGOL FLEET WAS BATTERED BY A *KAMIKAZE*--
--A DIVINE WIND THAT ROSE FROM THE SEA AND DESTROYED THE SHIPS.
KUBLAI KHAN HEARD OF THE FAILED INVASION--
--AND DECIDED TO SEND AN EVEN BIGGER FLEET.
AGAIN, THE PEOPLE OF JAPAN PRAYED TO *HACHIMAN.*
AND ONCE MORE, *HACHIMAN* ANSWERED.

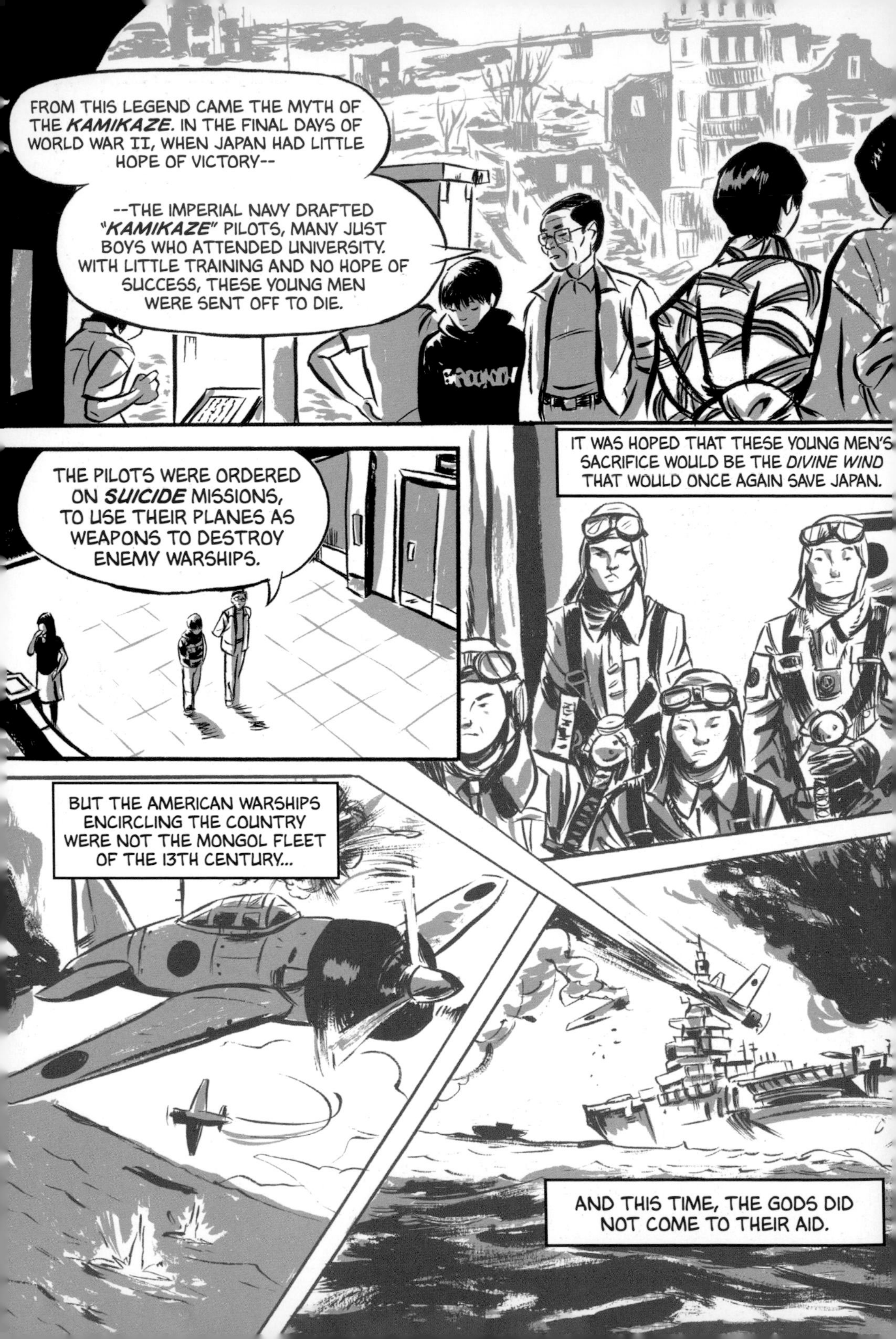
FROM THIS LEGEND CAME THE MYTH OF THE *KAMIKAZE.* IN THE FINAL DAYS OF WORLD WAR II, WHEN JAPAN HAD LITTLE HOPE OF VICTORY--
--THE IMPERIAL NAVY DRAFTED "*KAMIKAZE*" PILOTS, MANY JUST BOYS WHO ATTENDED UNIVERSITY. WITH LITTLE TRAINING AND NO HOPE OF SUCCESS, THESE YOUNG MEN WERE SENT OFF TO DIE.
THE PILOTS WERE ORDERED ON *SUICIDE* MISSIONS, TO USE THEIR PLANES AS WEAPONS TO DESTROY ENEMY WARSHIPS.
IT WAS HOPED THAT THESE YOUNG MEN'S SACRIFICE WOULD BE THE *DIVINE WIND* THAT WOULD ONCE AGAIN SAVE JAPAN.
BUT THE AMERICAN WARSHIPS ENCIRCLING THE COUNTRY WERE NOT THE MONGOL FLEET OF THE 13TH CENTURY...
AND THIS TIME, THE GODS DID NOT COME TO THEIR AID.

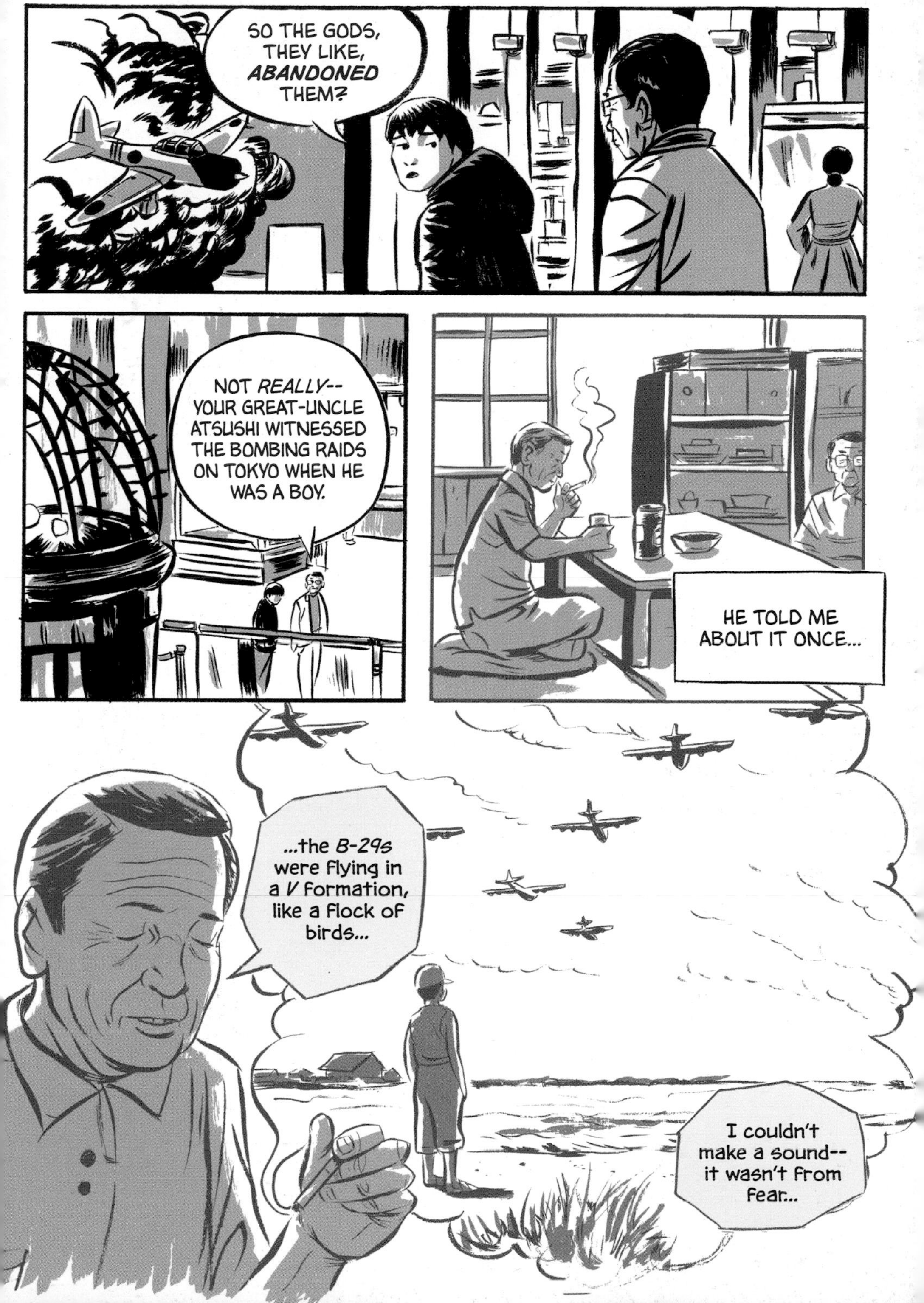
SO THE GODS, THEY LIKE, ABANDONED THEM?
NOT REALLY-- YOUR GREAT-UNCLE ATSUSHI WITNESSED THE BOMBING RAIDS ON TOKYO WHEN HE WAS A BOY.
HE TOLD ME ABOUT IT ONCE...
...the B-29s were flying in a V formation, like a flock of birds...
I couldn't make a sound-- it wasn't from fear...

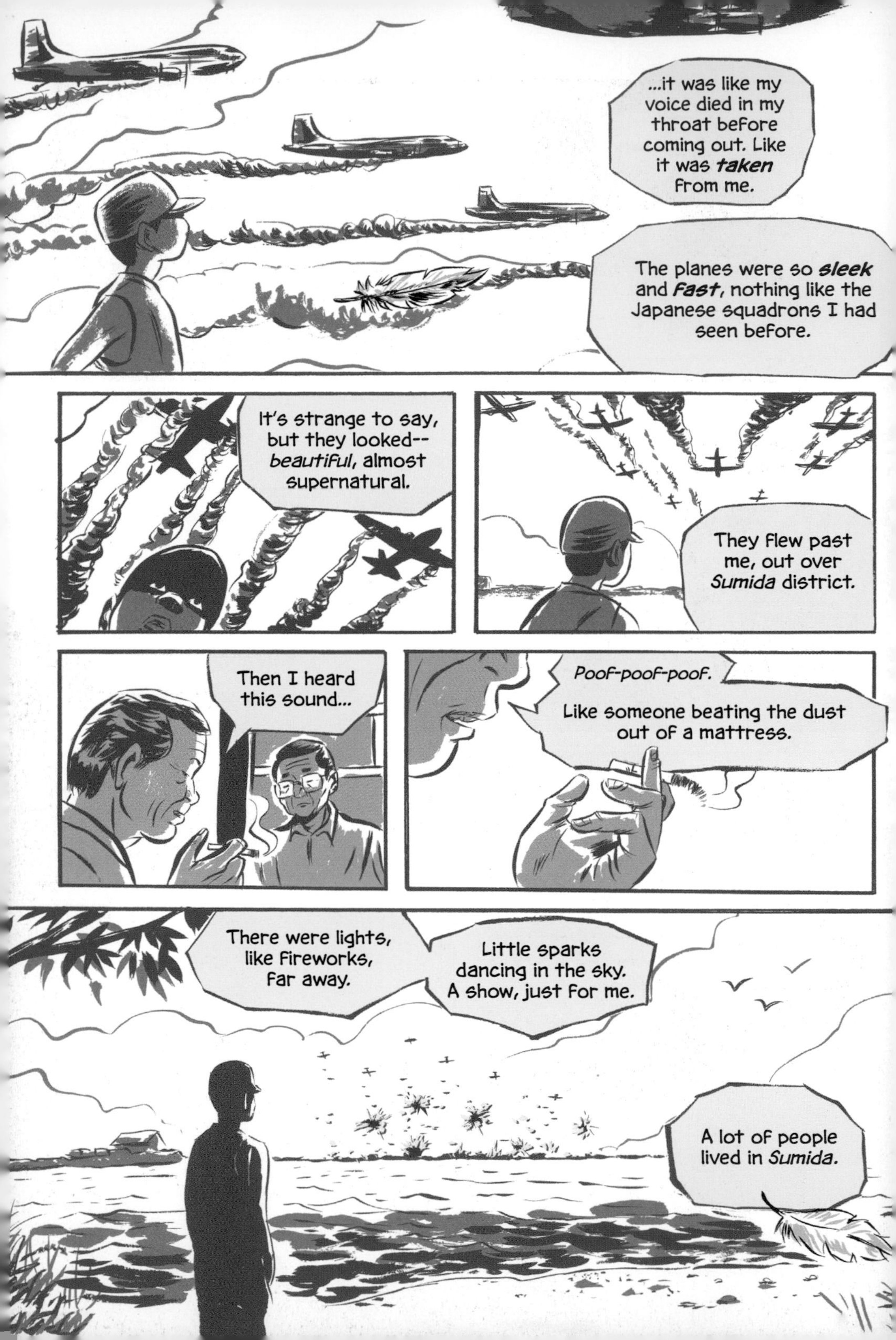
...it was like my voice died in my throat before coming out. Like it was *taken* from me.
The planes were so ***sleek*** and ***fast***, nothing like the Japanese squadrons I had seen before.
It's strange to say, but they looked-- *beautiful*, almost supernatural.
They flew past me, out over *Sumida* district.
Then I heard this sound...
Poof-poof-poof.
Like someone beating the dust out of a mattress.
There were lights, like fireworks, far away.
Little sparks dancing in the sky. A show, just for me.
A lot of people lived in *Sumida*.

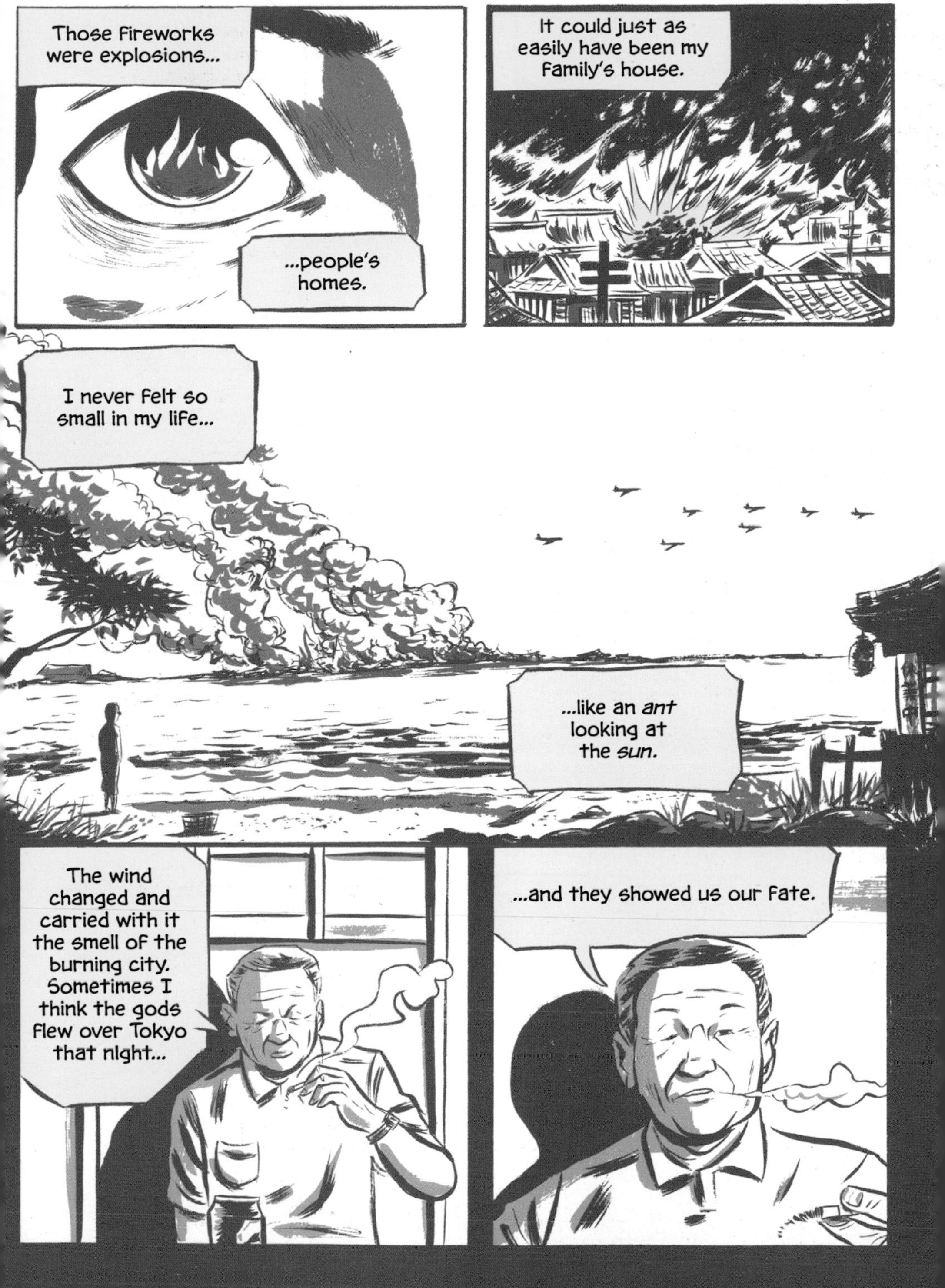
Those fireworks were explosions...
...people's homes.
It could just as easily have been my family's house.
I never felt so small in my life...
...like an *ant* looking at the *sun.*
The wind changed and carried with it the smell of the burning city. Sometimes I think the gods flew over Tokyo that night...
...and they showed us our fate.

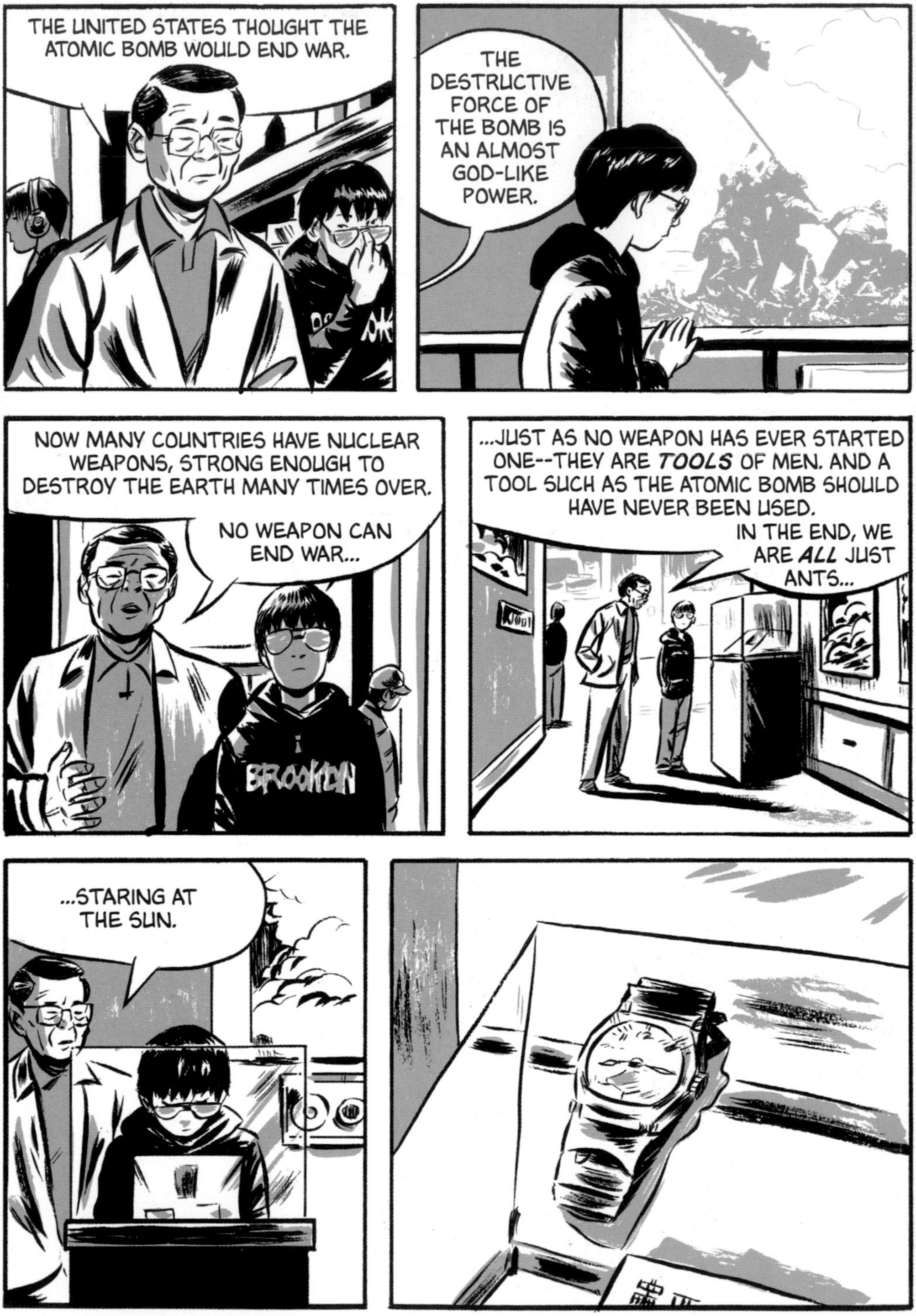
THE UNITED STATES THOUGHT THE ATOMIC BOMB WOULD END WAR.
THE DESTRUCTIVE FORCE OF THE BOMB IS AN ALMOST GOD-LIKE POWER.
NOW MANY COUNTRIES HAVE NUCLEAR WEAPONS, STRONG ENOUGH TO DESTROY THE EARTH MANY TIMES OVER.
NO WEAPON CAN END WAR...
BROOKLYN
...JUST AS NO WEAPON HAS EVER STARTED ONE--THEY ARE *TOOLS* OF MEN. AND A TOOL SUCH AS THE ATOMIC BOMB SHOULD HAVE NEVER BEEN USED.
IN THE END, WE ARE *ALL* JUST ANTS...
...STARING AT THE SUN.

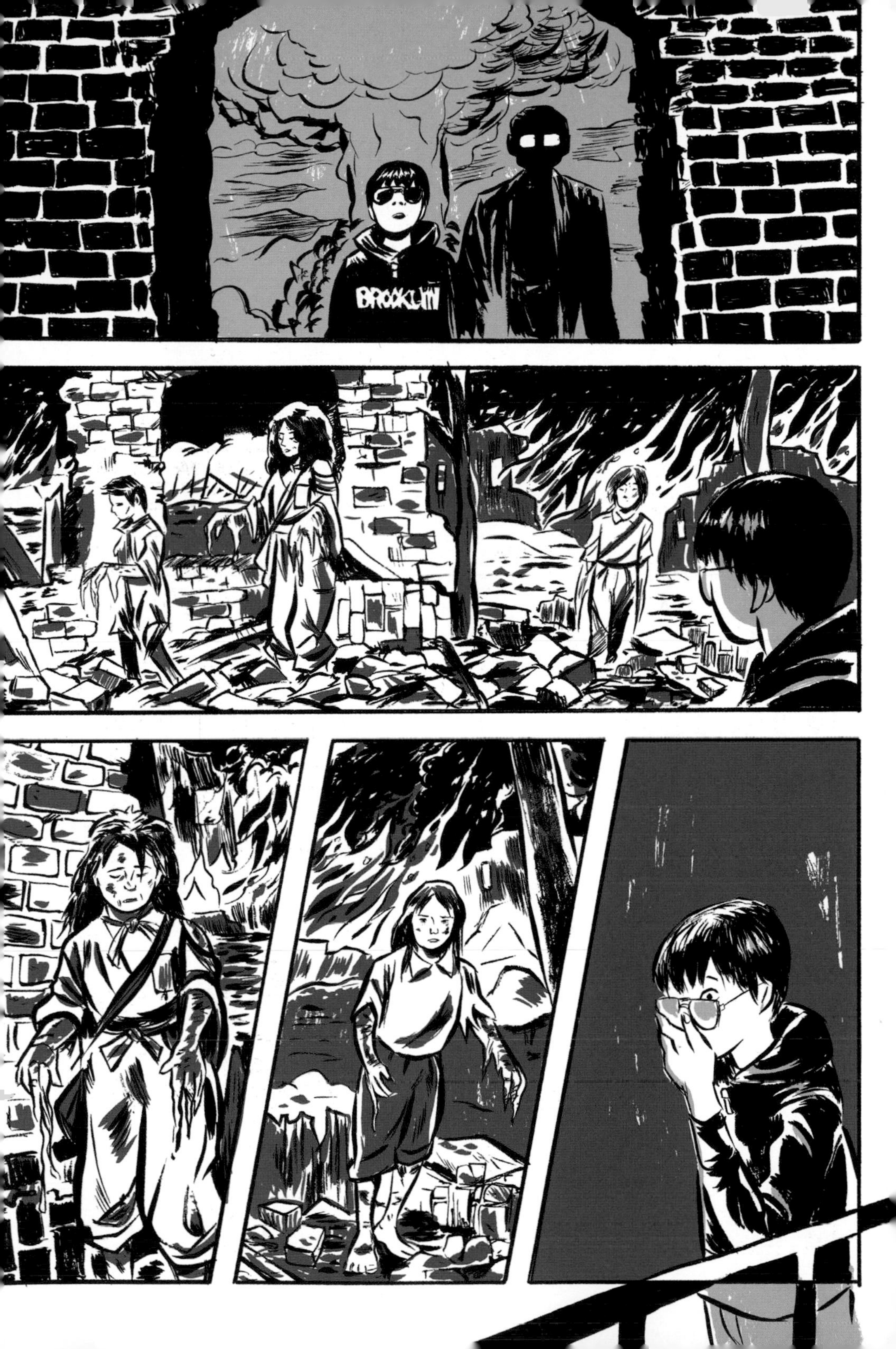
BROOKLYN

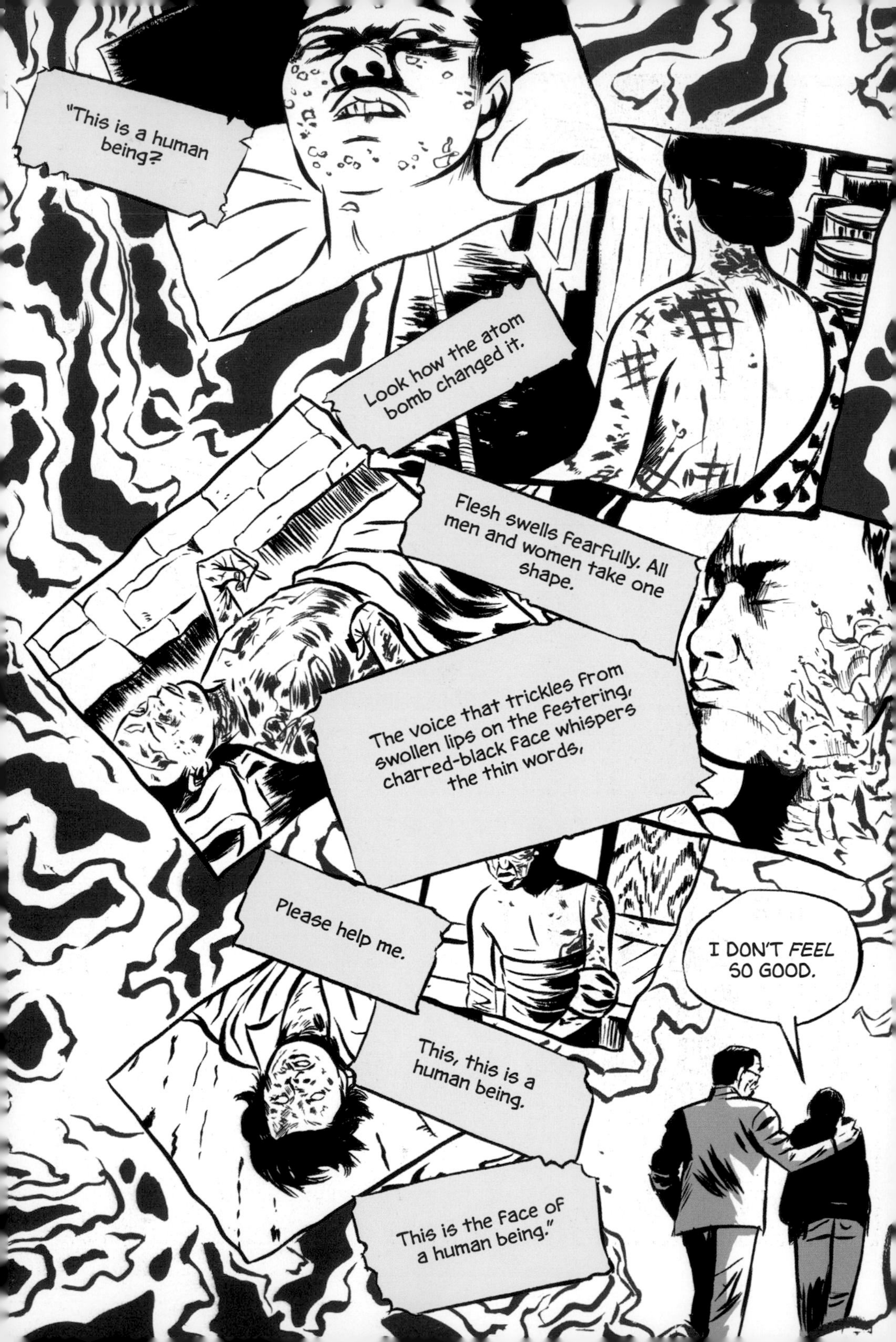
"This is a human being?
Look how the atom bomb changed it.
Flesh swells fearfully. All men and women take one shape.
The voice that trickles from swollen lips on the festering, charred-black face whispers the thin words,
Please help me.
I DON'T FEEL SO GOOD.
This, this is a human being.
This is the face of a human being."

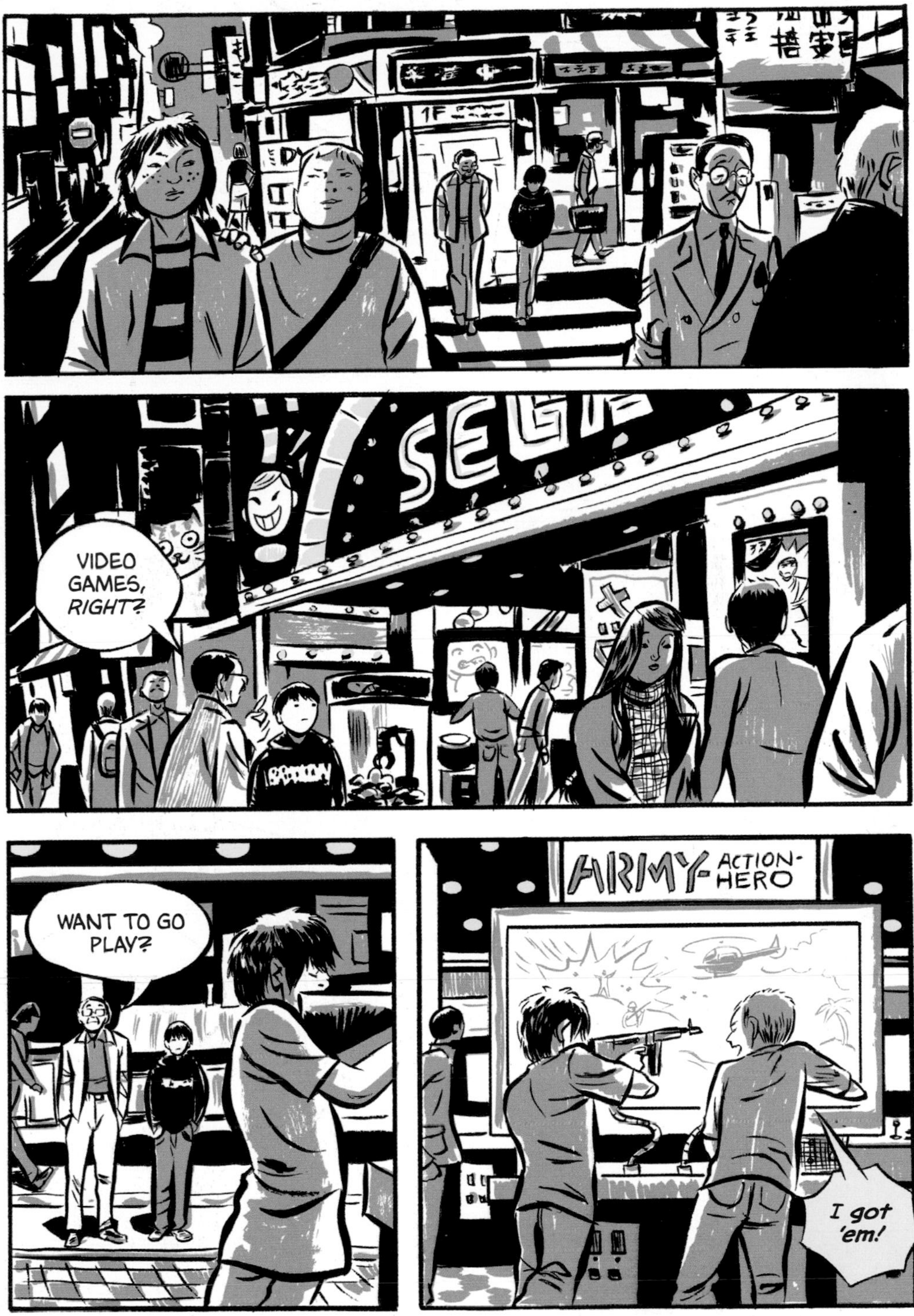
VIDEO GAMES, RIGHT?
WANT TO GO PLAY?
ARMY-ACTION-HERO
I got 'em!

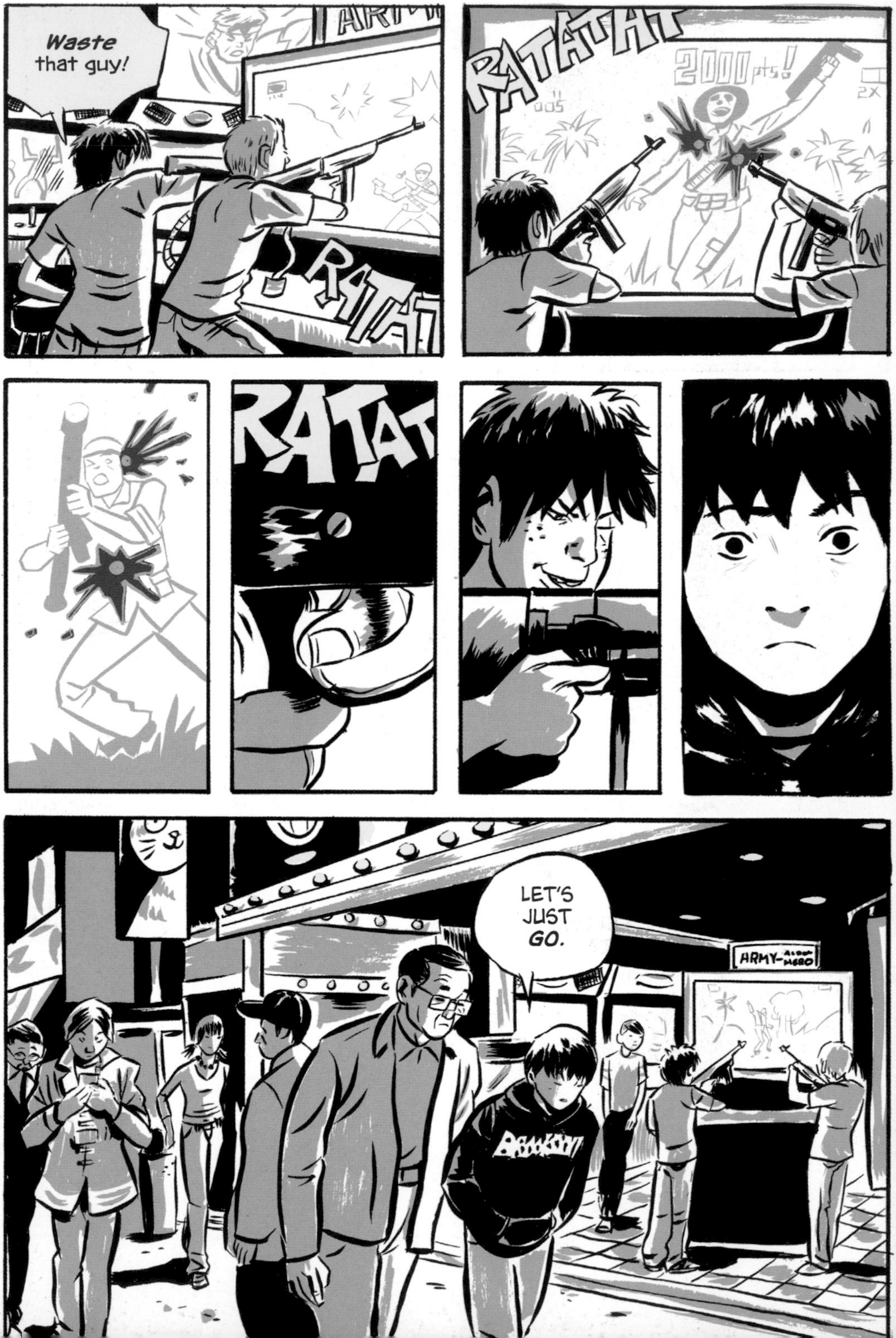
Waste that guy!
RATATAT
RATATAT
2000 pts!
2X
RATAT
LET'S JUST GO.
ARMY-

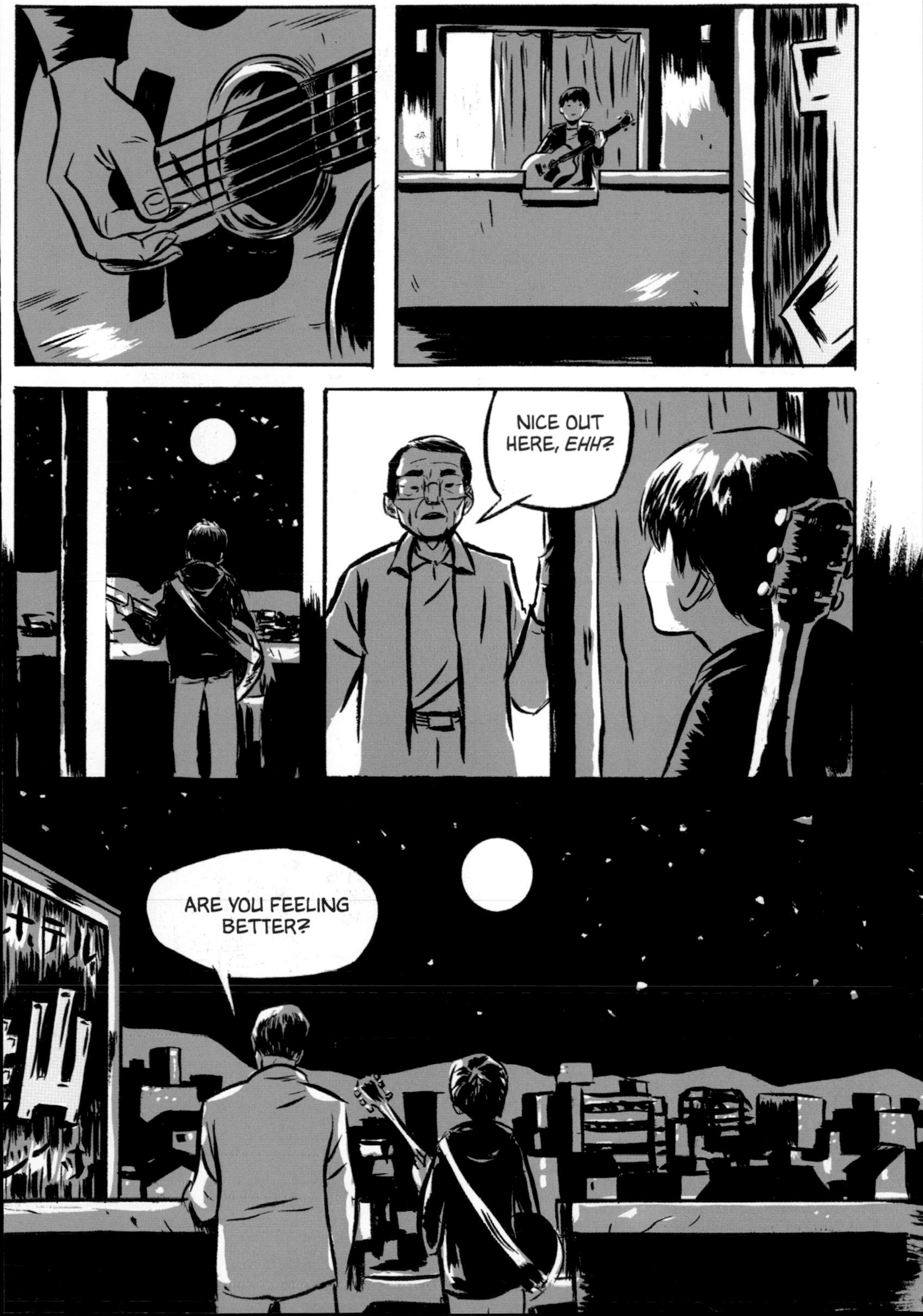
NICE OUT HERE, *EHH*?
ARE YOU FEELING BETTER?

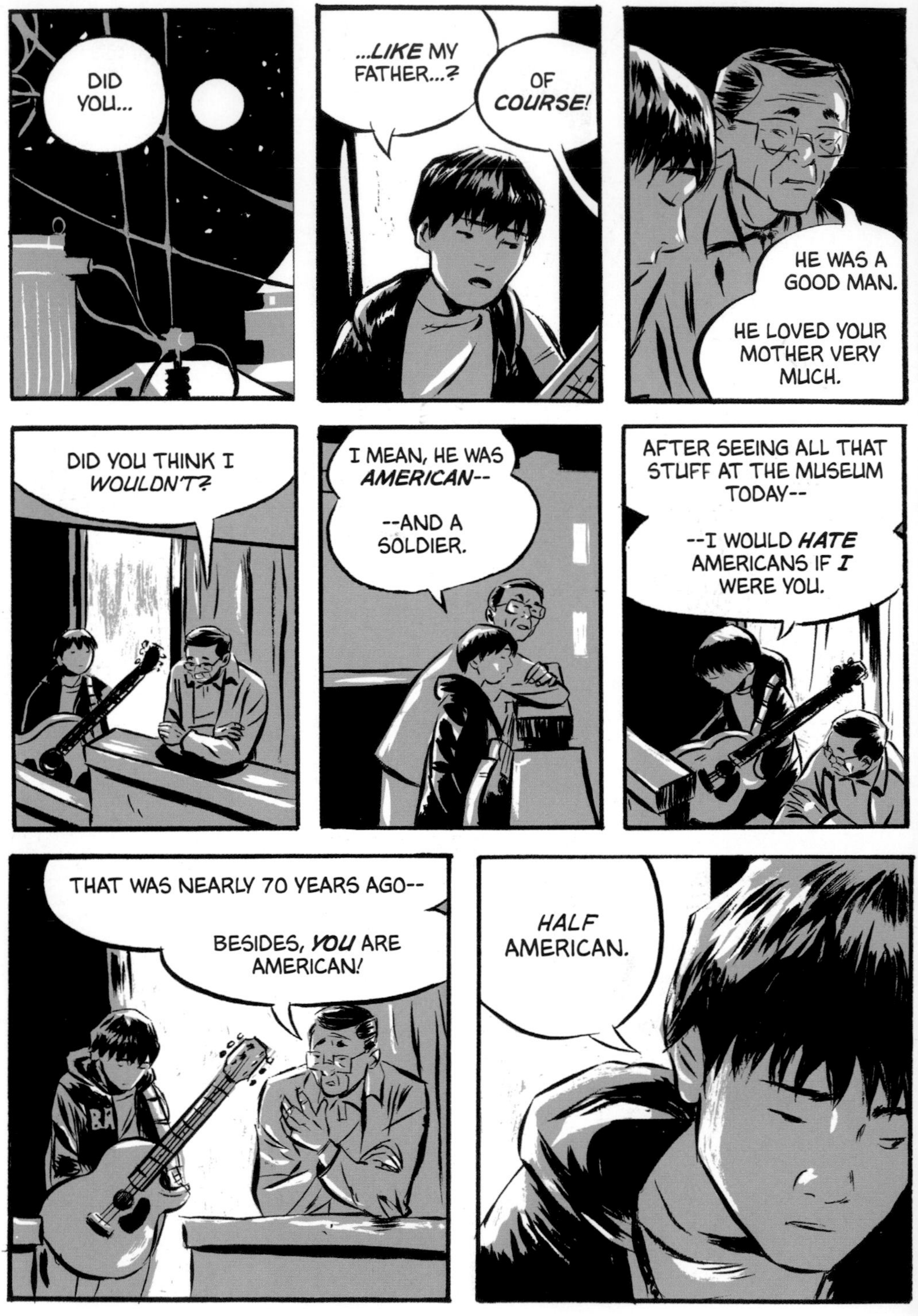
DID YOU...
...LIKE MY FATHER...?
OF COURSE!
HE WAS A GOOD MAN.
HE LOVED YOUR MOTHER VERY MUCH.
DID YOU THINK I WOULDN'T?
I MEAN, HE WAS AMERICAN--
--AND A SOLDIER.
AFTER SEEING ALL THAT STUFF AT THE MUSEUM TODAY--
--I WOULD HATE AMERICANS IF I WERE YOU.
THAT WAS NEARLY 70 YEARS AGO--
BESIDES, YOU ARE AMERICAN!
HALF AMERICAN.

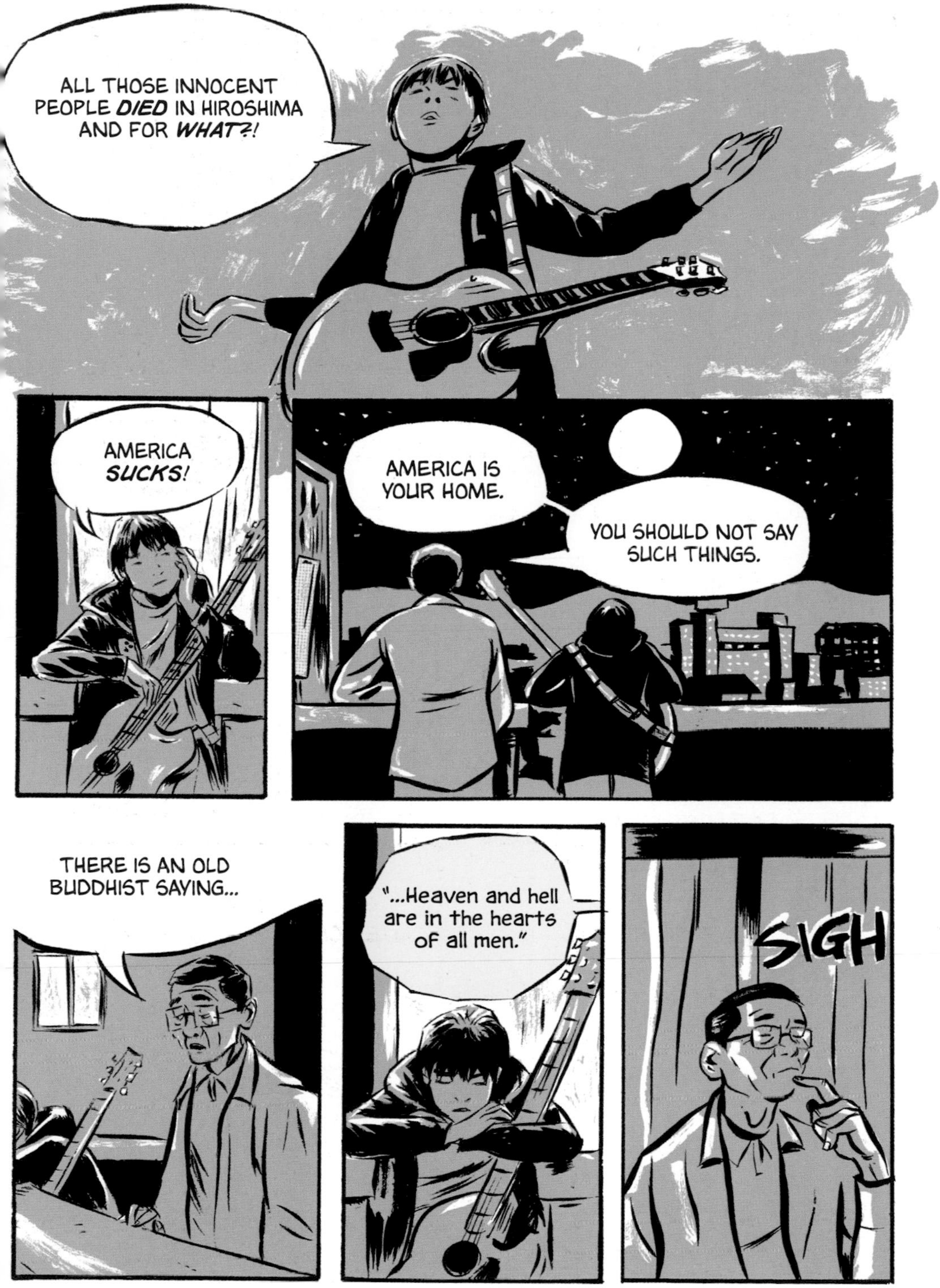
ALL THOSE INNOCENT PEOPLE DIED IN HIROSHIMA AND FOR WHAT?!
AMERICA SUCKS!
AMERICA IS YOUR HOME.
YOU SHOULD NOT SAY SUCH THINGS.
THERE IS AN OLD BUDDHIST SAYING...
"...Heaven and hell are in the hearts of all men."
SIGH

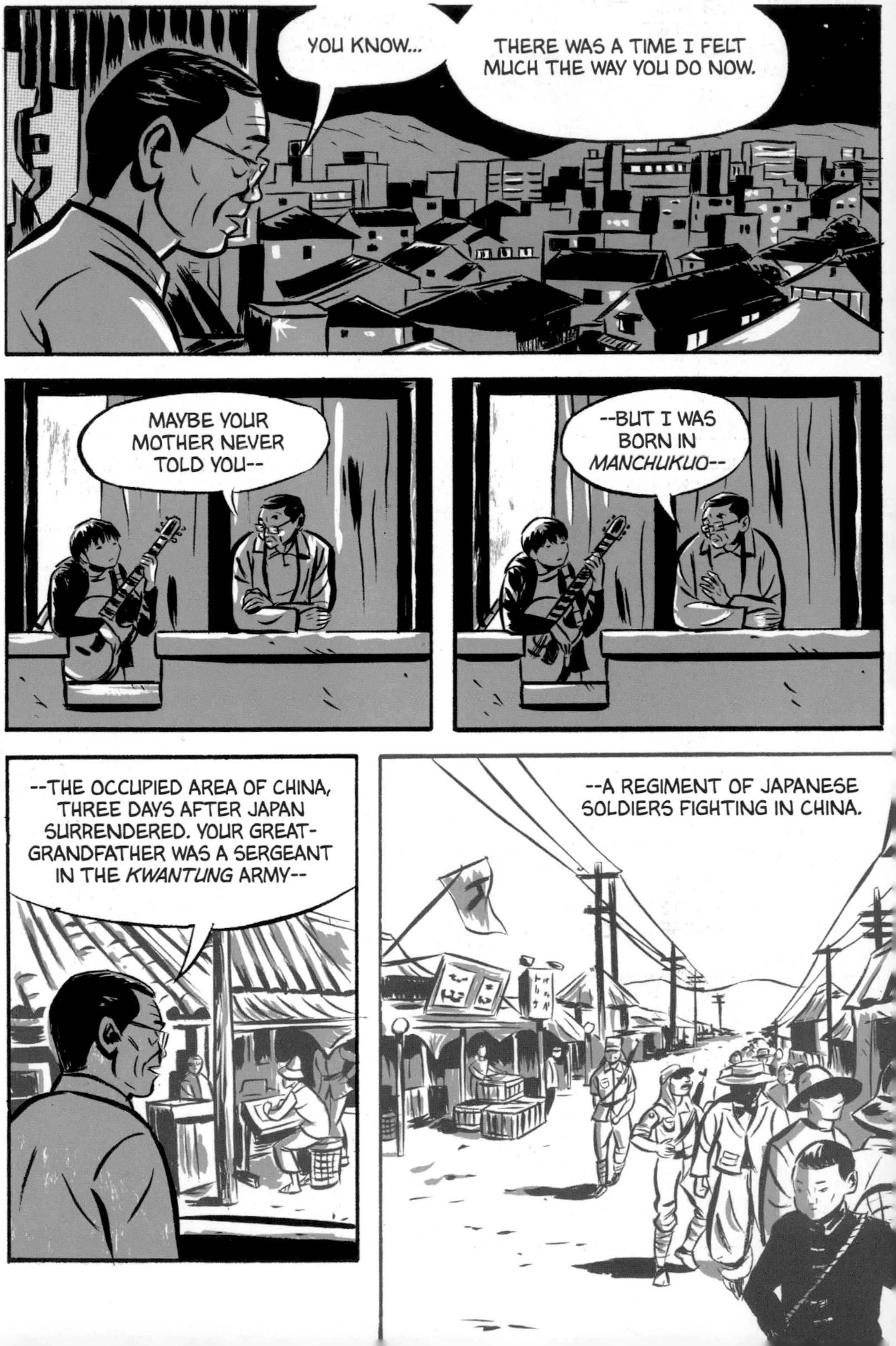
YOU KNOW...
THERE WAS A TIME I FELT MUCH THE WAY YOU DO NOW.
MAYBE YOUR MOTHER NEVER TOLD YOU--
--BUT I WAS BORN IN *MANCHUKUO*--
--THE OCCUPIED AREA OF CHINA, THREE DAYS AFTER JAPAN SURRENDERED. YOUR GREAT-GRANDFATHER WAS A SERGEANT IN THE *KWANTUNG* ARMY--
--A REGIMENT OF JAPANESE SOLDIERS FIGHTING IN CHINA.

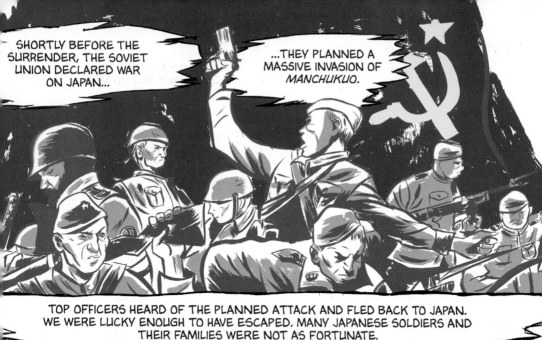

SHORTLY BEFORE THE SURRENDER, THE SOVIET UNION DECLARED WAR ON JAPAN...

...THEY PLANNED A MASSIVE INVASION OF *MANCHUKUO.*

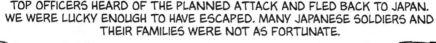

TOP OFFICERS HEARD OF THE PLANNED ATTACK AND FLED BACK TO JAPAN. WE WERE LUCKY ENOUGH TO HAVE ESCAPED. MANY JAPANESE SOLDIERS AND THEIR FAMILIES WERE NOT AS FORTUNATE.

I HAVE ALWAYS BEEN INTERESTED IN CHINESE HISTORY.

MAYBE IT IS BECAUSE EARLY JAPANESE SOCIETY WAS SO INFLUENCED BY CHINA...

...OR MAYBE BECAUSE I WAS BORN THERE.

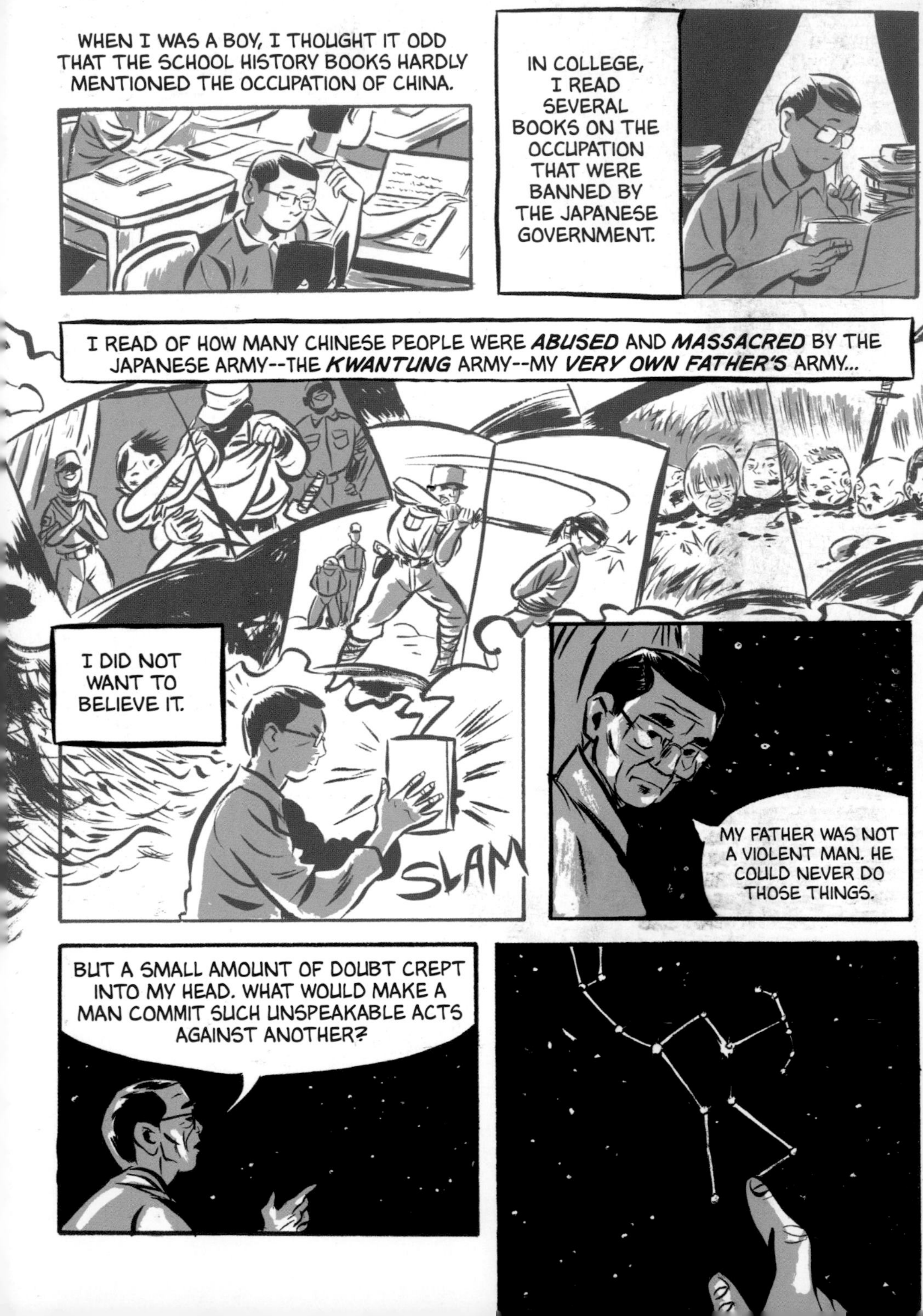
WHEN I WAS A BOY, I THOUGHT IT ODD THAT THE SCHOOL HISTORY BOOKS HARDLY MENTIONED THE OCCUPATION OF CHINA.
IN COLLEGE, I READ SEVERAL BOOKS ON THE OCCUPATION THAT WERE BANNED BY THE JAPANESE GOVERNMENT.
I READ OF HOW MANY CHINESE PEOPLE WERE ABUSED AND MASSACRED BY THE JAPANESE ARMY--THE KWANTUNG ARMY--MY VERY OWN FATHER'S ARMY...
I DID NOT WANT TO BELIEVE IT.
SLAM
MY FATHER WAS NOT A VIOLENT MAN. HE COULD NEVER DO THOSE THINGS.
BUT A SMALL AMOUNT OF DOUBT CREPT INTO MY HEAD. WHAT WOULD MAKE A MAN COMMIT SUCH UNSPEAKABLE ACTS AGAINST ANOTHER?

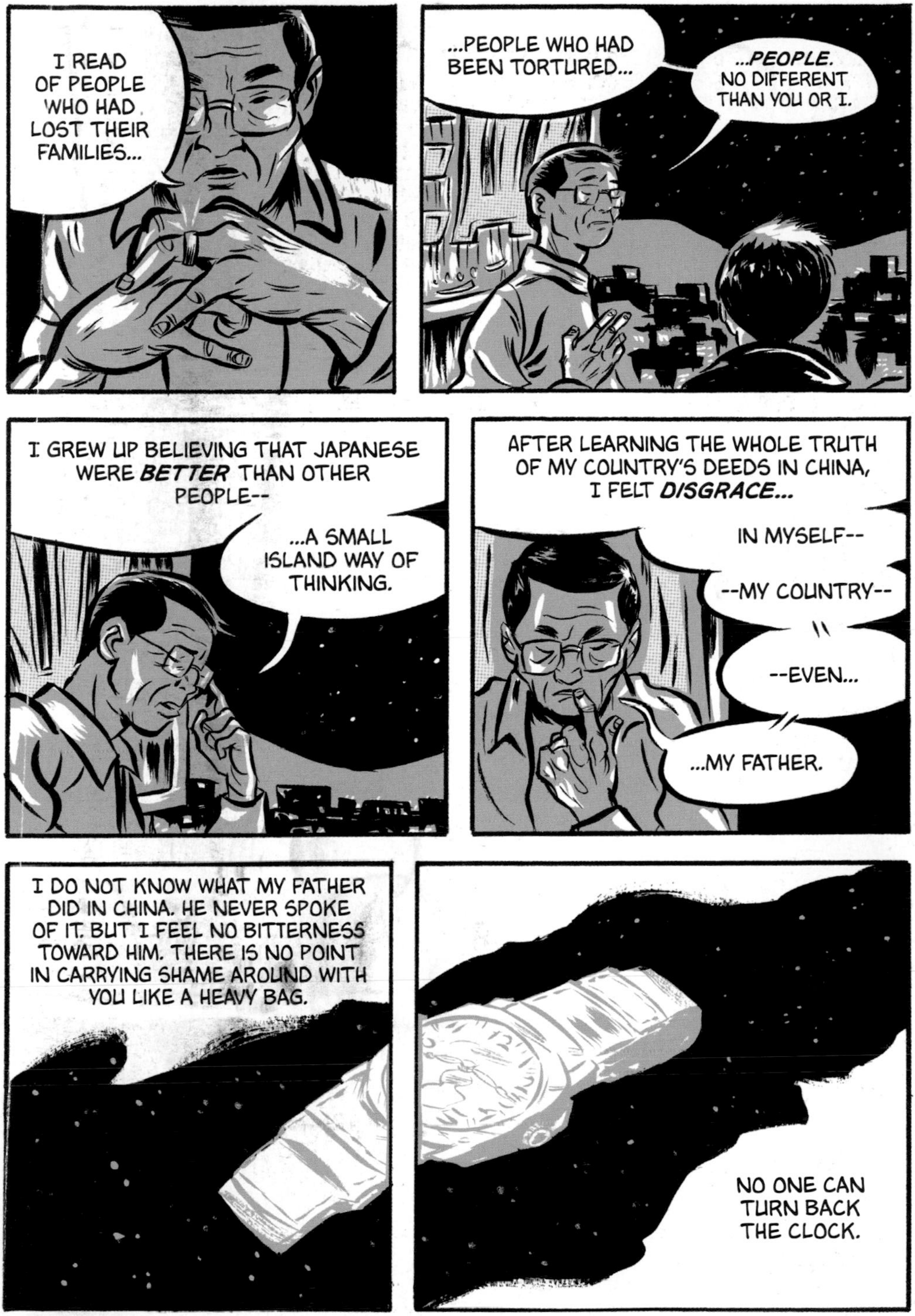
I READ OF PEOPLE WHO HAD LOST THEIR FAMILIES...
...PEOPLE WHO HAD BEEN TORTURED...
...PEOPLE. NO DIFFERENT THAN YOU OR I.
I GREW UP BELIEVING THAT JAPANESE WERE BETTER THAN OTHER PEOPLE--
...A SMALL ISLAND WAY OF THINKING.
AFTER LEARNING THE WHOLE TRUTH OF MY COUNTRY'S DEEDS IN CHINA, I FELT DISGRACE...
IN MYSELF--
--MY COUNTRY--
--EVEN...
...MY FATHER.
I DO NOT KNOW WHAT MY FATHER DID IN CHINA. HE NEVER SPOKE OF IT. BUT I FEEL NO BITTERNESS TOWARD HIM. THERE IS NO POINT IN CARRYING SHAME AROUND WITH YOU LIKE A HEAVY BAG.
NO ONE CAN TURN BACK THE CLOCK.

SOME PEOPLE DENY THIS PART OF OUR HISTORY.

THE TRUTH IS OFTEN HARD TO ACCEPT.

I AM PROUD TO BE JAPANESE...

...BUT WE ARE NOT PERFECT.

NOBODY IS.

WHAT'S THE POINT IN KNOWING ALL THIS BAD STUFF WHEN IT'S JUST GOING TO MAKE YOU FEEL *ROTTEN*?

YOU HAVE HEARD THE EXPRESSION "HISTORY REPEATS ITSELF"?

YEAH.

THAT IS WHY OLD MEN LIKE ME HAVE TO PASS DOWN THIS HISTORY TO THEIR GRANDSONS.

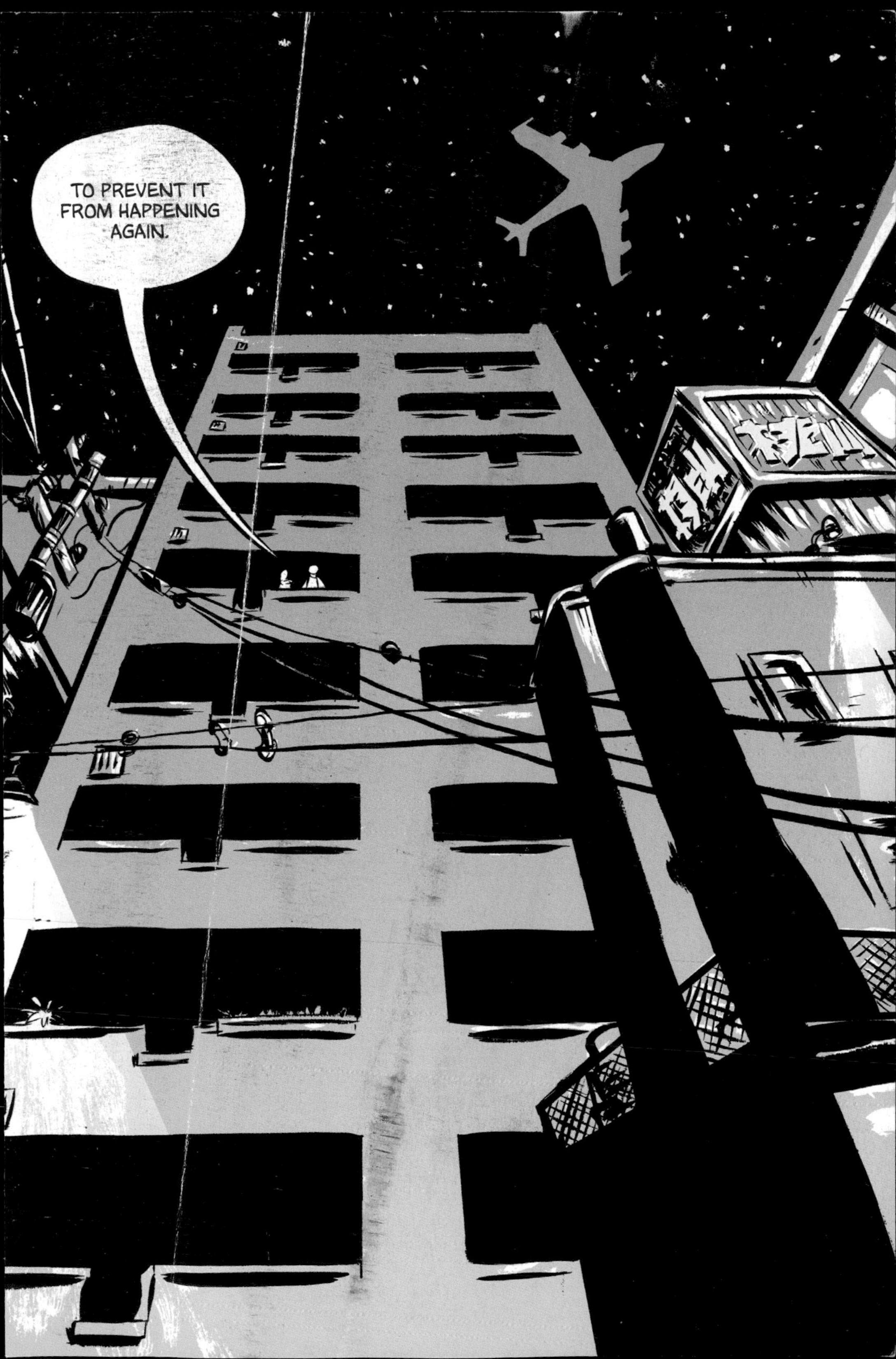
TO PREVENT IT FROM HAPPENING AGAIN.

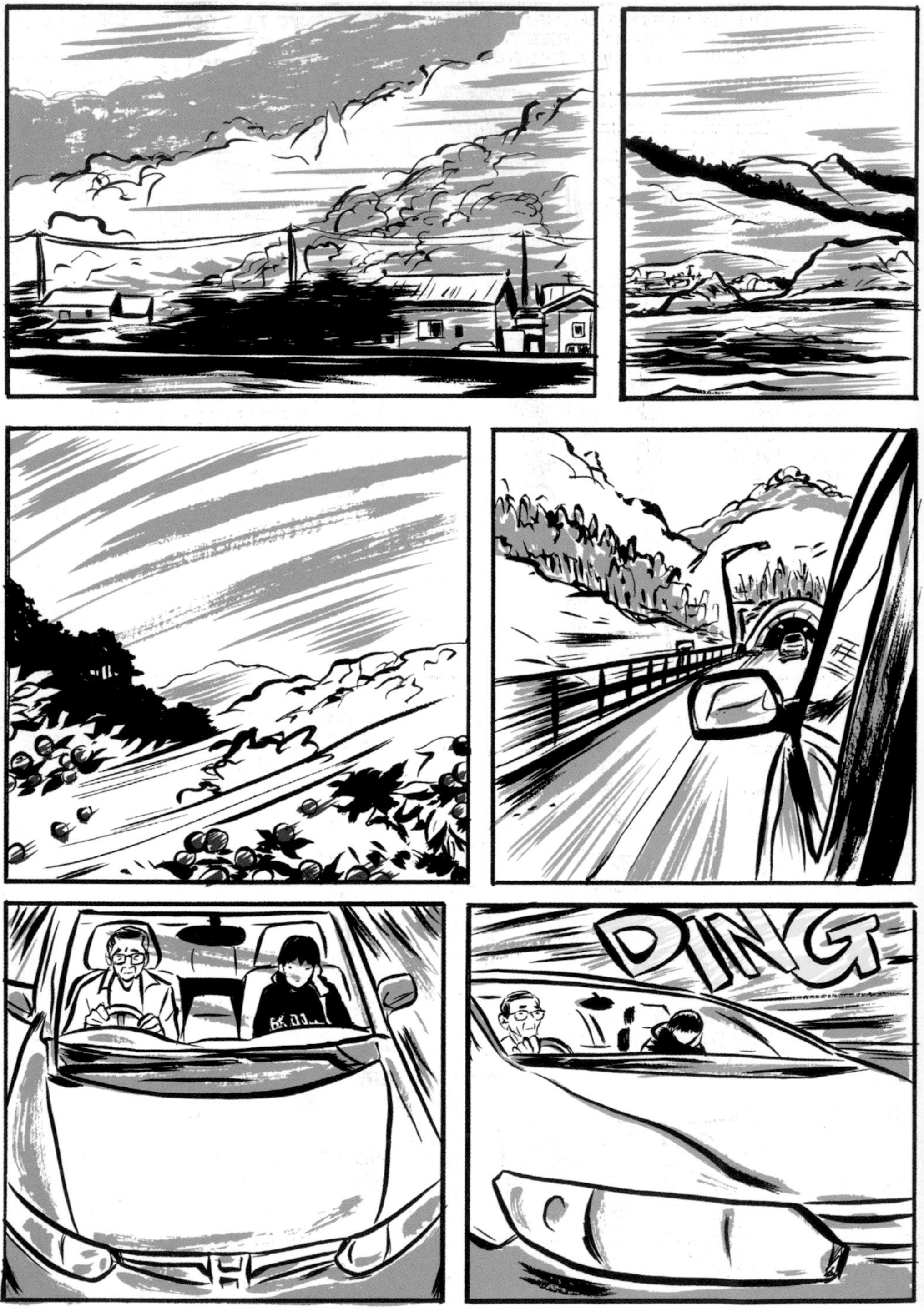
DING

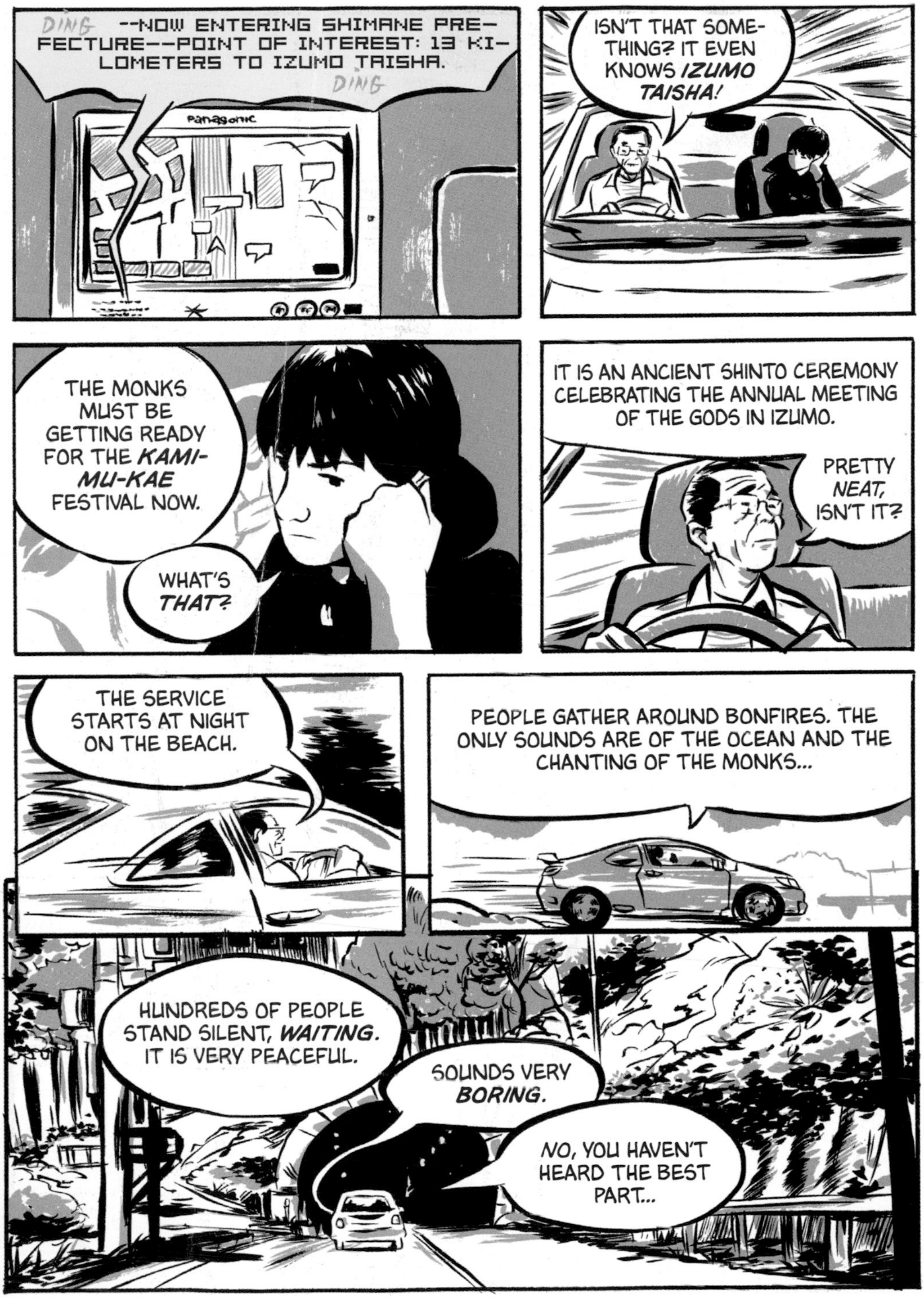
DING --NOW ENTERING SHIMANE PREFECTURE--POINT OF INTEREST: 13 KILOMETERS TO IZUMO TAISHA. DING
Panasonic
ISN'T THAT SOMETHING? IT EVEN KNOWS *IZUMO TAISHA!*
THE MONKS MUST BE GETTING READY FOR THE *KAMI-MU-KAE* FESTIVAL NOW.
WHAT'S *THAT?*
IT IS AN ANCIENT SHINTO CEREMONY CELEBRATING THE ANNUAL MEETING OF THE GODS IN IZUMO.
PRETTY *NEAT,* ISN'T IT?
THE SERVICE STARTS AT NIGHT ON THE BEACH.
PEOPLE GATHER AROUND BONFIRES. THE ONLY SOUNDS ARE OF THE OCEAN AND THE CHANTING OF THE MONKS...
HUNDREDS OF PEOPLE STAND SILENT, *WAITING.* IT IS VERY PEACEFUL.
SOUNDS VERY *BORING.*
NO, YOU HAVEN'T HEARD THE BEST PART...

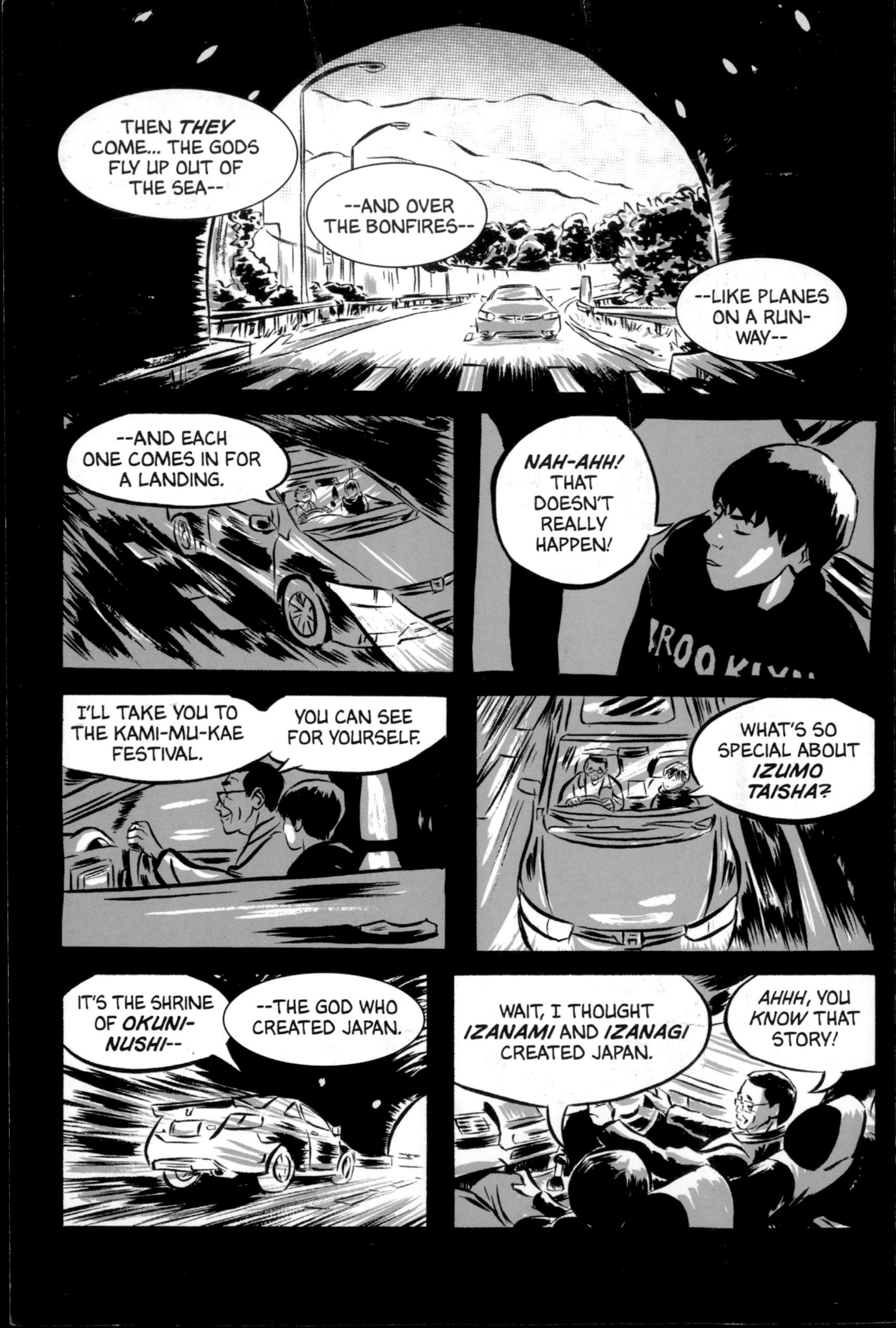
THEN *THEY* COME... THE GODS FLY UP OUT OF THE SEA--
--AND OVER THE BONFIRES--
--LIKE PLANES ON A RUN-WAY--
--AND EACH ONE COMES IN FOR A LANDING.
NAH-AHH! THAT DOESN'T REALLY HAPPEN!
I'LL TAKE YOU TO THE KAMI-MU-KAE FESTIVAL.
YOU CAN SEE FOR YOURSELF.
WHAT'S SO SPECIAL ABOUT *IZUMO TAISHA?*
IT'S THE SHRINE OF *OKUNI-NUSHI*--
--THE GOD WHO CREATED JAPAN.
WAIT, I THOUGHT *IZANAMI* AND *IZANAGI* CREATED JAPAN.
AHHH, YOU *KNOW* THAT STORY!

IZANAMI AND IZANAGI *BEGAN* TO CREATE THE LAND--

--BUT THEY DID NOT FINISH IT.

QUIT HALF-WAY THROUGH, HUH?

NO, IZANAGI AND IZANAMI DIDN'T *QUIT*, BUT--

--IT ENDED *BADLY* FOR THEM.

WHY?

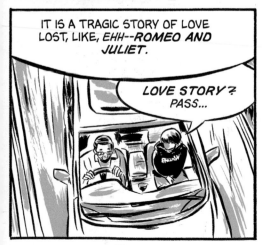

IT IS A TRAGIC STORY OF LOVE LOST, LIKE, EHH--*ROMEO AND JULIET*.

LOVE STORY? PASS...

THAT IS OK, YOU DON'T HAVE TO HEAR IT.

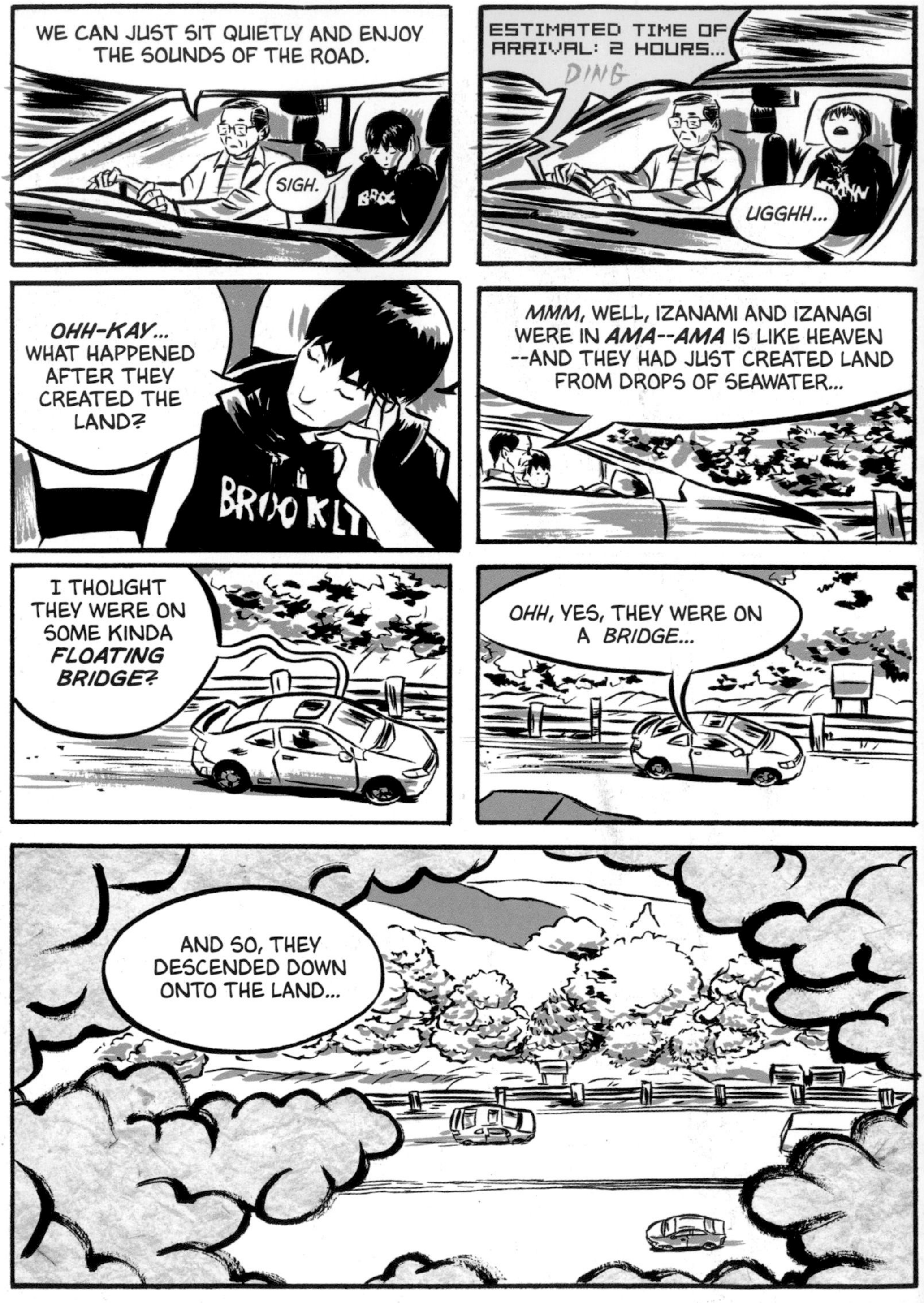
WE CAN JUST SIT QUIETLY AND ENJOY THE SOUNDS OF THE ROAD.
SIGH.
BROOK
ESTIMATED TIME OF ARRIVAL: 2 HOURS...
DING
UGGHH...
OHH-KAY... WHAT HAPPENED AFTER THEY CREATED THE LAND?
BROOKLY
MMM, WELL, IZANAMI AND IZANAGI WERE IN AMA--AMA IS LIKE HEAVEN --AND THEY HAD JUST CREATED LAND FROM DROPS OF SEAWATER...
I THOUGHT THEY WERE ON SOME KINDA FLOATING BRIDGE?
OHH, YES, THEY WERE ON A BRIDGE...
AND SO, THEY DESCENDED DOWN ONTO THE LAND...

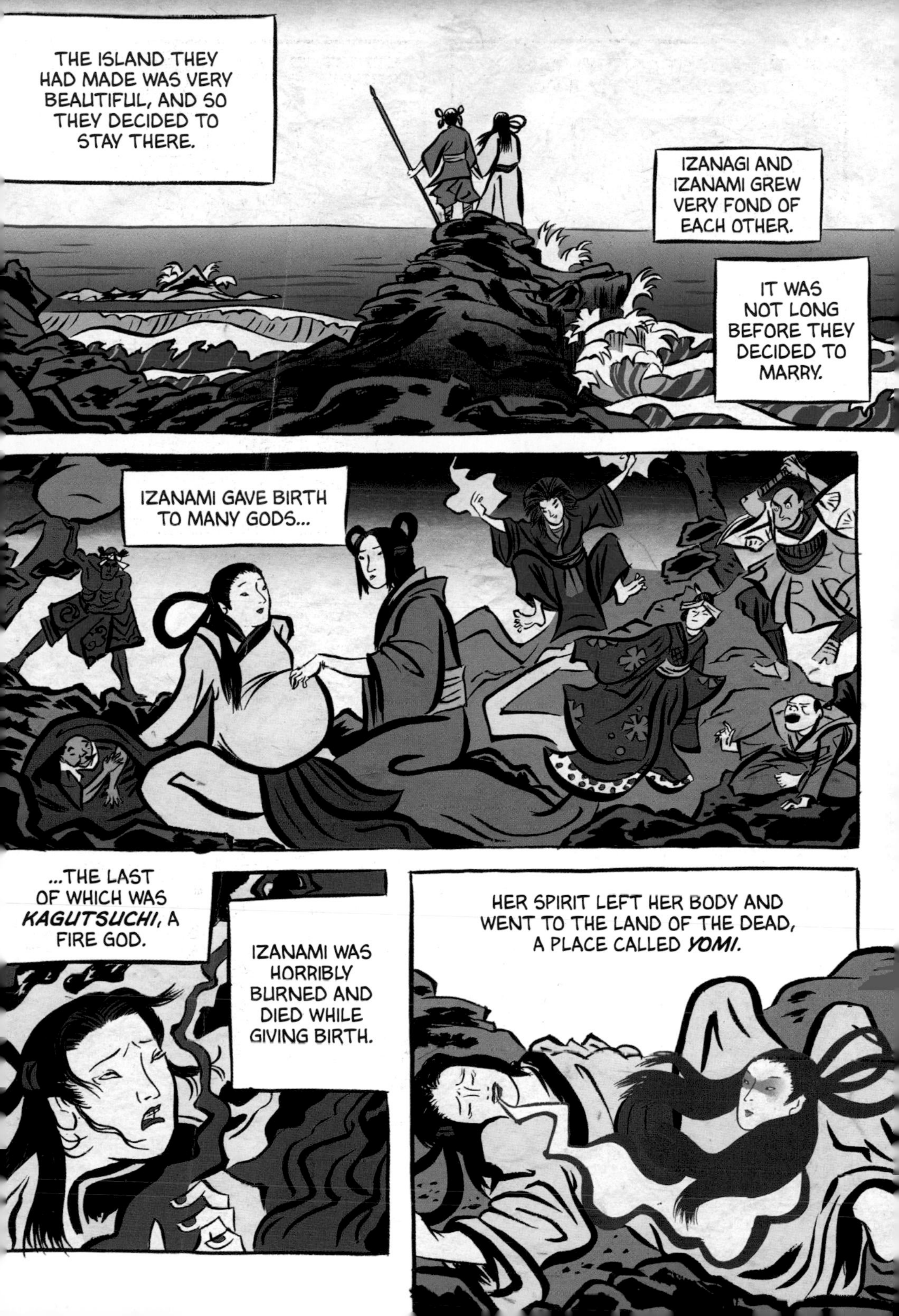
THE ISLAND THEY HAD MADE WAS VERY BEAUTIFUL, AND SO THEY DECIDED TO STAY THERE.
IZANAGI AND IZANAMI GREW VERY FOND OF EACH OTHER.
IT WAS NOT LONG BEFORE THEY DECIDED TO MARRY.
IZANAMI GAVE BIRTH TO MANY GODS...
...THE LAST OF WHICH WAS *KAGUTSUCHI*, A FIRE GOD.
IZANAMI WAS HORRIBLY BURNED AND DIED WHILE GIVING BIRTH.
HER SPIRIT LEFT HER BODY AND WENT TO THE LAND OF THE DEAD, A PLACE CALLED *YOMI*.

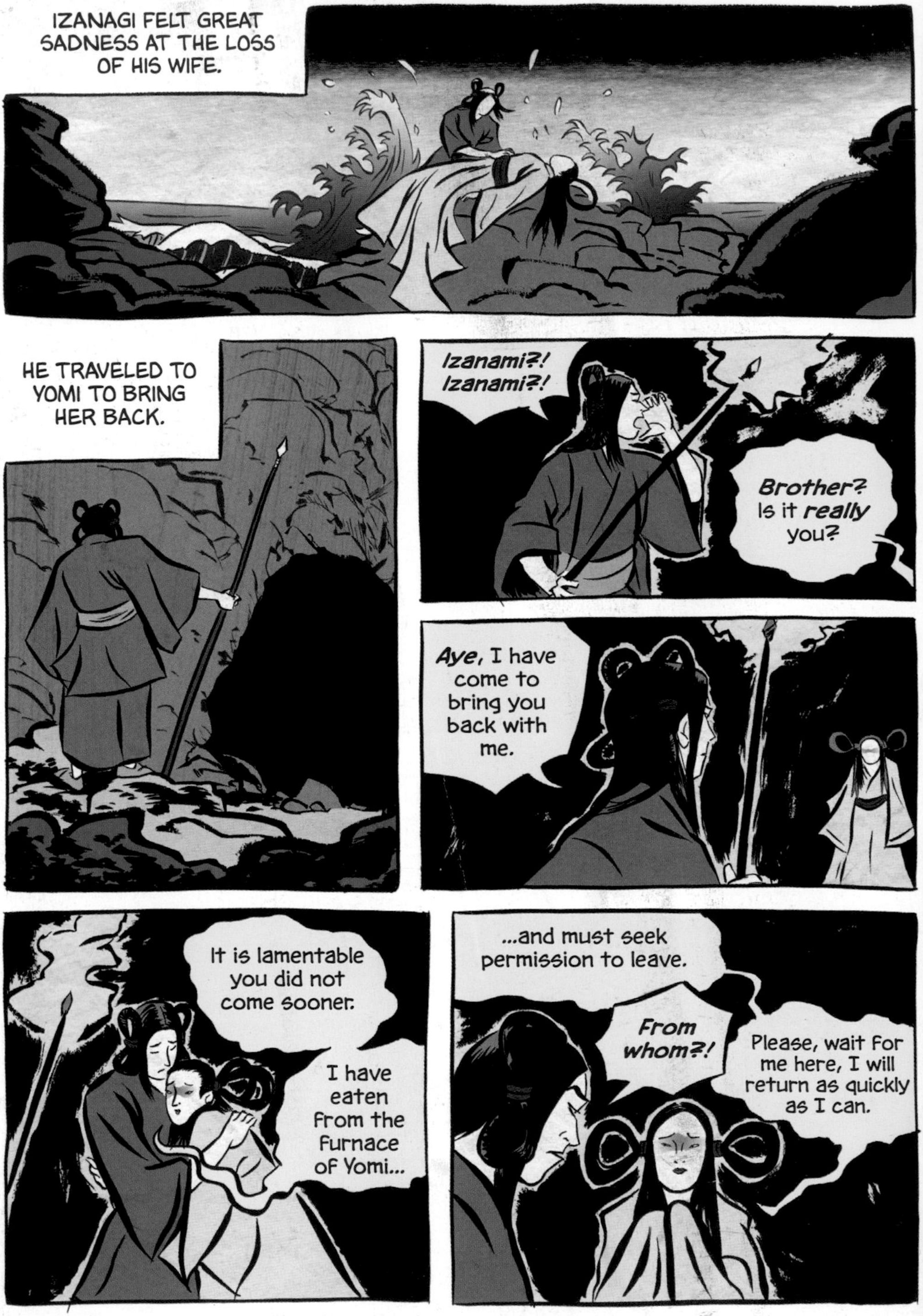
IZANAGI FELT GREAT SADNESS AT THE LOSS OF HIS WIFE.
HE TRAVELED TO YOMI TO BRING HER BACK.
Izanami?! Izanami?!
Brother? Is it really you?
Aye, I have come to bring you back with me.
It is lamentable you did not come sooner.
I have eaten from the furnace of Yomi...
...and must seek permission to leave.
From whom?!
Please, wait for me here, I will return as quickly as I can.

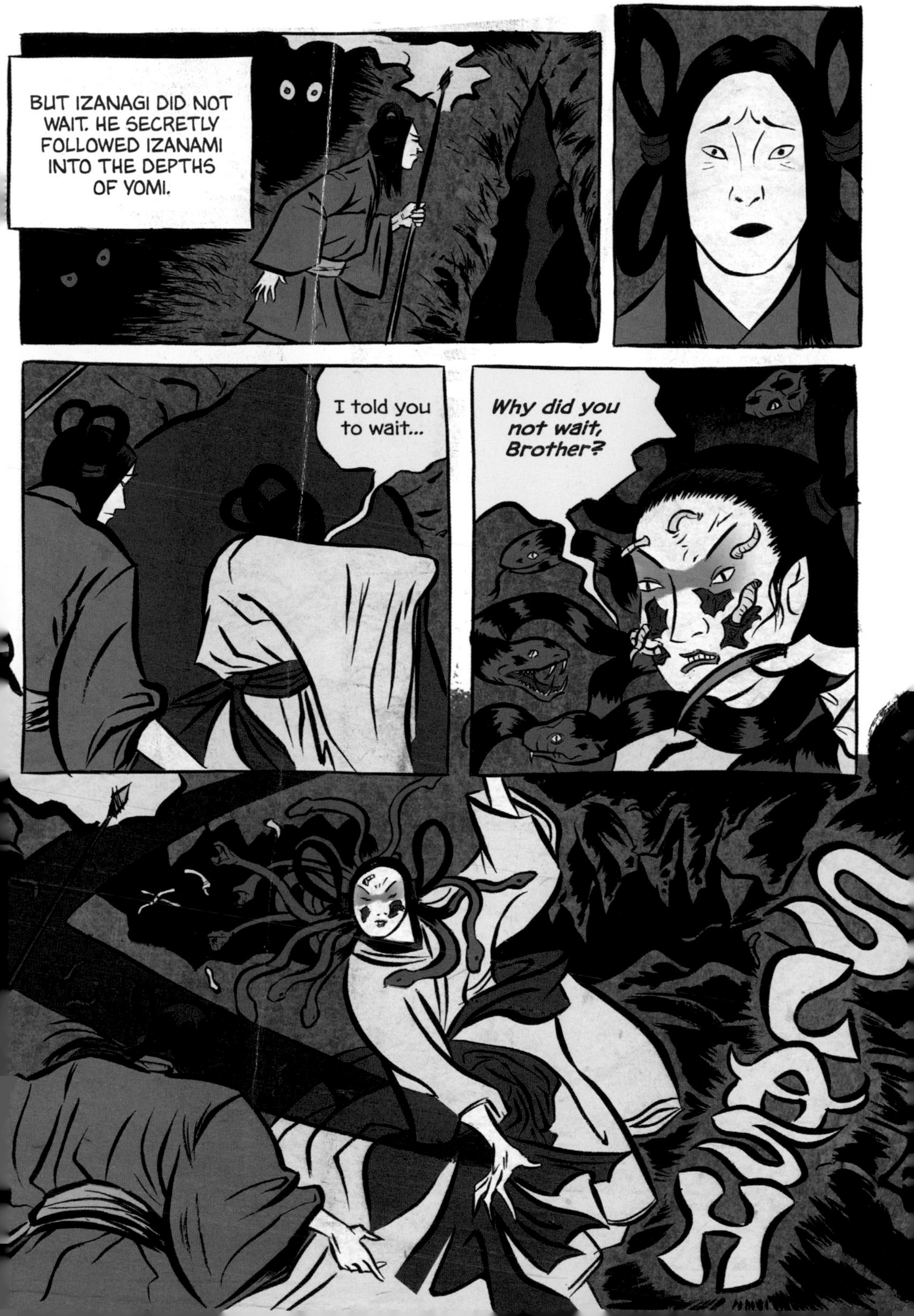
BUT IZANAGI DID NOT WAIT. HE SECRETLY FOLLOWED IZANAMI INTO THE DEPTHS OF YOMI.
I told you to wait...
Why did you not wait, Brother?

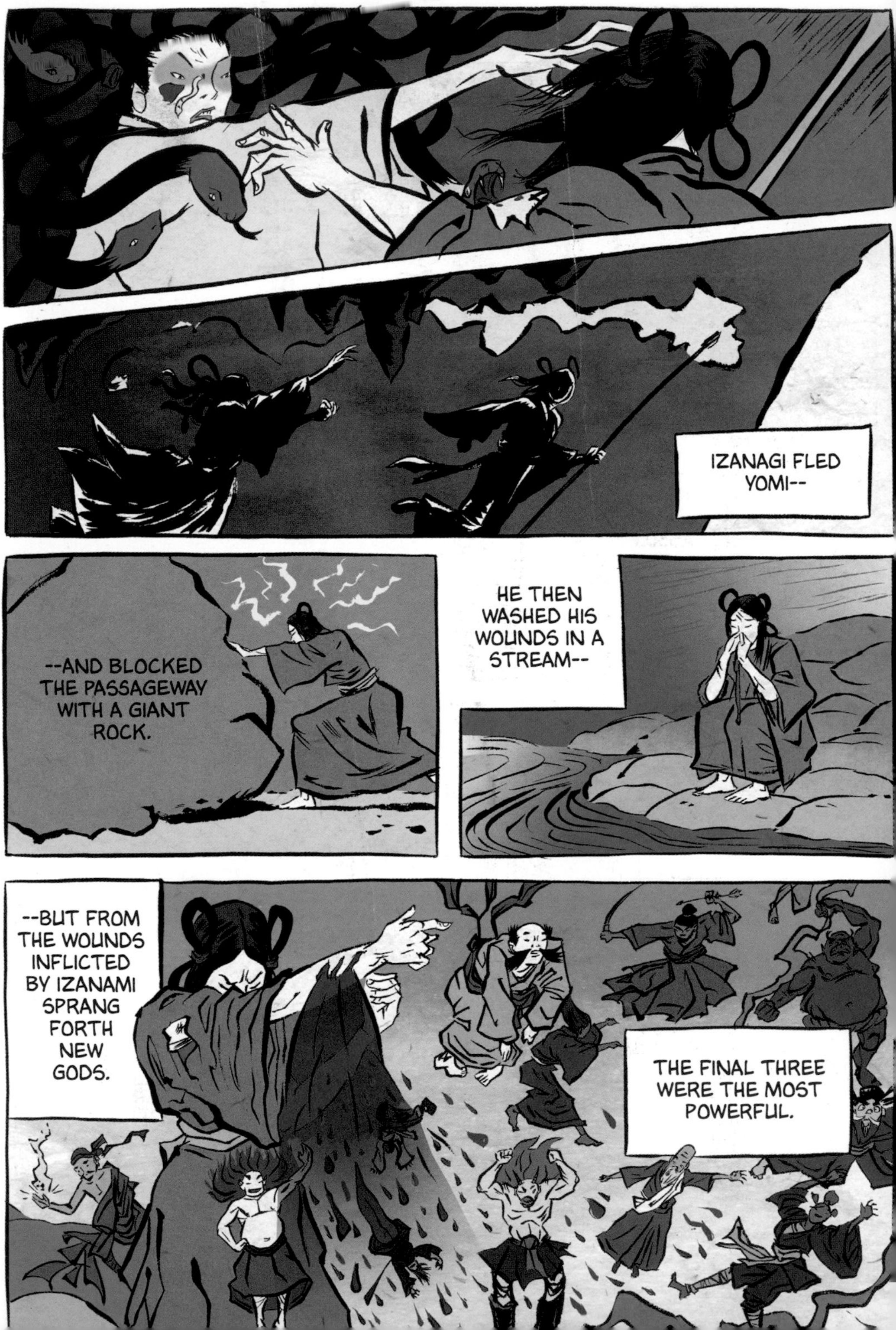
IZANAGI FLED YOMI--
--AND BLOCKED THE PASSAGEWAY WITH A GIANT ROCK.
HE THEN WASHED HIS WOUNDS IN A STREAM--
--BUT FROM THE WOUNDS INFLICTED BY IZANAMI SPRANG FORTH NEW GODS.
THE FINAL THREE WERE THE MOST POWERFUL.

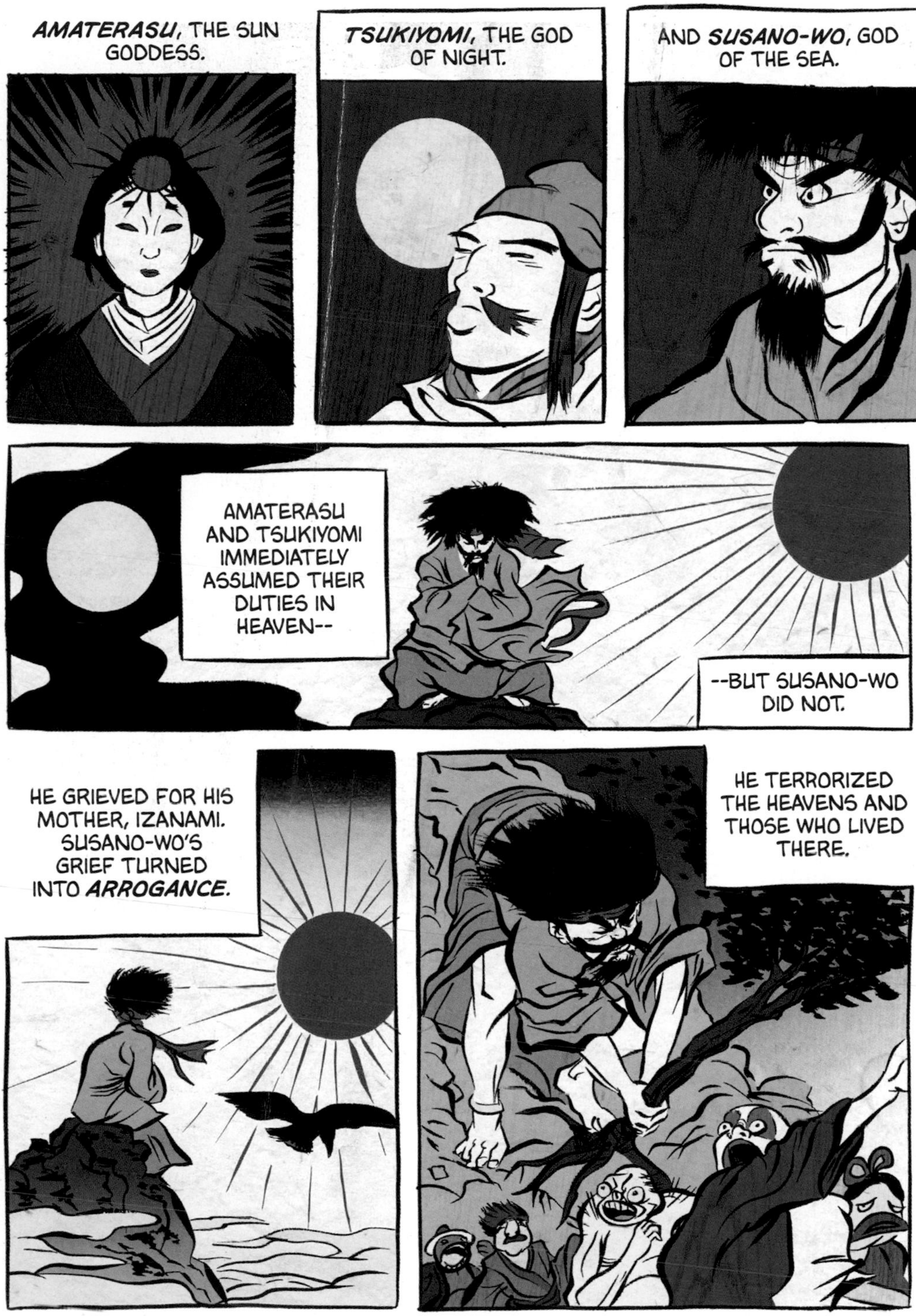
AMATERASU, THE SUN GODDESS.
TSUKIYOMI, THE GOD OF NIGHT.
AND SUSANO-WO, GOD OF THE SEA.
AMATERASU AND TSUKIYOMI IMMEDIATELY ASSUMED THEIR DUTIES IN HEAVEN--
--BUT SUSANO-WO DID NOT.
HE GRIEVED FOR HIS MOTHER, IZANAMI. SUSANO-WO'S GRIEF TURNED INTO ARROGANCE.
HE TERRORIZED THE HEAVENS AND THOSE WHO LIVED THERE.

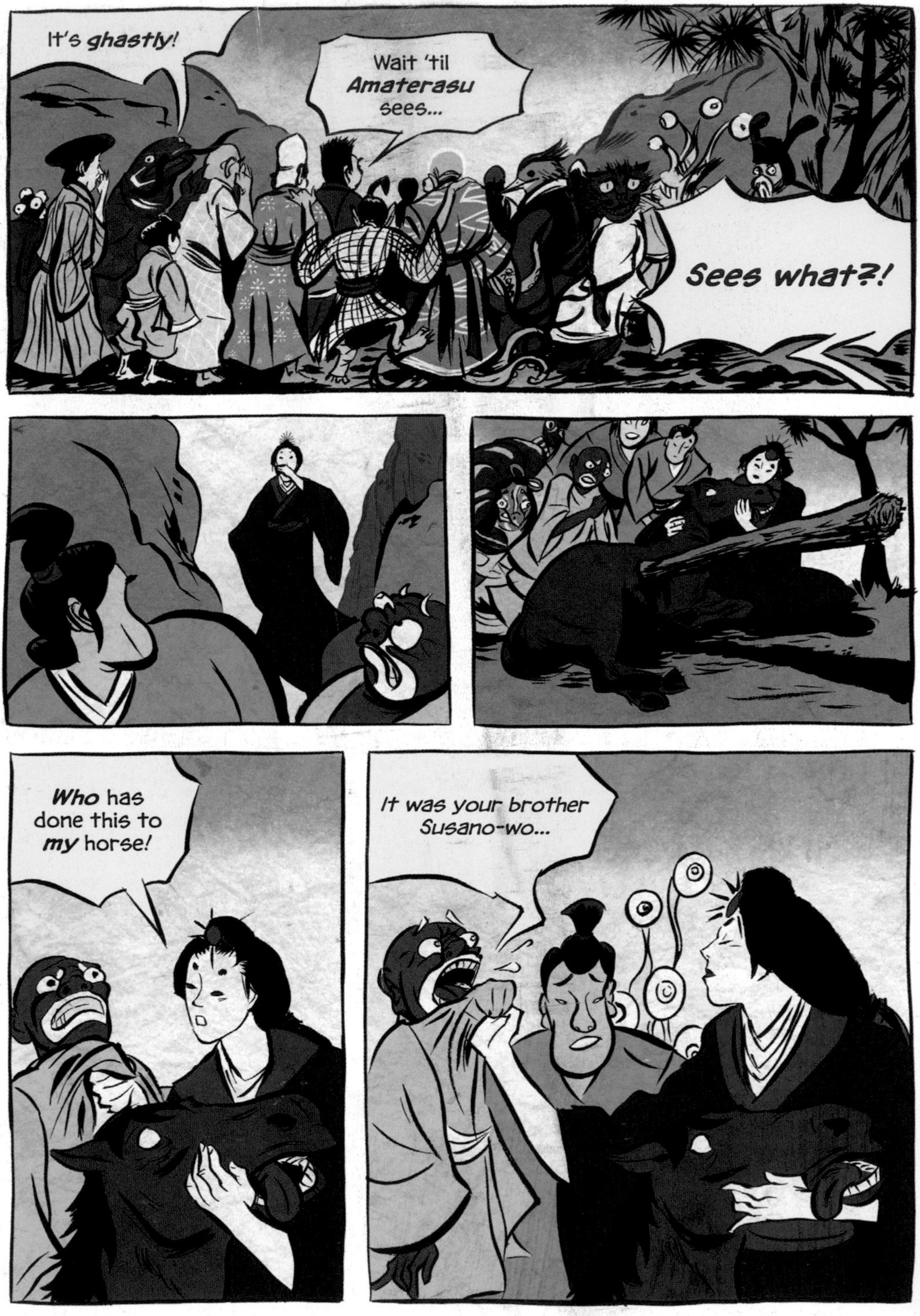

It's *ghastly*!
Wait 'til *Amaterasu* sees...
Sees what?!
Who has done this to *my* horse!
It was your brother Susano-wo...

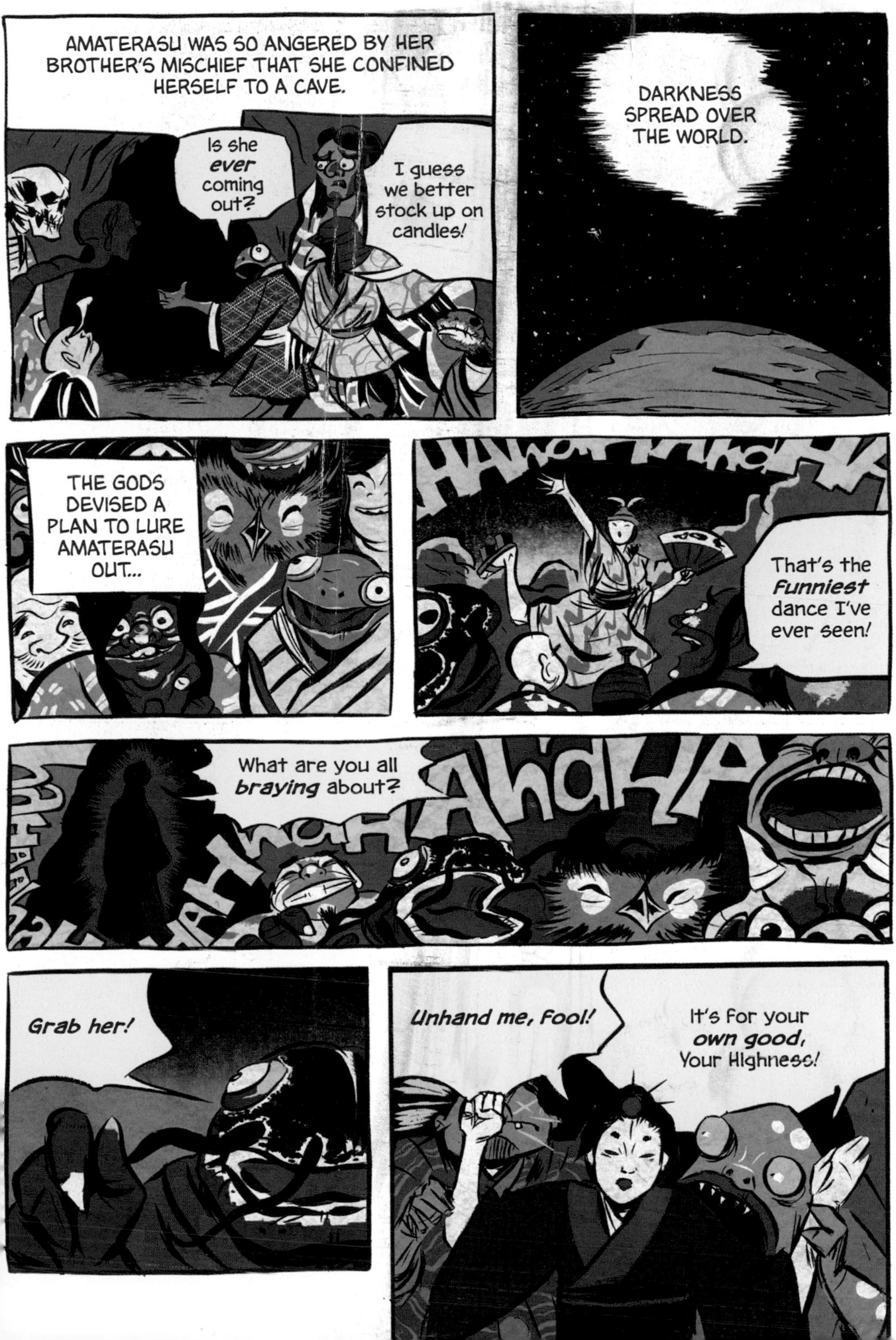

AMATERASU WAS SO ANGERED BY HER BROTHER'S MISCHIEF THAT SHE CONFINED HERSELF TO A CAVE.
Is she *ever* coming out?
I guess we better stock up on candles!
DARKNESS SPREAD OVER THE WORLD.
THE GODS DEVISED A PLAN TO LURE AMATERASU OUT...
That's the *funniest* dance I've ever seen!
What are you all *braying* about?
Grab her!
Unhand me, fool!
It's for your *own good,* Your Highness!

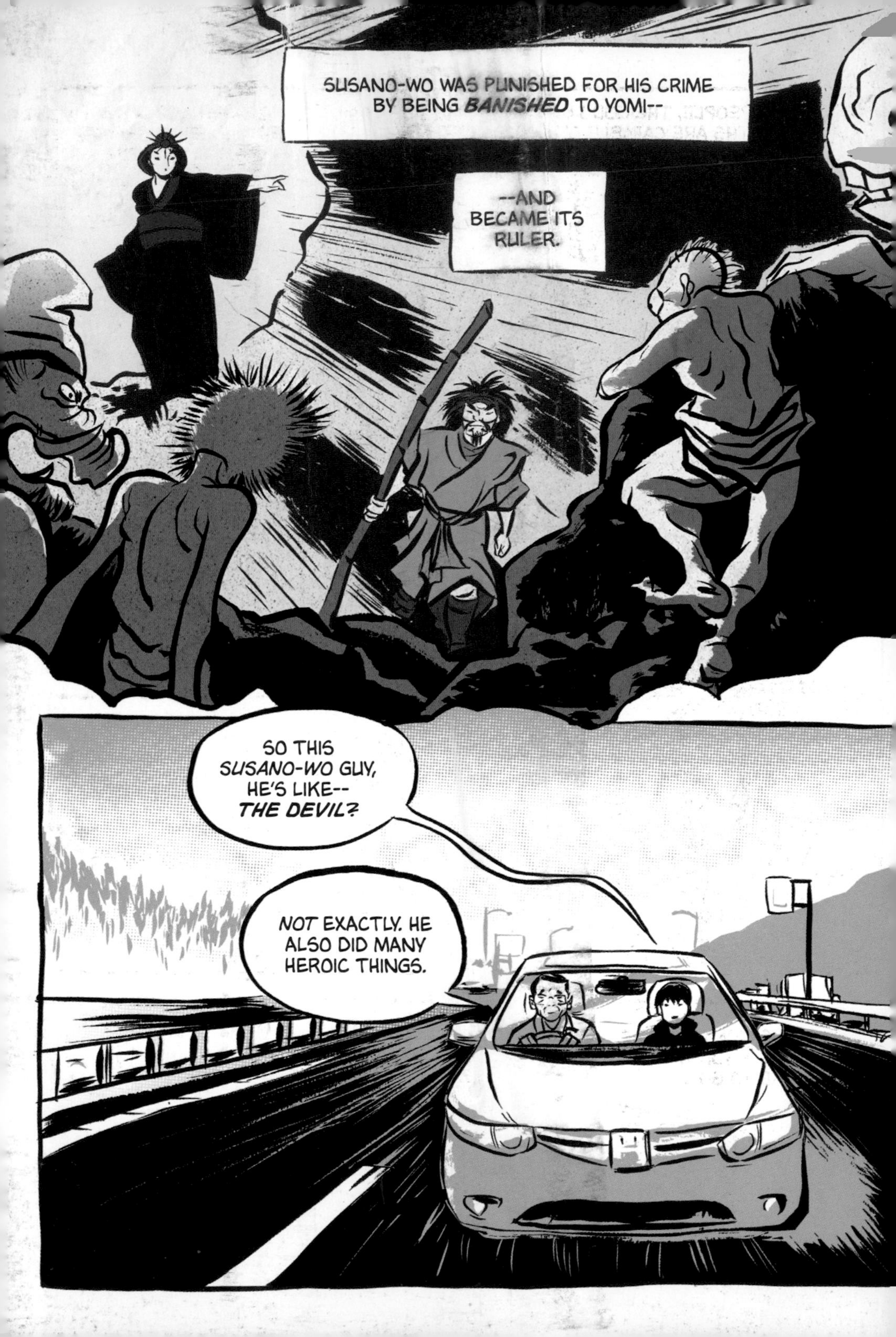
SUSANO-WO WAS PUNISHED FOR HIS CRIME BY BEING BANISHED TO YOMI--
--AND BECAME ITS RULER.
SO THIS SUSANO-WO GUY, HE'S LIKE-- THE DEVIL?
NOT EXACTLY. HE ALSO DID MANY HEROIC THINGS.

JUST LIKE PEOPLE, THE GODS IN SHINTO MYTHS ARE CAPABLE OF BOTH *GOOD* AND *EVIL.*

YOU SAID THAT IZANAGI AND IZANAMI WERE BROTHER AND SISTER--BUT, THEY HAD A BUNCH OF *KIDS?*

EHHHM, SO THE SHRINE I TOLD YOU ABOUT IN IZUMO, THEY ALL-- *UHHH...*

THAT MUST MEAN THEY *DID IT* TOGETHER...

...THAT IS, *ERR-EH-HEM,* ALL THE GODS ASSEMBLE THERE ONCE A YEAR TO DISCUSS THE FATE OF MANKIND...

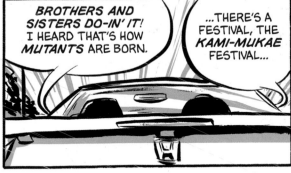

BROTHERS AND SISTERS DO-IN' IT! I HEARD THAT'S HOW *MUTANTS* ARE BORN.

...THERE'S A FESTIVAL, THE *KAMI-MUKAE* FESTIVAL...

...IT IS THIS MONTH. I CAN TAKE YOU, IF YOU WOULD LIKE TO GO...

GUESS THAT'S WHY THOSE SHINTO GODS ARE ALL *CRAZY-LOOK'N* IN PICTURES.

THEY'RE *MUTANTS!*

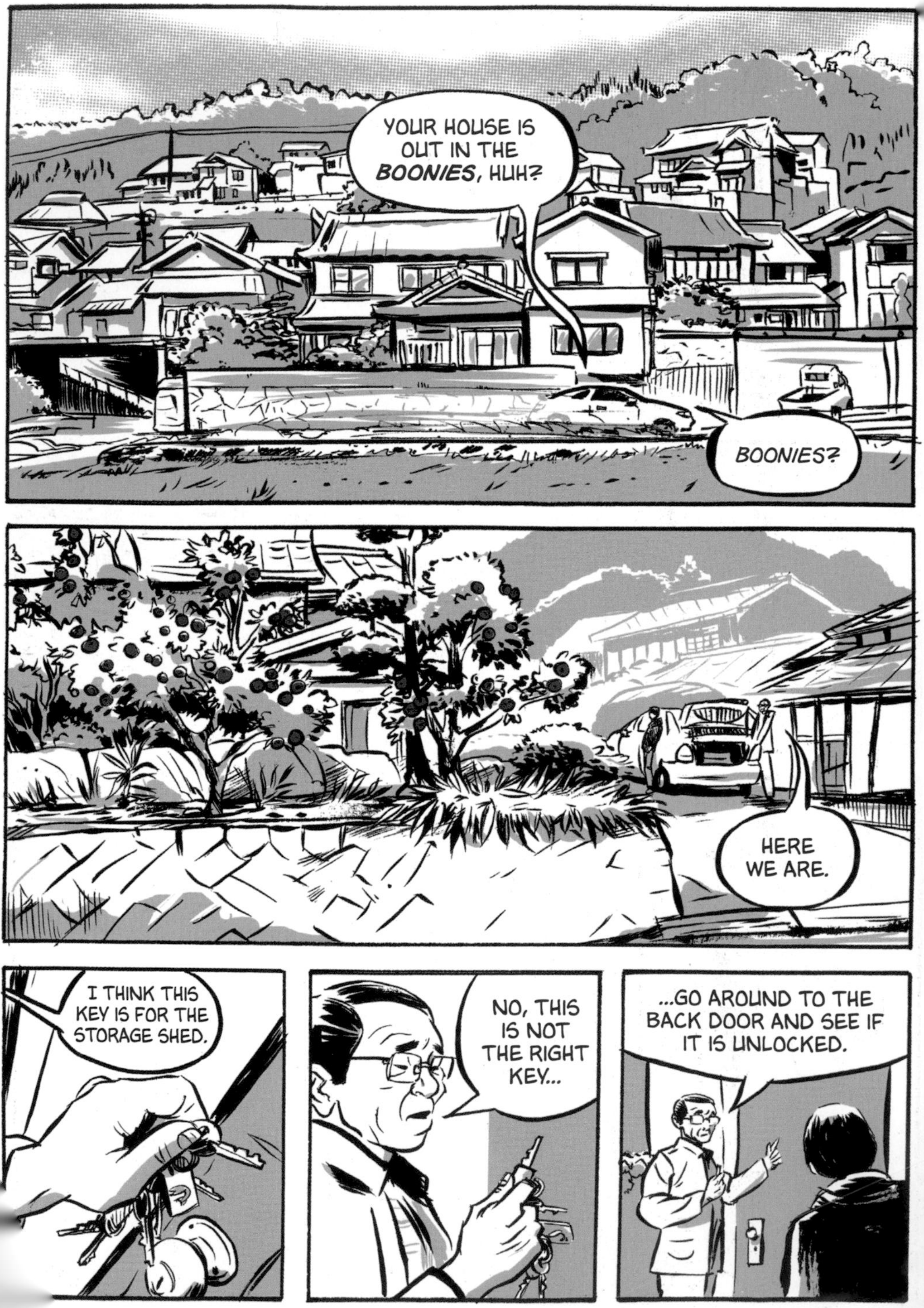
YOUR HOUSE IS OUT IN THE *BOONIES*, HUH?
BOONIES?
HERE WE ARE.
I THINK THIS KEY IS FOR THE STORAGE SHED.
NO, THIS IS NOT THE RIGHT KEY...
...GO AROUND TO THE BACK DOOR AND SEE IF IT IS UNLOCKED.

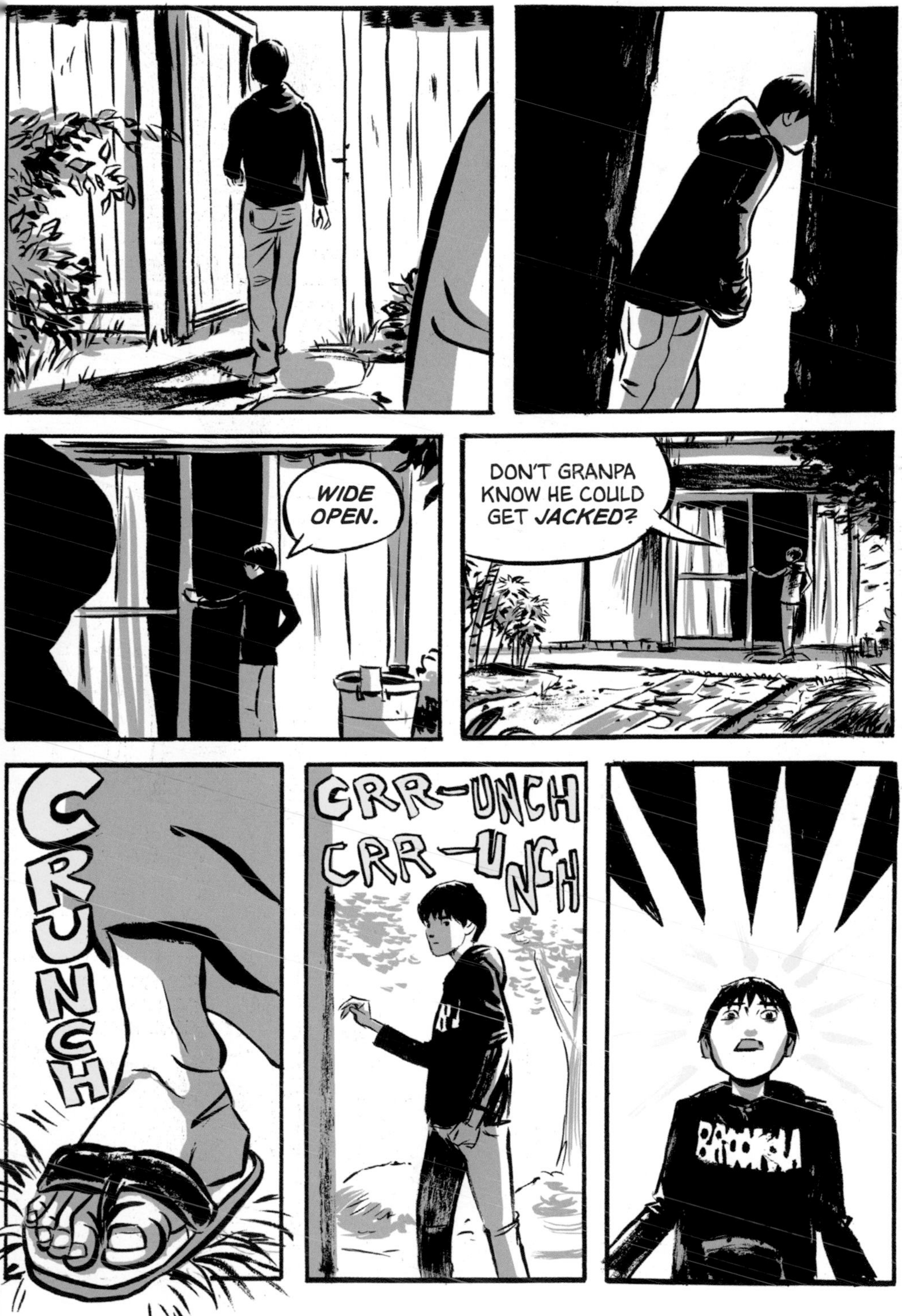
WIDE OPEN.
DON'T GRANPA KNOW HE COULD GET JACKED?
CRUNCH
CRR-UNCH CRR-UNCH

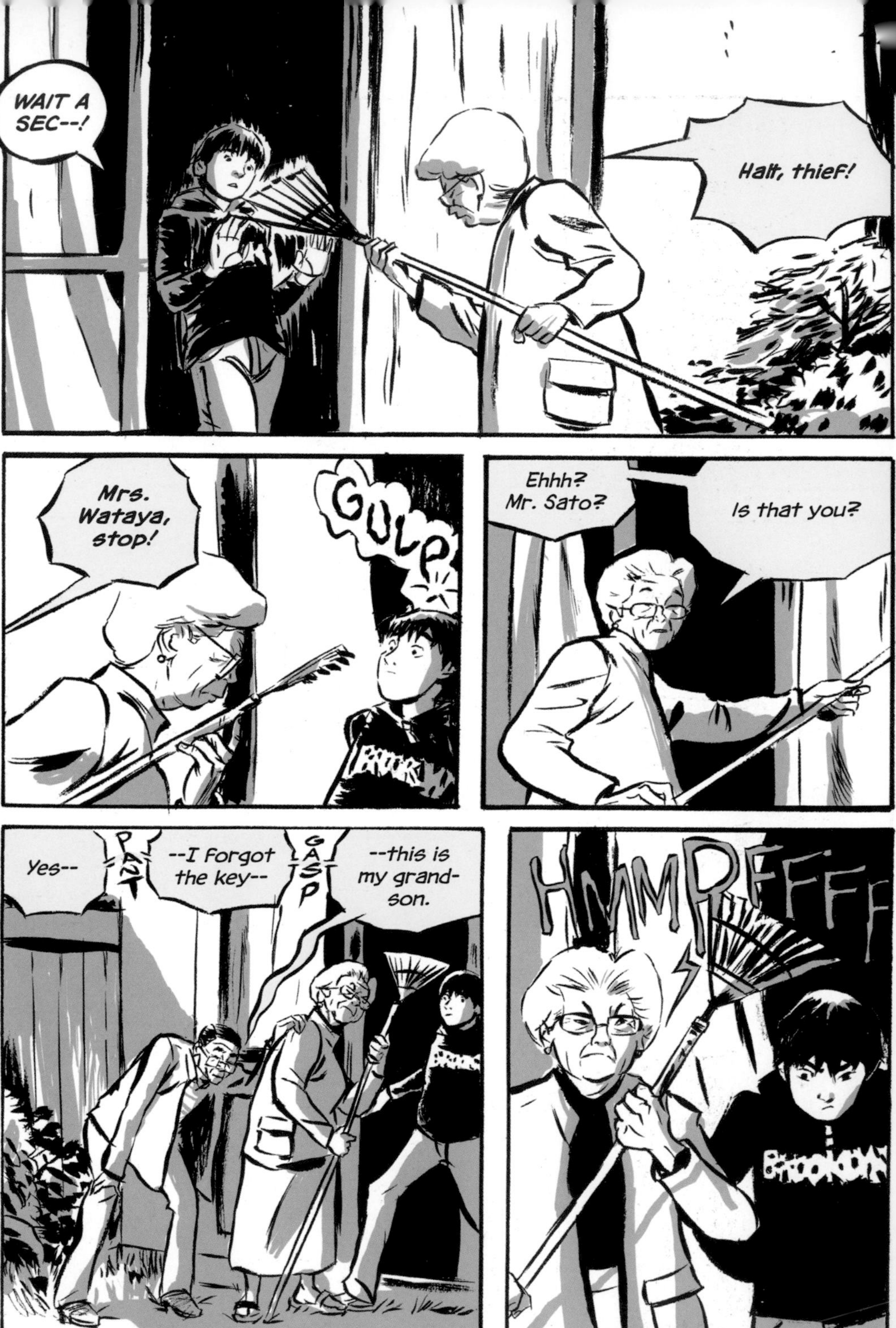
WAIT A SEC--!
Halt, thief!
Mrs. Wataya, stop!
GULP
Ehhh? Mr. Sato?
Is that you?
Yes--
PANT
--I forgot the key--
GASP
--this is my grand-son.
HMMPFFFF

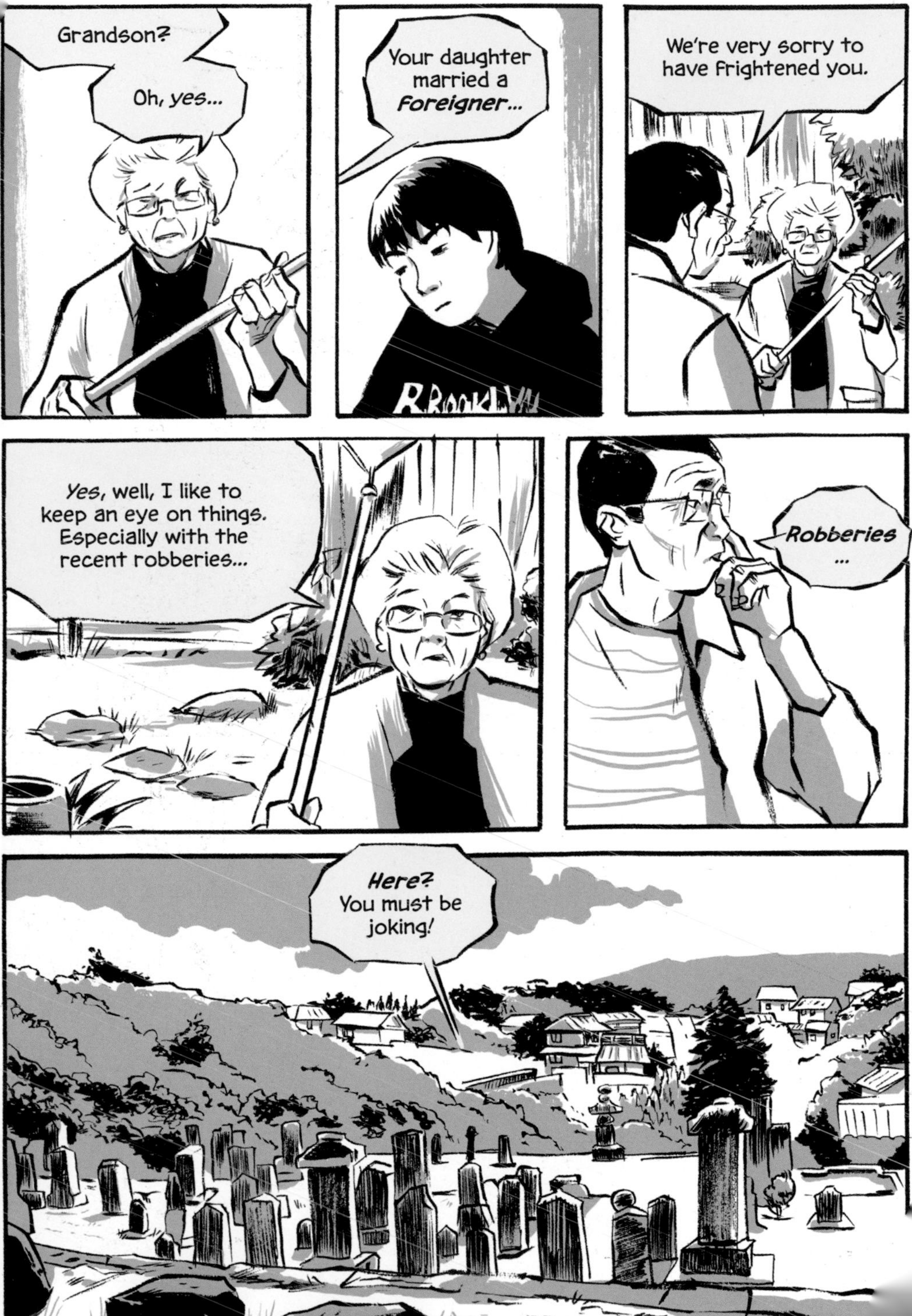
Grandson?
Oh, yes...
Your daughter married a *foreigner*...
BROOKLYN
We're very sorry to have frightened you.
Yes, well, I like to keep an eye on things. Especially with the recent robberies...
Robberies ...
Here? You must be joking!

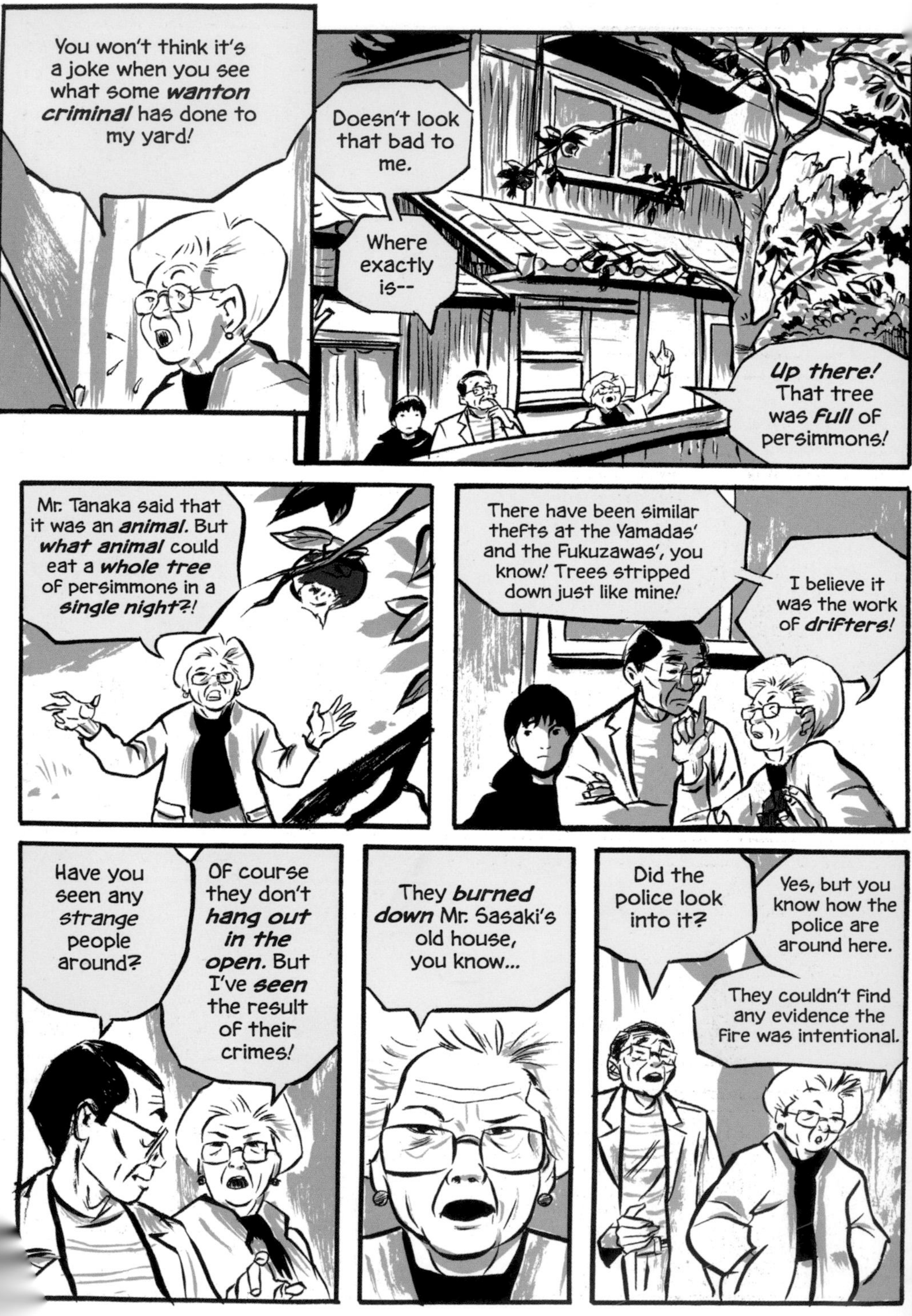
You won't think it's a joke when you see what some *wanton criminal* has done to my yard!
Doesn't look that bad to me.
Where exactly is--
Up there! That tree was *full* of persimmons!
Mr. Tanaka said that it was an *animal*. But *what animal* could eat a *whole tree* of persimmons in a *single night?!*
There have been similar thefts at the Yamadas' and the Fukuzawas', you know! Trees stripped down just like mine!
I believe it was the work of *drifters*!
Have you seen any *strange* people around?
Of course they don't *hang out in the open*. But I've *seen* the result of their crimes!
They *burned down* Mr. Sasaki's old house, you know...
Did the police look into it?
Yes, but you know how the police are around here.
They couldn't find any evidence the fire was intentional.

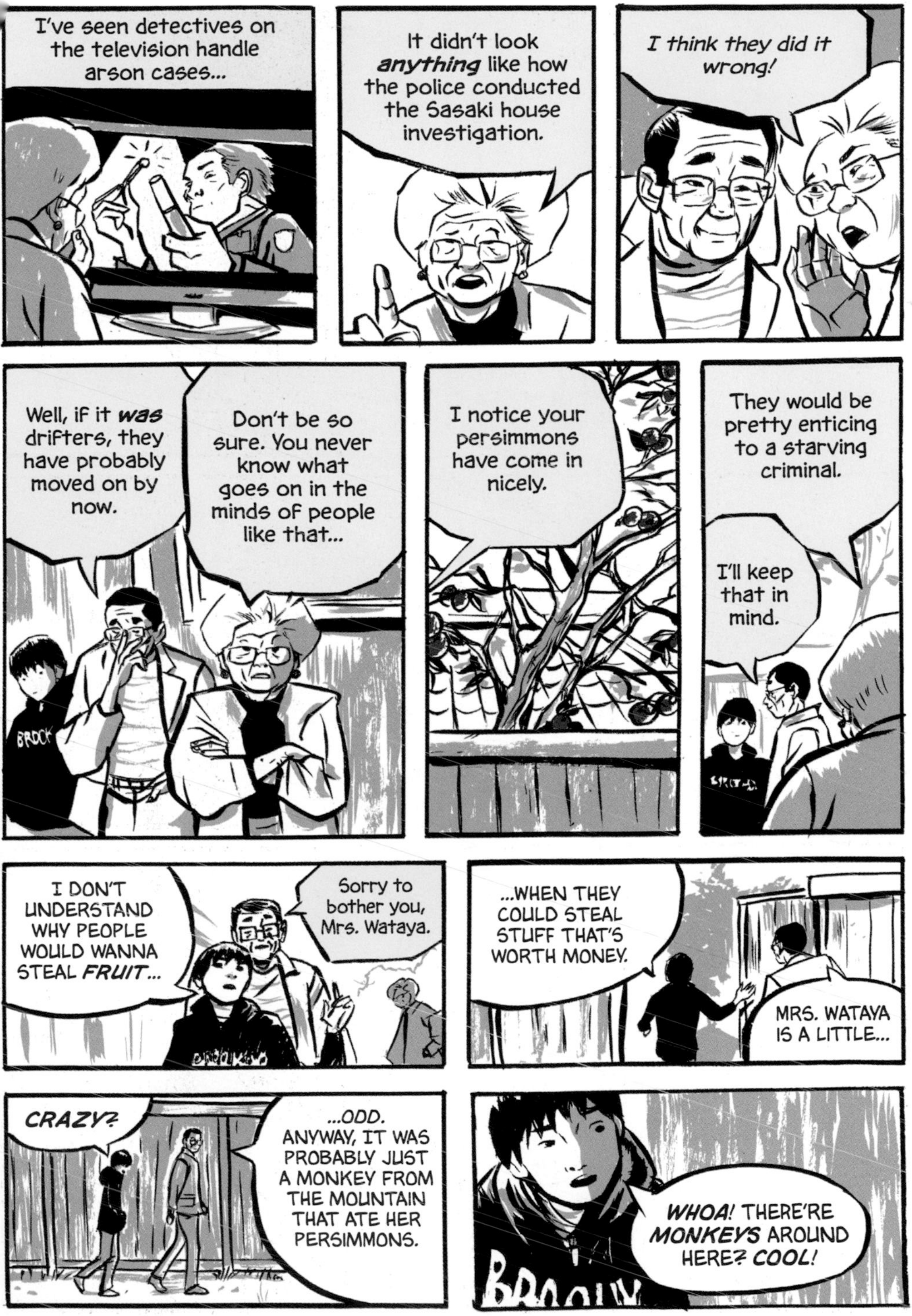
I've seen detectives on the television handle arson cases...
It didn't look *anything* like how the police conducted the Sasaki house investigation.
I think they did it wrong!
Well, if it *was* drifters, they have probably moved on by now.
Don't be so sure. You never know what goes on in the minds of people like that...
I notice your persimmons have come in nicely.
They would be pretty enticing to a starving criminal.
I'll keep that in mind.
I DON'T UNDERSTAND WHY PEOPLE WOULD WANNA STEAL *FRUIT*...
Sorry to bother you, Mrs. Wataya.
...WHEN THEY COULD STEAL STUFF THAT'S WORTH MONEY.
MRS. WATAYA IS A LITTLE...
CRAZY?
...ODD. ANYWAY, IT WAS PROBABLY JUST A MONKEY FROM THE MOUNTAIN THAT ATE HER PERSIMMONS.
WHOA! THERE'RE *MONKEYS* AROUND HERE? *COOL!*

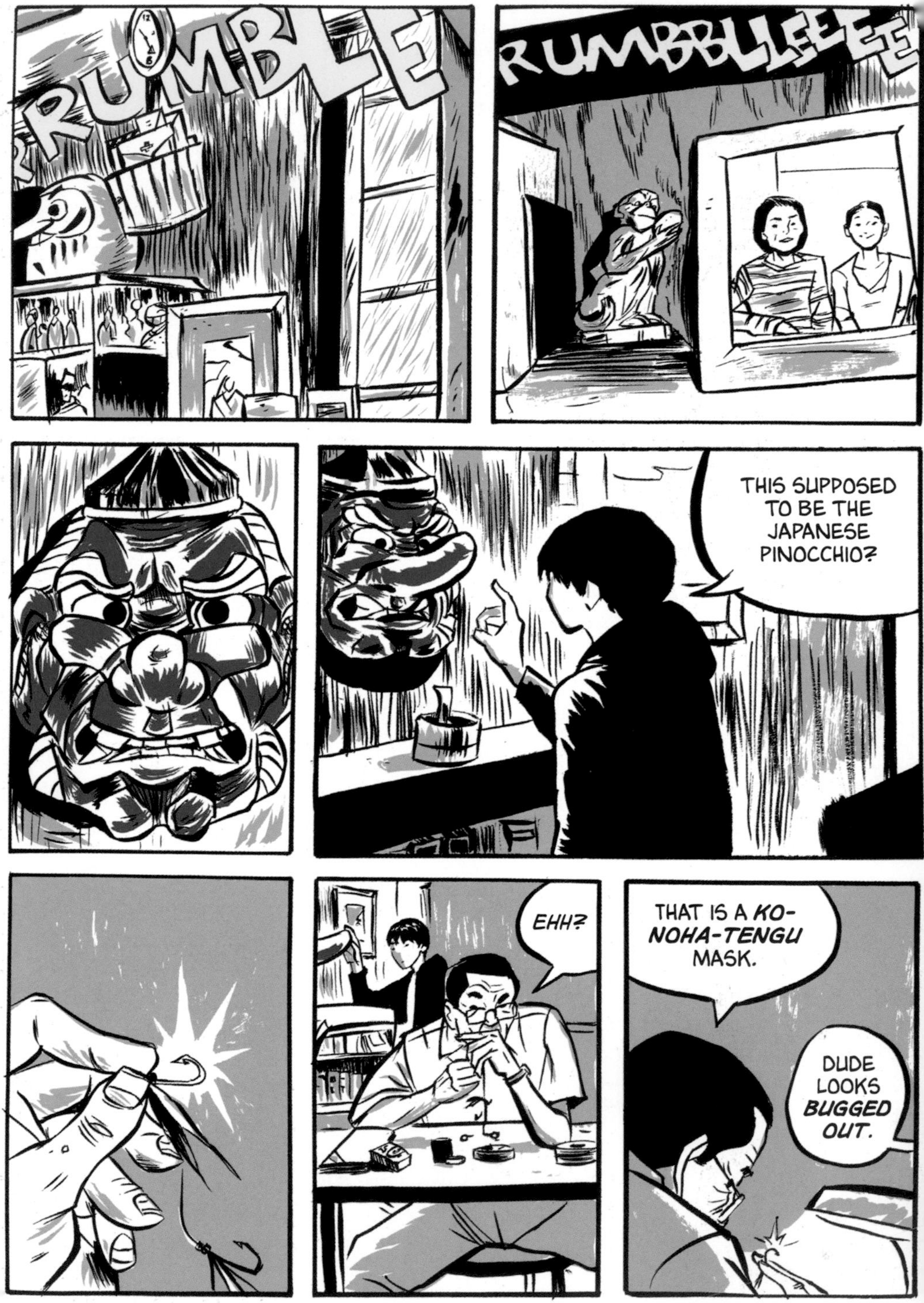
RUMBLE
RUMBBLLEEEE
THIS SUPPOSED TO BE THE JAPANESE PINOCCHIO?
EHH?
THAT IS A KO-NOHA-TENGU MASK.
DUDE LOOKS BUGGED OUT.

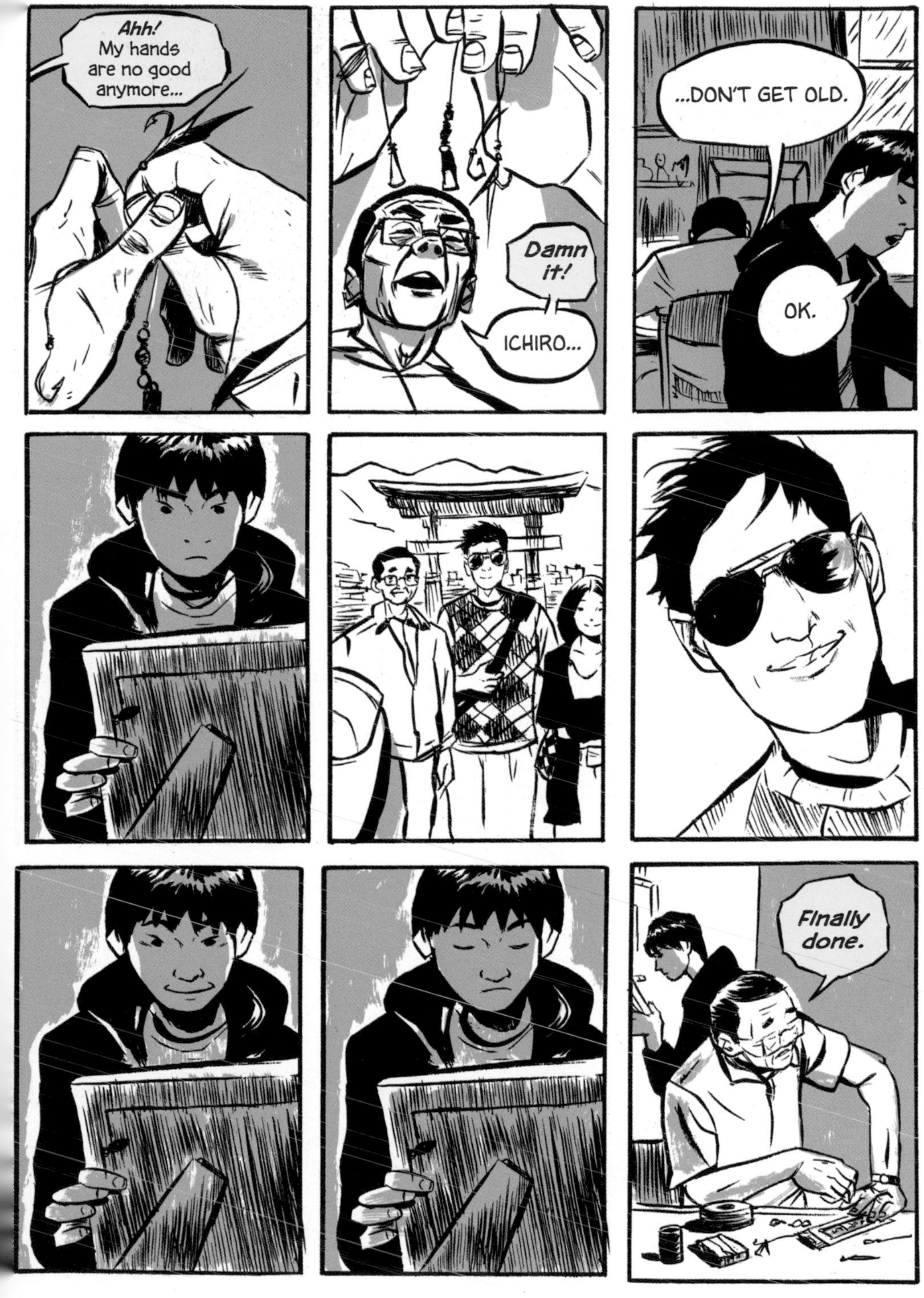
Ahh! My hands are no good anymore...
Damn it!
ICHIRO...
...DON'T GET OLD.
OK.
Finally done.

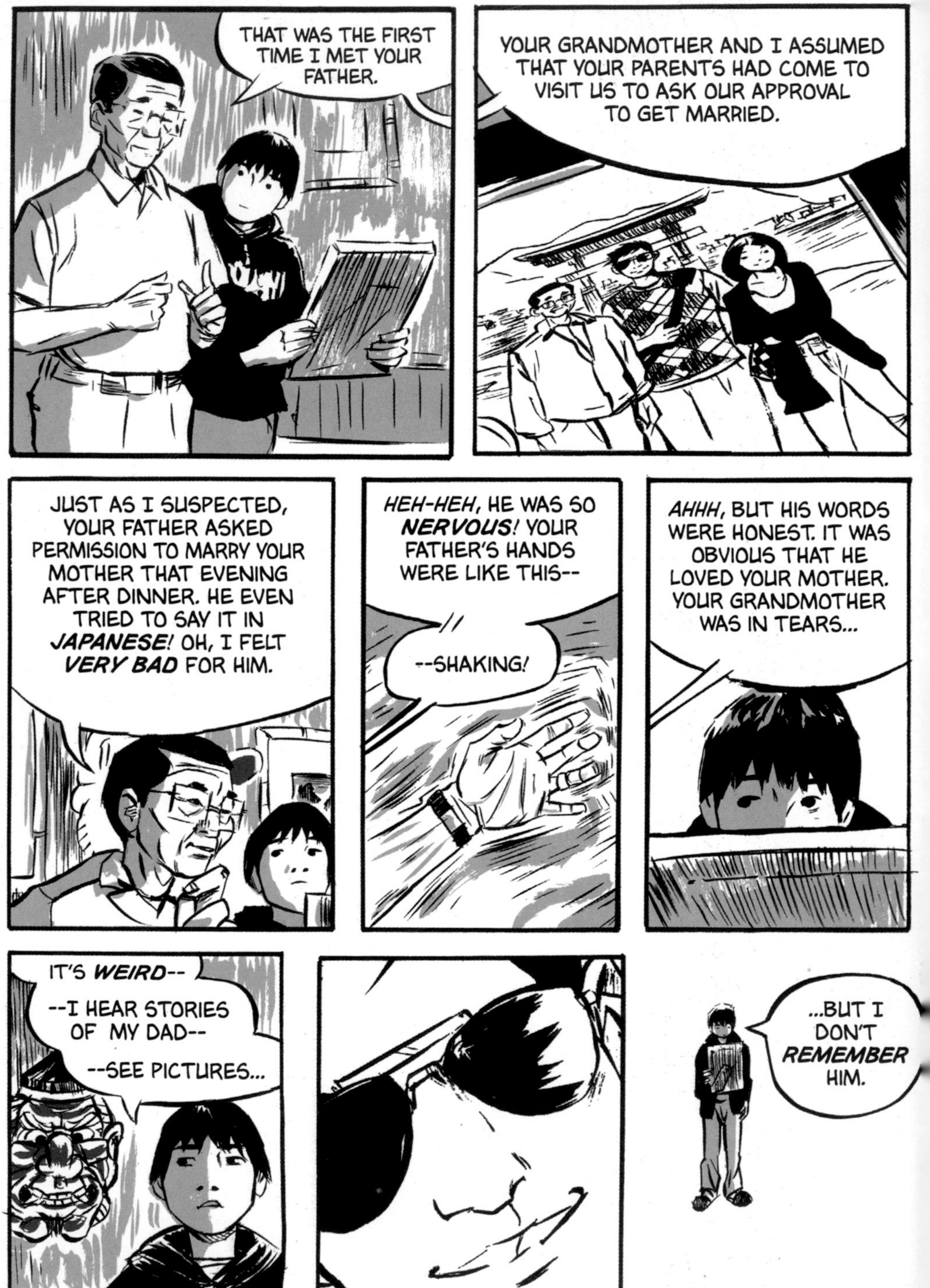
THAT WAS THE FIRST TIME I MET YOUR FATHER.
YOUR GRANDMOTHER AND I ASSUMED THAT YOUR PARENTS HAD COME TO VISIT US TO ASK OUR APPROVAL TO GET MARRIED.
JUST AS I SUSPECTED, YOUR FATHER ASKED PERMISSION TO MARRY YOUR MOTHER THAT EVENING AFTER DINNER. HE EVEN TRIED TO SAY IT IN *JAPANESE!* OH, I FELT ***VERY BAD*** FOR HIM.
HEH-HEH, HE WAS SO ***NERVOUS!*** YOUR FATHER'S HANDS WERE LIKE THIS--
--SHAKING!
AHHH, BUT HIS WORDS WERE HONEST. IT WAS OBVIOUS THAT HE LOVED YOUR MOTHER. YOUR GRANDMOTHER WAS IN TEARS...
IT'S ***WEIRD***--
--I HEAR STORIES OF MY DAD--
--SEE PICTURES...
...BUT I DON'T ***REMEMBER*** HIM.

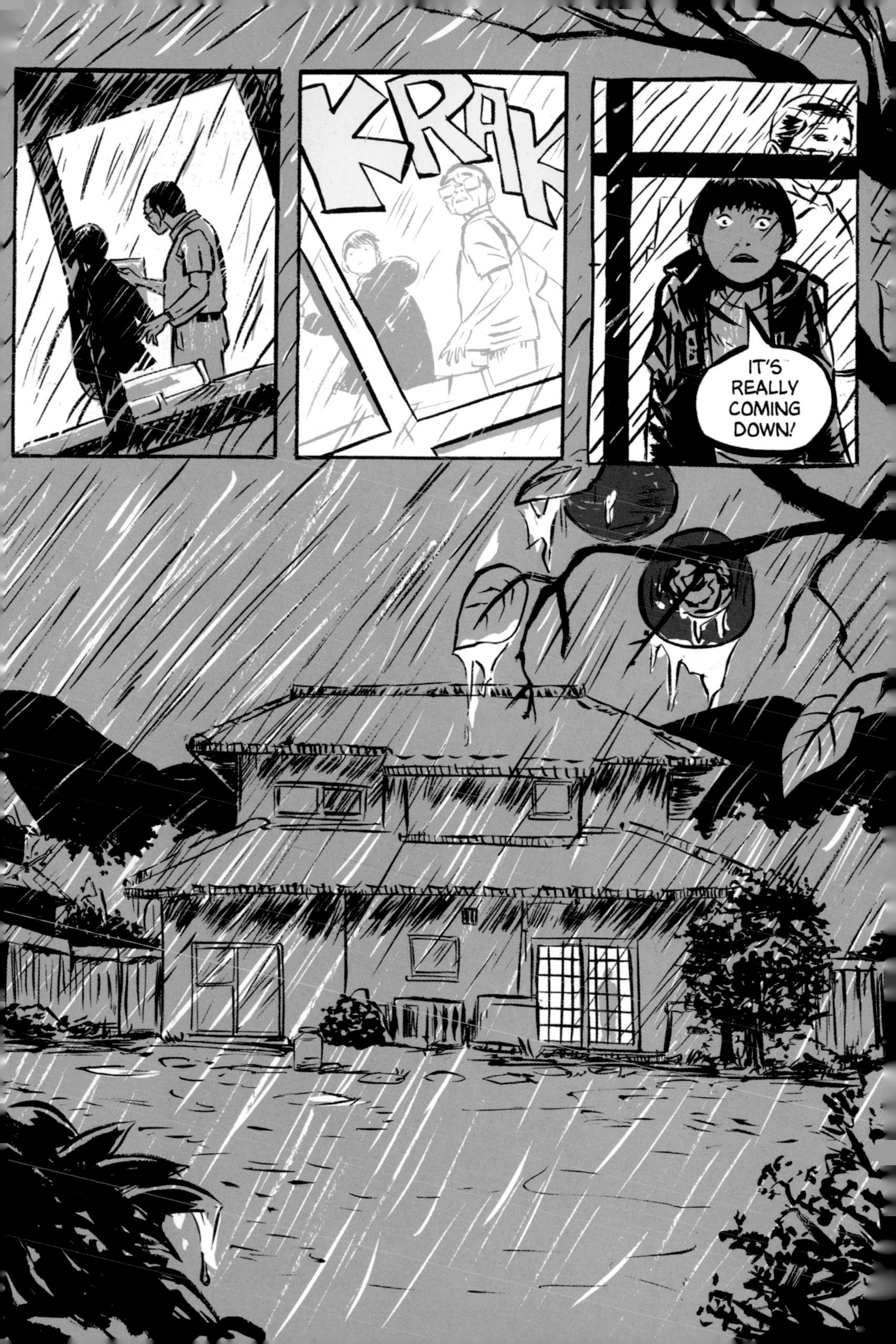
KRAK
IT'S REALLY COMING DOWN!

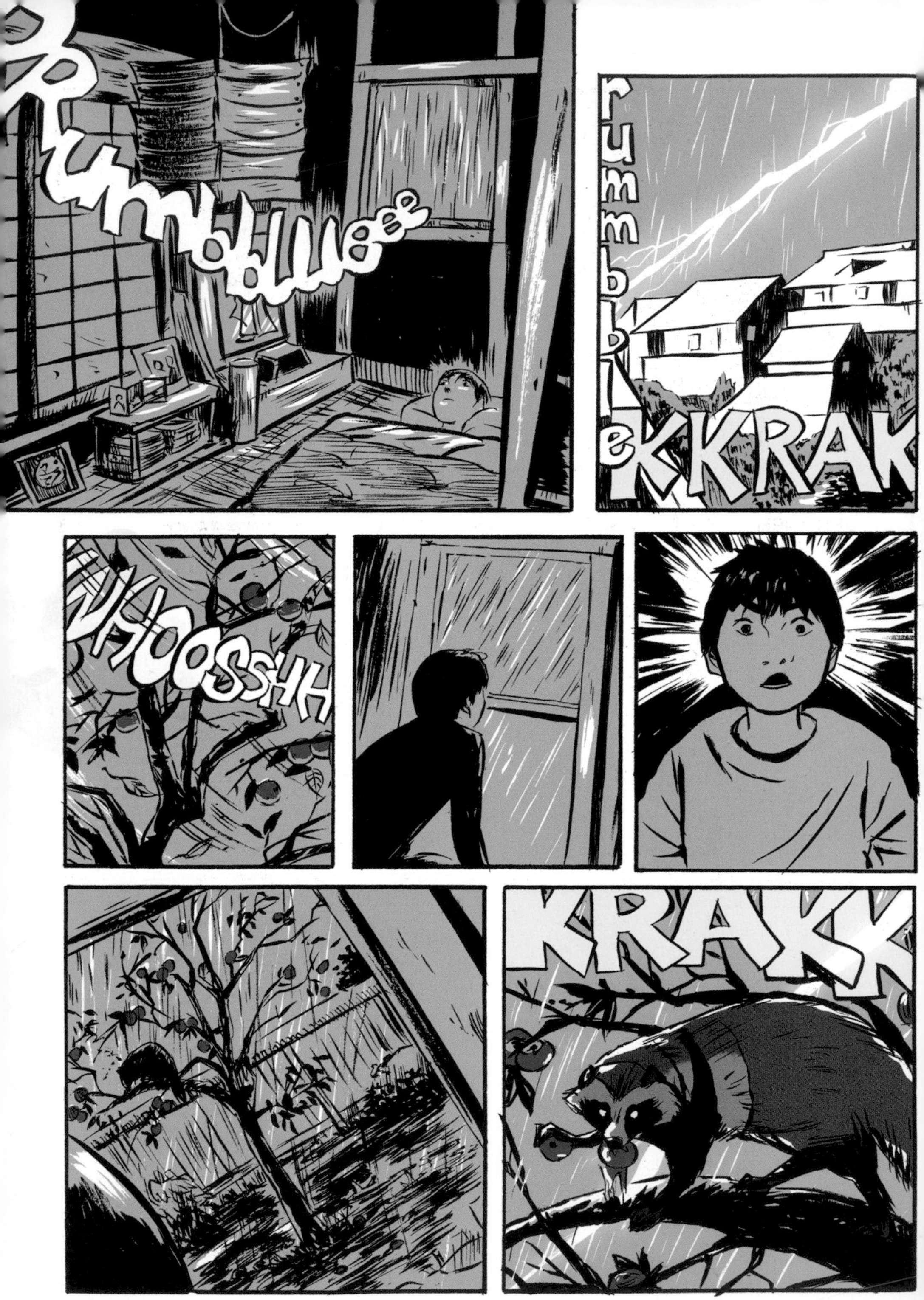
Rumbbllleee
rummbble
KKRAK
WHOOSSHH
KRAKK

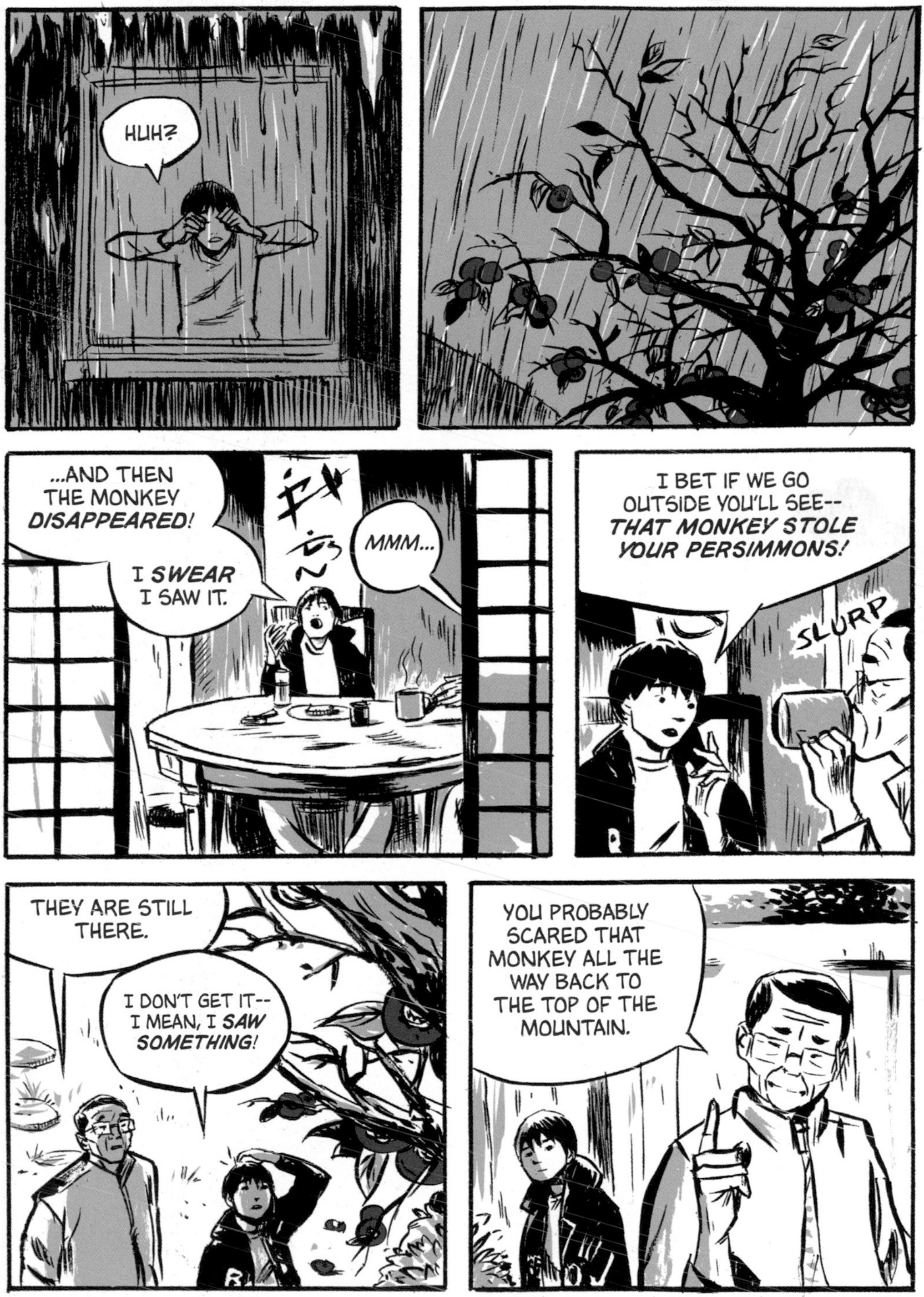
HUH?
...AND THEN THE MONKEY DISAPPEARED!
I SWEAR I SAW IT.
MMM...
I BET IF WE GO OUTSIDE YOU'LL SEE-- THAT MONKEY STOLE YOUR PERSIMMONS!
SLURP
THEY ARE STILL THERE.
I DON'T GET IT-- I MEAN, I SAW SOMETHING!
YOU PROBABLY SCARED THAT MONKEY ALL THE WAY BACK TO THE TOP OF THE MOUNTAIN.

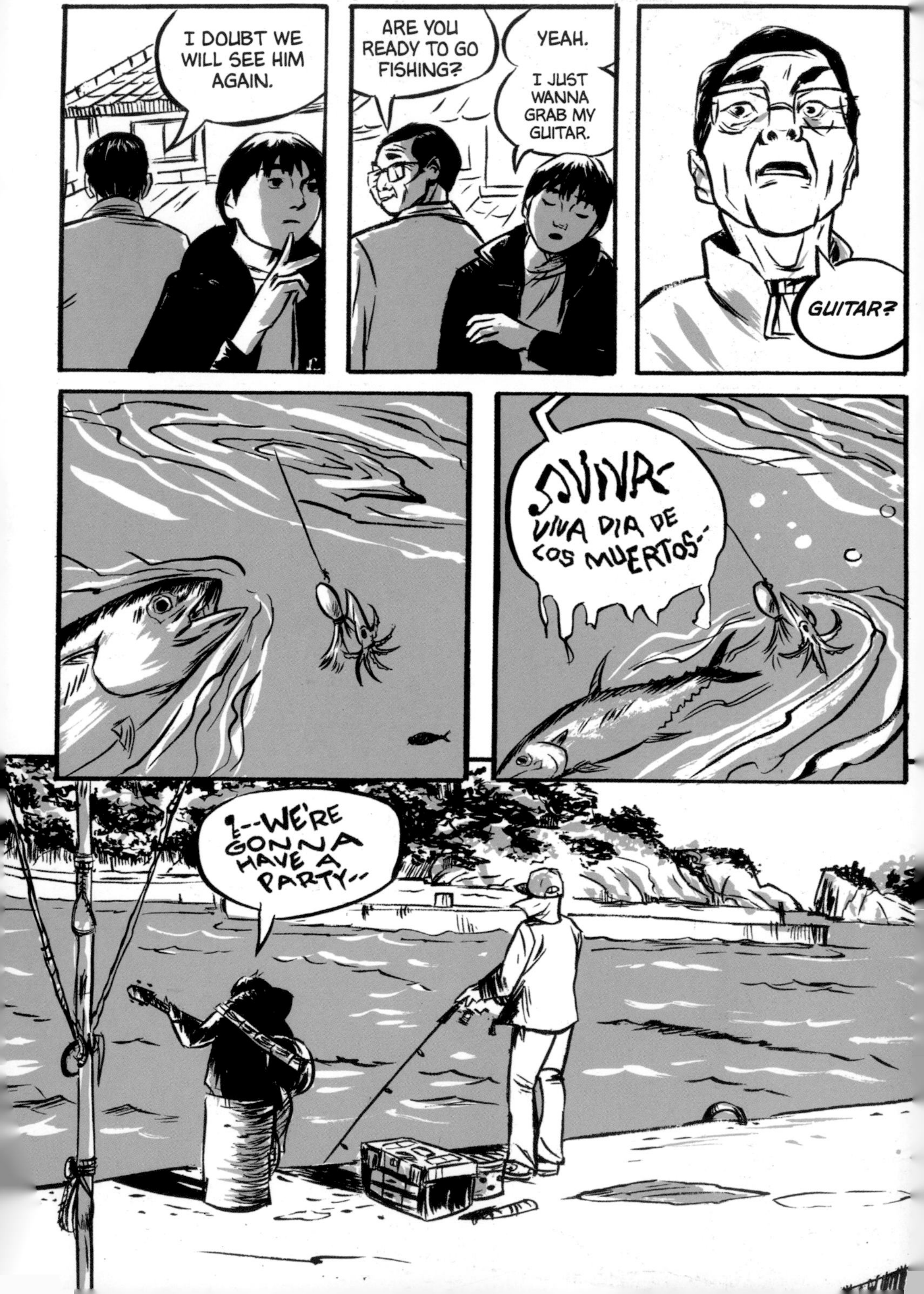
I DOUBT WE WILL SEE HIM AGAIN.
ARE YOU READY TO GO FISHING?
YEAH.
I JUST WANNA GRAB MY GUITAR.
GUITAR?
♪VIVA-
VIVA DIA DE LOS MUERTOS-
♪--WE'RE GONNA HAVE A PARTY--

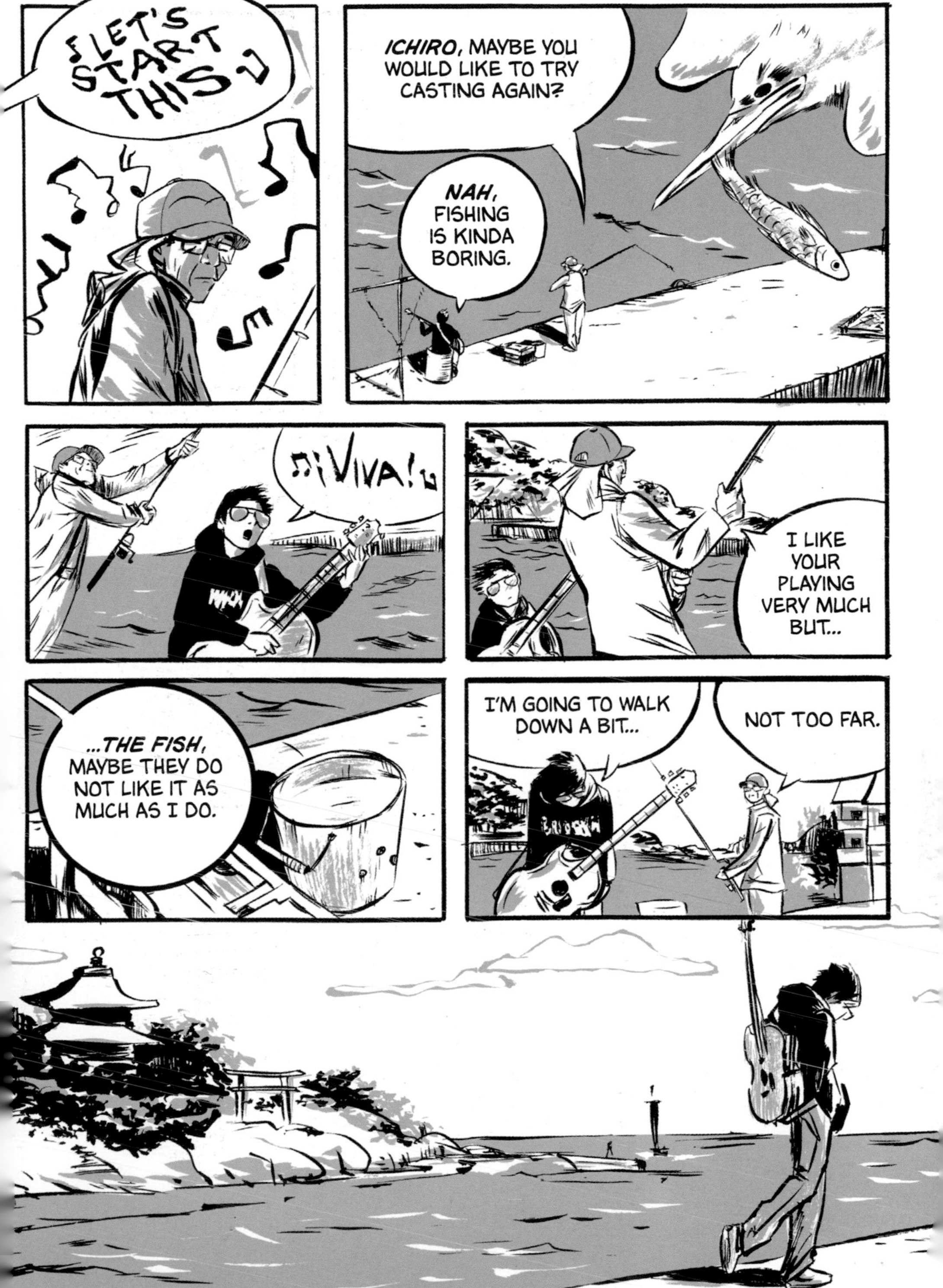
LET'S START THIS
ICHIRO, MAYBE YOU WOULD LIKE TO TRY CASTING AGAIN?
NAH, FISHING IS KINDA BORING.
¡VIVA!
I LIKE YOUR PLAYING VERY MUCH BUT...
...THE FISH, MAYBE THEY DO NOT LIKE IT AS MUCH AS I DO.
I'M GOING TO WALK DOWN A BIT...
NOT TOO FAR.

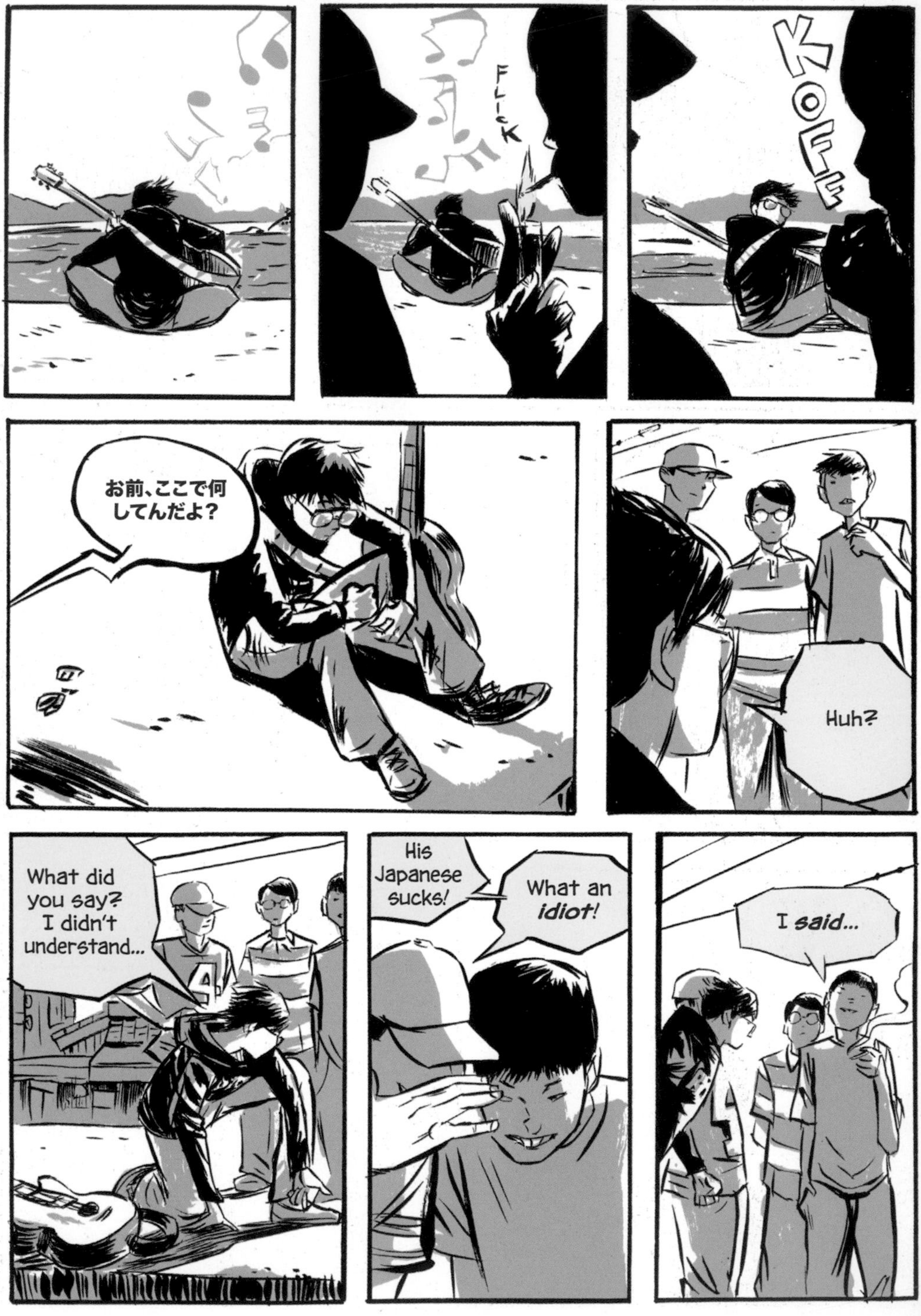

FLICK
KOFF
お前、ここで何してんだよ？
Huh?
What did you say? I didn't understand...
His Japanese sucks!
What an *idiot*!
I *said*...

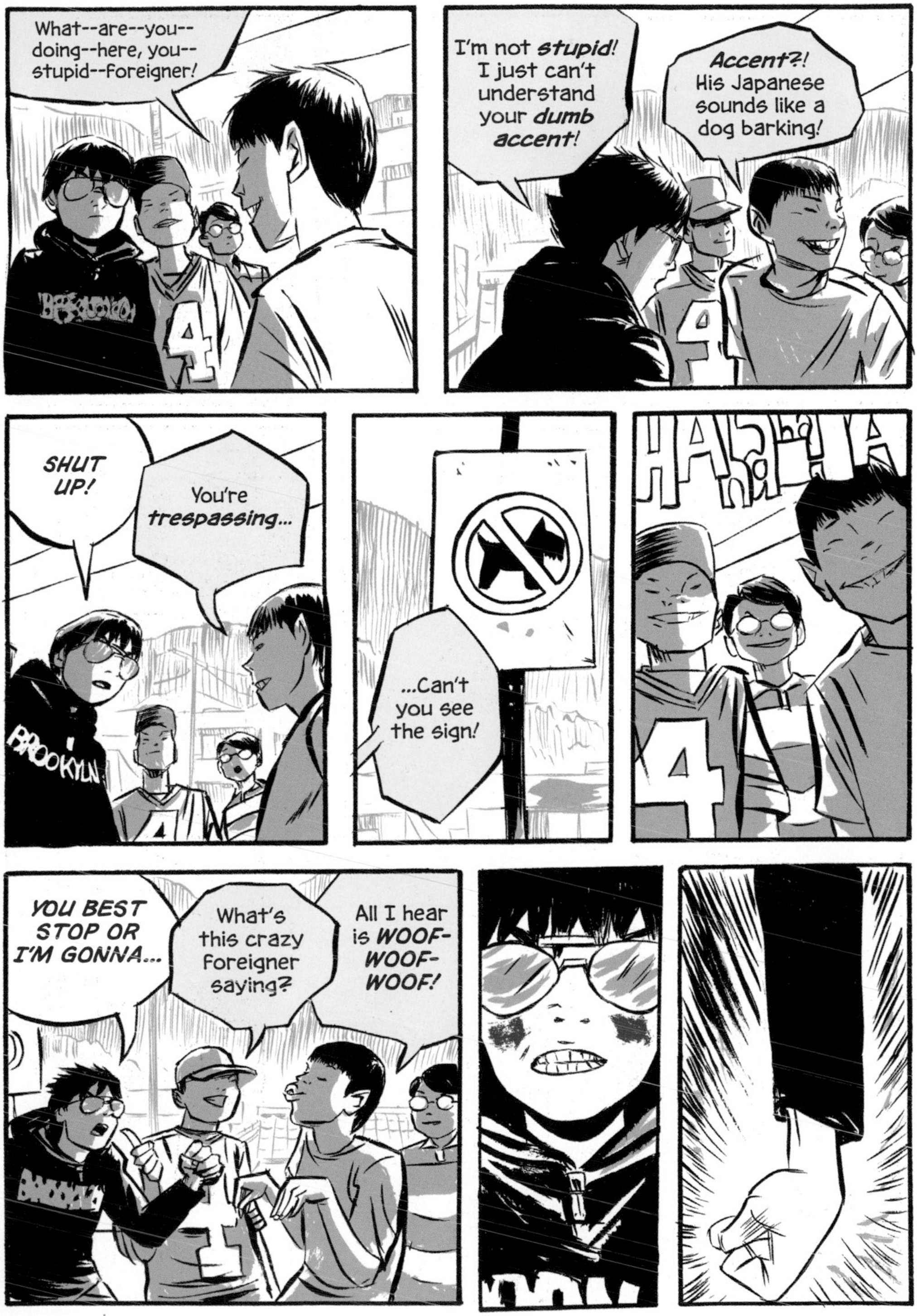
What--are--you--doing--here, you--stupid--foreigner!
I'm not *stupid*! I just can't understand your *dumb accent*!
Accent?! His Japanese sounds like a dog barking!
SHUT UP!
You're *trespassing...*
...Can't you see the sign!
HA HA HA HA
YOU BEST STOP OR I'M GONNA...
What's this crazy foreigner saying?
All I hear is *WOOF-WOOF-WOOF!*

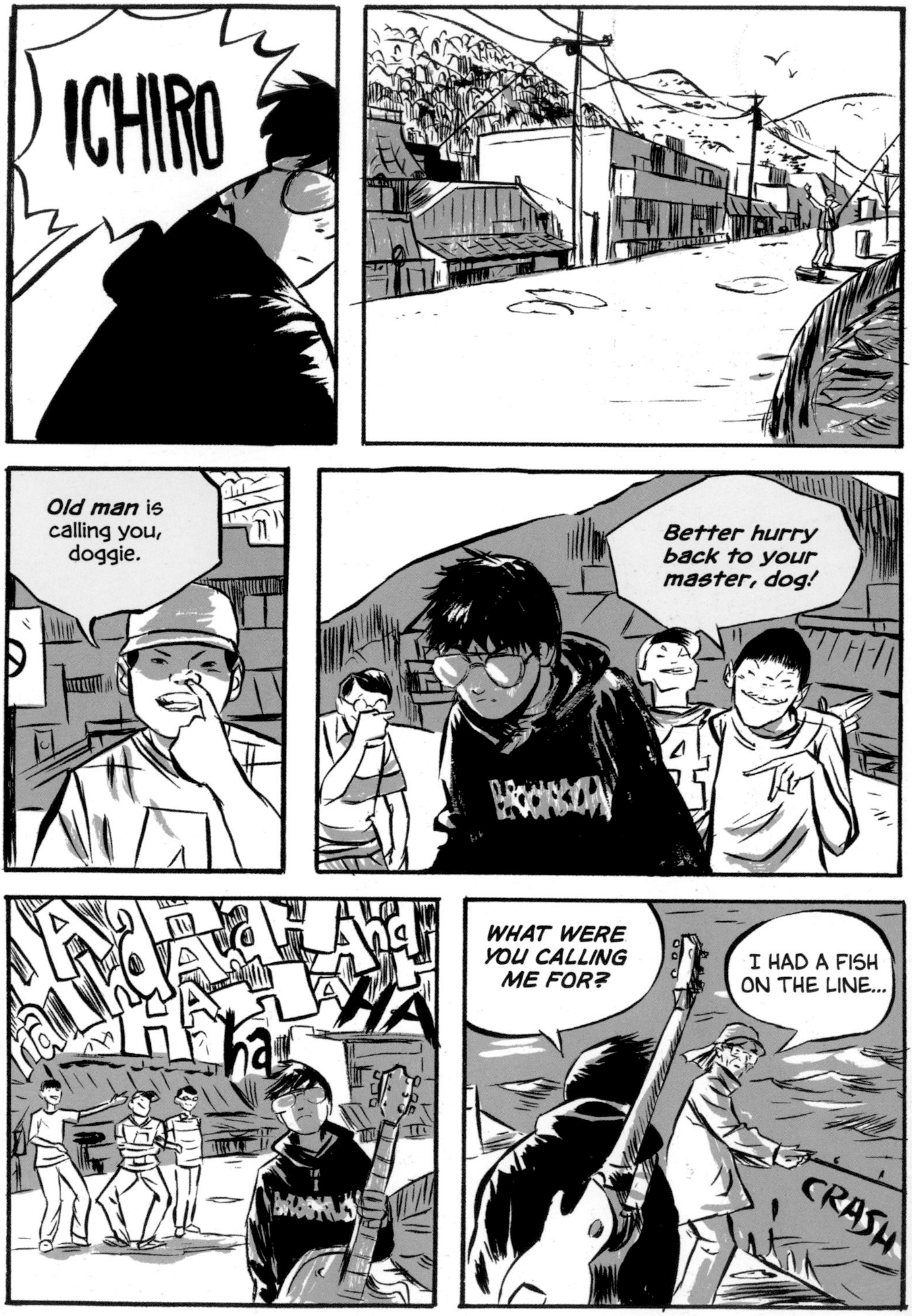
ICHIRO
Old man is calling you, doggie.
Better hurry back to your master, dog!
HA HA HA ha HA HA ha
WHAT WERE YOU CALLING ME FOR?
I HAD A FISH ON THE LINE...
CRASH

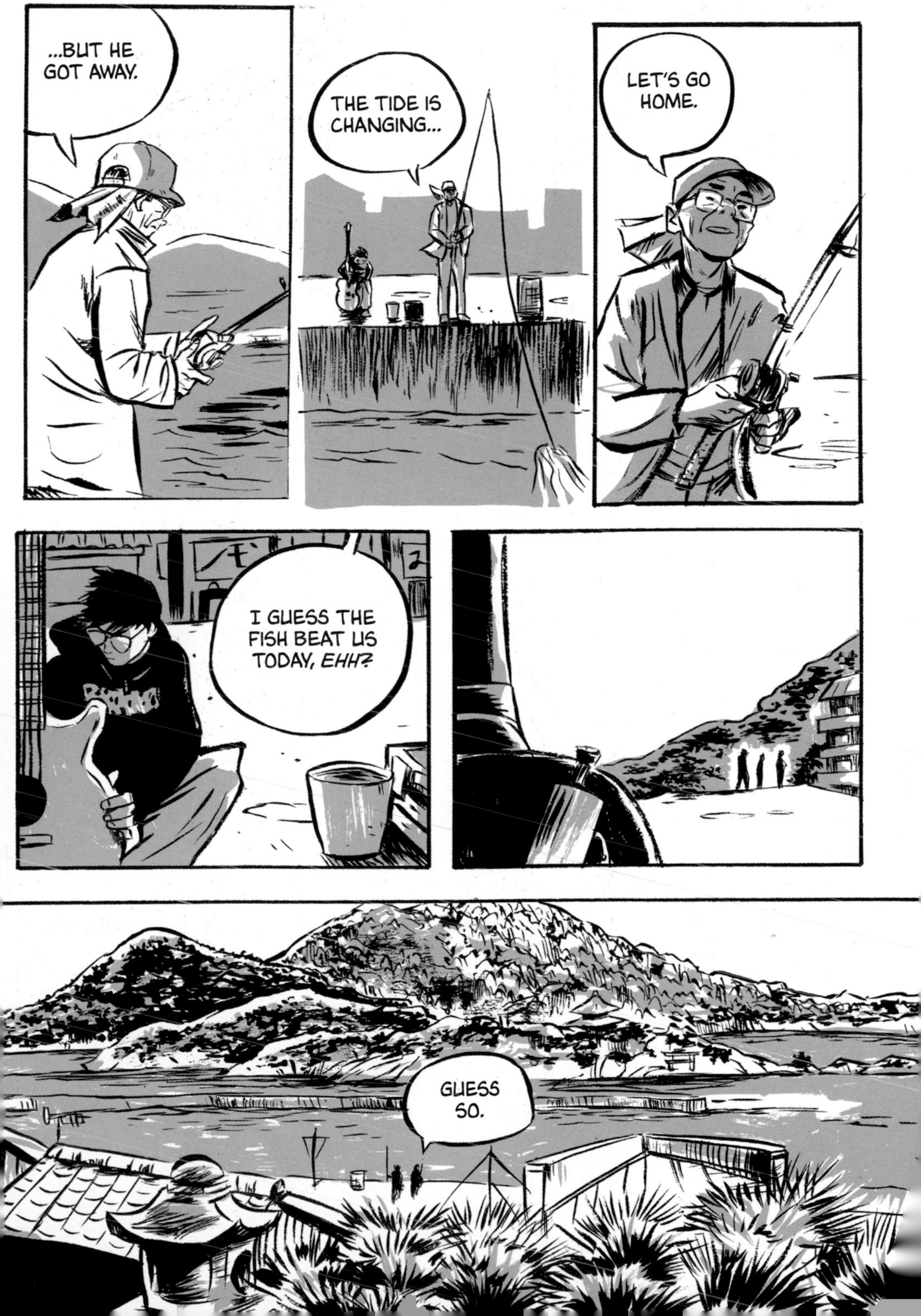
...BUT HE GOT AWAY.
THE TIDE IS CHANGING...
LET'S GO HOME.
I GUESS THE FISH BEAT US TODAY, *EHH?*
GUESS SO.

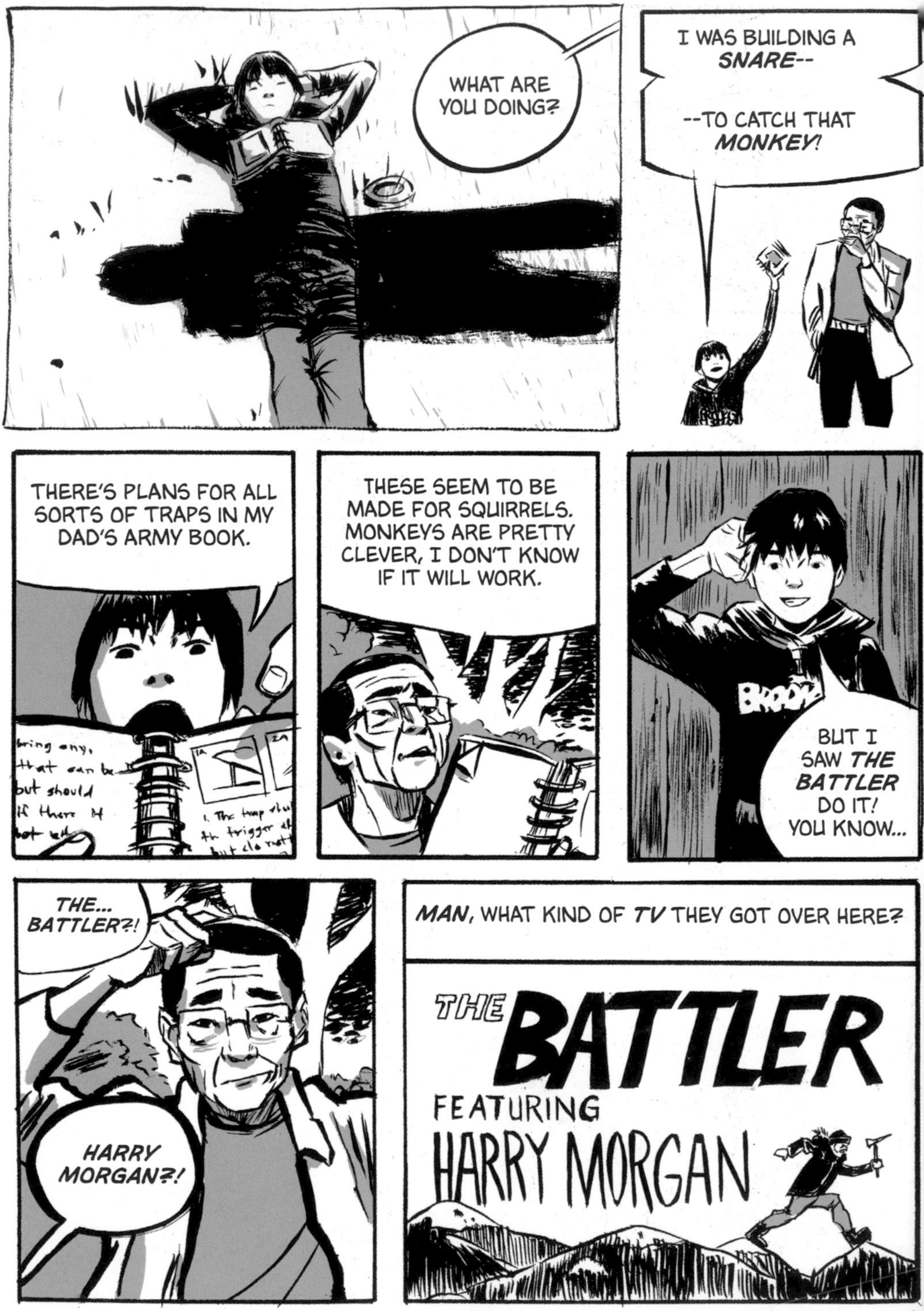
WHAT ARE YOU DOING?
I WAS BUILDING A SNARE--
--TO CATCH THAT MONKEY!
THERE'S PLANS FOR ALL SORTS OF TRAPS IN MY DAD'S ARMY BOOK.
THESE SEEM TO BE MADE FOR SQUIRRELS. MONKEYS ARE PRETTY CLEVER, I DON'T KNOW IF IT WILL WORK.
BUT I SAW THE BATTLER DO IT! YOU KNOW...
THE... BATTLER?!
HARRY MORGAN?!
MAN, WHAT KIND OF TV THEY GOT OVER HERE?
THE BATTLER
FEATURING
HARRY MORGAN

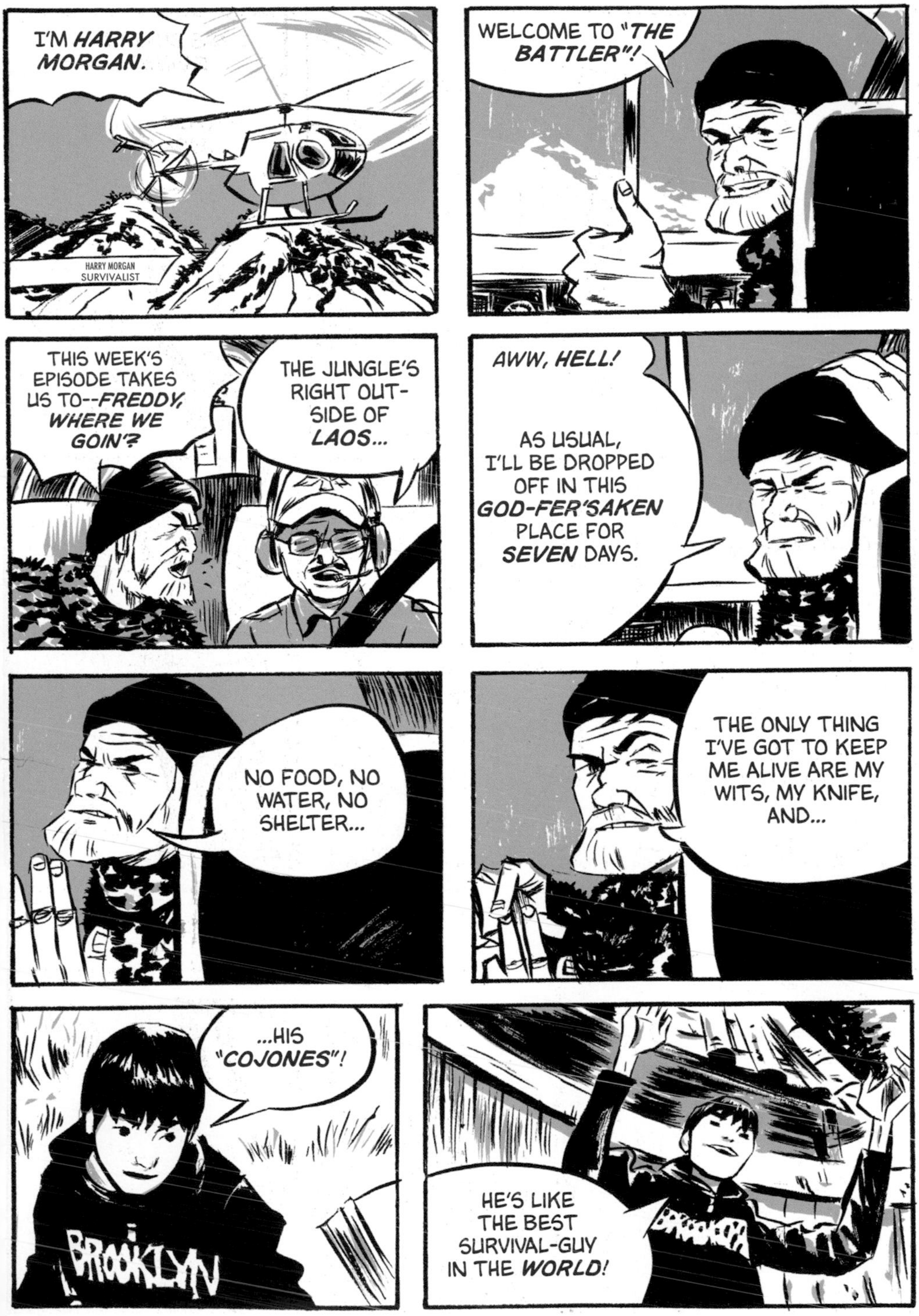
I'M HARRY MORGAN.
HARRY MORGAN SURVIVALIST
WELCOME TO "THE BATTLER"!
THIS WEEK'S EPISODE TAKES US TO--FREDDY, WHERE WE GOIN'?
THE JUNGLE'S RIGHT OUT-SIDE OF LAOS...
AWW, HELL!
AS USUAL, I'LL BE DROPPED OFF IN THIS GOD-FER'SAKEN PLACE FOR SEVEN DAYS.
NO FOOD, NO WATER, NO SHELTER...
THE ONLY THING I'VE GOT TO KEEP ME ALIVE ARE MY WITS, MY KNIFE, AND...
...HIS "COJONES"!
BROOKLYN
HE'S LIKE THE BEST SURVIVAL-GUY IN THE WORLD!
BROOKLYN

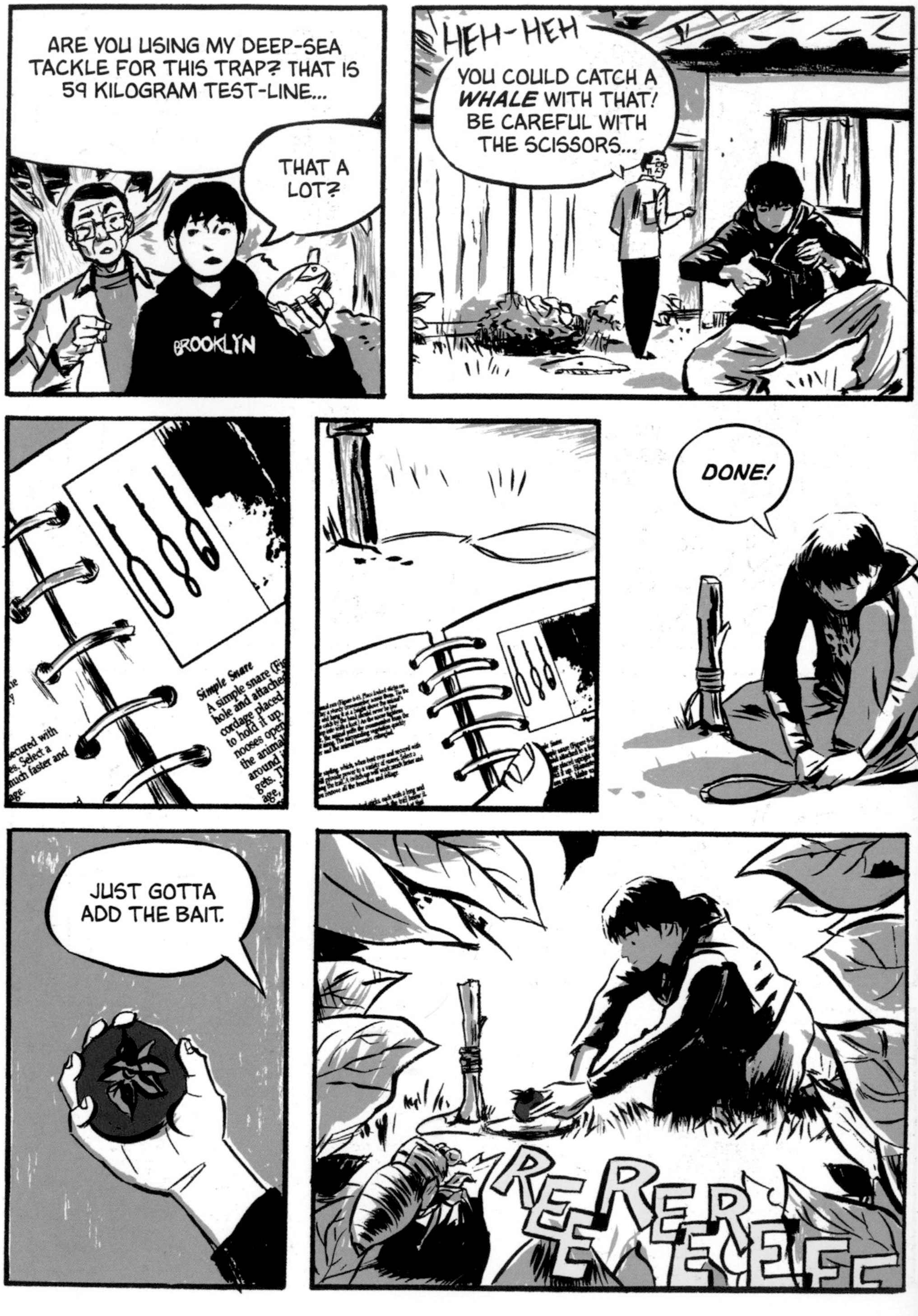

ARE YOU USING MY DEEP-SEA TACKLE FOR THIS TRAP? THAT IS 59 KILOGRAM TEST-LINE...
THAT A LOT?
HEH-HEH
YOU COULD CATCH A *WHALE* WITH THAT! BE CAREFUL WITH THE SCISSORS...
BROOKLYN
Simple Snare
DONE!
JUST GOTTA ADD THE BAIT.

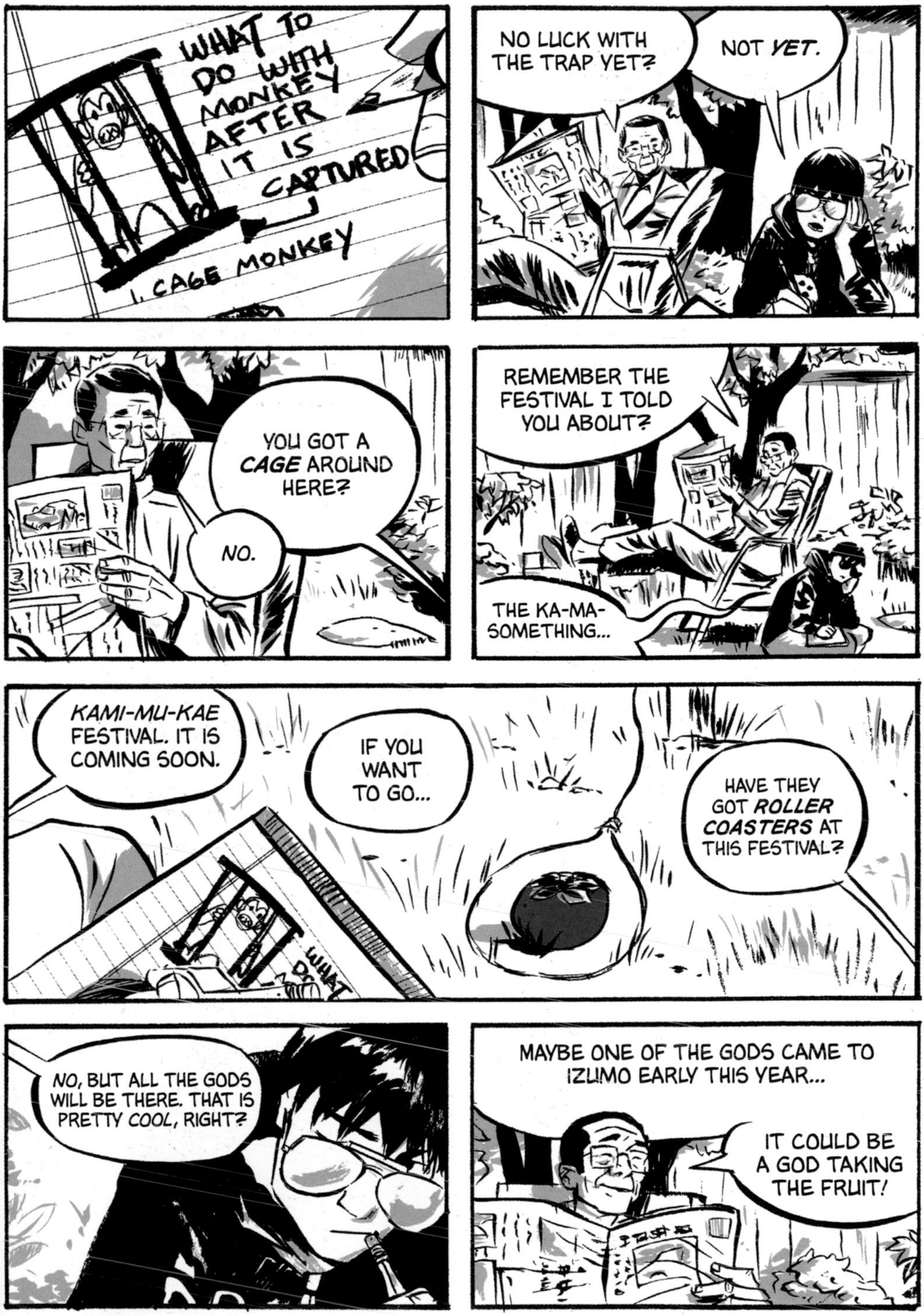

WHAT TO DO WITH MONKEY AFTER IT IS CAPTURED
1. CAGE MONKEY
NO LUCK WITH THE TRAP YET?
NOT *YET*.
YOU GOT A *CAGE* AROUND HERE?
NO.
REMEMBER THE FESTIVAL I TOLD YOU ABOUT?
THE KA-MA-SOMETHING...
KAMI-MU-KAE FESTIVAL. IT IS COMING SOON.
IF YOU WANT TO GO...
HAVE THEY GOT *ROLLER COASTERS* AT THIS FESTIVAL?
NO, BUT ALL THE GODS WILL BE THERE. THAT IS PRETTY *COOL*, RIGHT?
MAYBE ONE OF THE GODS CAME TO IZUMO EARLY THIS YEAR...
IT COULD BE A GOD TAKING THE FRUIT!

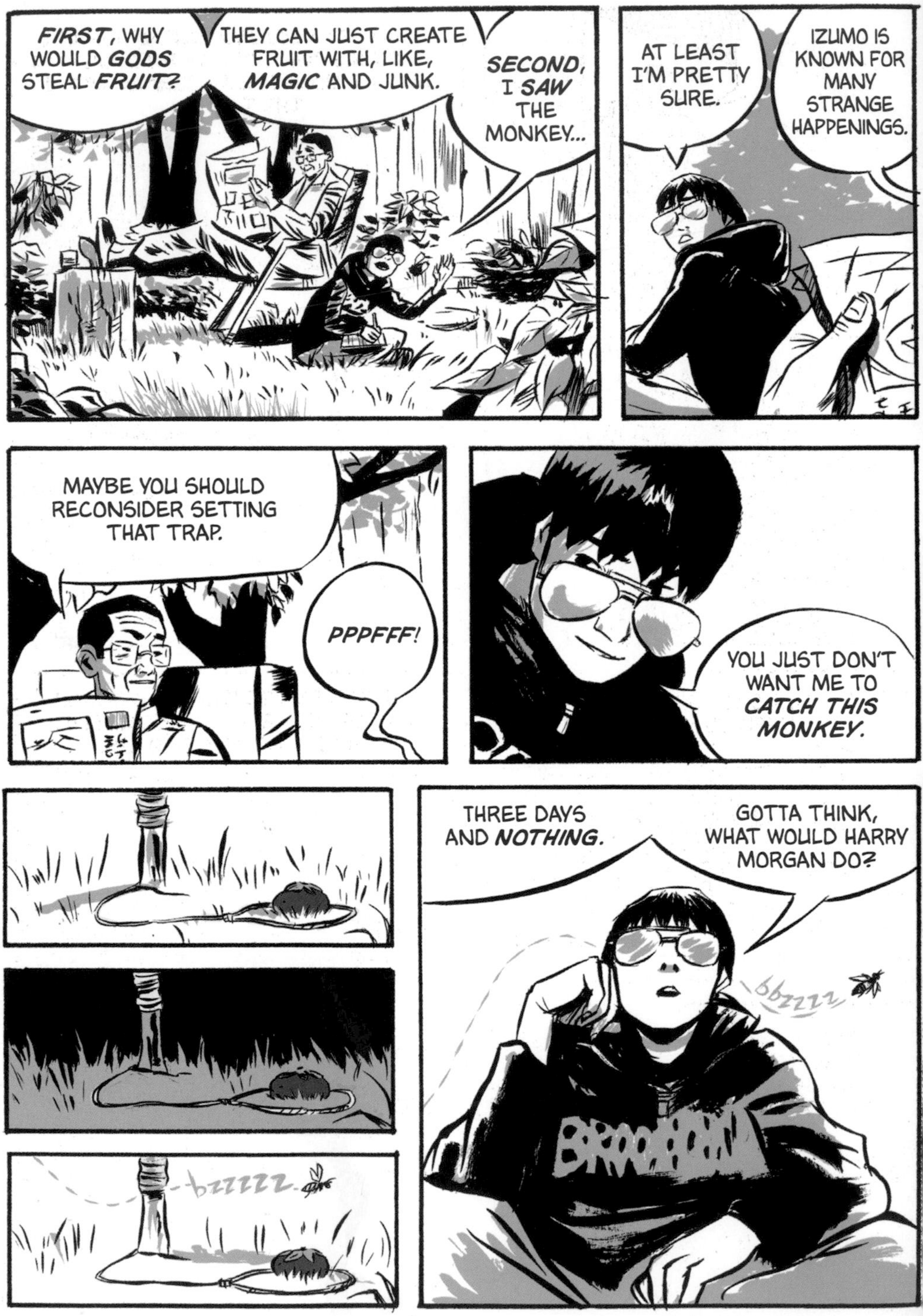
FIRST, WHY WOULD GODS STEAL FRUIT?
THEY CAN JUST CREATE FRUIT WITH, LIKE, MAGIC AND JUNK.
SECOND, I SAW THE MONKEY...
AT LEAST I'M PRETTY SURE.
IZUMO IS KNOWN FOR MANY STRANGE HAPPENINGS.
MAYBE YOU SHOULD RECONSIDER SETTING THAT TRAP.
PPPFFF!
YOU JUST DON'T WANT ME TO CATCH THIS MONKEY.
bzzzzz
THREE DAYS AND NOTHING.
GOTTA THINK, WHAT WOULD HARRY MORGAN DO?
bbzzzz

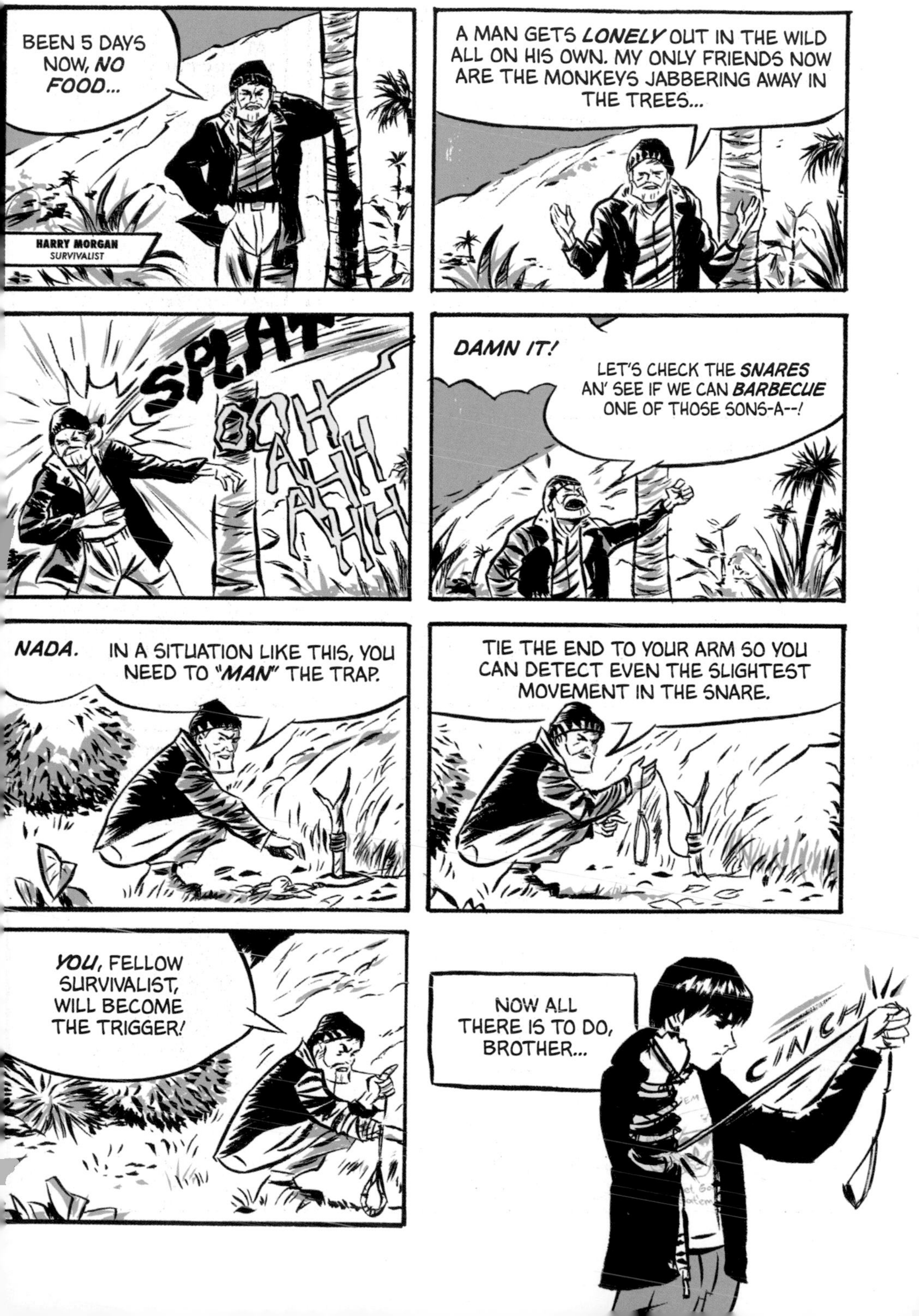
BEEN 5 DAYS NOW, NO FOOD...
HARRY MORGAN
SURVIVALIST
A MAN GETS LONELY OUT IN THE WILD ALL ON HIS OWN. MY ONLY FRIENDS NOW ARE THE MONKEYS JABBERING AWAY IN THE TREES...
SPLAT
OOH AHH AHH
DAMN IT!
LET'S CHECK THE SNARES AN' SEE IF WE CAN BARBECUE ONE OF THOSE SONS-A--!
NADA.
IN A SITUATION LIKE THIS, YOU NEED TO "MAN" THE TRAP.
TIE THE END TO YOUR ARM SO YOU CAN DETECT EVEN THE SLIGHTEST MOVEMENT IN THE SNARE.
YOU, FELLOW SURVIVALIST, WILL BECOME THE TRIGGER!
NOW ALL THERE IS TO DO, BROTHER...
CINCH

...IS *WAIT.*

Ehhhhhh?
What could
it be?

Americans
are so
strange!

RRREEREERRRR

RRREE EKEER
RR

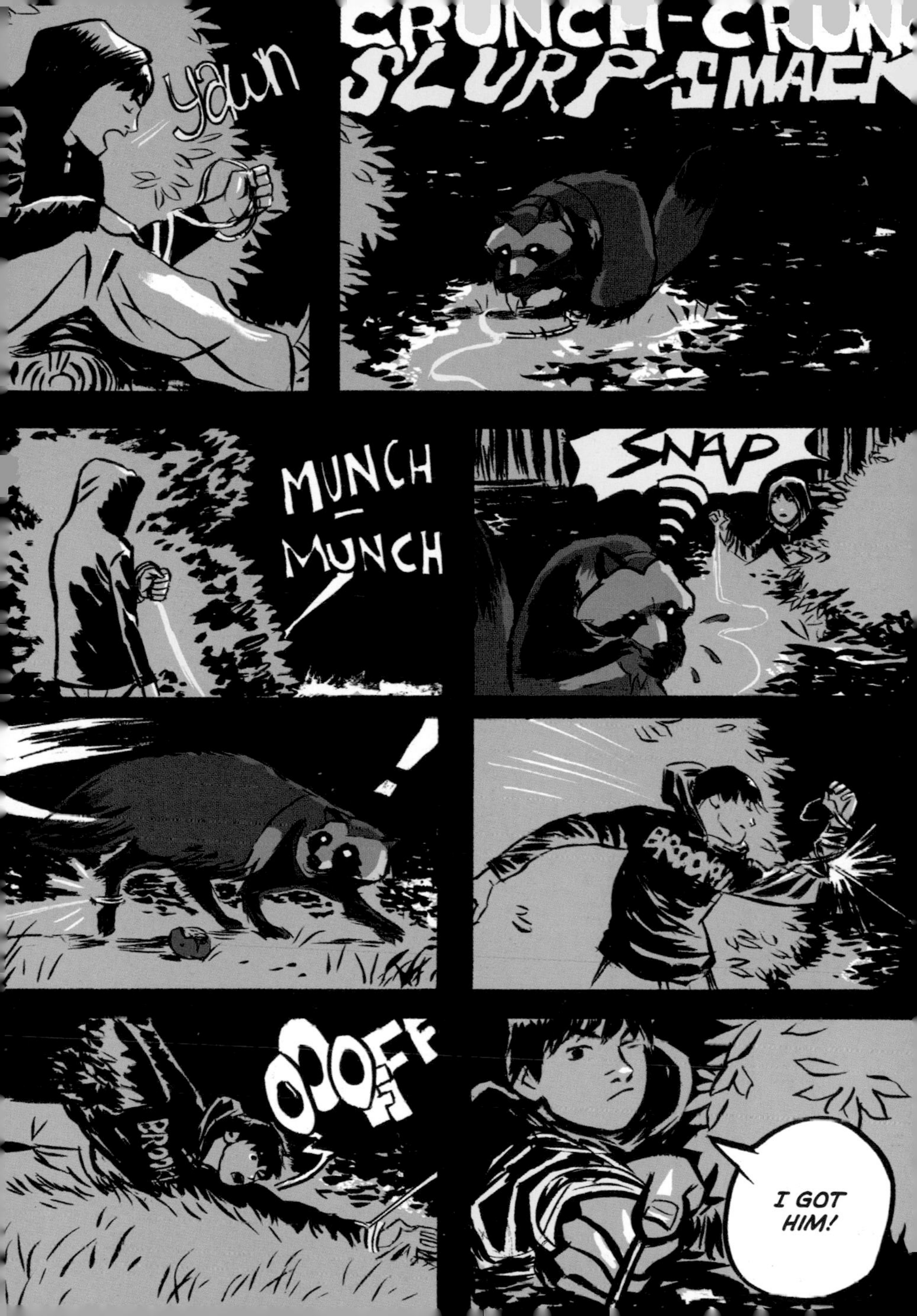
yawn
CRUNCH-CRUN
SLURP-SMACK
MUNCH-MUNCH
SNAP
!
OOOFF
I GOT HIM!

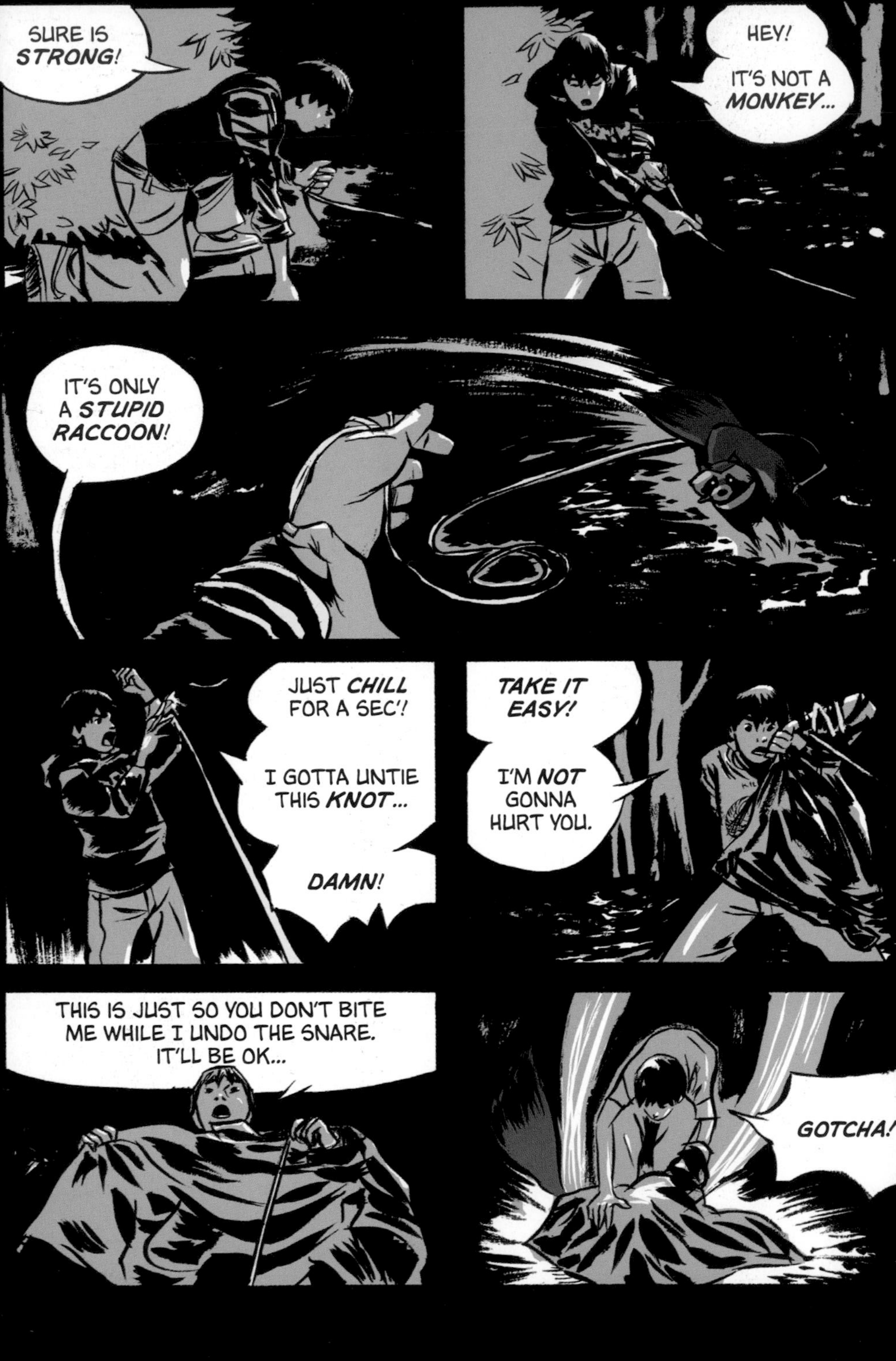
SURE IS STRONG!
HEY!
IT'S NOT A MONKEY...
IT'S ONLY A STUPID RACCOON!
JUST CHILL FOR A SEC'!
I GOTTA UNTIE THIS KNOT...
DAMN!
TAKE IT EASY!
I'M NOT GONNA HURT YOU.
THIS IS JUST SO YOU DON'T BITE ME WHILE I UNDO THE SNARE. IT'LL BE OK...
GOTCHA!

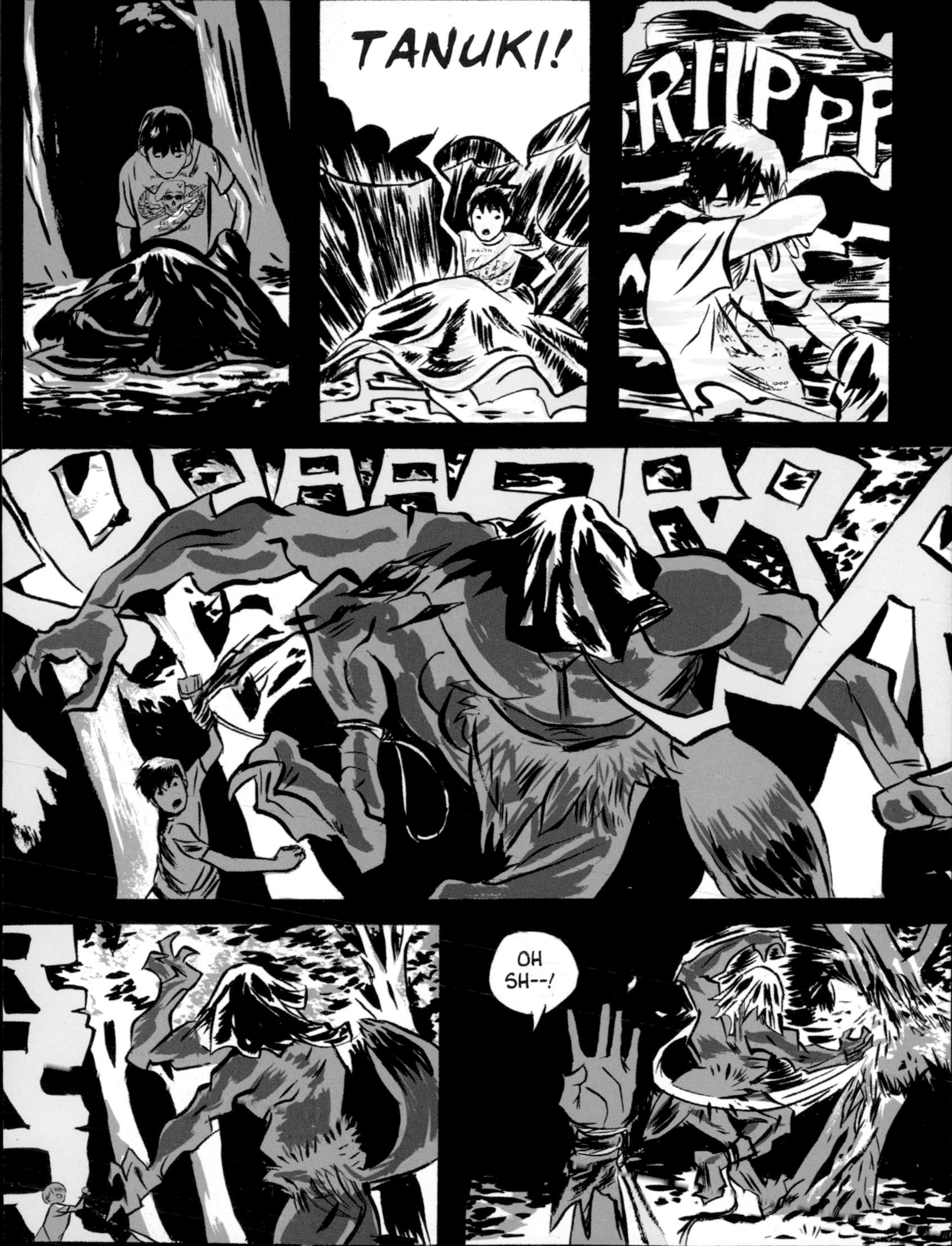
TANUKI!
RIIPPP
OH SH--!

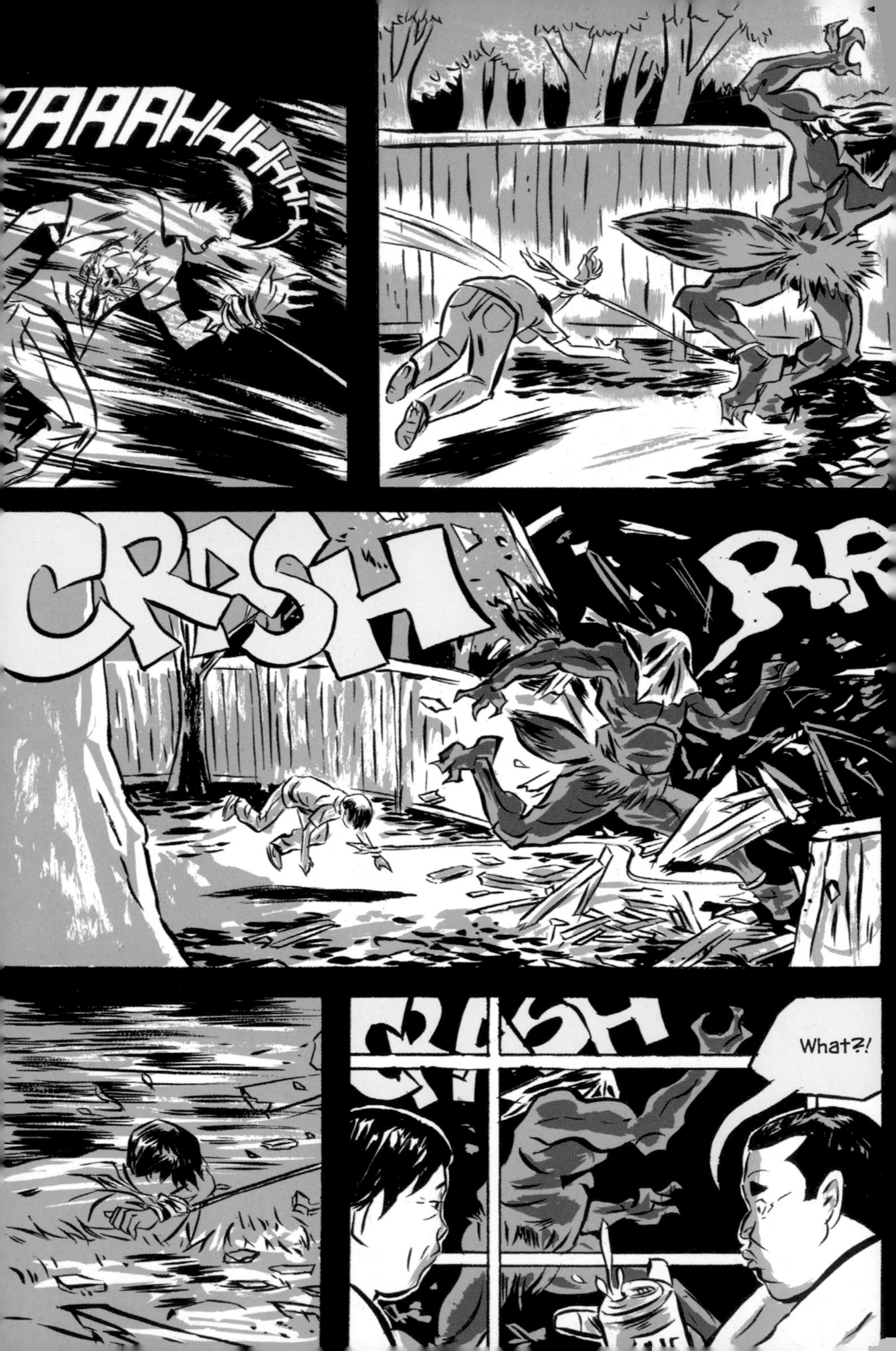
AAAAHHHHHH
CRASH
RR
CRASH
What?!

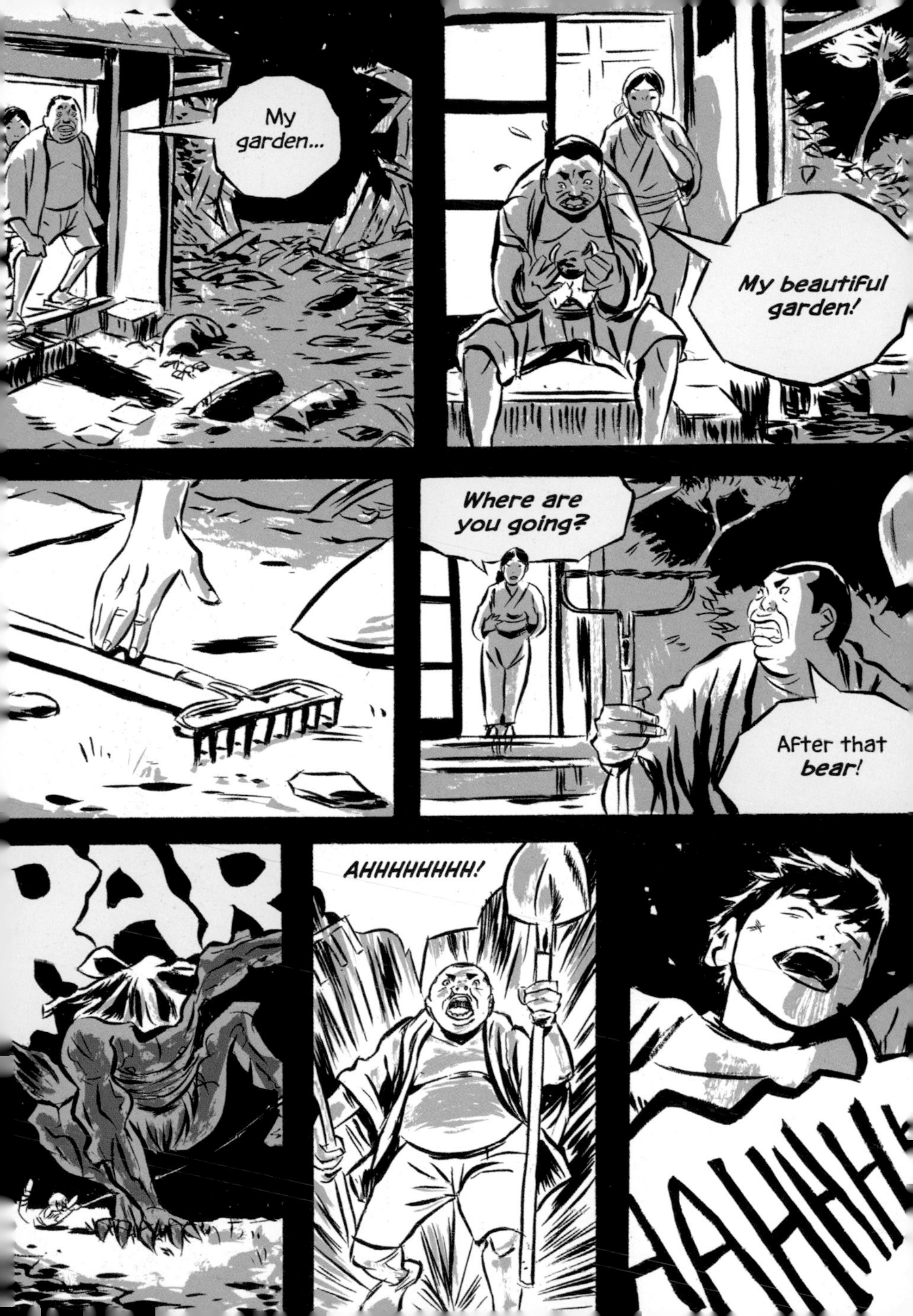
My garden...
My beautiful garden!
Where are you going?
After that *bear*!
AHHHHHHHH!

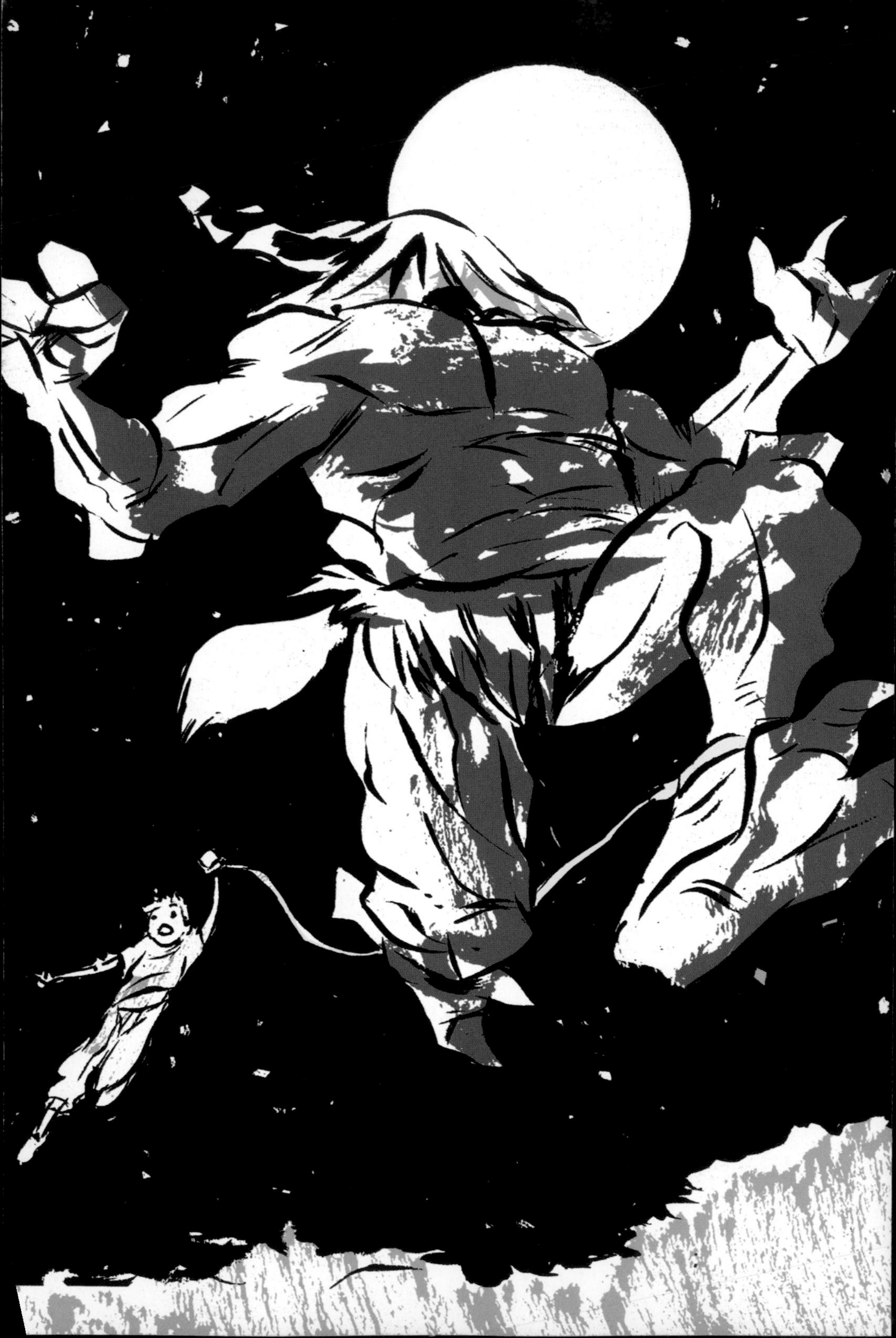

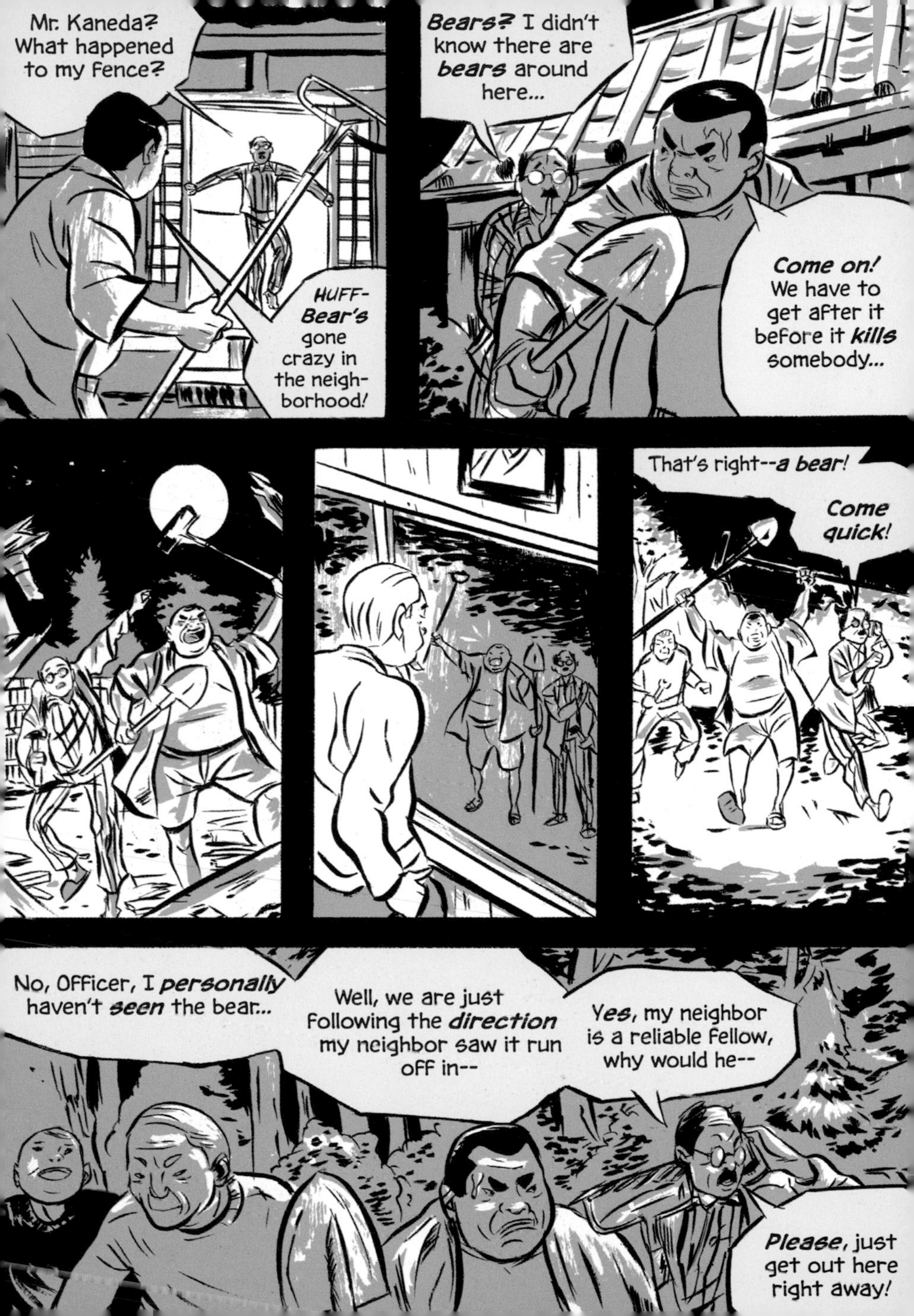

Mr. Kaneda? What happened to my fence?
HUFF- Bear's gone crazy in the neighborhood!
Bears? I didn't know there are bears around here...
Come on! We have to get after it before it kills somebody...
That's right--a bear!
Come quick!
No, Officer, I personally haven't seen the bear...
Well, we are just following the direction my neighbor saw it run off in--
Yes, my neighbor is a reliable fellow, why would he--
Please, just get out here right away!

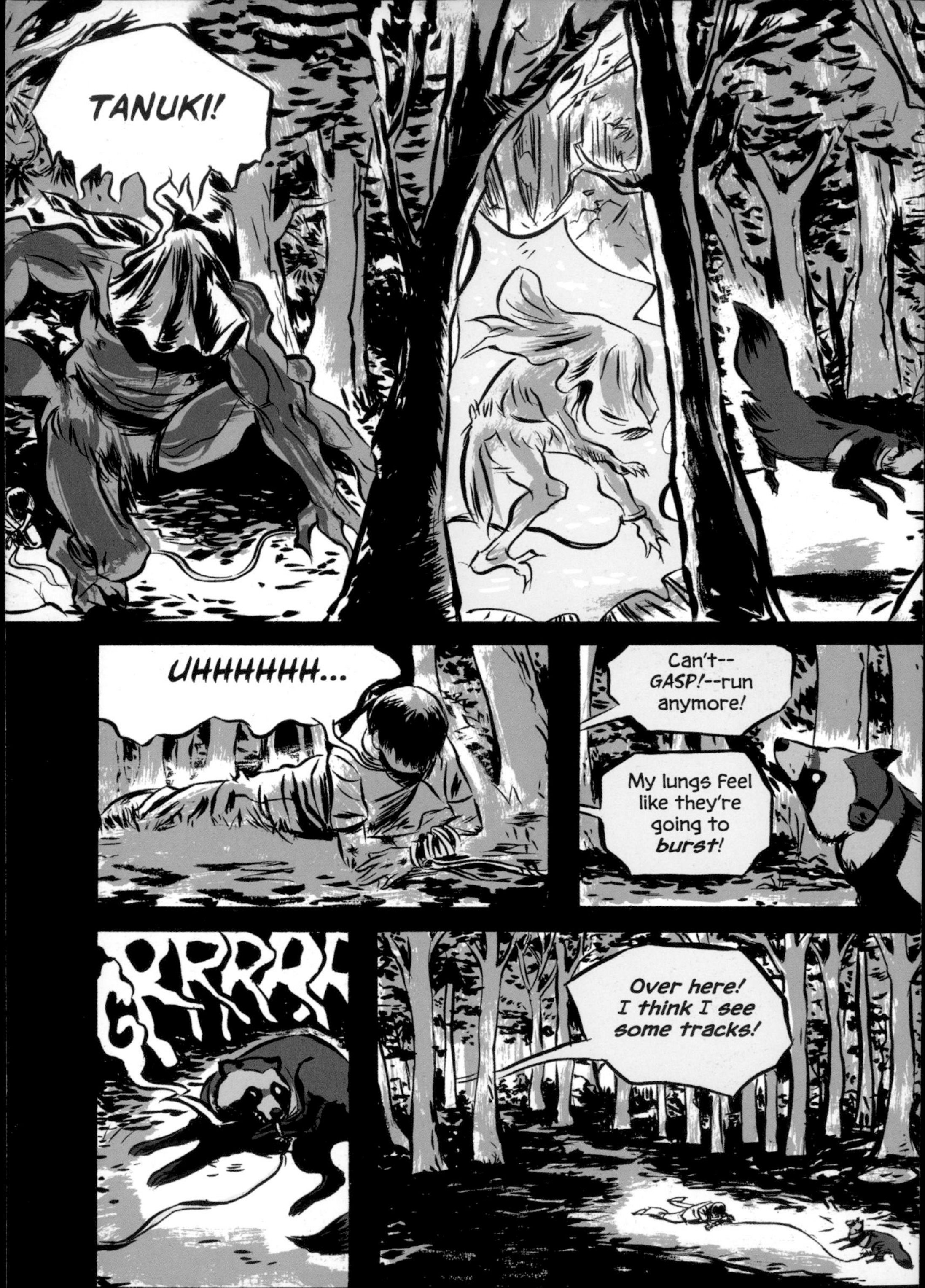
TANUKI!
UHHHHHH...
Can't--GASP!--run anymore!
My lungs feel like they're going to burst!
GRRRR
Over here! I think I see some tracks!

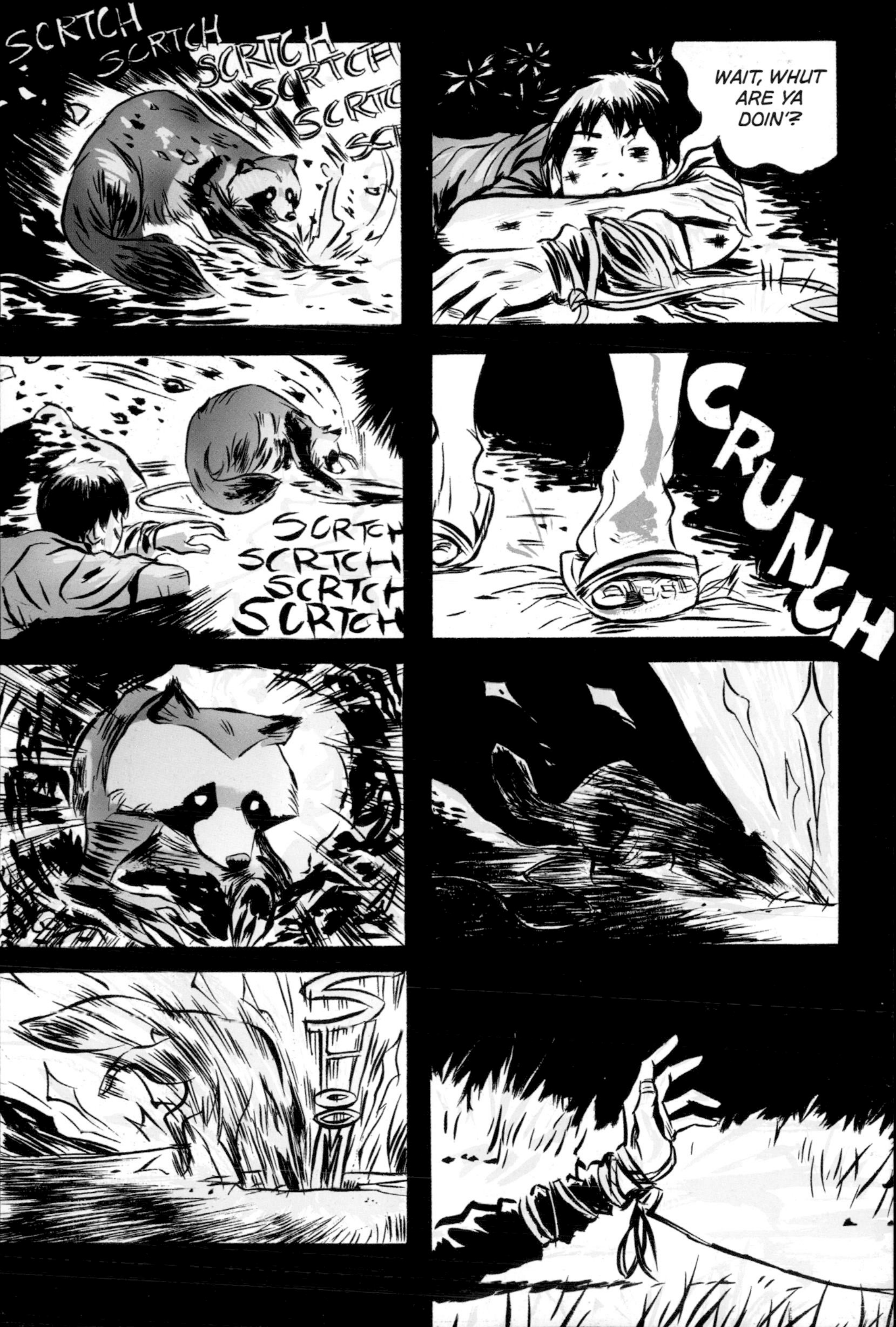
SCRTCH SCRTCH SCRTCH SCRTCH SCRTCH SCRTCH
WAIT, WHUT ARE YA DOIN'?
SCRTCH SCRTCH SCRTCH SCRTCH
CRUNCH

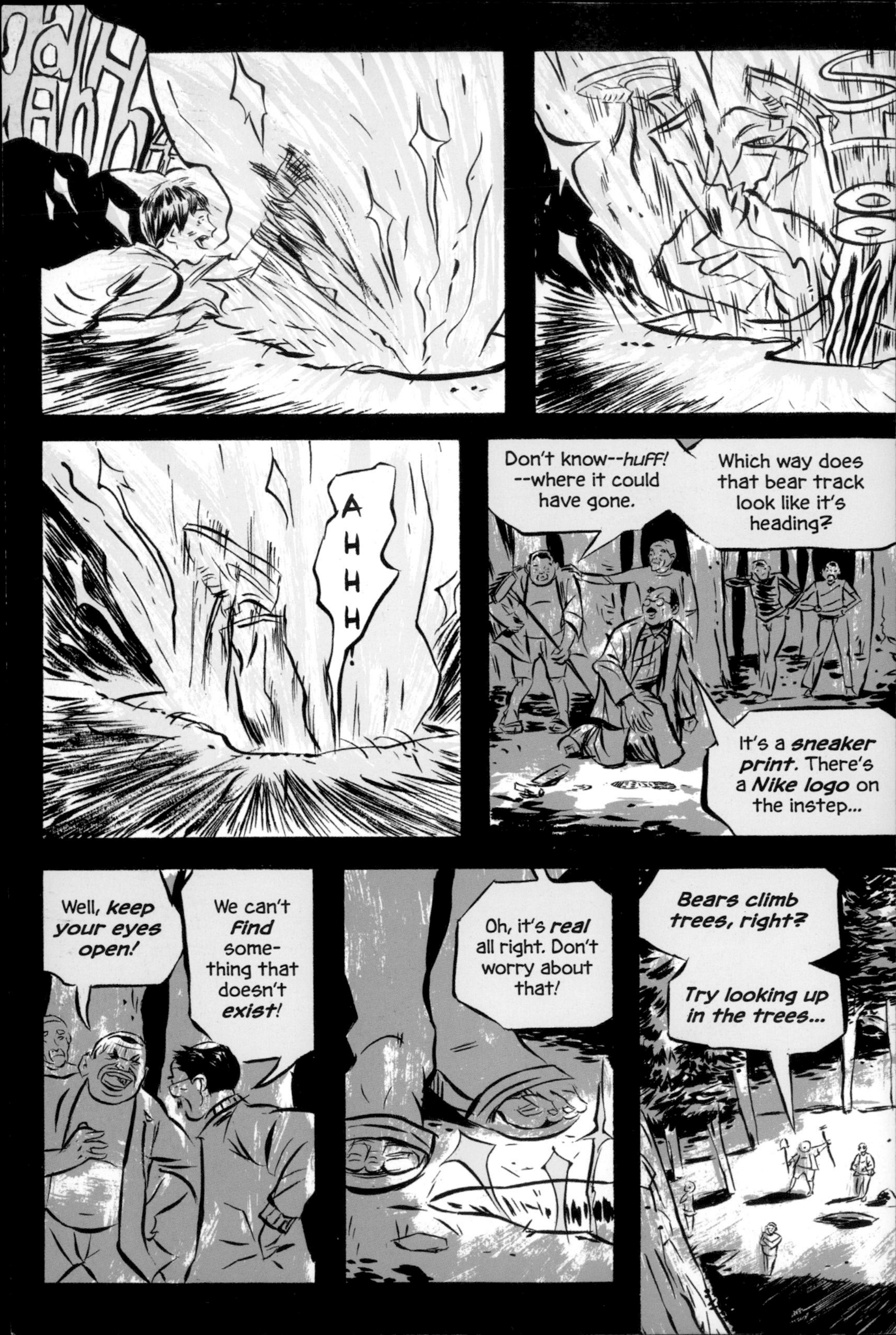
Aahhhh
AHHH!
Don't know--huff! --where it could have gone.
Which way does that bear track look like it's heading?
It's a sneaker print. There's a Nike logo on the instep...
Well, keep your eyes open!
We can't find some-thing that doesn't exist!
Oh, it's real all right. Don't worry about that!
Bears climb trees, right?
Try looking up in the trees...

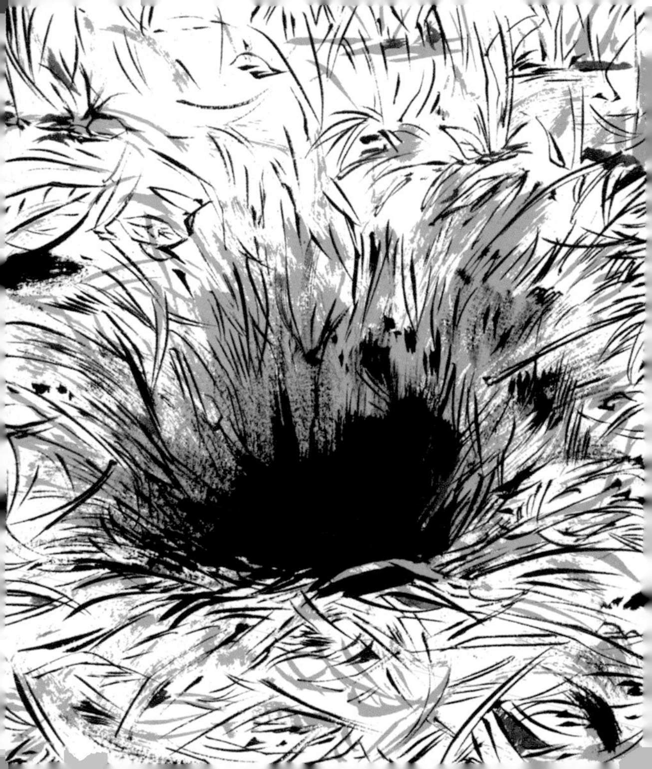

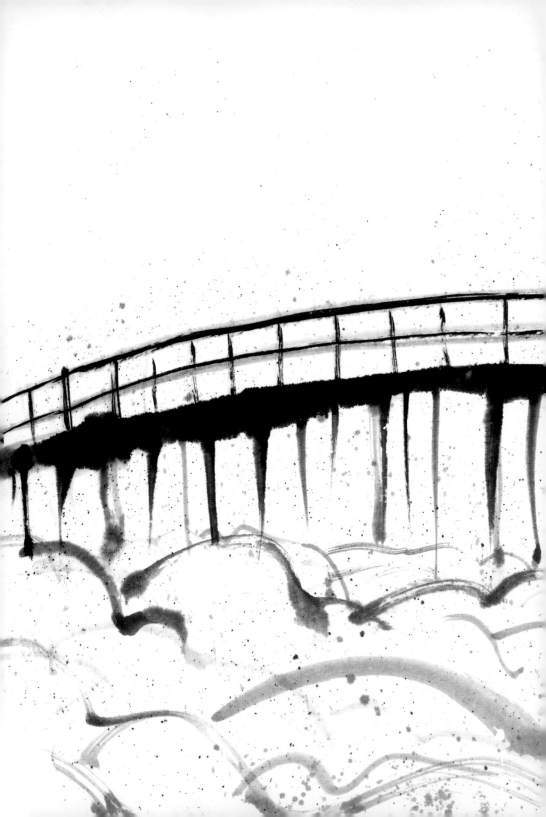

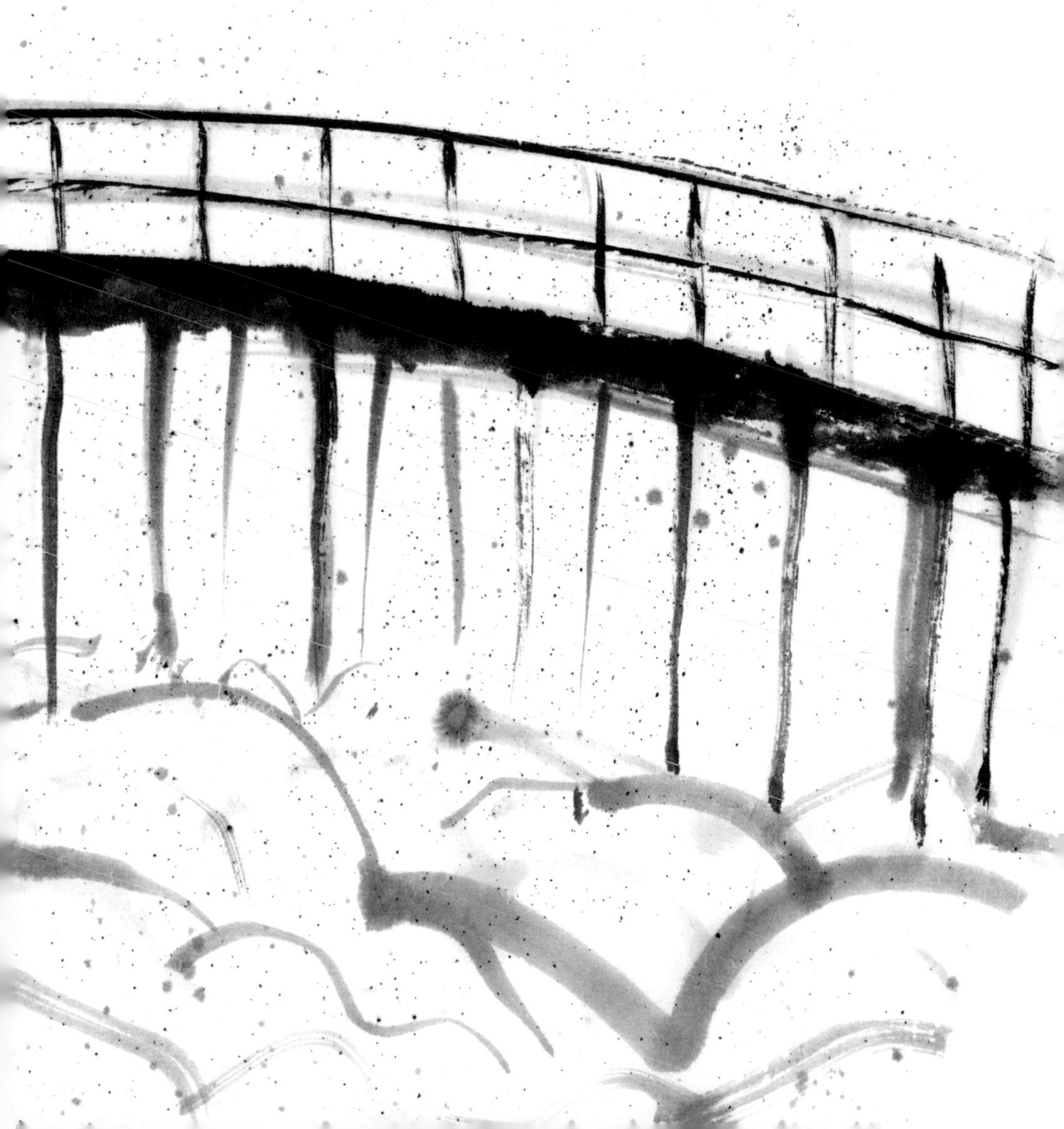

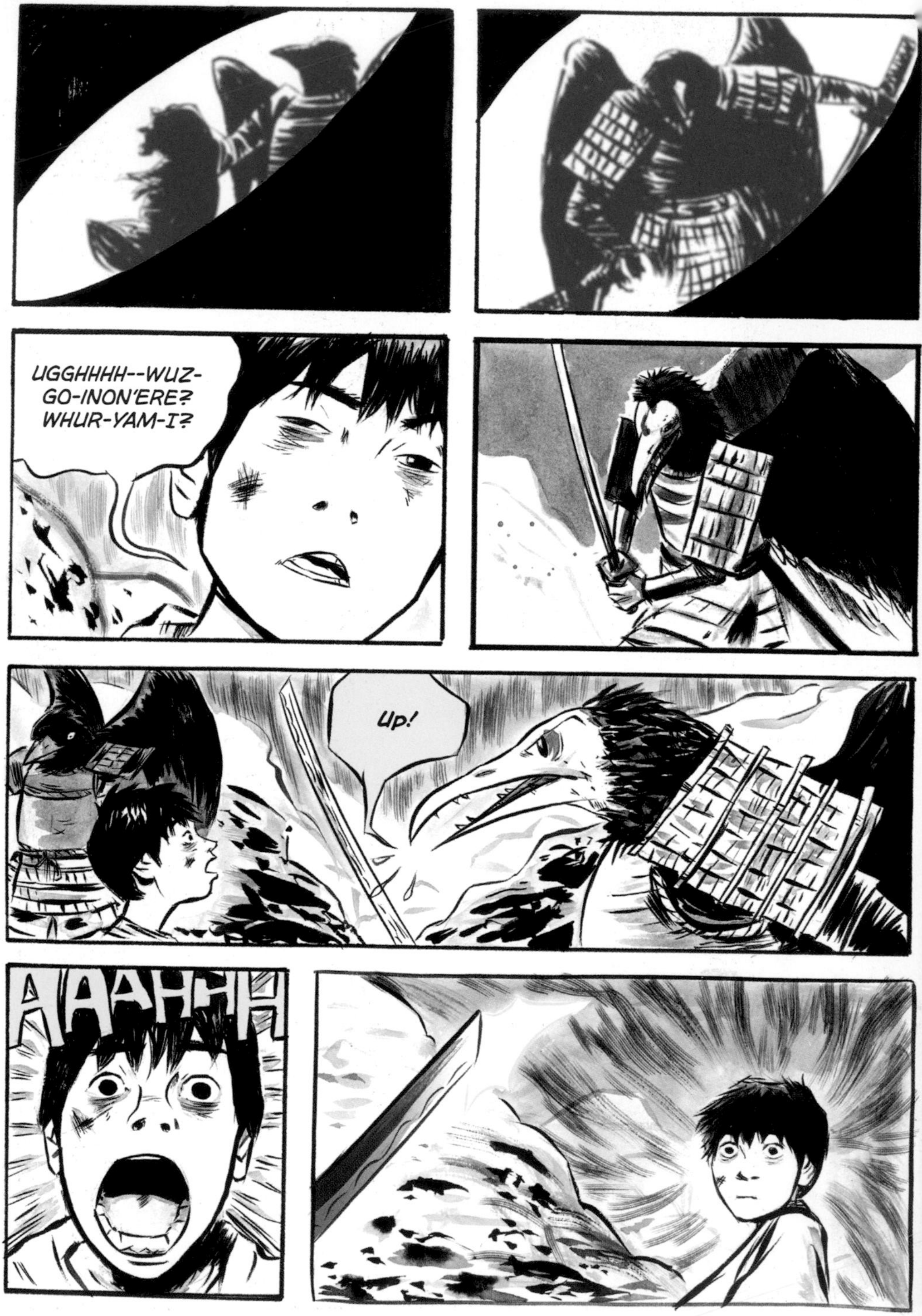
UGGHHHH--WUZ-GO-INON'ERE? WHUR-YAM-I?
Up!
AAAHHH

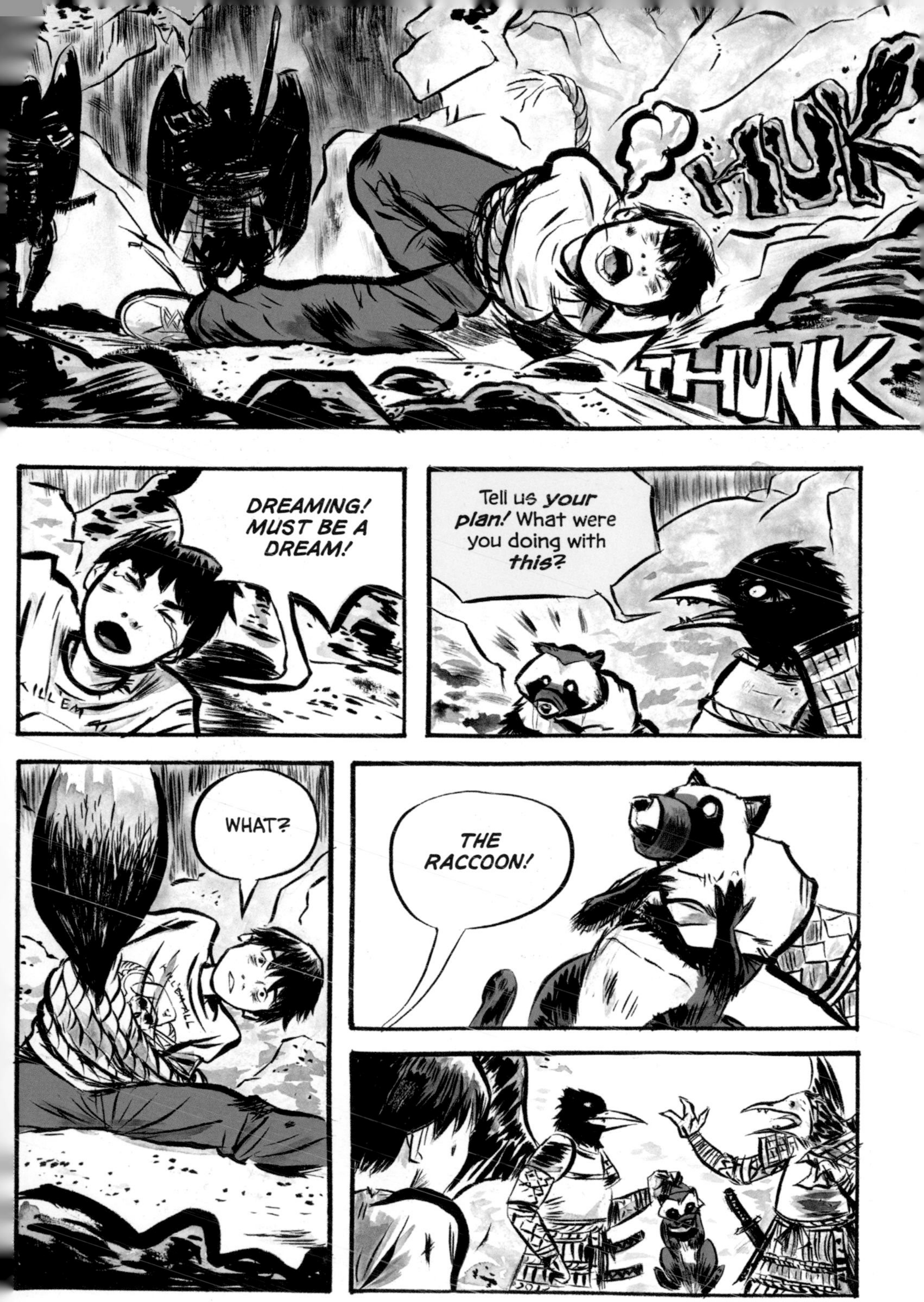
HUK
THUNK
DREAMING! MUST BE A DREAM!
KILL 'EM
Tell us your plan! What were you doing with this?
WHAT?
THE RACCOON!

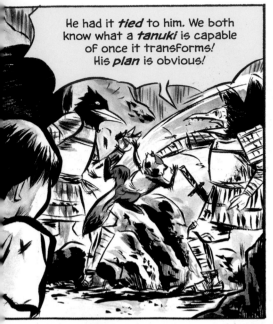

He had it *tied* to him. We both know what a *tanuki* is capable of once it transforms! His *plan* is obvious!

Who put you up to this?

Was it that scoundrel *Aobozu*?!

Useless!

Throw them in the prison!

But the jail in Yomi has reached *capacity*. We will have to take the prisoners to central holding in Ama.

Am I in *hell*? Is that what this place is?

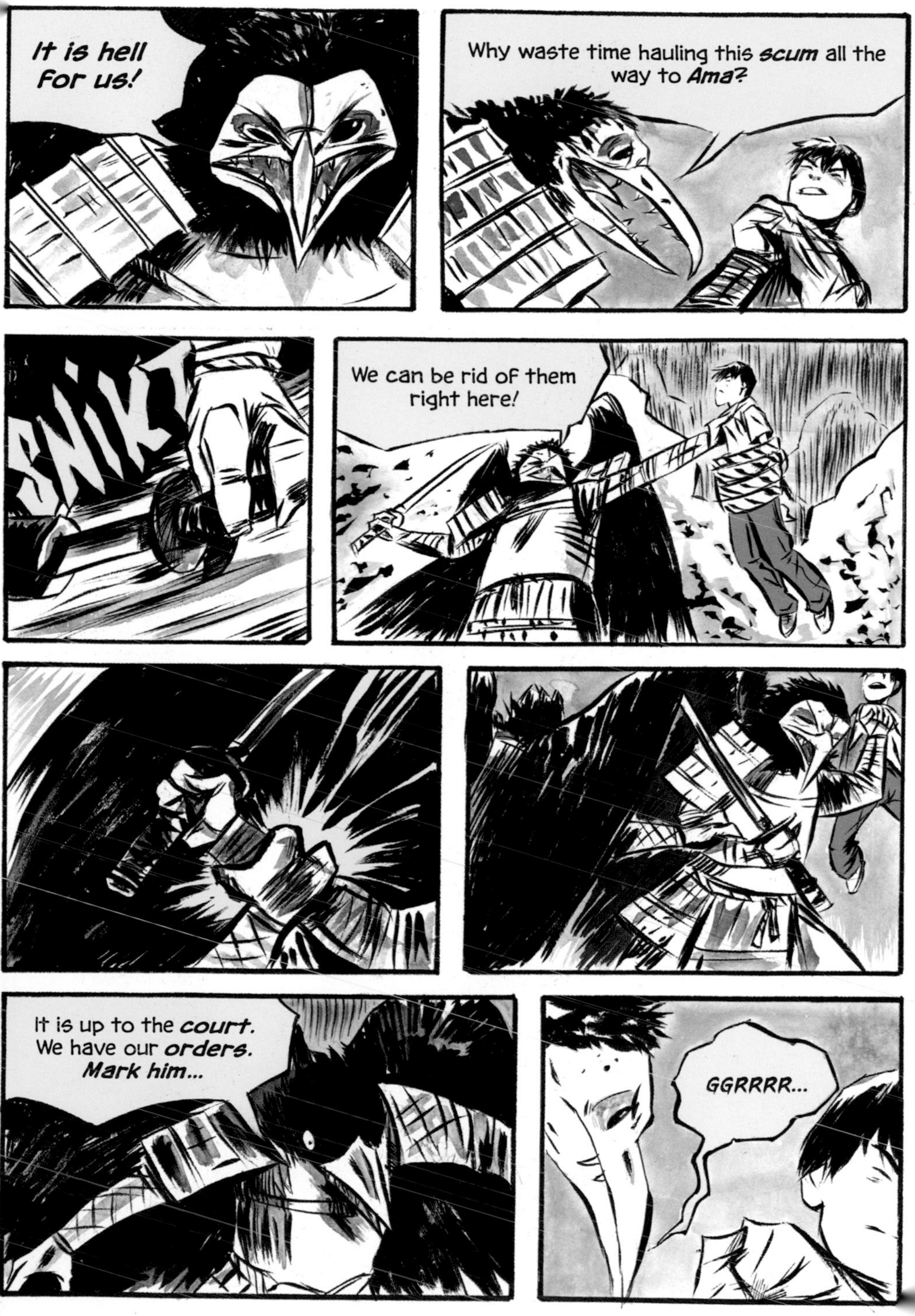
It is hell for us!
Why waste time hauling this scum all the way to Ama?
SNIKT
We can be rid of them right here!
It is up to the court. We have our orders. Mark him...
GGRRRR...

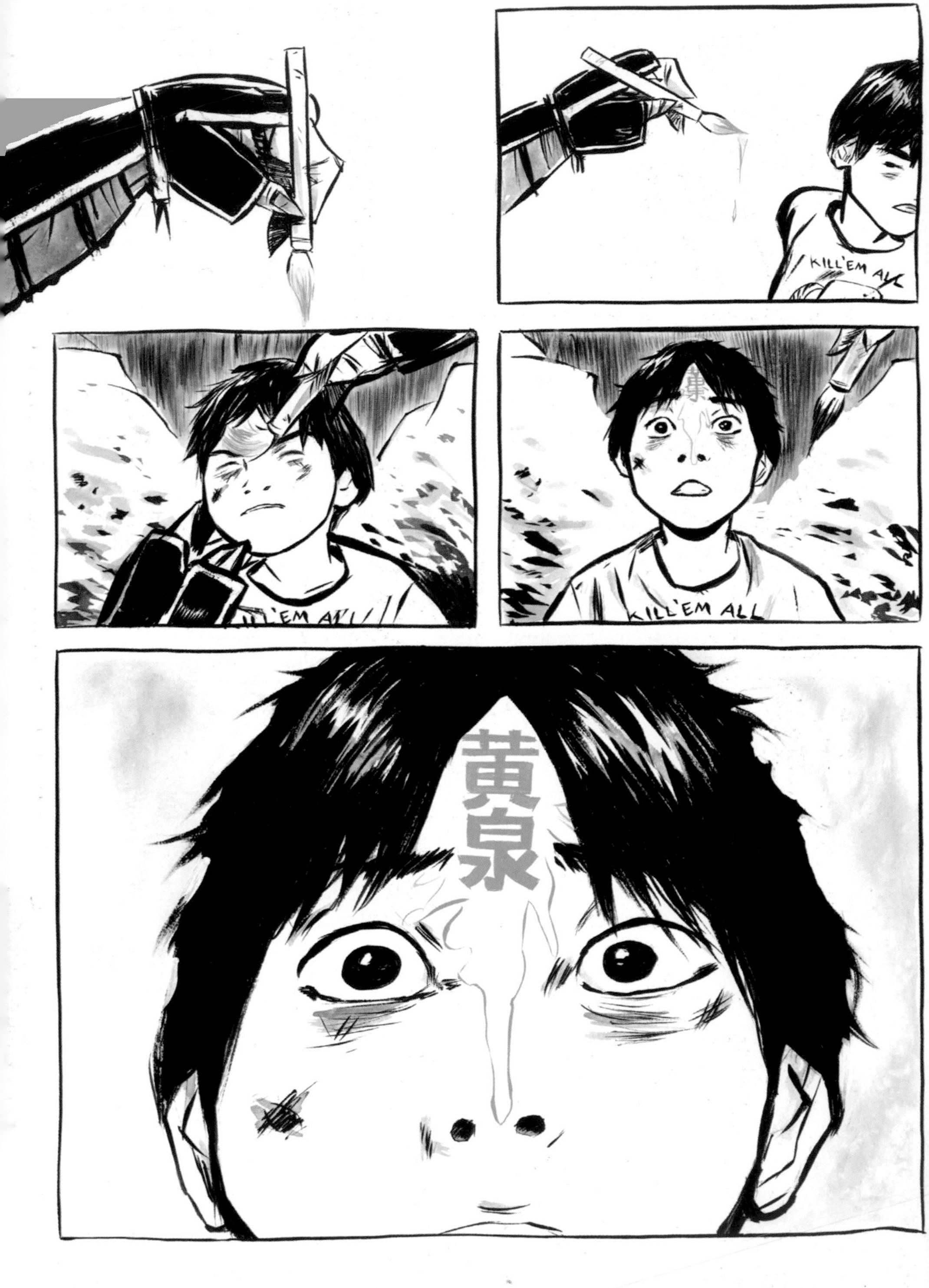

KILL'EM ALL
KILL'EM ALL
黄泉

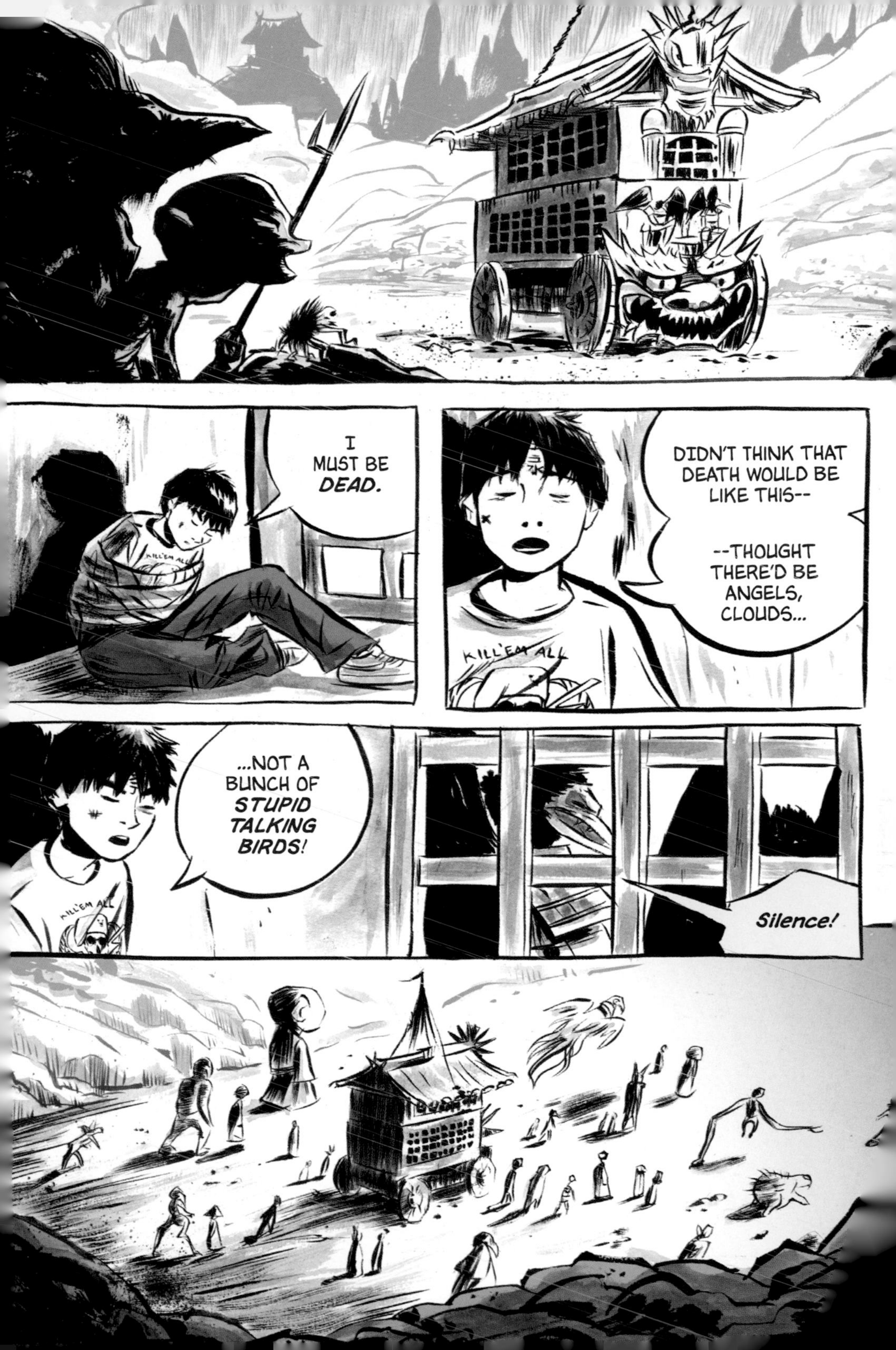
I MUST BE *DEAD.*
DIDN'T THINK THAT DEATH WOULD BE LIKE THIS--
--THOUGHT THERE'D BE ANGELS, CLOUDS...
KILL'EM ALL
...NOT A BUNCH OF *STUPID TALKING BIRDS!*
Silence!

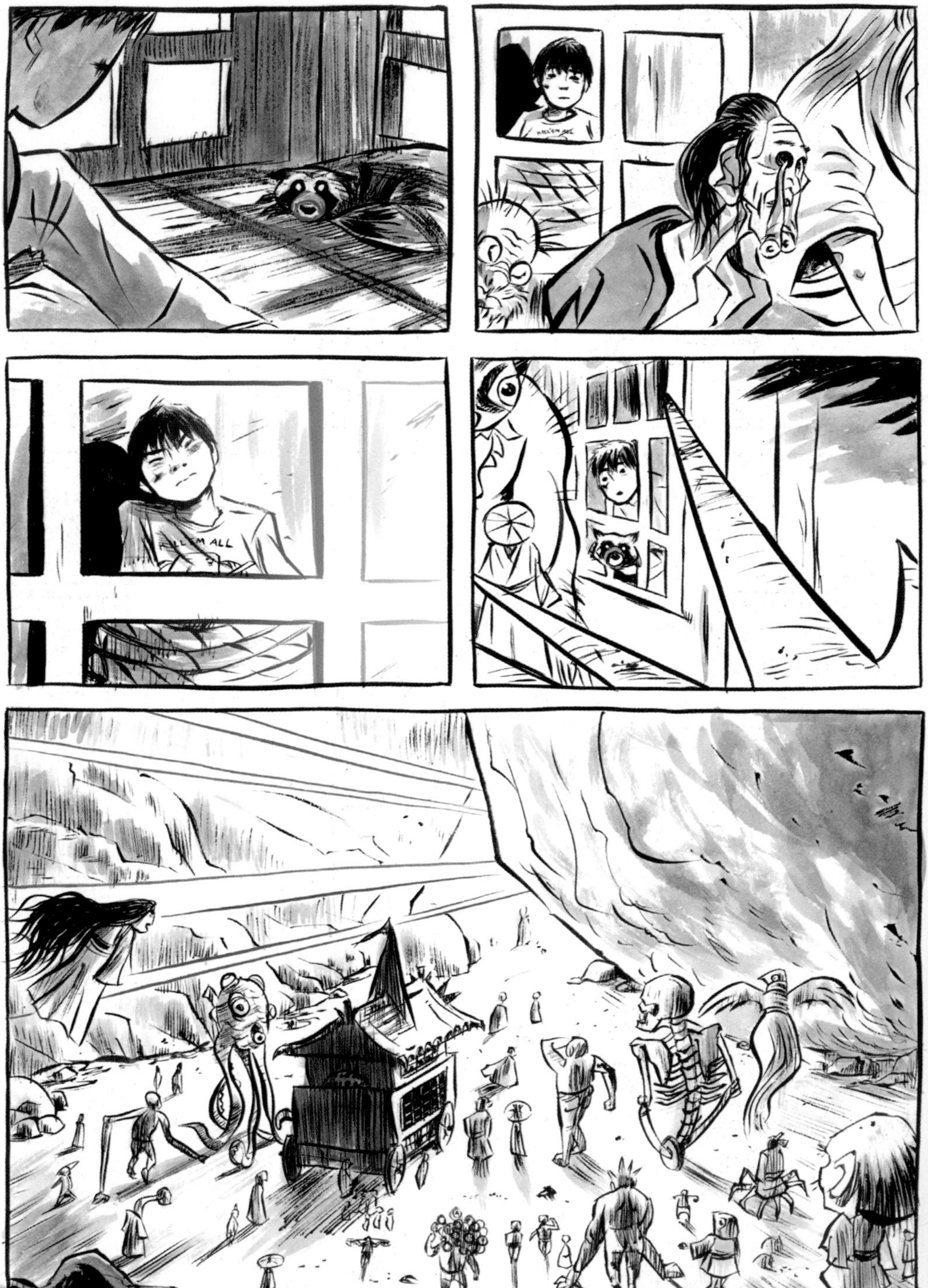

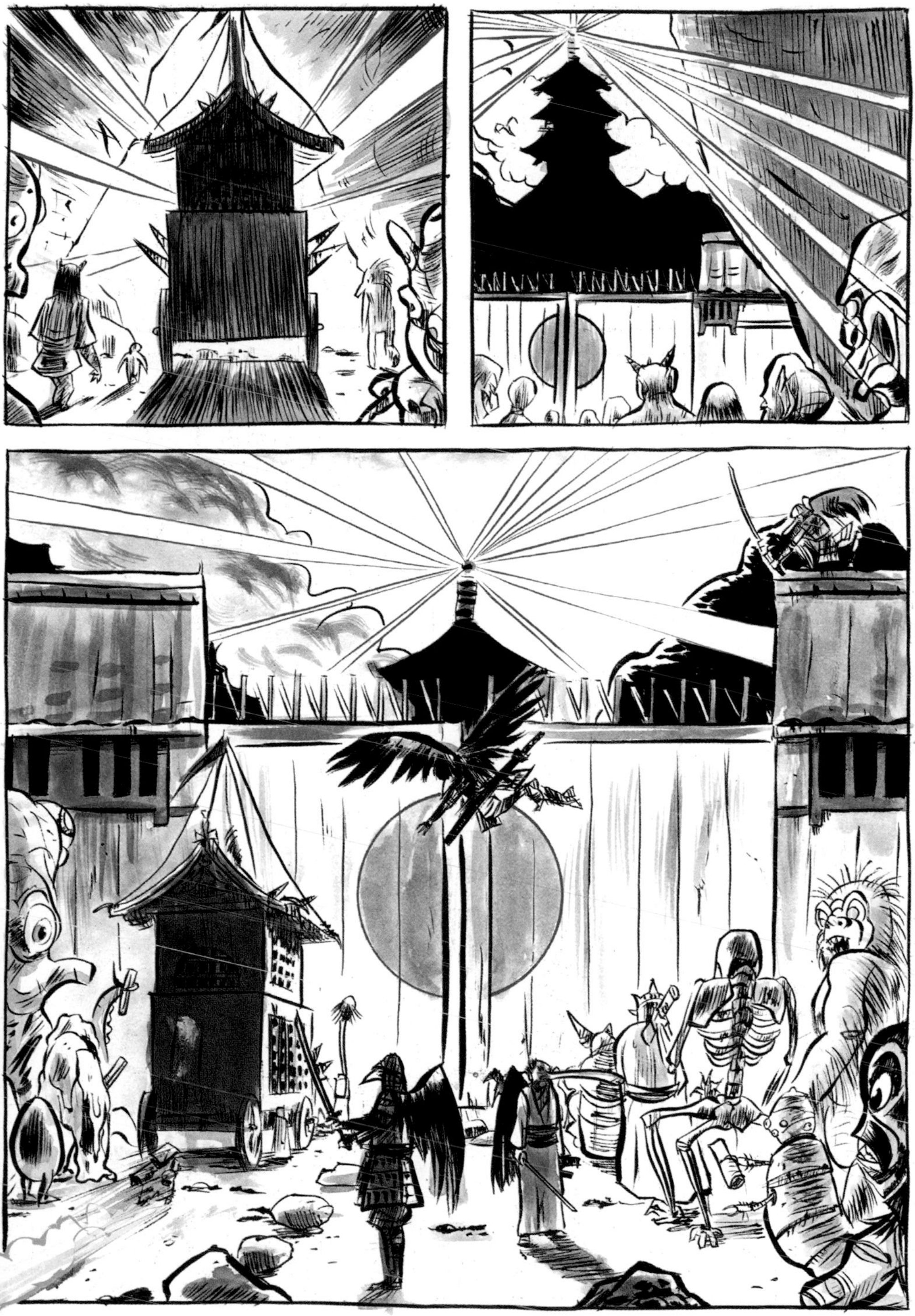

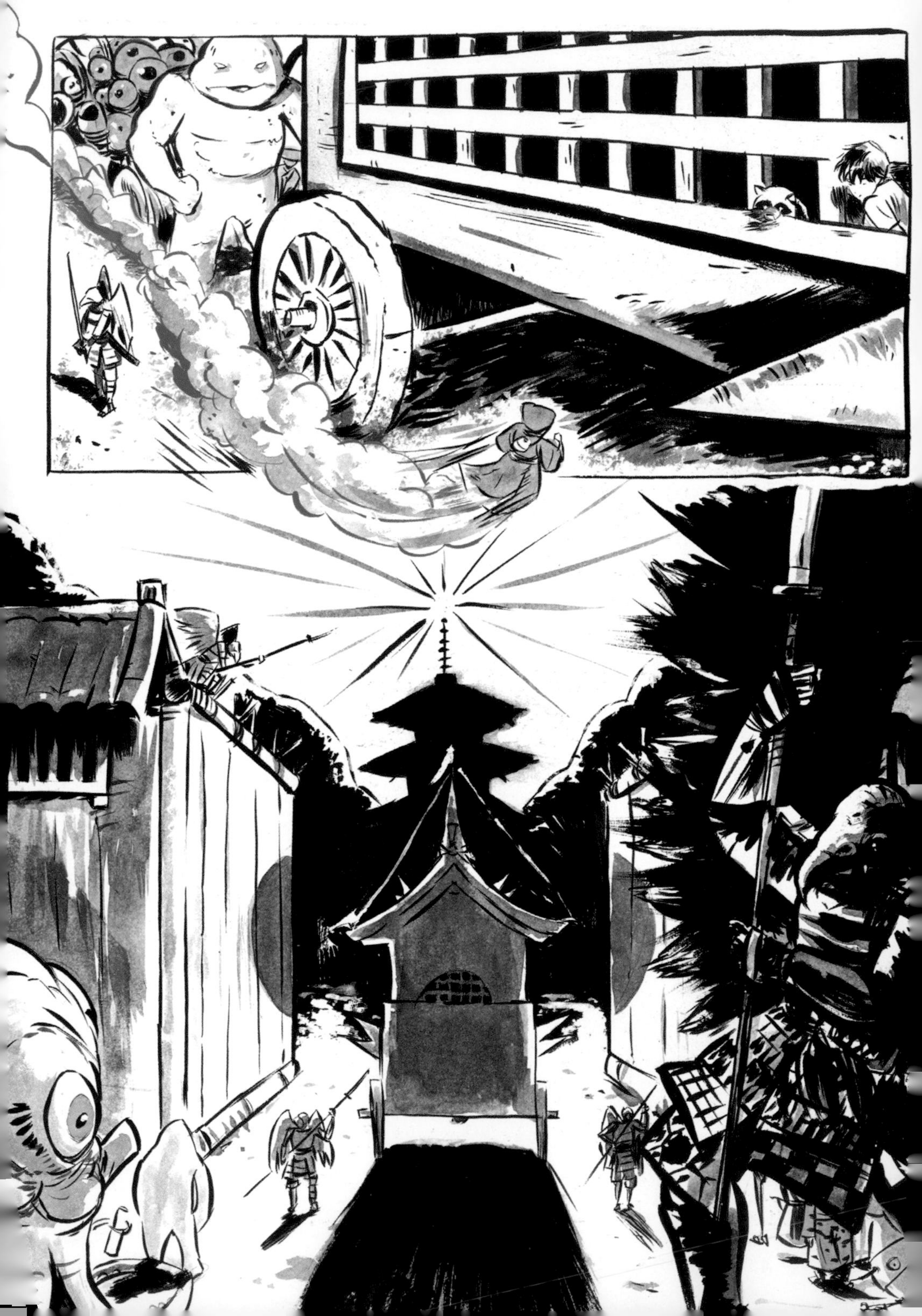

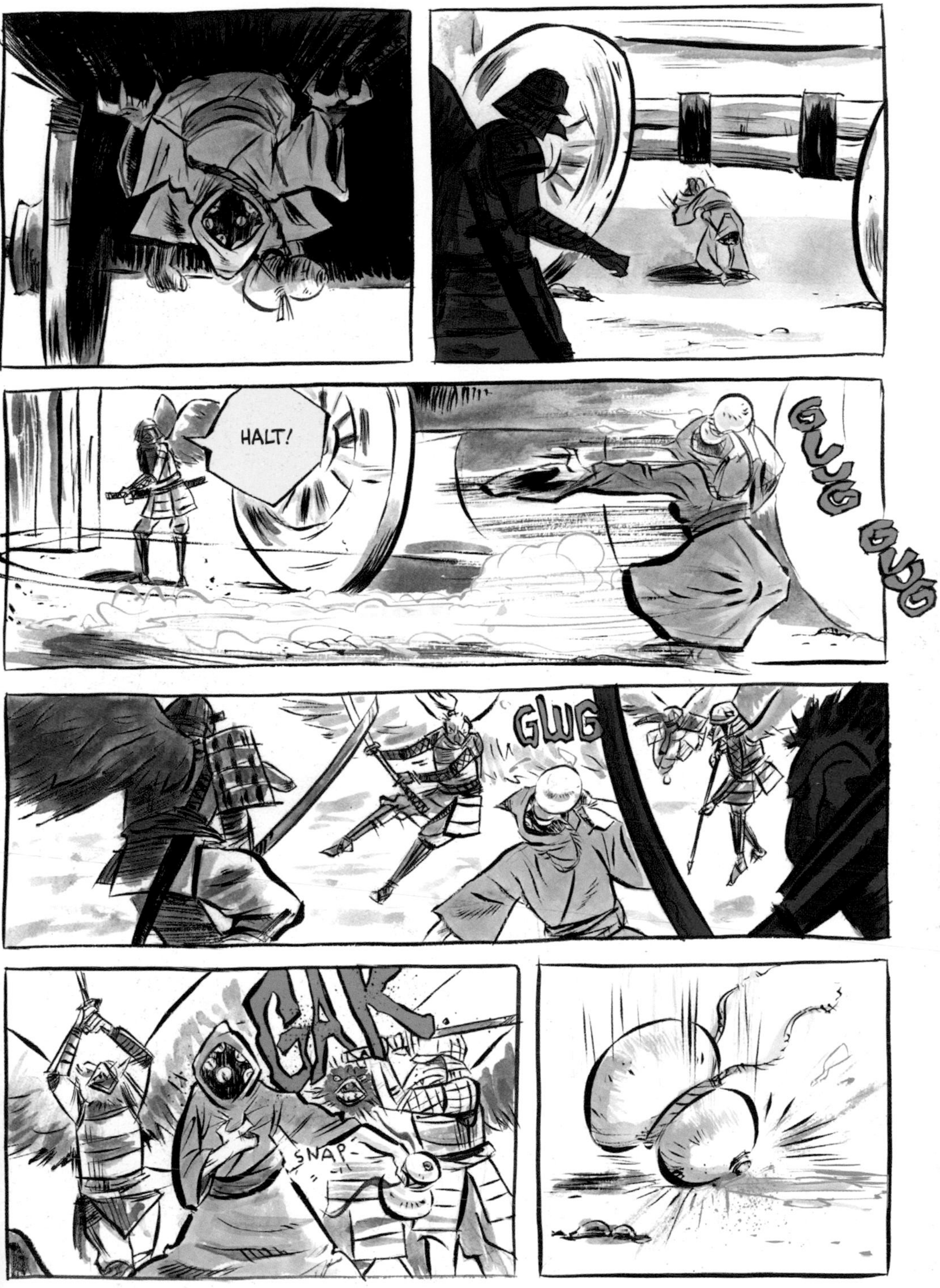
HALT!
GLUG GLUG
GLUG
CAK
SNAP

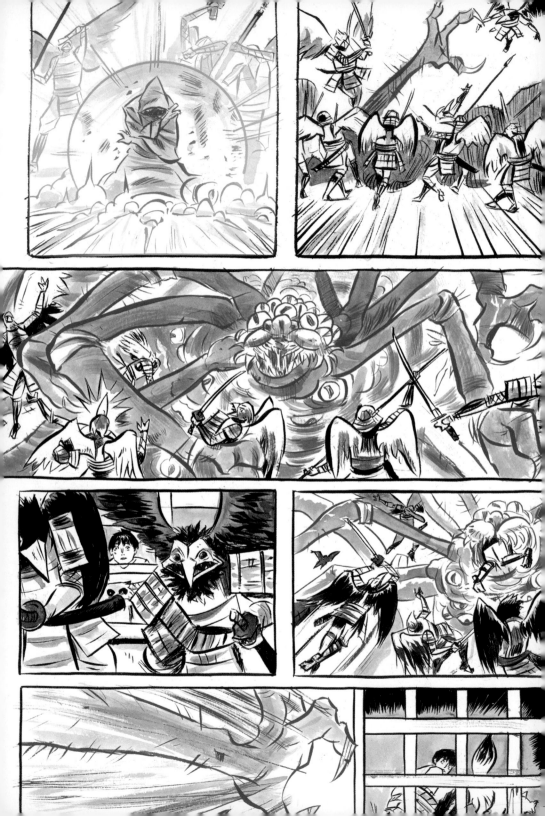

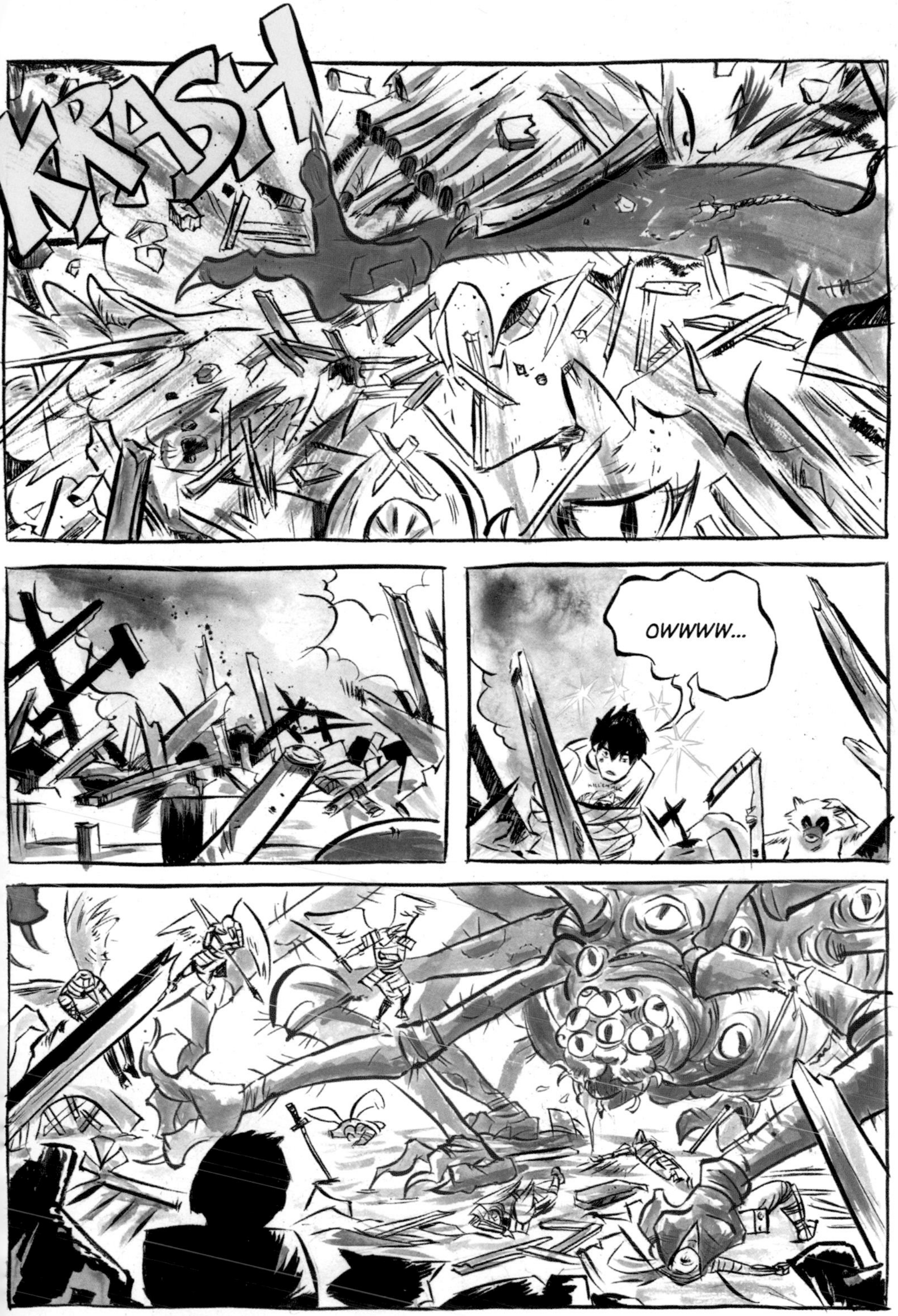
KRASH
OWWWW...

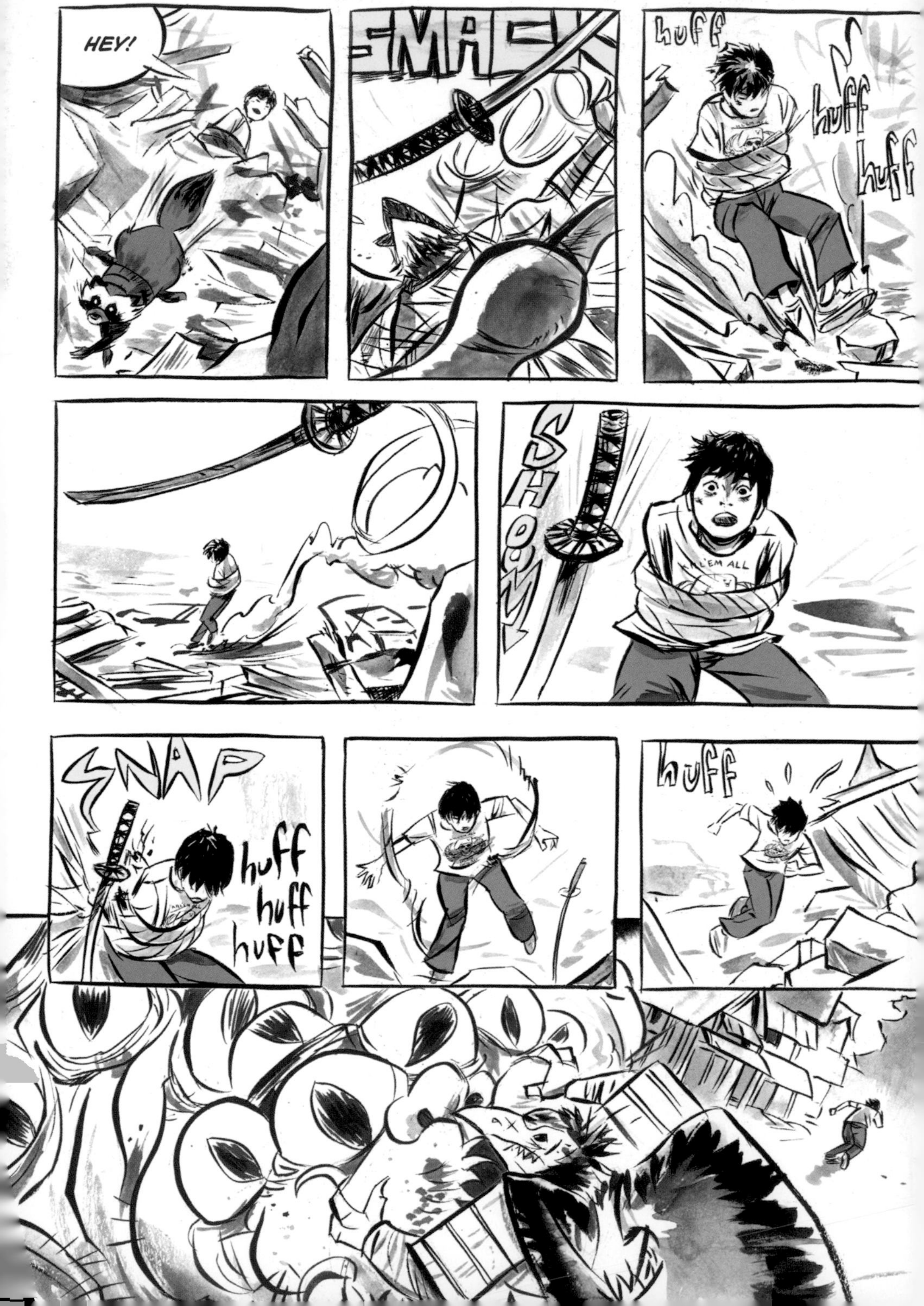
HEY!
SMACK
huff
huff
huff
huff
SHOOM
KILL 'EM ALL
SNAP
huff
huff
huff
huff

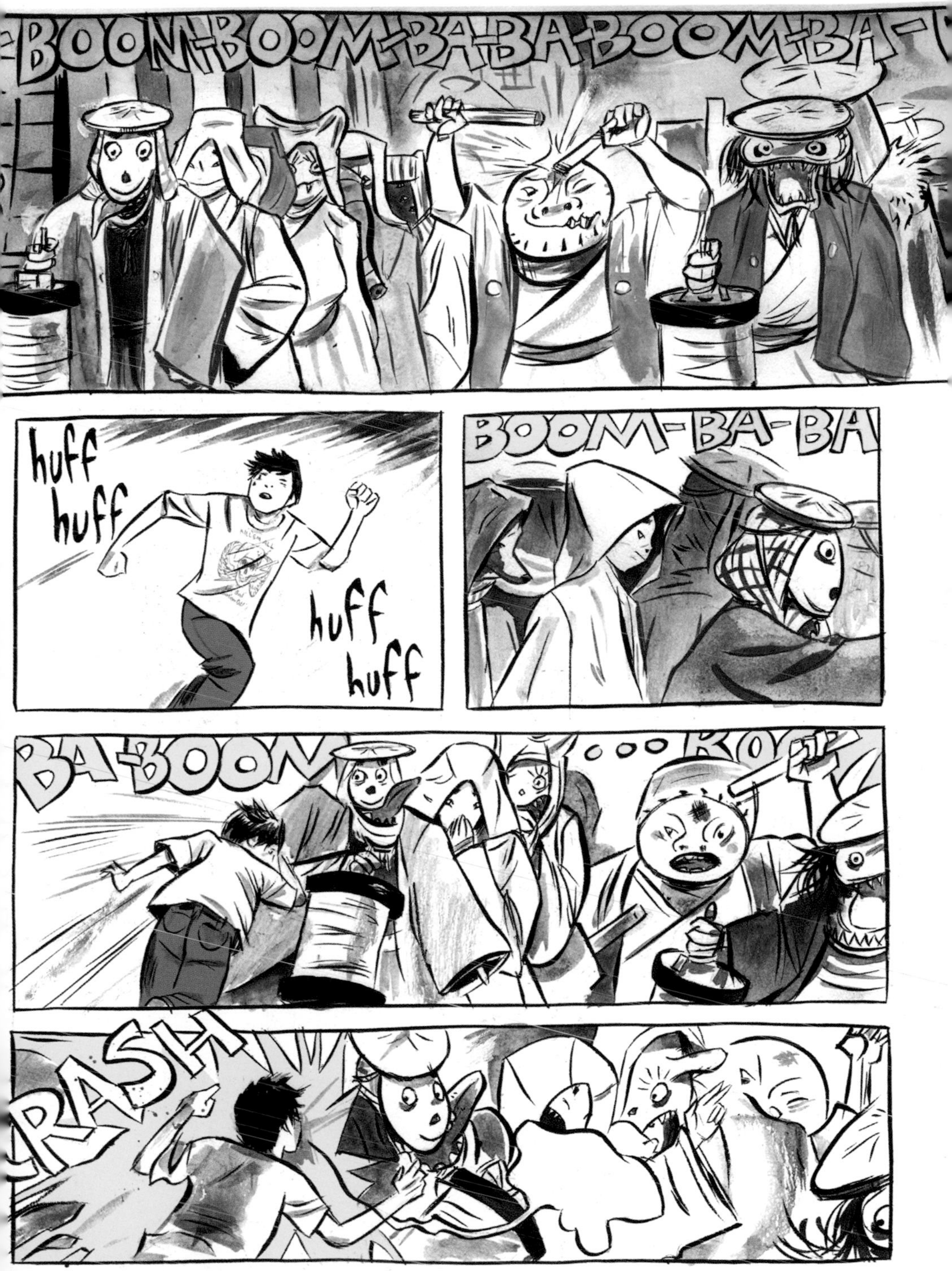
BOOM-BOOM-BA-BA-BOOM-BA-
huff
huff
huff
huff
BOOM-BA-BA
BA-BOO
...BOO
CRASH

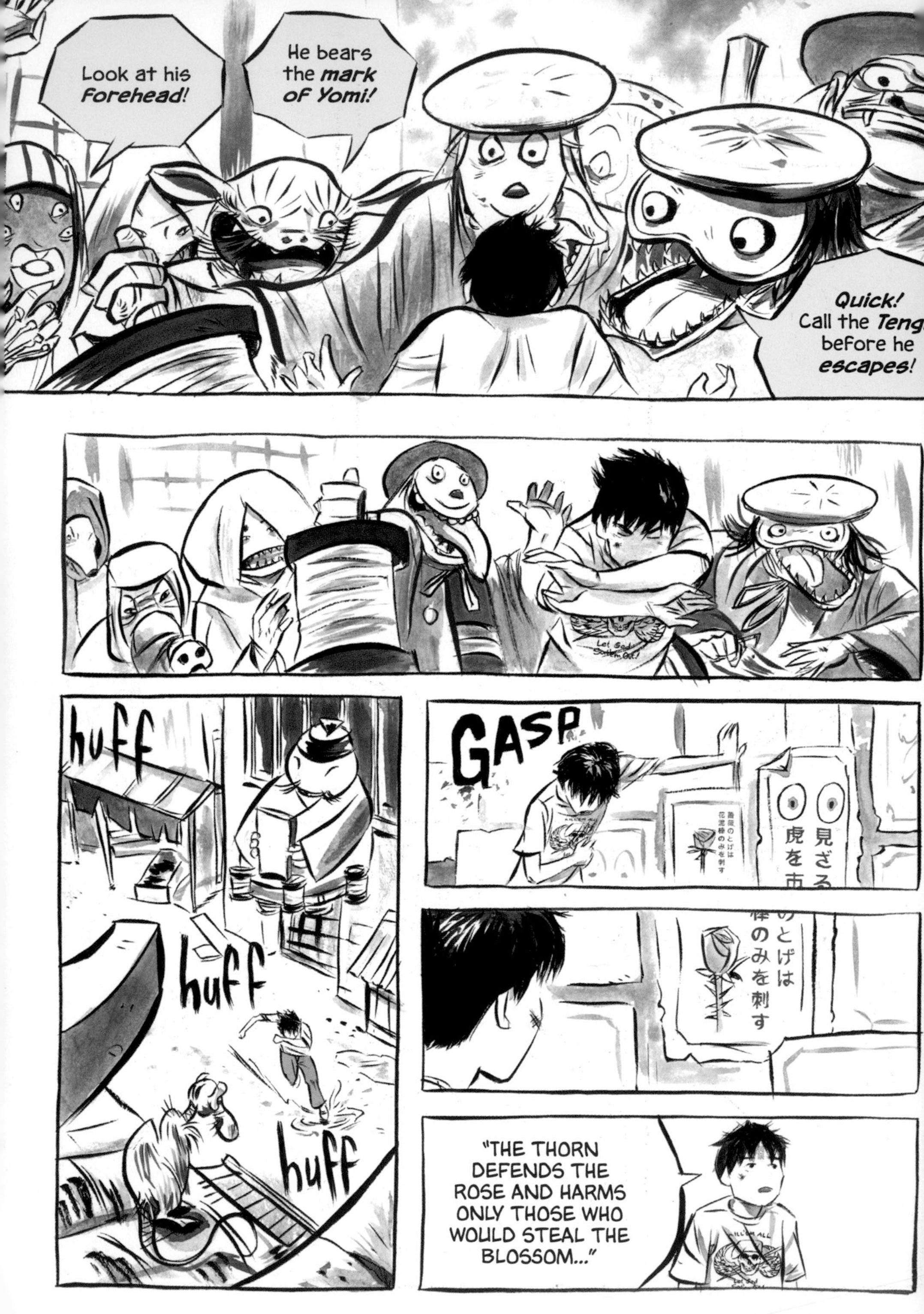

Look at his *Forehead!*
He bears the *mark of Yomi!*
Quick! Call the ***Tengu*** before he ***escapes!***
huff
huff
huff
GASP
見ざる
虎を市
のとげは
棒のみを刺す
"THE THORN DEFENDS THE ROSE AND HARMS ONLY THOSE WHO WOULD STEAL THE BLOSSOM..."

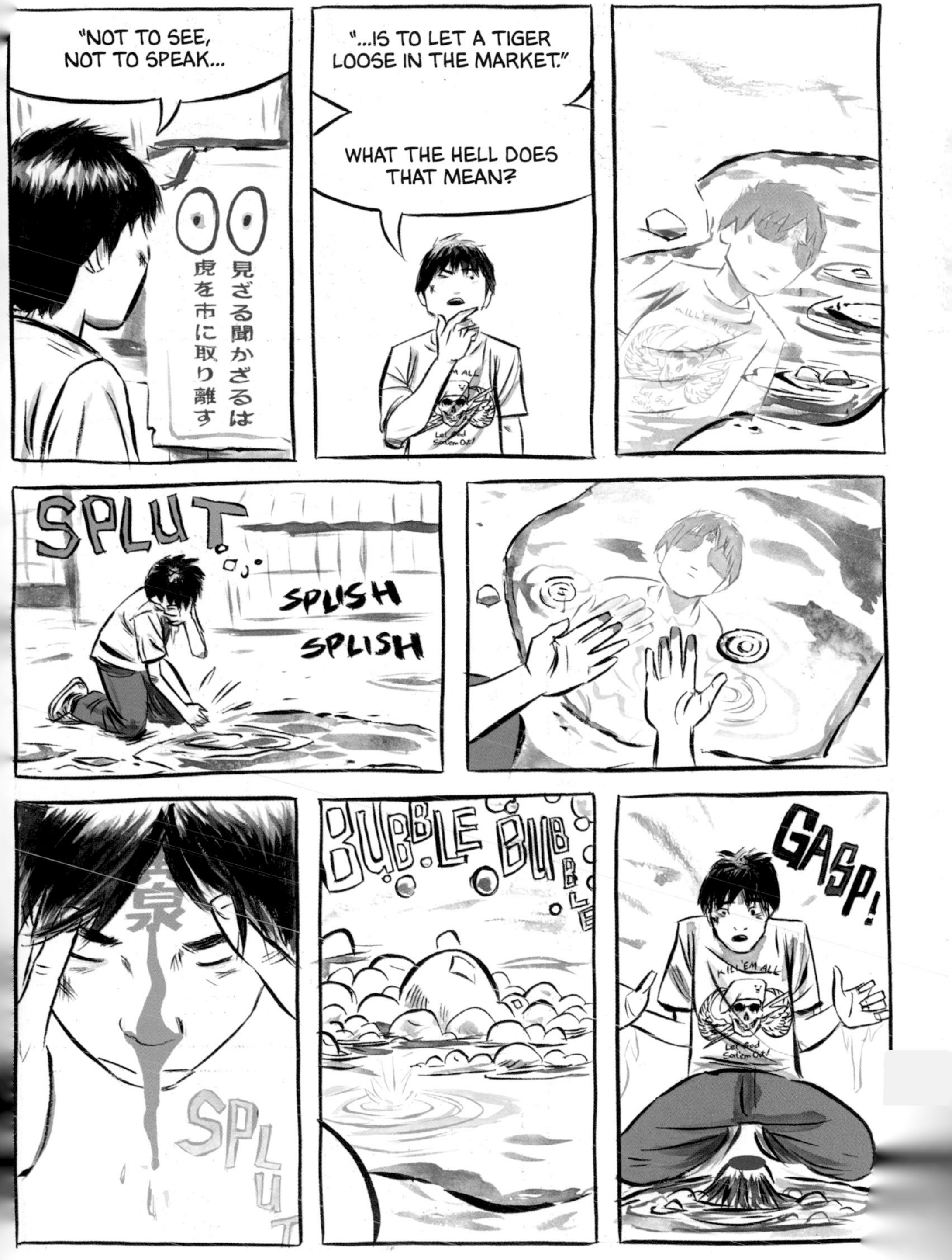
"NOT TO SEE, NOT TO SPEAK...
見ざる聞かざるは
虎を市に取り離す
"...IS TO LET A TIGER LOOSE IN THE MARKET."
WHAT THE HELL DOES THAT MEAN?
SPLUT
SPLUSH
SPLISH
SPLUT
BUBBLE BUBBLE
GASP!
KILL'EM ALL
Let God Sort'em Out!

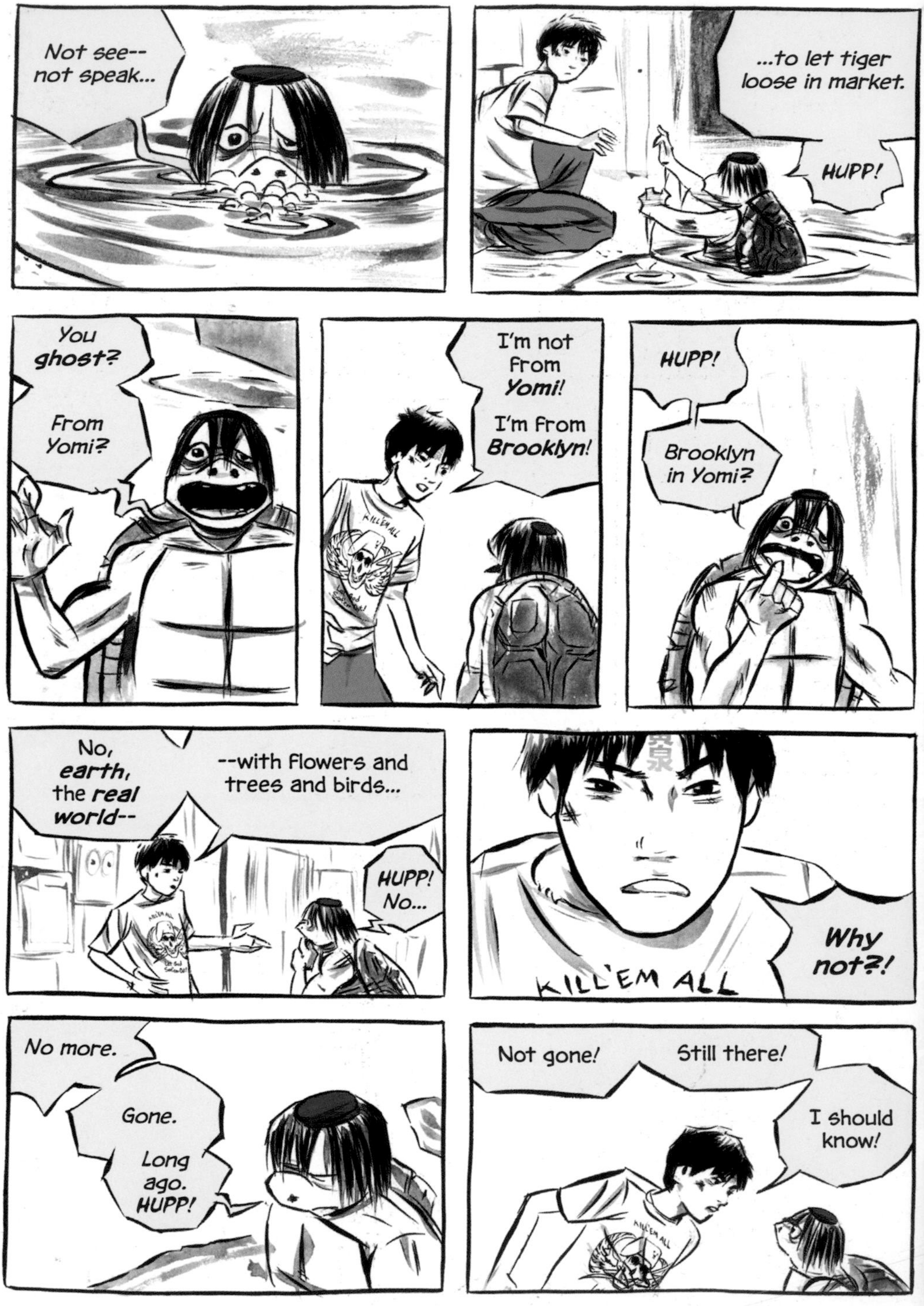

Not see-- not speak...
...to let tiger loose in market.
HUPP!
You ghost?
From Yomi?
I'm not from Yomi!
I'm from Brooklyn!
HUPP!
Brooklyn in Yomi?
No, earth, the real world--
--with flowers and trees and birds...
HUPP! No...
KILL'EM ALL
Why not?!
No more.
Gone.
Long ago. HUPP!
Not gone!
Still there!
I should know!

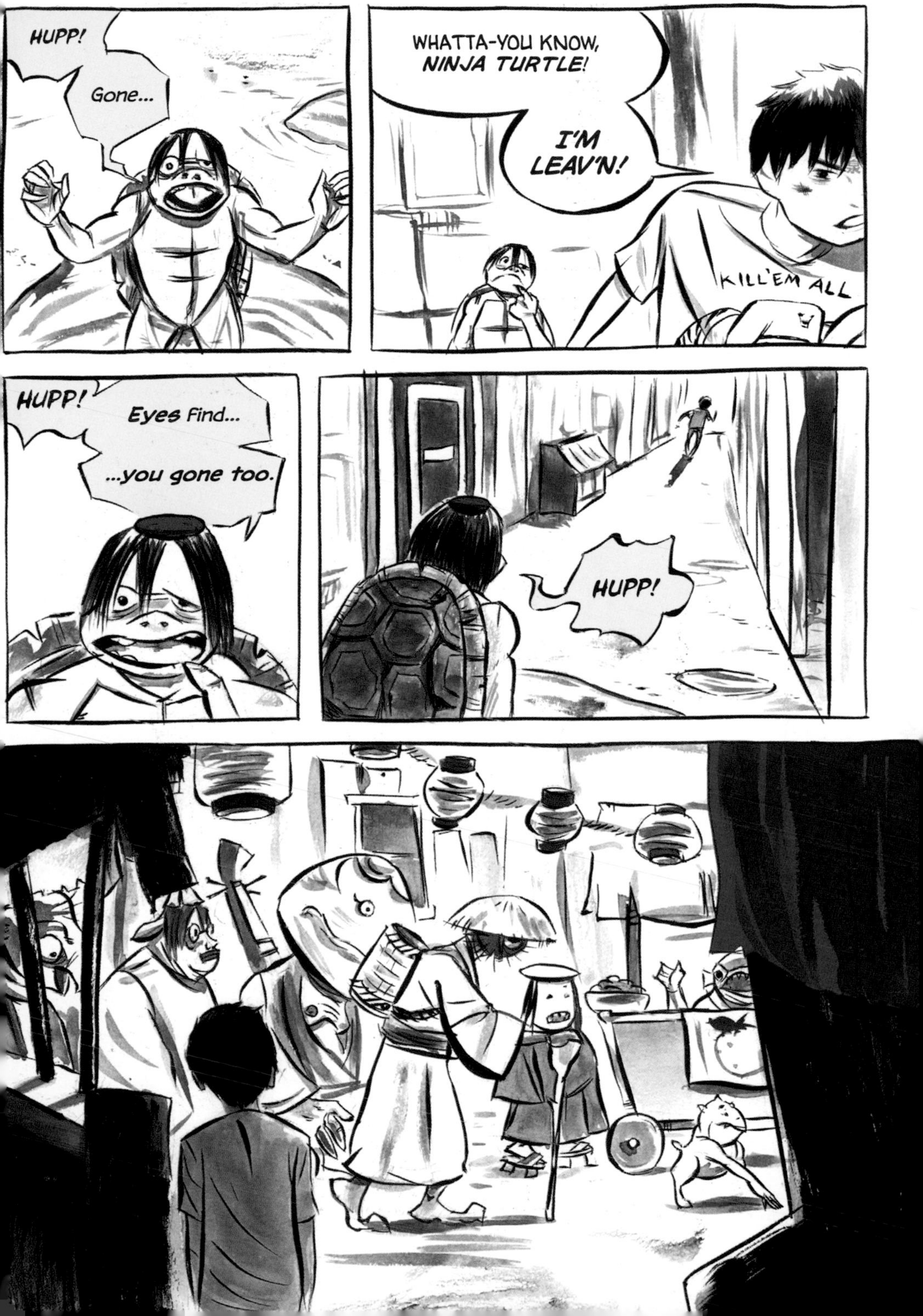
HUPP!
Gone...
WHATTA-YOU KNOW, NINJA TURTLE!
I'M LEAV'N!
KILL'EM ALL
HUPP!
Eyes find...
...you gone too.
HUPP!

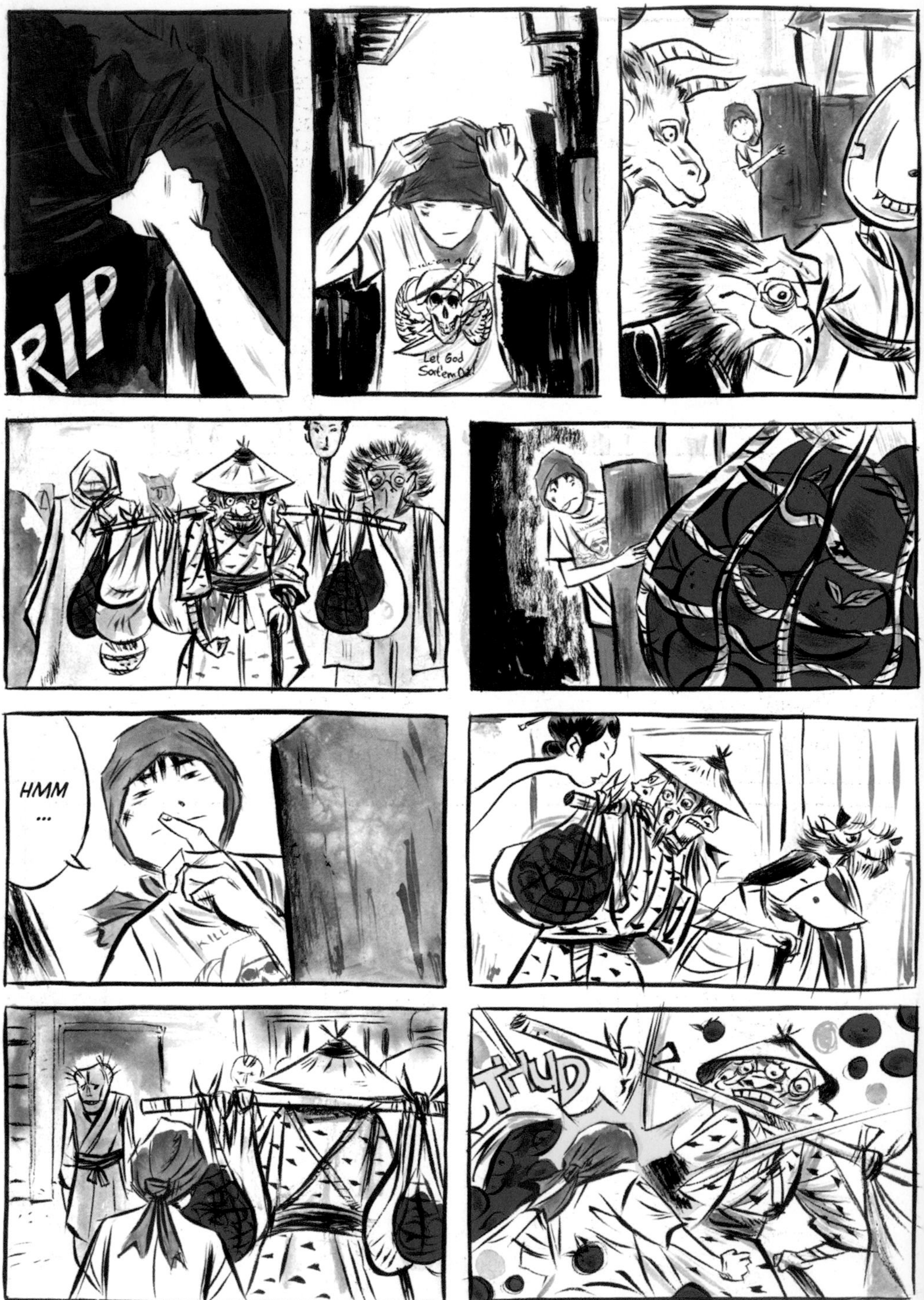
RIP
Let God Sort'em Out!
HMM ...
THUD

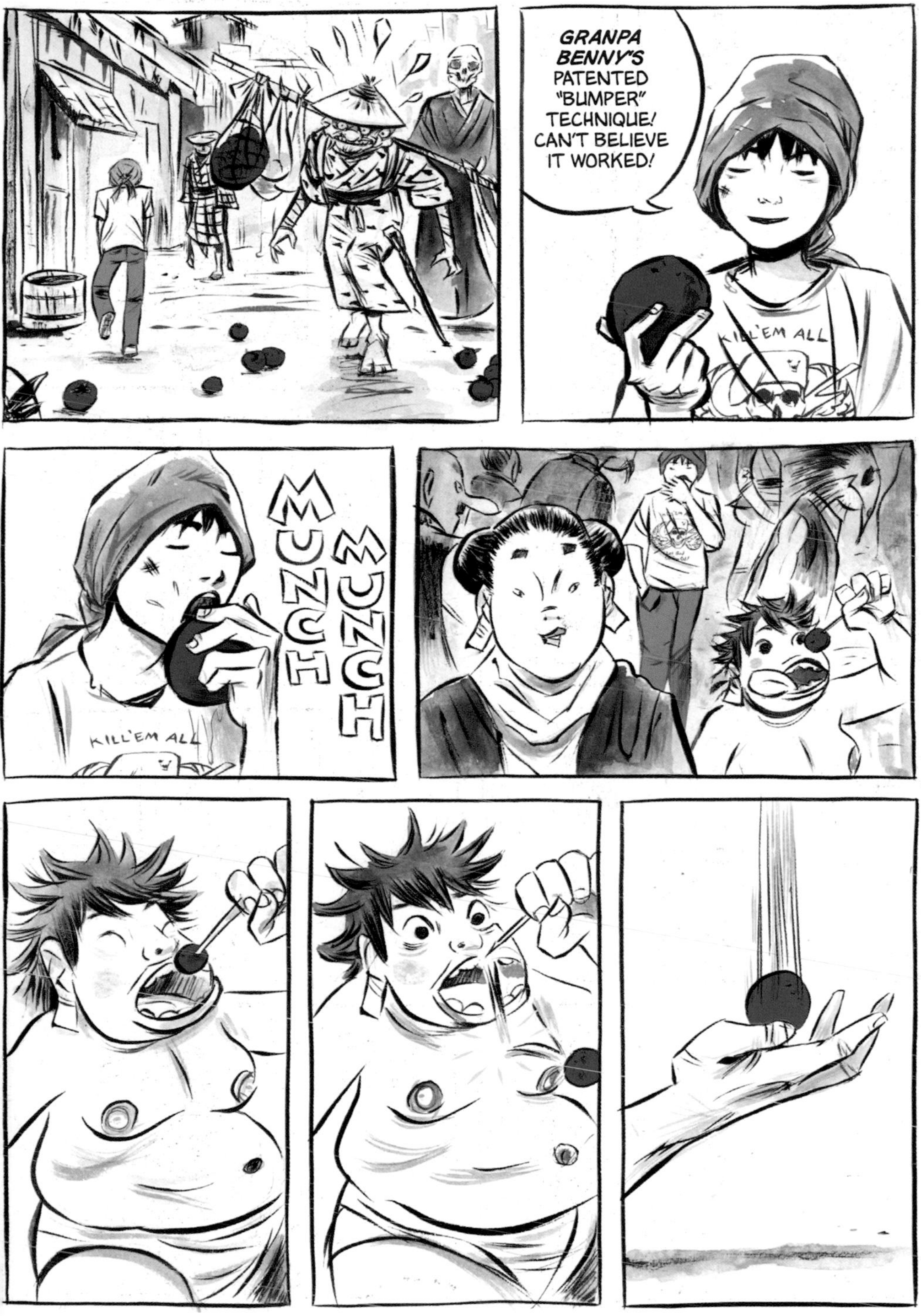
GRANPA BENNY'S PATENTED "BUMPER" TECHNIQUE! CAN'T BELIEVE IT WORKED!
KILL'EM ALL
MUNCH MUNCH
KILL'EM ALL

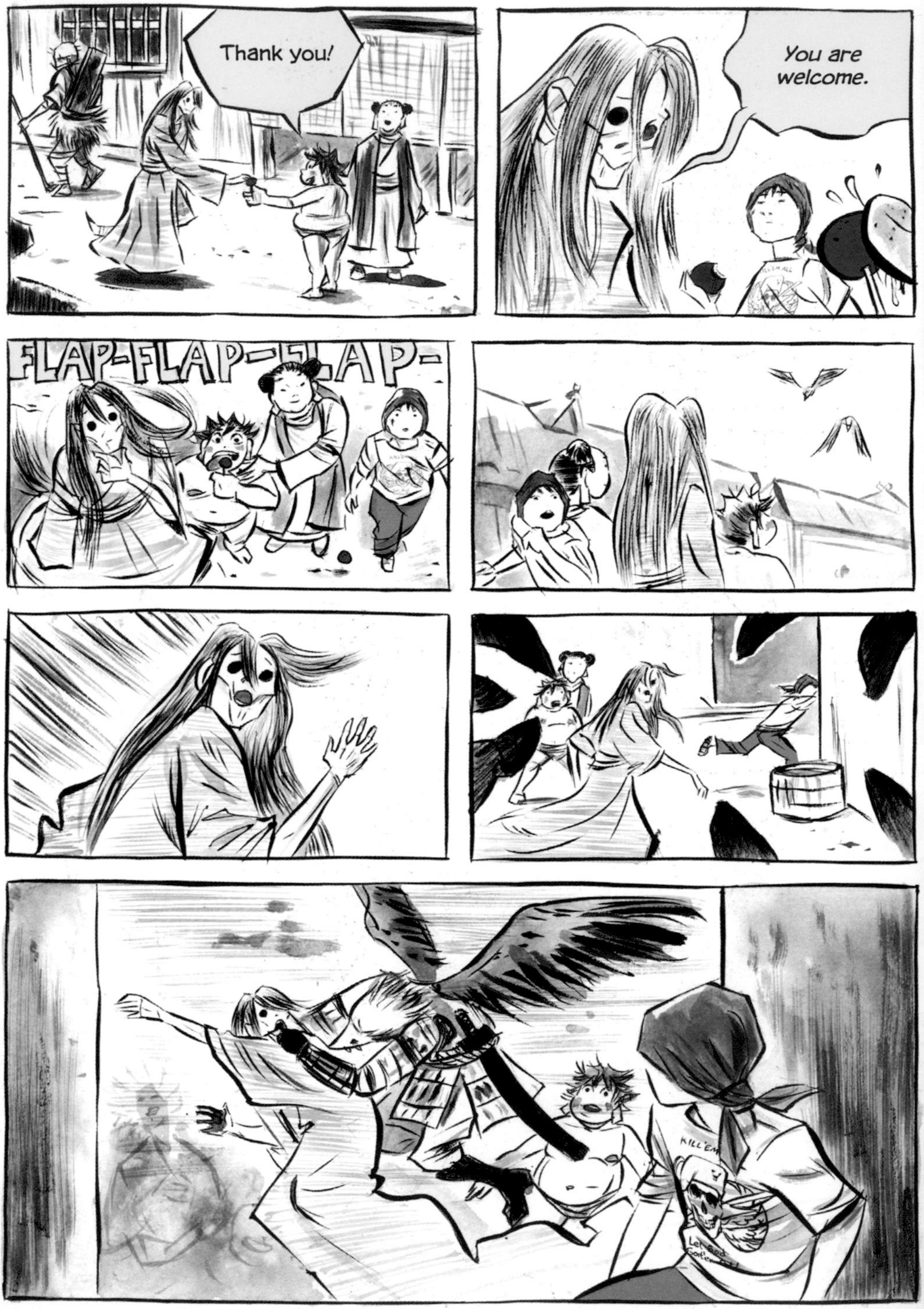
Thank you!
You are welcome.
FLAP-FLAP-FLAP-

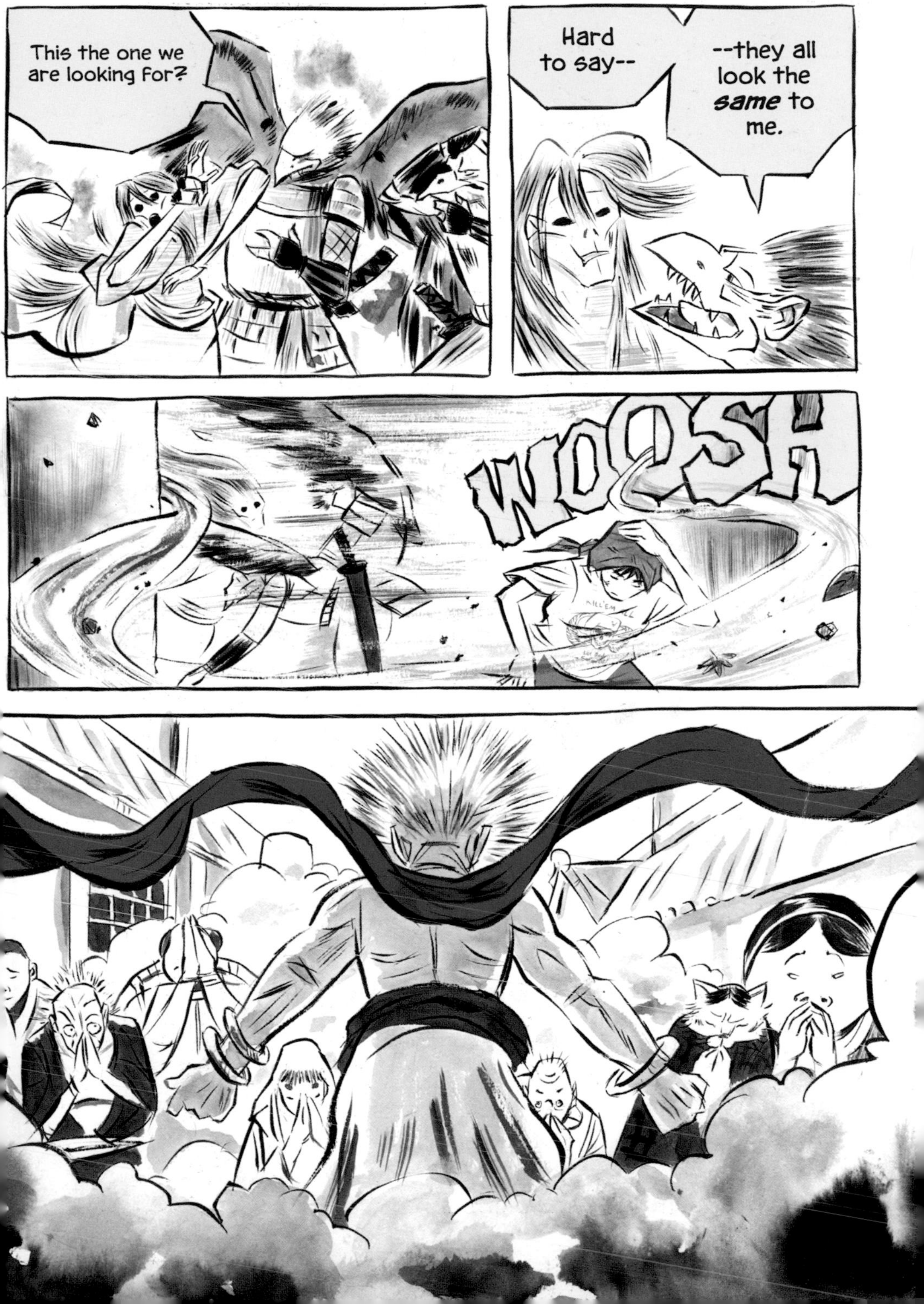
This the one we are looking for?
Hard to say--
--they all look the *same* to me.
WOOSH

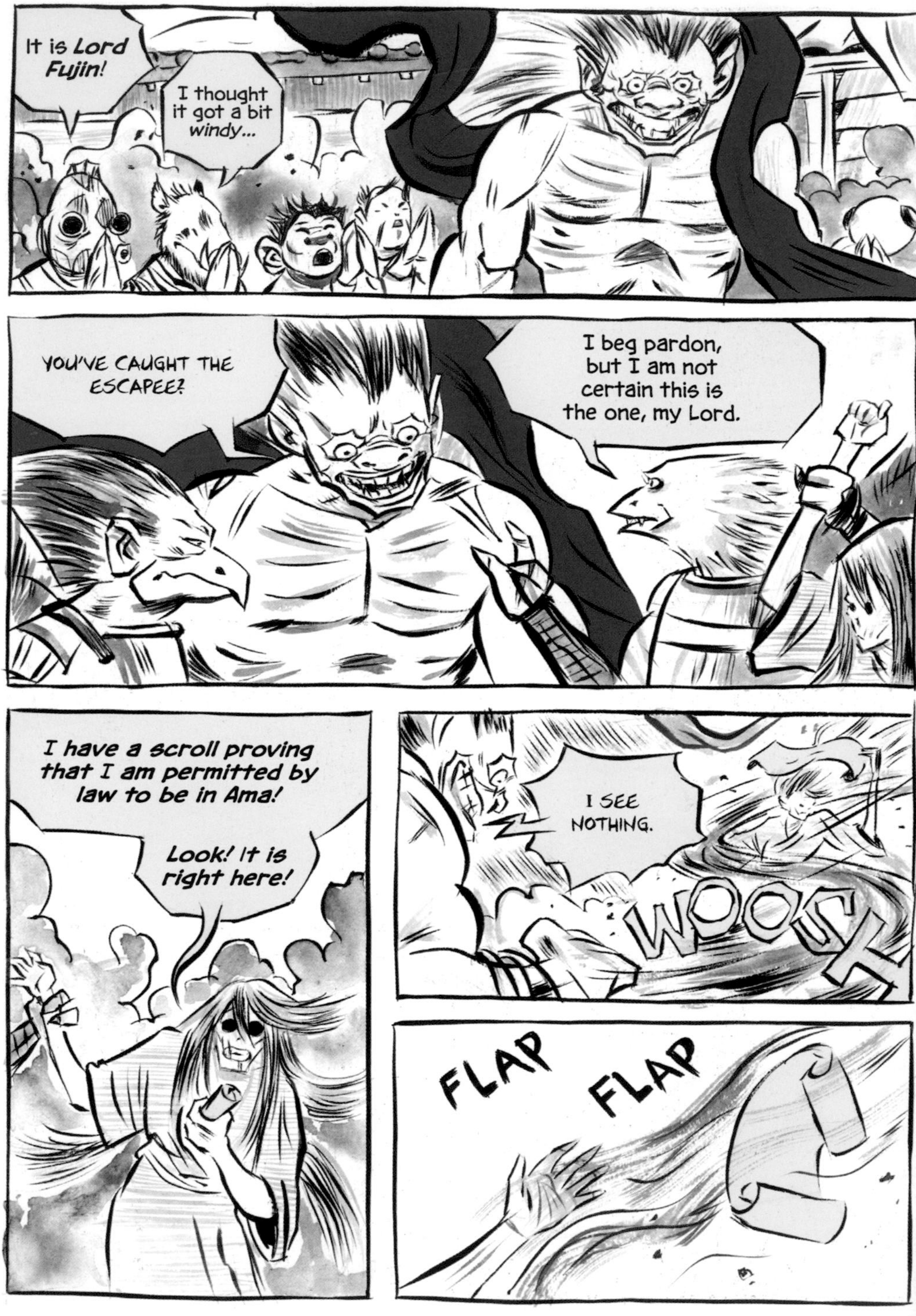

It is *Lord Fujin!*
I thought it got a bit windy...
YOU'VE CAUGHT THE ESCAPEE?
I beg pardon, but I am not certain this is the one, my Lord.
I have a scroll proving that I am permitted by law to be in Ama!
Look! It is right here!
I SEE NOTHING.
WOOSH
FLAP
FLAP

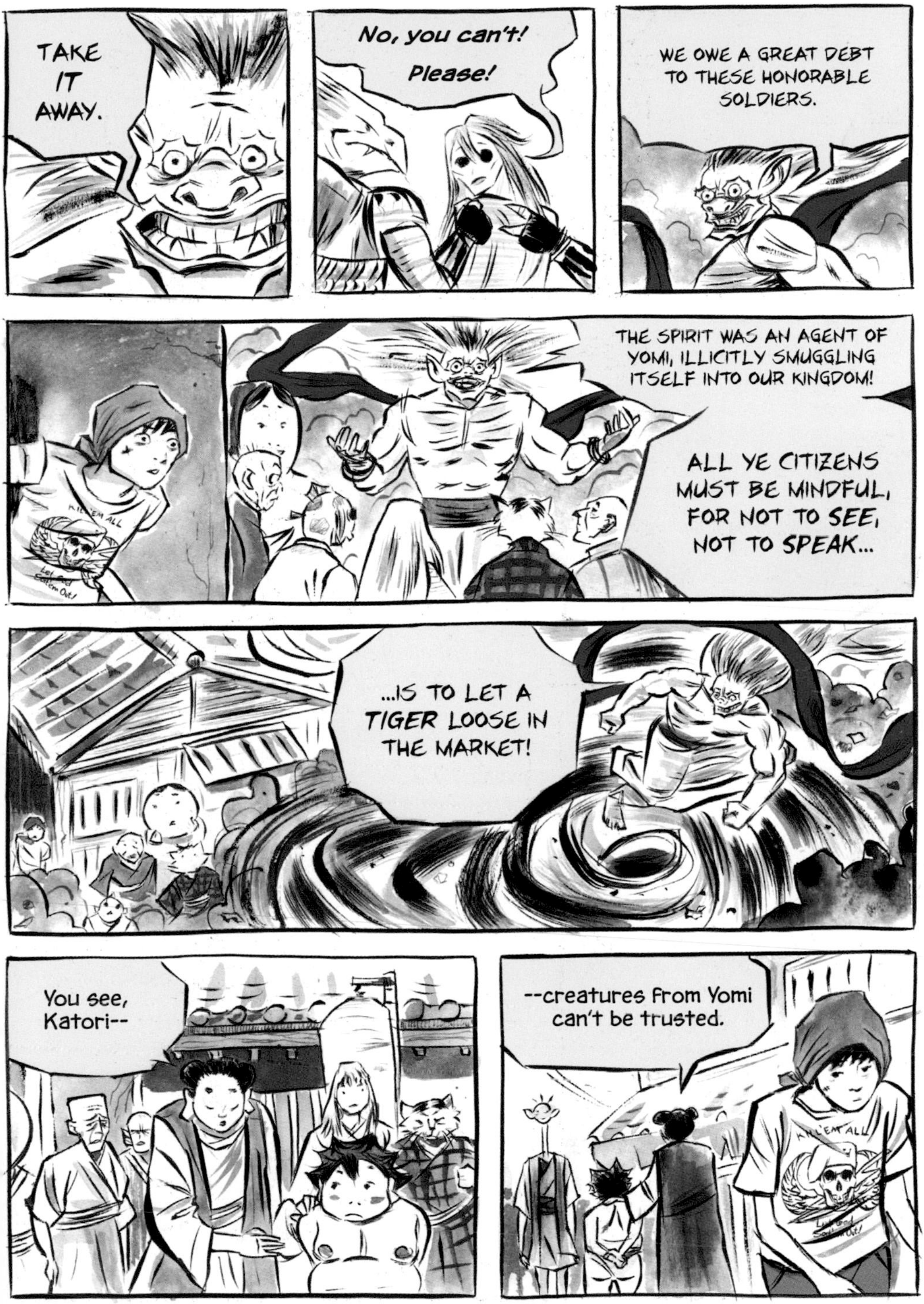
TAKE IT AWAY.
No, you can't!
Please!
WE OWE A GREAT DEBT TO THESE HONORABLE SOLDIERS.
THE SPIRIT WAS AN AGENT OF YOMI, ILLICITLY SMUGGLING ITSELF INTO OUR KINGDOM!
ALL YE CITIZENS MUST BE MINDFUL, FOR NOT TO SEE, NOT TO SPEAK...
...IS TO LET A TIGER LOOSE IN THE MARKET!
You see, Katori--
--creatures from Yomi can't be trusted.

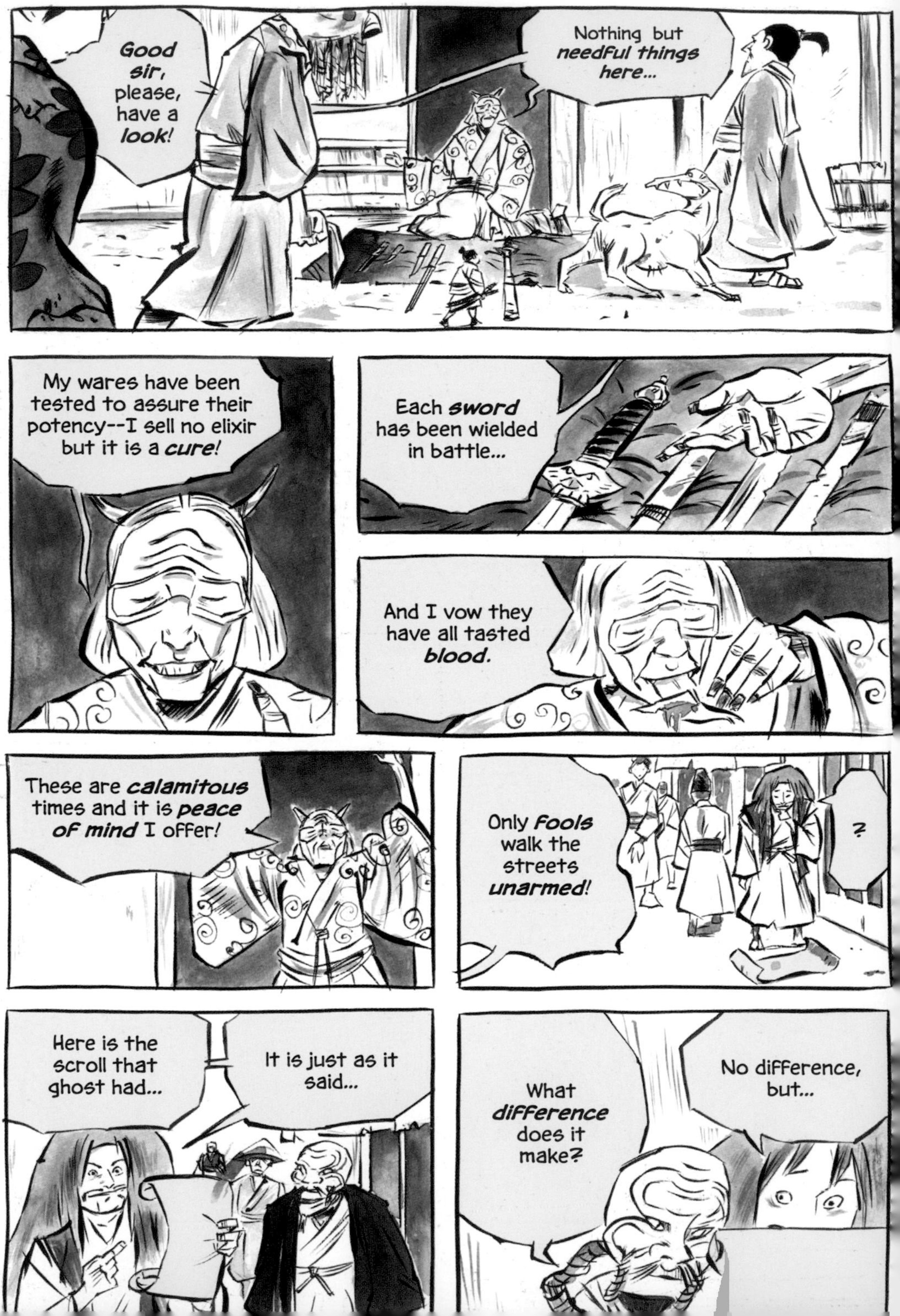

Good sir, please, have a look!
Nothing but needful things here...
My wares have been tested to assure their potency--I sell no elixir but it is a cure!
Each sword has been wielded in battle...
And I vow they have all tasted blood.
These are calamitous times and it is peace of mind I offer!
Only fools walk the streets unarmed!
?
Here is the scroll that ghost had...
It is just as it said...
What difference does it make?
No difference, but...

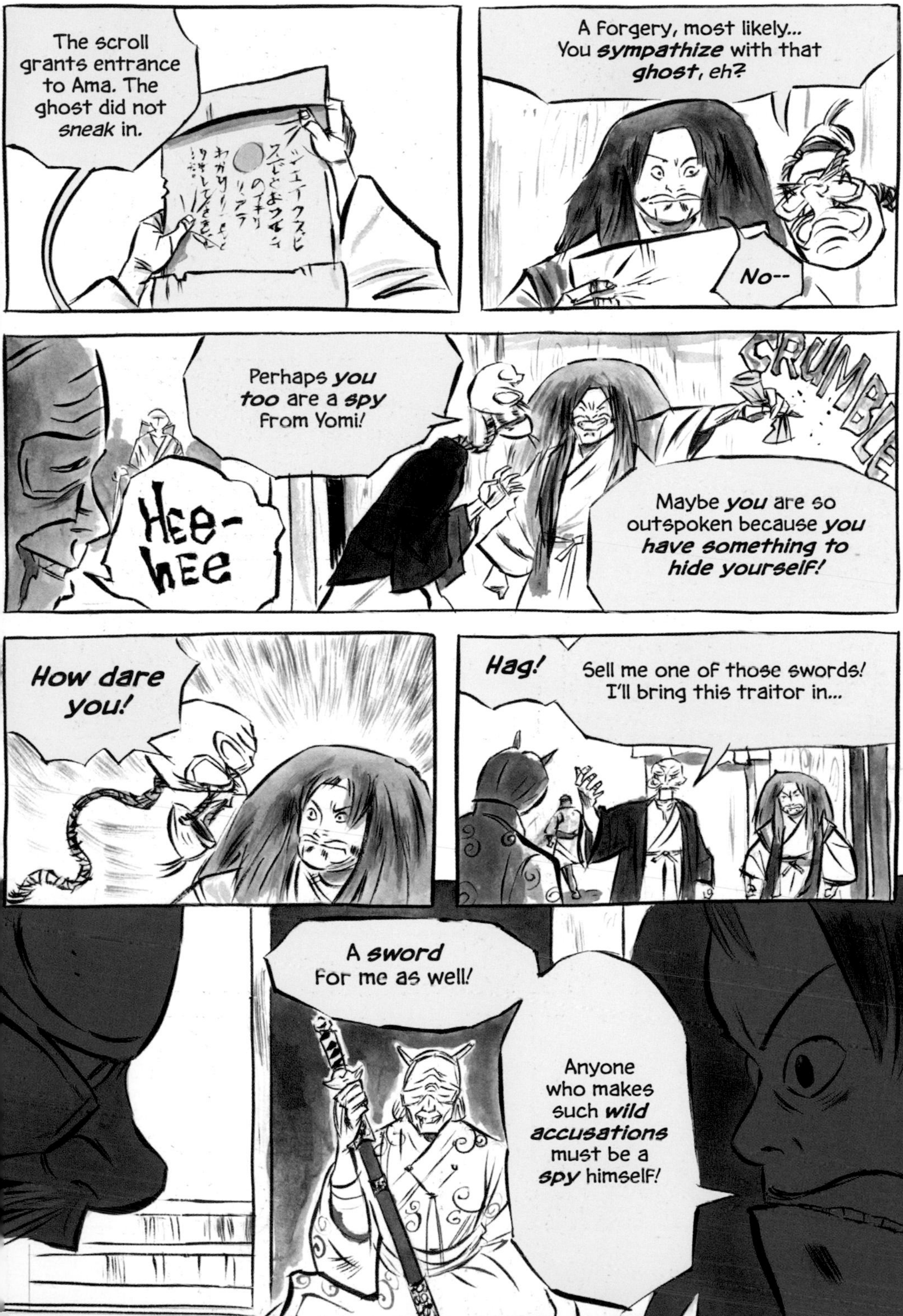
The scroll grants entrance to Ama. The ghost did not *sneak* in.
A forgery, most likely... You ***sympathize*** with that ***ghost***, eh?
No--
Perhaps ***you too*** are a ***spy*** from Yomi!
Hee-hee
CRUMBLE
Maybe ***you*** are so outspoken because ***you have something to hide yourself!***
How dare you!
Hag!
Sell me one of those swords! I'll bring this traitor in...
A ***sword*** for me as well!
Anyone who makes such ***wild accusations*** must be a ***spy*** himself!

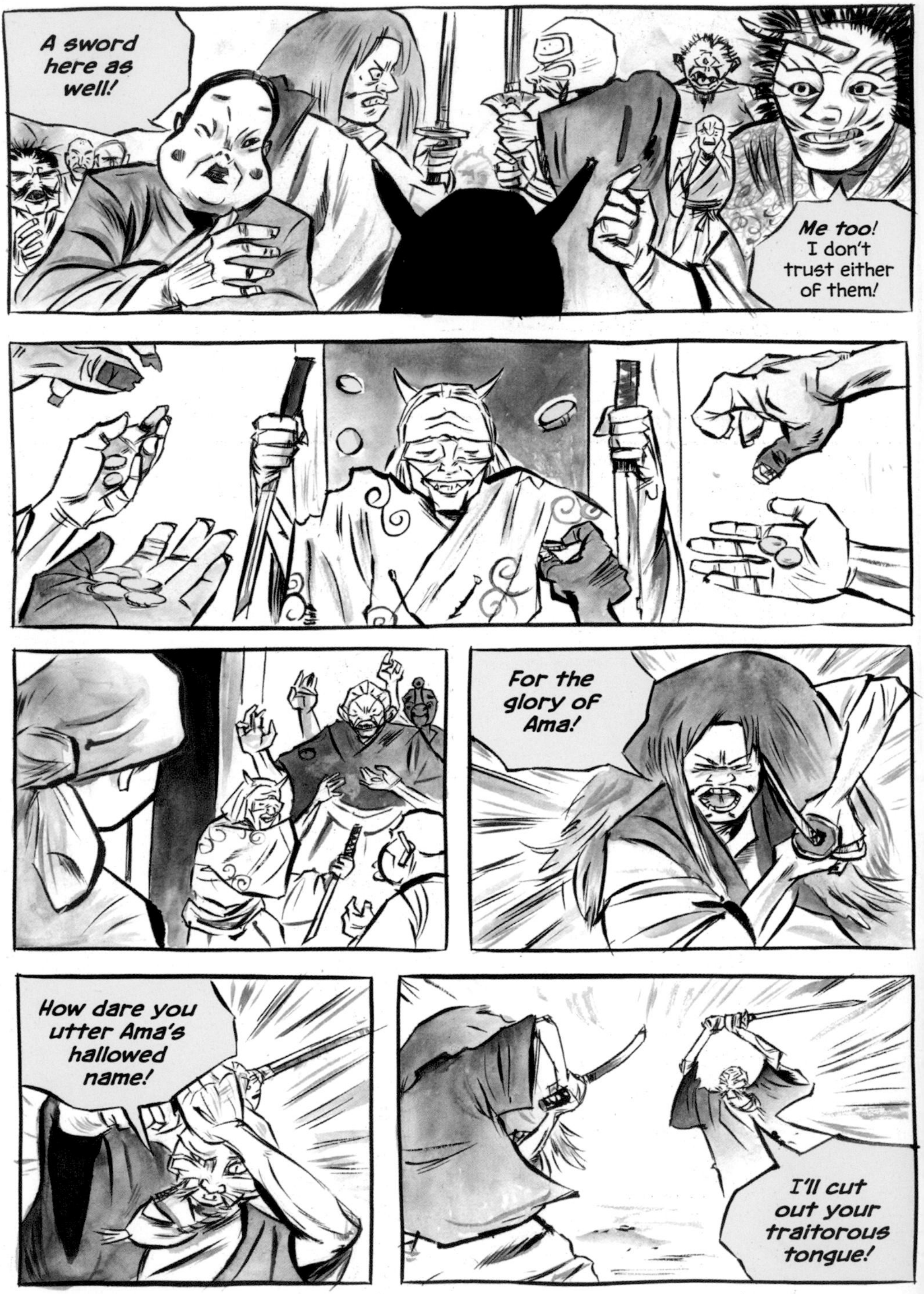
A sword here as well!
Me too! I don't trust either of them!
For the glory of Ama!
How dare you utter Ama's hallowed name!
I'll cut out your traitorous tongue!

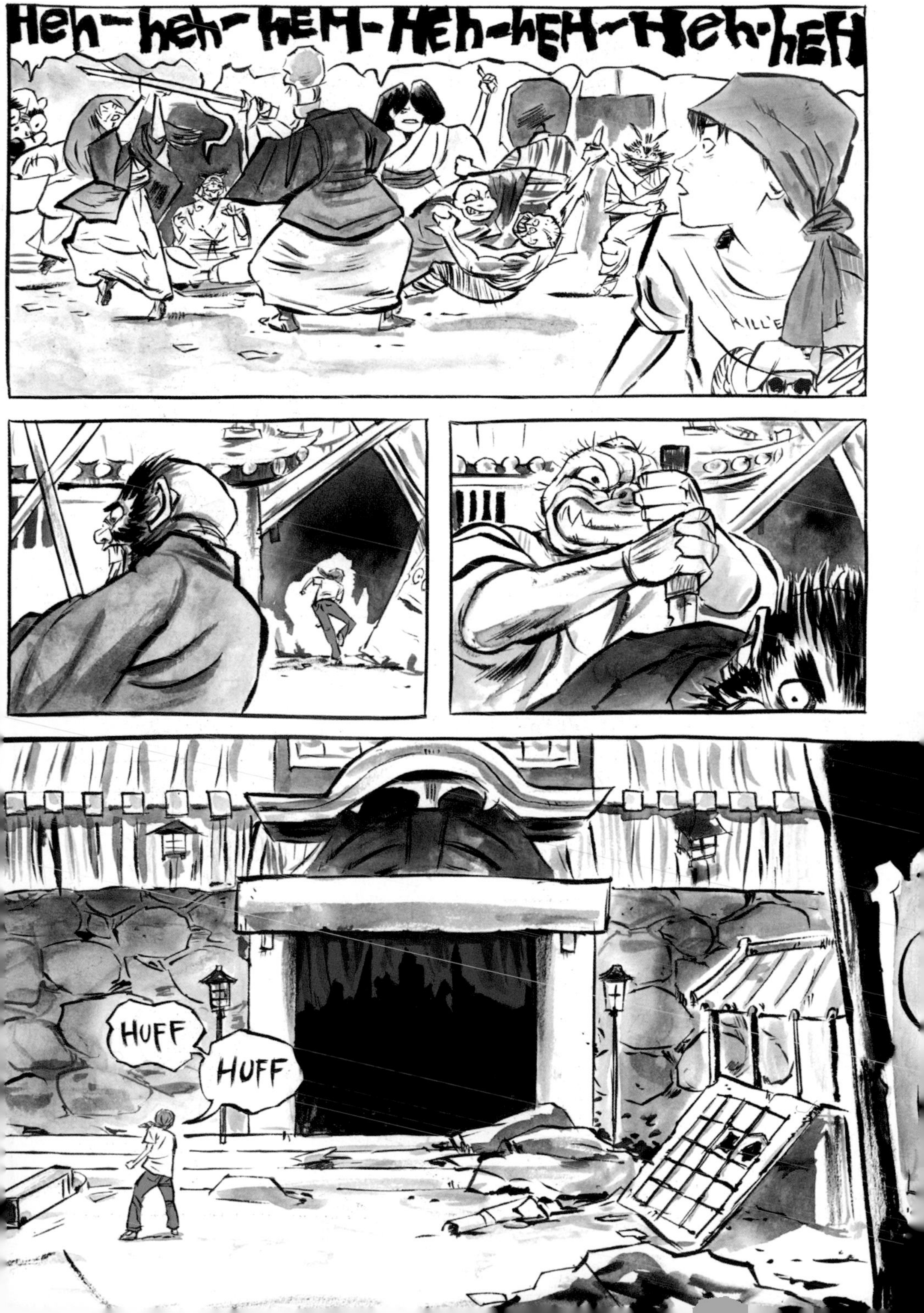
Heh-heh-HEH-HEH-HEH-Heh-HEH
KILL'E
HUFF
HUFF

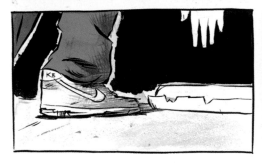

SO THIS IS WHERE THEY MADE THAT PRISON-WAGON I WAS IN...

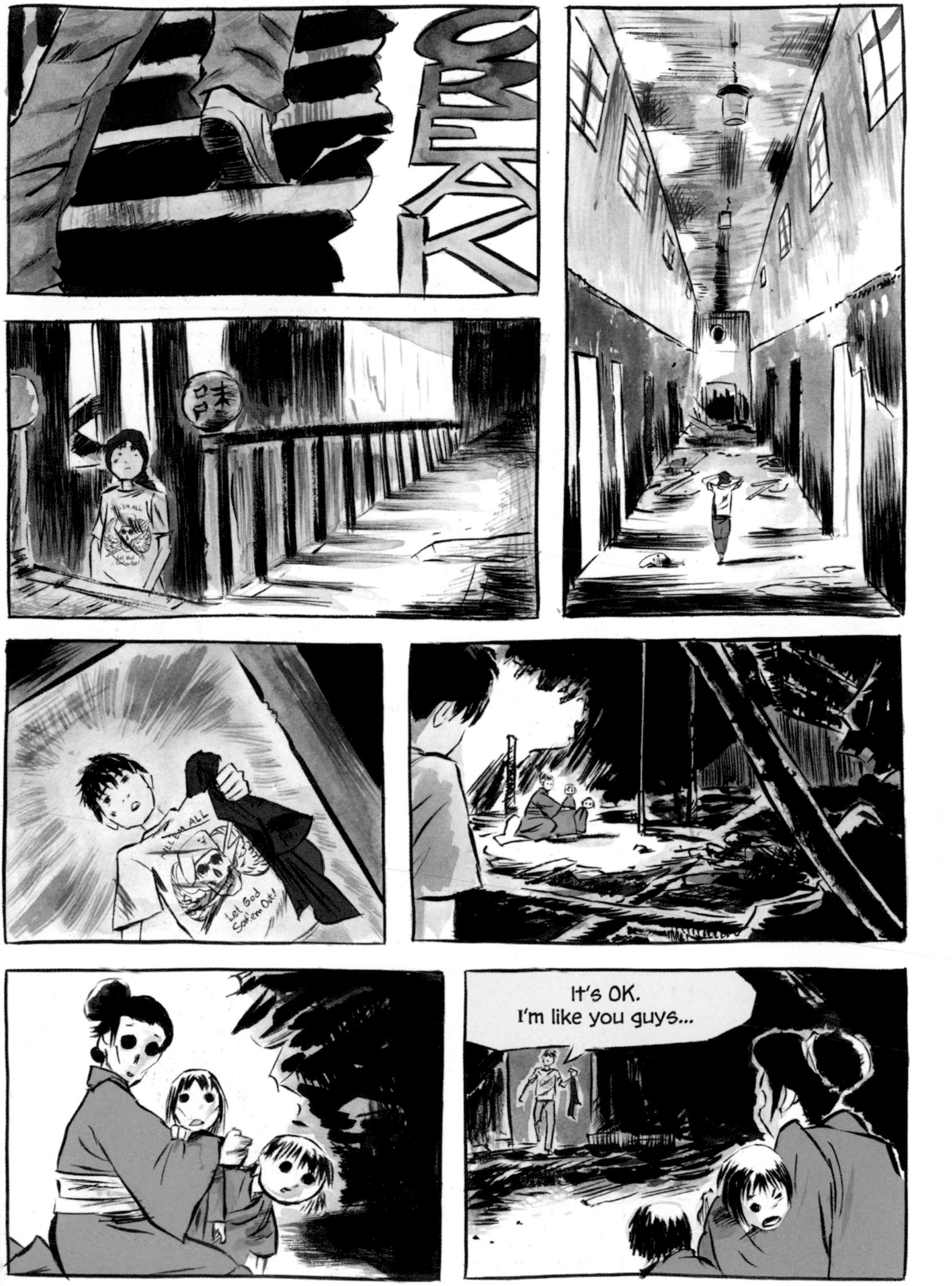
CREAK
It's OK. I'm like you guys...

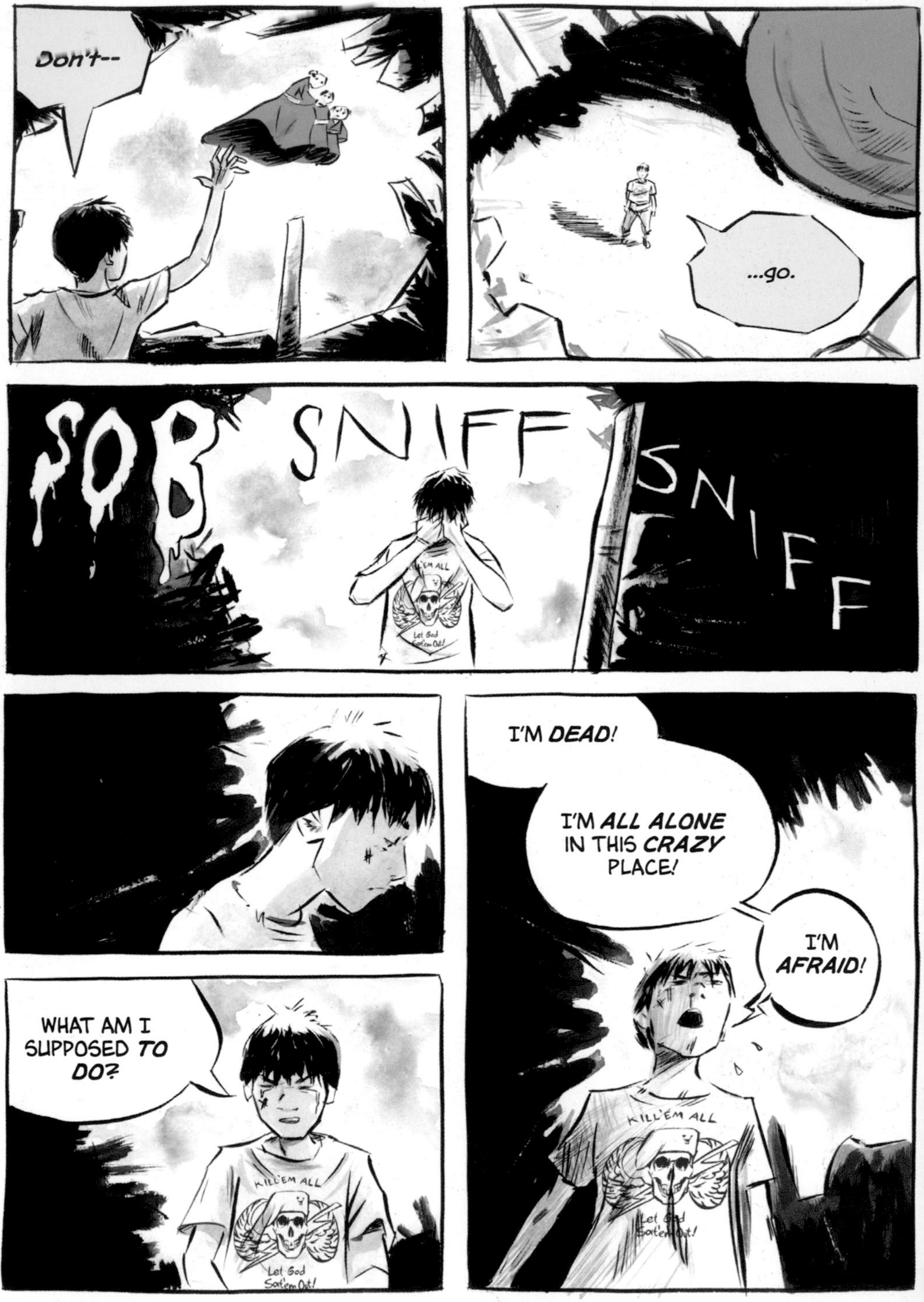
Don't--
...go.
SOB
SNIFF
SNIFF
I'M DEAD!
I'M ALL ALONE IN THIS CRAZY PLACE!
I'M AFRAID!
WHAT AM I SUPPOSED TO DO?
KILL'EM ALL
Let God Sort'em Out!

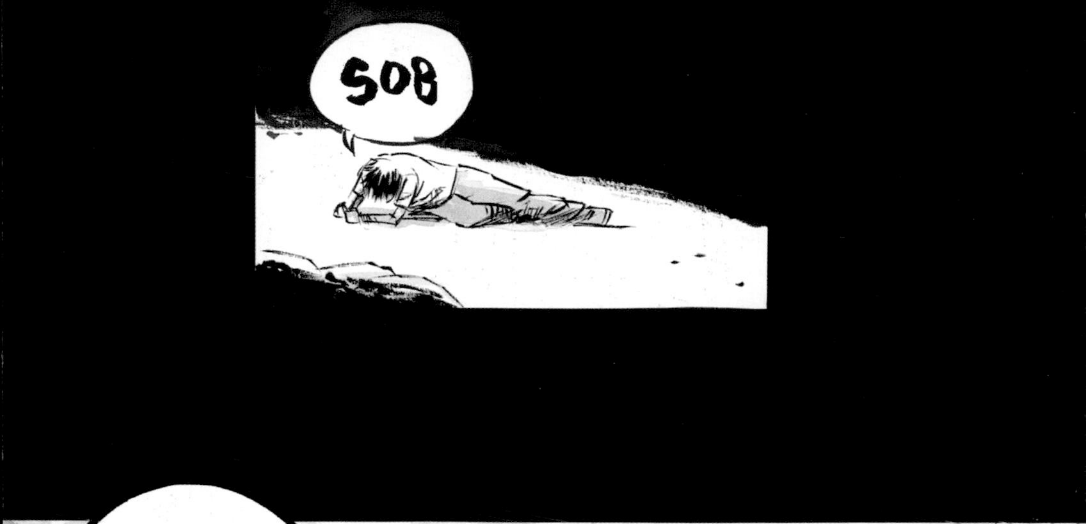
SOB

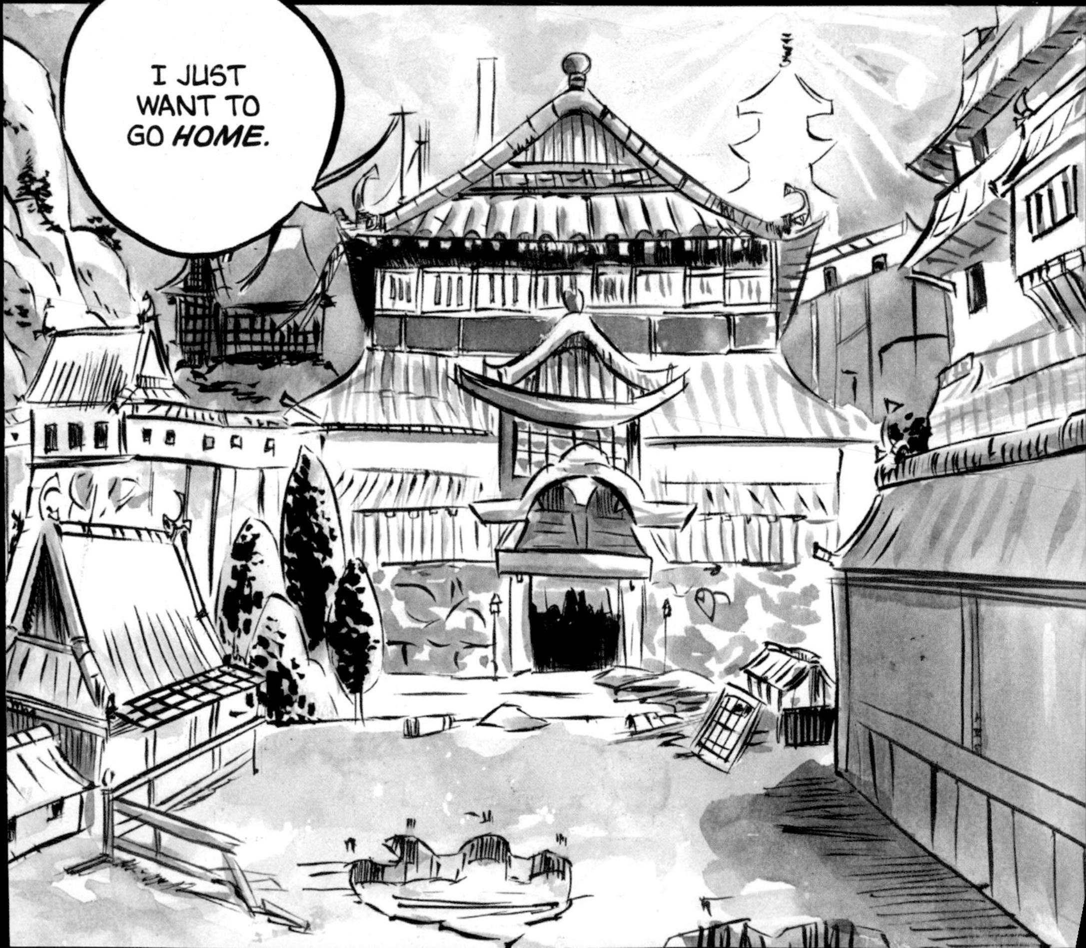
I JUST WANT TO GO *HOME*.

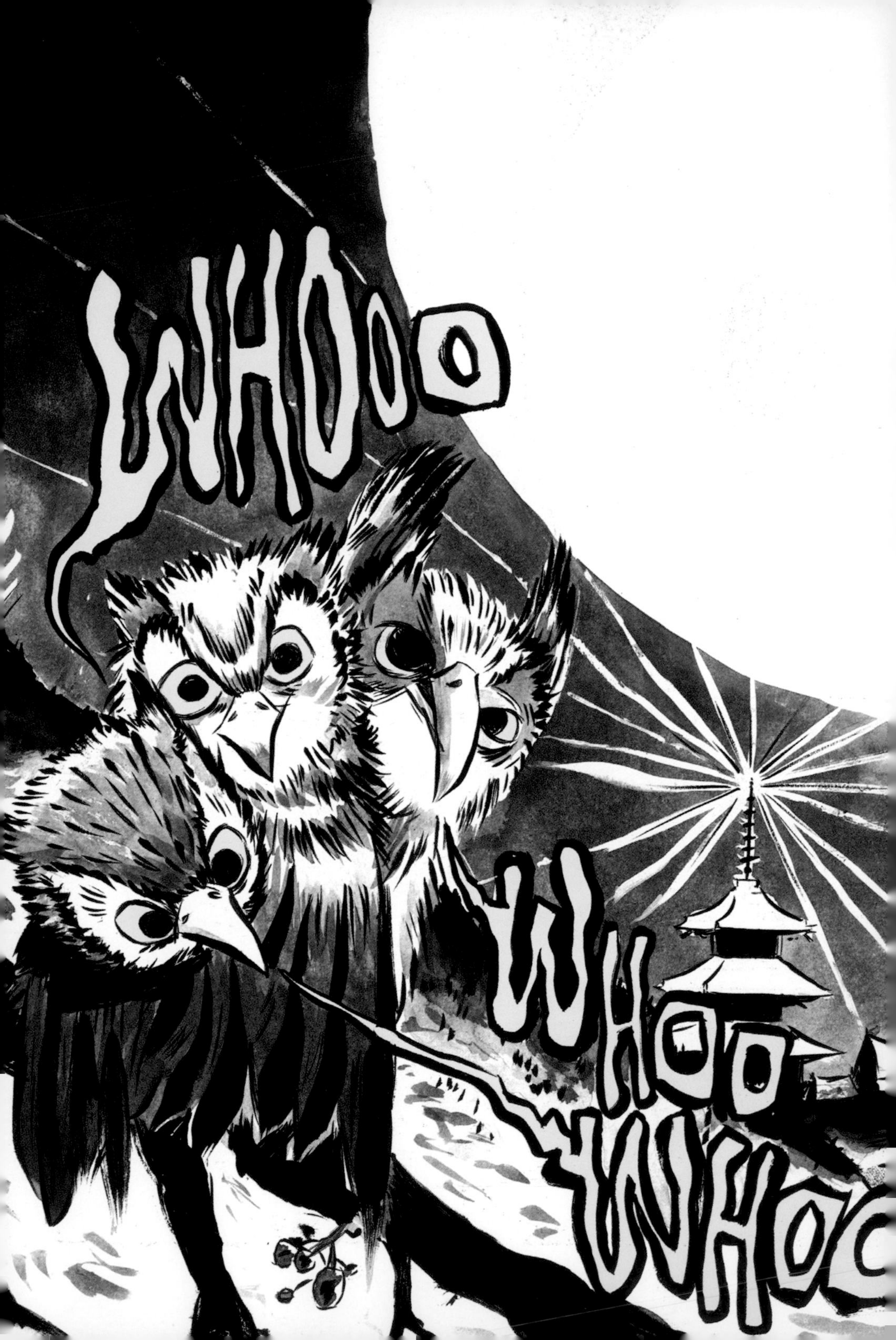
WHOOO
WHOO
WHO

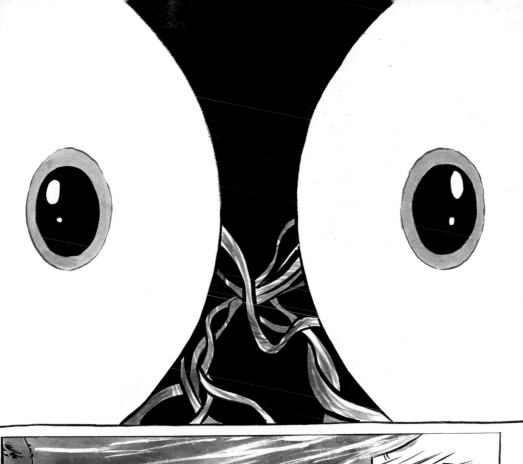

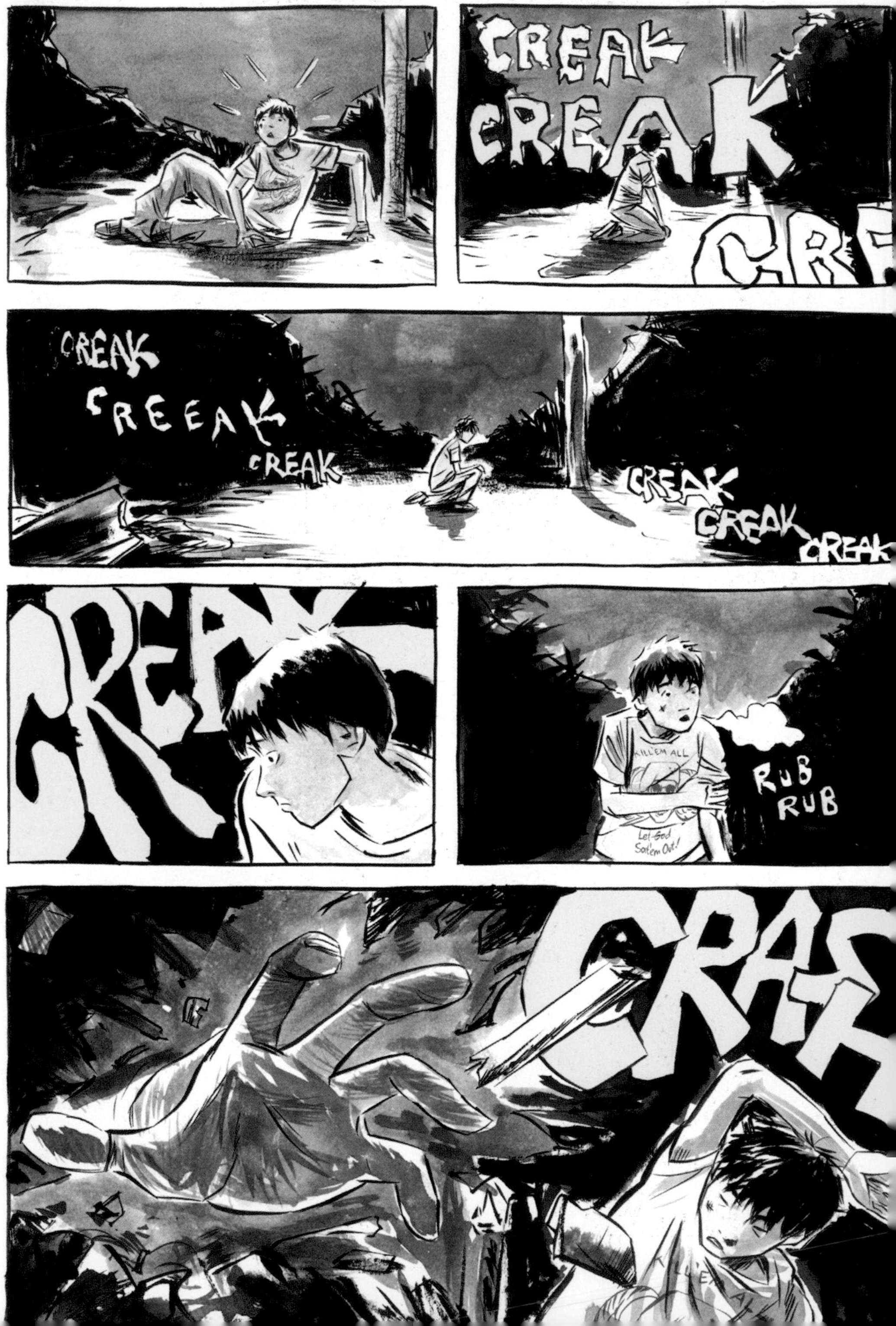
CREAK
CREAK
CREAK
CREEAK
CREAK
CREAK
CREAK
CREAK
KILL'EM ALL
RUB
RUB
Let God
Sort'em Out!

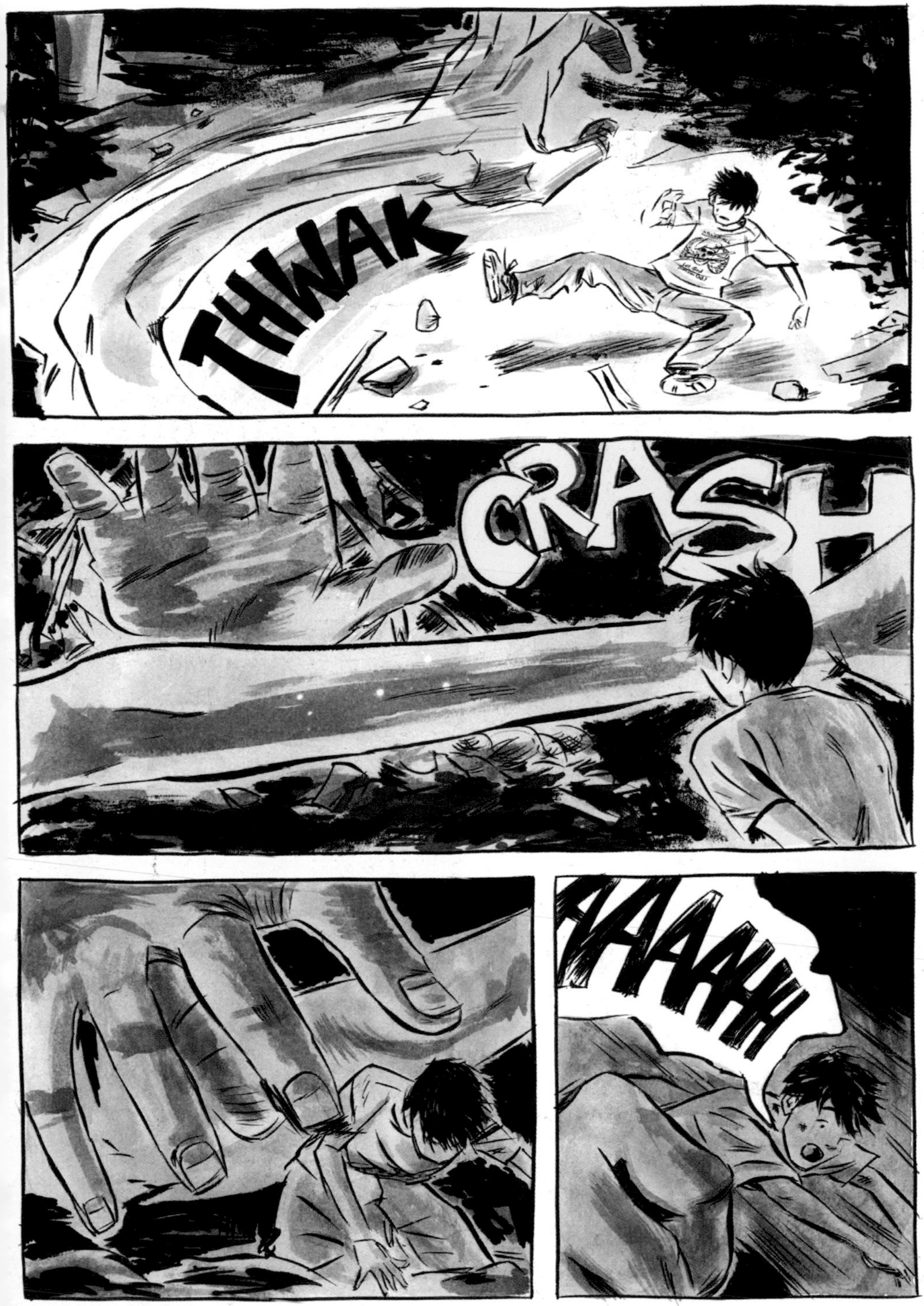
THWAK
CRASH
AAAAH

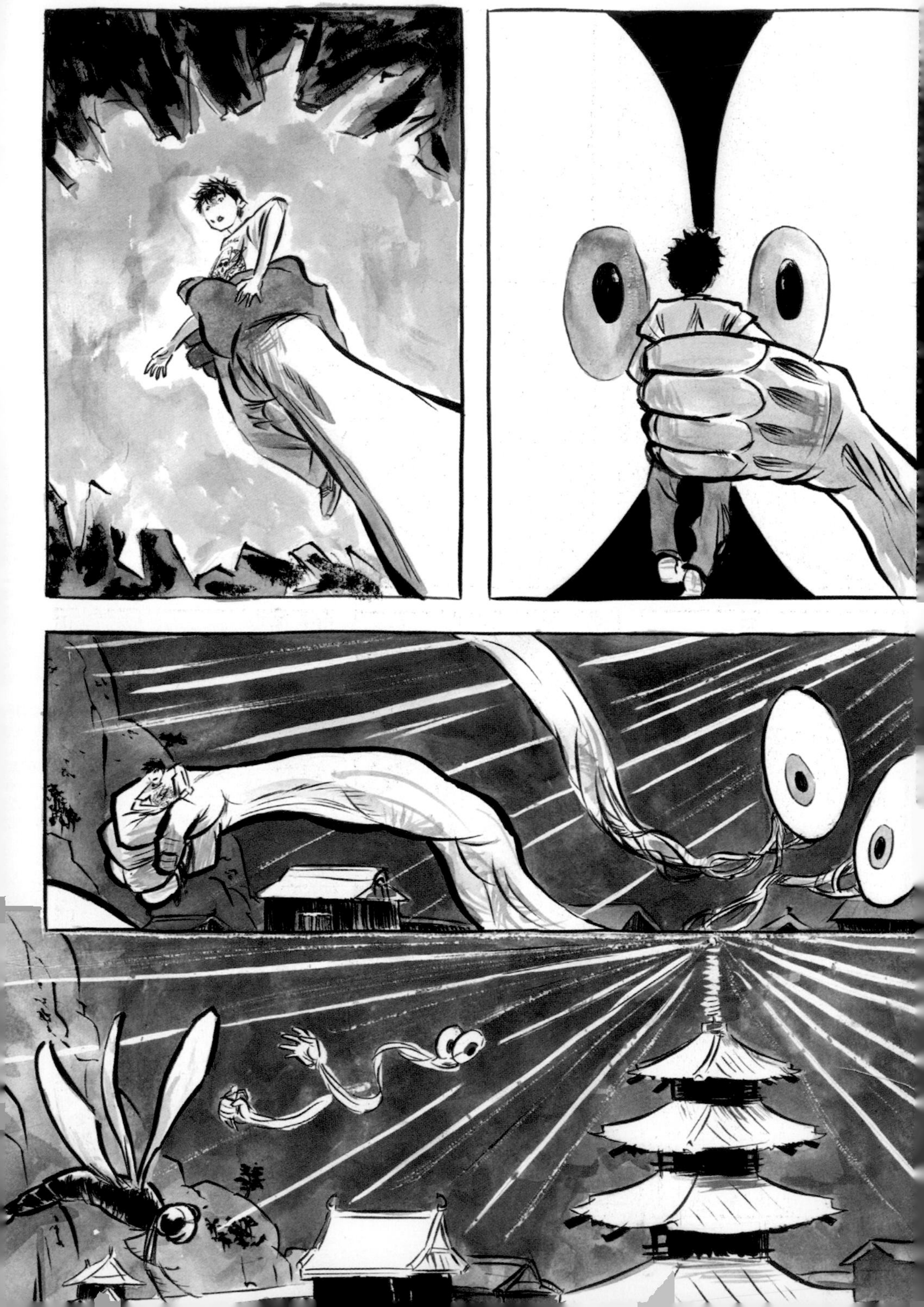

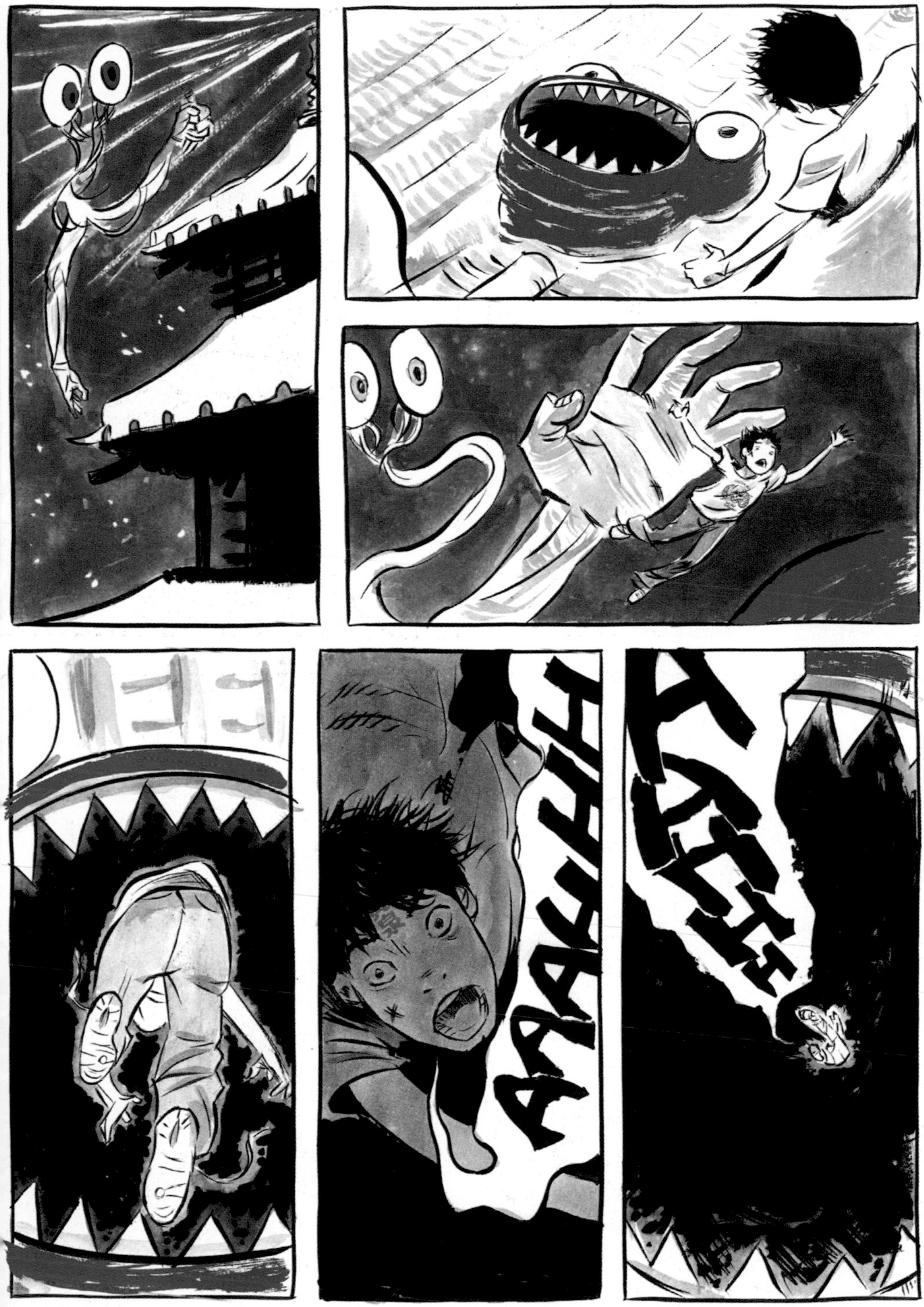
AAAHHH

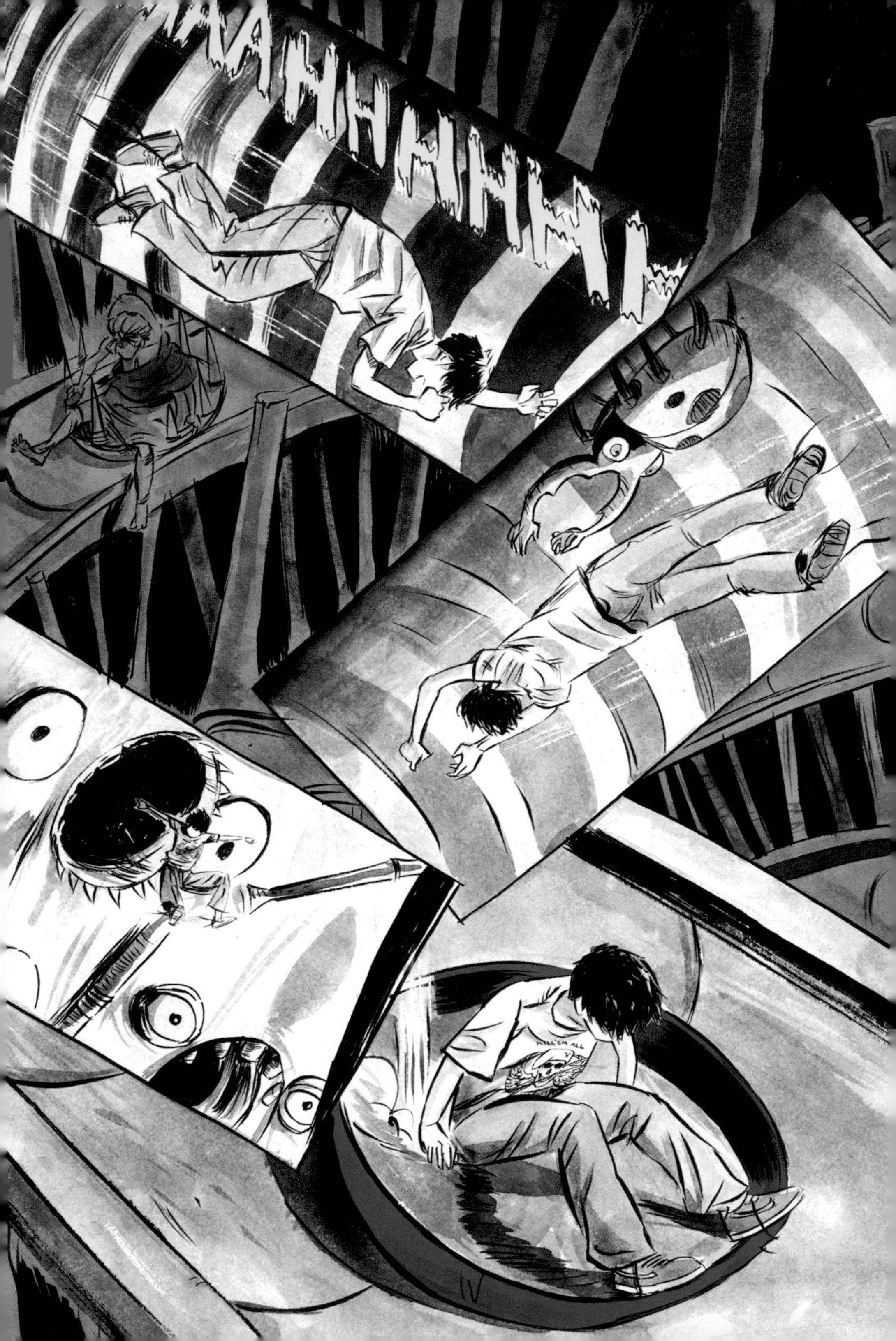
AHHHHHH!
KILL'EM ALL

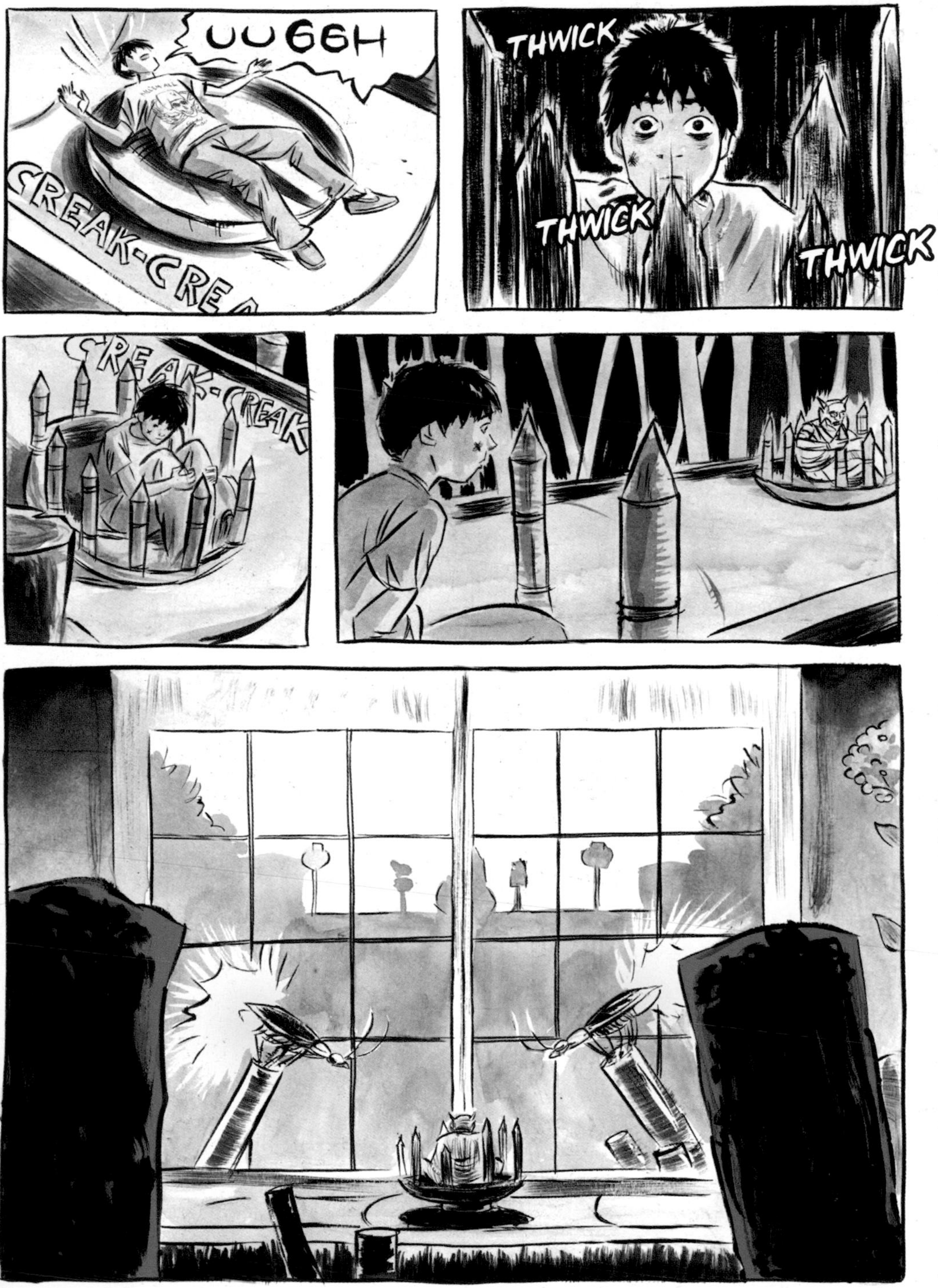
UUGGH
CREAK-CREA
THWICK
THWICK
THWICK
CREAK-CREAK

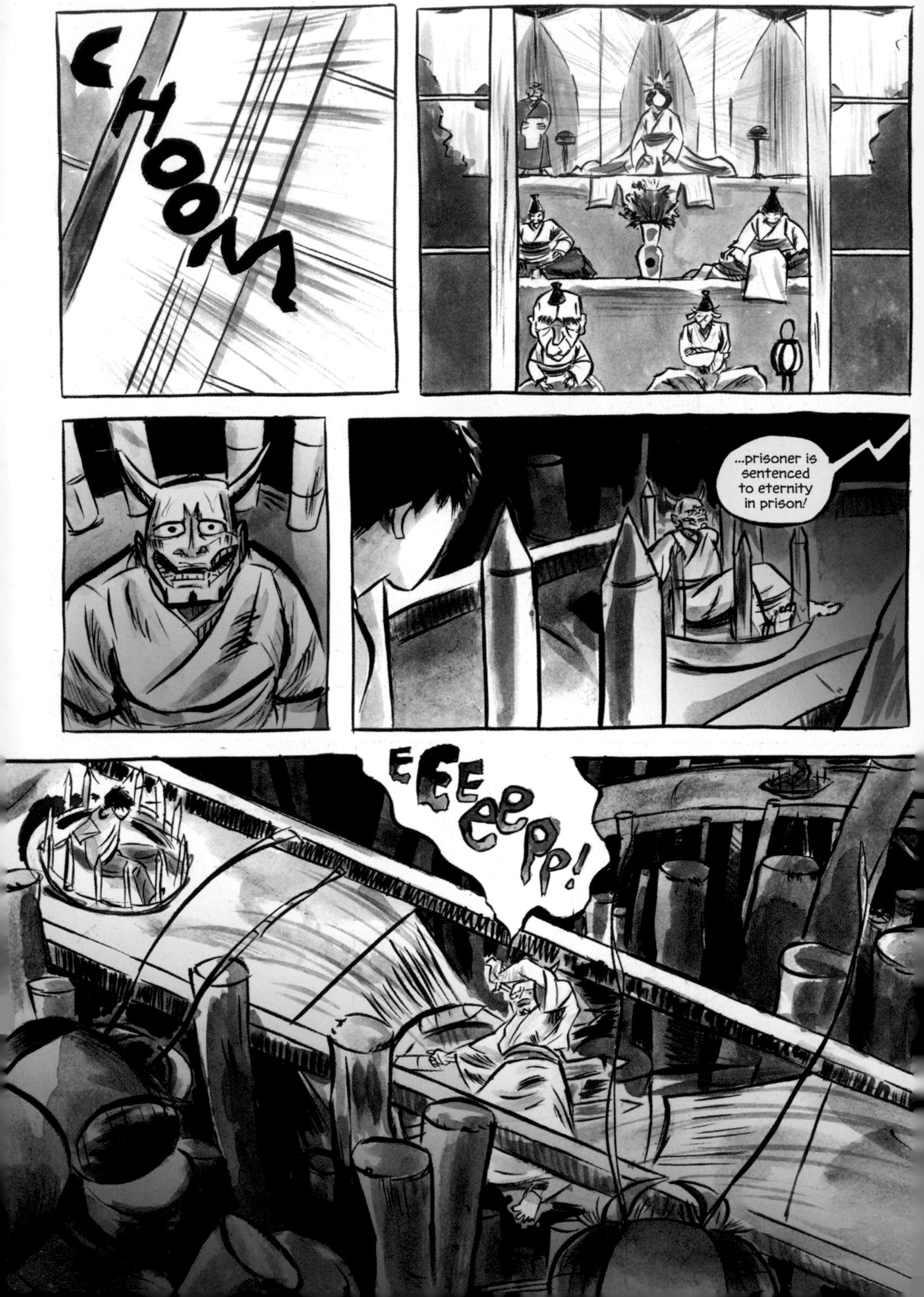
CHOOM
...prisoner is sentenced to eternity in prison!
EEEeePP!

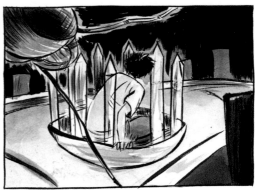

The prisoner is charged with attempting to destroy a garrison of the kingdom of Ama.

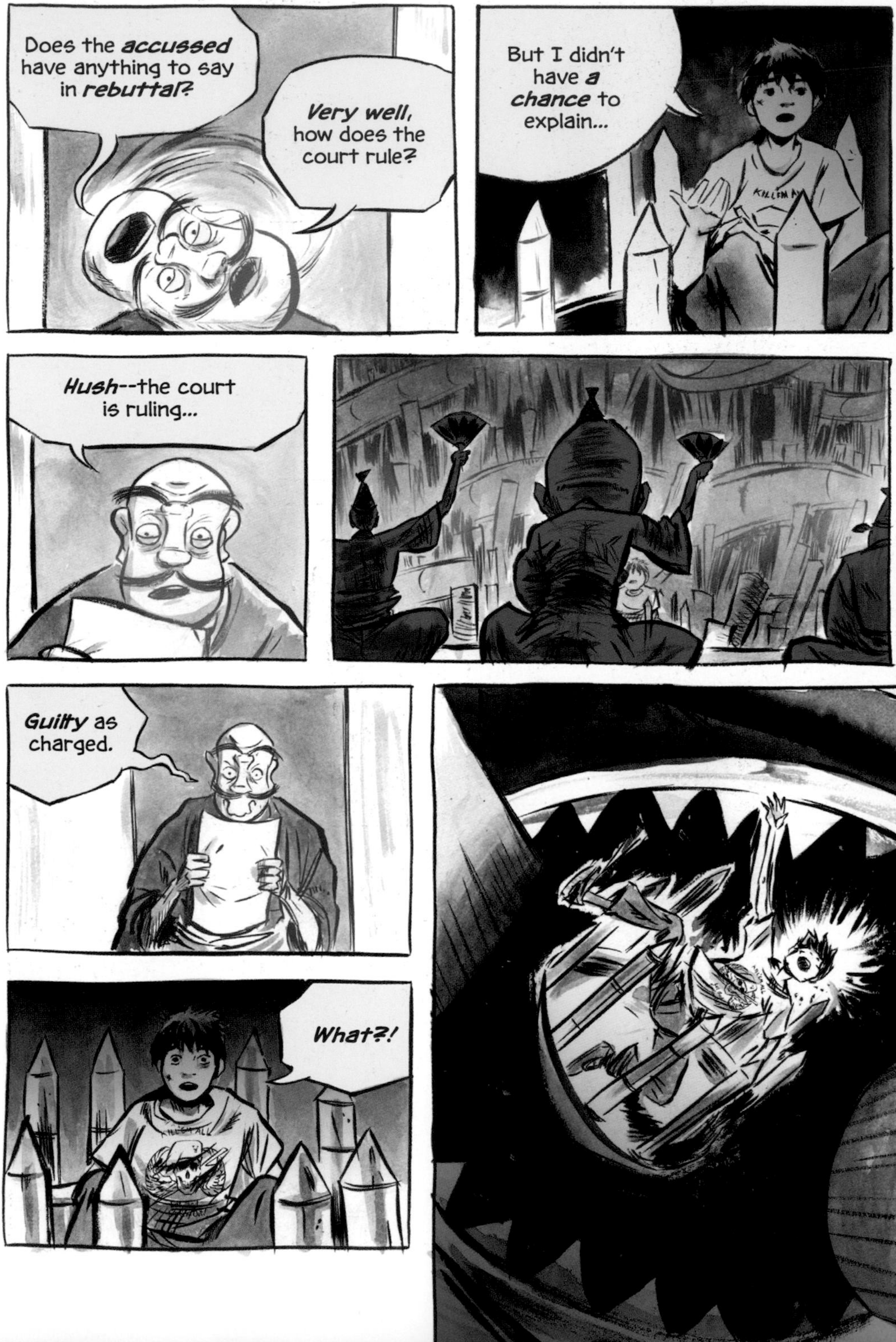
Does the *accussed* have anything to say in *rebuttal*?
Very well, how does the court rule?
But I didn't have *a chance* to explain...
Hush--the court is ruling...
Guilty as charged.
What?!

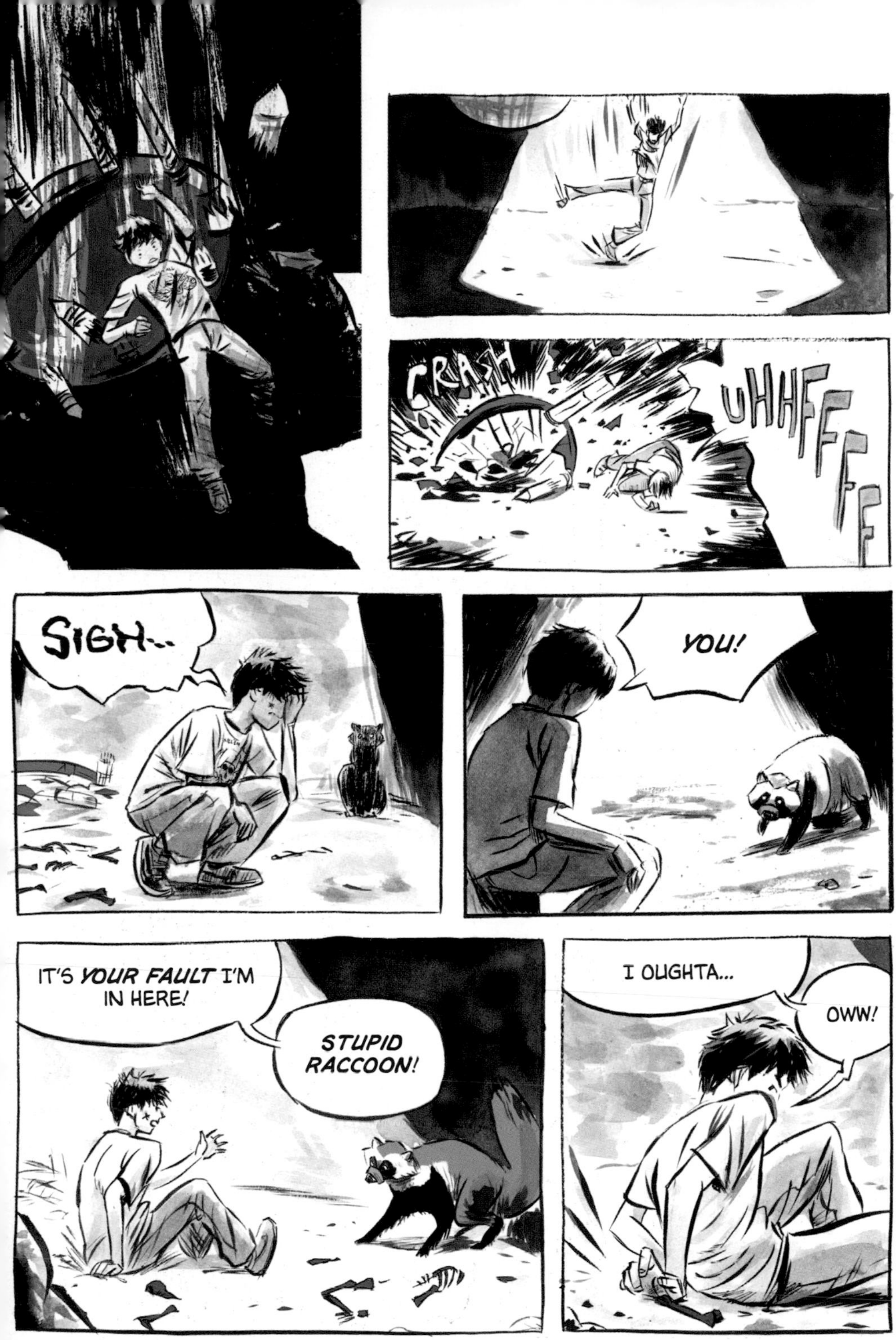

CRASH
UHHFFFFF
SIGH...
YOU!
IT'S YOUR FAULT I'M IN HERE!
STUPID RACCOON!
I OUGHTA...
OWW!

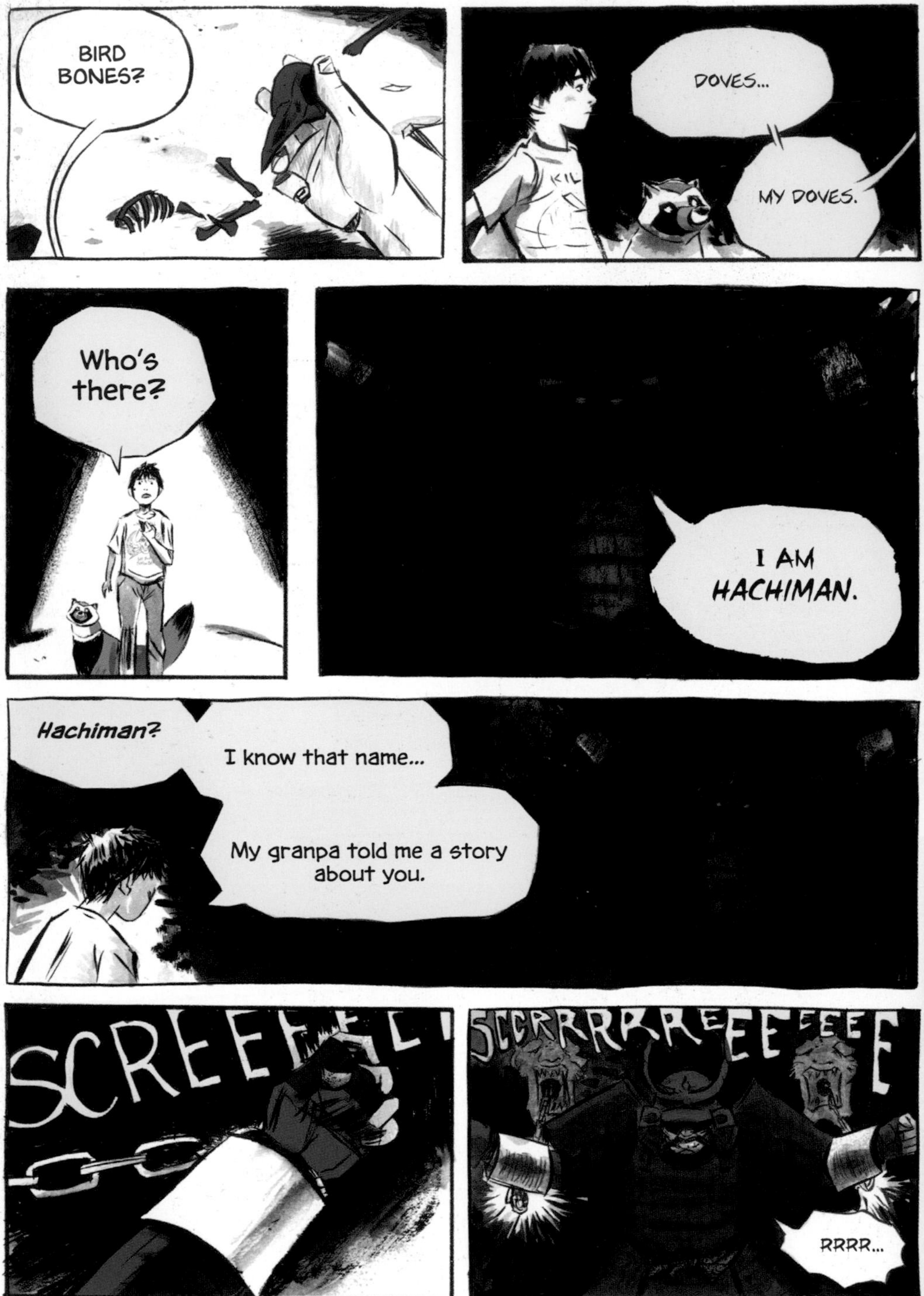
BIRD BONES?
DOVES...
MY DOVES.
Who's there?
I AM HACHIMAN.
Hachiman?
I know that name...
My granpa told me a story about you.
SCREEEEEE
SCRRRRRREEEEEEE
RRRR...

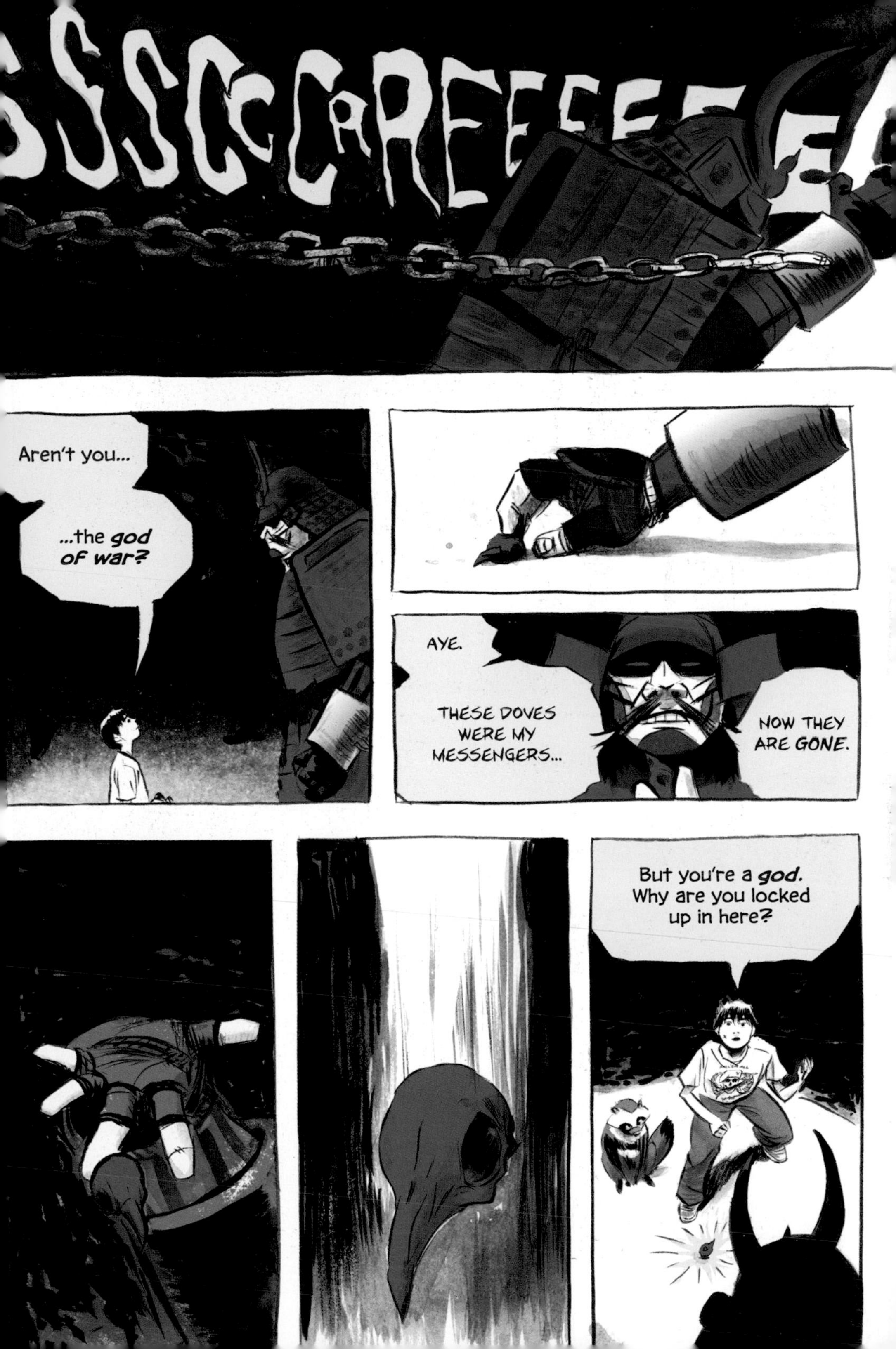
SSSCCRREEEEEE
Aren't you...
...the god of war?
AYE.
THESE DOVES WERE MY MESSENGERS...
NOW THEY ARE GONE.
But you're a god. Why are you locked up in here?

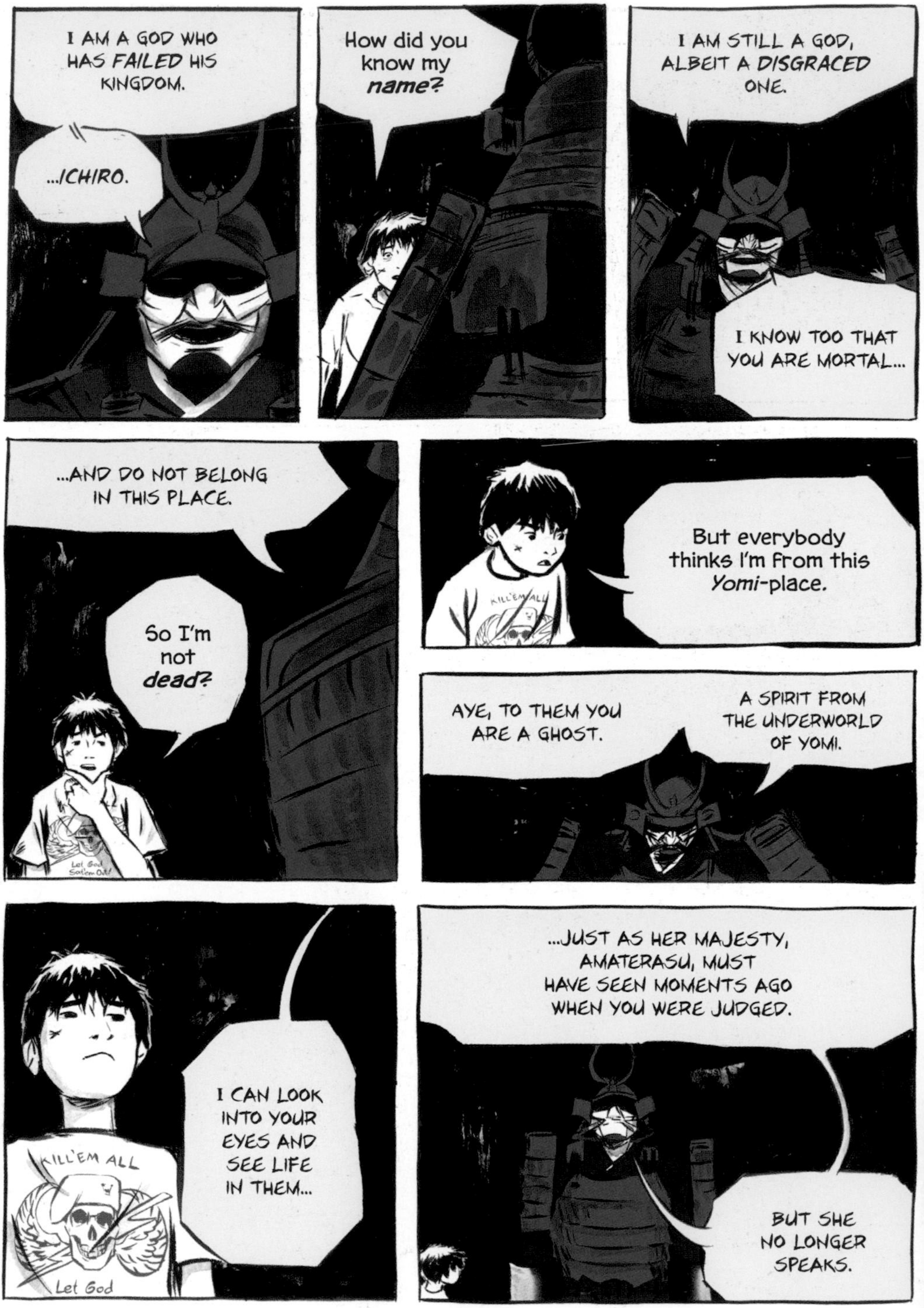

I AM A GOD WHO HAS FAILED HIS KINGDOM.
...ICHIRO.
How did you know my name?
I AM STILL A GOD, ALBEIT A DISGRACED ONE.
I KNOW TOO THAT YOU ARE MORTAL...
...AND DO NOT BELONG IN THIS PLACE.
So I'm not dead?
Let God Sort'em Out!
KILL'EM ALL
But everybody thinks I'm from this Yomi-place.
AYE, TO THEM YOU ARE A GHOST.
A SPIRIT FROM THE UNDERWORLD OF YOMI.
KILL'EM ALL
I CAN LOOK INTO YOUR EYES AND SEE LIFE IN THEM...
Let God
...JUST AS HER MAJESTY, AMATERASU, MUST HAVE SEEN MOMENTS AGO WHEN YOU WERE JUDGED.
BUT SHE NO LONGER SPEAKS.

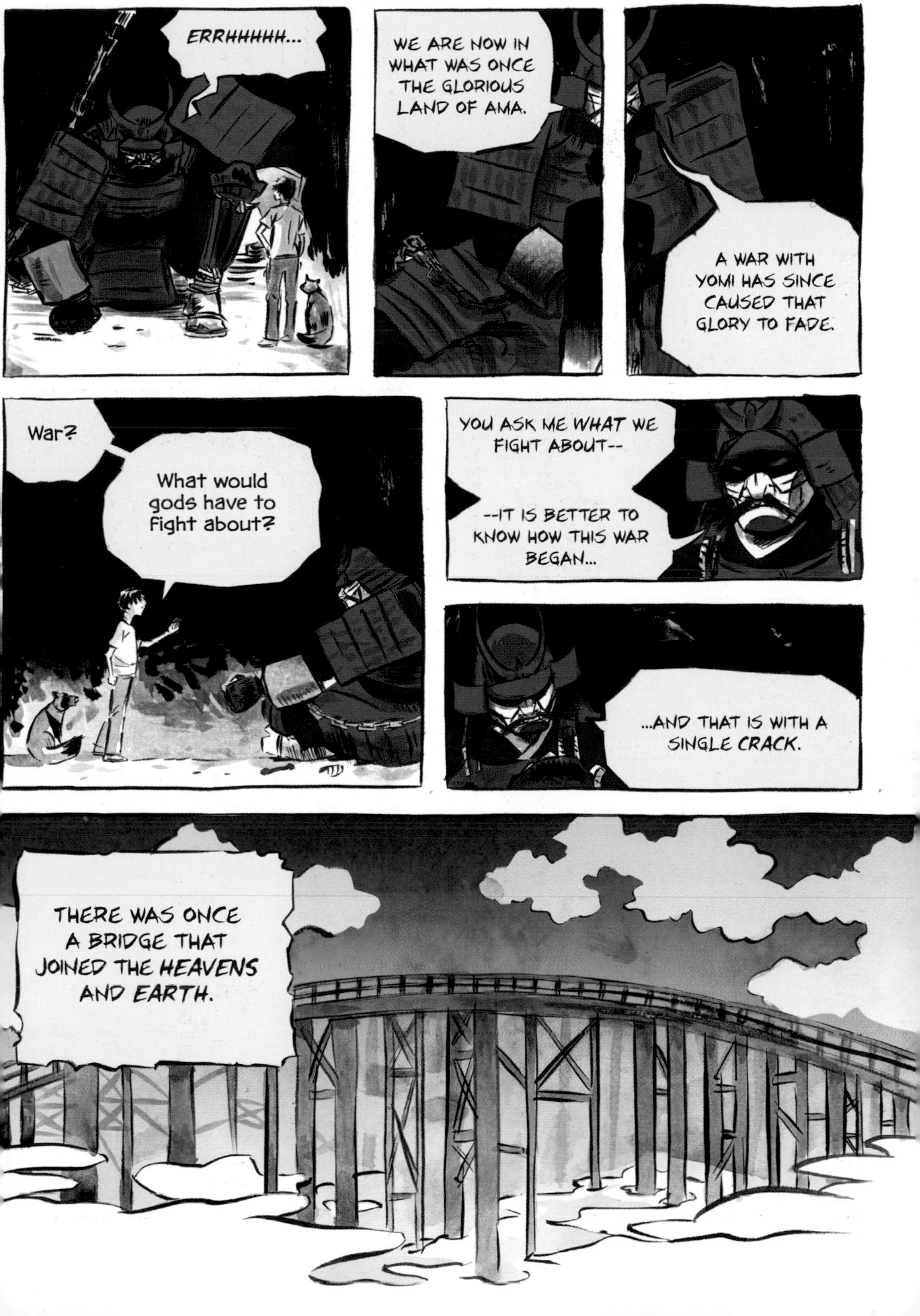

ERRHHHHH...
WE ARE NOW IN WHAT WAS ONCE THE GLORIOUS LAND OF AMA.
A WAR WITH YOMI HAS SINCE CAUSED THAT GLORY TO FADE.
War?
What would gods have to fight about?
YOU ASK ME WHAT WE FIGHT ABOUT--
--IT IS BETTER TO KNOW HOW THIS WAR BEGAN...
...AND THAT IS WITH A SINGLE CRACK.
THERE WAS ONCE A BRIDGE THAT JOINED THE HEAVENS AND EARTH.

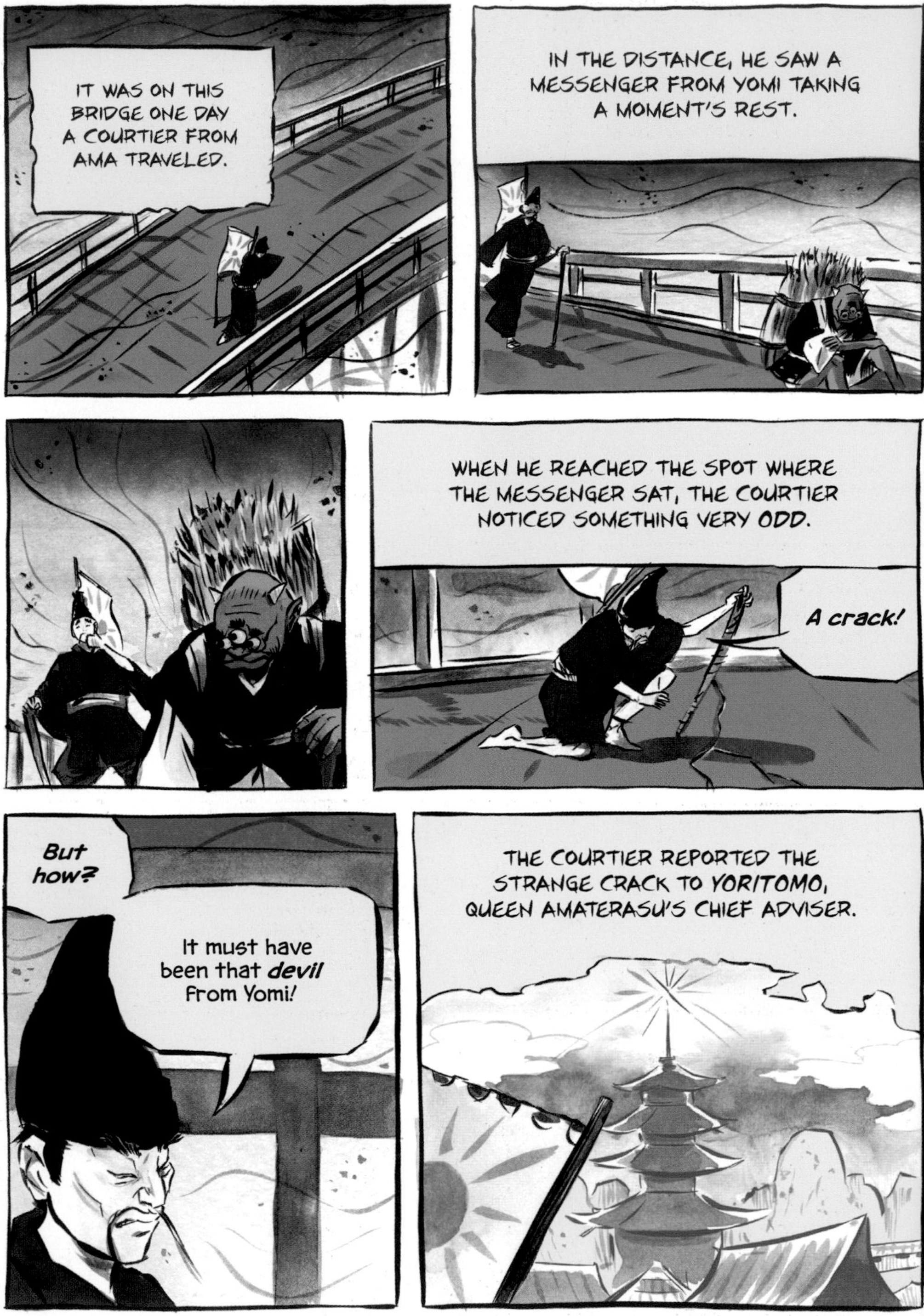

IT WAS ON THIS BRIDGE ONE DAY A COURTIER FROM AMA TRAVELED.
IN THE DISTANCE, HE SAW A MESSENGER FROM YOMI TAKING A MOMENT'S REST.
WHEN HE REACHED THE SPOT WHERE THE MESSENGER SAT, THE COURTIER NOTICED SOMETHING VERY ODD.
A crack!
But how?
It must have been that devil from Yomi!
THE COURTIER REPORTED THE STRANGE CRACK TO YORITOMO, QUEEN AMATERASU'S CHIEF ADVISER.

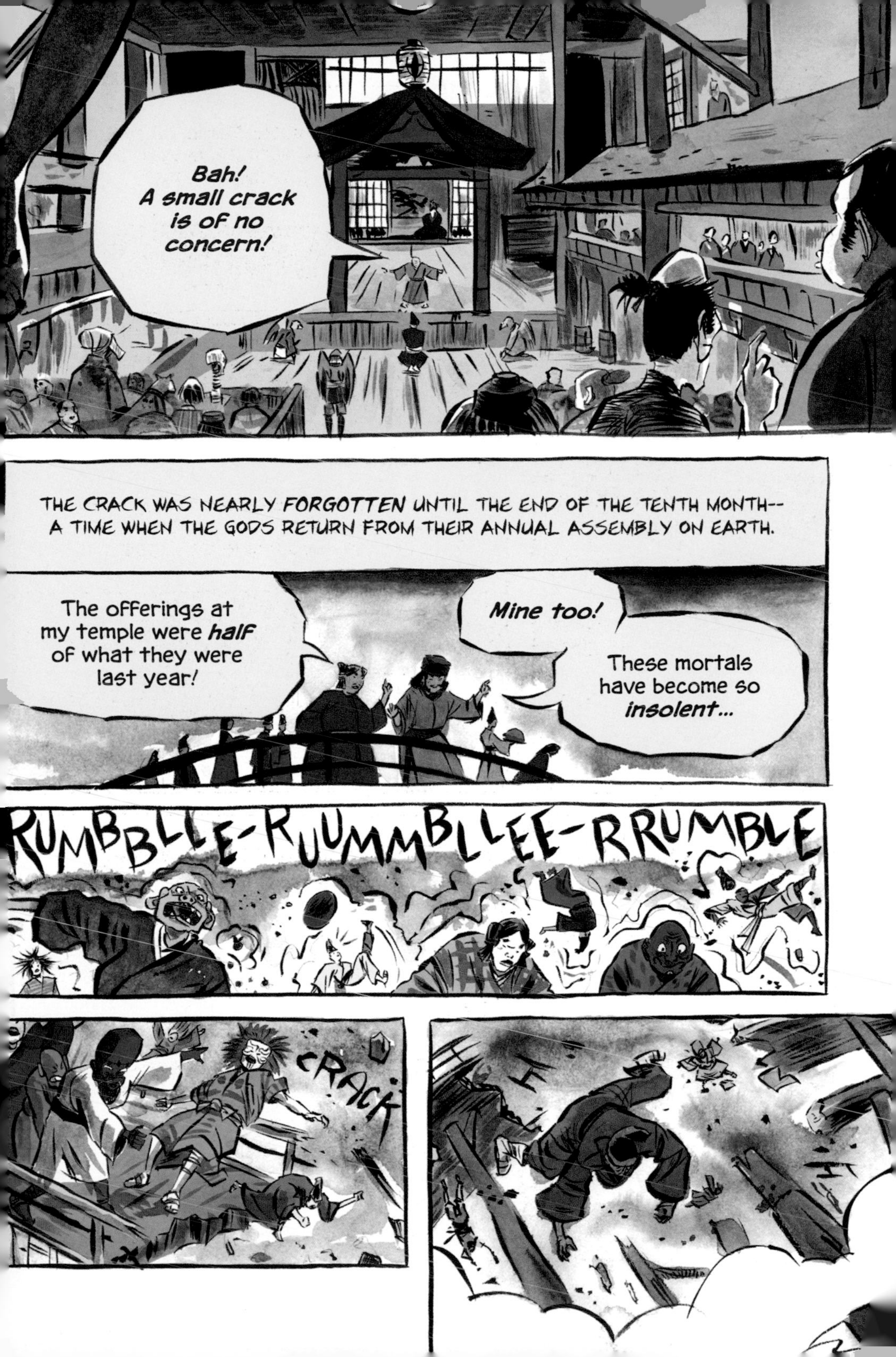
Bah! A small crack is of no concern!
THE CRACK WAS NEARLY FORGOTTEN UNTIL THE END OF THE TENTH MONTH-- A TIME WHEN THE GODS RETURN FROM THEIR ANNUAL ASSEMBLY ON EARTH.
The offerings at my temple were half of what they were last year!
Mine too!
These mortals have become so insolent...
RUMBBLLE-RUUMMBLLEE-RRUMBLE
CRACK

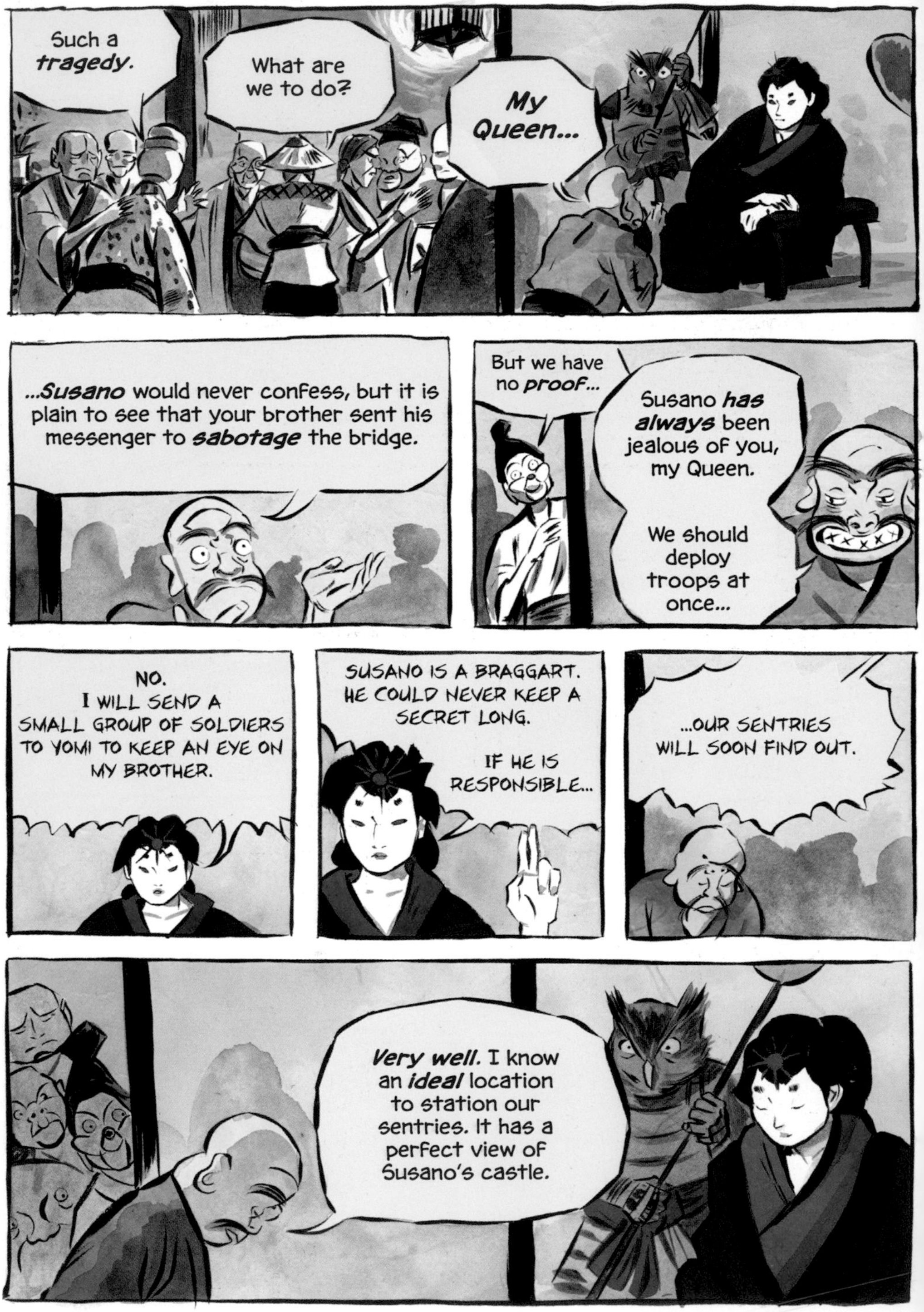
Such a *tragedy.*
What are we to do?
My Queen...
...Susano would never confess, but it is plain to see that your brother sent his messenger to *sabotage* the bridge.
But we have no *proof...*
Susano *has always* been jealous of you, my Queen.
We should deploy troops at once...
NO. I WILL SEND A SMALL GROUP OF SOLDIERS TO YOMI TO KEEP AN EYE ON MY BROTHER.
SUSANO IS A BRAGGART. HE COULD NEVER KEEP A SECRET LONG.
IF HE IS RESPONSIBLE...
...OUR SENTRIES WILL SOON FIND OUT.
Very well. I know an *ideal* location to station our sentries. It has a perfect view of Susano's castle.

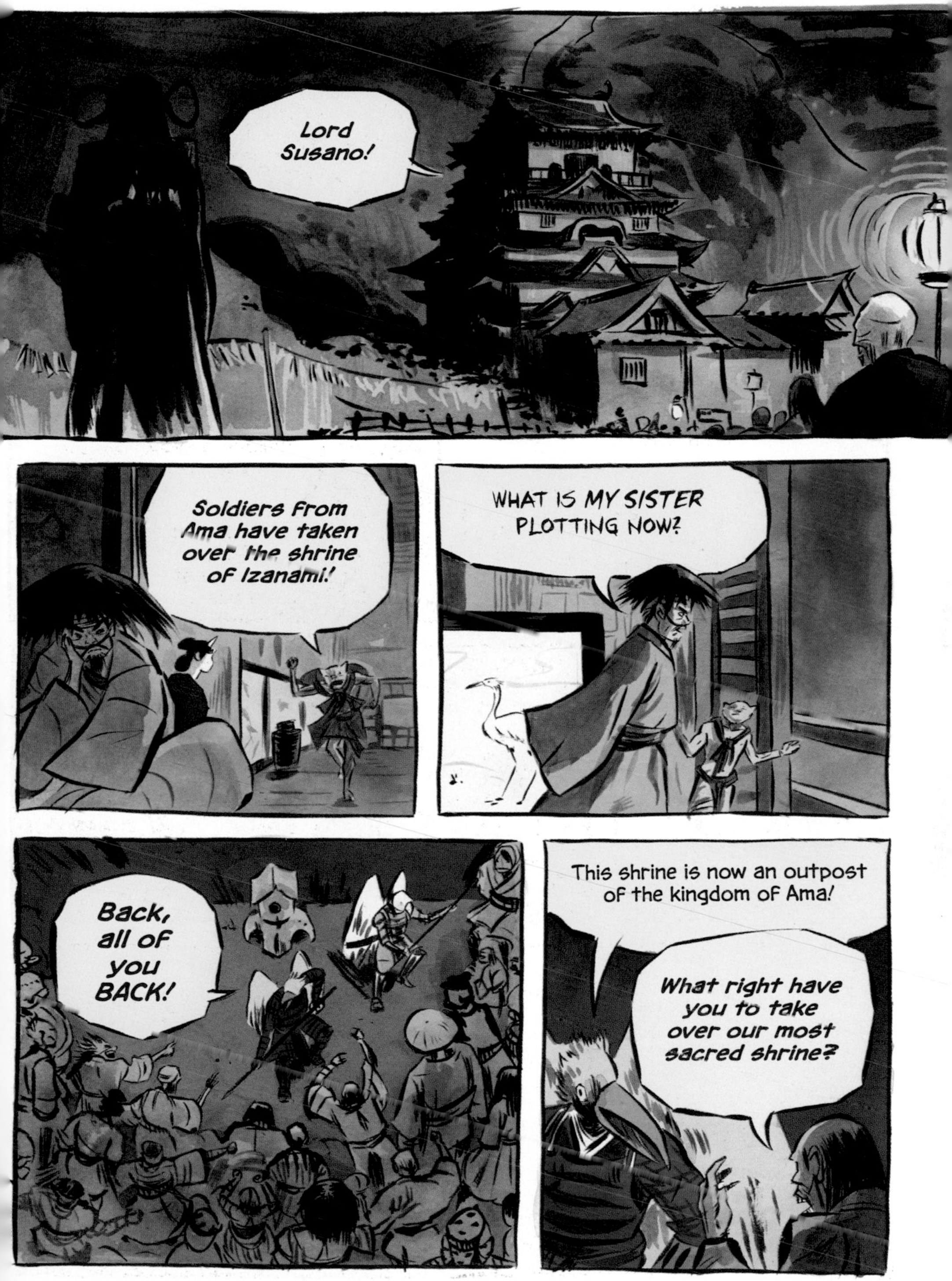
Lord Susano!
Soldiers from Ama have taken over the shrine of Izanami!
WHAT IS MY SISTER PLOTTING NOW?
Back, all of you BACK!
This shrine is now an outpost of the kingdom of Ama!
What right have you to take over our most sacred shrine?

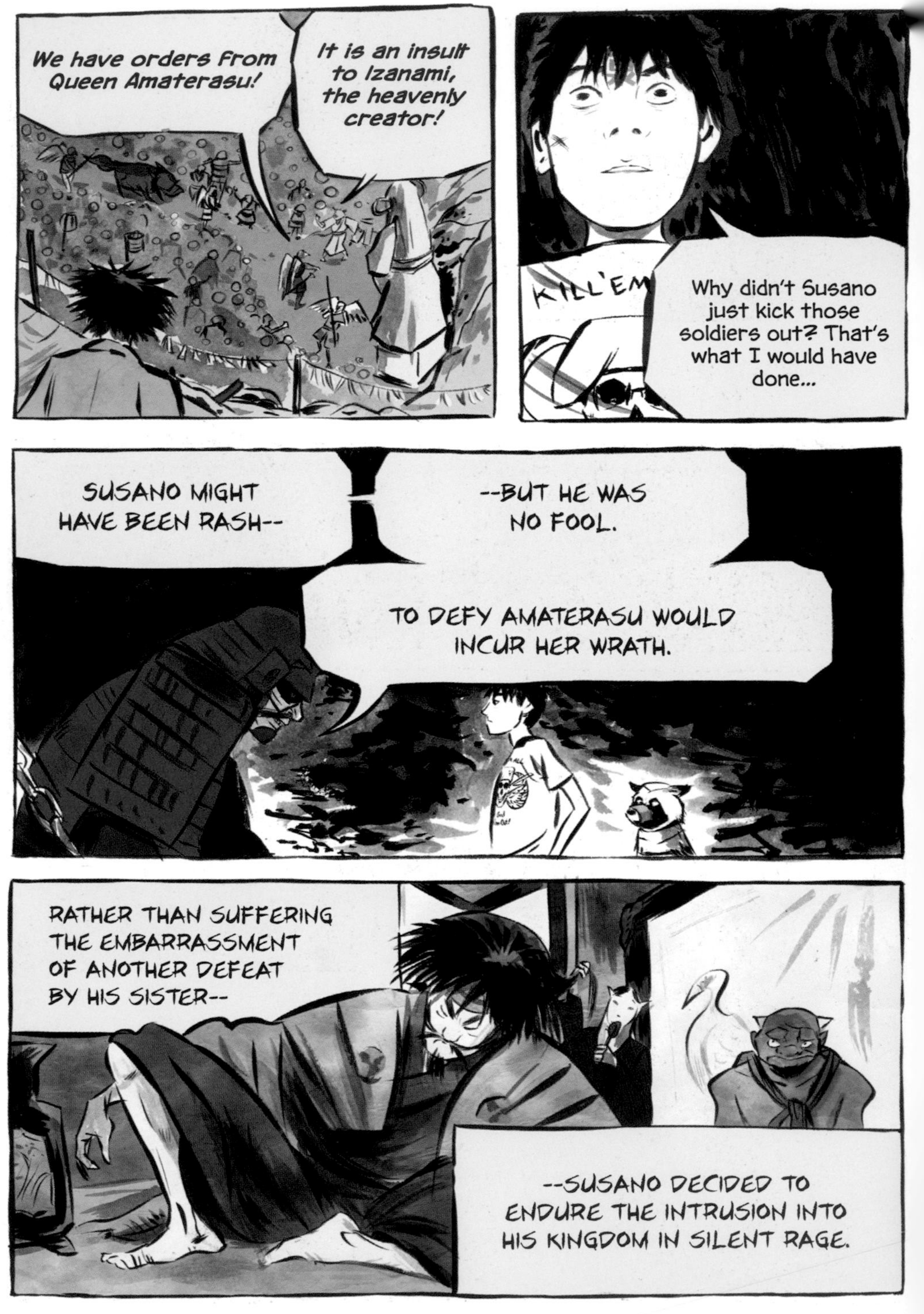
We have orders from Queen Amaterasu!
It is an insult to Izanami, the heavenly creator!
KILL'EM
Why didn't Susano just kick those soldiers out? That's what I would have done...
SUSANO MIGHT HAVE BEEN RASH--
--BUT HE WAS NO FOOL.
TO DEFY AMATERASU WOULD INCUR HER WRATH.
RATHER THAN SUFFERING THE EMBARRASSMENT OF ANOTHER DEFEAT BY HIS SISTER--
--SUSANO DECIDED TO ENDURE THE INTRUSION INTO HIS KINGDOM IN SILENT RAGE.

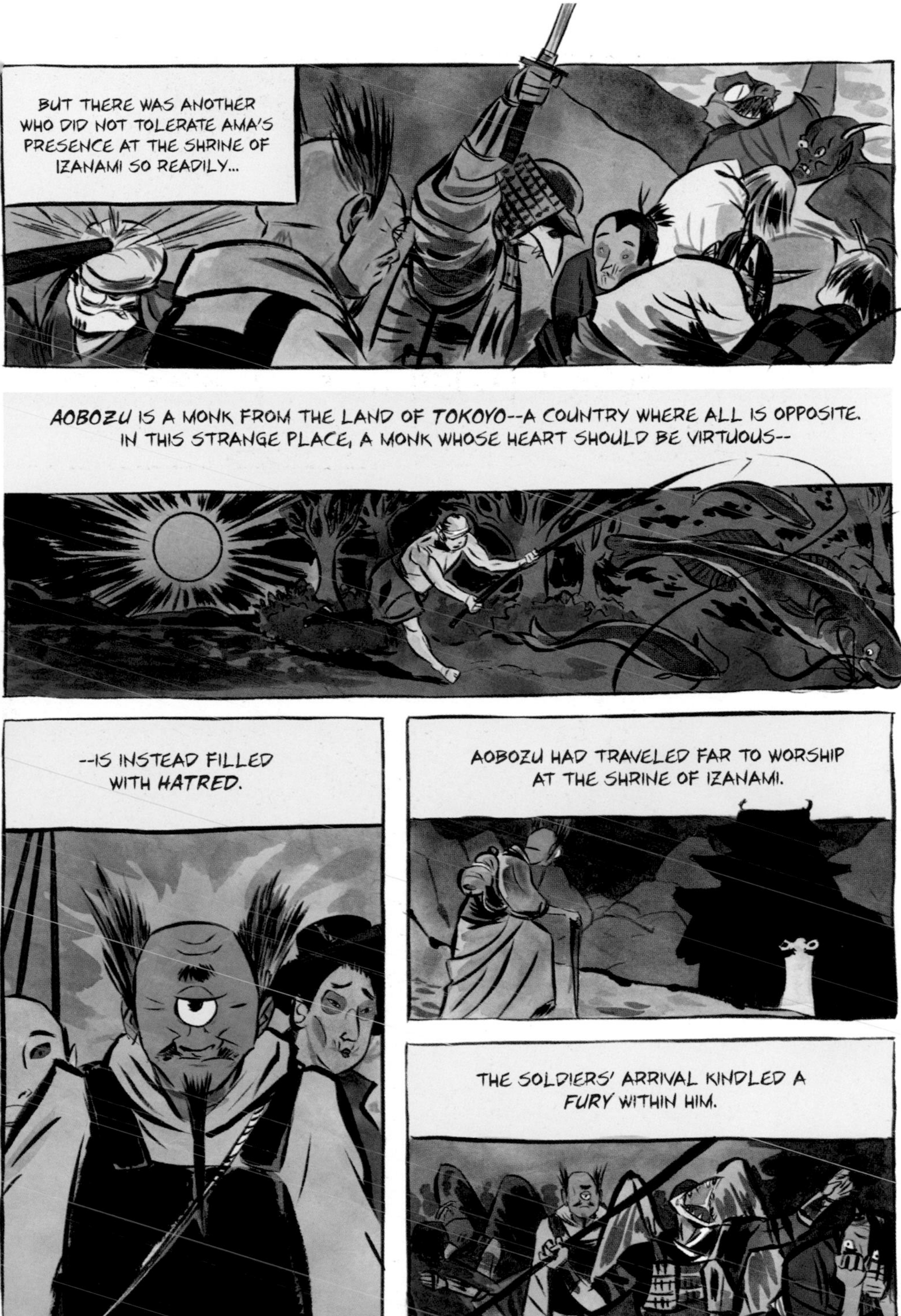
BUT THERE WAS ANOTHER WHO DID NOT TOLERATE AMA'S PRESENCE AT THE SHRINE OF IZANAMI SO READILY...
AOBOZU IS A MONK FROM THE LAND OF *TOKOYO*--A COUNTRY WHERE ALL IS OPPOSITE. IN THIS STRANGE PLACE, A MONK WHOSE HEART SHOULD BE VIRTUOUS--
--IS INSTEAD FILLED WITH *HATRED*.
AOBOZU HAD TRAVELED FAR TO WORSHIP AT THE SHRINE OF IZANAMI.
THE SOLDIERS' ARRIVAL KINDLED A *FURY* WITHIN HIM.

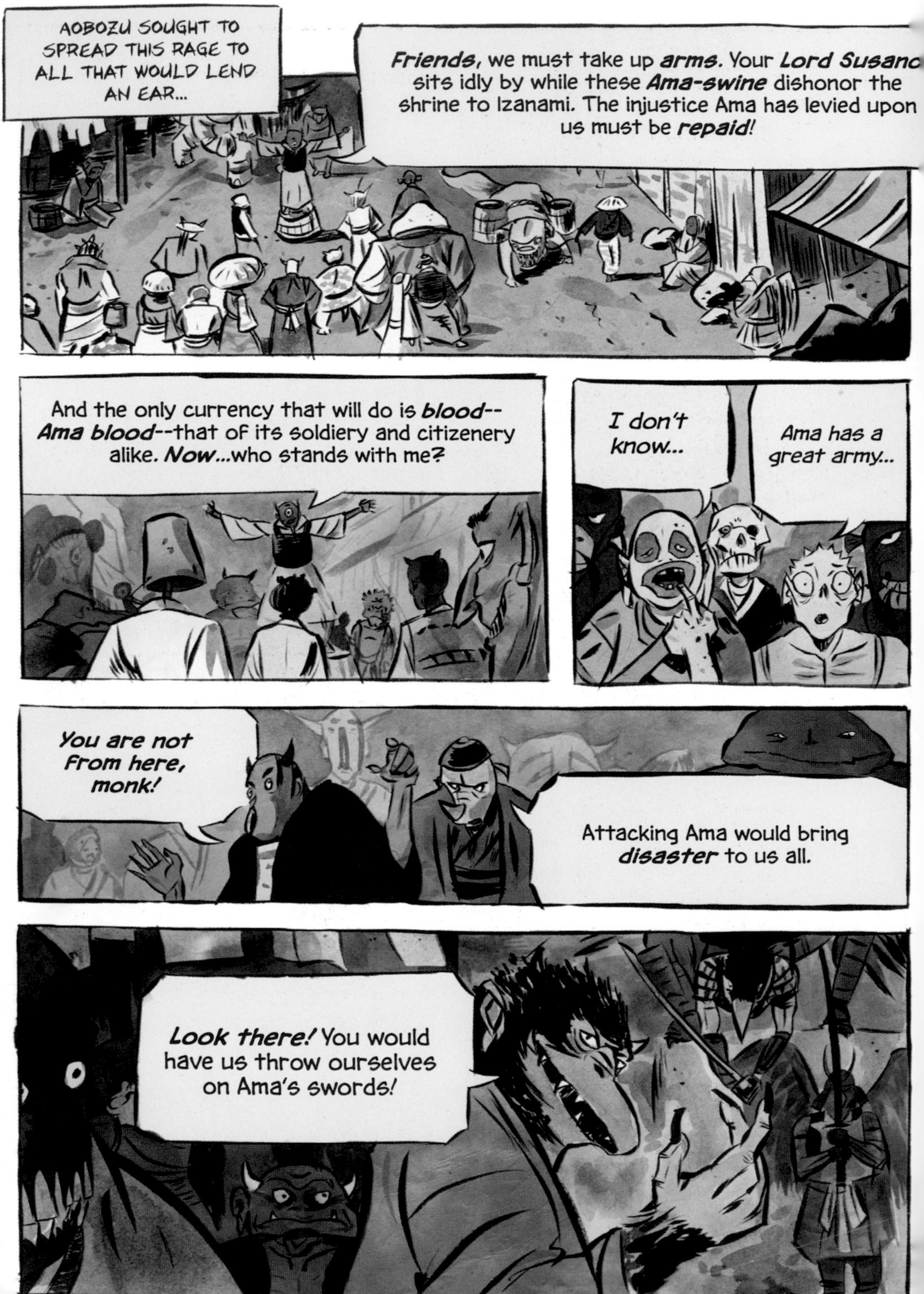
AOBOZU SOUGHT TO SPREAD THIS RAGE TO ALL THAT WOULD LEND AN EAR...
Friends, we must take up *arms*. Your *Lord Susano* sits idly by while these *Ama-swine* dishonor the shrine to Izanami. The injustice Ama has levied upon us must be *repaid*!
And the only currency that will do is *blood*--*Ama blood*--that of its soldiery and citizenery alike. *Now*...who stands with me?
I don't know...
Ama has a great army...
You are not from here, monk!
Attacking Ama would bring *disaster* to us all.
Look there! You would have us throw ourselves on Ama's swords!

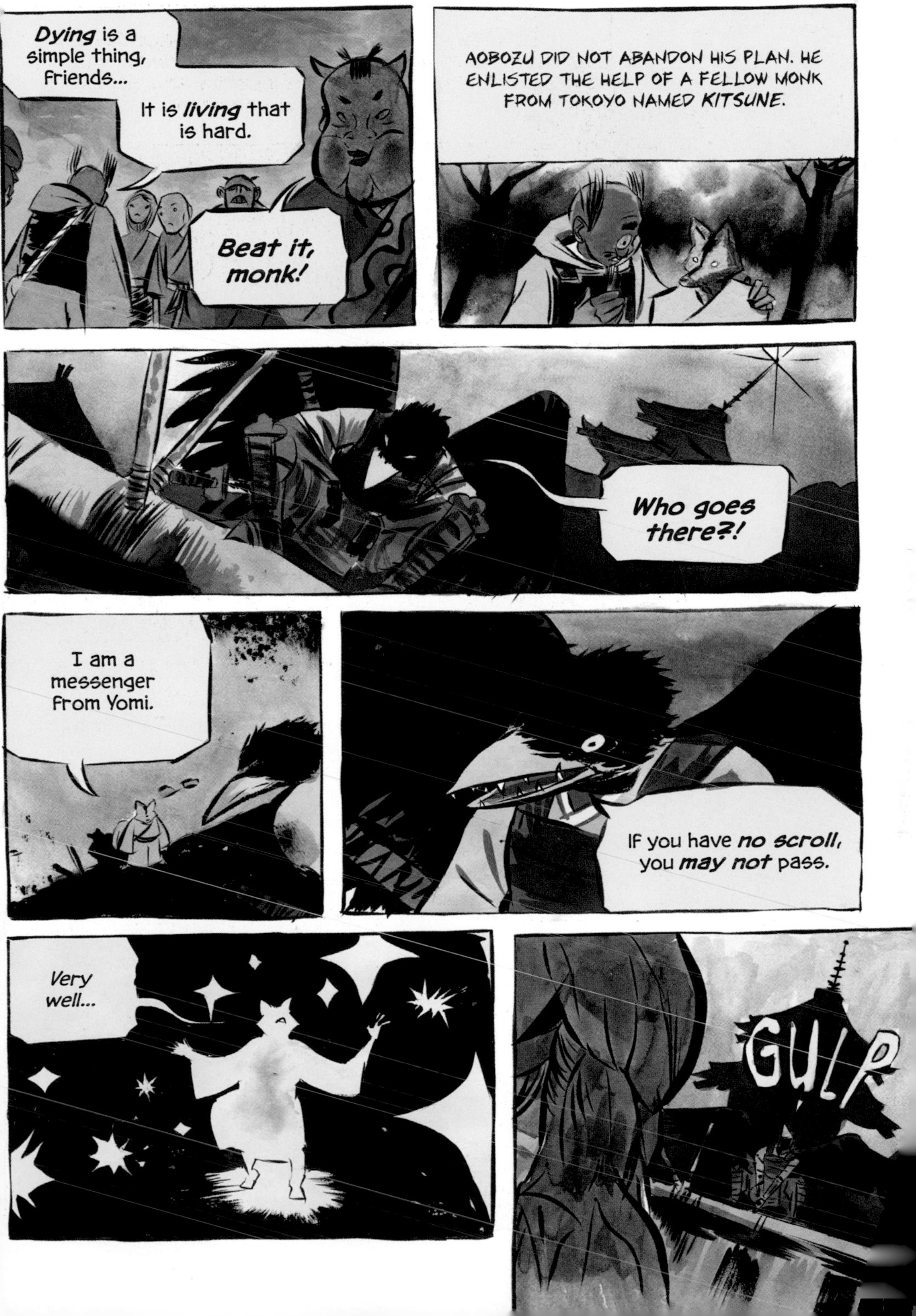
Dying is a simple thing, friends...
It is living that is hard.
Beat it, monk!
AOBOZU DID NOT ABANDON HIS PLAN. HE ENLISTED THE HELP OF A FELLOW MONK FROM TOKOYO NAMED KITSUNE.
Who goes there?!
I am a messenger from Yomi.
If you have no scroll, you may not pass.
Very well...
GULP

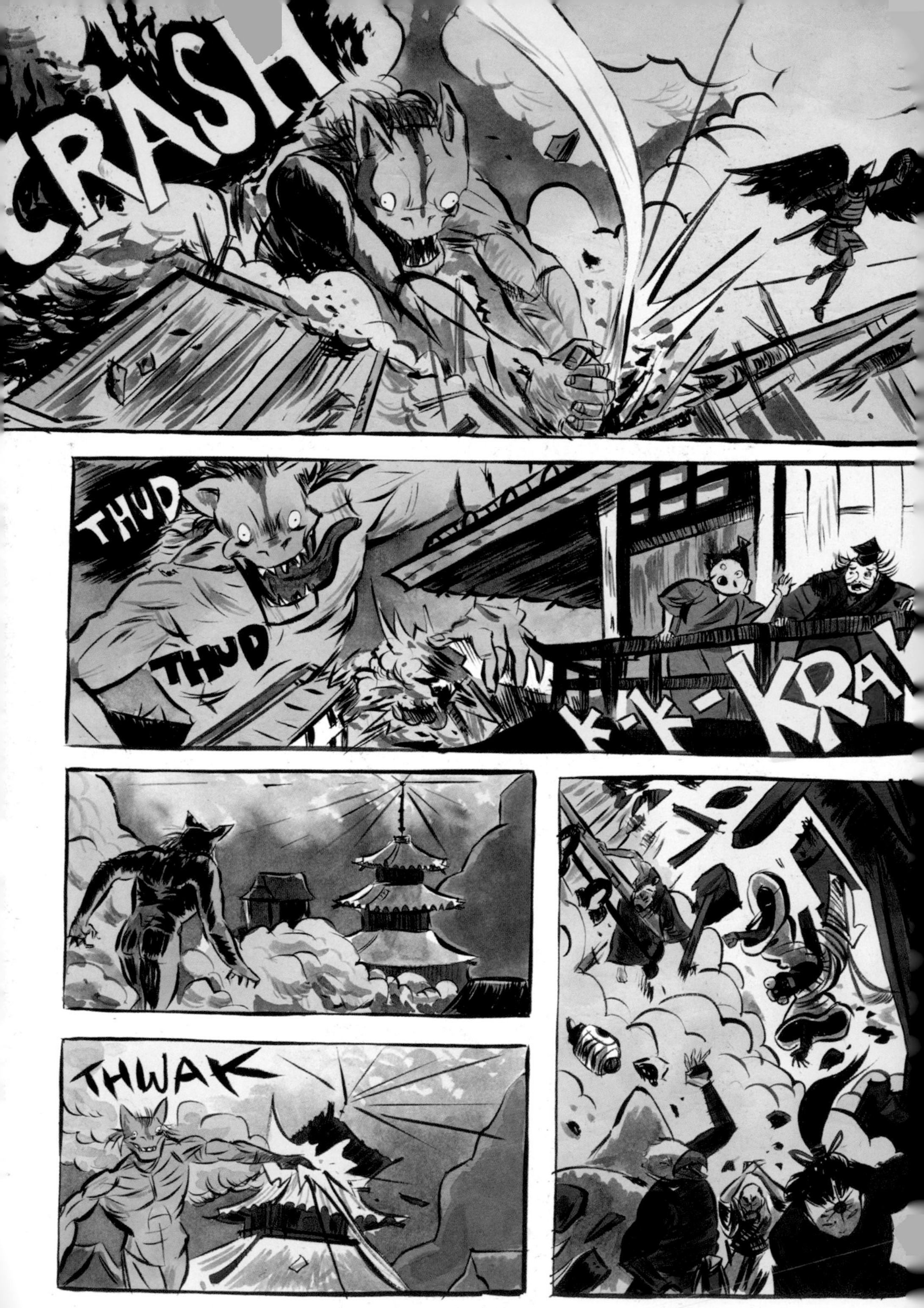
CRASH
THUD
THUD
K-K-KRA
THWAK

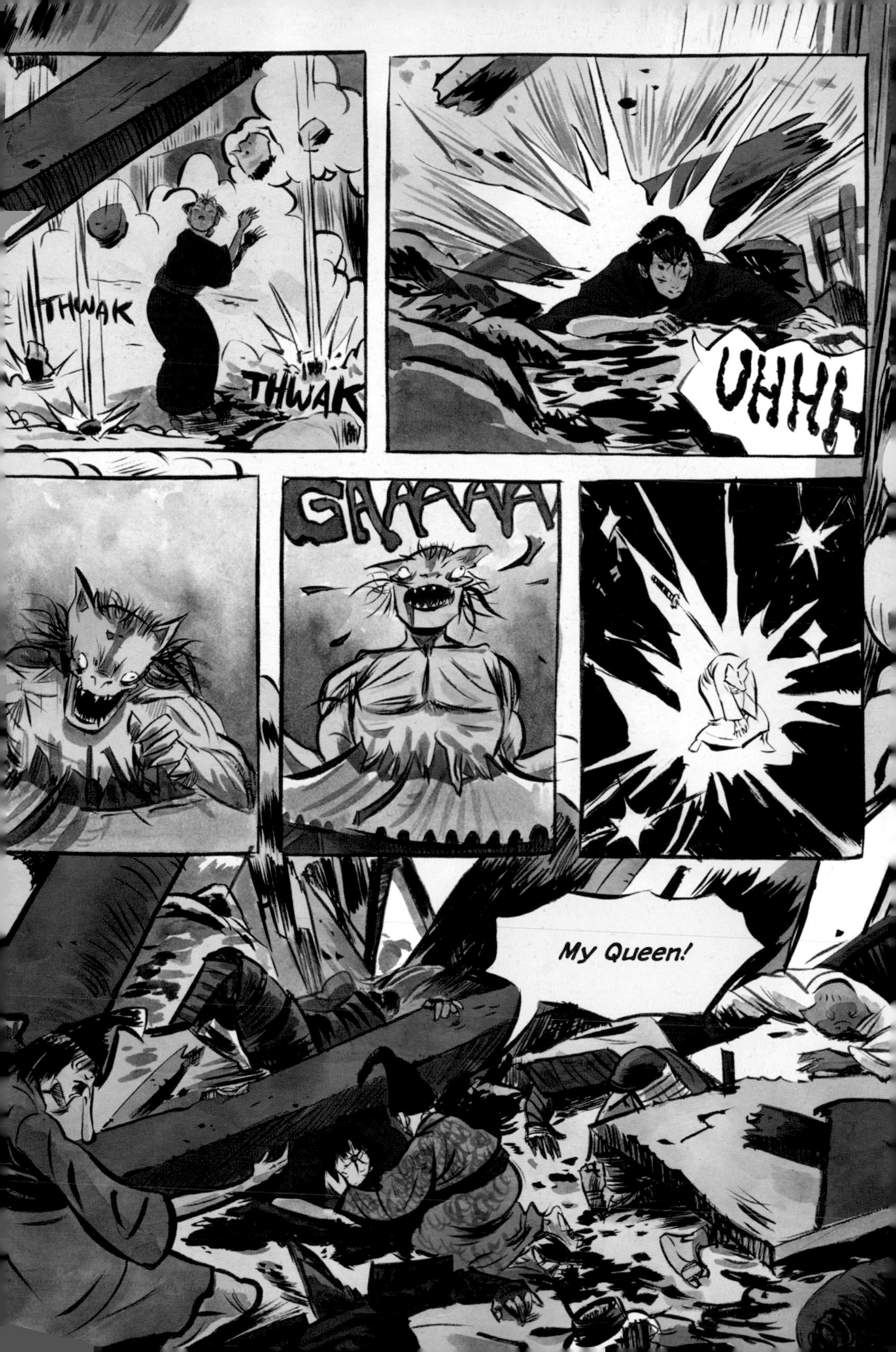
THWAK
THWAK
UHHH
GAAAAA
My Queen!

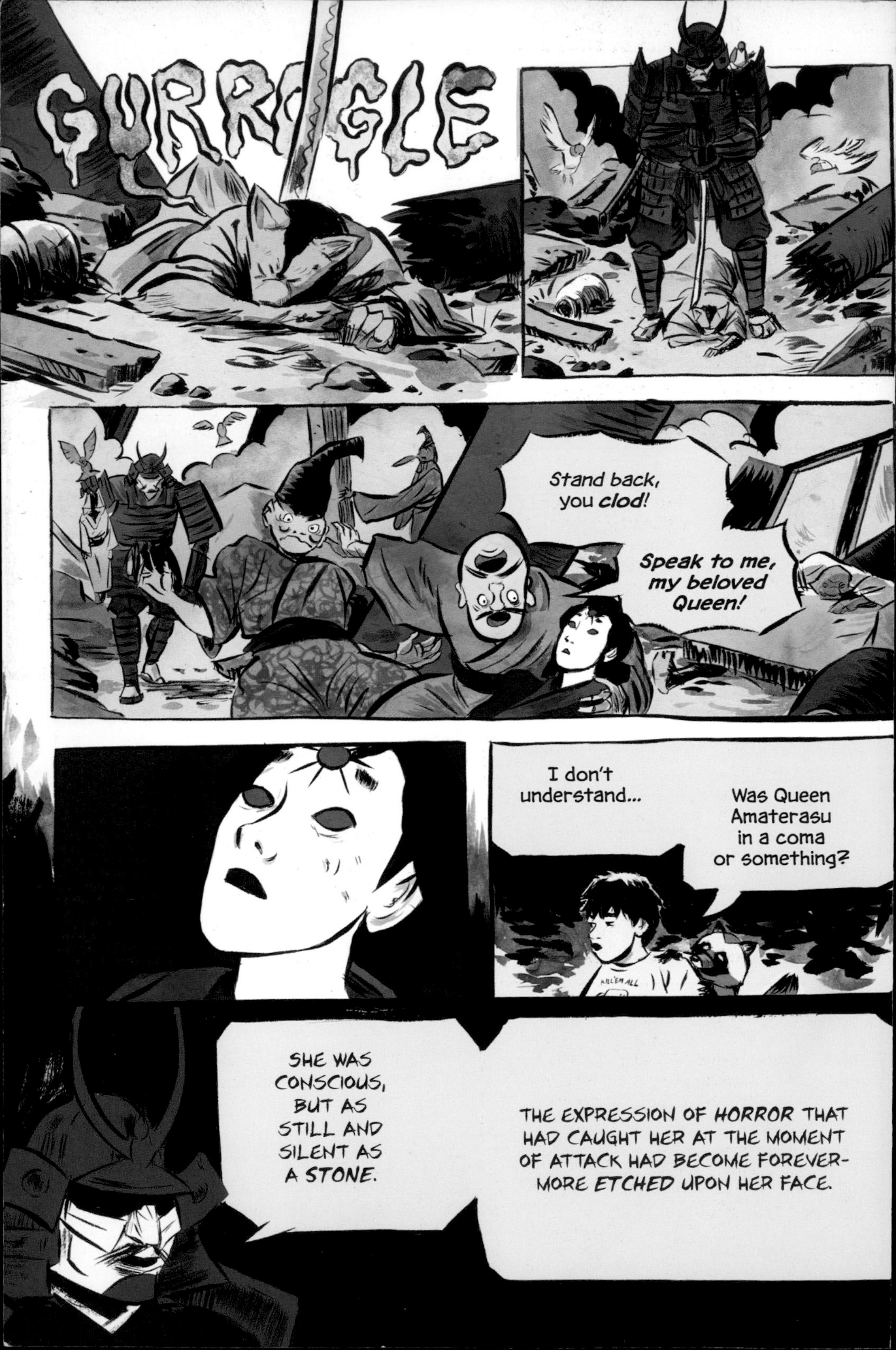
GURRGGLE
Stand back, you clod!
Speak to me, my beloved Queen!
I don't understand...
Was Queen Amaterasu in a coma or something?
SHE WAS CONSCIOUS, BUT AS STILL AND SILENT AS A STONE.
THE EXPRESSION OF HORROR THAT HAD CAUGHT HER AT THE MOMENT OF ATTACK HAD BECOME FOREVERMORE ETCHED UPON HER FACE.

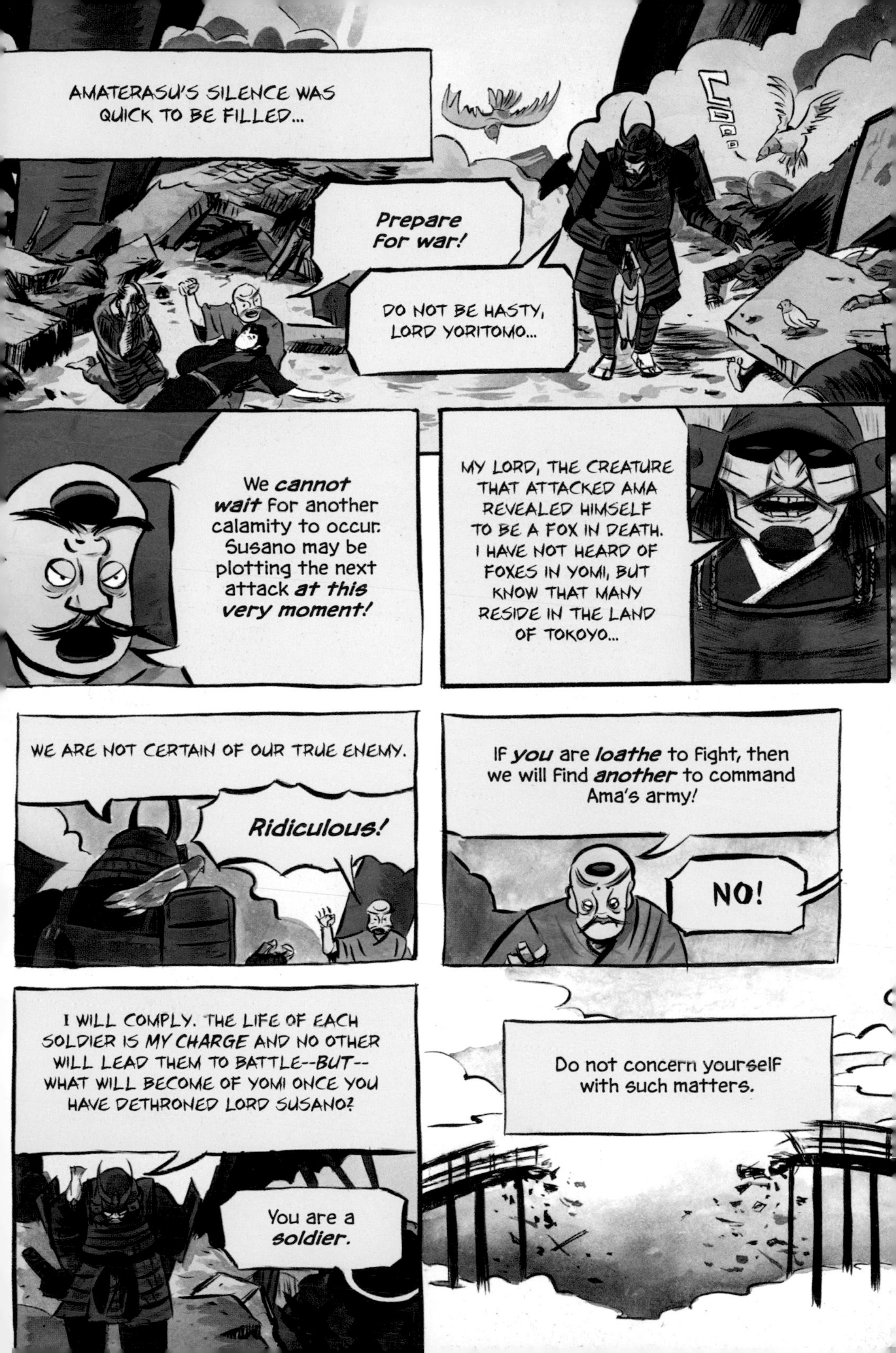
AMATERASU'S SILENCE WAS QUICK TO BE FILLED...
Prepare for war!
DO NOT BE HASTY, LORD YORITOMO...
We *cannot wait* for another calamity to occur. Susano may be plotting the next attack *at this very moment!*
MY LORD, THE CREATURE THAT ATTACKED AMA REVEALED HIMSELF TO BE A FOX IN DEATH. I HAVE NOT HEARD OF FOXES IN YOMI, BUT KNOW THAT MANY RESIDE IN THE LAND OF TOKOYO...
WE ARE NOT CERTAIN OF OUR TRUE ENEMY.
Ridiculous!
If *you* are *loathe* to fight, then we will find *another* to command Ama's army!
NO!
I WILL COMPLY. THE LIFE OF EACH SOLDIER IS *MY CHARGE* AND NO OTHER WILL LEAD THEM TO BATTLE--*BUT*--WHAT WILL BECOME OF YOMI ONCE YOU HAVE DETHRONED LORD SUSANO?
You are a *soldier*.
Do not concern yourself with such matters.

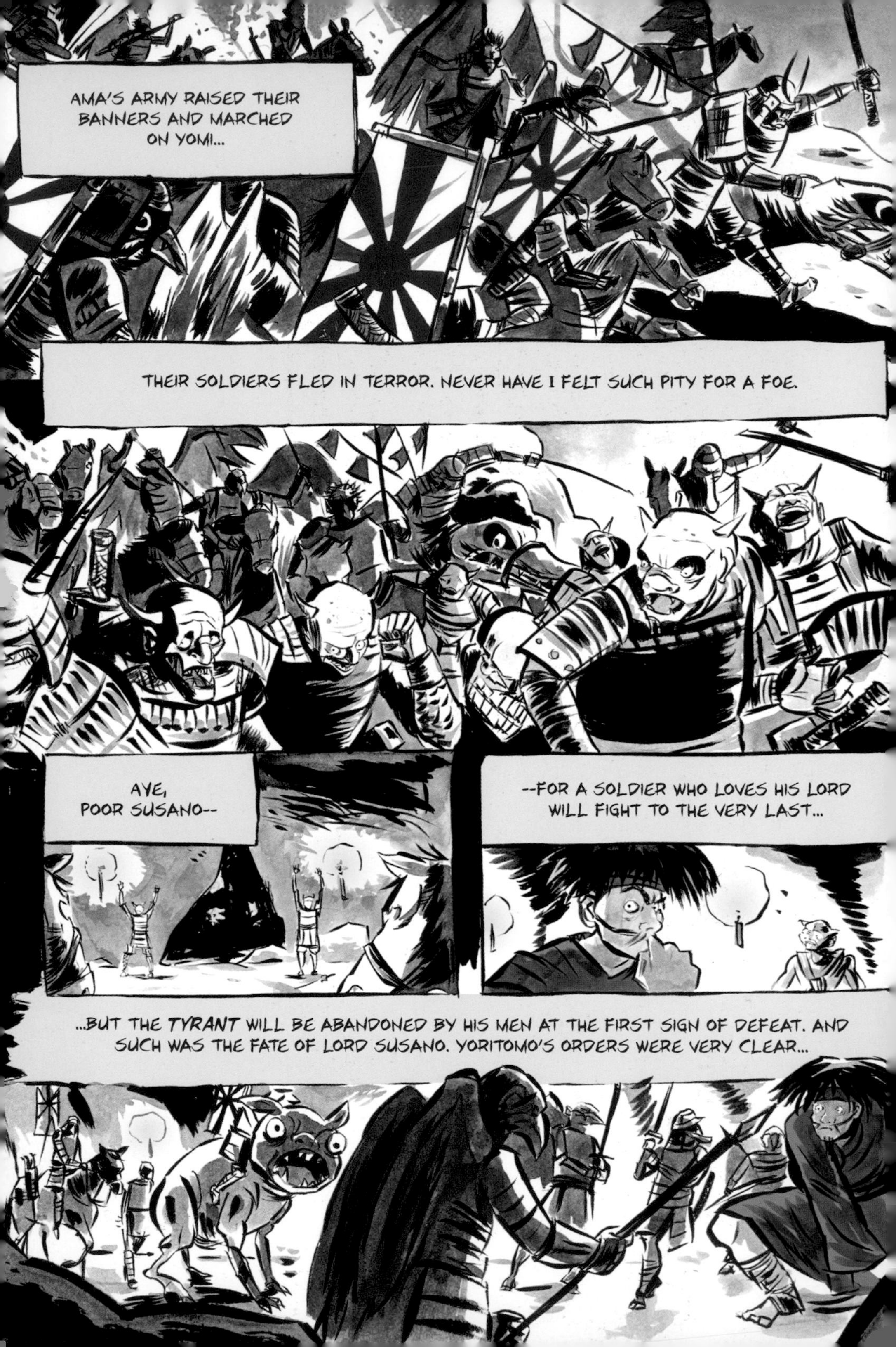
AMA'S ARMY RAISED THEIR BANNERS AND MARCHED ON YOMI...
THEIR SOLDIERS FLED IN TERROR. NEVER HAVE I FELT SUCH PITY FOR A FOE.
AYE, POOR SUSANO--
--FOR A SOLDIER WHO LOVES HIS LORD WILL FIGHT TO THE VERY LAST...
...BUT THE *TYRANT* WILL BE ABANDONED BY HIS MEN AT THE FIRST SIGN OF DEFEAT. AND SUCH WAS THE FATE OF LORD SUSANO. YORITOMO'S ORDERS WERE VERY CLEAR...

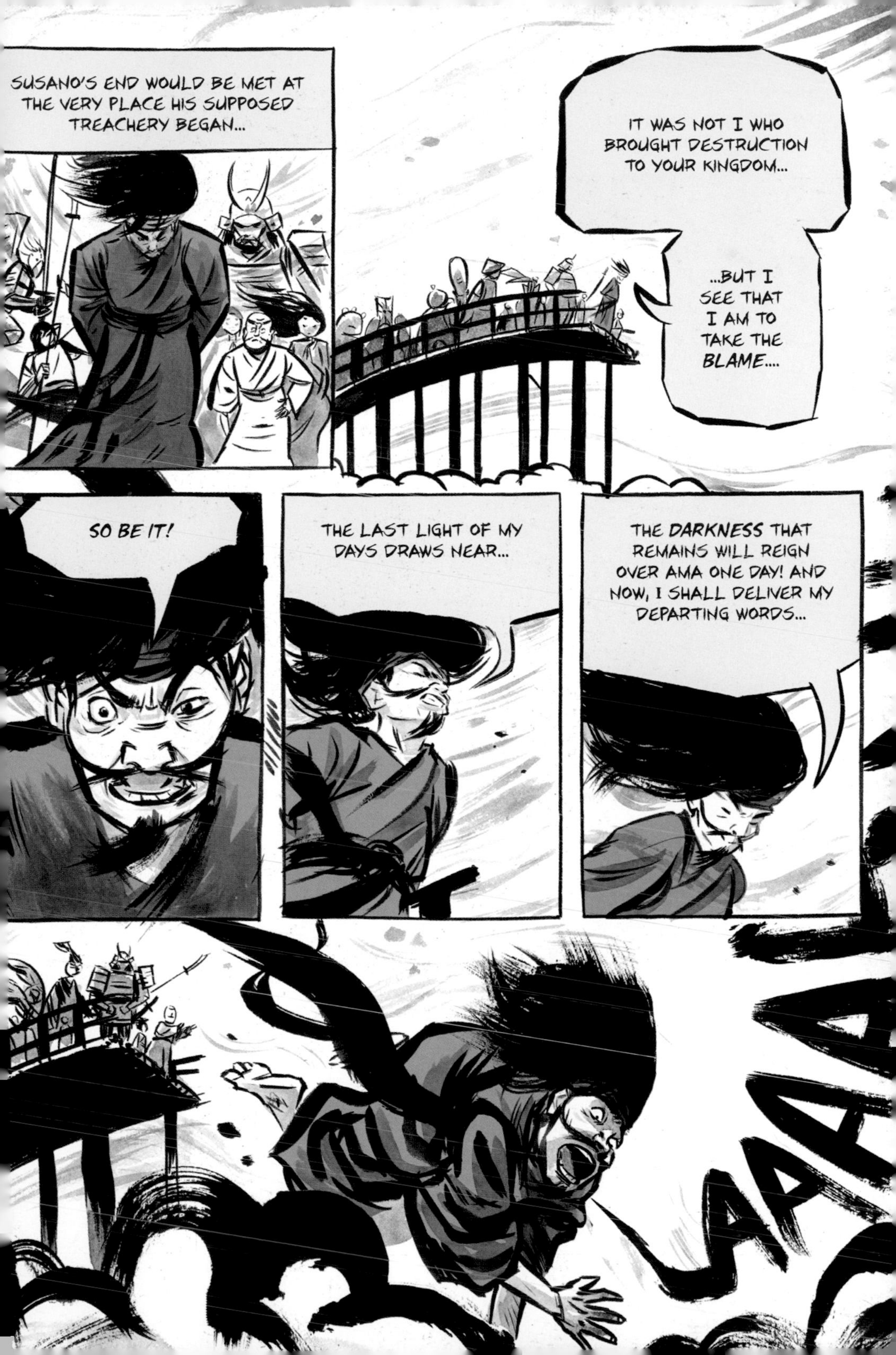

SUSANO'S END WOULD BE MET AT THE VERY PLACE HIS SUPPOSED TREACHERY BEGAN...
IT WAS NOT I WHO BROUGHT DESTRUCTION TO YOUR KINGDOM...
...BUT I SEE THAT I AM TO TAKE THE *BLAME*....
SO *BE IT!*
THE LAST LIGHT OF MY DAYS DRAWS NEAR...
THE *DARKNESS* THAT REMAINS WILL REIGN OVER AMA ONE DAY! AND NOW, I SHALL DELIVER MY DEPARTING WORDS...
AAAAA

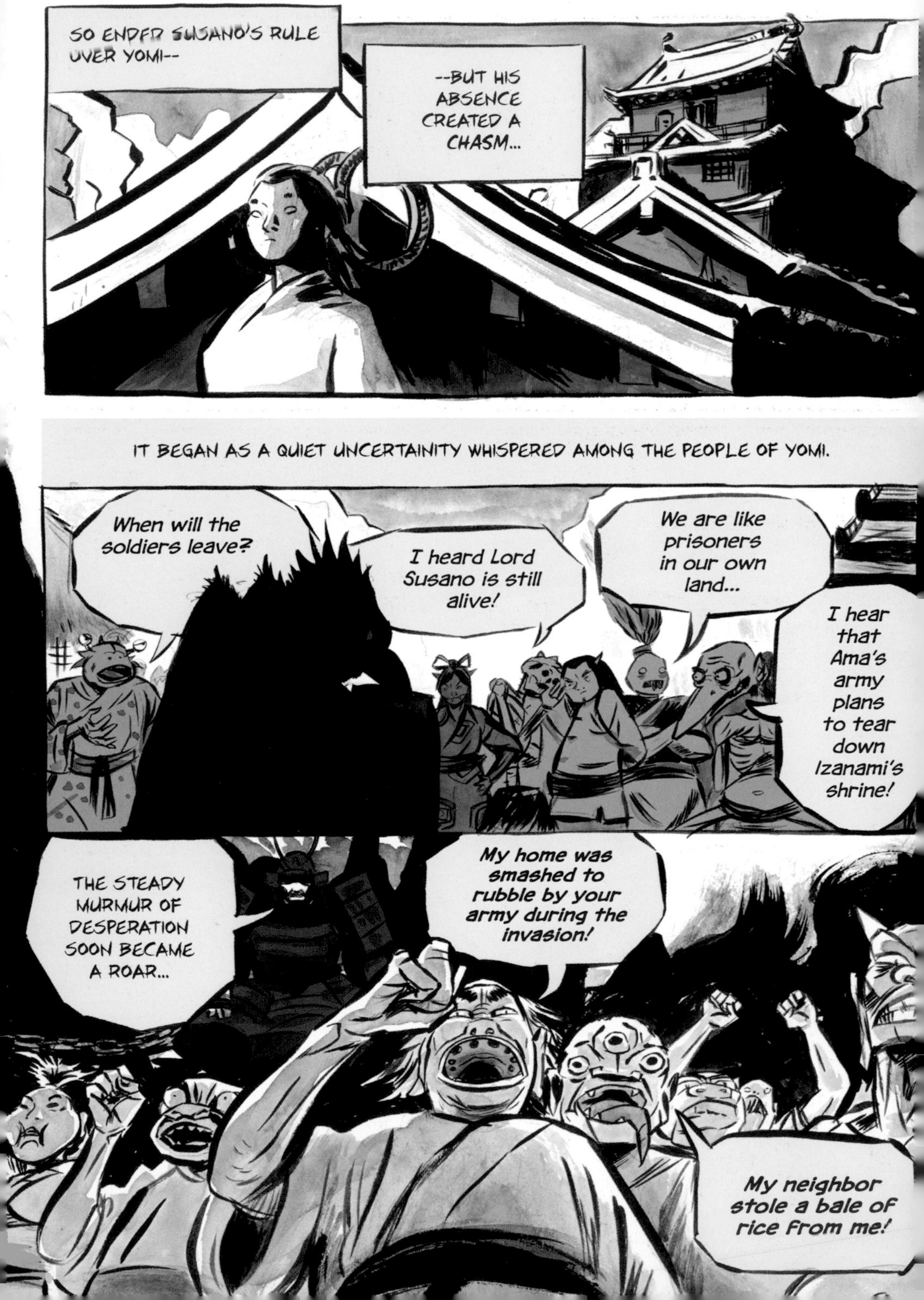
SO ENDED SUSANO'S RULE OVER YOMI--
--BUT HIS ABSENCE CREATED A CHASM...
IT BEGAN AS A QUIET UNCERTAINITY WHISPERED AMONG THE PEOPLE OF YOMI.
When will the soldiers leave?
I heard Lord Susano is still alive!
We are like prisoners in our own land...
I hear that Ama's army plans to tear down Izanami's shrine!
THE STEADY MURMUR OF DESPERATION SOON BECAME A ROAR...
My home was smashed to rubble by your army during the invasion!
My neighbor stole a bale of rice from me!

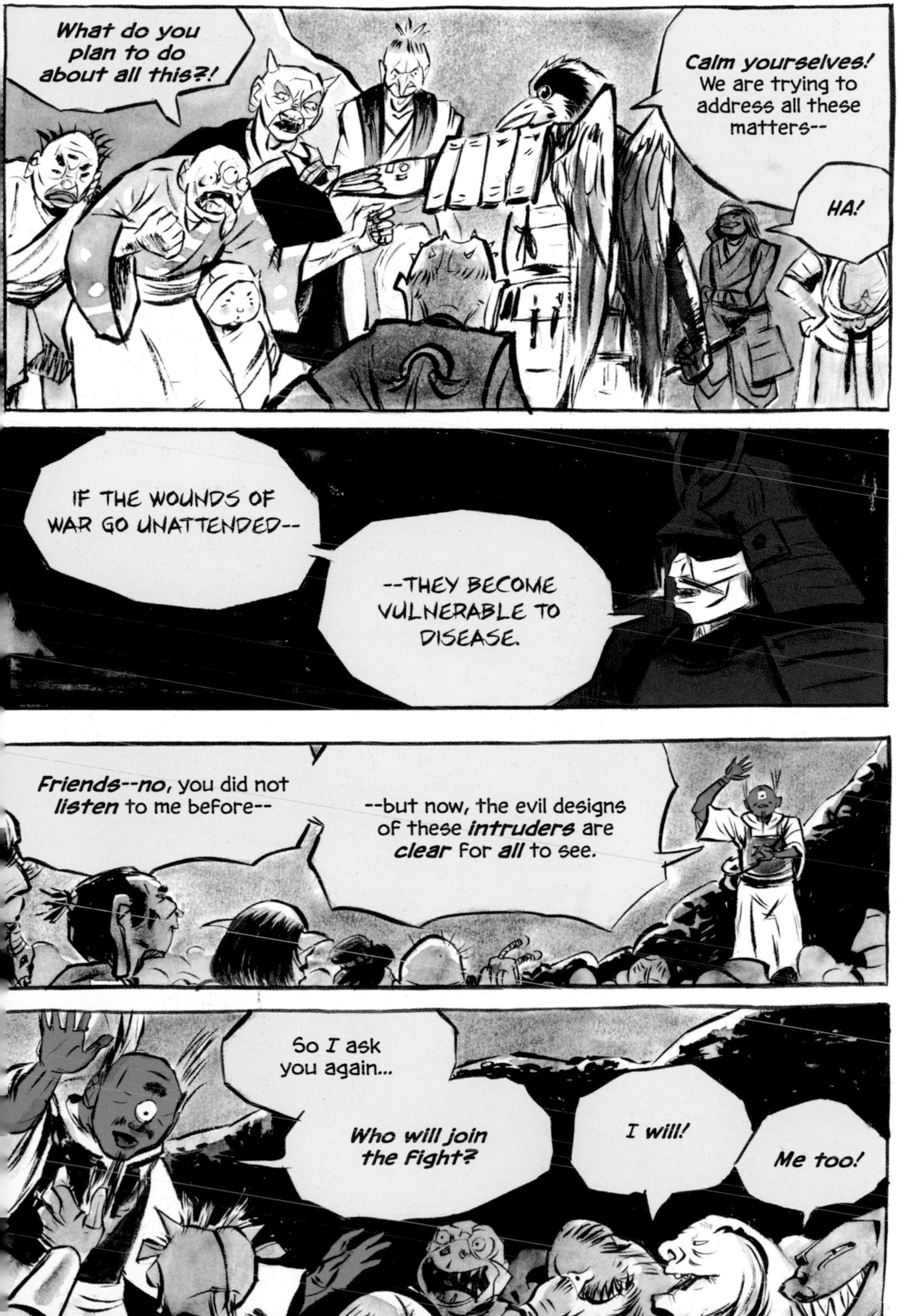
What do you plan to do about all this?!
Calm yourselves! We are trying to address all these matters--
HA!
IF THE WOUNDS OF WAR GO UNATTENDED--
--THEY BECOME VULNERABLE TO DISEASE.
Friends--no, you did not listen to me before--
--but now, the evil designs of these intruders are clear for all to see.
So I ask you again...
Who will join the fight?
I will!
Me too!

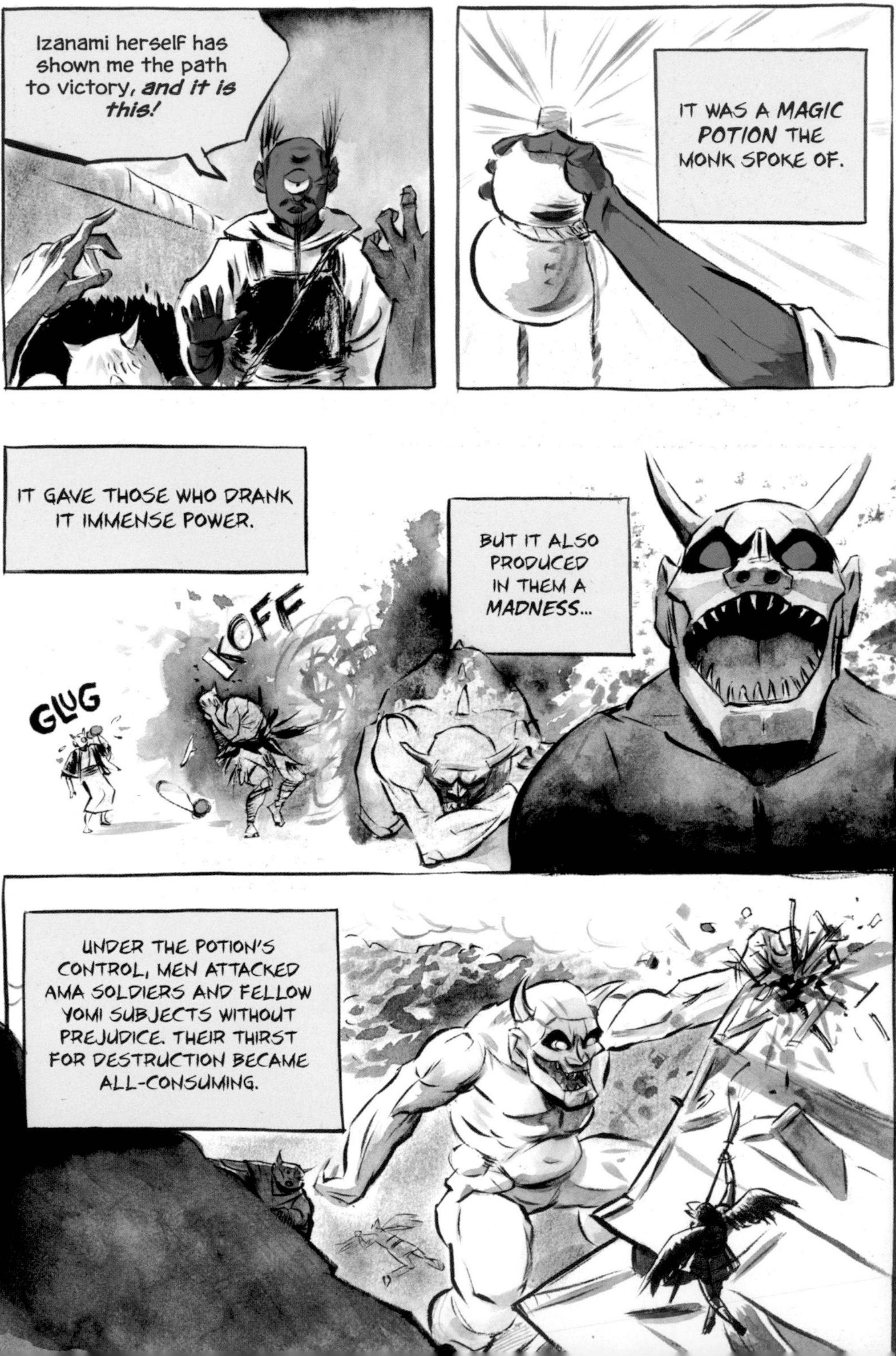
Izanami herself has shown me the path to victory, *and it is this!*
IT WAS A *MAGIC POTION* THE MONK SPOKE OF.
IT GAVE THOSE WHO DRANK IT IMMENSE POWER.
GLUG
KOFF
BUT IT ALSO PRODUCED IN THEM A *MADNESS*...
UNDER THE POTION'S CONTROL, MEN ATTACKED AMA SOLDIERS AND FELLOW YOMI SUBJECTS WITHOUT PREJUDICE. THEIR THIRST FOR DESTRUCTION BECAME ALL-CONSUMING.

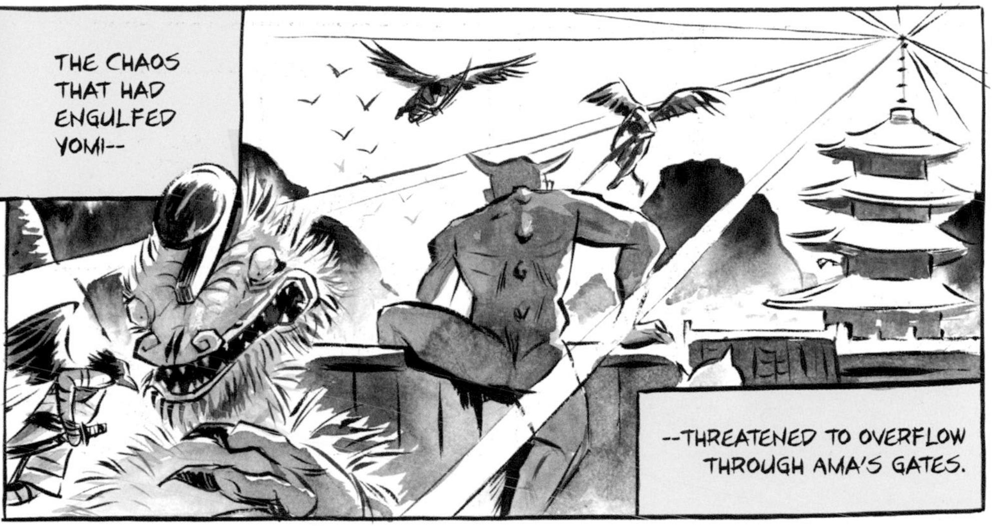
THE CHAOS THAT HAD ENGULFED YOMI--
--THREATENED TO OVERFLOW THROUGH AMA'S GATES.

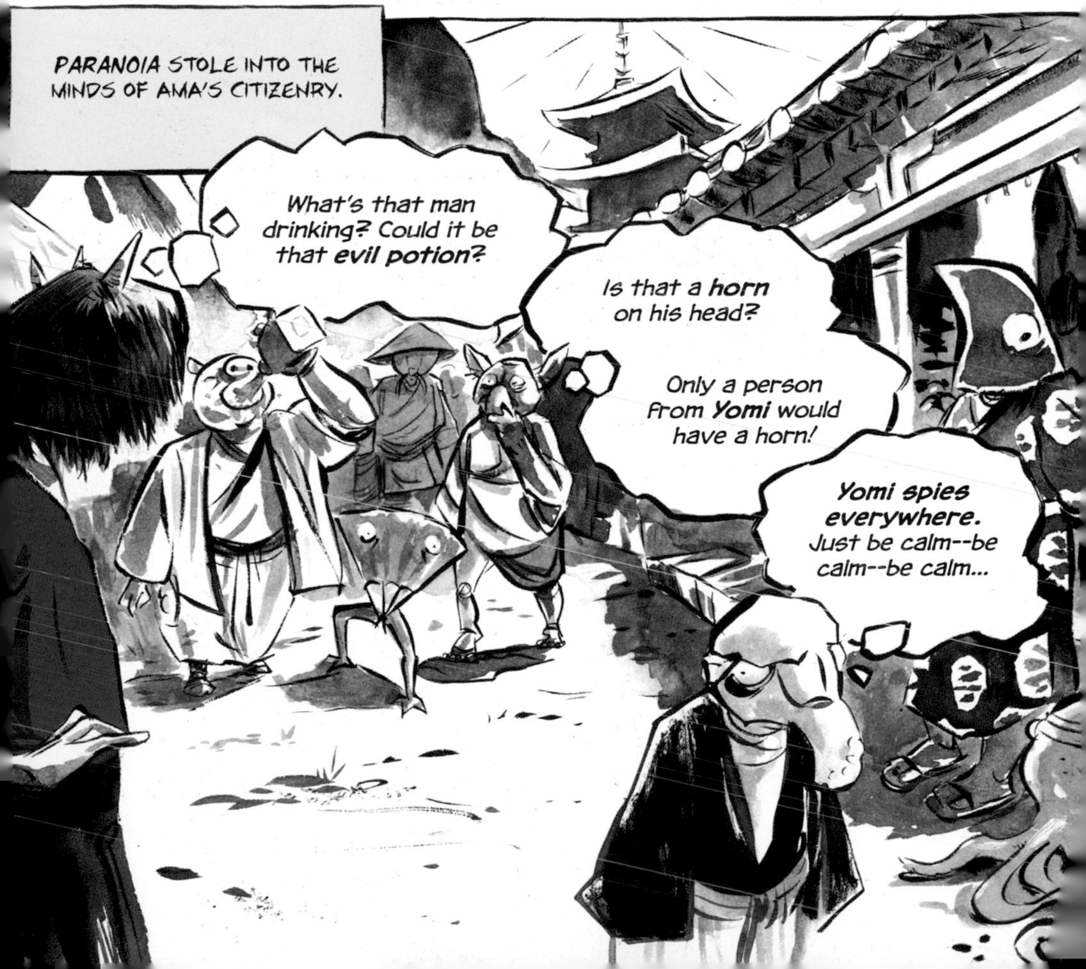
PARANOIA STOLE INTO THE MINDS OF AMA'S CITIZENRY.
What's that man drinking? Could it be that evil potion?
Is that a horn on his head?
Only a person from Yomi would have a horn!
Yomi spies everywhere. Just be calm--be calm--be calm...

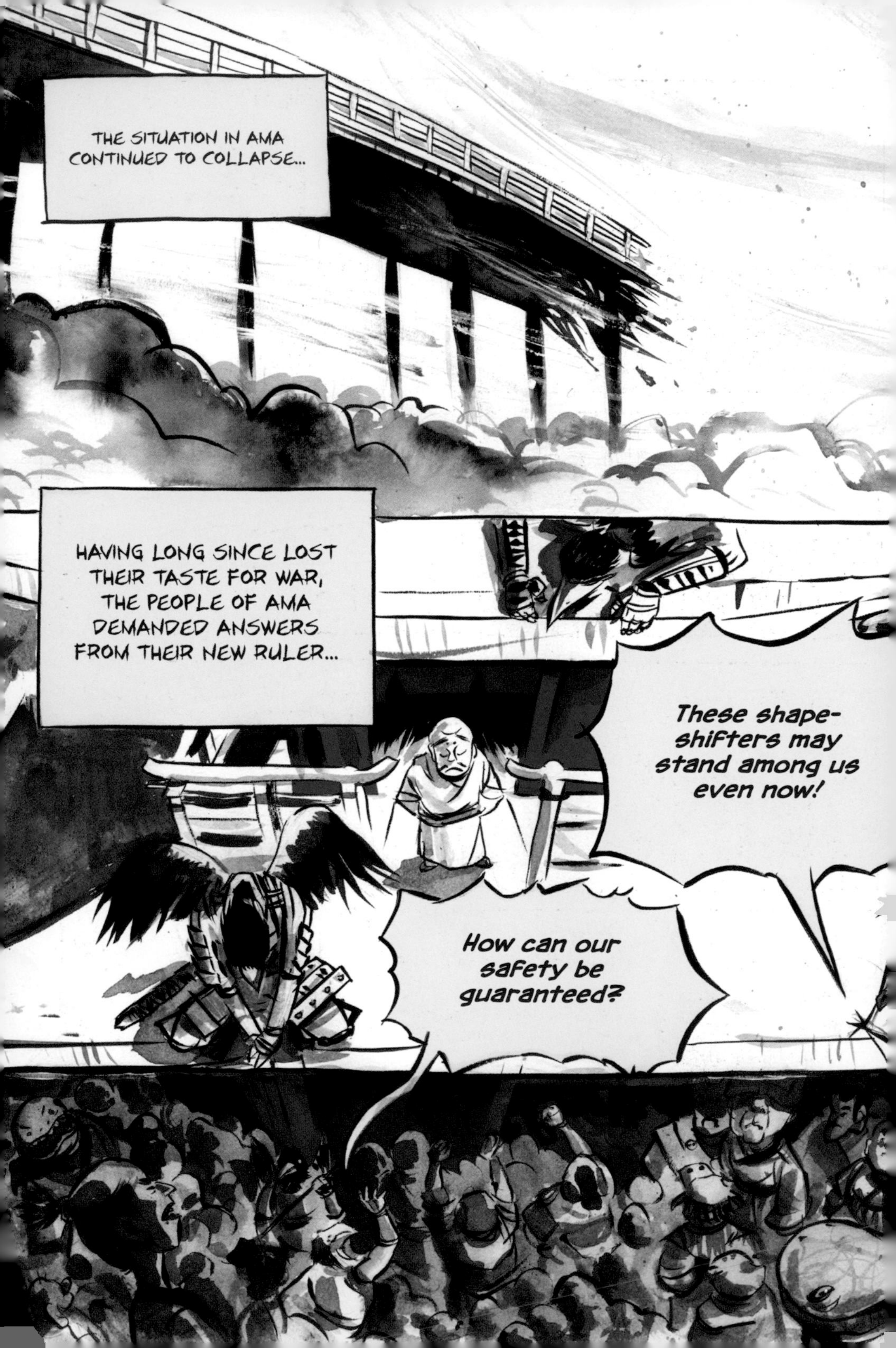
THE SITUATION IN AMA CONTINUED TO COLLAPSE...
HAVING LONG SINCE LOST THEIR TASTE FOR WAR, THE PEOPLE OF AMA DEMANDED ANSWERS FROM THEIR NEW RULER...
These shape-shifters may stand among us even now!
How can our safety be guaranteed?

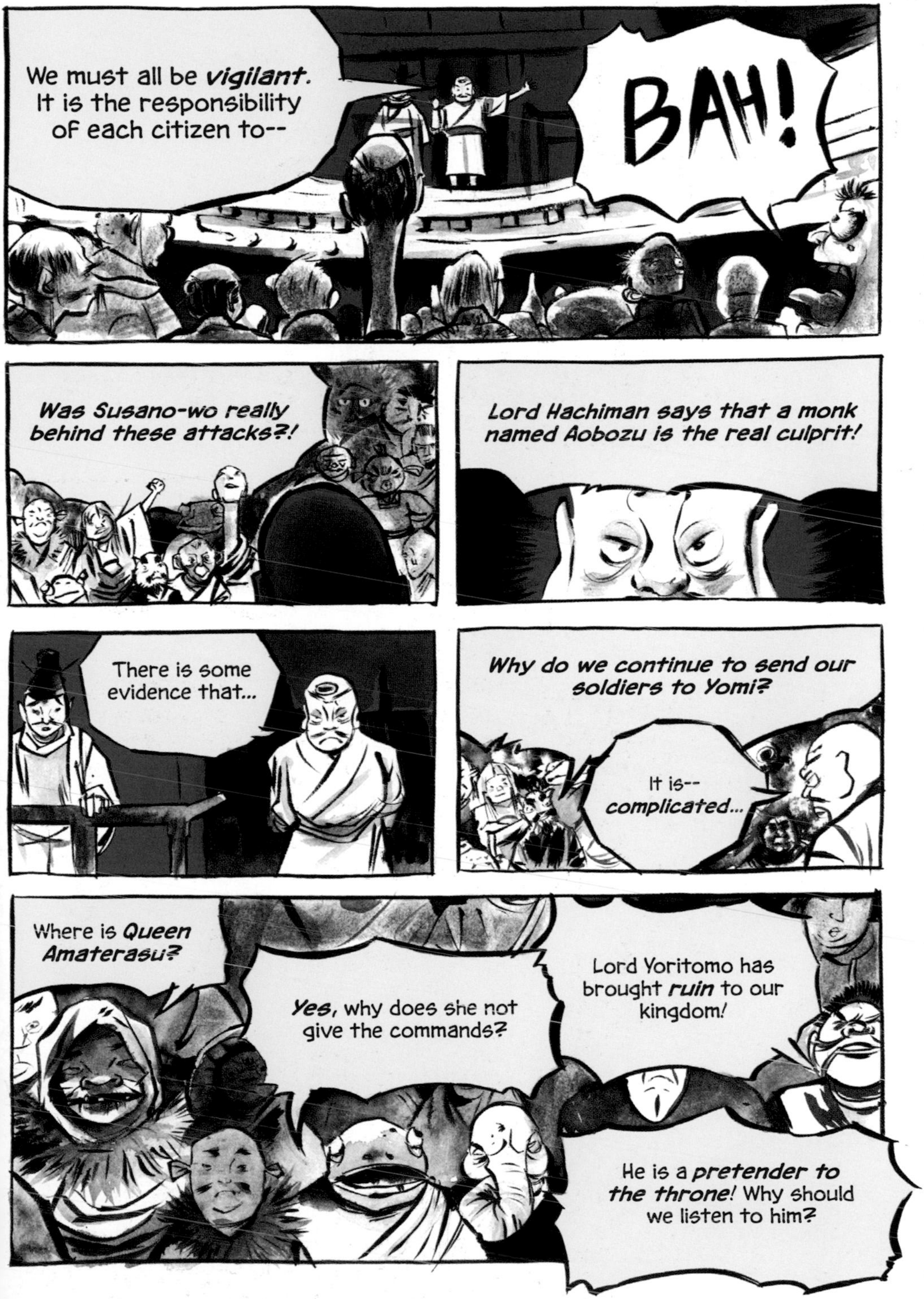
We must all be *vigilant.* It is the responsibility of each citizen to--
BAH!
Was Susano-wo really behind these attacks?!
Lord Hachiman says that a monk named Aobozu is the real culprit!
There is some evidence that...
Why do we continue to send our soldiers to Yomi?
It is-- *complicated...*
Where is *Queen Amaterasu?*
Yes, why does she not give the commands?
Lord Yoritomo has brought *ruin* to our kingdom!
He is a *pretender to the throne!* Why should we listen to him?

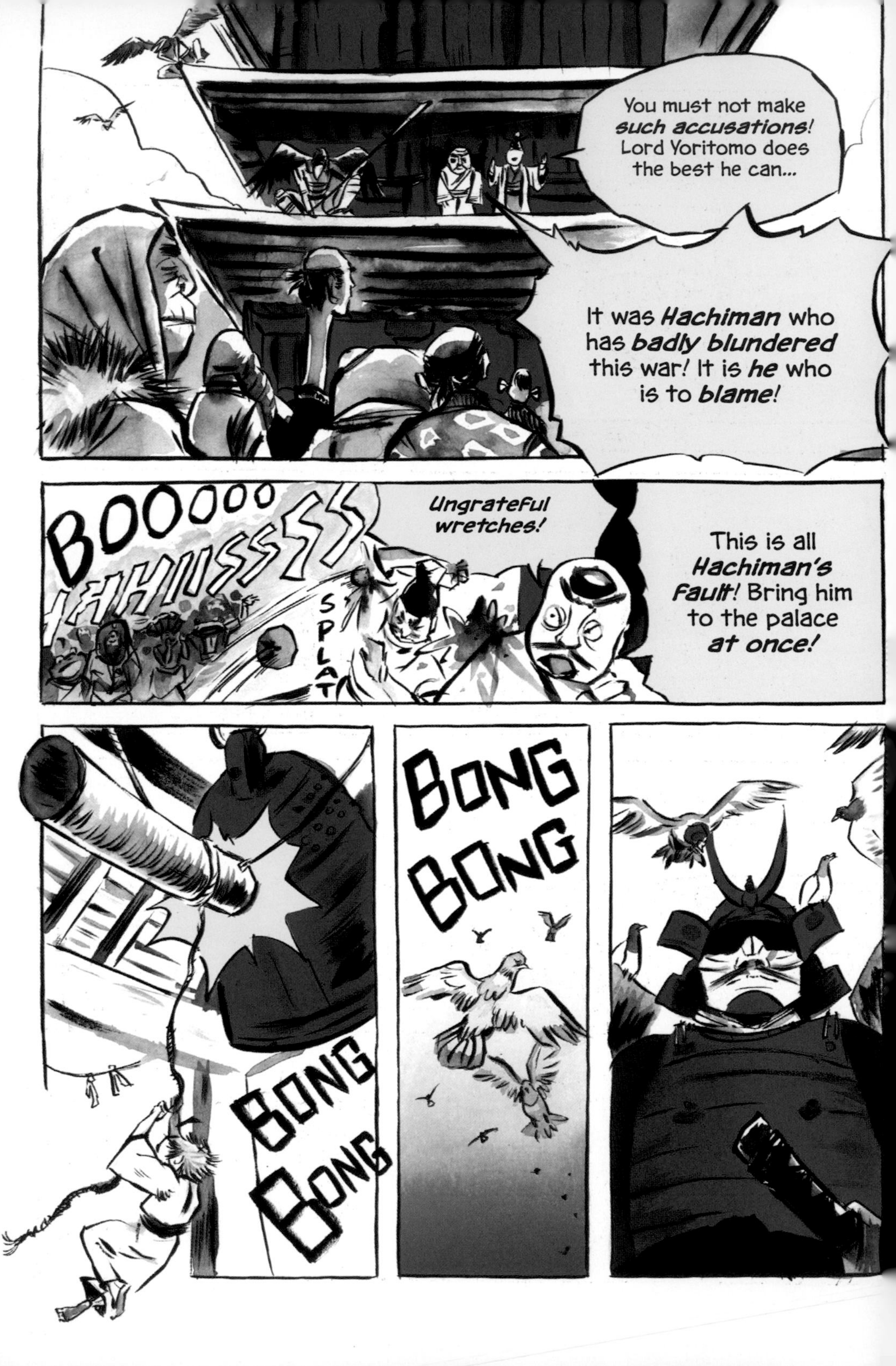
You must not make *such accusations*! Lord Yoritomo does the best he can...
It was *Hachiman* who has *badly blundered* this war! It is *he* who is to *blame*!
BOOOOOO
HHHISSSSS
Ungrateful wretches!
SPLAT
This is all *Hachiman's fault*! Bring him to the palace *at once!*
BONG
BONG
BONG
BONG

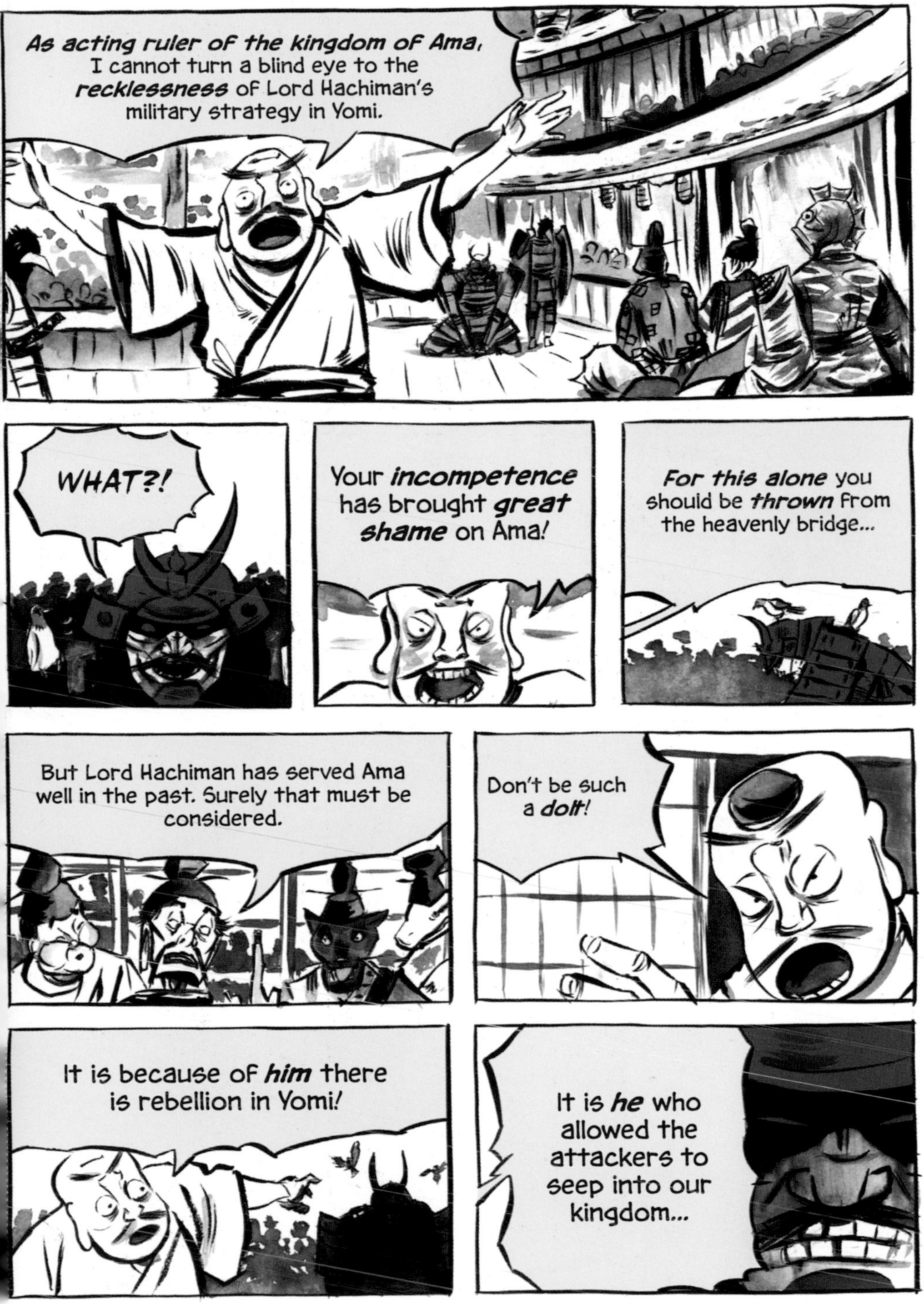
As acting ruler of the kingdom of Ama, I cannot turn a blind eye to the recklessness of Lord Hachiman's military strategy in Yomi.
WHAT?!
Your incompetence has brought great shame on Ama!
For this alone you should be thrown from the heavenly bridge...
But Lord Hachiman has served Ama well in the past. Surely that must be considered.
Don't be such a dolt!
It is because of him there is rebellion in Yomi!
It is he who allowed the attackers to seep into our kingdom...

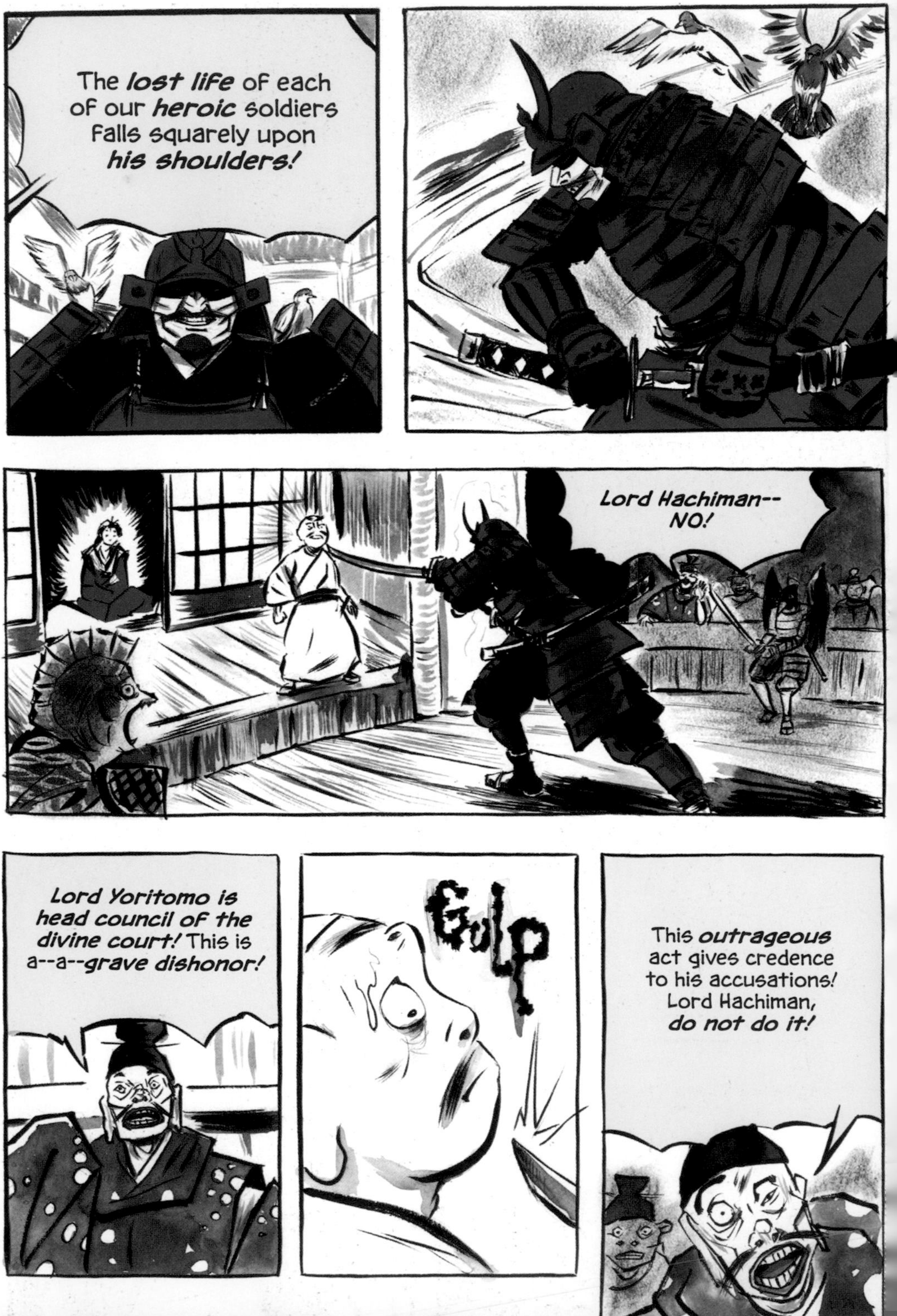

The *lost life* of each of our *heroic* soldiers falls squarely upon ***his shoulders!***
Lord Hachiman-- ***NO!***
Lord Yoritomo is head council of the divine court! This is a--a--***grave dishonor!***
Gulp
This ***outrageous*** act gives credence to his accusations! Lord Hachiman, ***do not do it!***

Whimper

Gulp...

Subdue Lord Hachiman! You will be *flung from the bridge* for this *outrage!*

I beg your pardon, my *great lord,* but--the court still must vote to decide Lord Hachiman's punishment.

Very well...

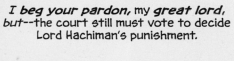

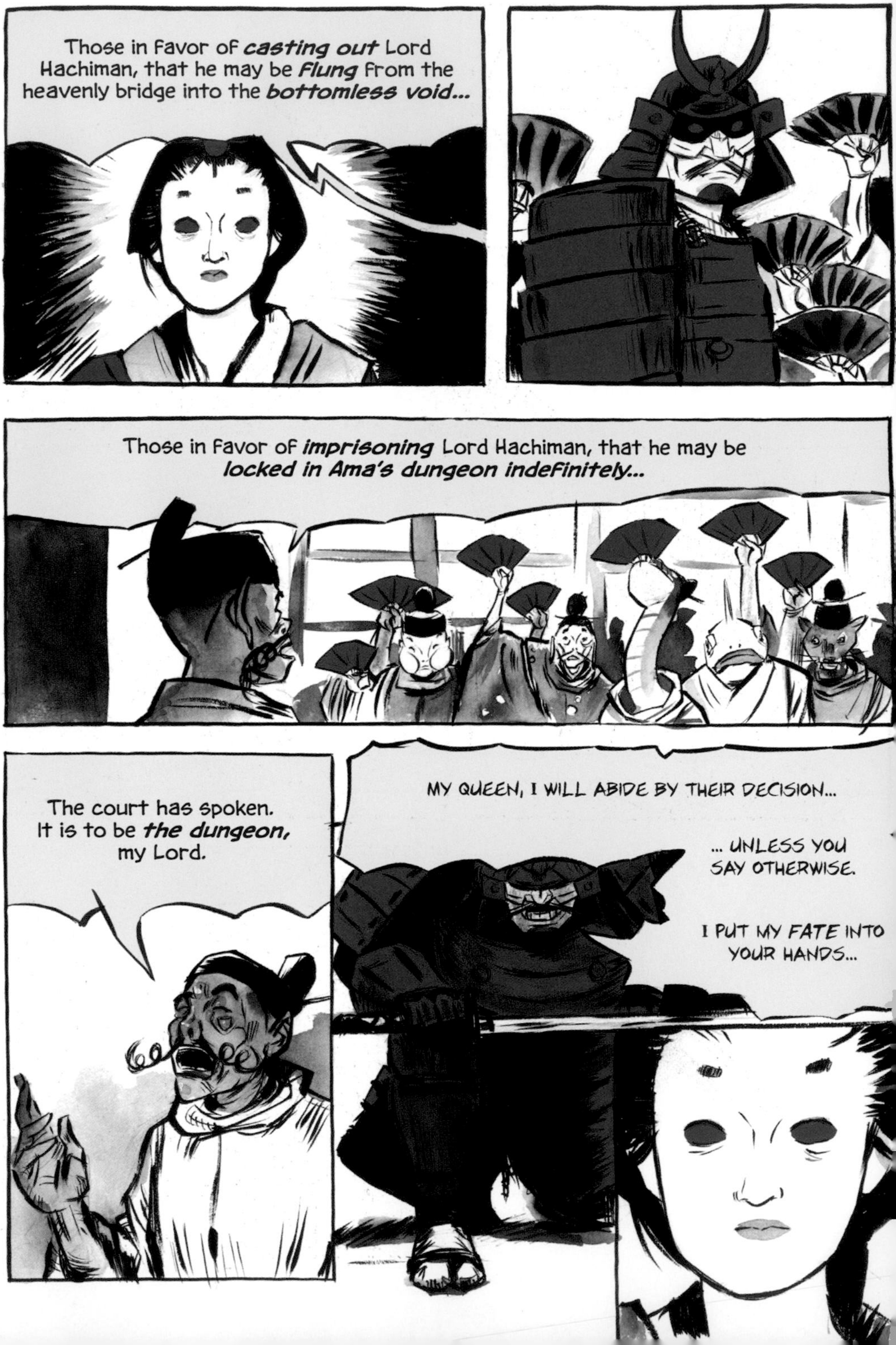

Those in favor of *casting out* Lord Hachiman, that he may be *flung* from the heavenly bridge into the *bottomless void...*
Those in favor of *imprisoning* Lord Hachiman, that he may be *locked in Ama's dungeon indefinitely...*
The court has spoken. It is to be *the dungeon,* my Lord.
MY QUEEN, I WILL ABIDE BY THEIR DECISION...
... UNLESS YOU SAY OTHERWISE.
I PUT MY *FATE* INTO YOUR HANDS...

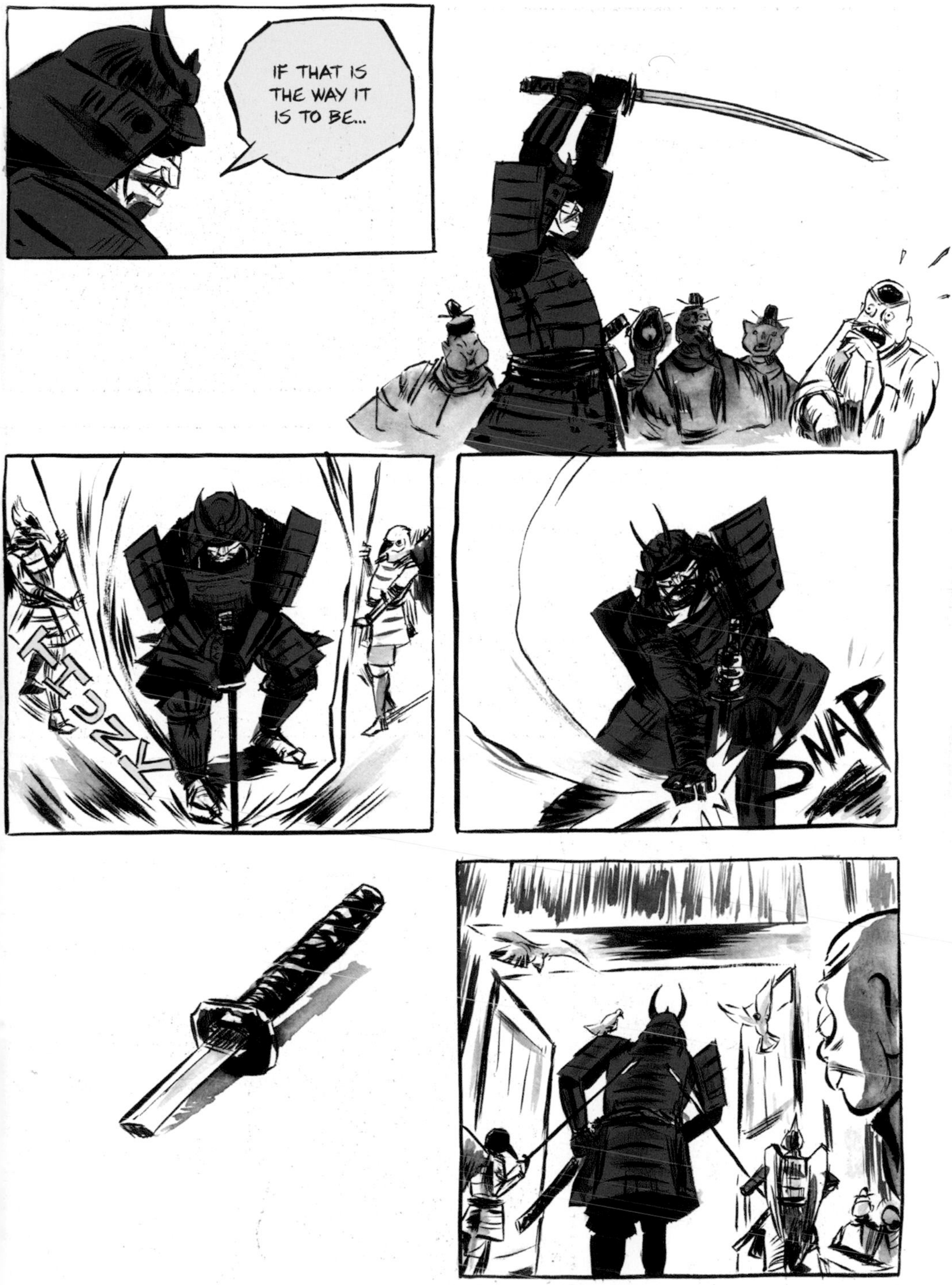
IF THAT IS THE WAY IT IS TO BE...
THUNK
SNAP

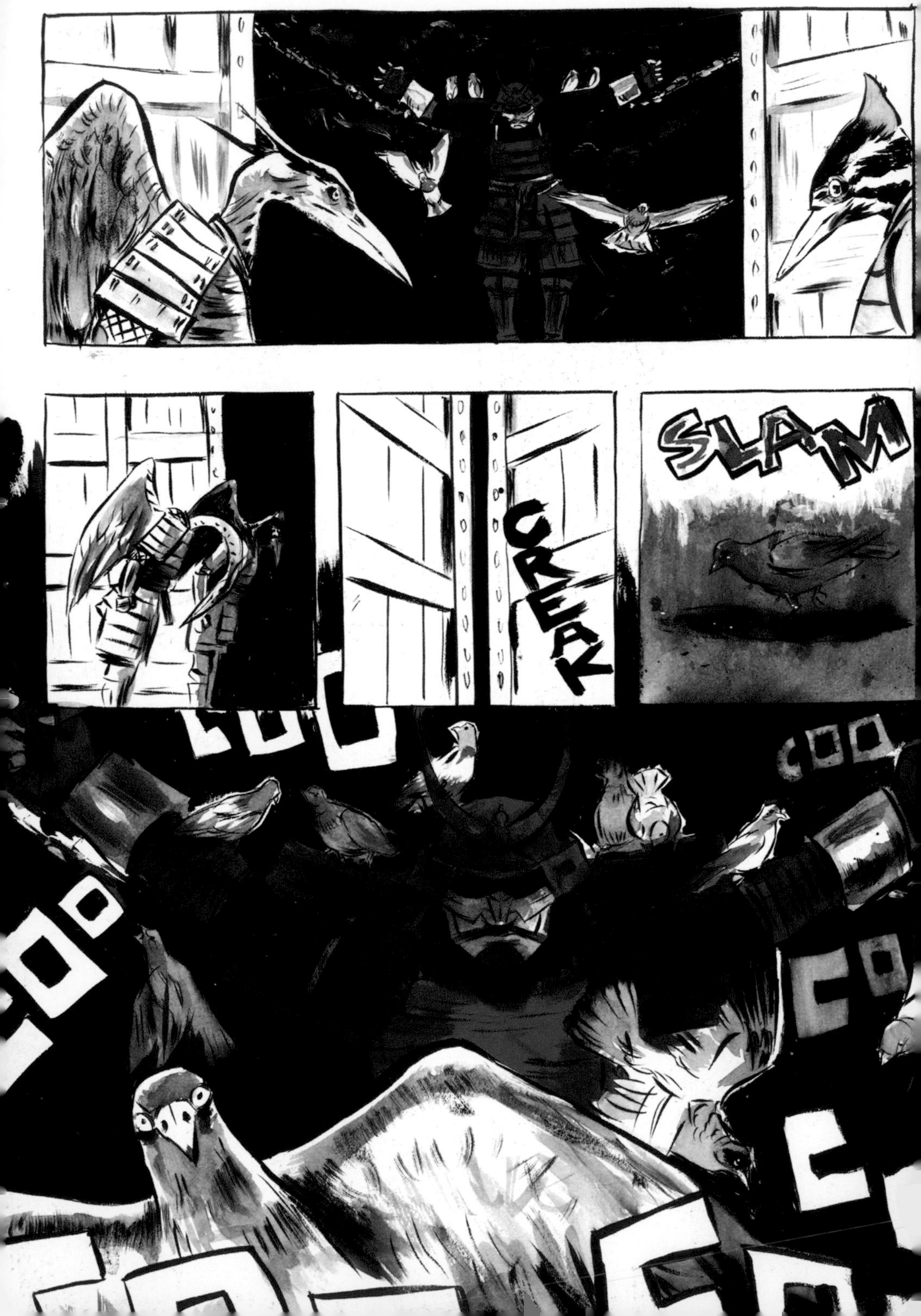
CREAK
SLAM
COO
COO
COO
COO
COO

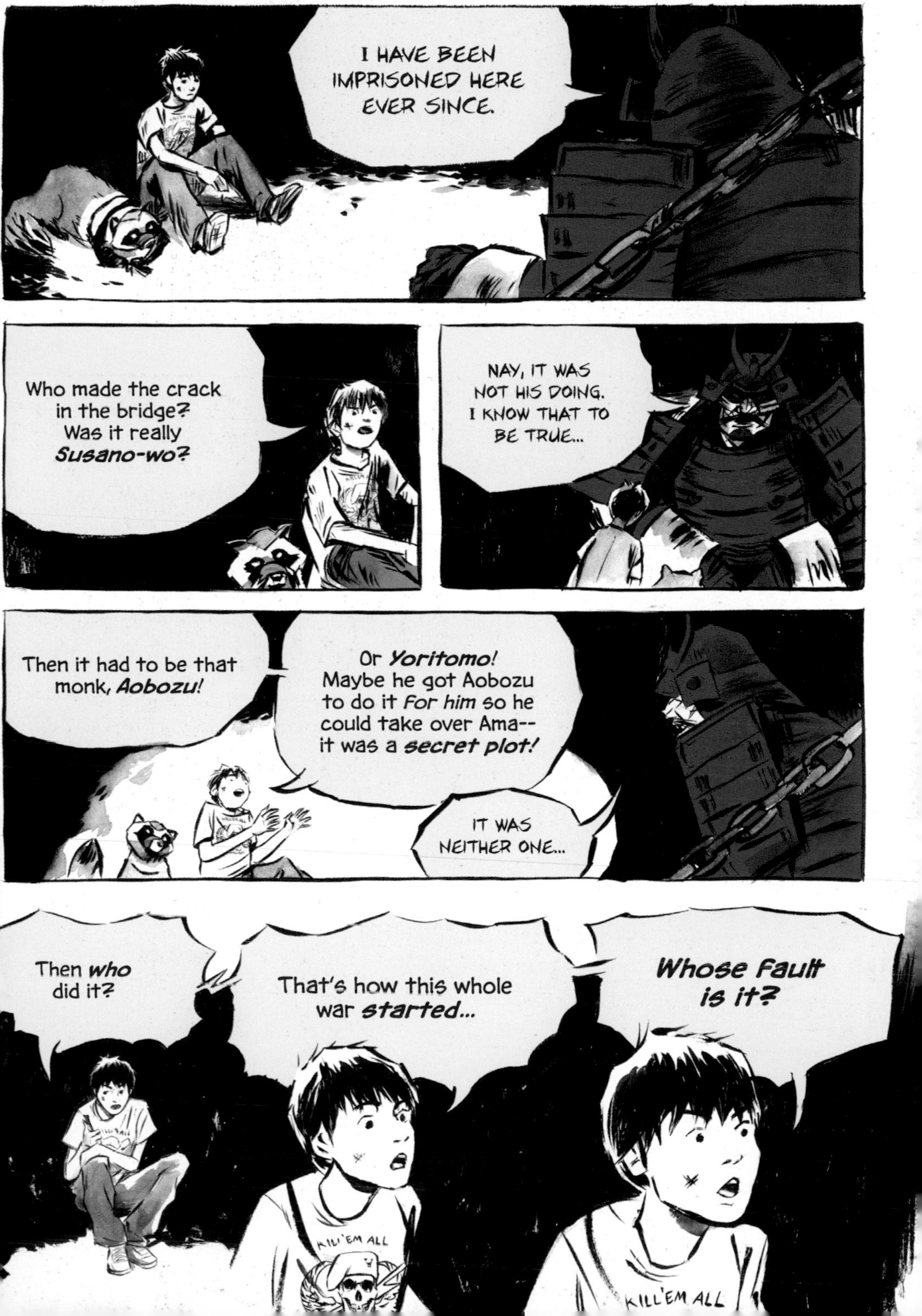
I HAVE BEEN IMPRISONED HERE EVER SINCE.
Who made the crack in the bridge? Was it really *Susano-wo?*
NAY, IT WAS NOT HIS DOING. I KNOW THAT TO BE TRUE...
Then it had to be that monk, *Aobozu!*
Or *Yoritomo!* Maybe he got Aobozu to do it *for him* so he could take over Ama-- it was a *secret plot!*
IT WAS NEITHER ONE...
Then *who* did it?
That's how this whole war *started...*
Whose fault is it?
KILL'EM ALL
KILL'EM ALL

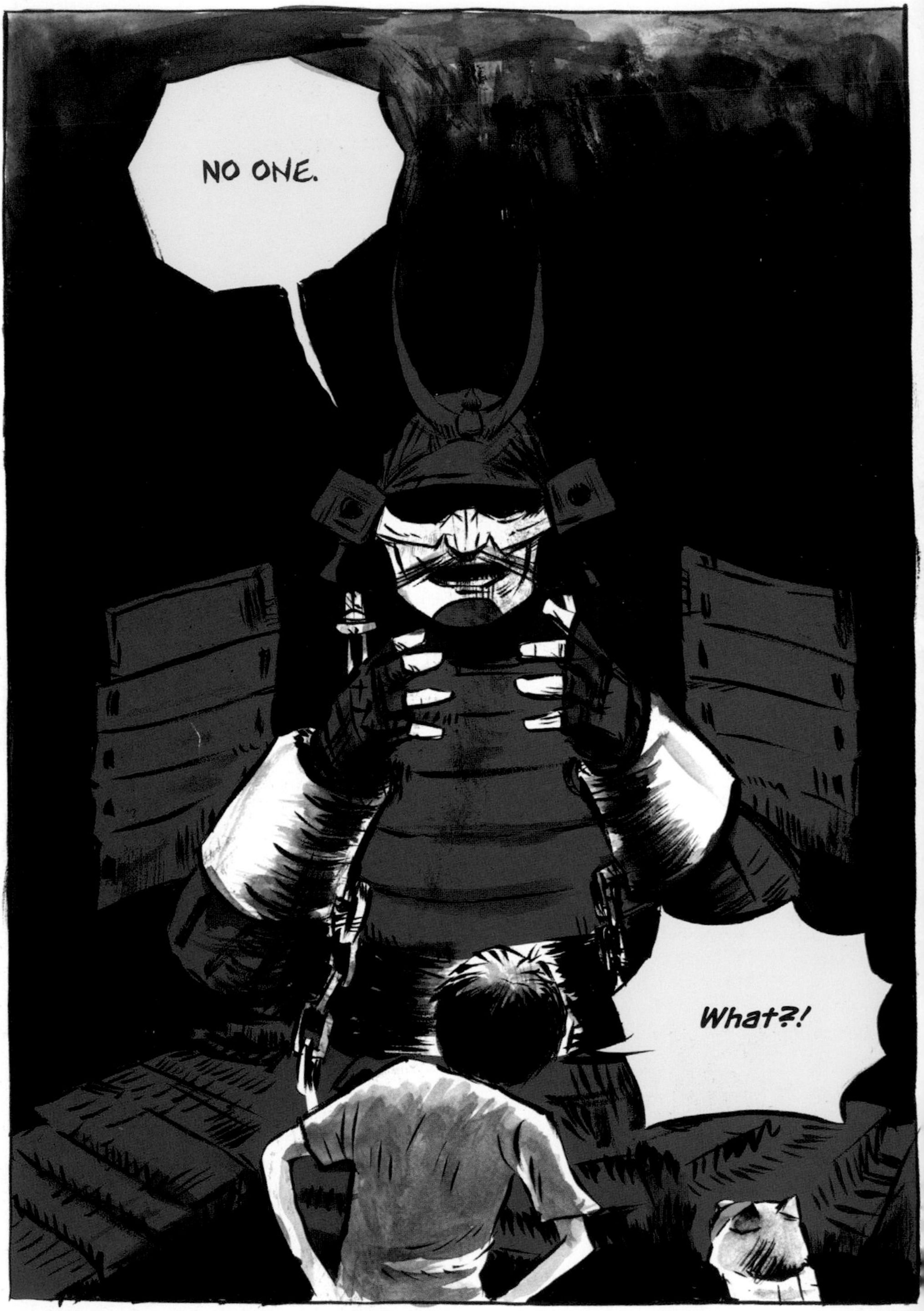
NO ONE.
What?!

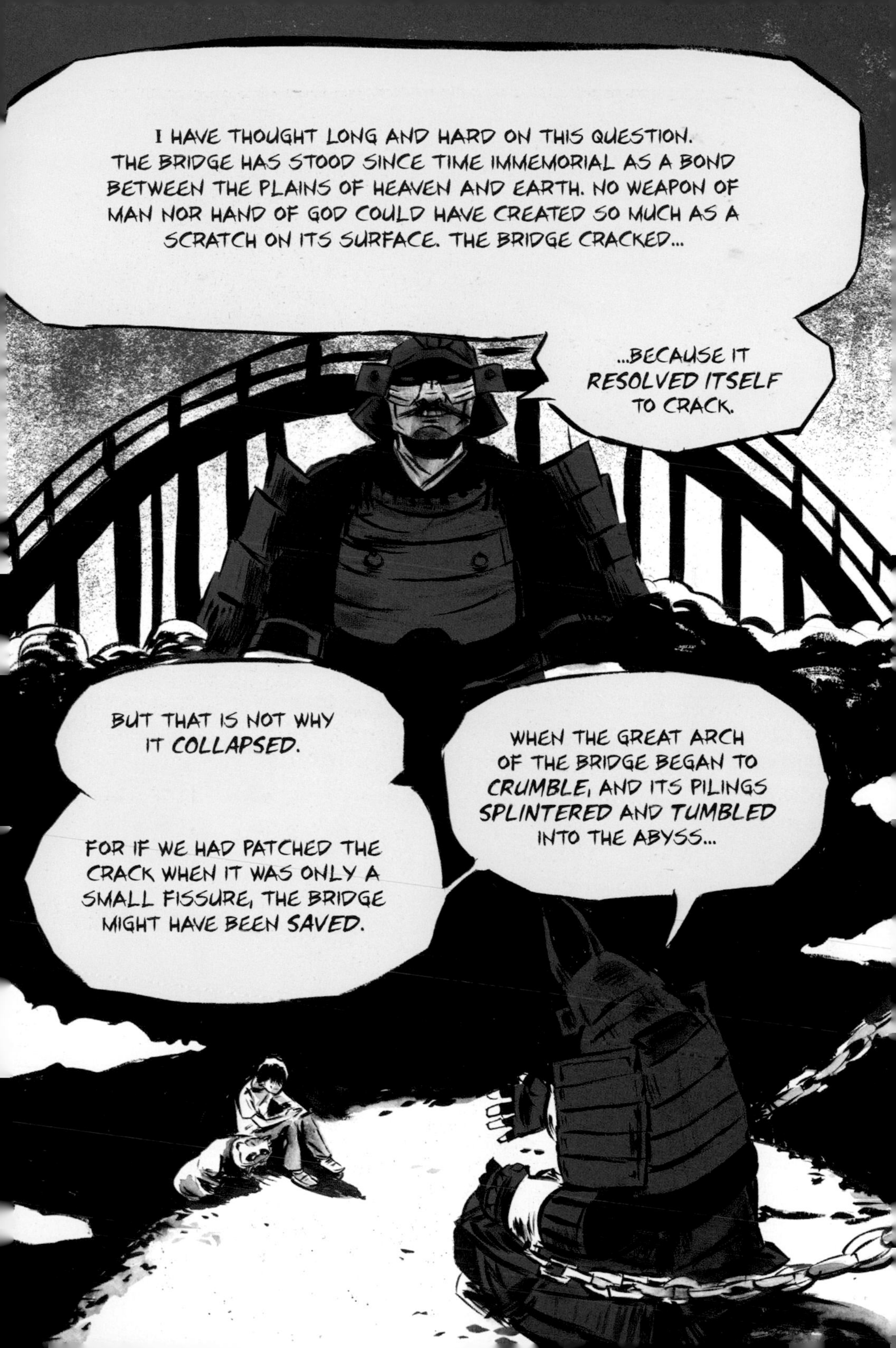
I HAVE THOUGHT LONG AND HARD ON THIS QUESTION. THE BRIDGE HAS STOOD SINCE TIME IMMEMORIAL AS A BOND BETWEEN THE PLAINS OF HEAVEN AND EARTH. NO WEAPON OF MAN NOR HAND OF GOD COULD HAVE CREATED SO MUCH AS A SCRATCH ON ITS SURFACE. THE BRIDGE CRACKED...
...BECAUSE IT **RESOLVED ITSELF** TO CRACK.
BUT THAT IS NOT WHY IT **COLLAPSED**.
FOR IF WE HAD PATCHED THE CRACK WHEN IT WAS ONLY A SMALL FISSURE, THE BRIDGE MIGHT HAVE BEEN **SAVED**.
WHEN THE GREAT ARCH OF THE BRIDGE BEGAN TO **CRUMBLE**, AND ITS PILINGS **SPLINTERED** AND **TUMBLED** INTO THE ABYSS...

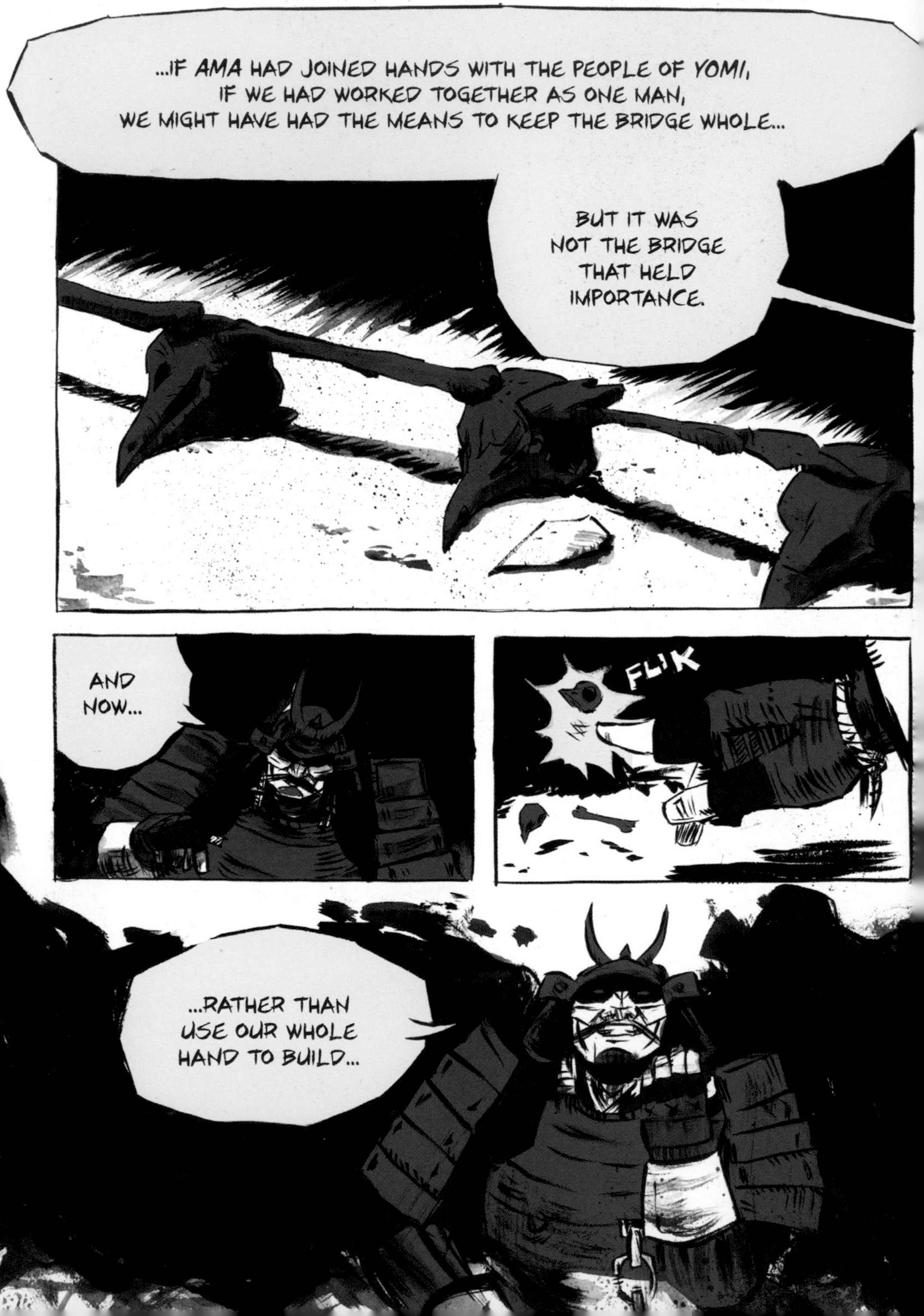
...IF AMA HAD JOINED HANDS WITH THE PEOPLE OF YOMI, IF WE HAD WORKED TOGETHER AS ONE MAN, WE MIGHT HAVE HAD THE MEANS TO KEEP THE BRIDGE WHOLE...
BUT IT WAS NOT THE BRIDGE THAT HELD IMPORTANCE.
AND NOW...
FLIK
...RATHER THAN USE OUR WHOLE HAND TO BUILD...

...WE USED ONLY A FINGER...

...TO ACCUSE.

WE DECIDED IT WAS BETTER TO BLAME THAN MEND...

...FIGHTING *MORE NOBLE* THAN FIXING.

THE WHEEL OF WAR WHEN SET TO SPIN...

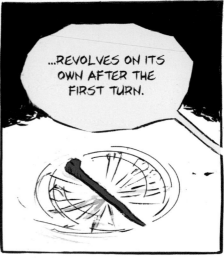

...REVOLVES ON ITS OWN AFTER THE FIRST TURN.

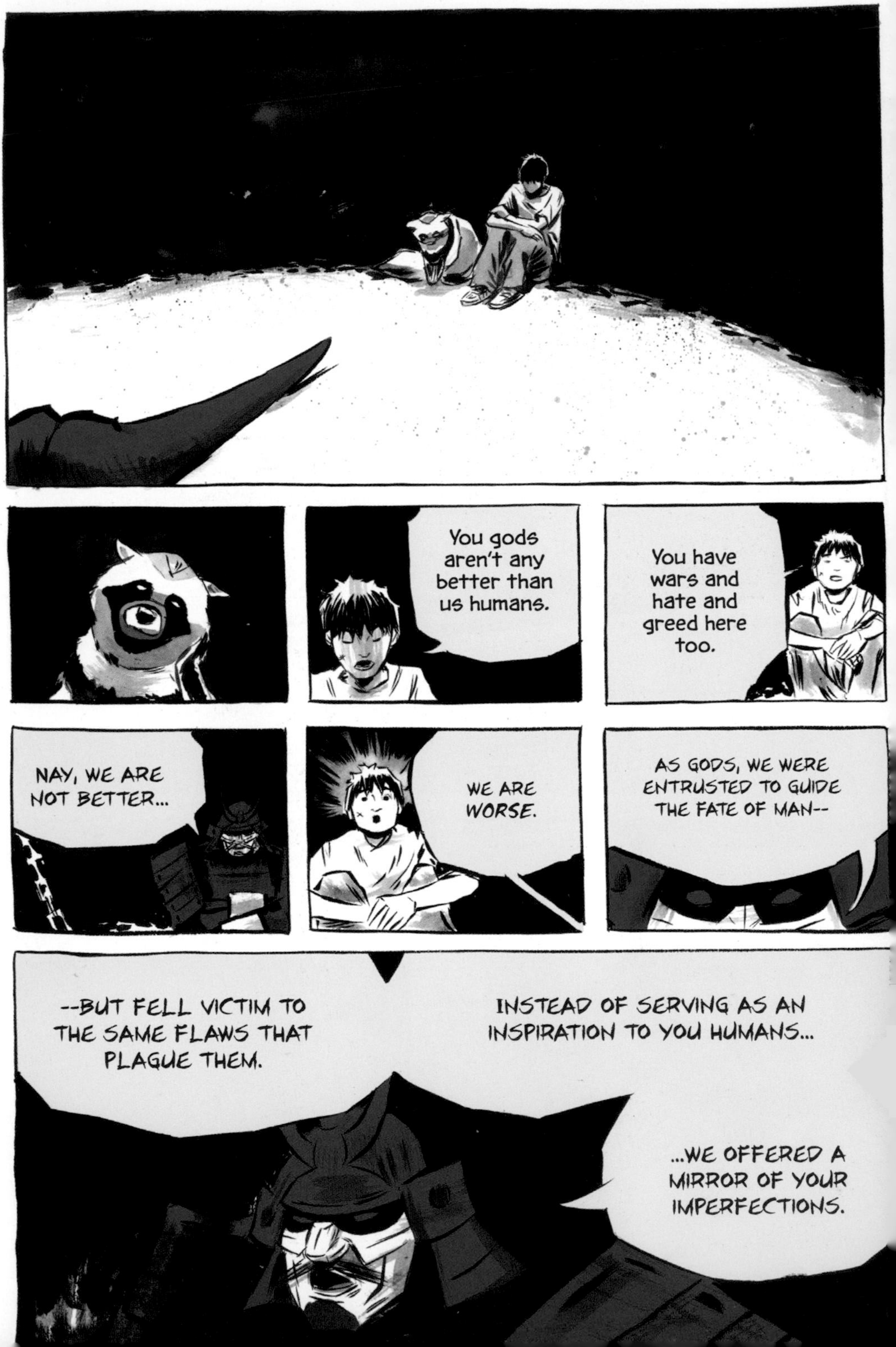
You gods aren't any better than us humans.
You have wars and hate and greed here too.
NAY, WE ARE NOT BETTER...
WE ARE WORSE.
AS GODS, WE WERE ENTRUSTED TO GUIDE THE FATE OF MAN--
--BUT FELL VICTIM TO THE SAME FLAWS THAT PLAGUE THEM.
INSTEAD OF SERVING AS AN INSPIRATION TO YOU HUMANS...
...WE OFFERED A MIRROR OF YOUR IMPERFECTIONS.

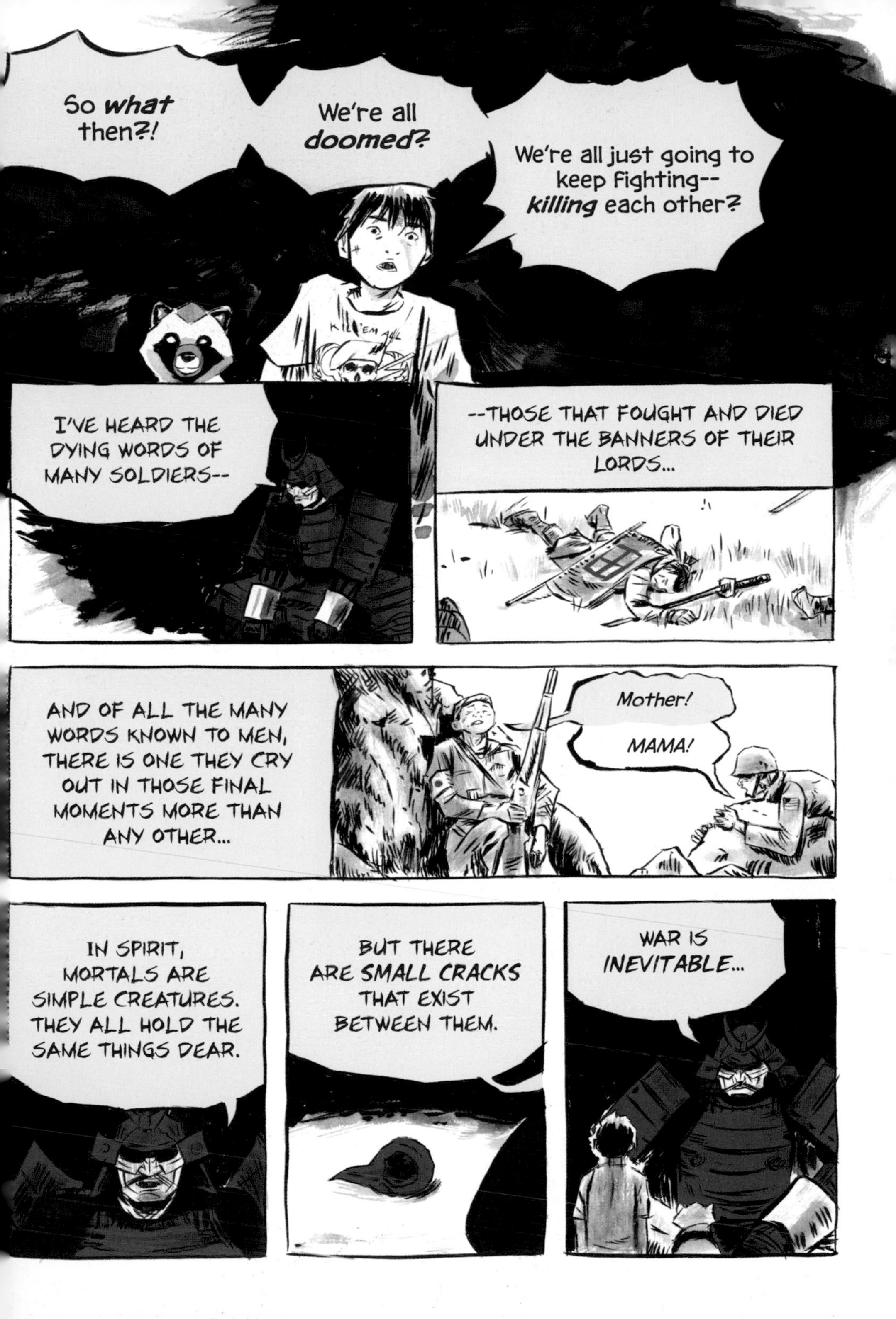
So what then?!
We're all doomed?
We're all just going to keep fighting-- killing each other?
KILL 'EM ALL
I'VE HEARD THE DYING WORDS OF MANY SOLDIERS--
--THOSE THAT FOUGHT AND DIED UNDER THE BANNERS OF THEIR LORDS...
AND OF ALL THE MANY WORDS KNOWN TO MEN, THERE IS ONE THEY CRY OUT IN THOSE FINAL MOMENTS MORE THAN ANY OTHER...
Mother!
MAMA!
IN SPIRIT, MORTALS ARE SIMPLE CREATURES. THEY ALL HOLD THE SAME THINGS DEAR.
BUT THERE ARE SMALL CRACKS THAT EXIST BETWEEN THEM.
WAR IS INEVITABLE...

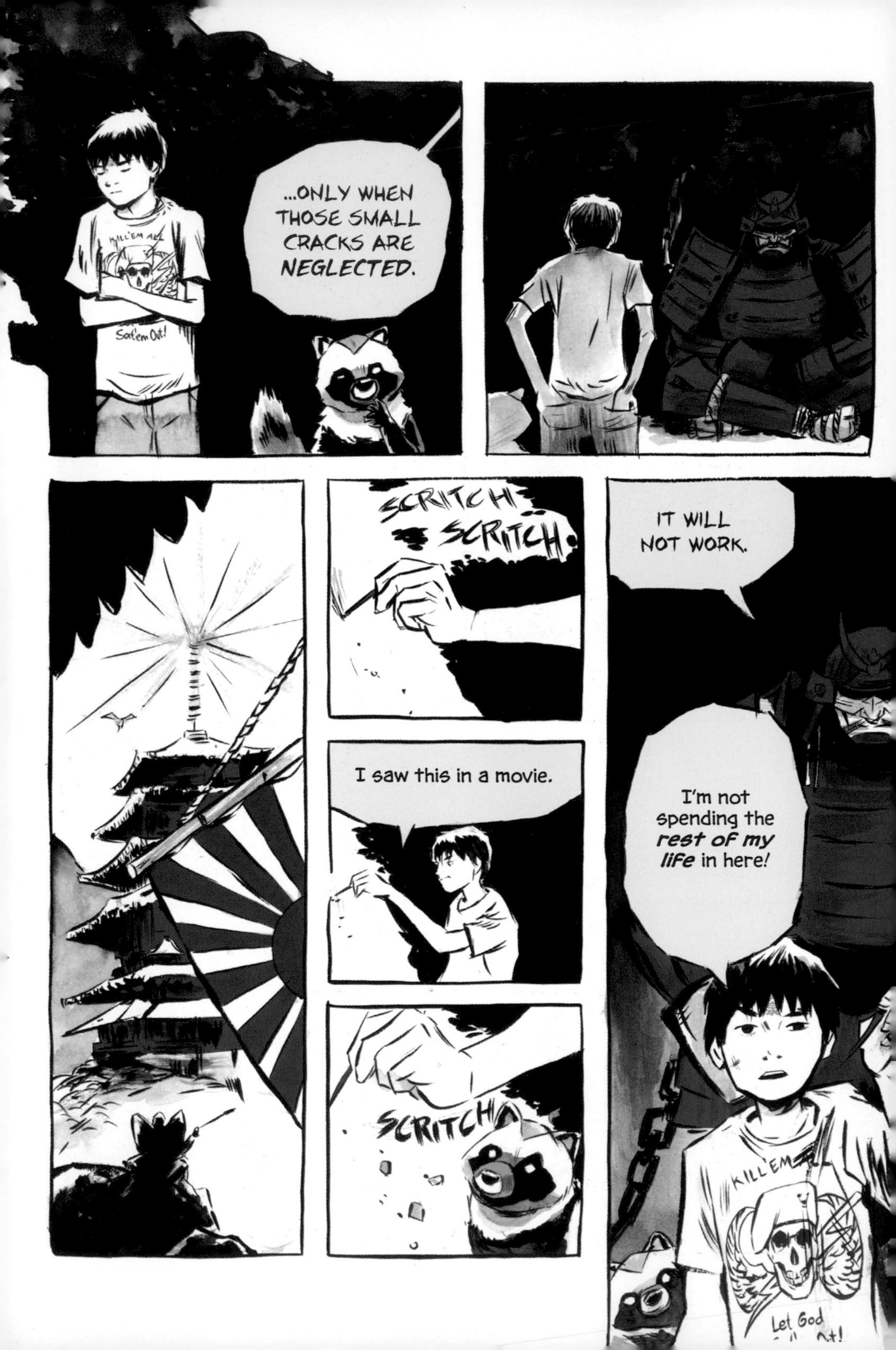
KILL'EM ALL
Sort'em Out!
...ONLY WHEN THOSE SMALL CRACKS ARE NEGLECTED.
SCRITCH
SCRITCH
I saw this in a movie.
SCRITCH
IT WILL NOT WORK.
I'm not spending the ***rest of my life*** in here!
KILL'EM
Let God

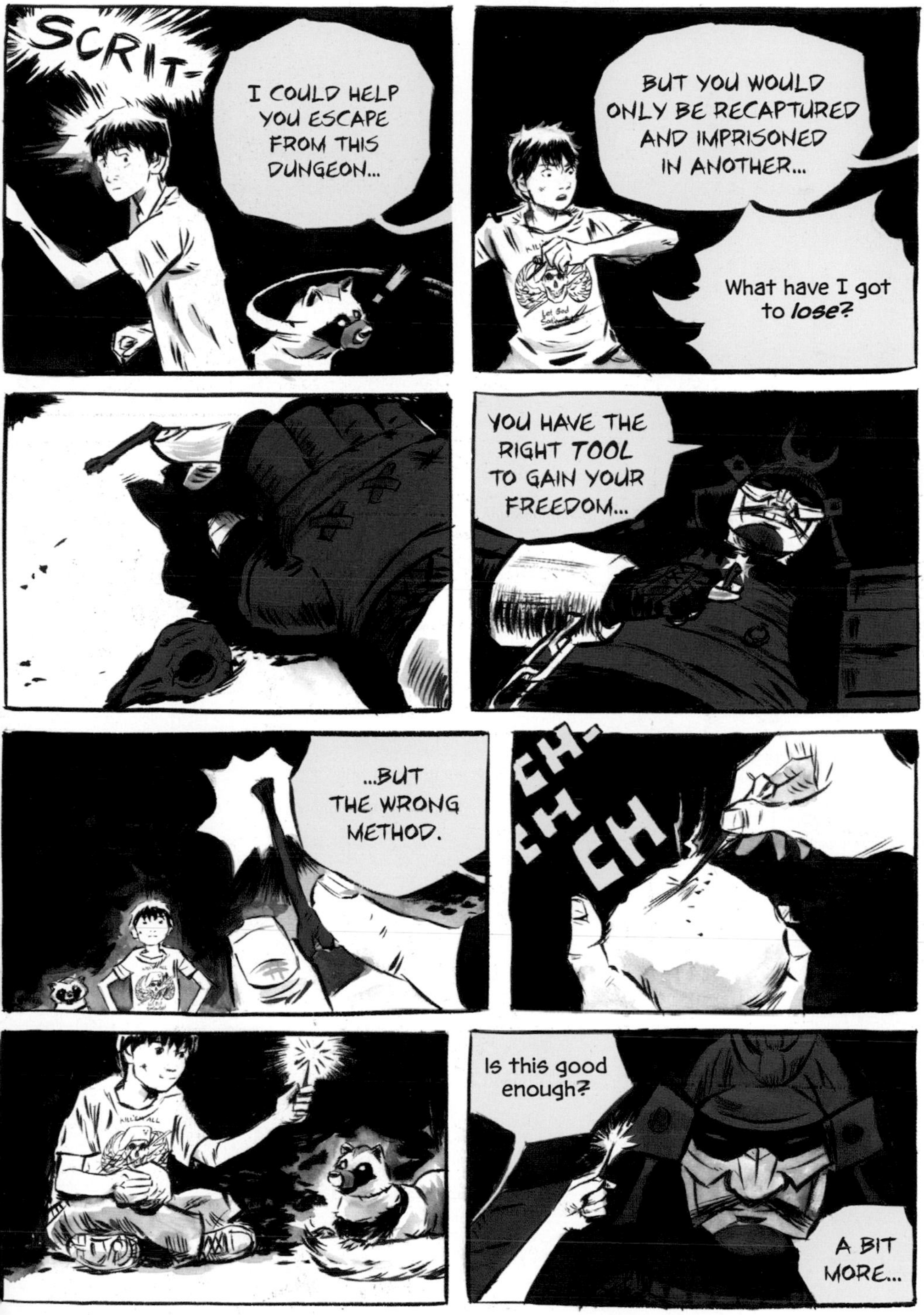
SCRIT-
I COULD HELP YOU ESCAPE FROM THIS DUNGEON...
BUT YOU WOULD ONLY BE RECAPTURED AND IMPRISONED IN ANOTHER...
What have I got to *lose*?
YOU HAVE THE RIGHT TOOL TO GAIN YOUR FREEDOM...
...BUT THE WRONG METHOD.
CH- CH CH
Is this good enough?
A BIT MORE...

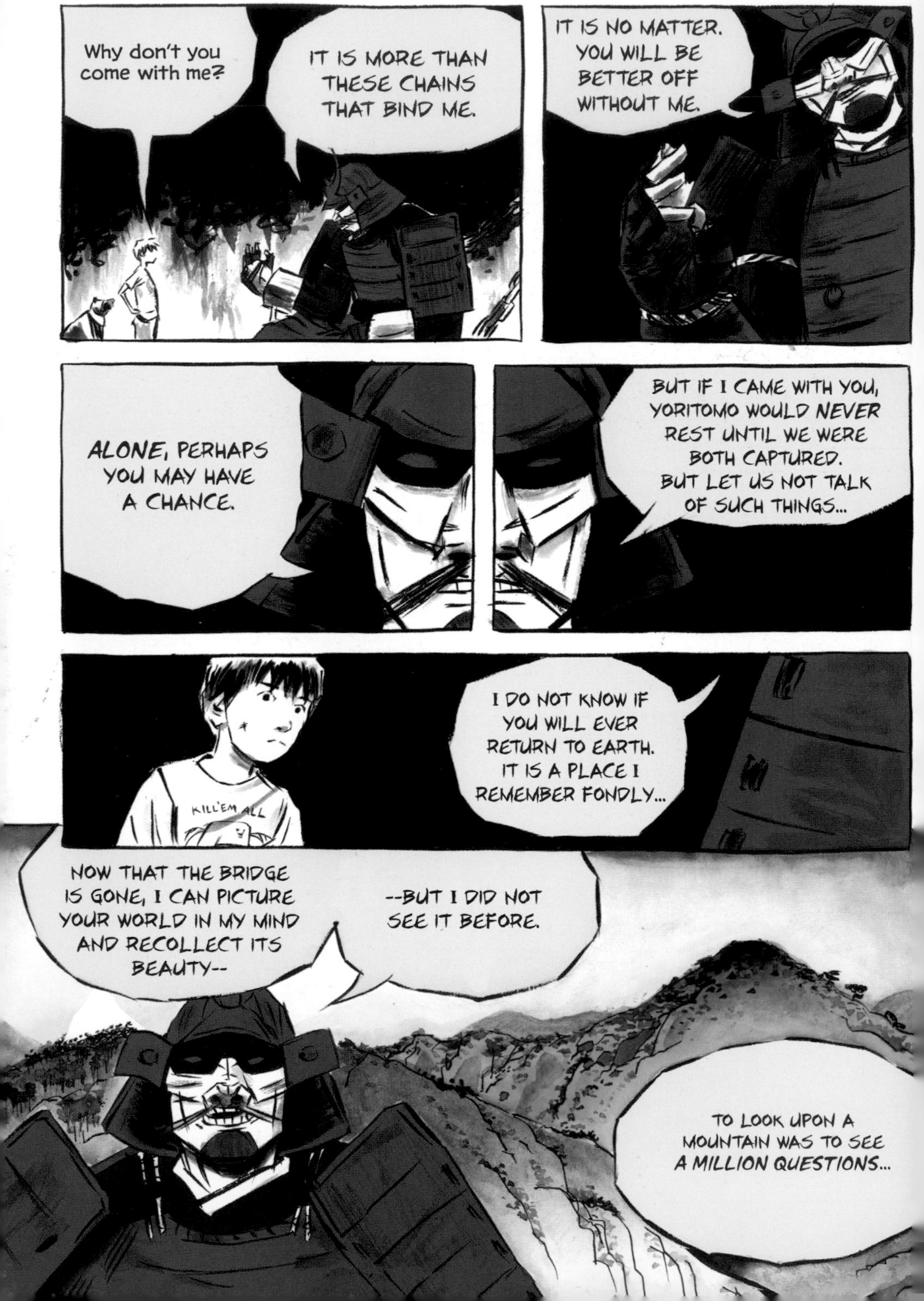
Why don't you come with me?
IT IS MORE THAN THESE CHAINS THAT BIND ME.
IT IS NO MATTER. YOU WILL BE BETTER OFF WITHOUT ME.
ALONE, PERHAPS YOU MAY HAVE A CHANCE.
BUT IF I CAME WITH YOU, YORITOMO WOULD NEVER REST UNTIL WE WERE BOTH CAPTURED. BUT LET US NOT TALK OF SUCH THINGS...
KILL'EM ALL
I DO NOT KNOW IF YOU WILL EVER RETURN TO EARTH. IT IS A PLACE I REMEMBER FONDLY...
NOW THAT THE BRIDGE IS GONE, I CAN PICTURE YOUR WORLD IN MY MIND AND RECOLLECT ITS BEAUTY--
--BUT I DID NOT SEE IT BEFORE.
TO LOOK UPON A MOUNTAIN WAS TO SEE A MILLION QUESTIONS...

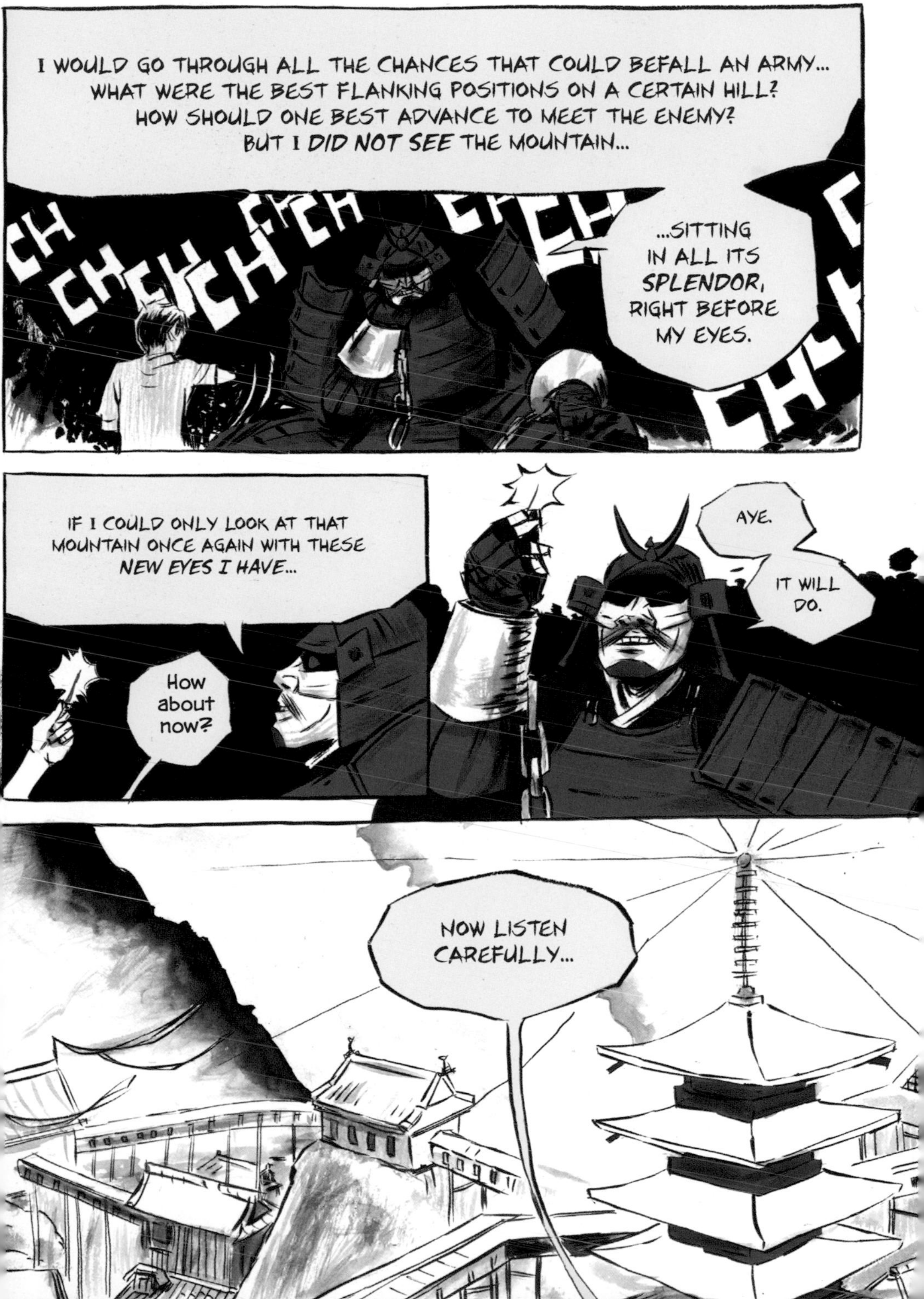
I WOULD GO THROUGH ALL THE CHANCES THAT COULD BEFALL AN ARMY... WHAT WERE THE BEST FLANKING POSITIONS ON A CERTAIN HILL? HOW SHOULD ONE BEST ADVANCE TO MEET THE ENEMY? BUT I *DID NOT SEE* THE MOUNTAIN...
...SITTING IN ALL ITS *SPLENDOR*, RIGHT BEFORE MY EYES.
IF I COULD ONLY LOOK AT THAT MOUNTAIN ONCE AGAIN WITH THESE *NEW EYES I HAVE*...
How about now?
AYE.
IT WILL DO.
NOW LISTEN CAREFULLY...

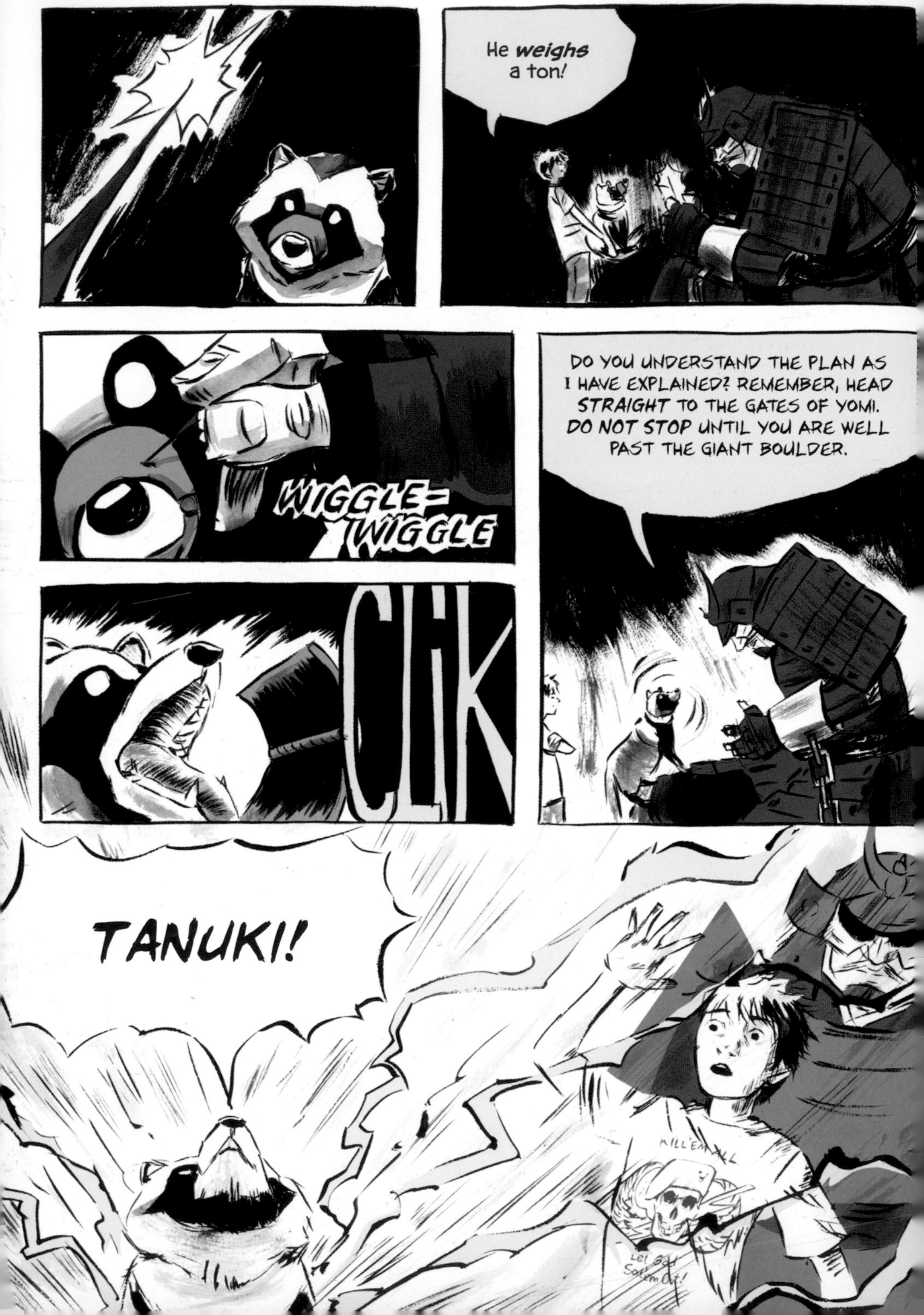
He *weighs* a ton!
DO YOU UNDERSTAND THE PLAN AS I HAVE EXPLAINED? REMEMBER, HEAD *STRAIGHT* TO THE GATES OF YOMI. DO NOT STOP UNTIL YOU ARE WELL PAST THE GIANT BOULDER.
WIGGLE-WIGGLE
CLIK
TANUKI!
KILL'EM ALL

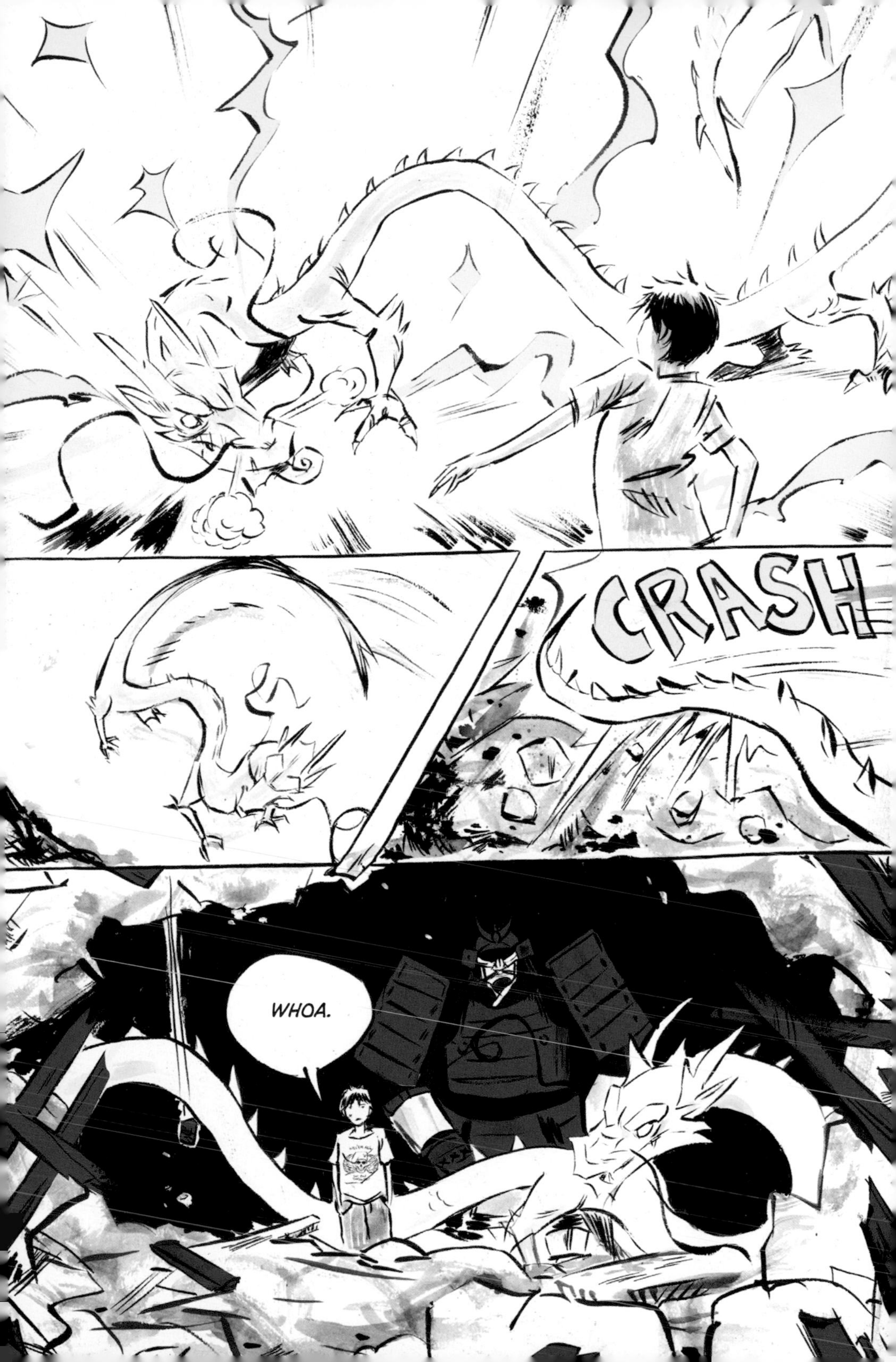
CRASH
WHOA.

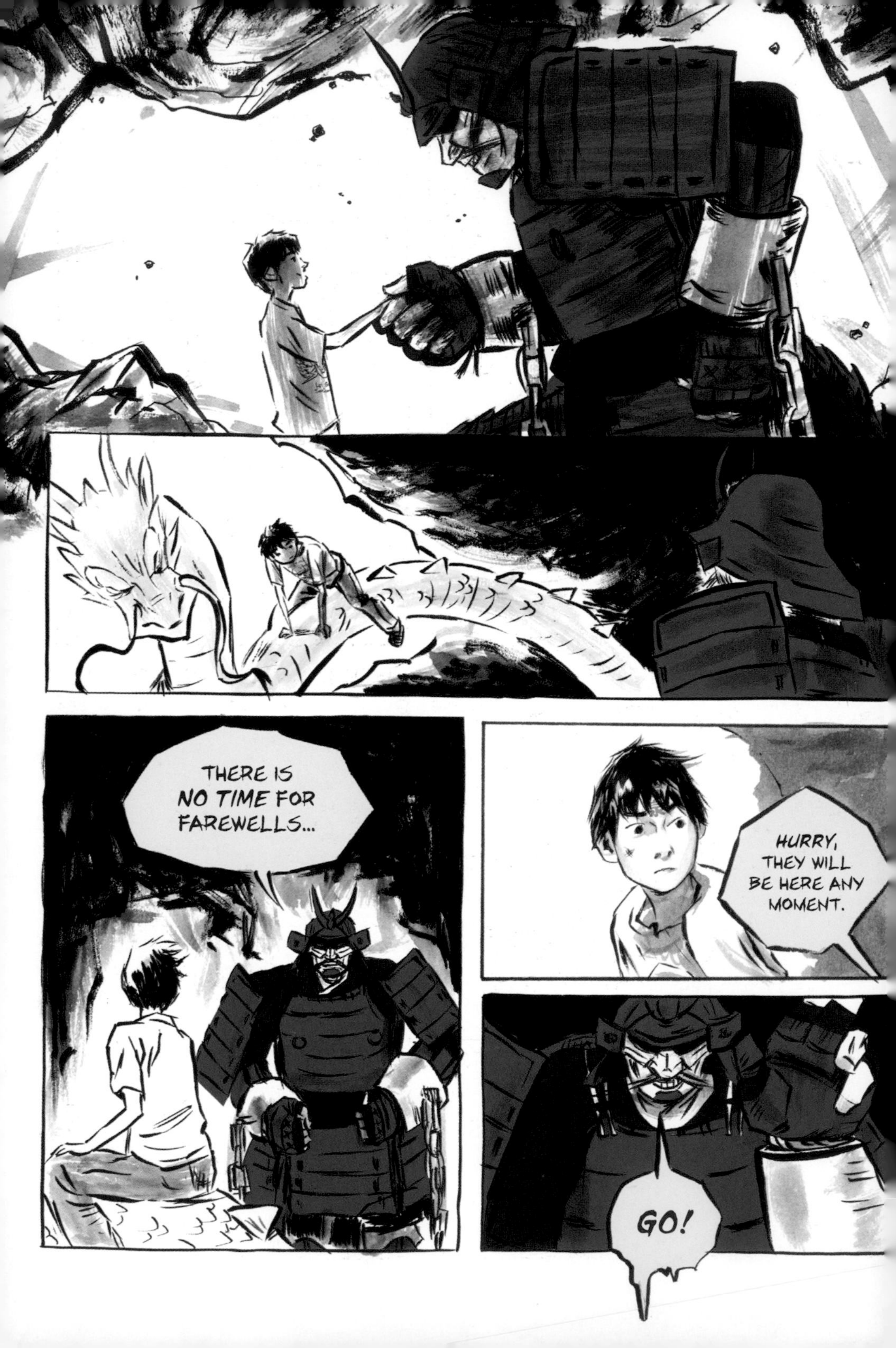
THERE IS NO TIME FOR FAREWELLS...
HURRY, THEY WILL BE HERE ANY MOMENT.
GO!

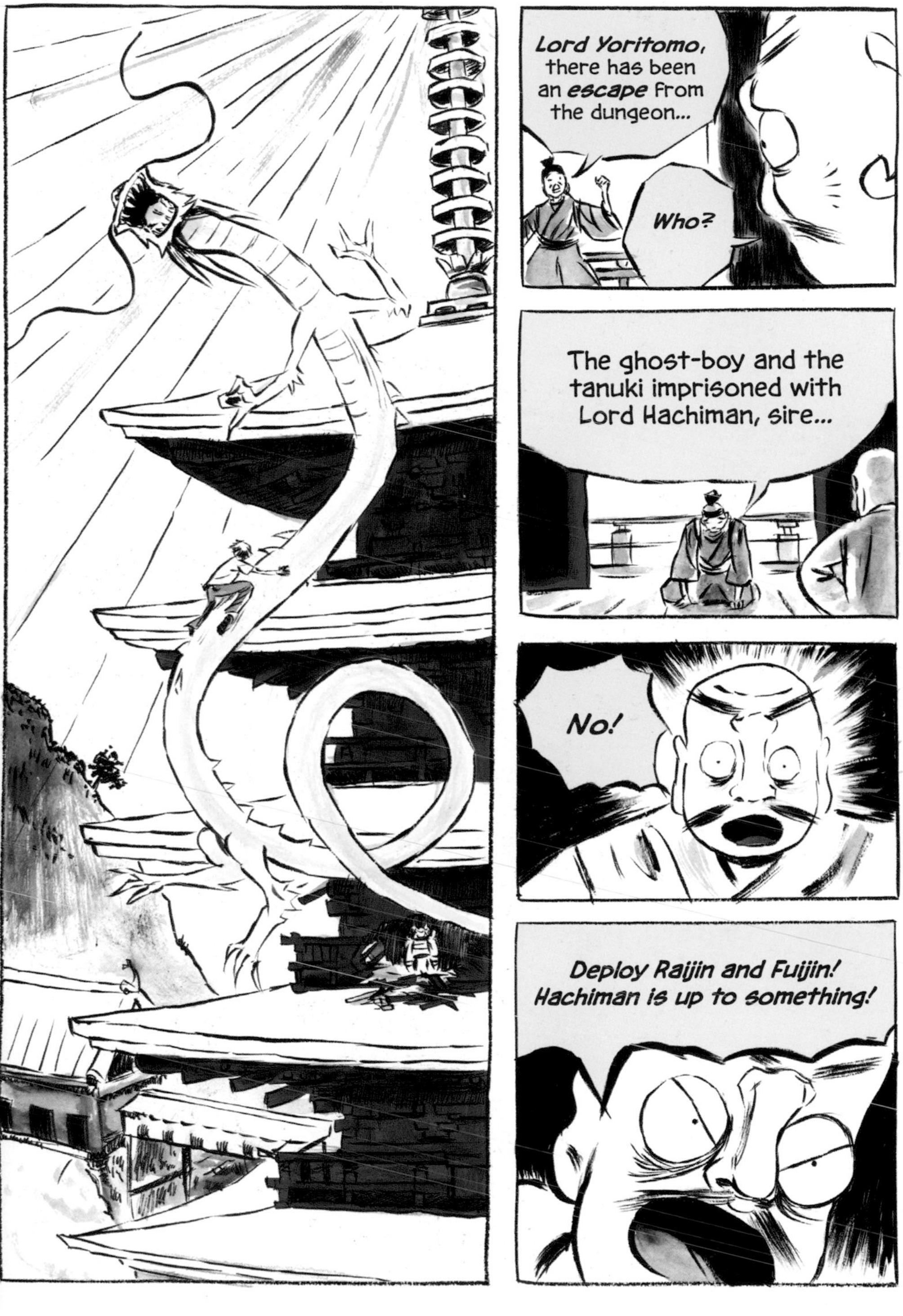
Lord Yoritomo, there has been an escape from the dungeon...
Who?
The ghost-boy and the tanuki imprisoned with Lord Hachiman, sire...
No!
Deploy Raijin and Fuijin! Hachiman is up to something!

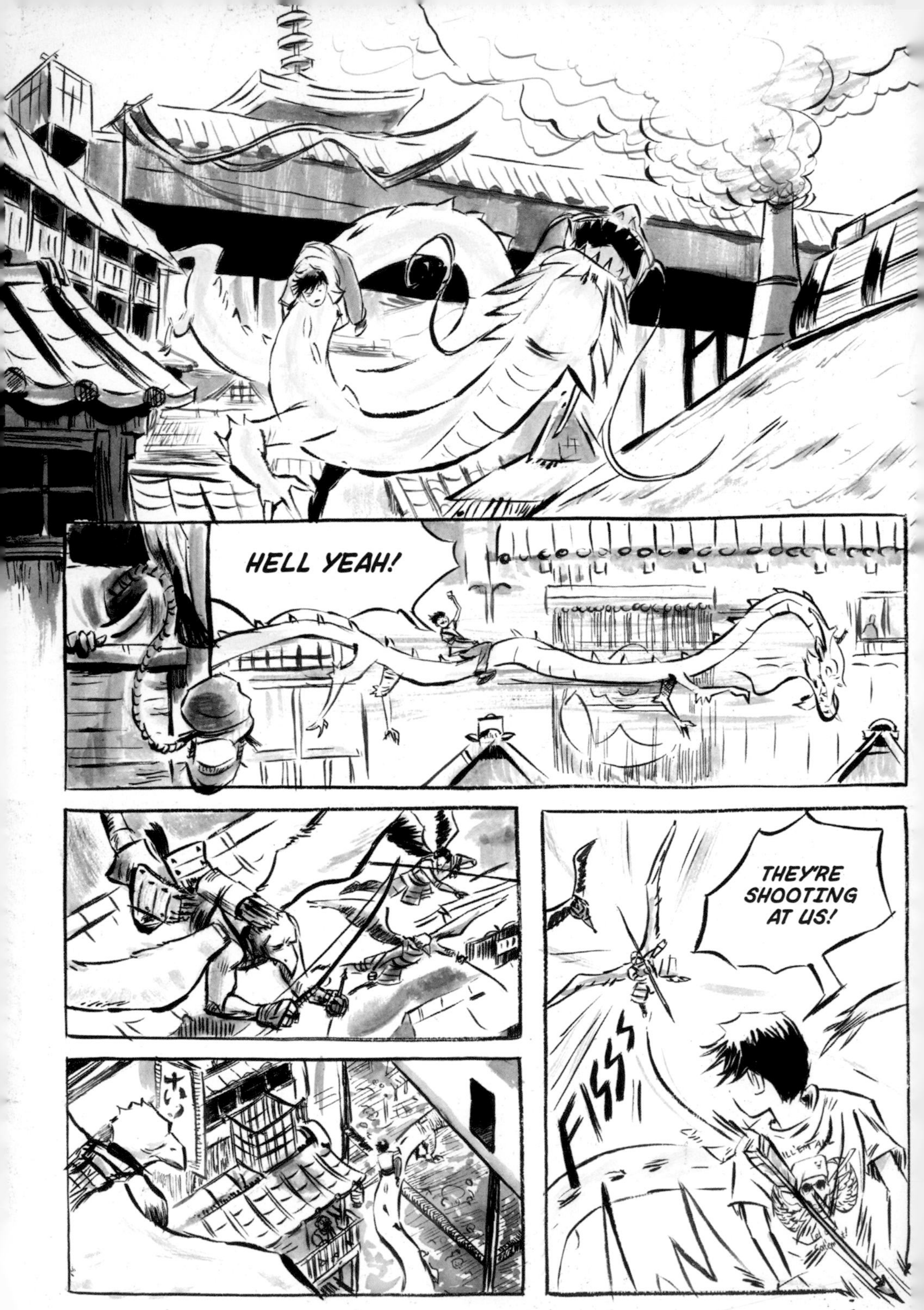
HELL YEAH!
THEY'RE SHOOTING AT US!
FISSS

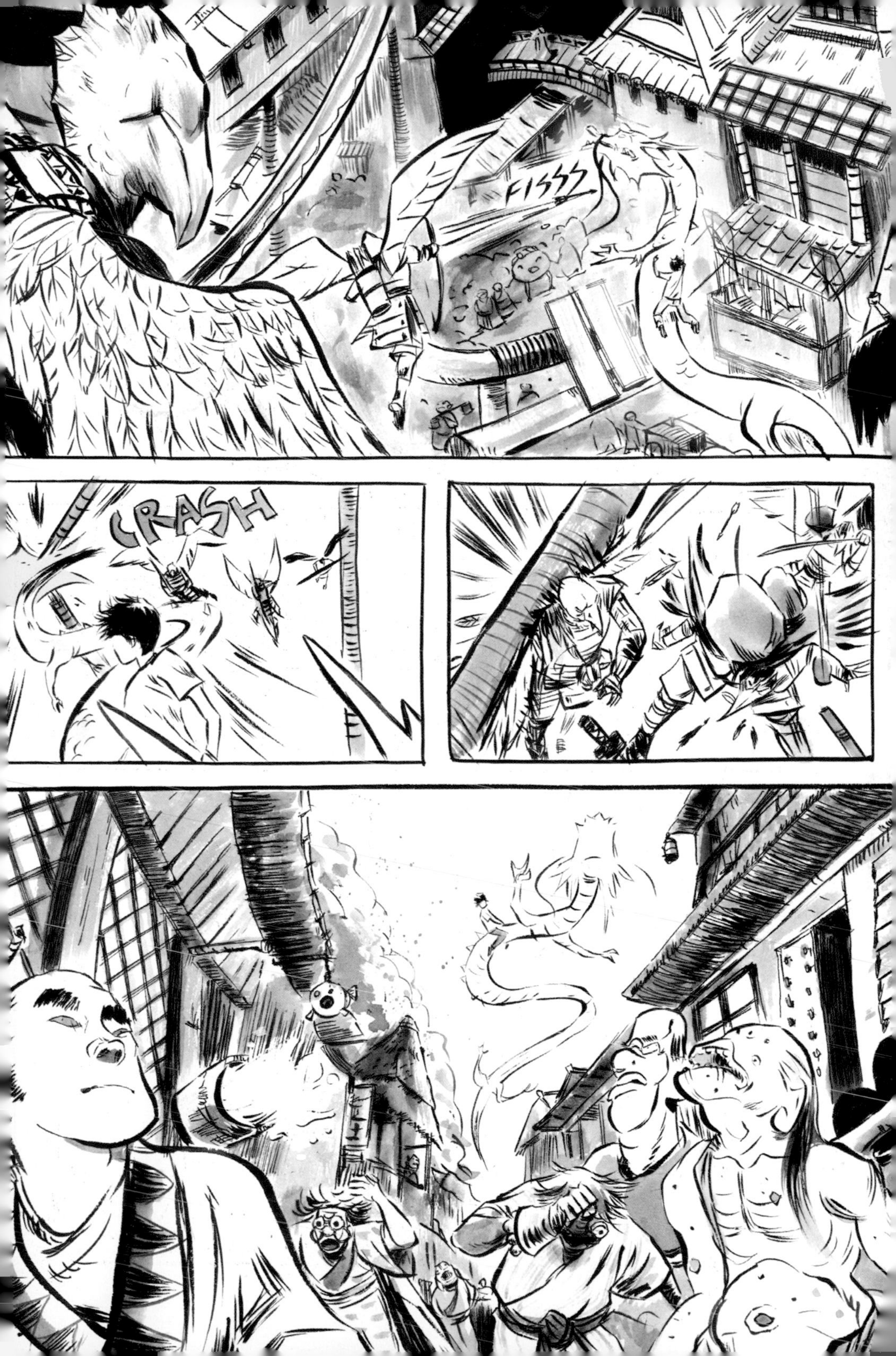
FISSS
CRASH

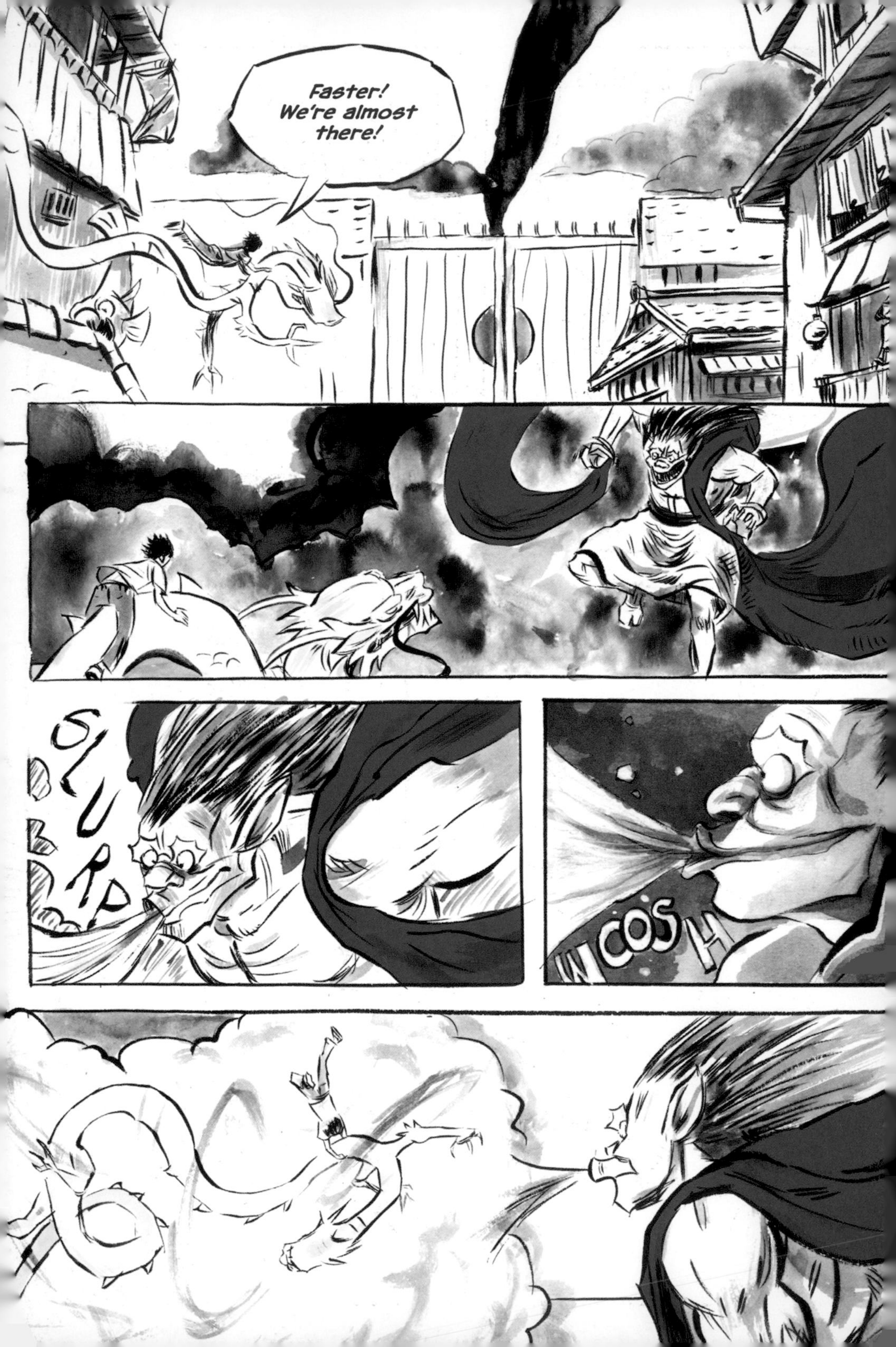

Faster! We're almost there!
SLURP
COSH

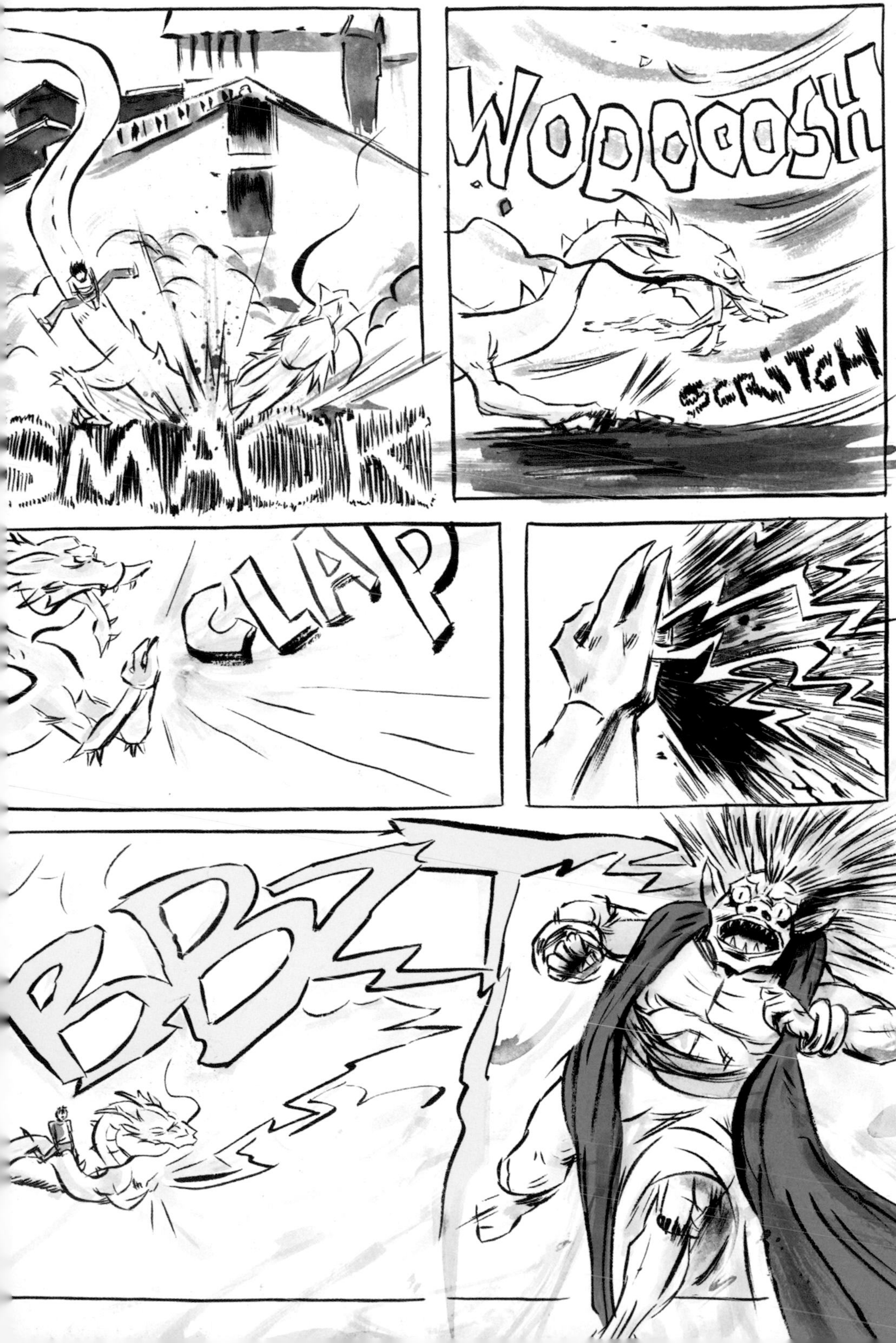
SMACK
WOOOOOSH
SCRITCH
CLAP
BBZT!

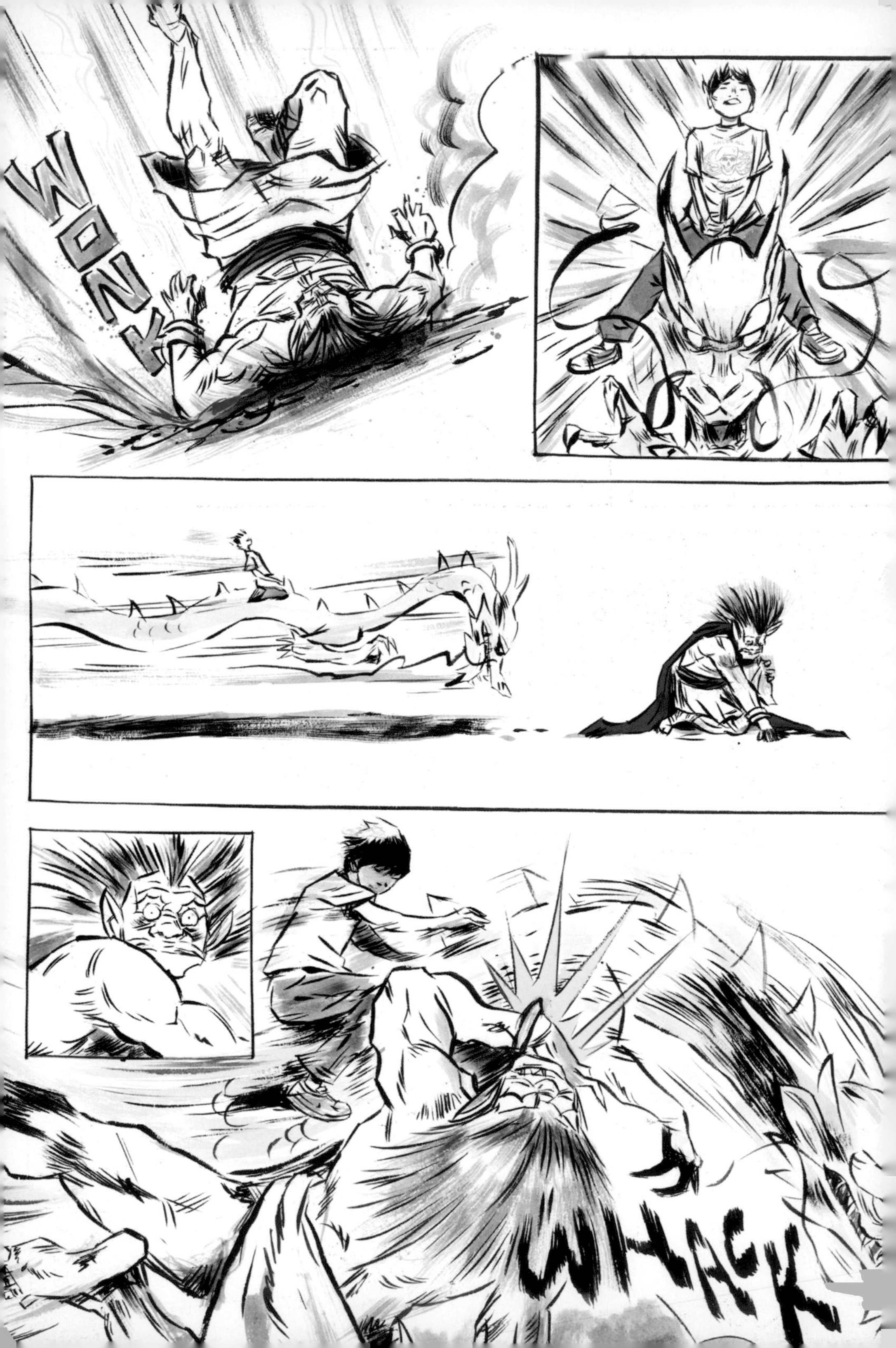
WONK
WHACK

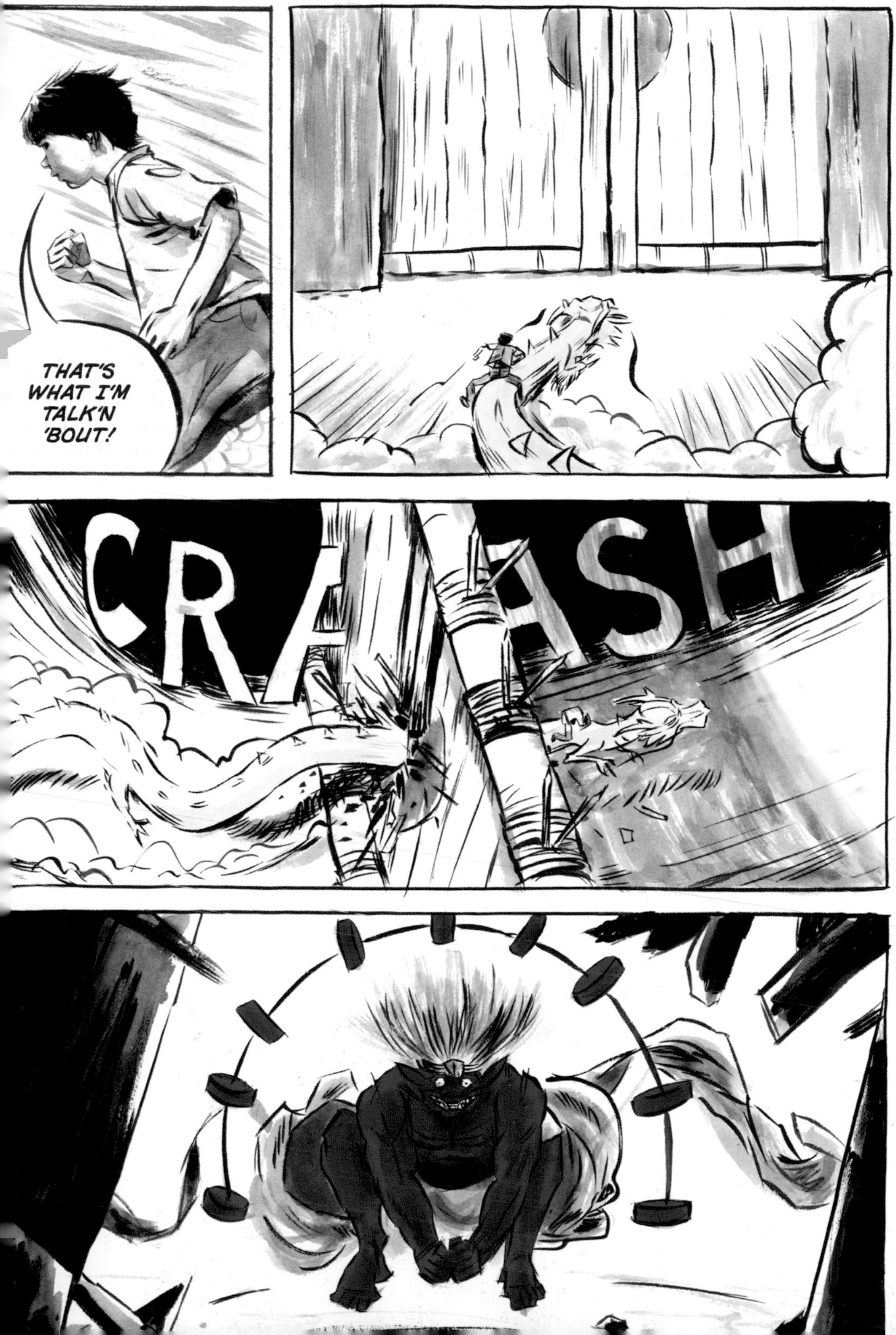
THAT'S WHAT I'M TALK'N 'BOUT!
CRASH

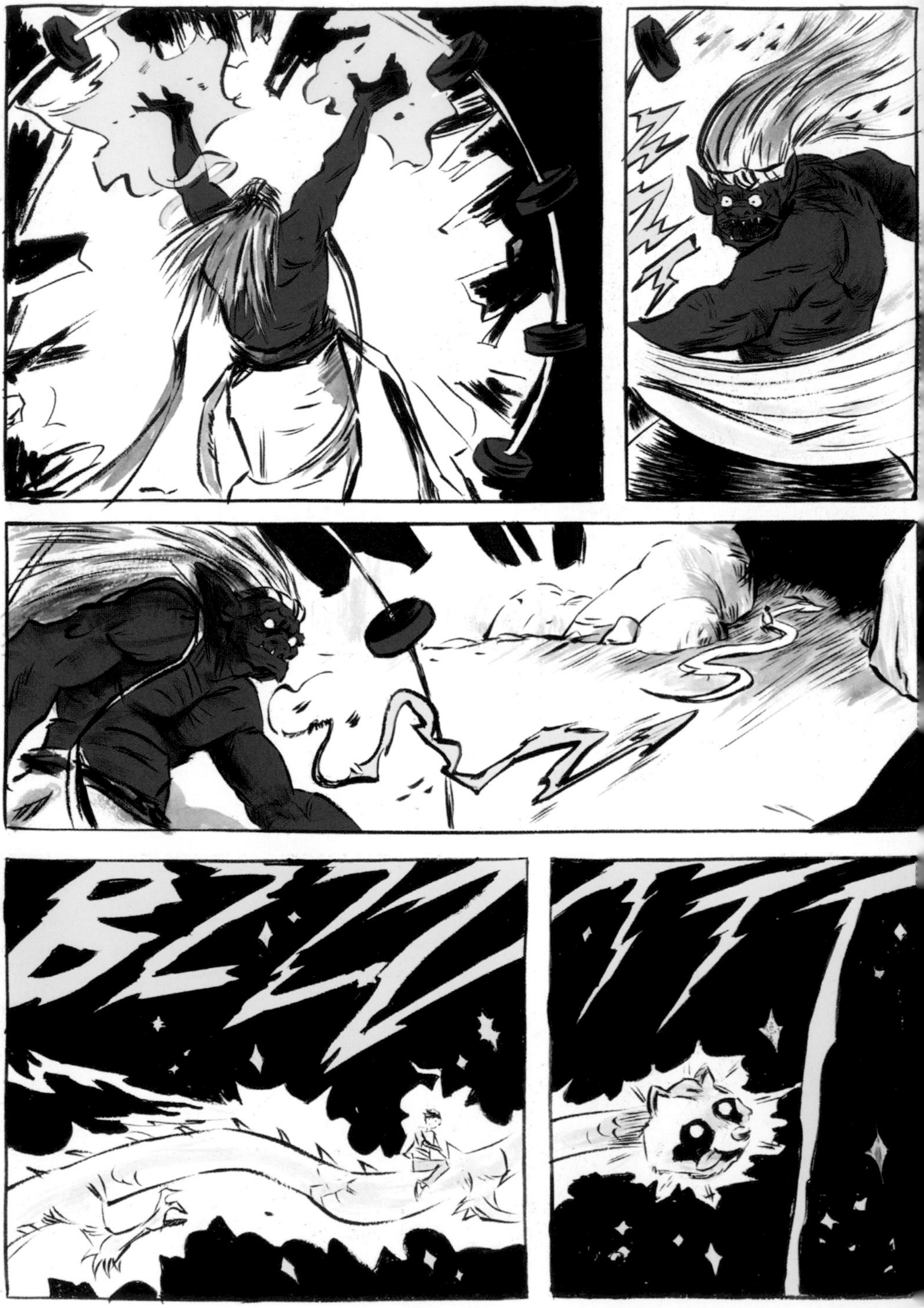
BZZZ

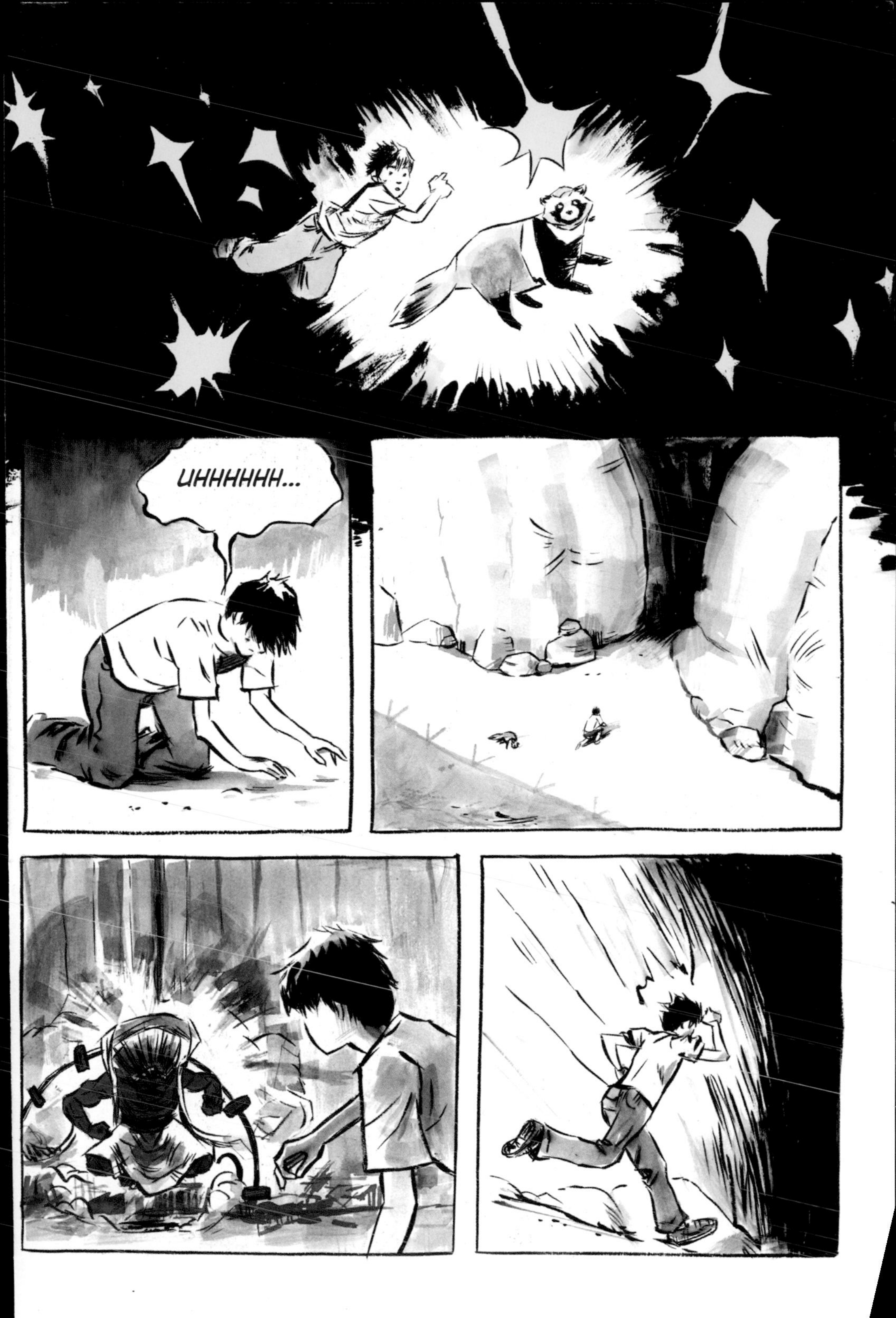
UHHHHHH...

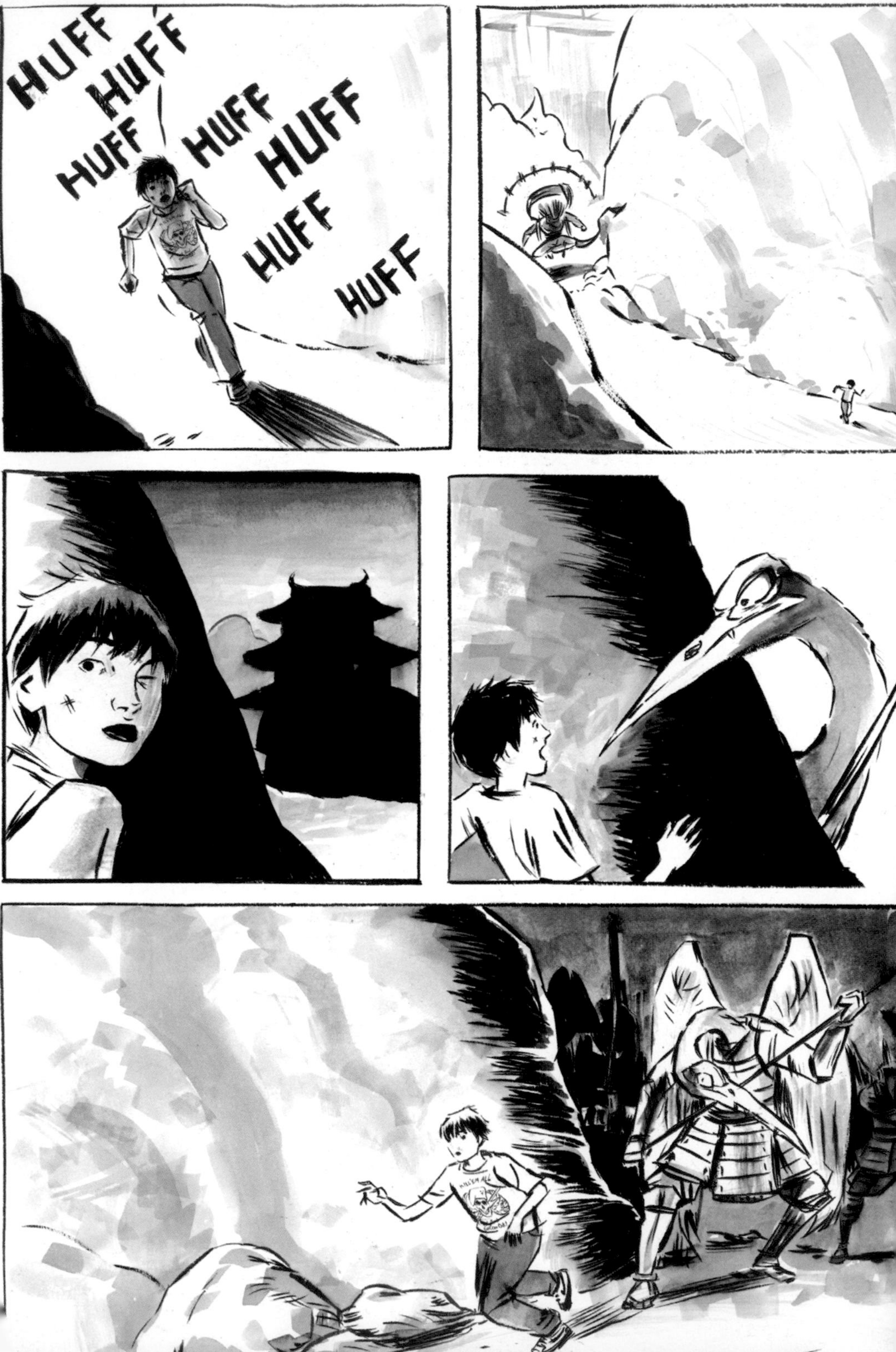
HUFF
HUFF
HUFF
HUFF
HUFF
HUFF
HUFF

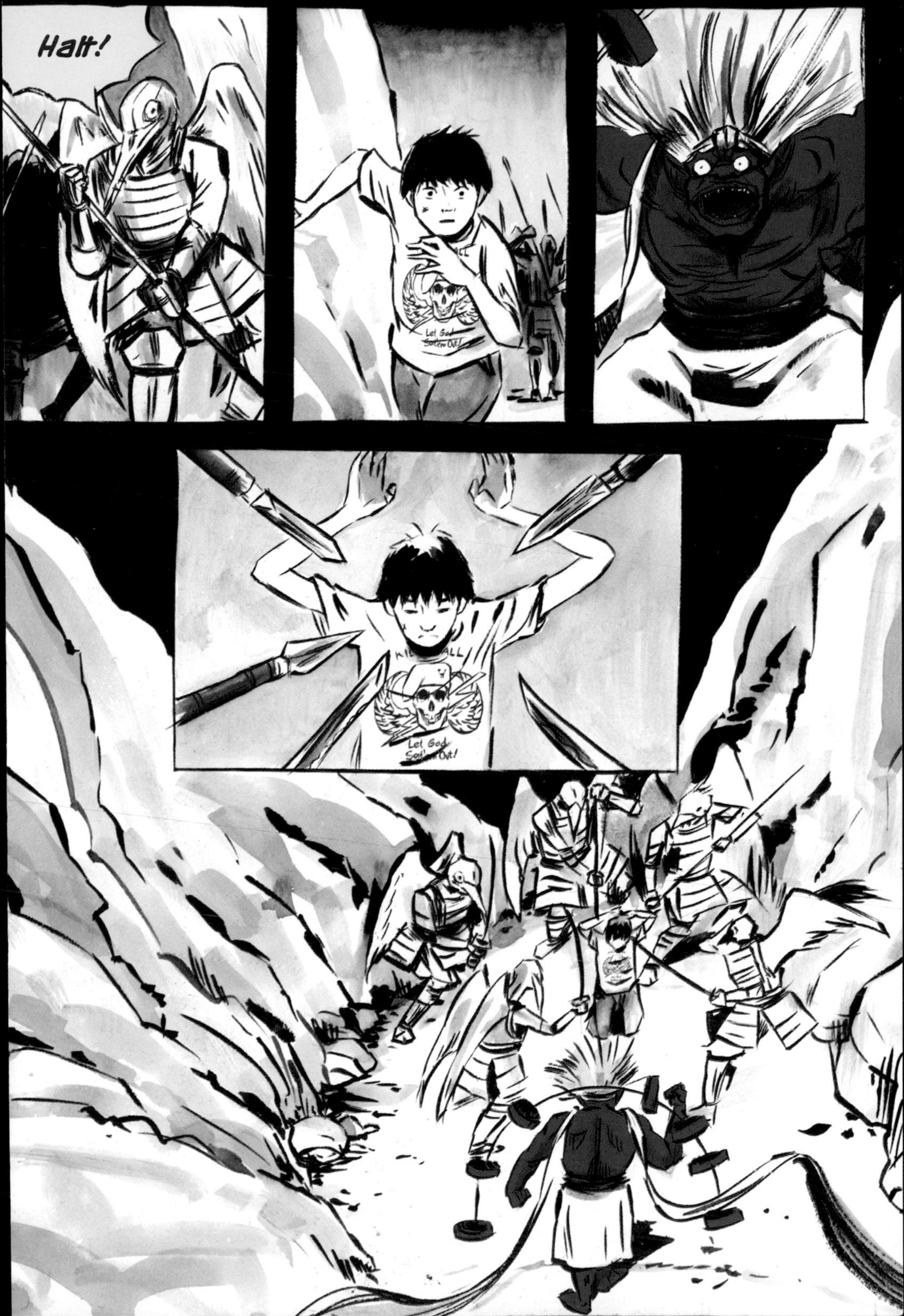
Halt!

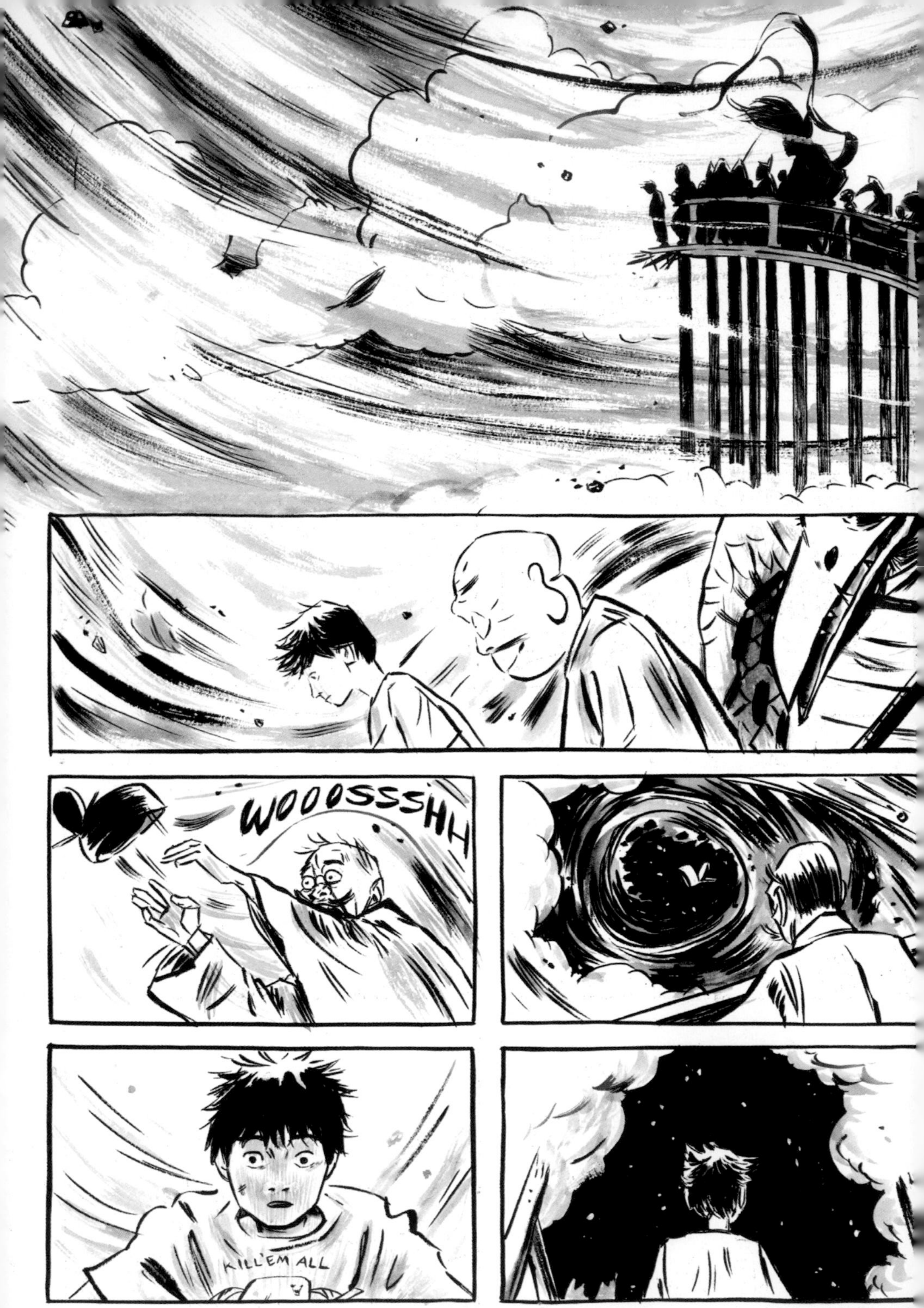
WOOOSSSSHH
KILL'EM ALL

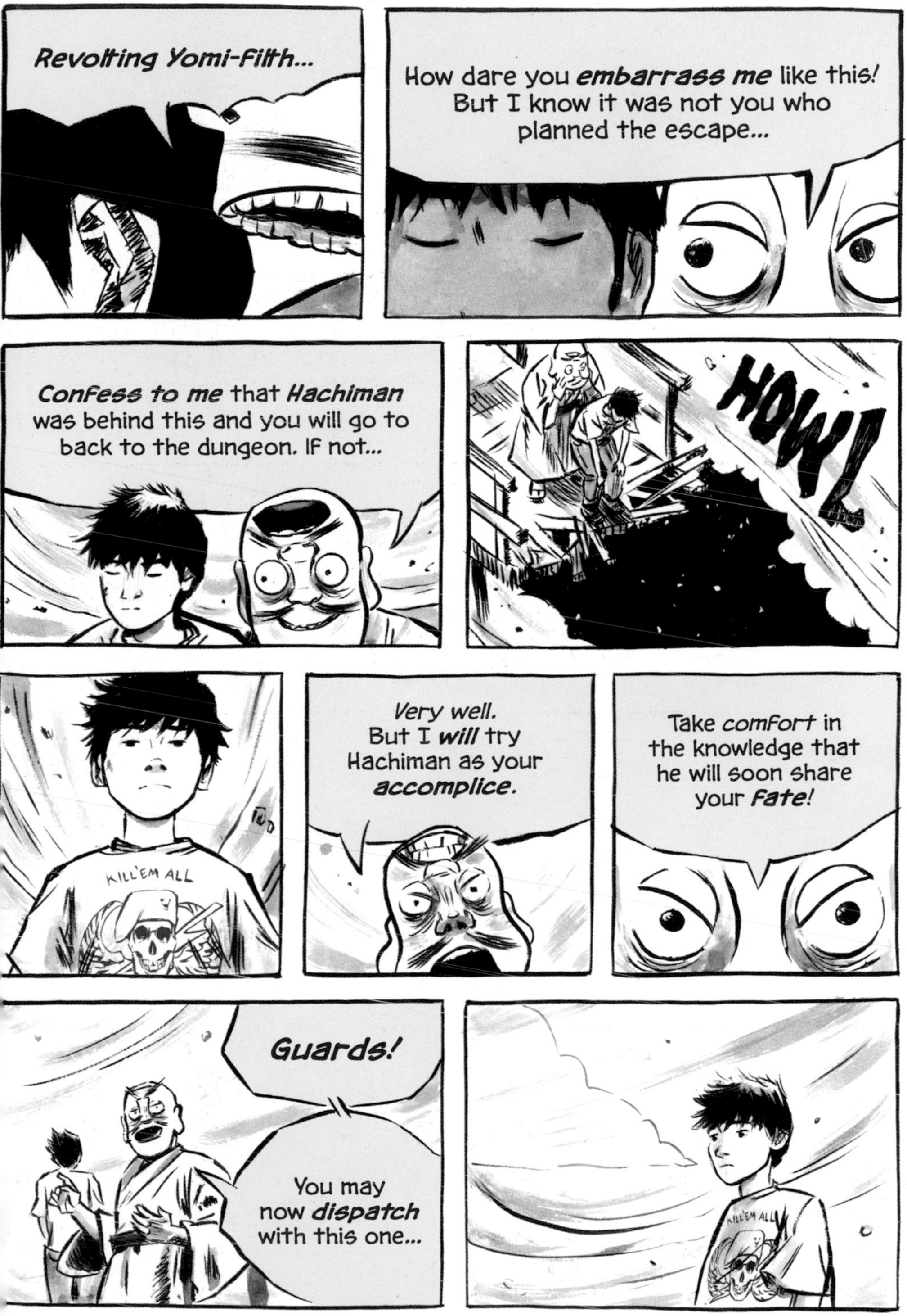
Revolting Yomi-Filth...
How dare you embarrass me like this! But I know it was not you who planned the escape...
Confess to me that Hachiman was behind this and you will go to back to the dungeon. If not...
HOW!
Very well. But I will try Hachiman as your accomplice.
Take comfort in the knowledge that he will soon share your fate!
Guards!
You may now dispatch with this one...
KILL'EM ALL

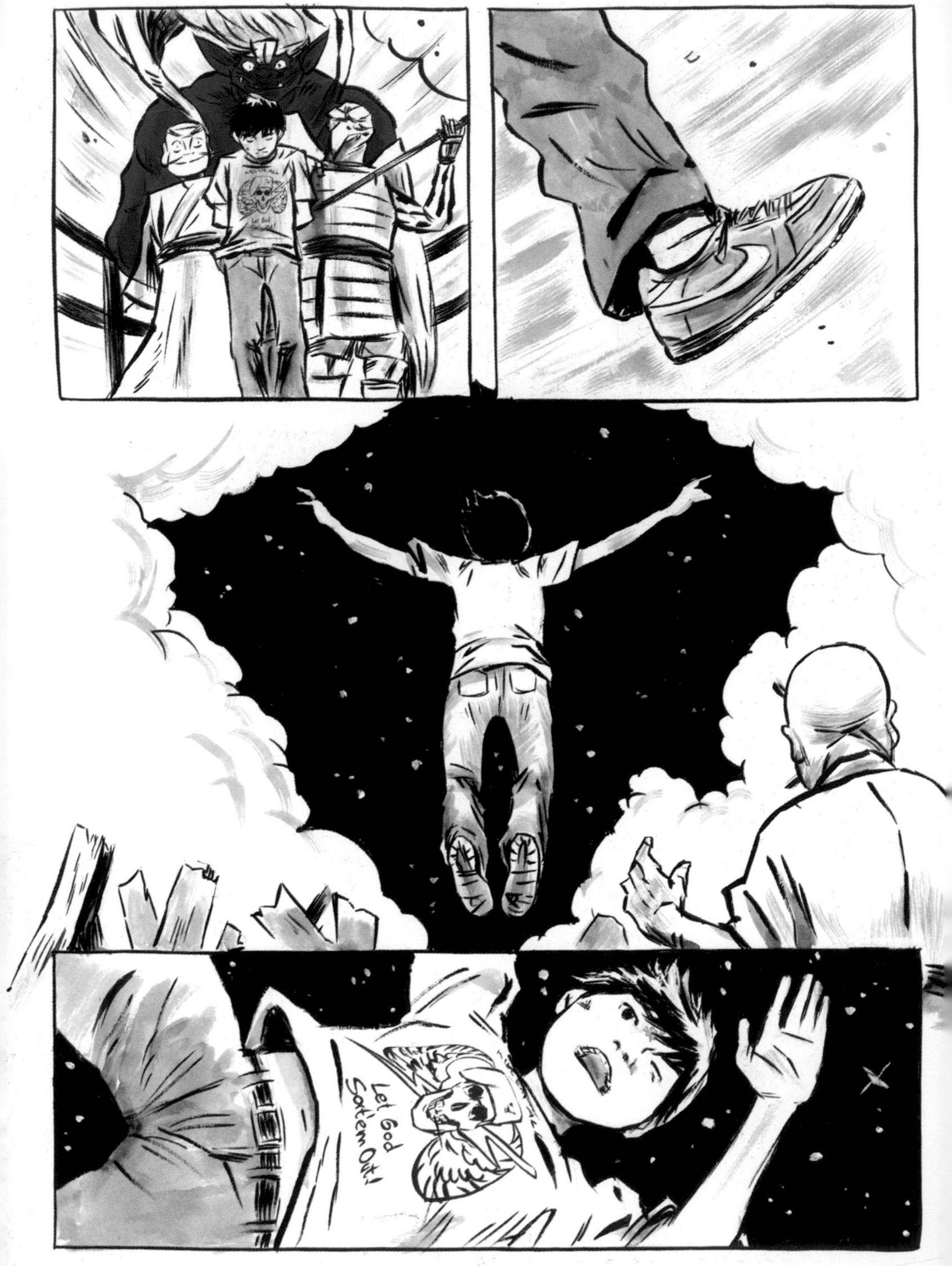
Let God
Sort'em Out!

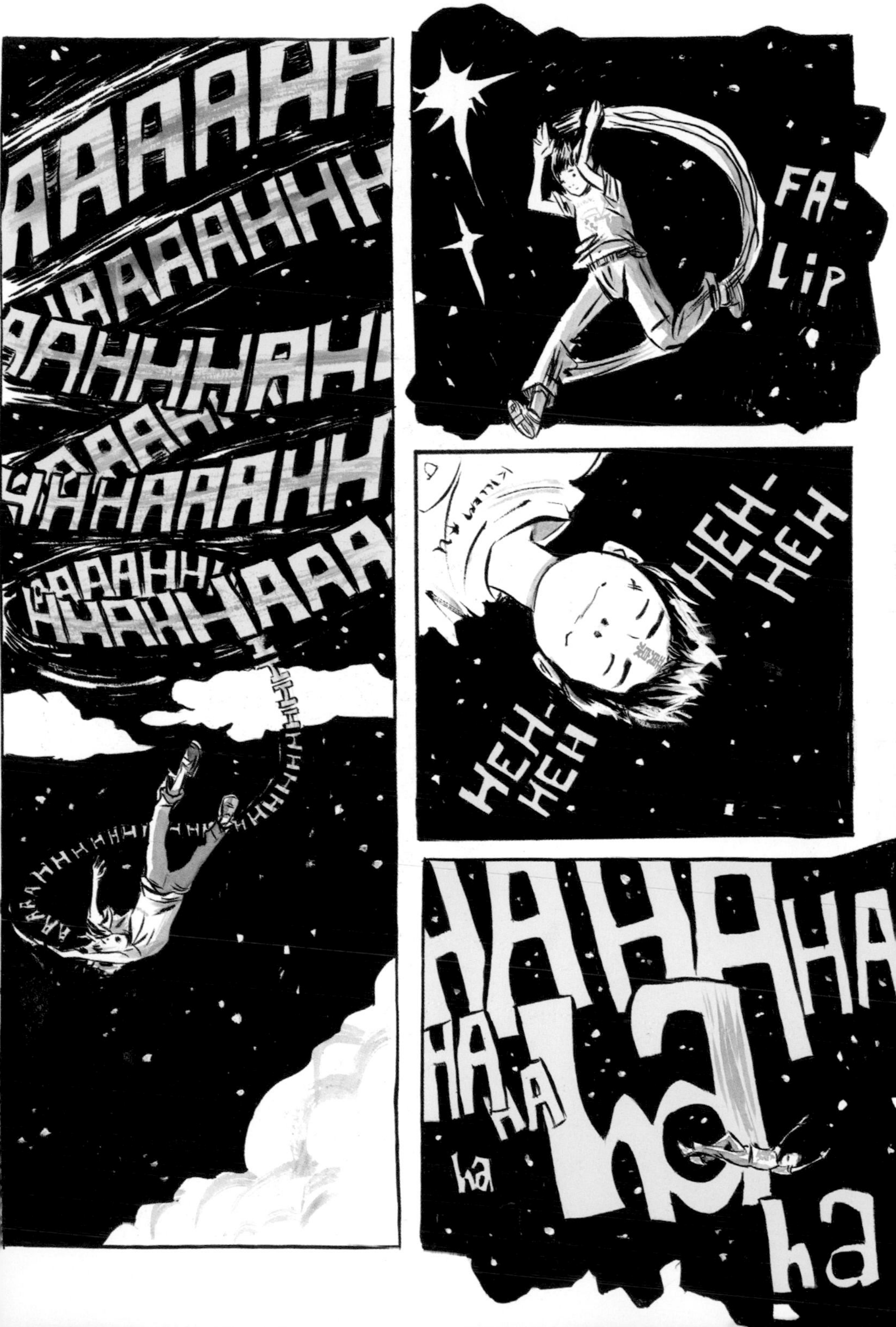
FA-
LIP
HEH-
HEH
HEH-
HEH
HA
HA
HA
HA
ha
ha
ha

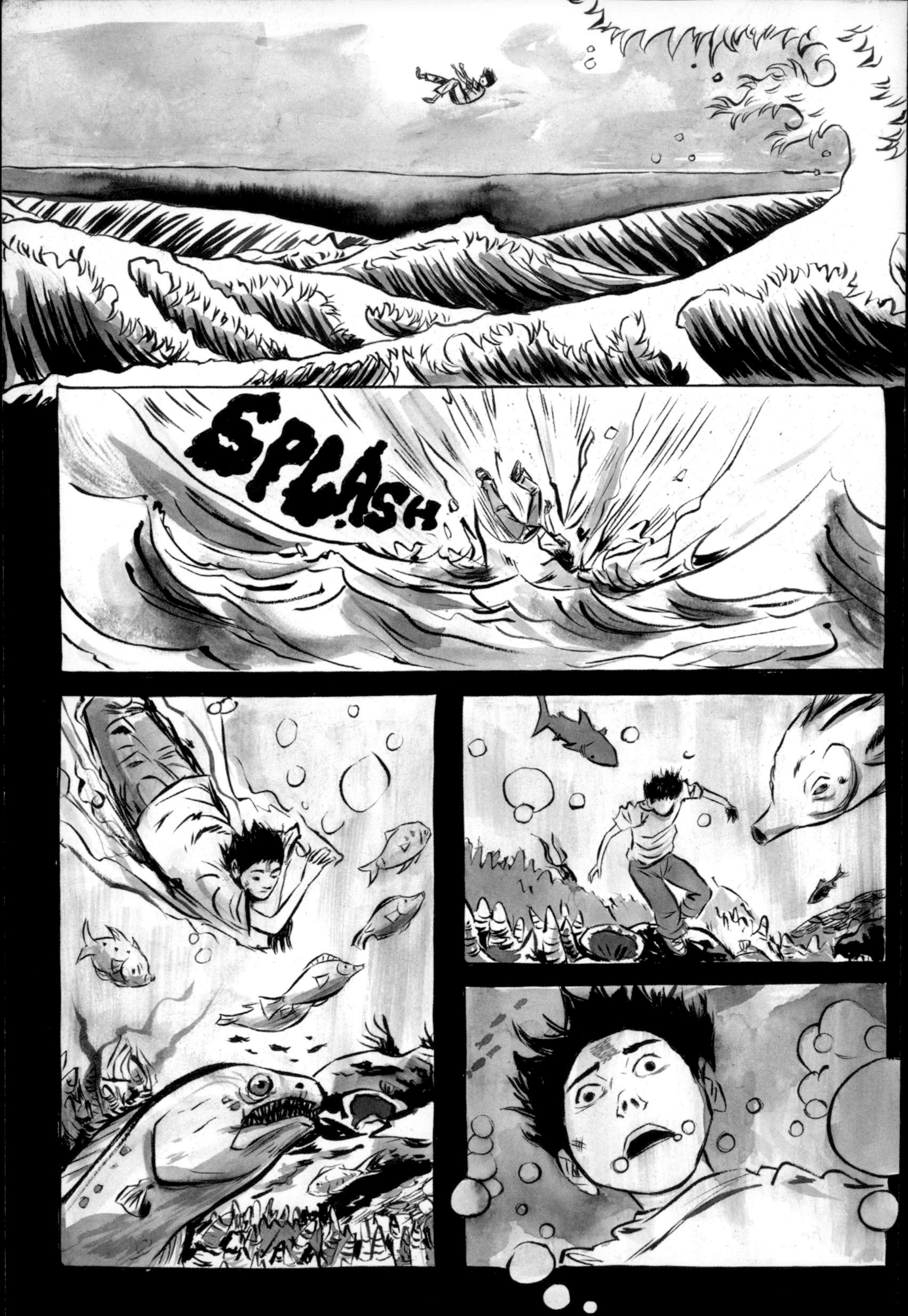
SPLASH

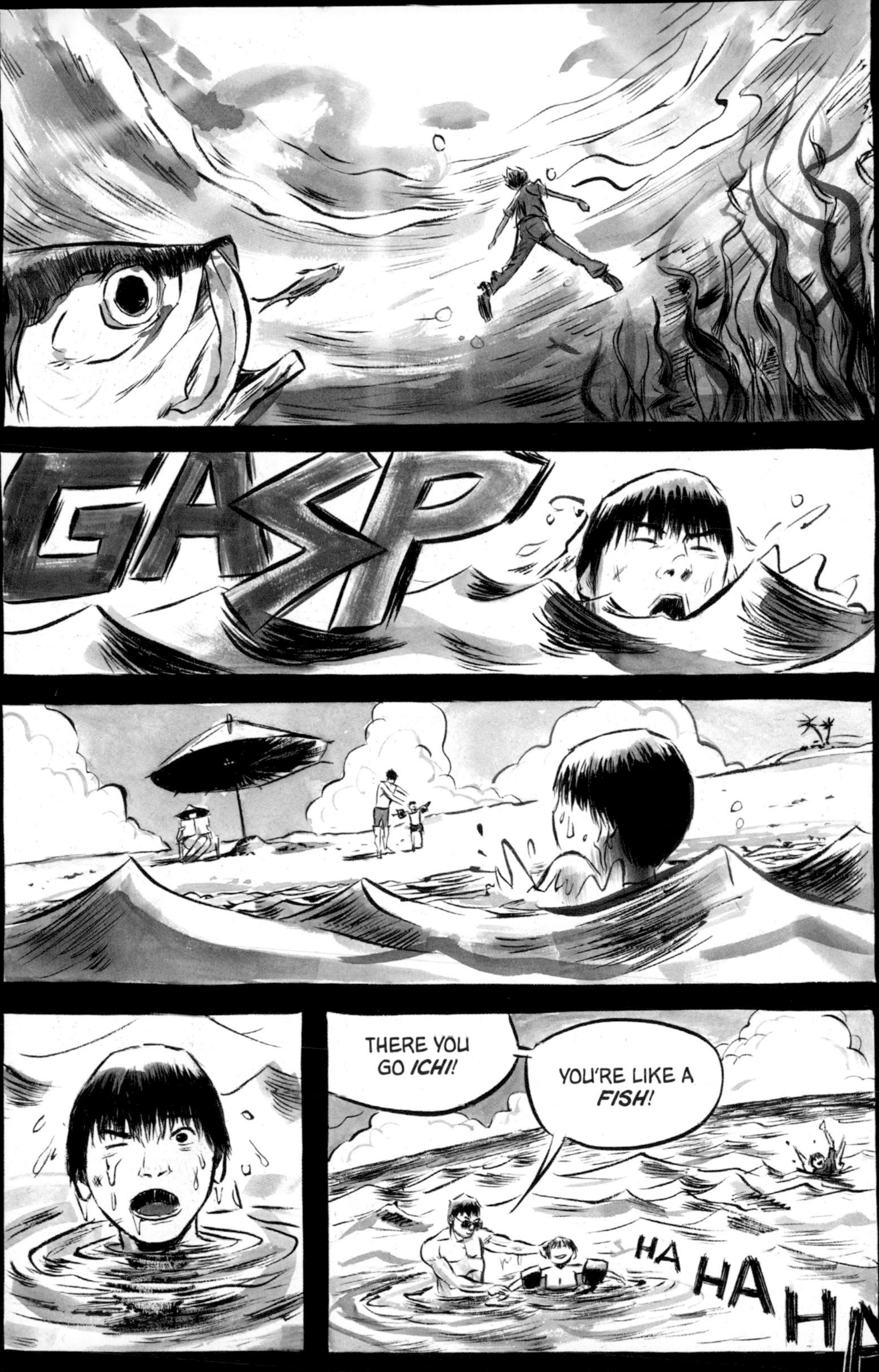
GASP
THERE YOU GO ICHI!
YOU'RE LIKE A FISH!
HA HA HA HA

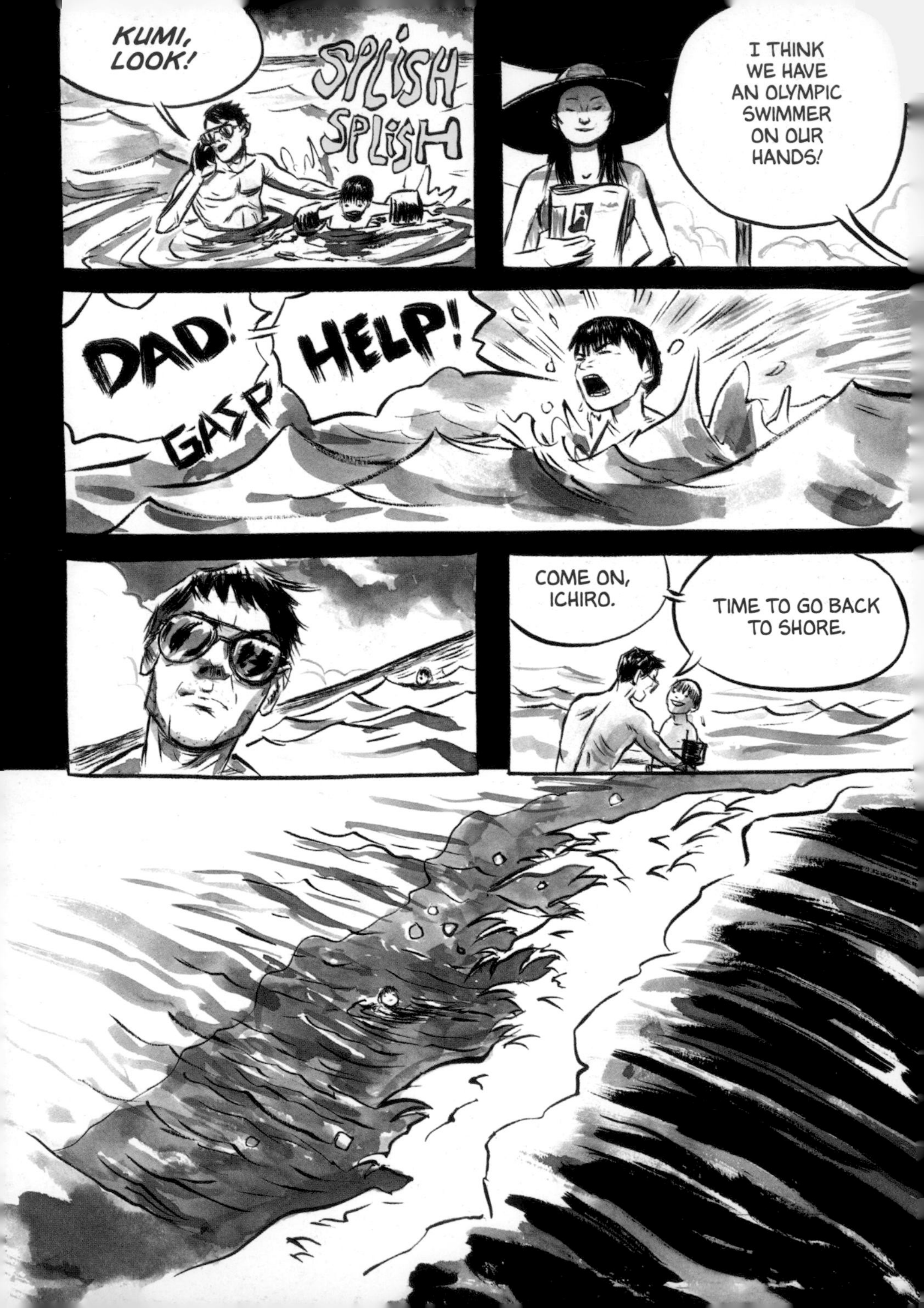
KUMI, LOOK!
SPLISH SPLISH
I THINK WE HAVE AN OLYMPIC SWIMMER ON OUR HANDS!
DAD!
GASP
HELP!
COME ON, ICHIRO.
TIME TO GO BACK TO SHORE.

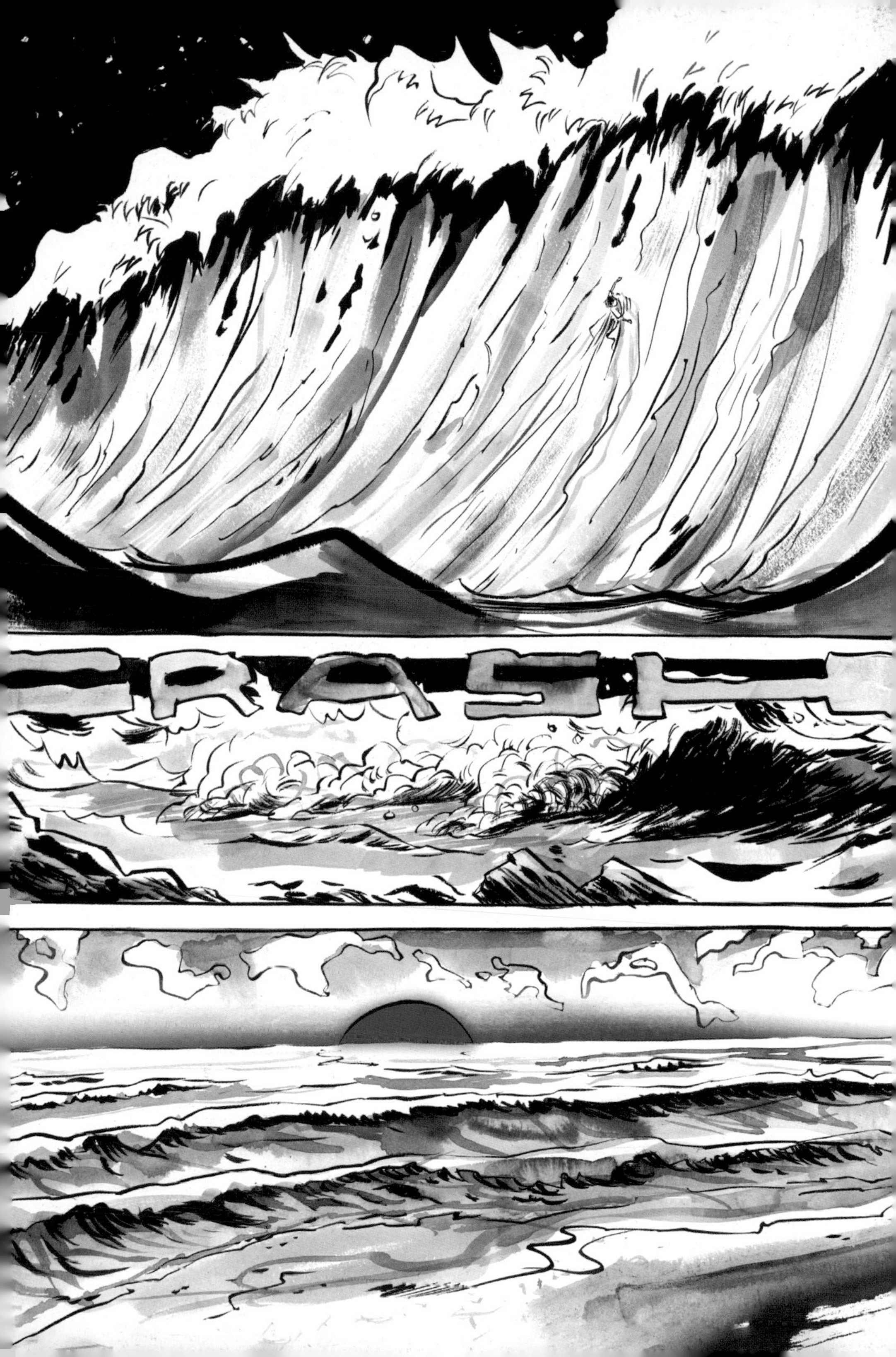
CRASH

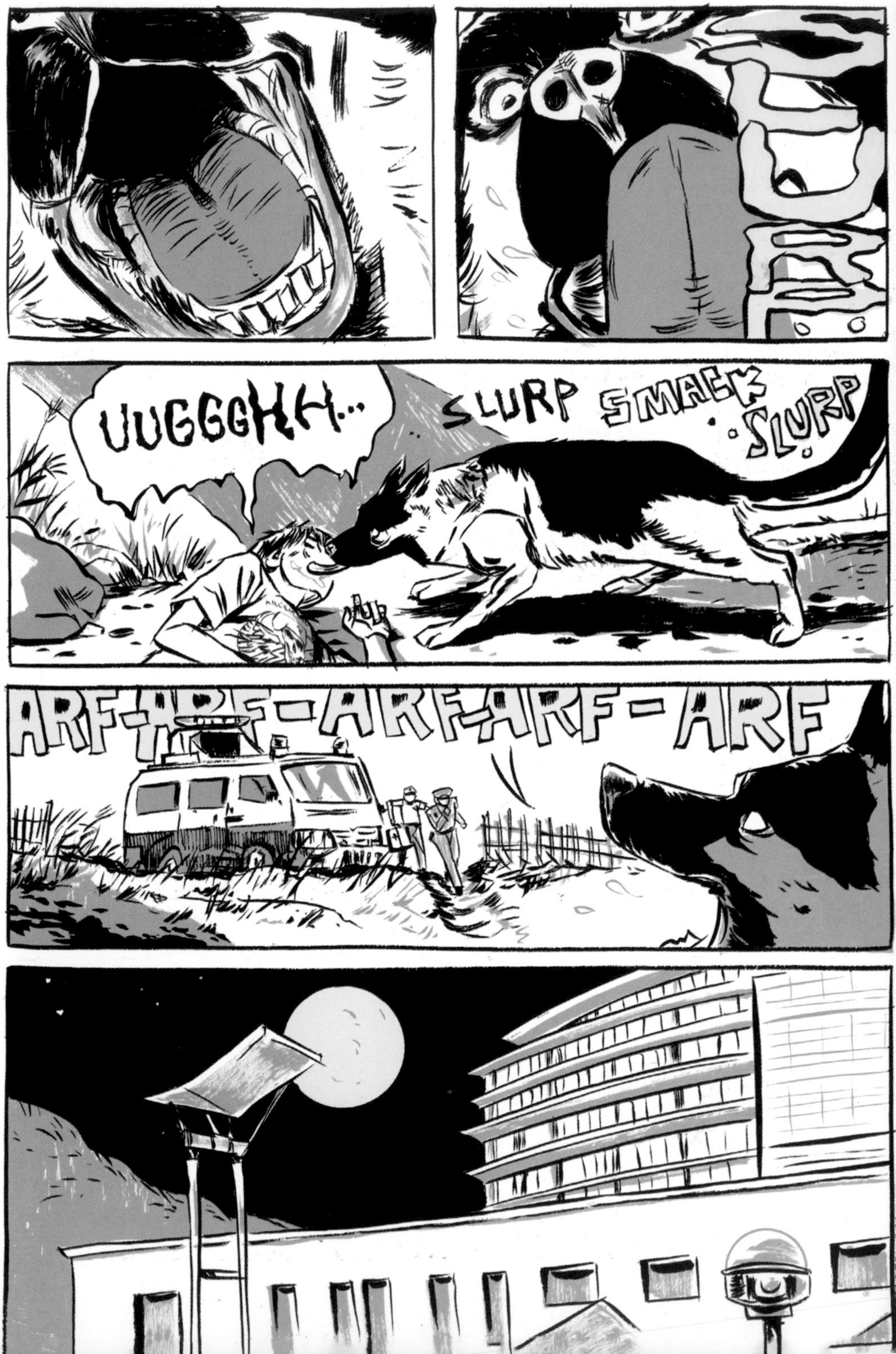
SLURP
UUGGGHH...
SLURP SMACK SLURP
ARF-ARF-ARF-ARF-ARF

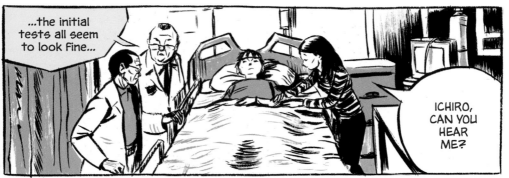

...the initial tests all seem to look fine...

ICHIRO, CAN YOU HEAR ME?

ARE YOU-- ARE YOU OK?

I'M *FINE*, MA. I'M NOT DYING OR ANYTHING.

I think it was just dehydration, but I would like to run some additional tests to be sure.

YOU HAD ME SO *WORRIED*!

I'M NEVER LEAVING YOU AGAIN!

MAAA, I'M OHH-KAY!

Give him some time to rest.

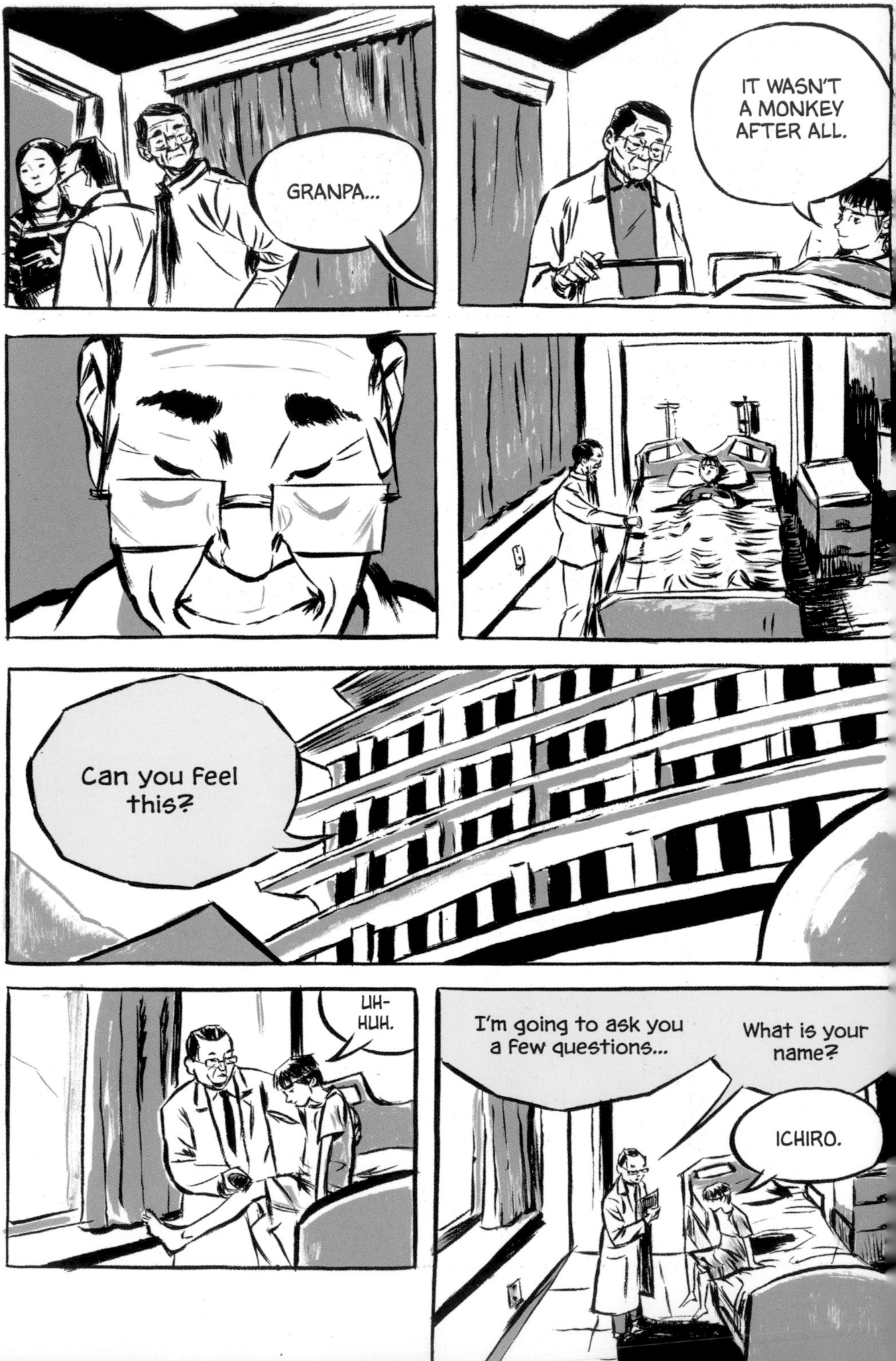
GRANPA...
IT WASN'T A MONKEY AFTER ALL.
Can you feel this?
UH-HUH.
I'm going to ask you a few questions...
What is your name?
ICHIRO.

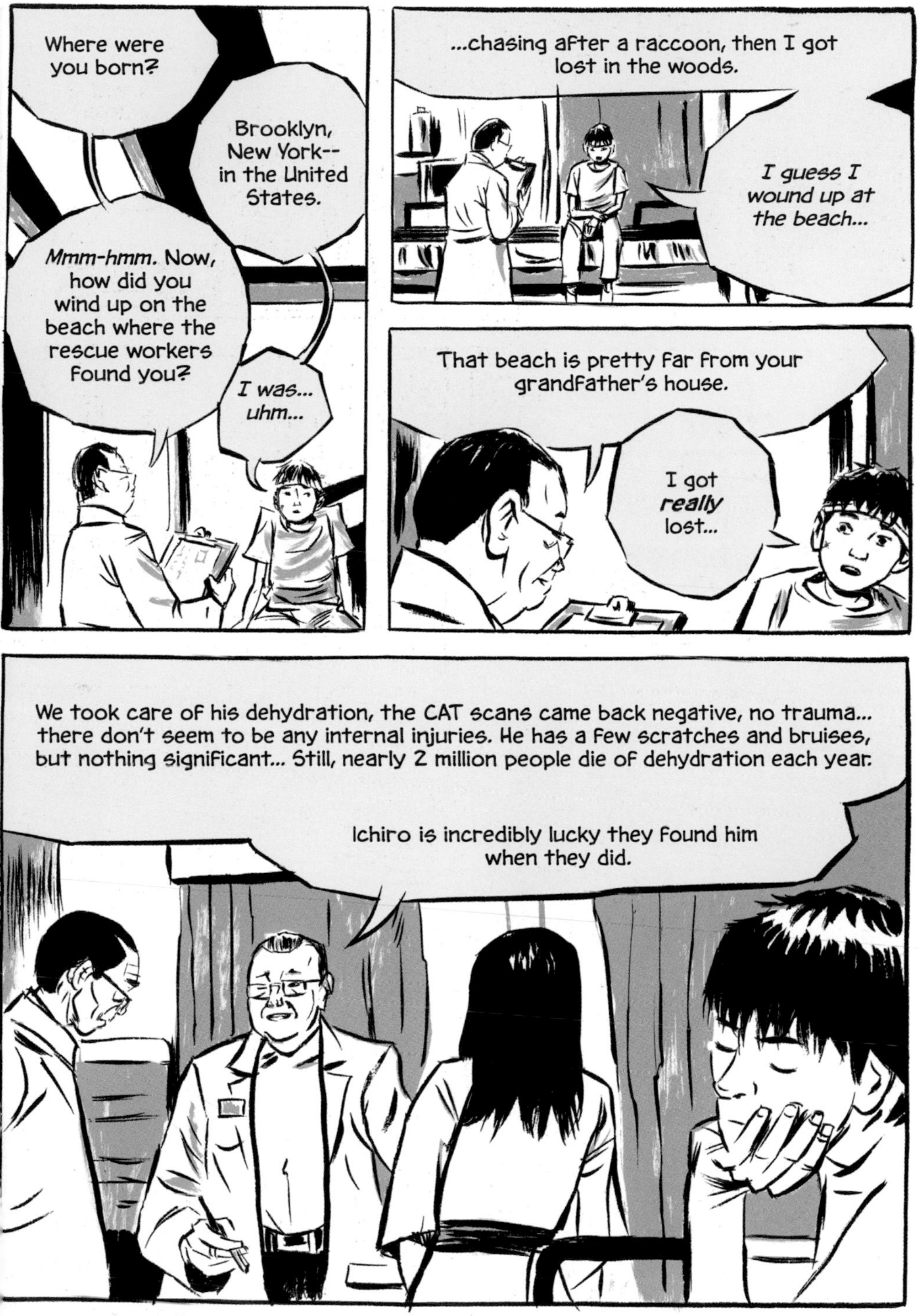
Where were you born?
Brooklyn, New York-- in the United States.
Mmm-hmm. Now, how did you wind up on the beach where the rescue workers found you?
I was... uhm...
...chasing after a raccoon, then I got lost in the woods.
I guess I wound up at the beach...
That beach is pretty far from your grandfather's house.
I got *really* lost...
We took care of his dehydration, the CAT scans came back negative, no trauma... there don't seem to be any internal injuries. He has a few scratches and bruises, but nothing significant... Still, nearly 2 million people die of dehydration each year.
Ichiro is incredibly lucky they found him when they did.

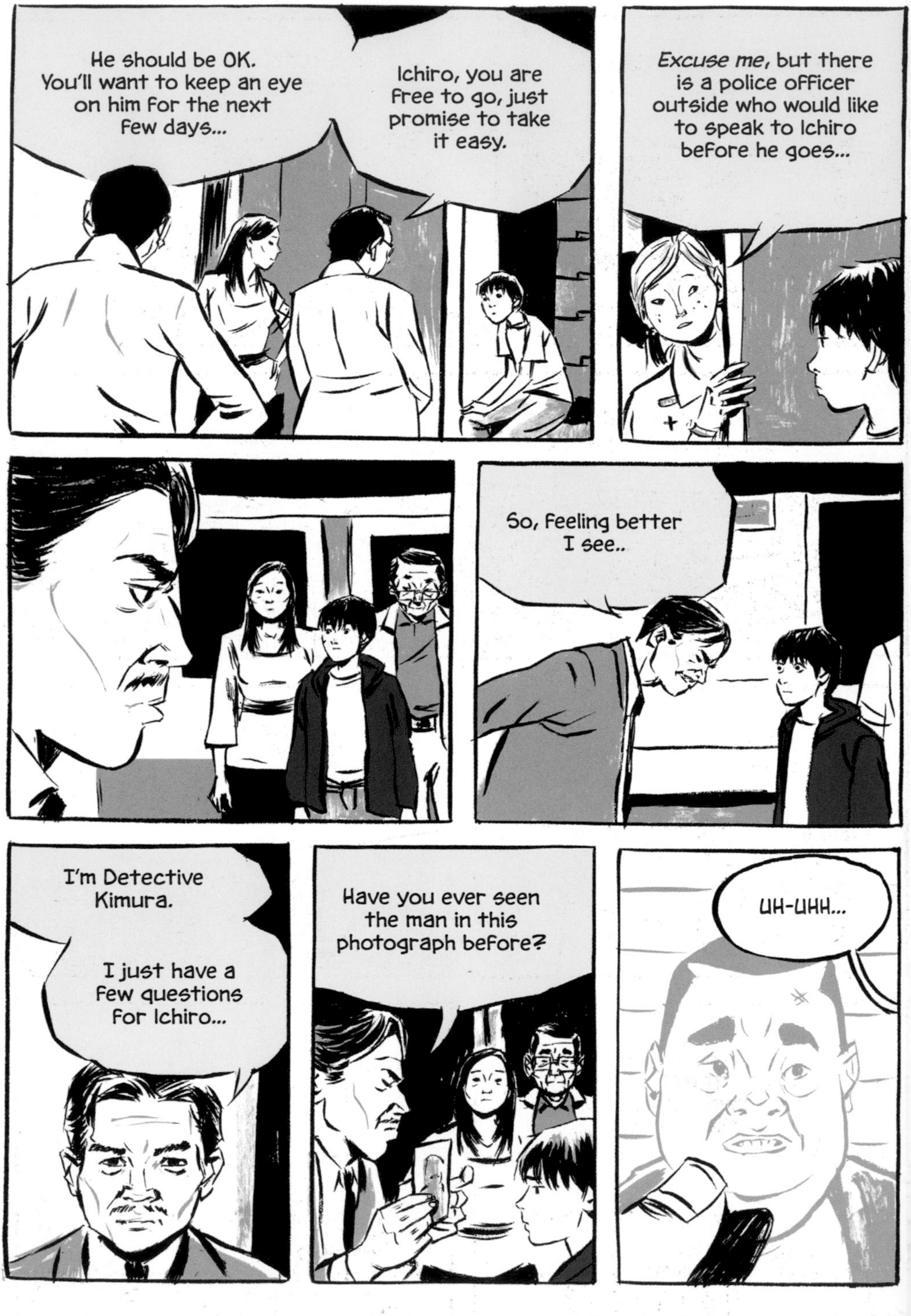
He should be OK. You'll want to keep an eye on him for the next few days...
Ichiro, you are free to go, just promise to take it easy.
Excuse me, but there is a police officer outside who would like to speak to Ichiro before he goes...
So, feeling better I see..
I'm Detective Kimura.
I just have a few questions for Ichiro...
Have you ever seen the man in this photograph before?
UH-UHH...

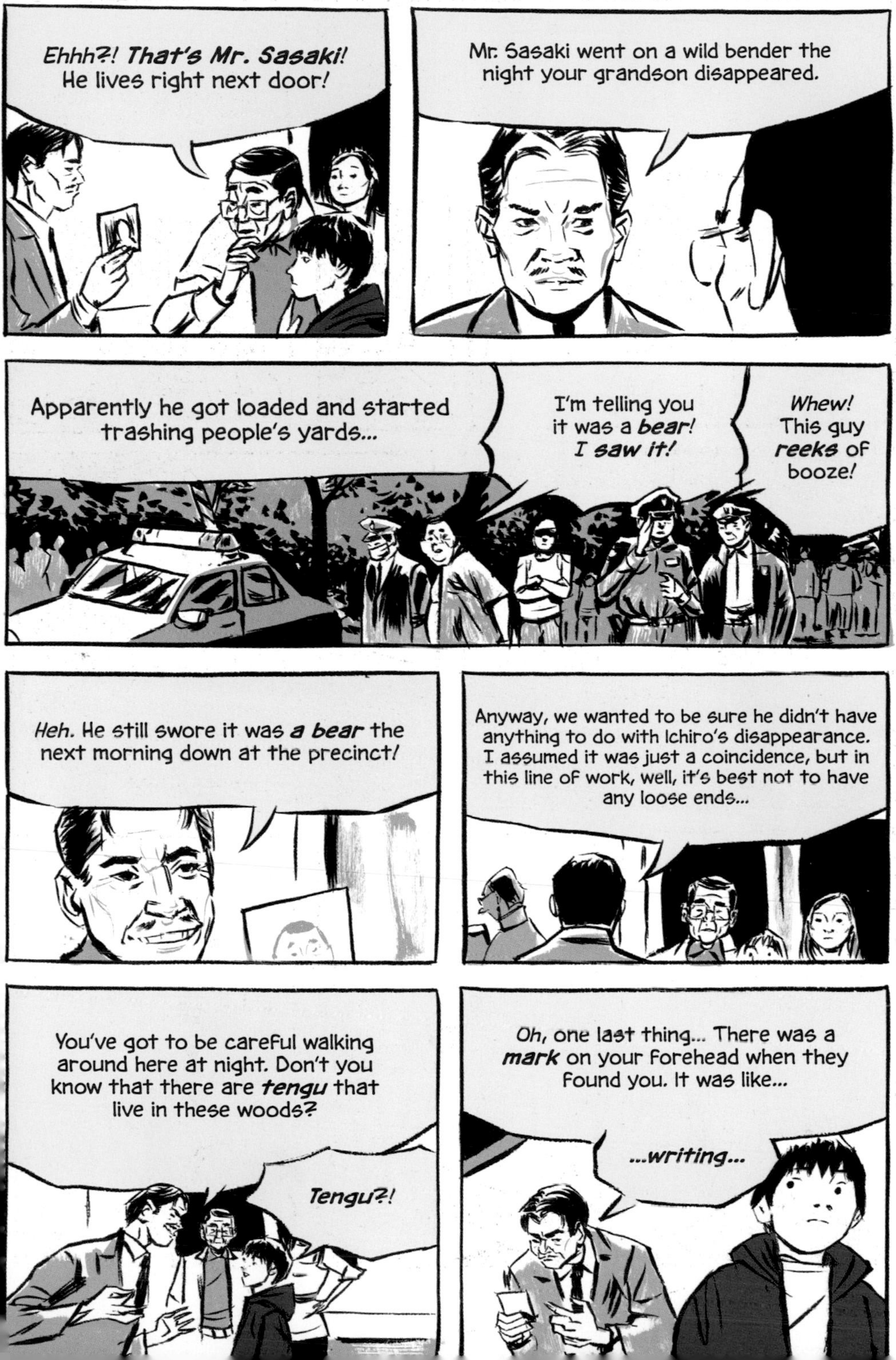
Ehhh?! That's Mr. Sasaki! He lives right next door!
Mr. Sasaki went on a wild bender the night your grandson disappeared.
Apparently he got loaded and started trashing people's yards...
I'm telling you it was a bear! I saw it!
Whew! This guy reeks of booze!
Heh. He still swore it was a bear the next morning down at the precinct!
Anyway, we wanted to be sure he didn't have anything to do with Ichiro's disappearance. I assumed it was just a coincidence, but in this line of work, well, it's best not to have any loose ends...
You've got to be careful walking around here at night. Don't you know that there are tengu that live in these woods?
Tengu?!
Oh, one last thing... There was a mark on your forehead when they found you. It was like...
...writing...

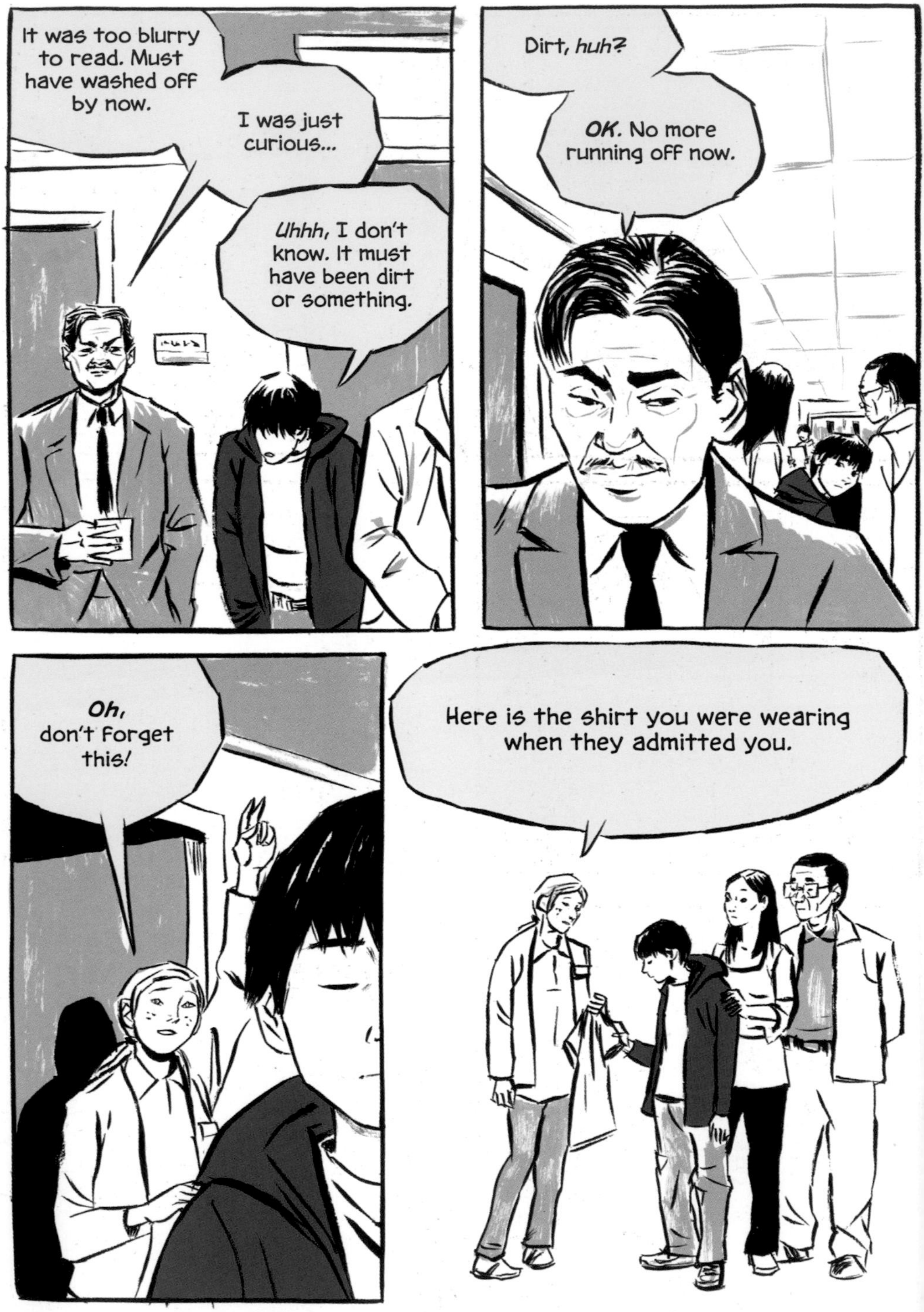
It was too blurry to read. Must have washed off by now.
I was just curious...
Uhhh, I don't know. It must have been dirt or something.
Dirt, *huh?*
OK. No more running off now.
Oh, don't forget this!
Here is the shirt you were wearing when they admitted you.

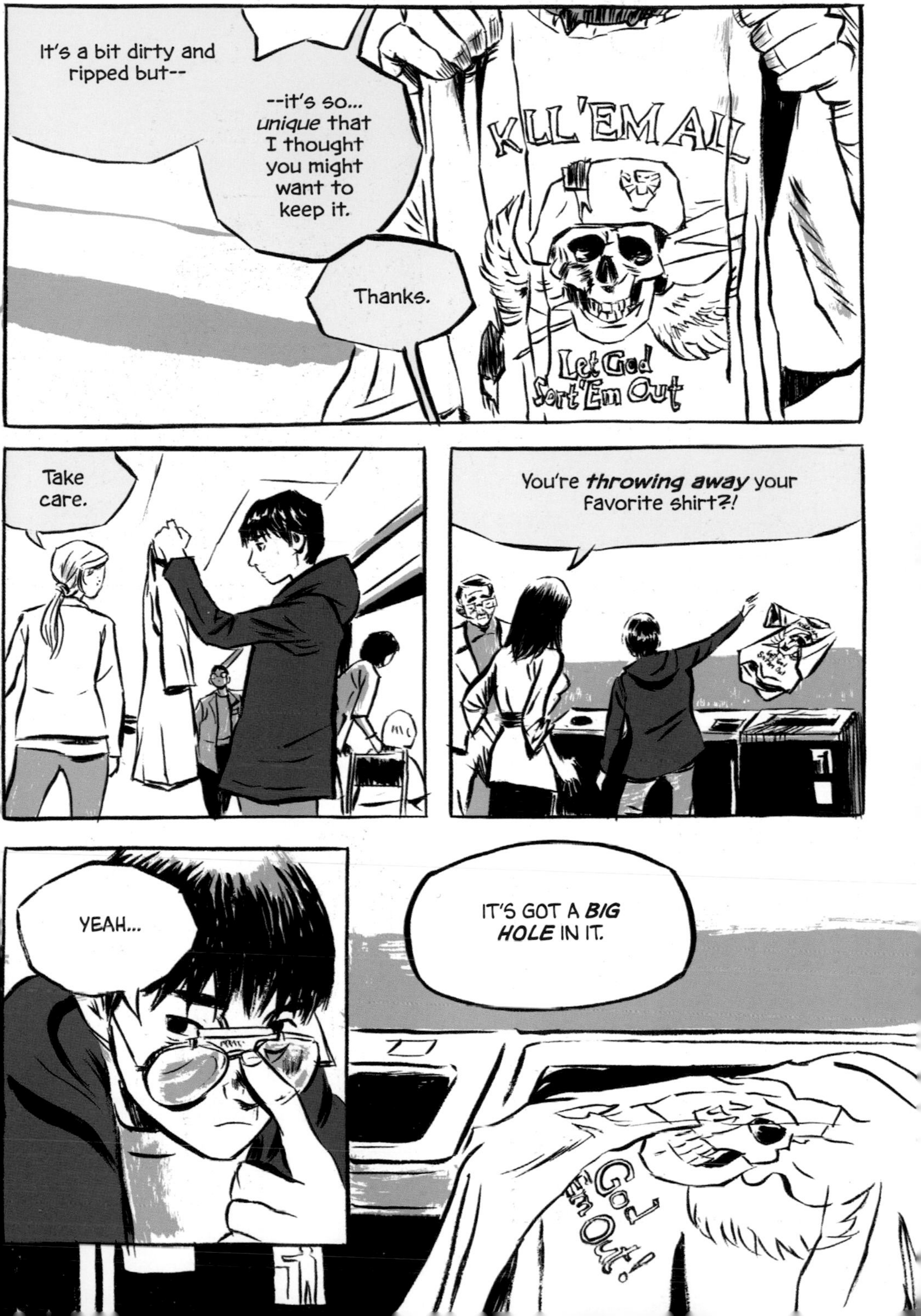
It's a bit dirty and ripped but--
--it's so... *unique* that I thought you might want to keep it.
Thanks.
KILL 'EM ALL
Let God Sort 'Em Out
Take care.
You're ***throwing away*** your favorite shirt?!
YEAH...
IT'S GOT A ***BIG HOLE*** IN IT.
God 'Em Out!

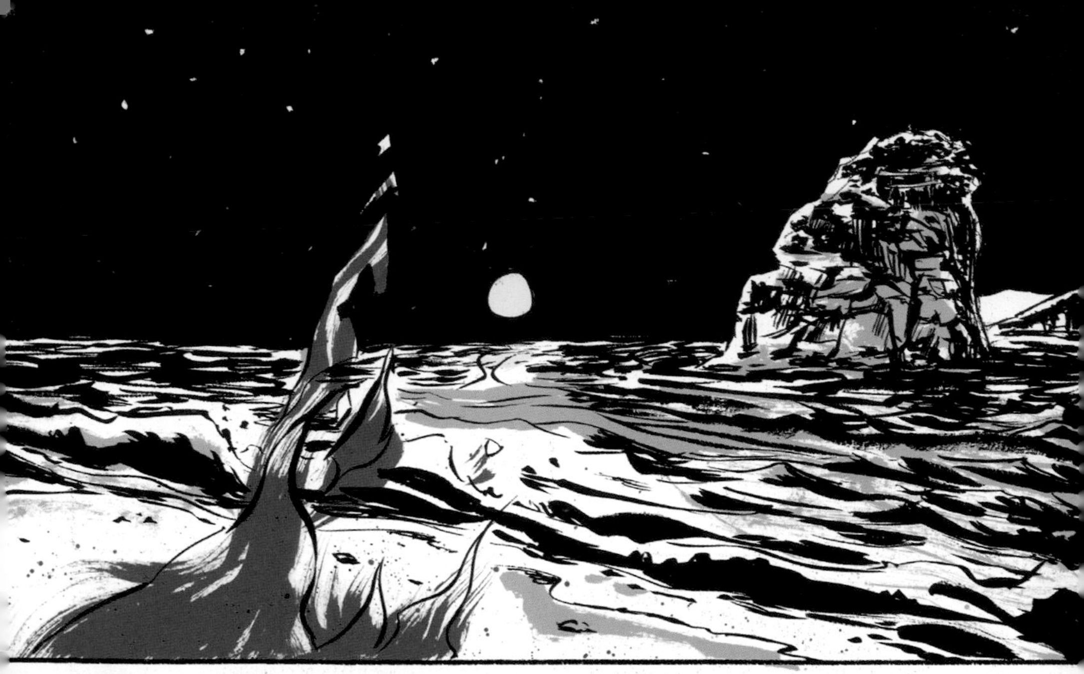

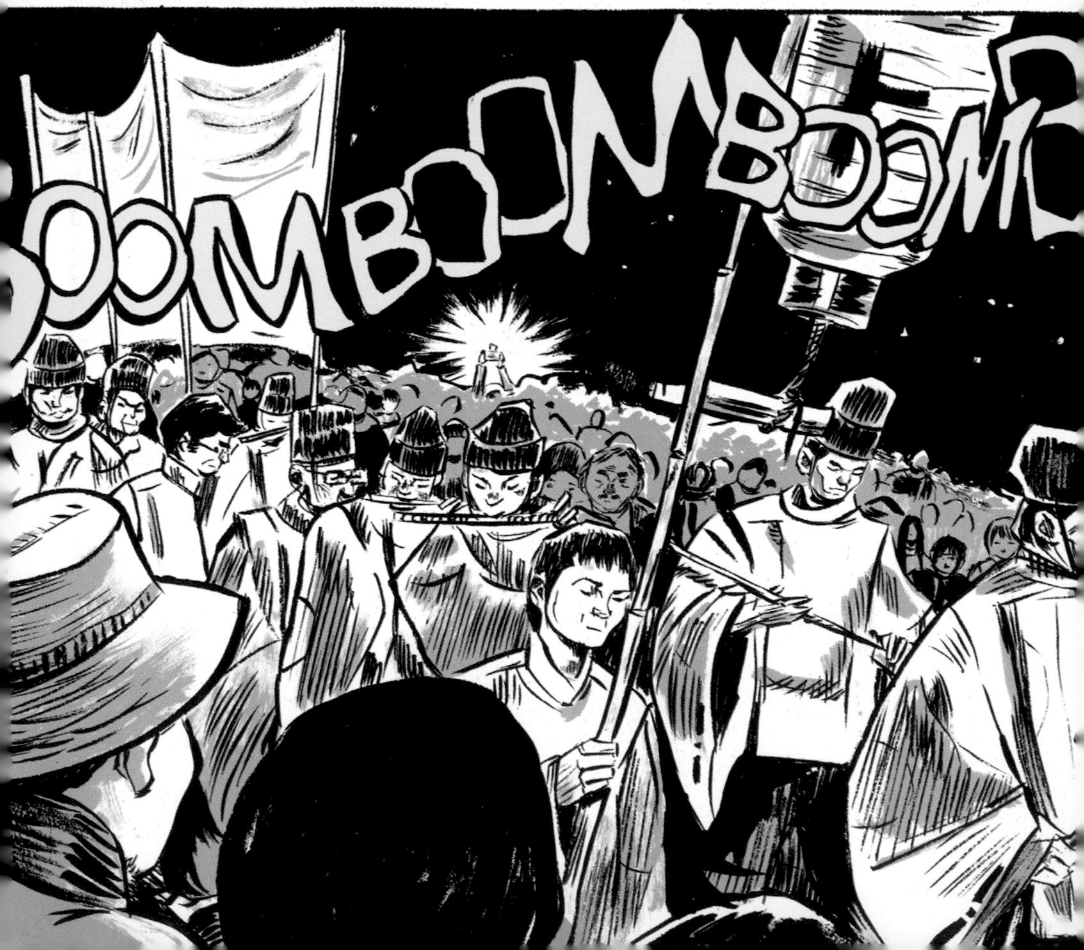
BOOMBOOMBOOM

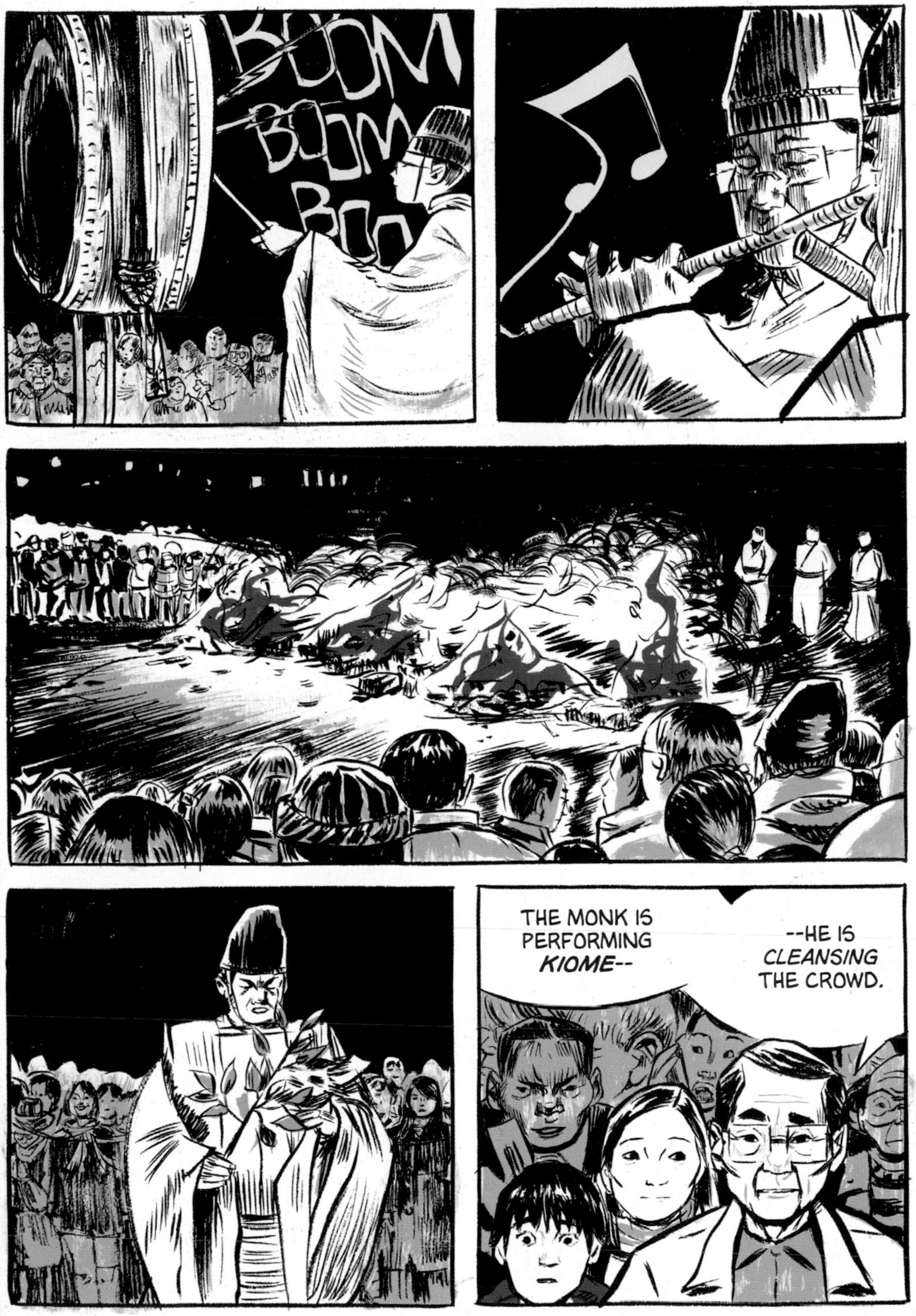
BOOM
BOOM
BOO
THE MONK IS PERFORMING *KIOME*--
--HE IS *CLEANSING* THE CROWD.

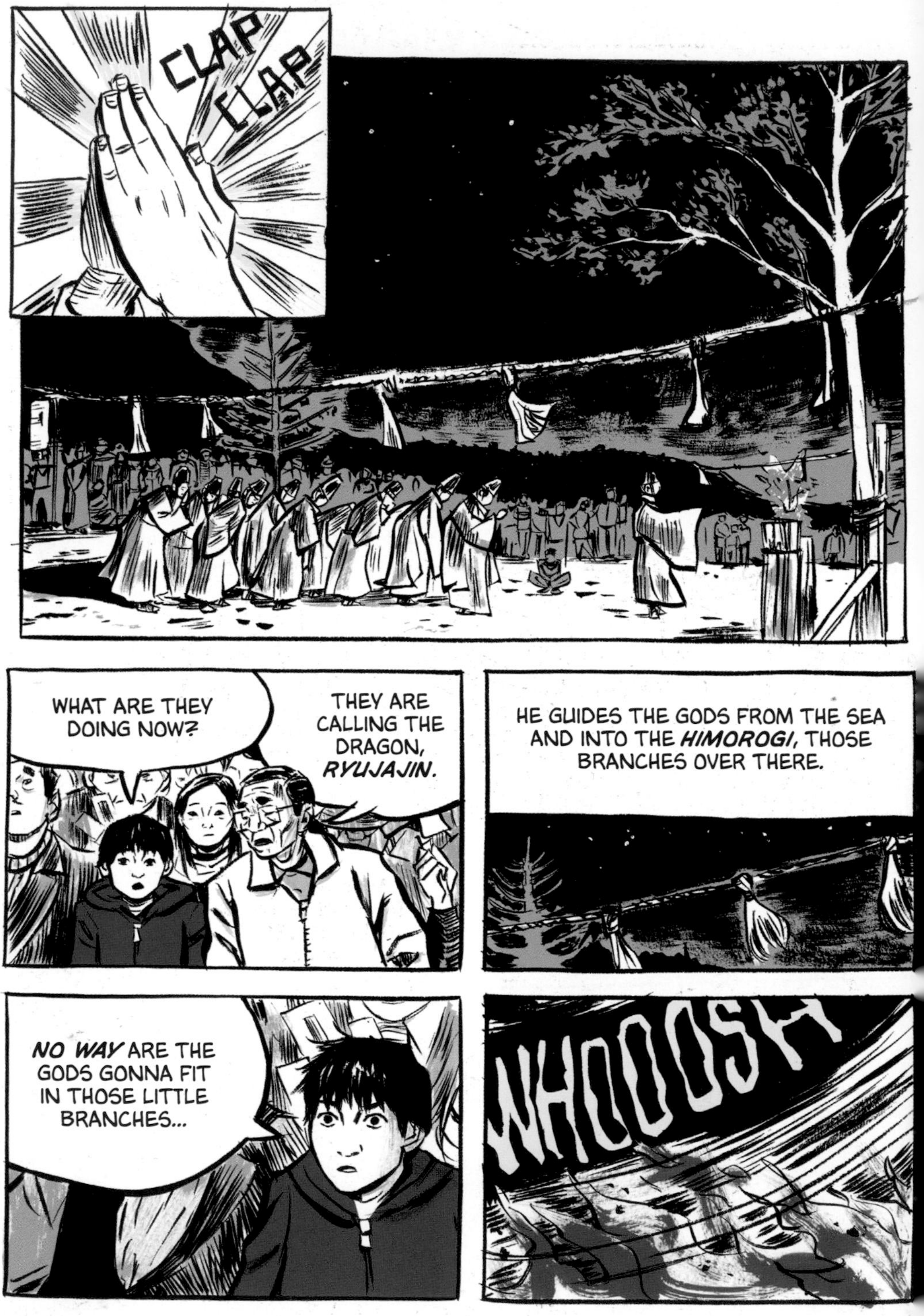
CLAP CLAP
WHAT ARE THEY DOING NOW?
THEY ARE CALLING THE DRAGON, *RYUJAJIN.*
HE GUIDES THE GODS FROM THE SEA AND INTO THE *HIMOROGI*, THOSE BRANCHES OVER THERE.
NO WAY ARE THE GODS GONNA FIT IN THOSE LITTLE BRANCHES...
WHOOOSH

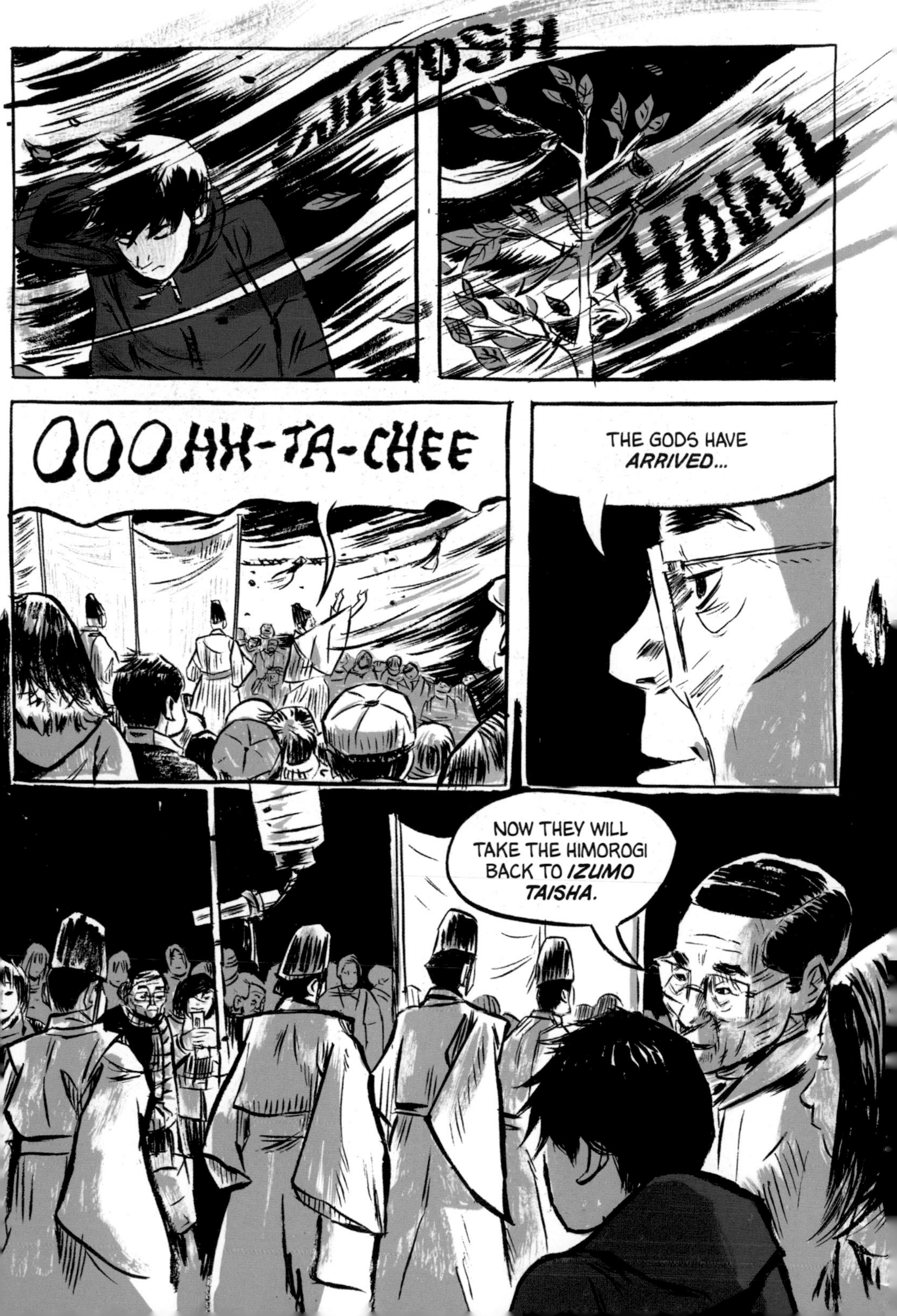
WHOOSH
HOWL
OOOHH-TA-CHEE
THE GODS HAVE ARRIVED...
NOW THEY WILL TAKE THE HIMOROGI BACK TO IZUMO TAISHA.

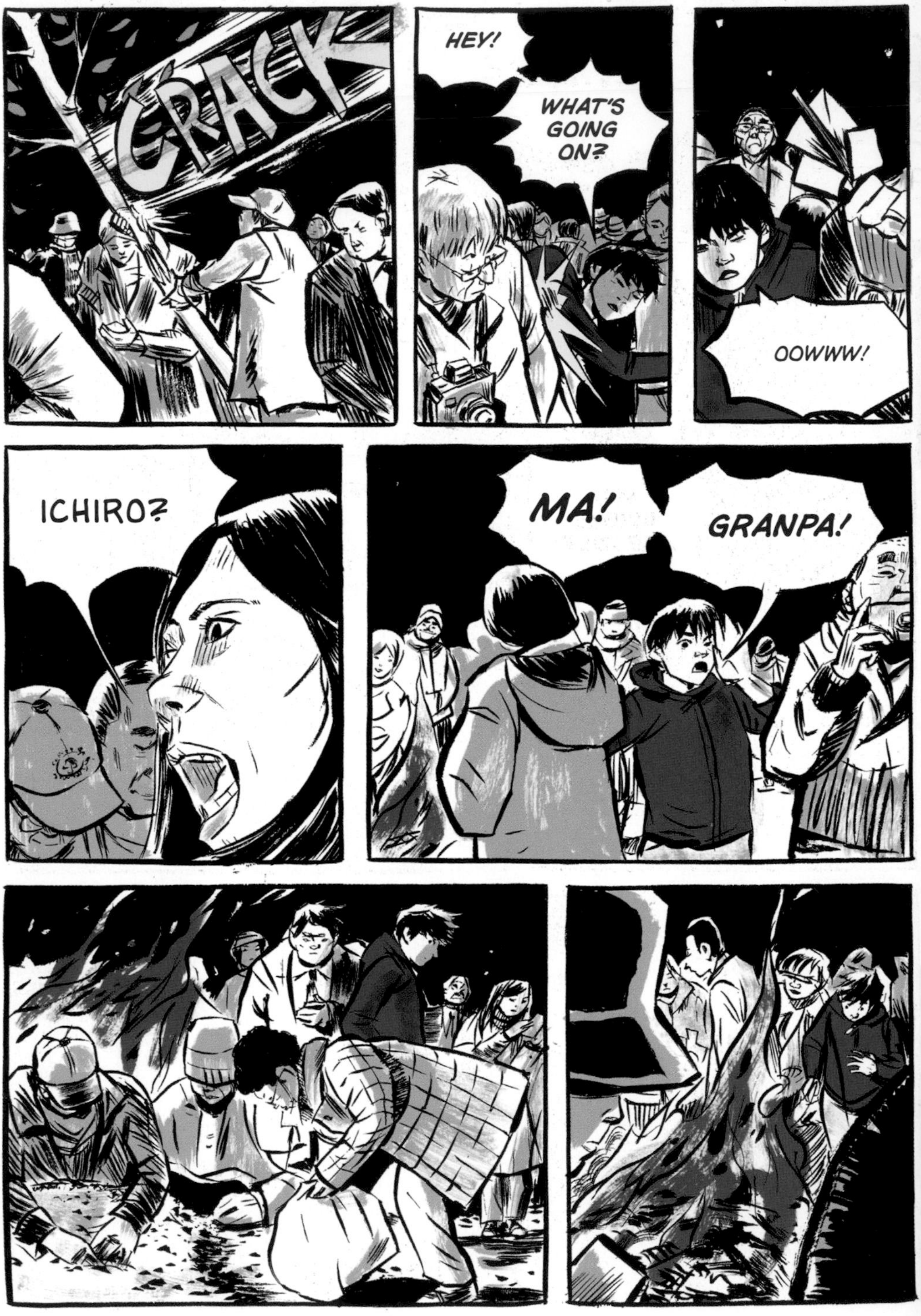
CRACK
HEY!
WHAT'S GOING ON?
OOWWW!
ICHIRO?
MA!
GRANPA!

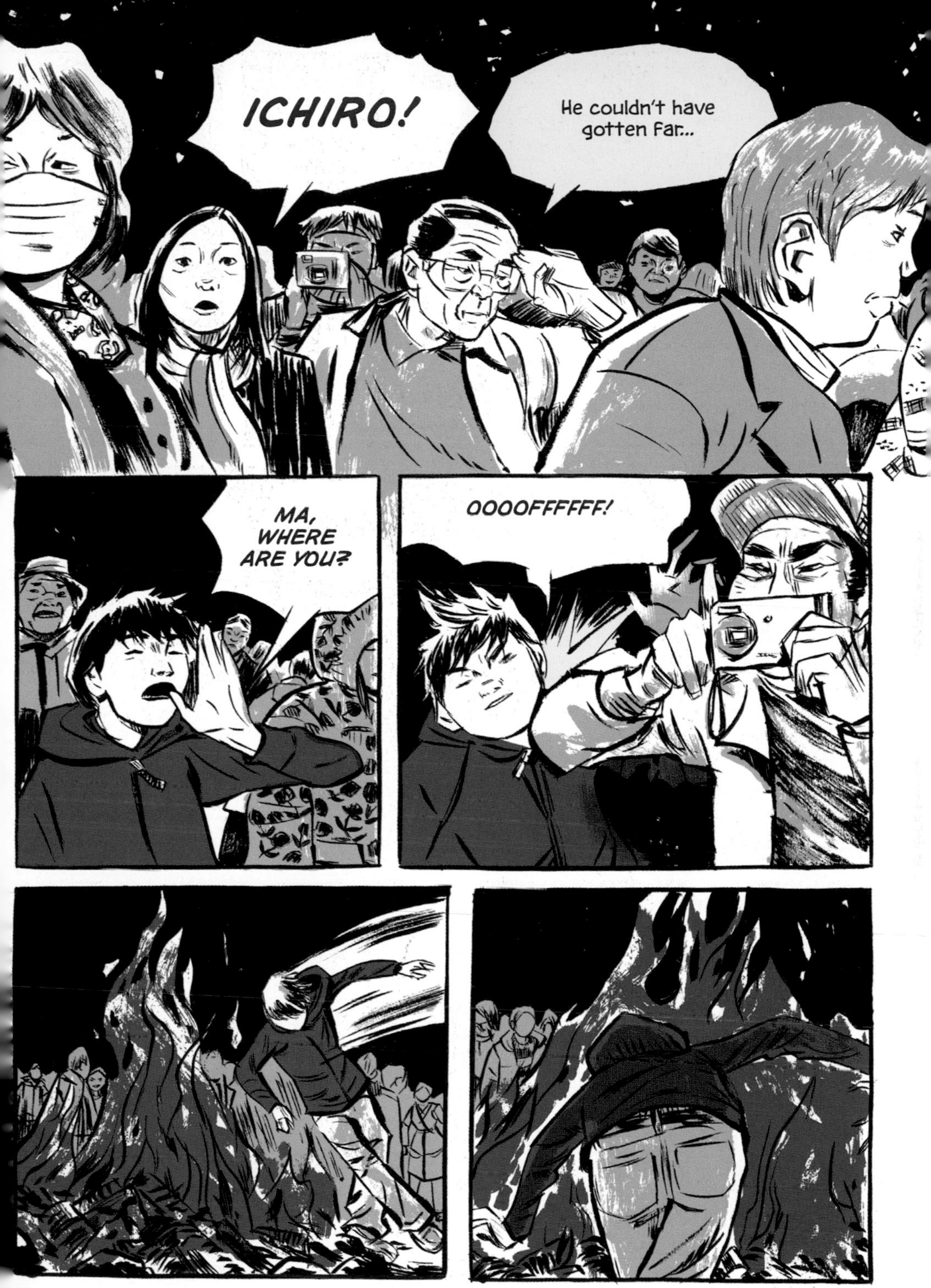
ICHIRO!
He couldn't have gotten far...
MA, WHERE ARE YOU?
OOOOFFFFFF!

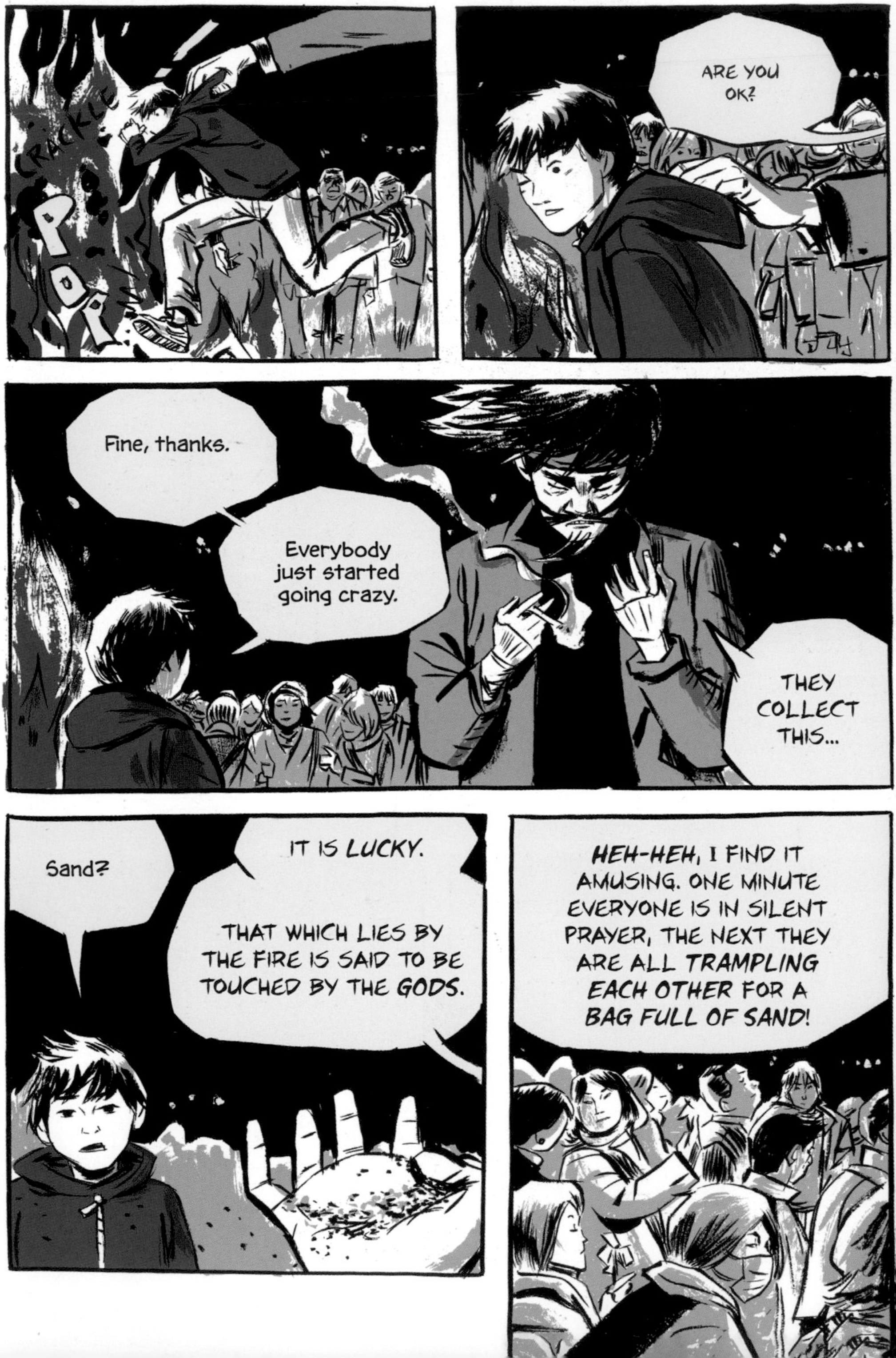
CRACKLE
POP
POP
ARE YOU OK?
Fine, thanks.
Everybody just started going crazy.
THEY COLLECT THIS...
Sand?
IT IS LUCKY.
THAT WHICH LIES BY THE FIRE IS SAID TO BE TOUCHED BY THE GODS.
HEH-HEH, I FIND IT AMUSING. ONE MINUTE EVERYONE IS IN SILENT PRAYER, THE NEXT THEY ARE ALL TRAMPLING EACH OTHER FOR A BAG FULL OF SAND!

IT IS AN ODD WAY TO HONOR THE GODS, BUT MAYBE IT IS FITTING.

You look familiar... Are you on TV?

MY CARD.

How did you...

TAKE CARE, ICHIRO.

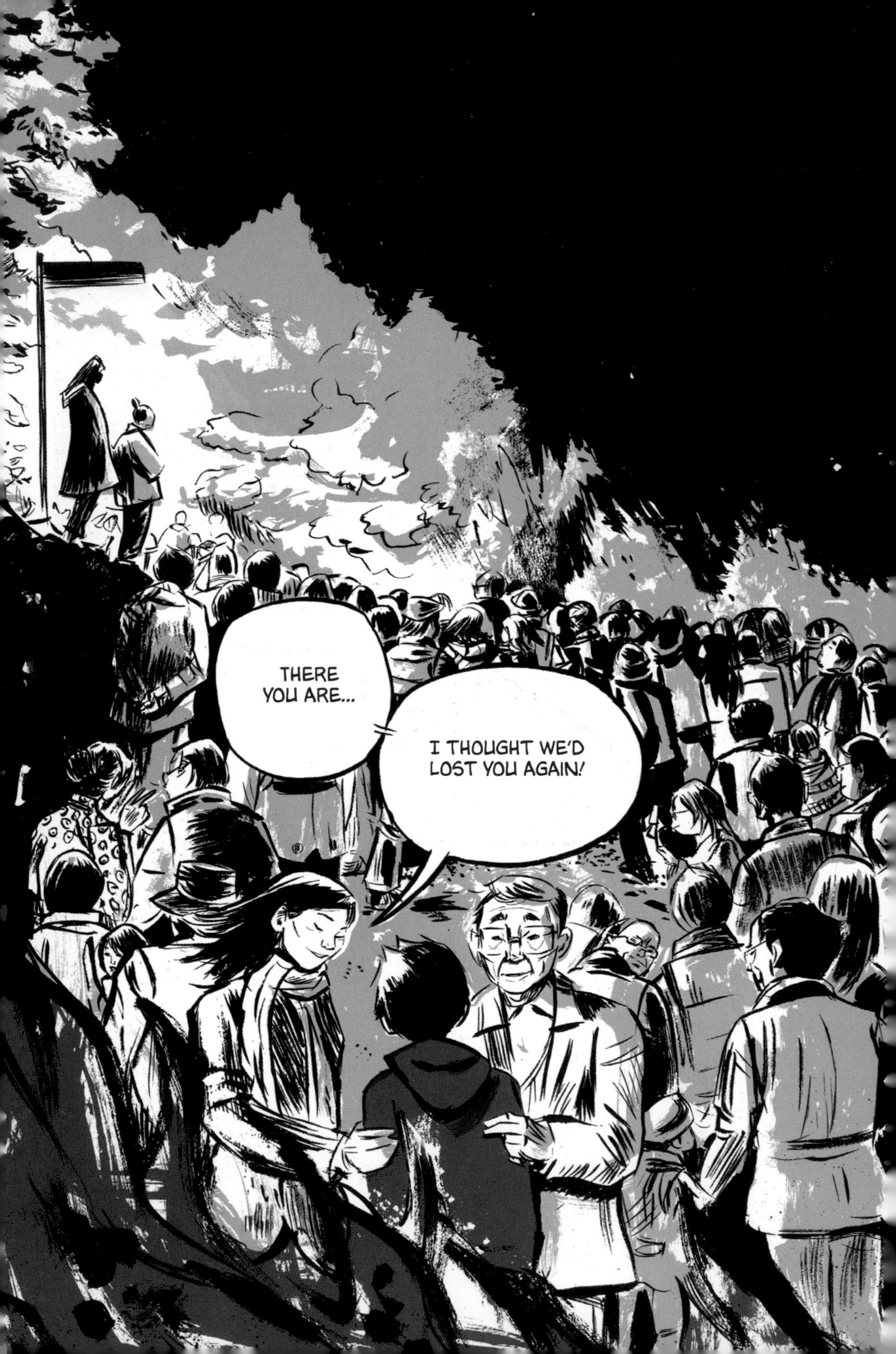
THERE YOU ARE...
I THOUGHT WE'D LOST YOU AGAIN!

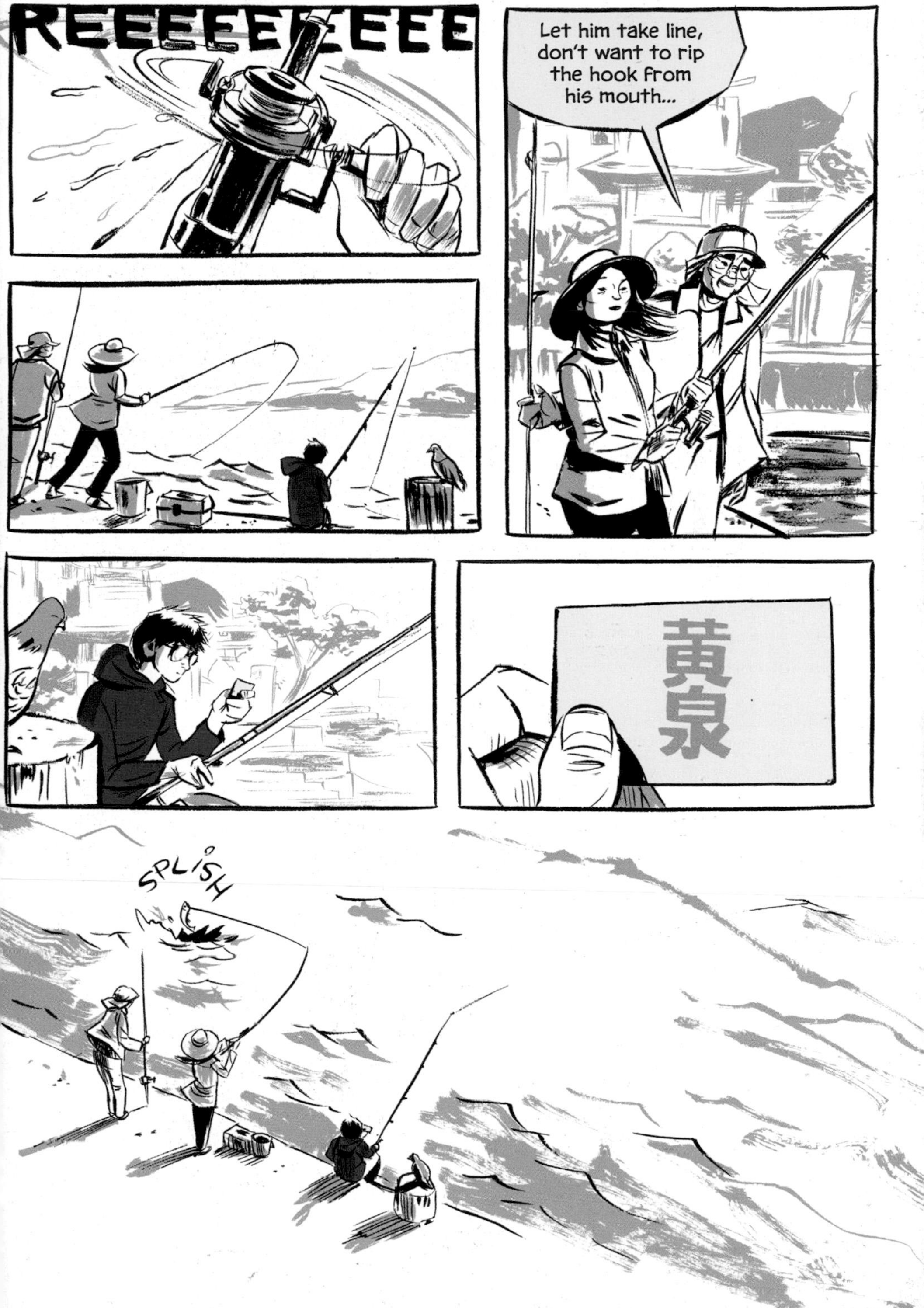
REEEEEEEEEE
Let him take line, don't want to rip the hook from his mouth...
黃泉
SPLISH

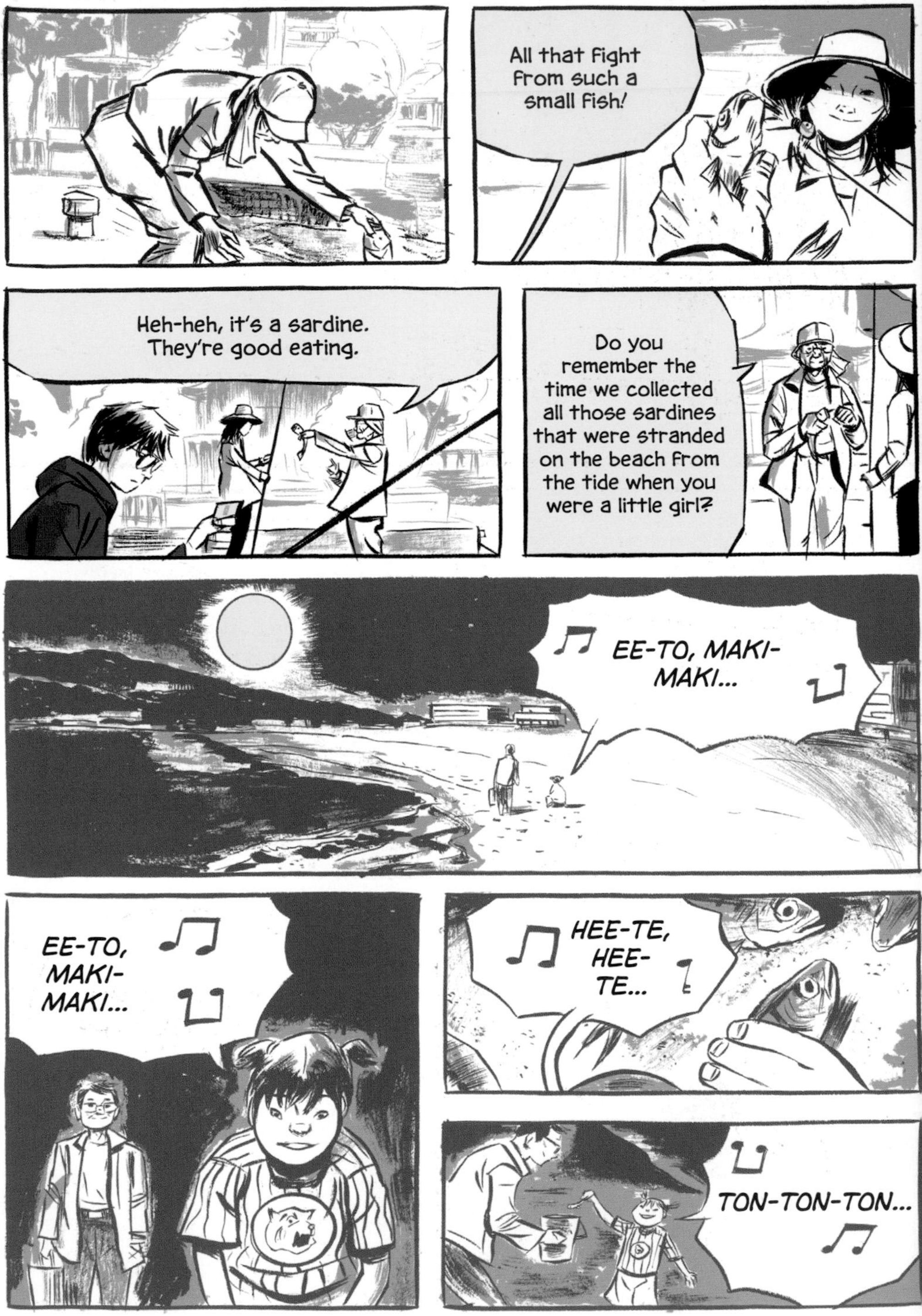
All that fight from such a small fish!
Heh-heh, it's a sardine. They're good eating.
Do you remember the time we collected all those sardines that were stranded on the beach from the tide when you were a little girl?
EE-TO, MAKI-MAKI...
EE-TO, MAKI-MAKI...
HEE-TE, HEE-TE...
TON-TON-TON...

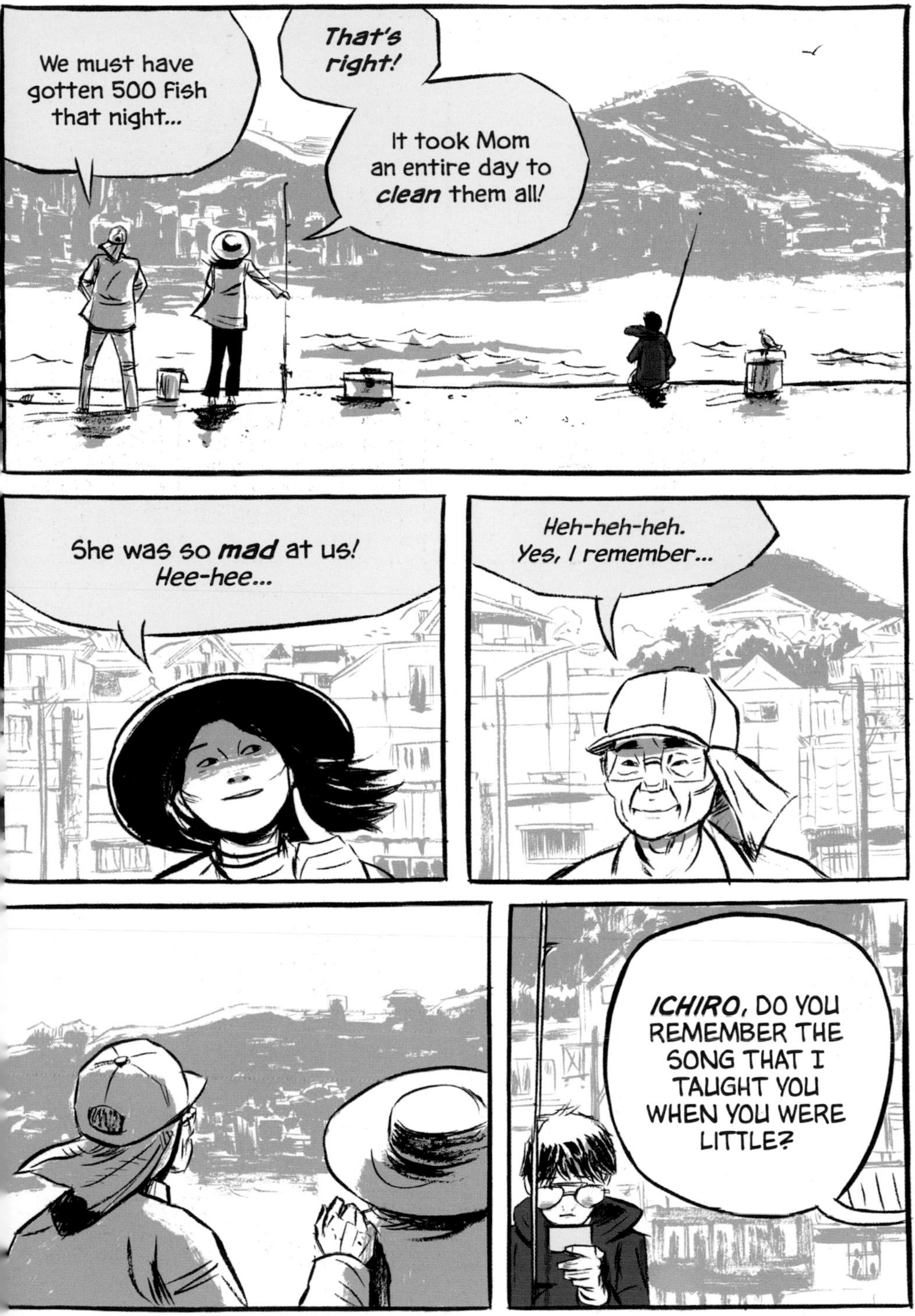
We must have gotten 500 fish that night...
That's right!
It took Mom an entire day to ***clean*** them all!
She was so ***mad*** at us! *Hee-hee...*
Heh-heh-heh. Yes, I remember...
ICHIRO, DO YOU REMEMBER THE SONG THAT I TAUGHT YOU WHEN YOU WERE LITTLE?

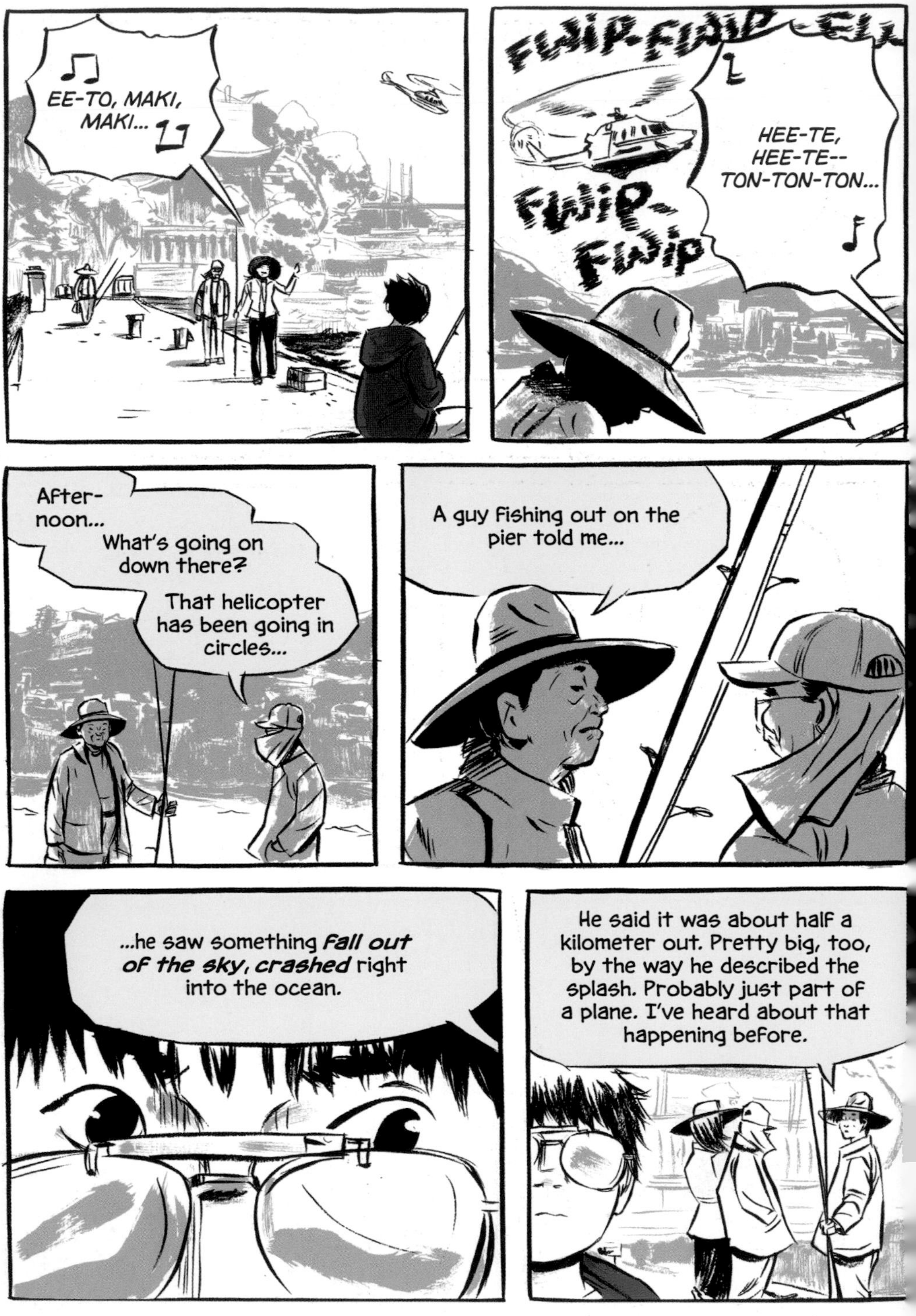

EE-TO, MAKI, MAKI...
FWIP-FWIP-FW
HEE-TE, HEE-TE-- TON-TON-TON...
FWIP-FWIP
After-noon...
What's going on down there?
That helicopter has been going in circles...
A guy fishing out on the pier told me...
...he saw something *fall out of the sky, crashed* right into the ocean.
He said it was about half a kilometer out. Pretty big, too, by the way he described the splash. Probably just part of a plane. I've heard about that happening before.

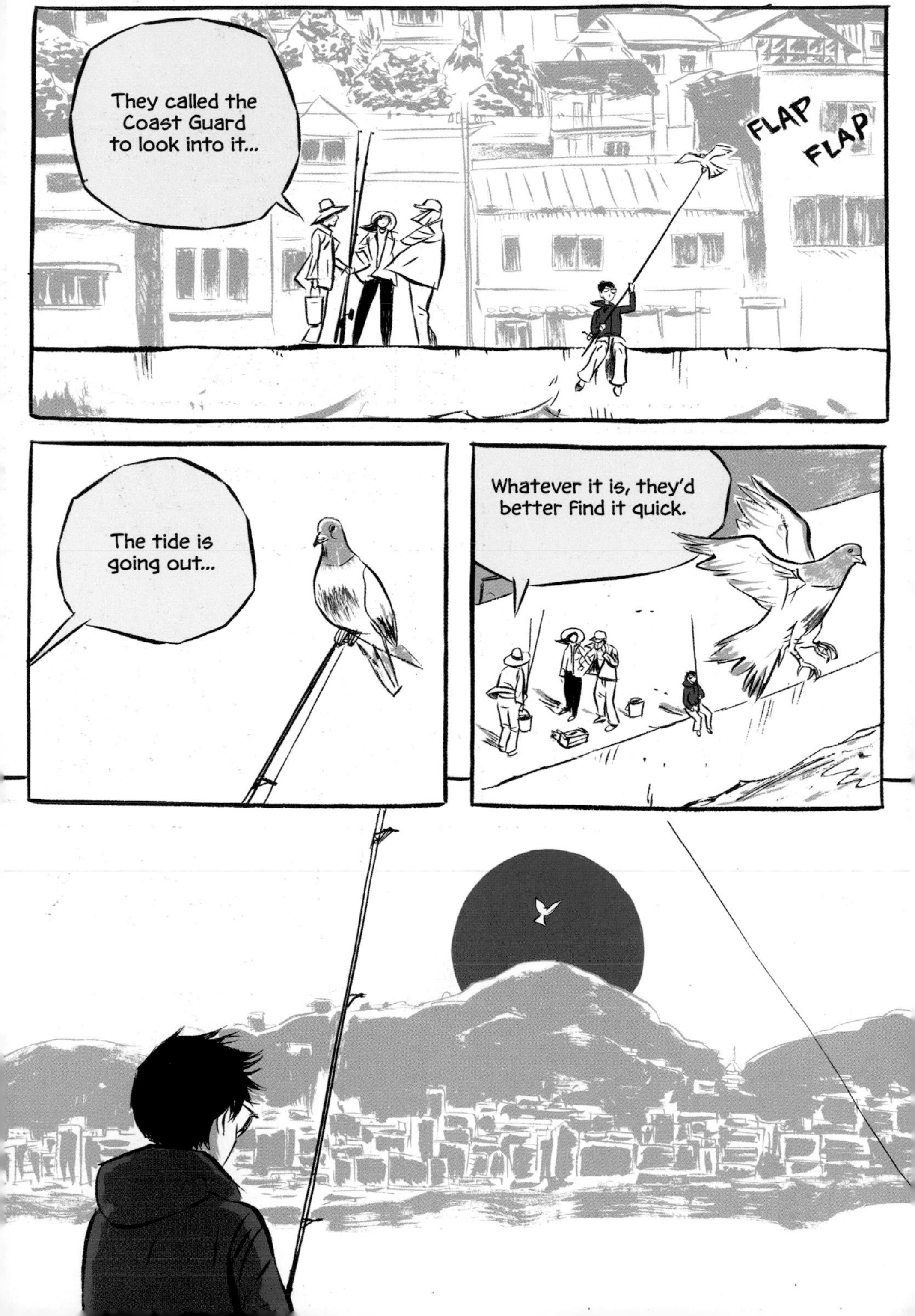
They called the Coast Guard to look into it...
FLAP
FLAP
The tide is going out...
Whatever it is, they'd better find it quick.

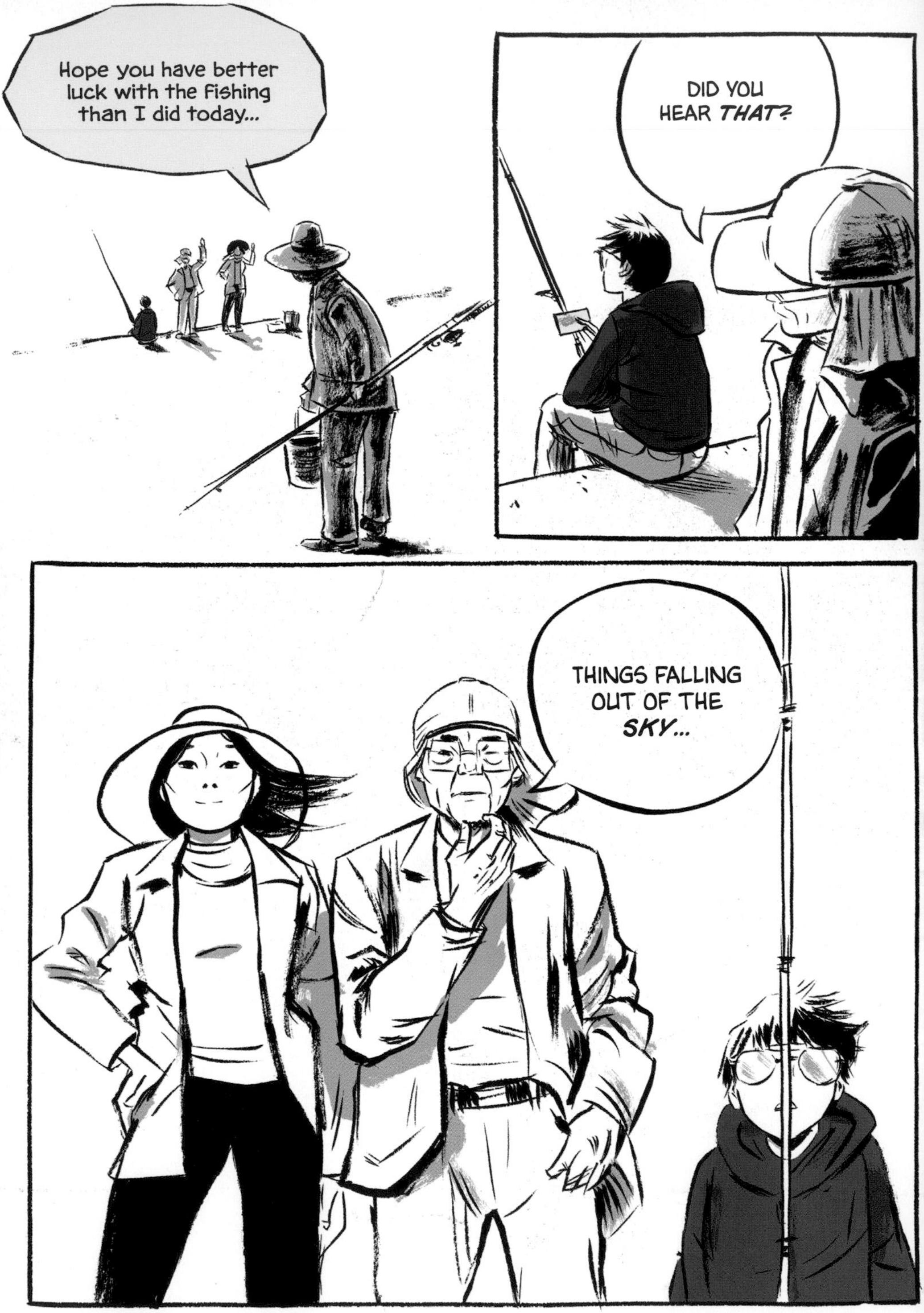
Hope you have better luck with the fishing than I did today...
DID YOU HEAR THAT?
THINGS FALLING OUT OF THE SKY...

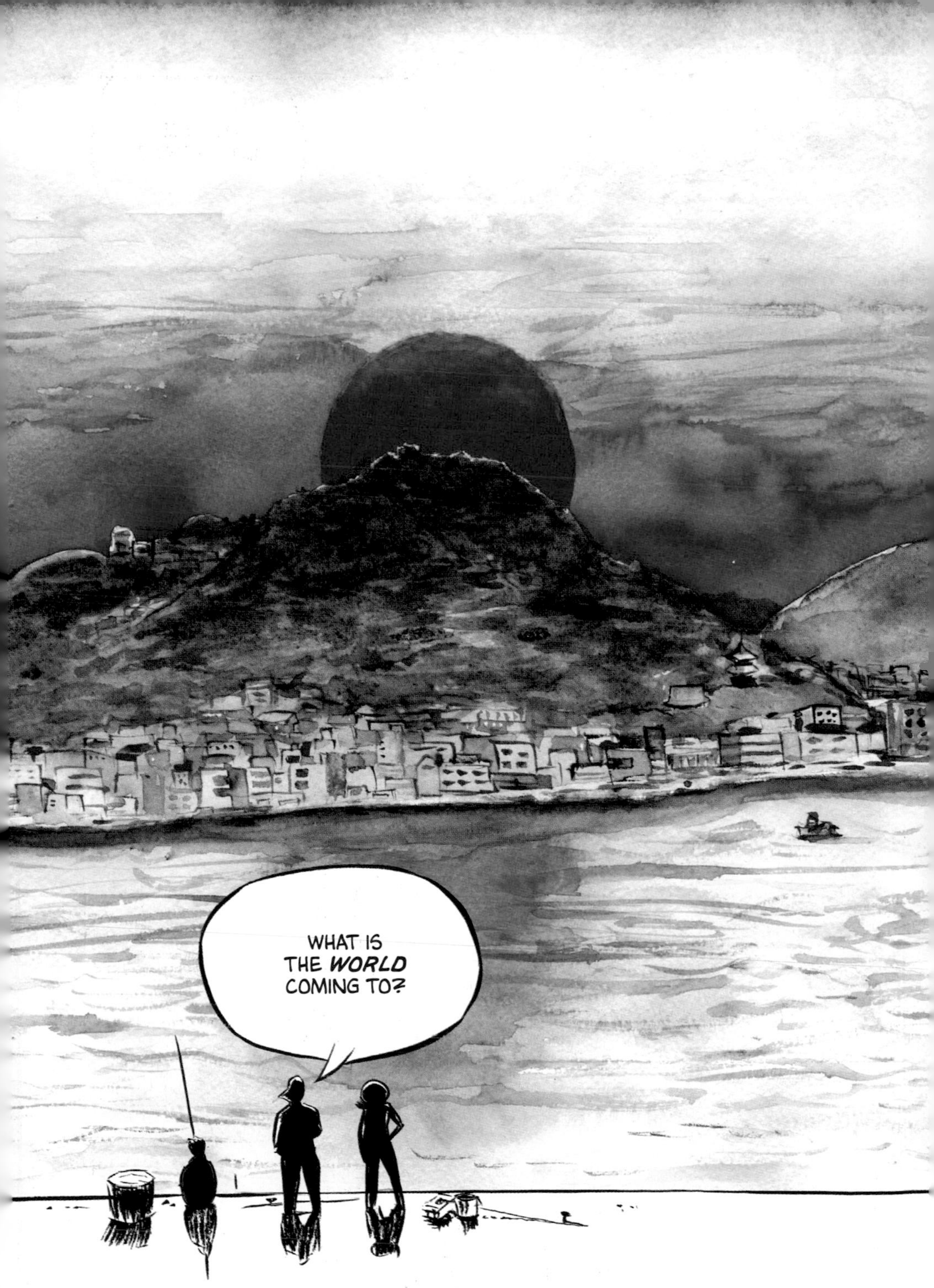
WHAT IS THE *WORLD* COMING TO?

MY DEEPEST GRATITUDE
TO THE EFFORTS OF
CAROL CHU AND JULIA RICHARDSON.
WITHOUT THEM,
THIS BOOK WOULD NOT
BE POSSIBLE.

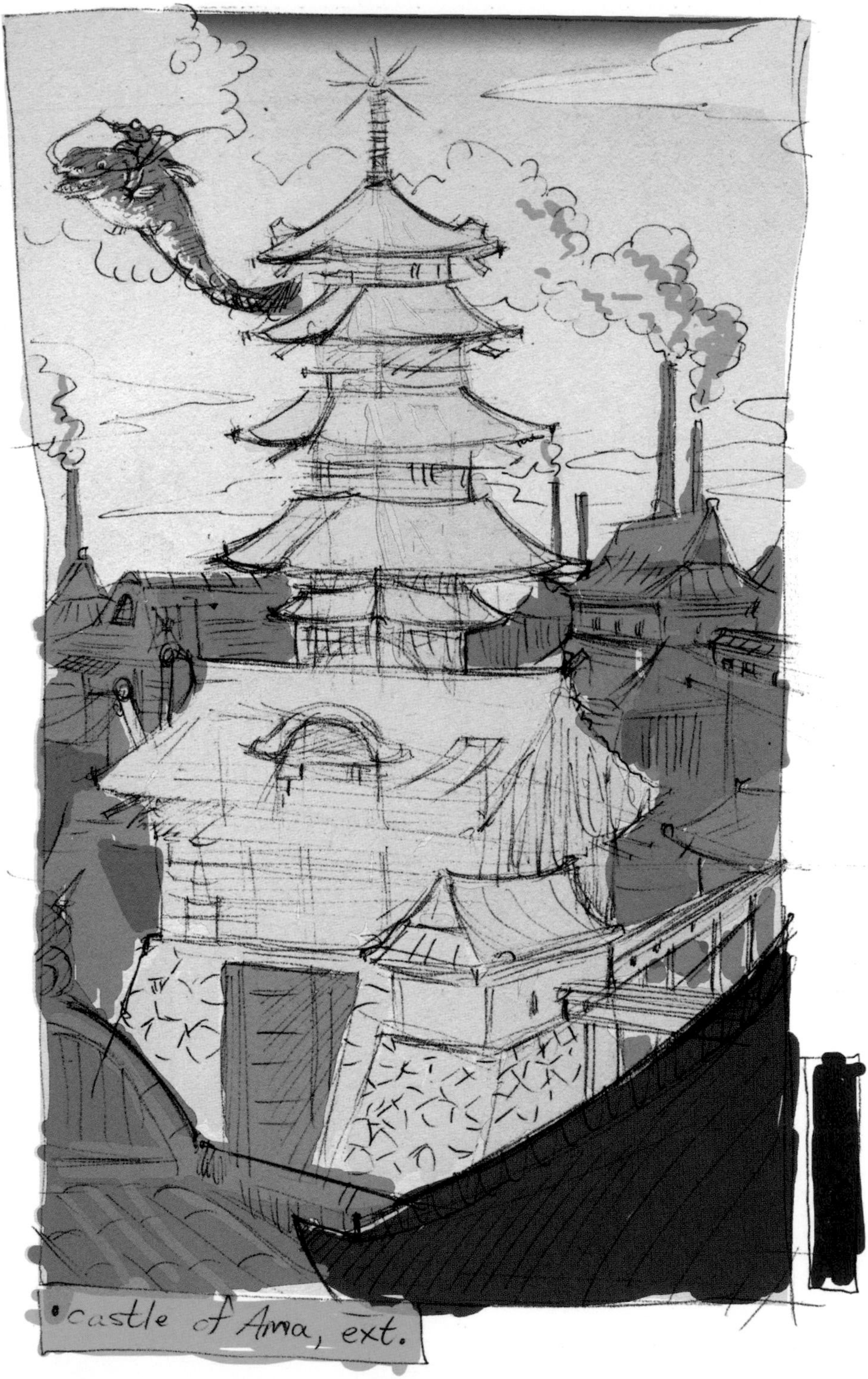
castle of Ama, ext.

THE MAKING OF
ICHIRO

INSPIRATION AND RESEARCH

I MADE TWO TRIPS TO JAPAN IN THE PROCESS OF CREATING *ICHIRO*. I KEPT SKETCHBOOKS AND NOTEBOOKS AND TOOK HUNDREDS OF PICTURES. A LOT OF THIS MATERIAL MADE IT INTO THE BOOK.

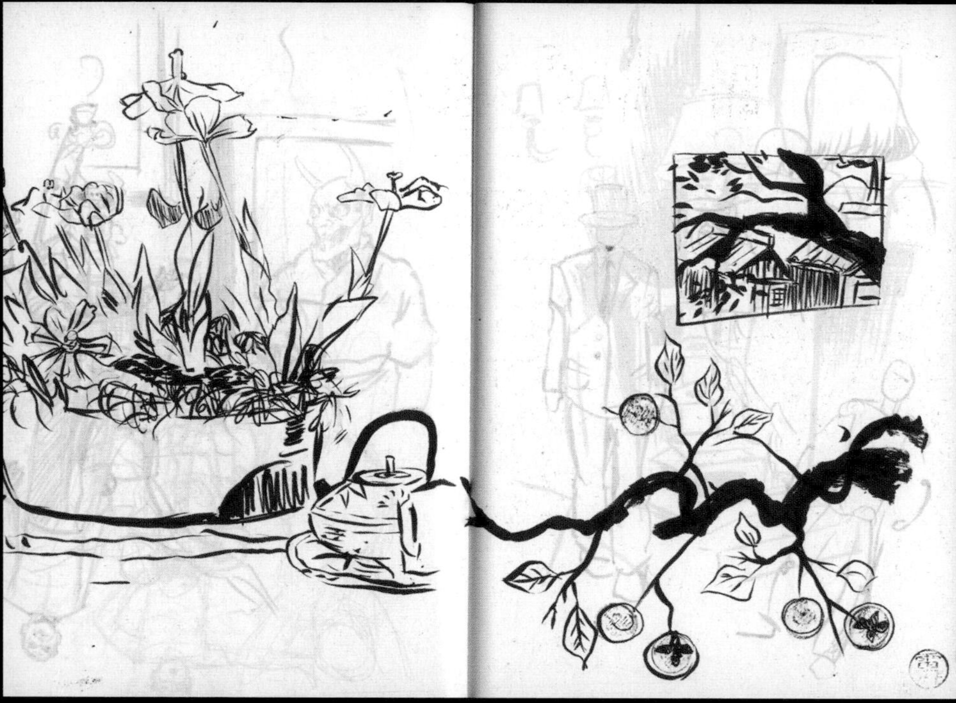

ABOVE LEFT: A SKETCH OF THE TEAPOT THAT THE TANUKI MORPHS INTO.
ABOVE RIGHT: A STUDY OF A PAINTING OF PERSIMMONS THAT I SAW AT THE ADACHI MUSEUM OF ART

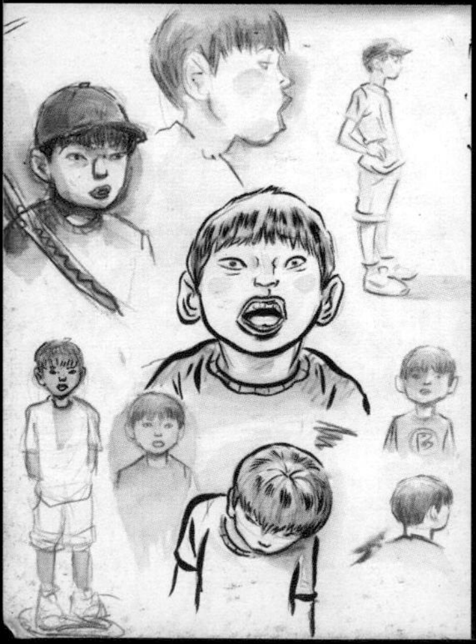

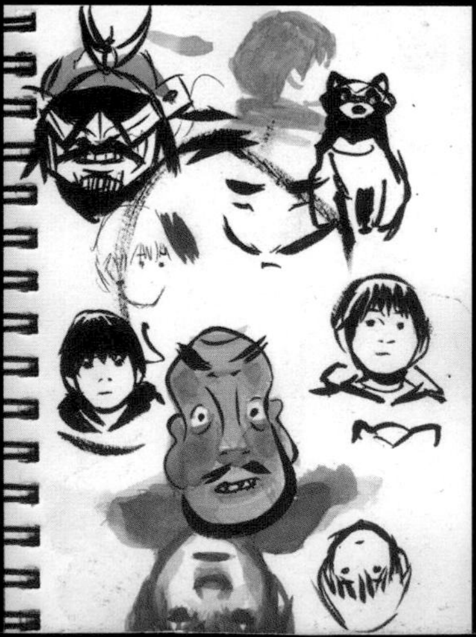

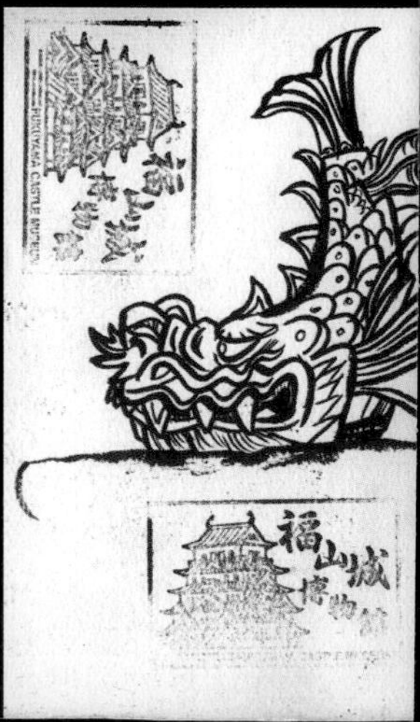
福山城博物館

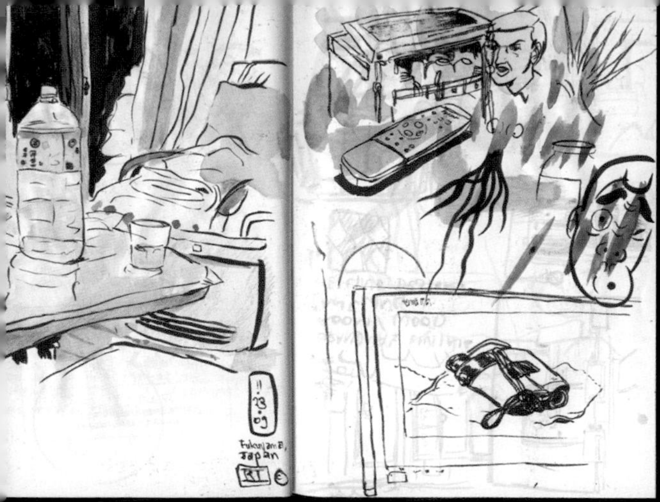

ASIDE FROM THE THINGS I SAW DURING MY TRAVELS, I FILLED PADS WITH CRAMPED NOTES FROM THE VARIOUS BOOKS, ONLINE RESOURCES AND DOCUMENTARIES I CONSULTED WHILE RESEARCHING FOR THE BOOK. ALL OF THIS MATERIAL WAS AT HAND AS I DOVE INTO WRITING AND SKETCHING THE SCRIPT.

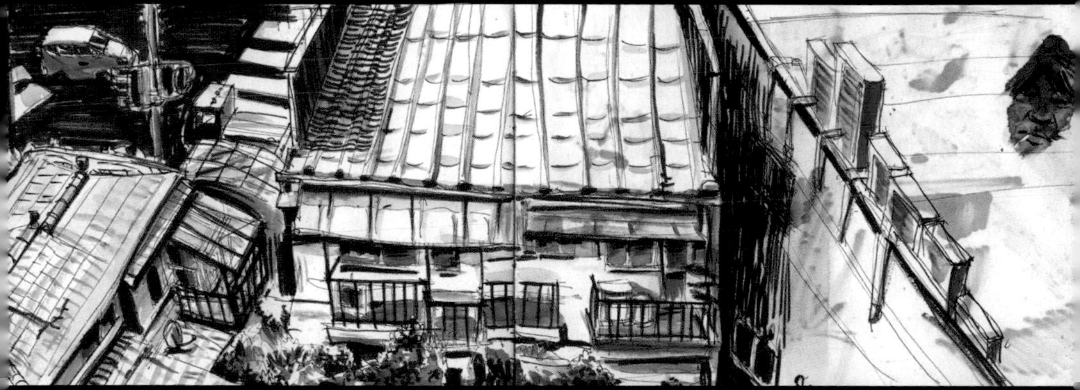

ABOVE: A BUILDING NEAR HIROSHIMA CITY I USED AS REFERENCE FOR GRANPA'S APARTMENT.

RIGHT: VARIOUS KAMI (GOD) MASKS WORN BY PERFORMERS OF NOH PLAYS. I USED THEM AS INSPIRATION FOR THE CHARACTERS IN *ICHIRO*'S MYTHOLOGICAL WORLD.

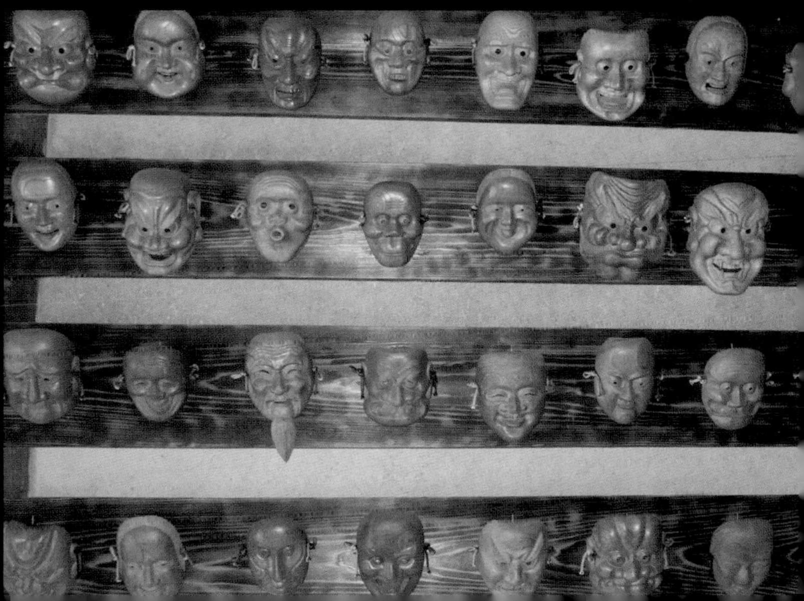

THIS TEMPLE IN NARA, JAPAN, INFLUENCED THE DESIGN OF AMA'S ARCHITECTURE.

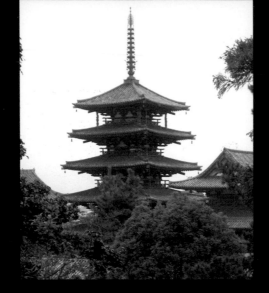

A TANUKI I ENCOUNTERED IN BROAD DAYLIGHT WALKING DOWN THE STREET ON A SMALL ISLAND IN SOUTHWEST JAPAN. ON THE RIGHT, AN EARLY CONCEPT SKETCH OF THE TANUKI CHARACTER.

Persimmon
TANUKI?
TANUKI

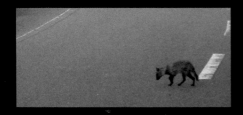

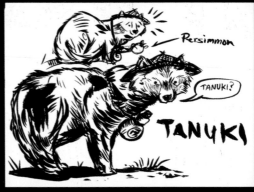

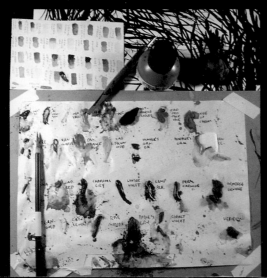

SOME OF THE ART MATERIALS I USED TO CREATE THE BOOK.

MEET THE CHARACTERS

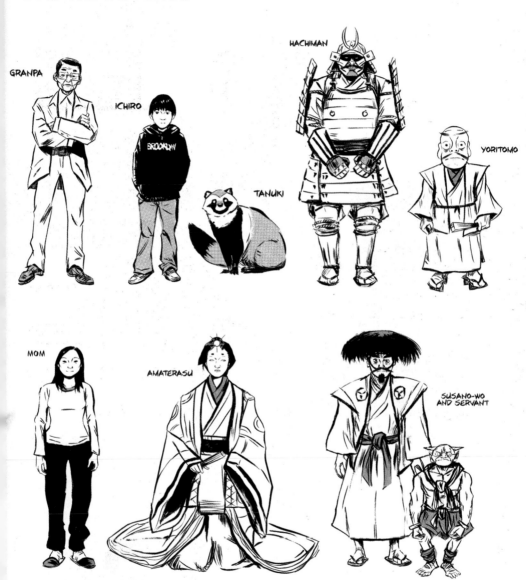

GRANPA

ICHIRO

TANUKI

HACHIMAN

YORITOMO

MOM

AMATERASU

SUSANO-WO AND SERVANT

AT THE BEGINNING OF THE PROCESS, I MADE
SOME STYLE SKETCHES OF THE MAIN AND SECONDARY CHARACTERS
THAT I COULD USE FOR REFERENCE.

A BREAKDOWN OF MY ART PROCESS

FOR *ICHIRO*, I WROTE A GENERAL OUTLINE OF THE STORY AND THEN SKETCHED THE THUMBNAILS AT THE SAME TIME I WROTE THE SCRIPT. THUMBNAILS ARE SMALL SKETCHES THAT PROVIDE THE FRAMEWORK FOR THE BOOK.

NEXT CAME THE PENCILS. SOME PAGES ARE ROUGHER THAN OTHERS--I TRY NOT TO OVER-DRAW AT THIS STAGE BECAUSE IT MAKES INKING OVER THEM LOOK LESS NATURAL.

THE MAJORITY OF THE INKING WAS DONE WITH A JAPANESE BRUSH CALLED A MENSO FUDE. THIS BRUSH ALLOWS FOR A WIDE VARIATION OF LINE WEIGHT IN A SINGLE STROKE. IN SOME SECTIONS, THE INKING WAS ALSO FOLLOWED BY GRAY WASHES.

ASIDE FROM A FEW SECTIONS PAINTED WITH GOUACHE AND WATER-COLORS, THE MAJORITY OF THE COLOR WAS DONE ON THE COMPUTER WITH PHOTOSHOP. USING THE LINE WORK AS A GUIDE, FLAT COLORS WERE LAID DOWN FIRST, WITH FURTHER RENDERING LAYERED ON TOP. PAINT AND PAPER TEXTURES WERE OVERLAID TO GIVE IT A LESS DIGITAL LOOK.

THUMBNAILS

PENCILS

INKS

INK WASH

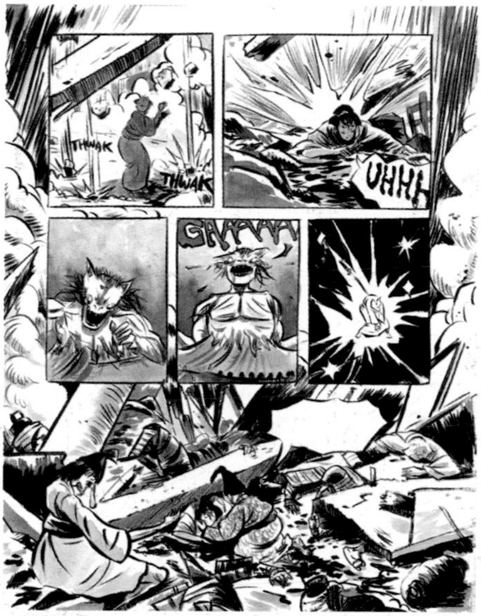
THWAK
THWAK
UHHH
GAAAAA

FLATS (THE FIRST STAGE OF DIGITAL COLORING)

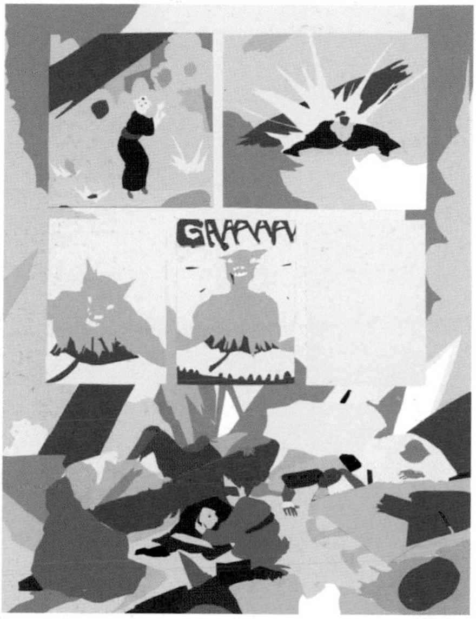
GAAAAA

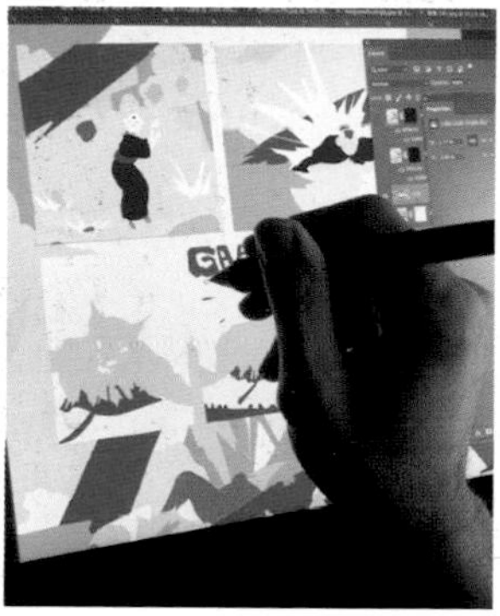

COLORING A PAGE

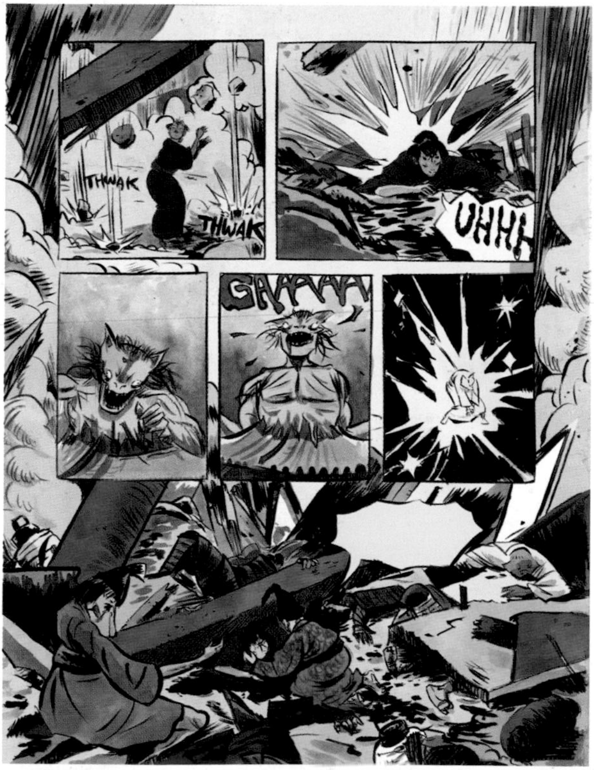
THWAK
THWAK
UHHH
GAAAAA

FINAL PAGE

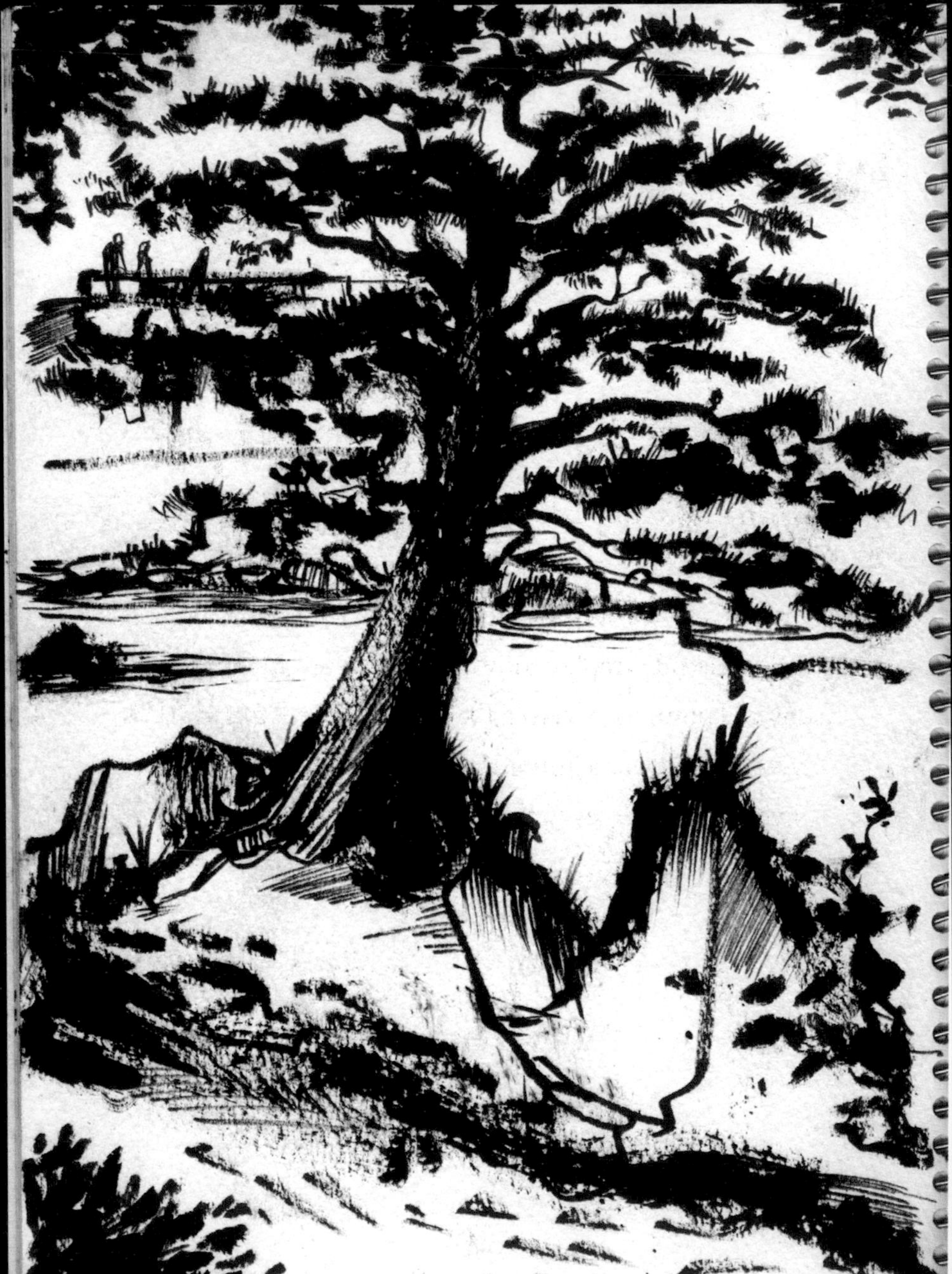

SKETCH OF KINKAKU-JI (GOLDEN PAVILION) IN KYOTO, JAPAN.